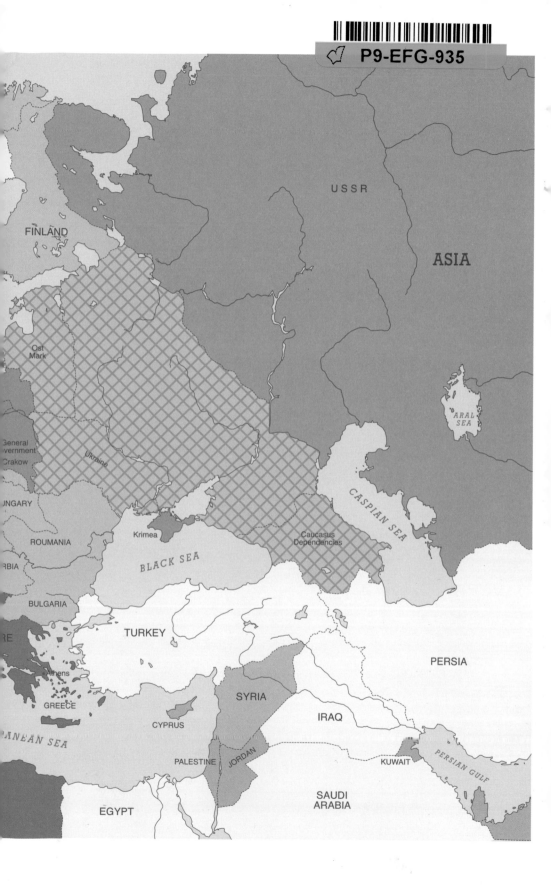

P9-EFG-935

FINLAND

USSR

ASIA

Ost
Mark

ARAL
SEA

General
Government
Crakow

Ukraine

CASPIAN SEA

UNGARY

Krimea

Caucasus
Dependencies

ROUMANIA

BLACK SEA

RBIA

BULGARIA

TURKEY

PERSIA

RE

Athens

GREECE

SYRIA

IRAQ

CYPRUS

RANEAN SEA

PALESTINE

JORDAN

KUWAIT

PERSIAN GULF

EGYPT

SAUDI
ARABIA

DOMINION

DOMINION

C. J. SANSOM

MULHOLLAND BOOKS

LITTLE, BROWN AND COMPANY

NEW YORK   BOSTON   LONDON

Copyright © 2012 by C. J. Sansom

Mulholland Books/Little, Brown and Company
Hachette Book Group
237 Park Avenue, New York, NY 10017
mulhollandbooks.com

First United States edition: January 2014

Originally published in Great Britain by Mantle, a division of Pan MacMillan, October 2012

Mulholland Books is an imprint of Little, Brown and Company, a division of Hachette Book Group, Inc. The Mulholland Books name and logo are trademarks of Hachette Book Group, Inc.

The publisher is not responsible for websites (or their content) that are not owned by the publisher.

The Hachette Speakers Bureau provides a wide range of authors for speaking events. To find out more, go to hachettespeakersbureau.com or call (866) 376-6591.

LCCN: 2013943520

10 9 8 7 6 5 4 3 2 1

RRD-C

Printed in the United States of America

To the memory of my parents,
TREVOR SANSOM (1921–2000)
and
ANN SANSOM (1924–1990),
who in 1939–1945 endured the hardships
and did their bit to defeat the Nazis.
And of
ROSALITA,
R.I.P. 19.2.2012

"The whole fury and might of the enemy must very soon be turned on us. Hitler knows that he will have to break us in this island or lose the war. If we can stand up to him all Europe may be free, and the life of the world will move forward into broad, sunlit uplands; but if we fail, then the whole world, including the United States, and all that we have known and cared for, will sink into the abyss of a new dark age made more sinister, and perhaps more prolonged, by the lights of a perverted science."

WINSTON CHURCHILL, 18 JUNE 1940

All events that take place after
5:00 p.m. on 9 May 1940
are imaginary.

DOMINION

PROLOGUE

The Cabinet Room, 10 Downing Street, London
4.30 p.m., 9 May 1940

Churchill was last to arrive. He knocked once, sharply, and entered. Through the tall windows the warm spring day was fading, shadows lengthening on Horse Guards Parade. Margesson, the Conservative Chief Whip, sat with Prime Minister Chamberlain and Foreign Secretary Lord Halifax at the far end of the long, coffin-shaped table which dominated the Cabinet room. As Churchill approached them Margesson, formally dressed as ever in immaculate black morning coat, stood up.

"Winston."

Churchill nodded at the Chief Whip, looking him sternly in the eye. Margesson, who was Chamberlain's creature, had made life difficult for him when he had stood out against party policy over India and Germany in the years before the war. He turned to Chamberlain and Halifax, the Prime Minister's right-hand man in the government's appeasement of Germany. "Neville. Edward." Both men looked bad; no sign today of the habitual half-sneer, nor of the snappy arrogance which had alienated Chamberlain's House of Commons during yesterday's debate over the military defeat in Norway. Ninety Conservatives had voted with the Opposition or abstained; Chamberlain had left the chamber followed by shouts of "Go!" The Prime Minister's eyes were red from lack of sleep or perhaps even tears—though it was hard to imagine Neville Chamberlain weeping. Last night the word around a feverish House of Commons was that his leadership could not survive.

Halifax looked little better. The Foreign Secretary held his enormously tall, thin body as erect as ever but his face was deathly pale, white skin stretched over his long, bony features. The rumor was that he was reluctant to take over, did not have the stomach for the premiership—literally, for at times of stress he was plagued with agonizing pains in his gut.

Churchill addressed Chamberlain, his deep voice somber, the lisp pronounced. "What is the latest news?"

"More German forces massed at the Belgian border. There could be an attack at any time."

There was silence for a moment, the tick of a carriage clock on the marble mantelpiece suddenly loud.

"Please sit down," Chamberlain said.

Churchill took a chair. Chamberlain continued, in tones of quiet sadness: "We have discussed yesterday's Commons vote at considerable length. We feel there are grave difficulties in my remaining as Prime Minister. I have made up my mind that I must go. Support for me within the party is hemorrhaging. If there should be a vote of confidence, yesterday's abstainers may vote against the government. And soundings with the Labour Party indicate they would only join a coalition under a new Prime Minister. It is impossible for me to continue with this level of personal antipathy." Chamberlain looked again at Margesson, almost as though seeking succor, but the Chief Whip only nodded sadly and said, "If we are to have a coalition now, which we must, national unity is essential."

Looking at Chamberlain, Churchill could find it in himself to pity him. He had lost everything; for two years he had tried to meet Hitler's demands, believing the Führer had made his last claim for territory at Munich only for him to invade Czechoslovakia a few months later, and then Poland. After Poland fell there had been seven months of military inaction, of "phony war." Last month Chamberlain had told the Commons that Hitler had "missed the bus" for a spring campaign, only for him suddenly to invade and occupy Norway, throwing back British forces. France would be next. Chamberlain looked between Churchill and Halifax. Then he spoke again, his voice still expressionless. "It is between the two of you. I would be willing, if desired, to serve under either."

Churchill nodded and leaned back in his chair. He looked at Halifax, who met his gaze with a cold, probing stare. Churchill knew Halifax held nearly all the cards, that most of the Conservative Party wanted him as the next Prime Minister. He had been Viceroy of India, a senior minister for years, a cool, steady, Olympian aristocrat, both trusted and respected. And most Tories had never forgiven Churchill his Liberal past, nor his opposition to his own party over Germany. They viewed him as an adventurer, unreliable, lacking in judgment. Chamberlain wanted Halifax, as did Margesson, together with most of the Cabinet. And so, Churchill knew, did Halifax's friend, the King. But Halifax had no fire in his belly, none. Churchill loathed Hitler but Halifax treated the Nazi leader with a sort of patrician contempt; he had once said the only people the Führer made life difficult for in Germany were a few trade unionists and Jews.

Churchill, though, had had the wind in his sails with the public since war was declared last September; Chamberlain had been forced to bring him back into the Cabinet when his warnings over Hitler had, finally, been proved right. But how to play that one card? Churchill settled more firmly into his chair. *Say nothing*, he thought, see where Halifax stands, whether he wants the job at all, and how much.

"Winston," Chamberlain began, his tone questioning now. "You were very rough on Labour in the debate yesterday. And you have always been their fierce opponent. Do you think this might be an obstacle for you?"

Churchill did not answer, but stood abruptly and walked over to the window, looking out into the bright spring afternoon. *Don't reply*, he thought. *Flush Halifax out.*

The carriage clock struck five, a high, pinging sound. As it finished Big Ben began booming out the hour. As the last note died away Halifax finally spoke.

"I think," he said, "that I would be better placed to deal with the Labour men."

Churchill turned and faced him, his expression suddenly fierce. "The trials to be faced, Edward, will be very terrible." Halifax looked tired, desperately unhappy, but there was determination in his face now. He had found steel in himself after all.

"That, Winston, is why I would like you at my side in a new, smaller War Cabinet. You would be Minister of Defense, you would have overall responsibility for conduct of the war."

Churchill considered the offer, moving his heavy jaw slowly from side to side. If he was in charge of the war effort, perhaps he could dominate Halifax, become Prime Minister in all but name. It all depended on who else Halifax put in place. He asked, "And the others? Who will you appoint?"

"From the Conservatives, you and I and Sam Hoare; I think that best reflects the balance of opinion within the party. Attlee for Labour, and Lloyd George to represent the Liberal interest, and as a national figure, the man who led us to victory in 1918." Halifax turned to Chamberlain. "I think you could be of most use now, Neville, as Leader of the Commons."

It was bad news, the worst. Lloyd George who, for all his recent back-pedaling, had spent the thirties idolizing Hitler, calling him Germany's George Washington. And Sam Hoare, the arch-appeaser, Churchill's old enemy. Attlee was a fighter, for all his diffidence, but the two of them would be in a minority.

"Lloyd George is seventy-seven," Churchill said. "Is he up to the weight that must be borne?"

"I believe so. And he will be good for morale." Halifax was sounding more resolute now. "Winston," he said, "I would very much like you beside me at this hour."

Churchill hesitated. This new War Cabinet would hobble him. He knew that Halifax had decided to take the premiership reluctantly and out of duty. He would do his best, but his heart was not in the struggle that was coming. Like so many, he had fought in the Great War and feared seeing all that bloodshed again.

For a moment Churchill thought of resigning from the Cabinet; but what good would that do? And Margesson was right; public unity was all important now. He would do what he could, while he could. He had thought, earlier that day, that his hour had come at last, but it was not to be after all, not yet. "I will serve under you," he said, his heart heavy.

CHAPTER ONE

November 1952

Almost all the passengers on the Tube to Victoria were, like David and his family, on their way to the Remembrance Sunday parade. It was a cold morning and the men and women all wore black winter coats. Scarves and handbags were also black, or muted brown, the only color the bright red poppies everyone wore in their buttonholes. David ushered Sarah and her mother into a carriage; they found two empty wooden benches and sat facing each other.

As the Tube rattled out of Kenton Station David looked around him. Everyone seemed sad and somber, befitting the day. There were relatively few older men—most of the Great War veterans, like Sarah's father, would be in central London already, preparing for the march past the Cenotaph. David was himself a veteran of the second war, the brief 1939–40 conflict that people called the Dunkirk campaign or the Jews' war, according to political taste. But David, who had served in Norway, and the other survivors of that defeated, humiliated army—whose retreat from Europe had been followed so quickly by Britain's surrender—did not have a place at the Remembrance Day ceremonies. Nor did the British soldiers who had died in the endless conflicts in India, and now Africa, that had begun since the 1940 Peace Treaty. Remembrance Day now had a political overtone: remember the slaughter when Britain and Germany fought in 1914–18; remember that must never happen again. Britain must remain Germany's ally.

"It's very cloudy," Sarah's mother said. "I hope it isn't going to rain."

"It'll be all right, Betty," David said reassuringly. "The forecast said it would just stay cloudy."

Betty nodded. A plump little woman in her sixties, her whole life was focused on caring for Sarah's father, who had had half his face blown off on the Somme in 1916.

"It gets very uncomfortable for Jim, marching in the rain," she said. "The water drips behind his prosthesis and of course he can't take it off."

Sarah took her mother's hand. Her square face with its strong round chin — her father's chin — looked dignified. Her long blond hair, curled at the ends, was framed by a modest black hat. Betty smiled at her. The Tube halted at a station and more people got on. Sarah turned to David. "There's more passengers than usual."

"People wanting to get a first look at the Queen, I imagine."

"I hope we manage to find Steve and Irene all right," Betty said, worrying again.

"I told them to meet us by the ticket booths at Victoria," Sarah told her. "They'll be there, dear, don't worry."

David looked out of the window. He was not looking forward to spending the afternoon with his wife's sister and her husband. Irene was good-natured enough, although she was full of silly ideas and never stopped talking, but David loathed Steve, with his mixture of oily charm and arrogance, his Blackshirt politics. David would have to try to keep his lip buttoned as usual.

The train ground to a jolting halt, just before the mouth of a tunnel. There was a hiss somewhere as brakes engaged. "Not today," someone said. "These delays are getting worse. It's a disgrace." Outside, David saw, the track looked down on rows of back-to-back houses of soot-stained London brick. Gray smoke rose from chimneys, washing was hanging out to dry in the backyards. The streets were empty. A grocer's window just below them had a prominent sign in the window, *Food Stamps Taken Here.* There was a sudden jolt and the train moved into the tunnel, only to judder to a halt again a few moments later. David saw his own face reflected back from the dark window, his head framed by his bulky dark coat with its wide lapels. A bowler hat hid his short black hair, a few unruly curls just visible. His unlined, regular features made him look younger than thirty-five; deceptively unmarked. He suddenly recalled a childhood memory, his mother's constant refrain to women visitors, "Isn't he a good-looking boy, couldn't you just eat him?" Delivered in her sharp Dublin brogue, it had made him squirm with embarrassment. Another memory came unbidden, of when he was seventeen and had won the inter-schools Diving Cup. He remembered standing on the high board, a sea of faces far below, the board trembling slightly beneath his feet. Two steps forward and then the dive, down into the great expanse of still water, the moment of fear and then the exhilaration of striking out into silence.

Steve and Irene were waiting at Victoria. Irene, Sarah's older sister, was also tall and blond but with a little dimpled chin like her mother's. Her black coat had a thick brown fur collar. Steve was good-looking in a raffish way, with a thin black mustache that made him look like a poor man's Errol Flynn. He wore a black fedora on his thickly brilliantined head — David could smell the chemical tang as he shook his brother-in-law's hand.

"How's the Civil Service, old man?" Steve asked.

"Surviving." David smiled.

"Still keeping watch over the Empire?"

"Something like that. How are the boys?"

"Grand. Getting bigger and noisier every week. We might bring them next year, they're getting old enough." David saw a shadow pass across Sarah's face and knew she was remembering their own dead son.

"We ought to hurry, get the Tube to Westminster," Irene said. "Look at all these people."

They joined the throng heading for the escalator. As the crowd pressed together their pace slowed to a silent shuffle, reminding David for a moment of his time as a soldier, shuffling with the rest of the weary troops onto the ships evacuating British forces from Norway, back in 1940.

They turned into Whitehall. David's office was just behind the Cenotaph; men walking past would still remove their hats as they passed it, respectfully and unselfconsciously, though fewer and fewer with each passing year—thirty-four now since the Great War ended. The sky was gray-white, the air cold. People's breath steamed before them as they jostled—quietly and politely—for places behind the low metal barriers opposite the tall white rectangle of the Cenotaph, a line of policemen in heavy coats in front. Some were ordinary constables in their helmets, but many were Special Branch Auxiliaries in their flat peaked caps and slimmer blue uniforms. When they were first created in the 1940s to deal with growing civil unrest David's father had said the Auxiliaries reminded him of the Black and Tans, the violent trench veterans recruited by Lloyd George to augment the police during the Irish Independence War. All were armed.

The ceremony had changed in the last few years; serving personnel no longer stood on parade around the Cenotaph, blocking the public view, and wooden boards had been laid on blocks behind the barriers to give people a better vantage point. It was part of what Prime Minister Beaverbrook called "demystifying the thing."

The family managed to get a good place opposite Downing Street and the big Victorian building which housed the Dominions Office where David worked. Beyond the barriers, forming three sides of a hollow square around the Cenotaph, the military and religious leaders had already taken their places. The soldiers were in full dress uniform, Archbishop Headlam, head of the section of the Anglican Church that had not split away in opposition to his compromises with the regime, in gorgeous green-and-gold vestments. Beside them stood the politicians and ambassadors, each holding a wreath. David looked them over; there was Prime Minister Beaverbrook with his wizened little monkey face, the wide fleshy mouth downturned in an expression of sorrow. For forty years, since he first came to England from Canada with business scandals hanging over him, Beaverbrook had combined building a newspaper empire with maneuvering in politics, pushing his causes of free enterprise, the Empire, and appeasement on the public and politicians. He was trusted by few, elected by none, and after the death of his immediate predecessor, Lloyd George, in 1945, the coalition had made him Prime Minister.

Lord Halifax, the Prime Minister who had surrendered after France fell, stood beside Beaverbrook, overtopping him by a foot. Halifax was bald now, his cadaverous face an ashen shadow beneath his hat, deep-set eyes staring over the crowd with a curious blankness. Beside him stood Beaverbrook's coalition colleagues: Home Secretary Oswald Mosley, tall and ramrod-straight, India Secretary Enoch Powell, only forty but seeming far older, black-mustached and darkly saturnine, Viscount Swinton, the Dominions Office Secretary and David's own minister, tall and aristocratic, Foreign Secretary Rab Butler with his pouched froggy face, and the Coalition Labour leader Ben Greene, one of the few Labour figures who had admired the Nazis in the 1930s. When Labour split in 1940 Herbert Morrison had led the Pro-Treaty minority that went into coalition with Halifax; he was one of those politicians for whom ambition was all-consuming. But he had resigned in 1943; the degree of British support for Germany had become too much for him, as it had for some other politicians like the Conservative Sam Hoare; all had retreated into private life with peerages.

Also standing in their dark coats were representatives of the Dominions; David recognized some of the High Commissioners from work, like the thickset, frowning Vorster of South Africa. Then behind them came ambassadors representing the other nations who had fought in the Great War: Germany's Rommel, Mussolini's son-in-law Ciano, the ambassadors of France and Japan, Joe Kennedy from America. Russia, though, had no representative; Britain, as Germany's ally, was still formally at war with the Soviet Union though she had no troops to spare for that giant meat-grinder, the German–Soviet war, which had gone on, over a 1,200-mile front, for eleven years now.

A little way off a group of men stood around an outside-broadcast camera, an enormous squat thing trailing thick wires, BBC emblazoned on the side. Beside it the heavy form of Richard Dimbleby could be seen speaking into a microphone, though he was too far off for David to hear anything.

Sarah shivered, rubbing her gloved hands together. "Golly, it's cold. Poor Dad will feel it standing around waiting for the march past to start." She looked at the Cenotaph, the bare white memorial. "God, it's all so sad."

"At least we know we'll never go to war with Germany again," Irene said.

"Look, there she is." Betty spoke in tones of hushed reverence.

The Queen had come out of the Home Office. Accompanied by the Queen Mother and her grandmother, old Queen Mary, equerries carrying their wreaths, she took her place in front of the Archbishop. Her pretty young face was ill suited to her black clothes. This was one of her few public appearances since her father's death early in the year. David thought she looked tired and afraid. Her expression reminded him of the late King's in 1940, when George VI rode down Whitehall in an open carriage beside Adolf Hitler, on the Führer's state visit after the Berlin Peace Treaty. David, still convalescing from frostbite caught in Norway, had watched the ceremony on the new television his father had bought, one of the first in the street, when the BBC resumed broadcasting. Hitler had looked in seventh heaven, beaming, flushed and rosy-cheeked, his dream of an alliance with the Aryan British at last fulfilled. He smiled and waved at the silent crowd, but the King had sat expressionless, only raising a hand occasionally, his body angled away from Hitler's. Afterwards David's father had said "enough," that was it, he was off to live with his brother in New Zealand, and David would come too if he knew what was good for him, never mind his Civil Service job. Thank God, he added feelingly, David's mother hadn't lived to see this.

Sarah was looking at the Queen. "Poor woman," she said.

David glanced over. He said very quietly, "She shouldn't have let them make her their puppet."

"What alternative did she have?"

David didn't answer.

People in the crowd glanced at their watches, then they all fell silent, removing hats and caps as, across Westminster, Big Ben boomed out eleven times. Then, shockingly loud in the still air, came the sound of a big gun firing, marking the moment the guns had stopped in 1918. Everyone bowed their heads for the two minutes' silence, remembering the terrible costs of Britain's victory in the Great War, or perhaps, like David, those of her defeat in 1940. Two minutes later the field-gun on Horse Guards Parade fired again, ending the silence. A bugler sounded the notes of "the last post," indescribably haunting and sad. The crowd listened, bareheaded in the winter cold, the only sound an occasional stifled cough. Every time he attended the ceremony David wondered that nobody in the crowd ever burst out crying, or, remembering the recent past, fell shrieking to the ground.

The last note died away. Then, to the sound of the "Funeral March" played by the band of the Brigade of Guards, the young Queen bore a wreath of poppies that looked too big for her to carry, laid it down on the Cenotaph, and stood with bowed head. She walked slowly back to her place and the Queen Mother followed. "So young to be a widow," Sarah said.

"Yes." David had noticed a faint smoky tang in the air and, looking up Whitehall for a moment, saw a slight haze. There would be fog tonight.

The rest of the Royal Family laid their wreaths, followed by the military leaders, the Prime Minister and politicians, and representatives of the Empire governments. The base of the stark, simple monument was now carpeted in the dark green wreaths with their red poppies. Then Germany's ambassador, Erwin Rommel, one of the victors of the 1940 campaign in France, stepped forward, trim and military, Iron Cross pinned to his breast, his handsome face stern and sad. The wreath he bore was enormous, larger even than the Queen's. In the center, on a white background, was a swastika. He laid the wreath and stood, head bowed, for a long moment before turning away. Behind him Joseph Kennedy, the veteran American ambassador, waited. It was his turn next.

Then, from behind David, came a sudden shouting. "End Nazi control! Democracy now! Up the Resistance!" Something sailed over the heads of the crowd and crashed at Rommel's feet. Sarah gasped. Irene and some of the other women in the crowd screamed. The steps of the

Cenotaph and the bottom of Rommel's coat were instantly streaked with red and for a moment David thought it was blood, that someone had thrown a bomb, but then he saw a paint-pot rattle down the steps onto the pavement. Rommel did not flinch, just stood where he was. Ambassador Kennedy, though, had jumped back in panic. Policemen were reaching for truncheons and pistols. A group of soldiers, rifles at the ready, stepped forward. David saw the Royal Family being hurried away.

"Nazis out!" someone called from the crowd. "We want Churchill!" Policemen were vaulting the barriers now. A couple of men in the crowd had also produced guns and looked fiercely around: Special Branch undercover men. David pulled Sarah to him. The crowd parted to let the police through, and he glimpsed a struggle off to his right. He saw a baton raised, heard someone call out, "Get the bastards!" encouragingly to the police.

Sarah said, "Oh God, what are they doing?"

"I don't know." Irene was holding Betty, the old woman weeping, while Steve was staring at the melee with a face like thunder. The whole crowd was talking now, a susurrating murmur from which the occasional shout could be heard. "Bloody Communists, beat their heads in!" "They're right, get the Germans out!"

A British general, a thin man with a sunburned face and gray mustache, climbed the steps of the Cenotaph, carrying a megaphone, picking his way through the wreaths, and called for order from the crowd.

"Did they get them?" Sarah asked David. "I couldn't see."

"Yes. I think there were just a few."

"It's bloody treason!" Steve said. "I hope they hang the buggers!"

The ceremony continued with the rest of the wreath-laying and then a short service led by Archbishop Headlam. He spoke a prayer, the microphone giving his voice an odd, tinny echo.

"*O Lord, look down on us as we remember the brave men who have died fighting for Britain. We remember the legions who fell between 1914 and 1918, that great and tragic conflict which still marks us all, here and across all*

Europe. Lord, remember the pain of those gathered here today who have lost loved ones. Comfort them, comfort them."

Then came the march past, the thousands of soldiers, many old now, marching proudly along in lines as the band played popular tunes from the Great War, each contingent laying a wreath. As always David and his family looked out for Sarah's father, but they didn't see him. The steps of the Cenotaph were still splotched with red, Rommel's swastika prominent among the wreaths. David wondered who the demonstrators had been. One of the independent pacifist groups perhaps; the Resistance would have shot Rommel, would have shot a lot of the Nazis stationed in Britain, but for the fear of reprisals. Poor devils, whoever they were; they would be getting a beating in a Special Branch Interrogation Centre now, or perhaps even in the basement of Senate House, the German embassy. As it had been an attack on Rommel, the British police might have handed the demonstrators over. He felt powerless. He hadn't even contradicted Steve. But he had to keep his cover intact, never step out of line, try to play the model civil servant. All the more because of Sarah's family's past. David felt a stab of unreasonable irritation against his wife.

His eyes were drawn back to the veterans. An old man of about sixty, his face stern and defiant, was marching past, his chest thrust out proudly. On one side of his coat was pinned a row of medals but on the other was sewn a large, bright yellow Star of David. Jews knew to stay out of the limelight now, not to attract attention, but the old man had defied common sense to go on the march wearing a prominent star, although he could have got away with the little Star of David lapel badge all Jews had to wear now, very British and discreet.

Someone in the crowd shouted out "Kike!" The old man did not flinch but David did, anger coursing through him. He knew that under the law he too should have worn a yellow badge, and should not be working in government service, an employment forbidden to Jews. But David's father, twelve thousand miles away, was the only other person who knew his mother had been that rare thing, an Irish Jew. And half a Jew was a Jew in Britain now; the penalty for concealing your identity was indefinite detention. In the 1941 census, when people were asked for the first time to state their religion, he had declared himself a Catholic. He had done the same thing whenever renewing his identity card, and the same again in the 1951 census, which this time also asked about Jewish parents or grandparents. But however often David pushed it all to the back of his mind, sometimes, in the night, he woke up terrified.

The rest of the ceremony went ahead without interruption, and afterwards they met up with Jim, Sarah's father, and went back to David and Sarah's mock-Tudor semi in Kenton, where Sarah would cook dinner for them all. Jim had known nothing about the paint-throwing until his family told him, though he had noticed the red stain on the Cenotaph steps. He said almost nothing about it on the journey back, and neither did Sarah or David, though Irene and especially Steve were full of outraged indignation. When they got back to the house Steve suggested they watch the news, see what it said about the attack.

David switched on the television, rearranging the chairs to face it. He didn't like the way that in most houses now the furniture was arranged around the set; over the last decade, ownership of what some still called the idiot-box had spread to half the population; having a television was a mark of the sharp dividing line between rich and poor. It was coming to take over national life. It wasn't quite time for the news; a children's serial was on, a dramatization of some Bulldog Drummond adventure story, featuring Imperial heroes and treacherous natives. Sarah brought them tea and David passed around the cigarette-box. He glanced at Jim. Despite his conversion to pacifism after the Great War, his father-in-law always took part in the Remembrance Day parade; however much he loathed war, he honored his old comrades. David wondered what he thought of the paint-throwing, but Jim's prosthetic mask was turned toward him. It was a good prosthesis, close-fitting and flesh-colored; there were even artificial eyelashes on the flat painted eye. Sarah confessed once that when she was small the crude mask he wore then, made from a thin sheet of metal, had frightened her and when he sat her in his lap on one occasion she'd burst into tears and Irene had to take her away. Her mother had called her a nasty, selfish girl but Irene, four years older, had held her and said, "You mustn't mind it. It's not Daddy's fault."

The news came on. They watched the young Queen paying her respects, and listened to Dimbleby's sonorous, respectful reporting. But the BBC did not show the incident with Rommel; they simply passed from the Dominion representatives' wreath-laying to Ambassador Kennedy's. There was a flicker on the screen that you wouldn't notice unless you were looking for it, and no break in the commentary — the BBC technicians must have done a re-recording later.

"Nothing," Irene said.

"They must have decided not to report it." Sarah had come in from the kitchen to watch, flushed from cooking.

"Makes you wonder what else they don't report," Jim said quietly.

Steve turned to him. He was wearing one of his glaringly bright sweaters, his plump stomach straining it unattractively. "They don't want people to be upset," he said. "Seeing something like that happen on Remembrance Day."

"People should know, though," Irene said fiercely. "They should see what these despicable terrorists do. In front of the Queen, too, poor girl! No wonder she's so seldom seen in public. It's a disgrace!"

David spoke up then, before he could stop himself. "It's what happens when people aren't allowed to protest against their masters."

Steve turned on him. He was still angry, looking for a scrap. "You mean the Germans, I suppose."

David shrugged noncommittally, though he would have liked to knock every tooth out of Steve's head. His brother-in-law continued. "The Germans are our partners, and jolly lucky for us they are, too."

"Lucky for those who make money trading with them," David snapped.

"What the devil's that supposed to mean? Is that a dig at my business in the Anglo-German Fellowship?"

David glowered at him. "If the cap fits."

"You'd rather have the Resistance people in charge, I suppose? Churchill — if the old warmonger's even still alive — and the bunch of

Communists he's got himself in with. Murdering soldiers, blowing people up—like that little girl who stepped on one of their mines in Yorkshire last week." He was beginning to get red in the face.

"Please," Sarah said sharply. "Don't start an argument." She exchanged a look with Irene.

"All right." Steve backed down. "I don't want to spoil the day any more than those swine have spoiled it already. So much for civil servants being impartial," he added sarcastically.

"What was that, Steve?" David asked sharply.

"Nothing." Steve raised his hands, palms up. "Pax."

"Rommel," Jim said, sadly. "He was a soldier in the Great War, like me. If only Remembrance Day could be less military. Then people mightn't feel the need to protest. There's rumors Hitler's very ill," he added. "He never broadcasts these days. And with the Democrats back in America, maybe changes will come." He smiled at his wife. "I always said they would, if we waited long enough."

"I'm sure they'd have told us if Herr Hitler was ill," Steve said dismissively. David glanced at Sarah, but said nothing.

Afterwards, when the rest of the family had driven off in Steve's new Morris Minor, David and Sarah argued. "Why must you get into fights with him, in front of everyone?" Sarah asked. She looked exhausted; she had been waiting on the family all afternoon, her hair was limp now, her voice ragged. "In front of Daddy, today of all days." She hesitated, then continued bitterly, "You were the one who told me to stay out of politics years ago, said it was safer to keep quiet."

"I know. I'm sorry. But Steve can't keep his damn trap shut. Today it was just—too much."

"How do you think these rows make Irene and me feel?"

"You don't like him any more than I do."

"We have to put up with him. For the family."

"Yes, and go visit him, look at that picture on the mantelpiece of him and his business pals with Speer, see his Mosley books and *The Protocols of the Elders of Zion* on the bookshelf," David said heavily. "I don't know why he doesn't join the Blackshirts and have done with it. But then he'd have to exercise, lose some of that fat."

Unexpectedly, Sarah shouted. "Haven't we been through enough? Haven't we?" She stormed out of the lounge; David heard her go into the kitchen, and the door banged shut. He got up and began gathering the dirty plates and cutlery onto the trolley. He wheeled it into the little hall. As he passed the staircase he could not help looking up, to the torn wallpaper at the top and bottom of the stairs, where the little gates had stood. He and Sarah had talked, since Charlie died, about getting new wallpaper. But like so much else, they had never got around to it. He would go to her in a minute, apologize, try to close the ever-growing gap a little. Though he knew it could not really be closed, not with the secrets he had to keep.

CHAPTER TWO

I t had begun two years before, with the results of the 1950 election, a few months after Charlie's death. Since the Hungarian banking crash of 1948, caused by the drain on Europe's economies from the endless German war in Russia, the economic and political news had been getting steadily worse. There were strikes and demonstrations in northern England and Scotland, India was in a seemingly permanent fervor of revolt, increasing numbers of arrests were being made under the never-repealed security legislation of 1939. People who had quietly assented to the 1940 Peace Treaty were starting to become angry, saying it was time Britain stood up to Germany a bit more and that after ten years it was time for a change of government, time to give Churchill and Attlee's United Democrat Party a chance. Despite the diet of pro-government propaganda from newspapers and the BBC, Beaverbrook was unpopular and there were rumors that the UDP might make big gains.

When the results were declared, though, the party had lost most of their hundred seats in Parliament, overtaken by British Union, Mosley's Fascist party, which rose from thirty seats to a hundred and four, and joined Beaverbrook's coalition of Treaty Conservative and Labour. Churchill had, finally, led his followers out of the Commons after a speech denouncing a "rigged election to return a gangster Parliament." So people whispered around the Whitehall corridors, although the newspapers and television reported that they had stormed out in a fit of pique. Shortly after, the United Democrats had been accused of fomenting political strikes and declared illegal. They went underground and a new name, "Resistance" after the French movement, began to appear on walls.

The new government swiftly moved even closer to Germany. German Jewish refugees had been returned under the Berlin Treaty in 1940 but despite growing anti-Semitism, restrictions on British Jews had been limited. Now the government claimed the Jews were implacable enemies of Britain's great ally, and elements of the German Nuremberg laws were to be brought in. David would wake sweating in the night at the thought of what might happen if his secret were found out. Everyone knew that Germany had been lobbying for years to have Britain's Jews, the last free Jews in Europe along with the remaining French ones, deported to the East. Perhaps now it would happen. David knew it was more important than ever to tell nobody, especially not Sarah, about his mother.

In the months that followed, though, David had begun to speak out, to Sarah and trusted friends, about other things: the continuing recession, the growing recruitment of "Biff-boys" from Mosley's Fascists as Special Branch Auxiliary Police to deal with unrest and strikes, the promise by Churchill to set Britain ablaze with "sabotage and resistance." Churchill and his people were denied radio or television time, of course, but there was talk of clandestine gramophone records circulated secretly, where he spoke of never surrendering, of the "dark tyranny that had descended over Europe." Something had snapped inside David after the election; perhaps even before, when Charlie died.

He had talked most of all to his oldest friend, Geoff Drax. Geoff had been with him at Oxford, and joined the Colonial Service at the same time as David joined the Dominions Office. Geoff had served in East Africa for six years, returning to work as a London desk officer in 1948. He had spoken even then of his shock at seeing at firsthand how Britain had turned into a drab, conformist German satellite state.

The years in Africa had changed Geoff. Under the thatch of fair hair his thin, bony face had new lines, and his mouth was pursed and unhappy. He had always had a sardonic sense of humor but now he was bitter, firing out caustic remarks, accompanied by a little barking laugh. He had spoken of an unhappy love affair in Kenya with a married woman. He had told David he hadn't managed to get over it, and envied his friend's settled life with Sarah and Charlie. He didn't like his desk work in the big new Colonial Office building at Church House, and when they met for lunch David thought how Geoff always looked uncomfortable in his black coat and pinstripe trousers, as though he should still be in baggy shorts and a pith helmet.

Geoff lived in Pinner, near David's Kenton home, and they would often meet for a swim and tennis on Saturday mornings. Afterwards they would sit in a corner of the tennis club bar, talking politics—quietly, for few in the club would have sympathized.

One Saturday in the summer of 1950, Geoff had been telling David about events in Kenya. "A hundred and fifty thousand settlers they've got there now," he said with quiet intensity. "It's bloody chaos. Unemployed families from Durham and Sheffield brought over with promises of free farms and unlimited native labor. They give them a three-month course in farming, then hand them a thousand acres of bush. They wouldn't have a clue if it weren't for the blacks. But it's the blacks' land. There's real trouble starting among the Kikuyu. Blood's going to get spilt. Some of these builders of this proposed new East African Dominion are going to wish they'd never left home." He gave one of his angry barks of laughter.

David hesitated, then spoke quietly. "Some of the Dominion governments are getting very concerned about what our new government's doing. The Canadians and New Zealanders are talking about leaving the Empire. They're very worried in the Office." David was being indiscreet, to a degree he would not have been even a year before. He went on to talk about protests from New Zealand about the latest British trade union bans. When David finished Geoff sat looking at him in silence, then whispered, "There's a friend of mine you might like to meet."

David felt a stab of anxiety as he realized he had been saying too much. "I think you'd find views in common," Geoff continued. "In fact I'm sure you would."

David looked back at him. Immediately he wondered if Geoff meant someone in the Resistance. With Geoff's angry restlessness, he recognized he might. "I don't know," he said. He thought of Sarah, at home, grieving for their dead son.

Geoff gave a tight little smile, waved an arm. "I'm not talking about committing to anything. Just talking to someone who—sees things the way we do. It helps to realize you're not alone."

Part of David wanted to say no, change the subject to sport or the weather, end the conversation. But then an angry impatience came over him, chasing away the fear.

Geoff introduced him to Jackson a week later. It was high summer, the sun hot in a cloudless sky. David met Geoff at Hampstead Heath Station and they walked to the top of Parliament Hill. Courting couples strolled along hand in hand, the women in bright, white-skirted summer dresses, the men in open-necked shirts and light jackets. There were families too; children were flying kites, bright colors against the blue sky.

David had been expecting Geoff's friend to be someone their age, but the man sitting on a bench was in his fifties, with iron-gray hair. He got up at their approach; he was tall and bulky but moved quickly. Geoff introduced him as Mr. Jackson and he shook David's hand with a firm grip. He had big, solid features and keen light-blue eyes. He gave David a broad smile.

"Mr. Fitzgerald." He spoke in a voice that Sarah's mother would have called la-di-da. "Delighted to meet you." His manner had the easy public-school confidence, what they called effortless superiority, that always made David, the grammar-school boy, feel slightly defensive.

"Let's take a turn," Jackson said cheerfully.

They walked toward Highgate Ponds. A group of teenage boys in Scout uniform were putting on a gymnastic display; three stood in a row, two more balanced on their shoulders, a sixth climbing slowly to form the pinnacle. Several people were watching. A scoutmaster gave instructions in a quiet voice. "Slowly now, distribute your weight carefully, that's the key."

Jackson stopped to watch. "Goodness me," he said quietly. "I remember when Scouts used to help old ladies across the road. It's all gymnastics and military exercises now. Of course they're afraid of a forced merger with the League of Fascist Youth."

"People wouldn't stand for that," David said. "They'd take their sons out."

Jackson laughed softly. "Who knows what some people will stand for, these days?" He turned away, striking out across the heath, Geoff and David following. Jackson, slowing down, spoke quietly to David. "Geoff tells me you're unhappy with the way the poor old country's going."

"Yes, I am." David hesitated, then thought, *to hell with it*. "They've got away with rigging the election. More and more people are getting arrested under Section 18a. And with Mosley as Home Secretary—the anti-Jew laws—we'll be as Fascist as the rest of Europe soon." He felt himself redden when he spoke of the anti-Jew laws, and glanced quickly at Jackson, but the older man didn't seem to have noticed. He just nodded, considered for a moment, and then said, "Felt like this for long?"

"I suppose I have. I know this has been building up for years. It's all caught up with me since the election."

Jackson looked reflective. "You lost a child recently, I believe. An accident."

David hadn't expected Geoff to tell him about Charlie. He answered "Yes," stiffly, giving Geoff a frown.

"I'm sorry to hear it."

"Thank you."

Jackson cleared his throat. "You served in the war, Geoff said."

"Yes, in Norway."

Jackson smiled sadly. "The Norway campaign finished Chamberlain. Some say if Churchill had got the premiership at that time, we'd have carried on the war after France fell. I wonder what would have happened then?"

They were walking briskly now; despite his size Jackson did not seem to be out of breath. David said, "Norway was a mess. I'd seen men die, the Germans seemed—invincible. After France fell I thought we had to make peace, I thought the Treaty was the only alternative to conquest."

"And Hitler promised to leave the Empire alone; many thought that generous. But Churchill said the Treaty would still lead to German dominion and he was right." He smiled at David then, a pleasant social smile although his eyes remained sharp. David knew that in a very English way he was being probed, tested. There was something about Jackson that made him guess this man was a civil servant like him, but very senior. He wondered where he was leading. Jackson smiled encouragingly. David took a breath and then dived right in, just as he had from the diving board as a boy.

"My wife's a pacifist," he said. "I used to agree with her. She still maintains that at least we stopped the war. Though she knows Britain's supporting what's going on in Russia. Endless bloody murder."

Jackson stopped and looked out over Highgate Ponds. In the same quiet voice he said, "The Germans can never win in Russia. They've been fighting for eleven years to realize their goal: a state of German settlement stretching from Archangel to Astrakhan, some capitalist semi-colonial Russian state beyond that in the Urals and Siberia. But they've never managed it. Every summer they edge a bit further east, they breach parts of the Volga line, every winter the Russians push them back with these new Kalashnikov rifles they're making beyond the Urals—millions of them, light and effective. And behind the lines, the partisans hold half the countryside. In some places the Germans just control the towns and the railway lines. Do you know what happened after they captured Leningrad ten years ago?"

"No one knows that, do they? All we hear is that the Germans keep slowly advancing."

"Well, they're not. As for Leningrad, the Germans didn't go in, they just surrounded the city and left the population to starve. Over three million people. There's been complete radio silence from Leningrad since 1942. Nothing, not a cheep. When they took Moscow they turned the population out, put them in camps, and left them to starve. Same with the European Jews. They're all supposed to have gone to labor camps, somewhere in the East. We've seen the newsreels, nice wooden huts with flowers in the window and lawns outside. But no English Jew has ever heard a word from friends or relatives who went there: not a letter, not a postcard. Nothing."

David stared at Jackson. *Does he know about me?* he thought. But nobody knew his secret, apart from his father. It was just that with the new laws people were talking about the Jews more. He said, "There were what, six million people, seven, sent to the labor camps?"

Jackson nodded gravely. "Yes. There's only ours and some of the French Jews left now. It's been a matter of national pride and independence not to let them go, despite German pressure. But Mosley wants them out and he counts more every month." He sighed. "Where are we going, do you think, Fitzgerald?"

"I think we're going to hell in a handcart."

A young couple walked by, the woman wearing white-framed sunglasses, a pink frock patterned with flowers. Between them they held the hands of a little girl, swinging her up in the air; she shrieked with delight. A collie dog ran around them, wagging its tail. Jackson smiled and the woman smiled back. The little family walked on, toward the water. When they were out of earshot Geoff said, "It's getting worse in India, too. Has been ever since Gandhi died in prison in '47. It doesn't matter how many leaders they lock up along with Nehru. It just goes on: the rent strikes, the boycott of British goods, strikes in the industries exporting to Britain. These mutinies of Indian regiments against their officers — that really could bring the whole thing tumbling down. And the irony is that the Berlin Treaty limited our trade with the continent — look at the duties we have to pay on imports and exports, just so Hitler can use Europe as a captive market for his own industries. But that's how Beaverbrook's people wanted it." Geoff paused. "Imperial free trade and tariffs on trade with everyone else. His lifelong dream."

"Well, now he's got it." Geoff gave one of his humorless barking laughs. "And we've had a Depression that's gone on over twenty years."

"I've heard around the office," David spoke hesitantly, "that Enoch Powell wants to recruit a couple of new English divisions to send to India. But that would push our army above the Treaty limit."

Jackson said, "Did you know, Hitler once offered to lend us a couple of SS divisions to sort out India." *How much does this man know?* David thought. *Who is he?*

Jackson looked at him. "You're in the Dominions Office, Geoff tells me."

"Yes." *This is going too fast.* He'd already said too much to Geoff.

"Principal in the Political Division, main job servicing the minister's weekly meetings with the Dominion High Commissioners." Jackson's tone had changed again, become brisk, businesslike.

"Yes." The weekly meetings between the minister and the High Commissioners for the Dominions—Canada, Australia, New Zealand, South Africa, and, since last year, Rhodesia—were organized and minuted by David's superior, with David doing much of the legwork.

"Present at most of the meetings?"

David didn't answer. There was a little silence, then Jackson continued, his tone conversational again. "You've been overseas, I believe, to New Zealand?"

"Yes. I was posted there from '44 to '46. My father has family in Auckland. He's gone to live with them, in fact. He thought we were going to hell in a handcart, too."

"And your mother?"

"She died when I was at school."

"You have Irish blood, from your name."

"My father's from a line of Dublin solicitors. He brought my mother and me over when I was three, during the Independence War."

Jackson smiled. "You have an Irish look, if you don't mind me saying."

"A lot of people think that."

"Any loyalties to Ireland?"

David shook his head. "To De Valera's republic? No. My father hated all that stern Catholic nationalism."

"Did you think of staying out in Kiwiland with your father?"

"Yes. But we decided to come back. This is still our country." And there had been no anti-Jew laws then; repression was still mild.

Jackson looked down across London, spread out under the blue sky. "Britain's become a dangerous place. If you step out of line, that is. But," he said quietly, "opposition's growing."

David looked at Geoff. His friend's nose was reddening in the sun. He wondered how, with his fair skin, Geoff had coped in Africa all that time. "Yes," David agreed, "it is."

"Fast."

David said, "A lot of people are being killed on both sides. Strikers. Soldiers. Policemen. It's getting worse."

"Churchill said we had to 'set Britain ablaze' after the last election was rigged."

"Is he still alive?" David asked. "I know there used be to be illicit recordings circulating of him urging us to resist, but nobody's heard of those for a while. He's getting on for eighty now. His wife Clementine's gone, they found her dead from pneumonia in that stately home in Lancashire last year. Life on the run, for old people like that?" He shook his head. "His son Randolph's a collaborator, been on TV supporting the government. And if Churchill's dead, who's in power in the Resistance now? The Communists?"

Jackson gave David a long, appraising look. "Churchill is alive," he said, quietly. "And the Resistance goes a great deal wider than the Communist Party." He gave a slow nod, then looked at his watch and said, suddenly, "Well, shall we walk back toward the station? My wife's expecting me home. One of her family get-togethers." And David realized that wherever Jackson was thinking of leading him, he wasn't going to go there just yet.

On the walk back to the station Jackson talked genially about cricket and rugger; he had been in the school XV at Eton. When they parted he shook David's hand, bestowed a rubicund smile, and walked away. In a rare gesture, Geoff squeezed David's arm. "He liked you," he said quietly.

"What's this about, Geoff? Why did you tell him so much about me?"

"I thought you might be interested in joining us."

"To do what?"

"Perhaps in time—help us." Geoff smiled his quick, anxious smile. "But it's up to you, David. The decision would have to come from you."

From the kitchen, David could hear Sarah doing the washing up, banging plates angrily on the draining board. He turned away from the staircase. Right from the beginning, from that first meeting with Jackson on Hampstead Heath, her safety had been his biggest worry. A wife, his handlers had told him later, could be told what her husband was doing only if she were totally committed as well. And although Sarah detested the government, her pacifism meant she couldn't support the Resistance, not after the bombings and shooting of policemen started. And ever since then David had felt resentment toward her, blamed her for the intolerable burden of yet another secret.

CHAPTER THREE

The following Sunday Sarah went into town to meet Irene and go to the pictures. They had spoken on the telephone during the week, and discussed what had happened on Remembrance Sunday. There had still been nothing about it on the news; it was as though the attack on Rommel and the arrests had never happened.

They went to the Gaumont in Leicester Square to see the new Marilyn Monroe comedy from America. Before the big feature the B film was the usual frothy German musical, and between the films they had to sit through one of the government-commissioned Pathé newsreels. The lights always came up then, to discourage Resistance supporters from booing if any Nazi leaders came on. First came a report of a European eugenics conference in Berlin: Marie Stopes talking with German doctors in a pillared hall. The next item was a vision of hell: a snow-covered landscape, an old woman swathed in ragged clothes weeping and shouting in Russian outside the smoking ruins of a hut, a German soldier in helmet and greatcoat trying to comfort her. Bob Danvers-Walker's voice turned stern: "In Russia, the war against communism continues. Soviet terrorists continue to commit fearful atrocities not just against Germans but against their own people. Outside Kazan a cowardly group of so-called partisans, skulking safely in the forests, fire a Katyusha rocket into a village whose inhabitants had dared to sell German soldiers some food." The camera panned outwards, from the ruined hut to the smashed and broken village. "Some Russians have chosen to forget what Germany rescued them from: the secret police and forced labor of Stalin's regime; the millions dumped in Arctic concentration camps." There followed familiar grainy footage of one of the camps discovered by the Germans in 1942, skeletal figures lying in deep snow, barbed wire, and watchtowers. Sarah looked away from the horrible scenes. The news-reader's voice deepened: "Never doubt Europe's eventual victory over this evil Asian doctrine. Germany beat Stalin and it will beat his successors." As a reminder, there followed the famous shots of Stalin after his capture when Moscow was taken in October 1941: a little man with a thick mustache, pockmarked, gray hair disheveled, scowling at the ground while his arms were held by laughing German soldiers. Later he had been hanged publicly in Red Square. Next there was footage of the new, giant German Tiger 4 tanks with their eighteen-foot guns smashing through a birch forest on a hunt for partisans, knocking over young trees like matchsticks while helicopters clattered overhead. Then came the launch of a V3 rocket, the camera following the huge pointed cylinder with its tail of fire as it rose into the sky on its way to the far side of the Urals. Optimistic martial music played. Then the newsreel switched to an item on Beaverbrook opening a shiny new television factory in the Midlands, before the lights finally dimmed again and the main feature opened with a clash of music and a bright wash of Technicolor.

When they came out of the cinema the short winter day was ending; lights were coming on in shops and restaurants, a faint yellow haze at their edges. "It's starting to get foggy," Sarah said. "The forecast said it might."

"We'll be all right on the Tube," Irene replied. "We've time for a coffee." She led the way across the road, pausing for a tram to jingle past. A couple of young men jostled them, wearing long drape jackets and drain-pipe trousers, their hair in high, greased quiffs. A little way off a police-man frowned at them from the open door of a police box.

"Don't they look ridiculous?" Irene said, "Jive Boys," her tone disgusted.

"They're just youngsters trying to look different."

"Those jackets —"

"Zoot suits." Sarah laughed. "They're American."

"What about that fight they had with the Young Fascists in Wandsworth last month?" Irene asked indignantly. "The knives and knuckledusters? People got badly hurt. I don't like boys getting the birch but they deserved it."

Sarah smiled to herself. Irene was always so indignant, so outraged. Yet Sarah knew it was all words; underneath her sister had a warm heart. The news item on the eugenics conference had reminded Sarah of the time, a few months before, when they had left another cinema to find a group of boys tormenting a Mongol child, telling him how he would be sterilized when the new laws came in. It was Irene, supporter of eugenics, who had waded in, shouting at the bullies and pushing them away.

"I don't know where we're going with all this terrorism," Irene said. "Did you hear about that army barracks the Resistance have blown up in Liverpool? That soldier killed?"

"I know. I suppose the Resistance would say they were fighting a war."

"Wars just kill people."

"You can't believe everything you're told about what the Resistance do. Look at how they hid what happened last Sunday."

They headed for a British Corner House, as all the Lyons Corner Houses were now known since the expropriation from their Jewish owners. The tearoom, all mirrors and bright chrome, was crowded with women shoppers, but they found an empty table for two and sat down. As the nippy, neat in white apron and cap, took their order Irene looked around her. "I'll have to start thinking about Christmas shopping soon. I can't decide what to give the boys. Steve's talking about getting them a big Hornby train set, but I know he just wants to play with it himself. Nanny says they want a whole army of toy soldiers."

"How is Nanny?"

"Still got that cough. I don't think the panel doctor she's with is any good, you know what they're like. I've made an appointment with our man. I worry about the children getting it, and you can see the poor girl's in discomfort."

"I'm dreading Christmas," Sarah said with sudden bleakness. "I have since Charlie died."

Irene reached over and put a hand on her sister's, her pretty face contrite. "I'm sorry, dear, I do go on so —"

"I can't expect people never to mention children in front of me."

Irene's blue eyes were full of concern. "I know it's hard. For you and David—"

Sarah took her cigarettes from her bag and offered one to her sister. She said, with sudden anger, "After more than two years you'd think it would get easier."

"No sign of another?" Irene asked.

Sarah shook her head. "No." She blinked away a tear. "I'm sorry David got into that argument with Steve on Sunday. He gets—moody."

"It doesn't matter. We were all upset."

"He said he was sorry afterwards. Not that he really meant it," she added heavily.

"You and David," Irene said hesitantly, "you find it hard to share the grief, don't you?"

"We used to be so close. But David's become—unreachable. When I think—when I think how we were when Charlie was alive." She looked her sister in the face. "I think he's having an affair."

"Oh, my dear," Irene said softly. "Are you sure?"

Sarah shook her head. "No. But I think so."

The nippy came with her silver-plated tray, set out the tea and biscuits. Irene poured and handed Sarah a cup. "Why do you think that?" she asked quietly.

"There's a woman at work he's friendly with. Carol. She's a clerk in the Dominions Office Registry. I've met her a couple of times at functions, she's quite plain but very smart, went to university. She's got a bright personality." Sarah gave a brittle laugh. "Good God, they used to say that about me." She hesitated. "David goes into work at weekends sometimes, he has for over a year. That's where he is today. He claims they're very busy, which I suppose they are, with relations with the Dominions being so tricky. But sometimes he goes out in the evening, too, he tells me he goes to the tennis club to play with his friend Geoff. They have an indoor court now. He says it relaxes him."

"Maybe it does."

"More than being at home with me, I suppose. Damn him," Sarah said, angry again, then shook her head. "No, I don't mean that."

35

Irene hesitated. "What makes you think he's interested in this woman?"

"She's interested in him, I could see that when we met."

Irene smiled. "David's a very good-looking man. But he's never—well—strayed before, has he? Not like Steve."

Sarah blew out a cloud of smoke. "You told me last time that you threatened to leave him, take the boys with you."

"Yes. I think that's stopped him, you know how he loves the boys. Me too, in his way. Sarah, you're not thinking of leaving David?"

She shook her head. "No. I love him more than ever. Pathetic, isn't it?"

"Of course not. But, dear, it doesn't sound like you've any real reason to suspect anything." She looked at her sister sharply. "Or have you? It was strange perfume on his collar that gave Steve away last time."

"A few weeks ago, when the weather was getting colder, David asked me to take his winter coat to the cleaners. I emptied out the pockets, like I usually do—he leaves handkerchiefs in there sometimes. I found a used ticket, for one of those lunchtime concerts they give in churches around Whitehall. There was a name on the back—her name, Carol Bennett. She must have reserved them."

"Maybe a whole group of them went. Did you ask him about it?"

"No." Sarah shook her head. "I'm a coward," she added quietly.

"You've never been a coward," Irene answered emphatically. "Was it a Saturday concert?"

"No. It was during the week." Sarah took a deep breath. "Then last Thursday evening, when David was supposed to be playing tennis, I rang the club to speak to him, just to check if he was there. Spying on him, I suppose. Well, he wasn't."

"Oh, darling," Irene said. "What are you going to do? Confront him?"

"Perhaps I should, but you see..." Sarah picked at the uneaten biscuit on her plate. "I'm frightened that if I'm right it could be the end of us. And if I'm wrong, confronting him could drive us further apart than ever. So you see, I *am* a coward." She frowned. "But there's only so much I'll take. It goes around and around in my head, being stuck alone in that bloody house all day."

"Have you thought any more about going back to teaching?"

"They won't take married women." Sarah sighed. "Well, at least I've got my charity work. The Christmas toys for children of the unemployed committee starts meeting next week. That'll get me out of the house. But it won't stop me worrying."

"Darling, you can't just let suspicion eat away at you. Believe me, that's what it does."

"I'm keeping track of him. I will say something, but I have to be sure." She looked at her sister in appeal. "I could be risking everything."

It was dark when they left the Corner House, a slight fog in the air. Wet tram rails glittered in the streetlights. They embraced and parted. Sarah walked to the Tube station; if the trains were running normally she should have dinner cooked by the time David came home at seven thirty. The streets were getting crowded, everyone wrapped up in coats, men in bowlers and caps and Homburgs, women in headscarves or the large saucer-shaped hats with feathers that were fashionable this year. Outside the entrance to Leicester Square Tube station some workmen were scrubbing at a whitewashed letter "V," one of the Resistance symbols. V for victory. Someone must have painted it there secretly during the night.

When Sarah arrived home the house was cold. She stood in the little hall, with its coat stand and the big table where the telephone sat, next to a large, colorful Regency vase that had belonged to David's mother. They had had to lock it away for safety when Charlie started toddling.

When she was growing up between the wars Sarah had thought of herself as an independent woman, a teacher. Before she met David she had begun to worry, at twenty-three, whether she might turn into a spinster, not because men didn't find her attractive, but because she found so many of them dull. She had wondered, during the 1939–40 war, whether women would become more independent, with their husbands away, but everything had gone back to normal afterwards, and government policy now was for wives to stay at home, keep what jobs there were for the men.

Irene was the beauty in the family but Sarah was pretty too, with blue eyes and a straight little nose, and her square chin gave her face a strong look. She had never been in love before she met David at the tennis-club dance in 1942. He had swept her off her feet, as they said in the romantic novels. A year later she was married and then she had gone with him on his two-year posting to New Zealand. When she returned she found she was pregnant with Charlie. She missed her work sometimes but she loved their baby, already looked forward to others following on.

Charlie was a bright, excitable, cheerful boy, quick to walk and learn. He had Sarah's blond hair and her features, but occasionally his expression would turn serious and solemn, in a way that reminded her of a look she caught on her husband's face sometimes; though with his son David was playful, childlike in a way that clutched at her heart. He would come home as early as possible from work and they would hold hands watching Charlie play on the floor beside them.

The stairs in the house were quite steep, and they had put child gates at the top and bottom, though they made the active little boy howl, resenting the restriction on his freedom. One day when he was nearly three Sarah had gone into the bedroom to put on some makeup before going to the shops. She had taken Charlie upstairs with her, closing the latch on the gate behind them. Outside it had been snowing—the tree in their little front garden and the privet hedge were thickly dusted with white—and Charlie was desperate to get out in it. He had gone out into the upstairs hall and called back, "Mummy, Mummy, want to see the snow!"

"In a minute. Be patient, sweetheart!"

Then there came a series of little bumps and tiny cries and a thud, followed by a silence so sudden and complete she could hear the blood thumping in her ears. She had sat rigid for a second, then called, "Charlie!" and ran into the hall. The gate at the top was still closed, but when she looked down Charlie was lying at the bottom of the stairs, limbs spread-eagled. She and David had said only a couple of days before that he was getting big and they would have to watch he didn't climb over.

Sarah ran downstairs, hoping against hope, but before she reached the bottom she could see from the complete stillness of Charlie's eyes and the angle of his head that he was dead, his neck broken. She lifted his little body and held it. It was still warm and she carried on hugging it, with a wild, mad feeling that if she held him to her own warm body, so long as he did not grow cold, somehow he might come back to life. Later, after she had at last telephoned 999, after David had been sent home from the office, she had told him why she had held him for so long, and David had understood.

Sarah shook herself, took off her coat, and switched on the central heating. She lit the coal fire, then went into the kitchen and turned on the radio, cheerful dance music on the Light Program breaking the silence. She began to prepare dinner. Despite what she had said to Irene, she knew she couldn't face it, she couldn't confront David yet.

CHAPTER FOUR

D avid had also traveled into London that Sunday afternoon, the key and the camera taken out of their locked drawer and slipped into his inside jacket pocket next to his ID card. Two years as a spy had strengthened him, hardened him, even though, tangled in all the lies, part of him felt totally at sea.

There were not many others traveling, a few shift workers and people going in to meet friends. David wore a sports jacket and flannel trousers under his coat; if staff came in to work at the Office at the weekend they were allowed to dress informally.

Opposite him a woman sat reading *The Times*. It had been bought by Beaverbrook to add to his newspaper empire just before he took the premiership; he owned almost half the country's newspapers now, and Lord Rothermere's *Daily Mail* stable had swallowed up a large chunk of the rest. "*What Now for America?*" a headline asked, above a picture of the newly elected Adlai Stevenson, his face serious and scholarly. "*For twelve years, America has minded its own business under Republican presidents. Will Stevenson, like Roosevelt, be tempted to naive interference in European affairs?*" They'll be worried, David thought with satisfaction. Nothing was going right for them now. Another article speculated that the Queen's Coronation next year might be in some way combined with celebrations of the twentieth anniversary of Herr Hitler's accession to power in Germany, where huge celebrations were planned, greater even than the Italian festivities earlier in the year to mark Mussolini's thirty years in power.

He arrived at Westminster and turned into Whitehall. It was a raw, chilly afternoon. The few people about walked along in their drab clothes, huddled into themselves. David had watched for over ten years, people growing slowly shabbier, looking more alone. A poster from last year's Festival of Empire at Greenwich hung, soot-smeared, on a hoarding; a young couple helping a child feed a calf against a background of hills. "*A Prosperous New Life in Africa.*"

The Dominions Office was on the corner of Downing Street. David could see the policeman standing outside Number 10. Nearby the pile of wreaths at the foot of the Cenotaph was looking sad and tatty now. He walked up the office steps. There was a frieze above the doors showing a panorama of Empire: Africans with spears, turbaned Indians, and Victorian statesmen all jumbled together, black with London grime. Inside, the wide vestibule was empty. Sykes, the porter, nodded to him. He was elderly, but sharp-eyed.

"Afternoon, Mr. Fitzgerald. Working Sunday again, sir?"

"Yes. Duty calls, I'm afraid. Anyone else in?"

"The Permanent Secretary, up on the top floor. Nobody else. People sometimes come in to work on Saturday, but seldom on Sundays." He smiled at David. "I remember, sir, when I started here. Assistant Secretaries often didn't come in till eleven. Nobody here at weekends except the Resident clerks." He shook his head.

"The trials of Empire," David said, returning the smile. He signed the day book. Sykes reached back to the row of numbered keys on the board behind him, and handed David the one to his office, on its metal tag. David walked to the lift. It was ancient and sometimes marooned people between floors. He wondered if one day the hundred-year-old cables might break, sending everyone inside to perdition. Creaking, it rose slowly to the second floor. He pulled aside the heavy gates and got out. In front of him was the Registry, where during the week clerks endlessly checked files in and out from behind a long counter, the clacking of typewriters audible beyond the door of the typing pool. At the far end of the counter Carol's desk stood empty, in front of a door with its smoked glass panels marked *Authorized Personnel Only*. David looked at it for a second, then turned and walked down the long narrow passage. It was strange how footsteps echoed in here when you were alone.

His office was half of a big Victorian room, an elegant cornice cut off by a partition. He saw, in the center of his desk, the fat High Commissioners' Meetings file, the draft agenda he had prepared for Hubbold pinned to the front with a note in his superior's tiny scrawl. *We spoke. Let us discuss further, on Monday.*

David took off his coat, then retrieved the tiny silver camera from his pocket. It was, ironically, German, a Leica; not much bigger than a Swan Vestas matchbox, you could photograph dozens of documents just by the light of a lamp. The camera had seemed an extraordinary thing when he was first given it, like something out of a science-fiction story, but he was used to it now. He lit a cigarette to steady himself.

After that first meeting on Hampstead Heath, the next time David saw Geoff at the tennis club he had asked, "That man Jackson, he's in the Civil Service, isn't he?"

A spasm had crossed Geoff's face, annoyance and guilt mixed together. "I can't answer that, old boy; you have to realize, I can't."

"Jackson knew a lot about me. Is he interested in me for some particular reason?"

"I can't tell you. You have to decide first whether you're willing to support us."

"I do support you. You mean, am I willing to *do* things for you?"

"*With* us. Things are hotting up, now we're illegal." Geoff gave his quick sardonic smile. "You may have noticed."

David had heard the radio broadcasts saying the British Resistance was a treasonous organization, the public under a duty to report its activities. He had seen the new posters, a picture of Churchill when he was a minister during the 1939–40 war, dressed in a dark suit and Homburg and holding a machine gun, the caption underneath, *"Wanted Dead or Alive."* He moved closer to Geoff and asked quietly, "The news reports about illegal strikers carrying guns, about that armored police car being blown up in Glasgow, are they true?"

"They rigged the election," Geoff said heavily. "And they declared war on us. You know what war is."

"I've never been a pacifist like Sarah." David shook his head. "But if I worked with you I'd be putting everything on the line. My whole life. My wife's life."

"Not if she didn't know." There was a long silence. "It's all right, David," Geoff said. "You've got responsibilities, I know."

"I hate it all," he said quietly.

Geoff looked at him. "Would you like to see Jackson again?"

David took a long, long breath. "Yes," he said finally.

It was several meetings later, toward the end of 1950, that Jackson told David he wanted him to be the Resistance spy in the Dominions Office. The two of them were in a private room in an exclusive Westminster club.

"We need information, intelligence on what the government's thinking and doing. Not just in home policy, but foreign and Imperial policy, too. After all, the core agreement of the 1940 Treaty was that Hitler took Europe and we kept the Empire. And developed it, too, to an extent we hadn't bothered about before, to make up for the loss of markets in Europe." He smiled sadly. "The retreat into Empire. The old dream of the political right, Beaverbrook's dream."

"But we've made the Empire hate us."

"Yes, we have, haven't we?" That sad smile again. Then Jackson gave David one of his long, slow looks. "The Resistance have people in the India Office and the Colonial Office. There have been three famines in Bengal since 1942, for example, that we've never been told about. We need someone who can tell us how it's going with the Dominions. The White Empire. We know Canada and Australia and New Zealand aren't happy with political developments here, though the South Africans don't mind. We want to know how the big African settlement programs are going, the plans for the new East African and Rhodesian Dominions. You could supply us with that information, papers too. You'd meet periodically with me, our man from the India Office, and our Colonial Office fellow."

"Geoff's the Colonial Office man, isn't he?" David said. *And you're from the Foreign Office,* he thought. Jackson didn't answer.

"I'm too junior to be allowed to take papers from the office."

Jackson nodded his big gray head and smiled in that way he had, half confidential, half condescending. "There are ways."

"What ways?" David asked. Looking back, he realized that was the moment when he had made the final, irrevocable commitment.

Jackson said, "So you're joining us?"

David hesitated, then nodded. "Yes."

Jackson smiled, a smile of real warmth. "Thank you," he said. He shook David's hand firmly.

And so, bit by bit, David learned how the Resistance had people everywhere, in factories, offices, the countryside, organizing protests and poster campaigns, strikes and demonstrations. There were even small areas, mining villages and remote country districts, where they were in charge, where the police dared not venture except in force. Passive resistance was over; the police and army and their buildings were all legitimate targets. They had links with other Resistance groups throughout the continent. And they had spies everywhere, "sleepers" working in institutions all over the country, awaiting the call.

Shortly after, when they met in the club again, Jackson said, "Time to introduce you to the Soho flat."

"Why Soho?"

"Soho's a good place to meet, full of all sorts." He smiled. "If we bump into someone from the Service in the streets, he'll think we're on the same business as he is, and he's hardly going to talk about it, now is he?"

David visited the flat for the first time the following week, one evening after work. It felt strange, getting off the Tube at Piccadilly Circus and walking into Soho. The address he had been given was in a narrow alley, a door with peeling paint beside an Italian coffee shop. Inside two Jive Boys stood beside a jukebox, which was belting out some of the horrible new American rock 'n' roll. The papers said the jukebox craze would kill live music, that they should be banned. He knocked. He heard footsteps descending stairs and the door opened. A dark-haired woman stood there; even in the dim light from within David saw she was attractive.

She wore a shapeless smock covered in splashes of paint. She gave him a direct look from green, slightly Oriental eyes, and said, "Come up," brusquely. She had a slight accent that he couldn't place.

He followed her up a narrow staircase, smelling of damp and old vegetables, into a studio flat, a big single room with pictures stacked against the wall and on easels, a narrow bed and tiny kitchen at one end. The pictures were oils, well done. Some were urban scenery, narrow streets and baroque churches, others snow-covered landscapes with mountains in the distance. In one, figures were lying on the snow, covered with red splashes; blood, David realized. At once he was reminded of Norway, German planes strafing the column of British soldiers stumbling terrified through the snow.

Geoff and Jackson were sitting on either side of an electric fire. Geoff smiled awkwardly. The woman spoke first. "Welcome, Mr. Fitzgerald. I am Natalia." Her smile was pleasant but somehow closed. In the light she looked a little older than he had thought, in her mid-thirties perhaps, tiny crow's feet beside those eyes, slightly narrowed and upturned at the corners. She had long, straight brown hair and a wide mouth above a pointed chin.

"This is where we will meet, our little Imperial group." Jackson looked at Natalia with a respect that surprised David. "Natalia is to be trusted absolutely," he said. "When I'm not here, she is in charge. We meet together, and never with anyone else, apart from our Indian Office man."

"I understand."

"So." Jackson put his hands on his knees. "Tea, everyone? Natalia, would you mind doing the honors?"

The first thing they discussed, that night at the end of 1950, was how David could gain access to the room in which the confidential department files were kept. David could think of no way to get in there, as the only people with keys were the Registrar, Dabb, and the woman in charge of the secret files room, Miss Bennett, and both had to hand their keys in to the porter whenever they left the building.

"We don't need the key," Jackson said briskly, "just the number on the tag. You know there's a number stamped on all of them, four digits, so that if a key gets lost they can match the numbering with their records at the Department of Works."

"All Civil Service filing cabinets, and the keys, are made by Works Department locksmiths," Geoff explained. "When the '48 rules came in forbidding Jews from working in the Civil Service all Jewish employees had to leave. For security reasons."

"Yes." David remembered lying awake at night beside his sleeping wife as Parliament passed yet another anti-Jew law, fists clenched, eyes wide.

Jackson said, "One of the locksmiths was an old Jew who was kicked out then. He's come over to us, and brought the specifications for all the keys with him. All you need is the number on the key to the secret room and he can make a copy." He smiled. "These stupid Jew laws actually help us sometimes."

"But how do I get it?" David asked.

Jackson exchanged a look with Geoff. "Tell me about Miss Bennett."

"She's one of the 1939–40 intake, when they allowed women into the administrative grades because of the war."

Jackson nodded. "I often think those women who stayed after the Treaty must feel very out of place. Unmarried, of course, or they would've had to leave. What's Miss Bennett like?"

David hesitated. "A nice woman. Bored, I think, wasted in that job." He thought of Carol, her desk behind the counter with the buff files with red crosses marked "Top Secret," a cigarette usually burning in her ashtray.

"Attractive?" Jackson asked him.

David could suddenly see where this might be going, and felt something sink in his chest. "Not really." Carol was tall and thin, with large brown eyes and dark hair, a long nose and chin. She always dressed well, always with a touch of color, a brooch or a bright scarf, in tiny defiance of the convention that women in the Service should dress conservatively. But he had never been remotely attracted to her.

"Interests? Hobbies? Boyfriend? What sort of life does she have outside the office?"

"I've only spoken to her a few times. I think she likes concerts. She's got a nickname, like a lot of the junior staff." He hesitated. "They call her the bluestocking."

"So, possibly lonely." Jackson smiled encouragingly. "How about if you became friendly with her, took her out to lunch a couple of times, say. She might be flattered by the attention from a handsome educated fellow like yourself. You might be able to contrive a way of seeing the key."

"Are you suggesting I . . ." He looked around the small group. Natalia was smiling at him a little sadly.

"Seduce the girl?" she said. "Ideally no. That could lead to gossip and even trouble, given you're married."

Jackson looked at him. "But you could make friends with her, lead her along a little."

David was silent. Natalia said, "We all must do things we do not like now."

And so David made friends with Carol, going toward her end of the long counter if he had papers to book out or return, taking the opportunity to chat. It had been easy. Carol wasn't popular in the dusty, conservative atmosphere of the Registry and was pleased to have someone to talk to. He remarked casually that he had heard she had been to Oxford, like him. She told him she had read English at Somerville, that her real love was music but she had been hopeless at any instrument she tried. He learned how lonely she was, with only a couple of women friends and her elderly, difficult mother, whom she looked after.

They had told him to take his time, but it was Carol who, a month later, diffidently took the initiative. She said that sometimes she went to lunchtime concerts at local churches and wondered if he might like to come to one. He had pretended an interest in music and he could see the hesitant hope in her eyes.

And so they went to a recital. Snatching a quick lunch in a British Corner House afterwards Carol asked, "Doesn't your wife like music?"

"Sarah doesn't like going out much just now." David hesitated. "We lost a little boy, at the start of the year. An accident in the house."

"Oh, no." She looked genuinely distressed. "I'm so sorry."

David couldn't answer; he felt suddenly choked. Tentatively, Carol put out a hand to touch David's. He withdrew it sharply, and she reddened a little. "Sorry," he said.

"I understand."

"It helps to get away from things at lunchtime, do something different."

"Yes. Yes, of course."

There were more recitals, more quick lunches, after that. She told him of her problems with her mother. And sitting together at the concerts, she would try to make sure their bodies touched. He hated what he might be doing to her. But his commitment to the Resistance was hardening and so, slowly, was he. He learned, in Soho, more of the truth behind the propaganda in the press and on the BBC; the strikes and riots in Scotland and the North of England, the chaos in India, the endless savagery of the German war in Russia. He saw the increasing confidence of the Blackshirts on the streets as the Jews, marked by their yellow badges, shuffled along, eyes on the ground.

It was January before he managed to see the key. Watching her, David had seen that at work Carol kept it in her handbag, always giving it to the porter before they went out. At their last concert David had noticed she seemed a little distracted. She told him over lunch that her mother was being especially difficult, and had accused her daughter of taking money from her purse, which was absurd because it was Carol's salary that kept them both. She feared the old lady might be going senile.

He worked out how he might do it. The following week he suggested another concert, in Smith Square. Carol agreed enthusiastically. He said he would get the tickets on his way home. On the day of the recital, bringing a file into Registry, he went over to her desk. She was splitting one of the secret files into two, carefully moving documents from one folder to another. As usual, David was careful to avoid glancing at them; she was well trained and whatever Carol felt about him she would have noticed that. "Looking forward to the concert?" he asked.

He saw that sparkle in her eyes. "Yes. It should be good."

"What seats are we in?"

She gave him a puzzled smile. "You've got the tickets."

"No, no. I gave them to you."

She stared at him. "When?"

"Yesterday. I'm sure I did."

She closed the files carefully, picked up her handbag, and, as he had hoped, opened it on the desk. She took out her purse, then bent her head to look through the compartments. The bag lay open. David looked around quickly but no one was watching them; their friendship was stale gossip now and Dabb, the Registrar, was busy checking a file. David bent over a little, enough to see into the bag. There was a powder-puff, a packet of cigarettes, and the key on its metal tab. Squinting, he made out the numbers stamped onto it: 2342. He stepped away just as Carol looked up from her purse.

"They're jolly well not here." There was anxiety in her voice.

David took out his wallet, checking. With an expression of surprise, he pulled out the tickets. "I'm terribly sorry. They were here all along. I am sorry, Carol."

She sighed with relief. "For a moment I was frightened I was going potty, with all this worry over Mother."

Walking back to his own office David had to stop at the gents. He went into a cubicle and was violently sick. He crouched, breathing heavily; the vomiting relieved the almost unbearable tension he had felt since getting the number, but did nothing to assuage his shame.

And so he began to come in at weekends and photograph papers from the secret files. At least once a month he met in Soho with Jackson, Geoff—who was indeed the Resistance agent in the Colonial Office—and Boardman, a tall, thin man from the India Office, an old Etonian like Jackson. The quiet discussions in the squalid Soho flat went on for hours, while next door a prostitute—another Resistance supporter—plied her trade, cries and bumps occasionally audible through the wall.

David learned more and more about the fragility of Fascist Europe. The Depression and the demands on her economies to feed the gigantic,

endless German war effort in Russia were sucking the continental countries dry, while labor conscription to Germany was sending young men
in France and Italy and Spain literally running to the hills. On the other
side of the world Japan was as deadlocked in its war with China as Germany was in Russia. Its strategy toward the Chinese was the same as the
Germans' toward the Russians, summed up in their policy of the "three
alls": kill all, burn all, destroy all. Recently Jackson—who David knew
now was in the Foreign Office—had told them the rumors that Germany was in political trouble were true. The reason Hitler never
appeared in public was that he was seriously incapacitated by Parkinson's
disease, barely lucid enough to take decisions, hallucinating about Jews
with skullcaps and sidelocks grinning at him from the corner of the
room; hallucinations were sometimes a symptom of the latest and sever-
est stage of the disease. Following Göring's death from a stroke the year
before Goebbels was his nominated successor but he had many enemies.
Factions representing the army, the Nazi Party, and the SS were all cir-
cling and plotting.

He learned more about the Resistance, too, an alliance of Socialists
and Liberals with old-fashioned Conservatives like Jackson and Geoff,
who loathed Fascist authoritarianism and who had come, sadly, to realize the Imperial mission had failed. Their numbers were growing all the
time, and violence had become necessary to destabilize the police state.

Natalia was always there; listening avidly, always smoking. David didn't
know what her politics were, knew only that she was a refugee from Slovakia, a far corner of Eastern Europe of which he had barely heard. At meetings she said little, though what she said was always to the point. As time
passed he began to see her look at him in the way Carol did, and Sarah
once had. He didn't respond, but something in the way she was both
focused and committed, yet somehow rootless, stirred him unexpectedly.

He stubbed out his cigarette. This Sunday he had to copy some papers
for the next High Commissioners' meeting detailing possible South
African military assistance to Kenya. Then he had to photograph a
secret paper which he had heard of but not seen—about the Canadians

supplying uranium to the United States for their nuclear weapons program. It was known the Germans were working on nuclear weapons, too, but with little success. Apart from anything else they lacked uranium; they were mining it in the former Belgian Congo but had lost a huge consignment which the Belgians had shipped to the United States just before the colony was annexed by Germany in the peace treaty with Belgium in 1940. He also had to find anything he could on New Zealand's threats to leave the Empire. That made him think of his father; he was happy there, kept asking David and Sarah to join him. With a sigh, David put the camera in his pocket, picked up the bulky High Commissioners' file, and went out.

He walked along the corridor, stepping quietly. He could have photographed the High Commissioners' file in his office, but papers were best copied in bright artificial light, and the room where the secret files were kept had an Anglepoise lamp. In the Registry, he opened the flap of the counter and walked over to Carol's desk. There was a pile of stubs in her overflowing ashtray. He went up to the frosted-glass door, took out his duplicate key, and opened it.

The room was quite small, with a table in the center and files on shelves. He knew his way around the filing system intimately now. The Anglepoise lamp with its powerful bulb stood on the desk.

He laid the High Commissioners' file on the table and began taking the buff envelopes, each with a red diagonal cross, out of their places. It took an hour to find the documents he wanted, rapidly scanning them to check their relevance, then extracting them and laying each one neatly on the desk with the papers he needed from the High Commissioners' file. He worked efficiently, calmly, very quietly, always with one ear cocked for sounds from outside. Then he switched on the Anglepoise lamp and carefully photographed the documents, one by one. When he was finished David switched off the light, replaced the camera in his jacket pocket and started returning the secret papers to the files piled on the table, stringing them quickly through the tail-tags.

He was halfway through when he heard a loud voice beyond the door speak his name. He froze, one of the secret papers still in his hand.

"Fitzgerald's not in his office." It was the deep voice of his superior, Archie Hubbold. "I've come down to the Registry, you know my office phone isn't working. I *have* mentioned it." David realized Hubbold was talking to the porter on the Registry telephone, speaking, as he always did to non-administrative staff, as though to a half-witted child. "Are you sure you saw him come in?" He heard a couple of grunts and then, "All right. Good-bye." There were a few dreadful seconds of silence before he heard, faintly, Hubbold's footsteps padding away.

There was a chair by the desk and David sat down. He forced himself to be calm. Hubbold occasionally came in to work at weekends, and the porter must have told him David was in. He must have gone to David's office, then come down to the Registry to telephone.

He had to get back to his room fast; finding him absent, Hubbold would probably have left a note. He would have to tell him he had been in the toilet; Hubbold was too fastidious to look for someone in there. Moving as rapidly as he could, David replaced the remaining papers in the files. He always liked to double-check everything was in order but there wasn't time now. He re-tagged the papers from the High Commissioners' file and then, with a deep breath, unlocked the door, stepped out, and locked it again.

Back in the office, Hubbold had indeed left a note for him. *Heard you were in. Could I have a final look at the HC file please. AH.* David put the file back under his arm and hurried out, walking rapidly up the stairs to Hubbold's office on the floor above.

Archie Hubbold was a short, stocky man with thinning white hair. Thick glasses magnified his eyes, making his expression unreadable. He and David had moved to the Political Division at the same time, three years ago. It had been a sideways move for David, though he was overdue for promotion. But David knew that although he was regarded as reliable and conscientious he was thought to lack the spike of ambition. Hubbold, though, had relished his promotion to Assistant Under-Secretary. He was vain, pompous, and pernickety, but sharp and watchful, too. When policy issues were discussed, like many in the Service he enjoyed paradoxes, playing one view off against another.

David knocked on Hubbold's door. A deep voice called, "Enter," and he forced himself to smile casually as he went in.

Hubbold waved his junior to a chair. "So you're working overtime as well."

"Yes, Mr. Hubbold. Just wanted to check all was well on the agenda. I got your note. Sorry, I was in the gents." David patted the file under his arm. "You wished to see this?"

Hubbold smiled generously. "If you've been checking it over, I'm sure it'll be all right." He reached into his pocket and pulled out a small silver box, tapping two little spots of brown powder onto the back of his hand. Many senior civil servants liked to cultivate some personal eccentricity, and Hubbold's was that he took snuff, like an eighteenth-century gentleman. He sniffed quickly, then sighed with mild pleasure and looked at David. "You mustn't make a habit of weekend work, Fitzgerald. What will your wife think of us, keeping your nose to the grindstone all the time?"

"She doesn't mind now and then." Hubbold had met Sarah at a couple of office social functions. He had been there with his own wife, a brash, tactless woman who had hogged the conversation, to her husband's obvious annoyance.

"Spending time together is *de bene esse* of a good marriage, you know." Hubbold, like so many in the Civil Service, loved peppering his conversation with Latin tags.

"Yes, sir," David answered, an unintended coldness coming into his voice.

Hubbold said, in a more formal tone, "There's a meeting we've been asked to arrange. A bit delicate. Some of the SS officials at the German embassy want to meet with appropriate staff from South Africa House, to look at whether aspects of apartheid might be useful in organizing the Russian population. I wonder if you could arrange that tomorrow. It's just bilateral liaison, low-level at this stage. Keep it quiet, would you?"

David thought he saw a flicker of distaste cross Hubbold's face when he mentioned the SS. But he had no idea where Hubbold stood politically, if anywhere; anybody politically suspect had been weeded out of the Civil Service years ago, along with the Jews. Civil servants had always discussed politics between themselves in a detached, superior way but these days they tended to avoid even the hint of commitment to anything at all unless speaking with friends they trusted.

"I'll speak to the South Africans tomorrow." He left, his hands shaking slightly as he walked down the corridor.

He arrived home just before six. Sarah was sitting knitting in front of the fire. He held out a large bunch of Michaelmas daisies he had bought from a stall on the way home. "Peace offering," he said. "For last Sunday. I was a pig."

She got up and kissed him. "Thanks. Good afternoon's tennis?"

"Not bad. I left my kit to be washed there."

"How's Geoff?"

"All right."

"You look tired."

"Just the exercise. What was the film like?"

"Very good."

"It's getting foggy out." He hesitated. "How was Irene?"

"She's all right." Sarah smiled. "We saw some Jive Boys in Piccadilly, and that got her going a bit."

"I can imagine." The two of us speak so stiffly now, he thought. On an impulse, he said, "Look, why don't we re-wallpaper those stairs?"

Her body seemed to relax with relief. "Oh, David, I wish we could."

He hesitated, then said, "Somehow I've felt—if we did it then we might come to forget him."

She came across and hugged him. "We won't ever forget. You know that. Never."

"Perhaps everything's forgotten, in time."

"No. Even if one day we managed to have another baby, we'd never forget Charlie."

David said, "I wish I believed in God, could believe Charlie still existed, in some afterlife."

"I wish that too."

"But there's only this life, isn't there?"

"Yes," she said. She smiled bravely. "Only one. And we have to do the best we can with it."

CHAPTER FIVE

Frank sat looking through the window at the grounds of the mental hospital, the sodden lawn and empty flowerbeds. It had been raining since early morning, hard and steady. The drug they gave him, the Largactil, made him feel calm and sleepy most of the time. In the Admissions Block he had been on a large dose, but after he was stabilized and had moved to a main ward, they reduced the dose and in his mind now the periods of dull calmness were sometimes broken by violent flashes of memory: the school; Mrs. Baker and her spirit guide; how his hand had become crippled. He suspected he was getting used to the drug, lessening its effect, but he did not want to go back on a larger dose because he needed his mind to be clear enough to keep his secret.

He had come into a little side room off the main ward that Monday morning, the quiet room as it was called, partly because the other patients frightened him, and also to get away from the overwhelming smell of cigarettes. Frank had never smoked. At school he knew he couldn't dare join the other boys smoking behind the boiler room; tobacco had passed him by like so much else. The patients were constantly wheedling the staff for tobacco, a Woodbine or just a dog-end. The hospital ceilings were all brown with it. He sat in an armchair, which, like all the hospital furniture, was huge, old, and heavy. His right hand hurt, as it often did when it rained, pain coursing through the two damaged fingers, shrunken and claw-like.

It had surprised Frank, when he arrived at the hospital three weeks before, that there were no bars on the windows. But as the police car that brought him drove through the gates he had glimpsed beyond the high wall, on the inner side, a broad ditch full of water, screened from view from the hospital by privet hedges. One of the patients on the admissions ward, a middle-aged man with lined, chalk-white features and wild hair, had told him he planned to escape, swim the ditch, and climb the wall. The law said if you escaped from a loony bin and weren't recaptured in fourteen days you were free. Frank looked at the man in a gray wool hospital suit that was even more shapeless than Frank's own. Even if escape were possible, which he doubted, there was nowhere for him to go now. After what had happened at his flat his neighbors would alert the police as soon as they set eyes on him again.

It had been like that at school, nowhere to run. The gates were always open, but he knew if ever he ran away, got off that bleak Scottish hillside and somehow managed to get home to Esher, his mother would simply bring him back. The mental hospital reminded him constantly of the horrors of school—the dormitory with its iron beds, the uniformed inmates who most of the time ignored him. And an all-male world; like all mental hospitals this one was divided into a men's side and women's side, the sexes kept entirely apart. From the looks he sometimes got Frank could tell the patients knew what he had done, perhaps were even afraid of him. The staff, too, reminded him of his teachers, with their sharp military manner and quick brutality if someone got difficult. Frank had tried to avoid thoughts of school for years but now he was constantly reminded; though school had been worse than here.

That afternoon Frank had an appointment with Dr. Wilson, the Medical Superintendent, in his office in the Admissions Building. He didn't want to go, he just wanted to stay in the quiet room. Sometimes other patients came in but he was alone today. He hoped he might be forgotten—patients' appointments were forgotten now and then—but after an hour the door opened and a young man in the peaked cap and brown serge uniform of a senior attendant came in. Frank hadn't seen him before. He was short and stocky, with a thin face and a prominent nose which at some time had been badly broken. His brown eyes were alert. He was carrying a big, rolled-up umbrella. He gave Frank a nod and a friendly smile. Frank was surprised; mostly the attendants treated the patients like recalcitrant children.

"Frank Muncaster?" the attendant asked in a broad Scottish accent. "How're ye daen?" Frank's face spasmed into a wide rictus, showing all his teeth, his chimp grin. Hearing a Scottish accent could unnerve him, because it reminded him of the school. But the attendant's accent was very different from the elongated vowels and rolling "R"s of middle-class Edinburgh that had prevailed at Strangmans; he spoke quickly, the words running together, a more guttural but, to Frank, less threatening accent.

The attendant's eyes widened a little; everyone's did when they saw that grin of Frank's for the first time. He said, "I'm Ben. I've come to take you to Dr. Wilson. They said in the day room you'd be here."

Reluctantly Frank followed Ben out, through the day room, where several patients sat slumped in front of the television. *Children's Hour* was on, a puppet in a striped uniform dancing manically on the end of its strings.

They walked along the echoing corridors to the main door, then out into the rain. Ben raised his umbrella and motioned Frank to stand under it with him. They splashed along the path between the lawns. Ben said, conversationally, "Expect you saw Dr. Wilson on the admissions ward."

"Yes. I saw him last week, too. He said he wants me to have some treatment." Frank looked sidelong at Ben; he had said little to anyone since his admission but this attendant seemed friendly.

"What sort of treatment?"

Frank shrugged. "I don't know."

"He likes new treatments, Dr. Wilson. I suppose some of his ideas aren't bad—this new drug Largactil, it's better than the old phenobarb and the paraldehyde—Jesus, how that stuff used to stink."

"I told him I wanted to leave, go back to work, but he said I wasn't nearly ready. He asked if I'd like to talk about my parents; I don't know why."

"Aye, he does that." Ben's voice was amused, half-contemptuous.

"I said what was the point, my father died before I was born and Mother's dead, too, now. He looked cross with me."

"You were a scientist afore you came here, weren't you?"

"Yes." A touch of pride entered Frank's voice. "I'm a research associate at Birmingham University. Geology department."

"I would have thought you could have afforded the Private Villa then. Ye get yer own room there."

Frank shook his head sadly. "Apparently as I've been certified I've lost the right to control my money. And there's no one to be a trustee."

Ben shook his head sympathetically. "The almoner should sort that out. You should ask Wilson."

They reached the Admissions Block, a square, two-story rectangle, redbrick like all the asylum buildings. In the doorway Ben shook out the umbrella. Frank glanced back at the enormous main building. It stood on a little hill; across the countryside, on a clear day, you could see the haze over Birmingham in the distance. From outside, the asylum, with its many-windowed front and neat grounds, looked like a country house; inside it was quite different, a thousand patients packed into cavernous wards with dilapidated furniture and peeling paint. Two nurses from the women's wing, capes over their starched uniforms, came out of the block. "Good morning, Mr. Hall," one said cheerfully to Ben. "Filthy day."

"Aye, it is."

The nurses raised umbrellas and walked quickly down the drive to the locked gates. Frank watched them go. Ben touched his arm. "Come on, pal, wake up," he said gently.

"I wish I could get out."

"Not after what you did, Frank," Ben said gravely. "Come on, let's get ye inside."

Frank's mind shied away from the event that had led him here. But sometimes, when the effects of the Largactil were wearing off, he would think about it.

It had started with his mother's death, a month before. She was past seventy, a little, bent, querulous old woman living alone in the house in Esher. Frank visited her a couple of times a year, out of duty. His older brother, Edgar, only saw her on his rare visits from California. When

Frank went to see her, Mrs. Muncaster would compare him unfavorably with his brother, as she had all her life. There Edgar was, married with children, a physicist in a great American university, while Frank had been stuck in the same boring job for ten years. She lived for Edgar's letters, she said. Frank didn't think his mother saw anyone apart from him these days, as her involvement with spiritualism had ended five years before when Mrs. Baker, her spiritual guru, had died, and the weekly séances in the dining room had ended.

The police had phoned Frank at work to tell him his mother had had a stroke while out shopping, and died two hours later in hospital. Frank sent a telegram to Edgar, who replied, to Frank's surprise, at once, saying he would come over for the funeral. Frank did not want to see Edgar, he loathed him; but though he didn't like train journeys, he had traveled from Birmingham to Esher to meet Edgar at the house where they had been brought up. On the journey he wondered what his brother would be like. He was an American citizen now. The letters their mother showed him were always full of his busy life at Berkeley, how he loved San Francisco, how his wife and three children were getting on.

But when he'd visited his mother at Easter he had found that Edgar, for the first time in his life, had upset her. He had written to her to say that he and his wife were getting a divorce. Mrs. Muncaster had been shocked, wringing her gnarled hands and telling Frank she hadn't liked Edgar's wife the one time he'd brought her to England: she was brassy and full of herself, a typical American. His mother had cried then, saying she would never see her grandchildren, adding bitterly that Frank was hardly likely to give her any now. Frank wondered if all the shock and distress had led to her stroke.

The crowds on the train frightened him; he was glad to get off at Esher. He walked to the house. It was a cold, misty afternoon. A boy on one of the new Vespa scooters buzzed past him, making him jump. When he entered the house he was aware of an emptiness, a new silence. Mrs. Baker would have said it was because a spirit had gone over. Frank shivered slightly. There was dust everywhere, peeling wallpaper, damp patches. Somehow he hadn't noticed how badly his mother had let the house go.

Edgar arrived a few hours later. He'd put on weight since Frank had last seen him. He was forty now, bespectacled and red-faced, his hair receding, the youthful handsomeness Frank had envied just a memory. "Well, Frank," he said heavily. "So, she's gone then." Just as Edgar's voice had taken on a Scottish accent while he was at Strangmans, so now he spoke with an American twang.

Frank took Edgar around the house. "It's in a bad state," Edgar said. "Some of these rooms don't look like anyone's been in them for years." They went into the dining room. There were mouse droppings on the floor. "Hell," Edgar said irritably. "I don't know how she could've lived like this. Didn't you try to get her to move?"

Frank didn't answer. He was looking at the big dining table. The electric light above still had the cheesecloth shawl draped over it; Mrs. Baker had needed muted light to commune with the spirit world.

Edgar pursed his lips thoughtfully. "What are house prices like in England these days?"

"Going down. The economy's not doing well."

"Best thing we can do is get shot of this place as soon as we can. Sell to some developer."

Frank touched the table. "Remember the séances?"

"Lot of bloody nonsense." Edgar laughed scoffingly. "They were all nuts. Mum, too. Believing Dad came through to her every week, just for her to tell him off about going to war and leaving her in 1914."

"I don't think she ever forgave him for going away to fight the war."

Edgar looked at his brother, considering. "Maybe that's why she didn't like you much, cos you looked so much like him."

That evening Edgar suggested they go out to eat so they walked to a restaurant a few streets away. It wasn't much of a place. They had beef stew with potatoes and Brussels sprouts, all swimming in watery gravy. Edgar ordered a beer. Frank, as usual, drank little but he noticed Edgar was drinking fast, one beer after another.

"The food in this country's still bloody awful," Edgar said. "In California, you can get anything you want, well cooked and lots of it." He shook his head. "This country looks more miserable and downtrodden every time I come."

"Did you go to the San Francisco Olympics in the summer?"

"No. It made getting around difficult, I can tell you. The next ones are in Rome, aren't they? Old Mussolini will mess it up, the Wops can't organize for toffee. By the way, I keep seeing the letters V and R painted on walls. What's that all about?"

"The Resistance signs. R for Resistance, Churchill's V for Victory sign."

"I'd give him a V sign." Edgar laughed. "How's Beaverbrook? Still licking the Germans' arses?"

Frank said, "Yes, yes, he is."

"Thank God Britain lost the war and Roosevelt lost the election in 1940, and Taft did his deal with the Japs. Though if that do-gooding leftie Adlai Stevenson wins the election in November he could start sticking his nose into Europe again."

"Do you think so?" Frank asked, perking up a little.

Edgar gave him a sharp look. "I hear these Resistance people are making trouble here. Stealing weapons from police stations, arming strikers, blowing things up, even killing people."

Frank said, daringly, "Maybe Stevenson should stick his nose in here, sort it all out."

"America needs to mind its own business. Nobody's going to make trouble for us," Edgar added complacently. "Not now we've got the atom bomb."

Four years earlier, in 1948, the Americans claimed to have exploded an atomic bomb, and there was even a film released of it going off in the New Mexico desert. The Germans said it had been faked. "I've never been sure those stories are true," Frank said. "I know the atom bomb's theoretically possible, but the amount of uranium you'd need is so colossal. I've heard the Germans are trying to build one, too, but they haven't got anywhere. If they had we'd have heard about it." He looked at his brother, scientist to scientist. "What do you think?"

Edgar gave him a hard stare. "We've got the atom bomb. We've other things, too, new types of incendiary bomb, chemical weapons—in a few years we'll have intercontinental missiles. The Germans probably will, too, by then, but we'll have atom bombs on top of ours."

"And then where will we all be?" Frank asked sadly.

"I don't know about you, but we'll be safe."

"While Britain's tied to Germany." Frank shook his head. He had always hated the Nazis and Blackshirts, the whole pack of bully-boy thugs. He had wished Britain hadn't surrendered even back in 1940.

Edgar had never liked Frank talking back to him. He frowned as he took another gulp of beer. "Got a girlfriend yet?" he asked.

"No."

"Never had one, have you?"

Frank didn't answer. "Women are bloody bitches," Edgar announced suddenly, so loud that people at neighboring tables stared. "So I had a fling with my secretary, so bloody what? Now Ella's taking half my salary for alimony."

"I'm sorry."

"I could do with my share of the money from Mum's house."

"I don't mind. We can sell up if you like." So that was why Edgar had really come over; he wanted his inheritance.

Edgar looked relieved. "Are the deeds at the house?" he asked.

"Yes. In a drawer. With Mum's bank books."

"I'll take those, if you don't mind. For—what do you call it—probate?"

"If you like."

Edgar asked, "You still working at that lab assistant job at Birmingham University?"

"I'm not a lab assistant. I'm a research associate."

"What are you researching, then?" Edgar's tone was belligerent; Frank realized he was very drunk. He remembered a lecturer at Birmingham who had got divorced and turned to drink; he had quietly been given premature retirement.

"The structure of meteorites," he answered. "How their elements bond together."

"Meteorites!" Edgar laughed.

"What are you working on?"

Edgar tapped the side of his nose in a ridiculous drunk's gesture, setting his glasses askew, then lowered his voice. "Government work. Can't tell you. They weren't that happy about my coming over here for the funeral. I have to report to the embassy every day." He picked up the menu. "What've they got for pudding? Jesus, spotted dick."

Mrs. Muncaster's funeral took place a few days later. Frank arranged it with the local vicar, careful not to tell him of Mrs. Muncaster's religious views. Apart from Frank and Edgar, only a couple of women from the days of the séances came; Frank had found their details in his mother's address book. They were old now, sad and faded. After the service one of them came up to the brothers and said their mother was with her husband on the other side now, walking through the gardens of the spirit world. Frank thanked her politely though Edgar flashed her a look of distaste. As they walked away from the cemetery Edgar said, "Talking of spirits, I could do with a drink."

They went to a pub in Esher High Street. Edgar drank heavily, but this time didn't get aggressive. To Frank the service had just been a rite, a performance like the séances, but it seemed to have affected Edgar. He said, "Strange to think mother's gone. God, she was an odd one."

"Yes, she was." There, at least, the brothers could agree.

"I have to go back soon, I'm needed at Berkeley. But I could stay on a few days." He looked at his brother. "It would help me if we could get the house on the market."

Frank had had more than enough of Edgar; he had been counting the hours till the funeral was over. "You do that if you want," he said. "I need to get back to Birmingham today."

"You could stay here a day or two. I don't know when we'll meet up again. Jesus," he said again, "Mum's gone. Everyone in my life's bloody gone," he added self-pityingly.

Frank spoke quickly. "I said I was going back to work tomorrow." He stood up. "I'm sorry, Edgar, I have to go now, really, if I'm to get back in time."

Edgar's mouth set in a sulky pout. He stared at Frank through his glasses. Then he held out a big meaty hand. Frank took it. "Well," Edgar said heavily. "That's that." Then a nasty glint came into his eyes as he nodded at Frank's hand, the damaged outer fingers. "How's that, nowadays?" he asked.

"A bit painful in bad weather."

"It was a strange accident, wasn't it?"

Frank met his brother's eyes and realized that Edgar knew what had really happened. He'd been at university by then but he kept up with friends from Strangmans and someone must have told him. Frank stood up. "Good-bye, Edgar," he said, and walked quickly away.

He went back to Birmingham and returned to work. It was a beautiful October, sunny mellow days succeeding each other, yellow leaves falling gently from the trees.

For the last ten years Frank had lived in a big Victorian villa divided into leasehold flats. He had four rooms on the second floor. The building was not well maintained, the paint on the front door and the windows peeling, half the sash windows rotten. One Sunday, ten days after his mother's funeral, he was sitting reading *Twenty Thousand Leagues Under the Sea* when his doorbell rang. He started violently, then went downstairs and opened the front door. Edgar was standing there, obviously the worse for wear, although it was only three in the afternoon. Frank stared at him blankly.

"Surprised to see me?" Edgar asked. "Aren't you going to invite me in?"

"Yes. Sorry." Frank turned and went back upstairs, Edgar following. Frank's heart was racing. Why had he come? What did he want? They went back into the flat, which Frank had furnished from junk shops when he moved in.

"Jeez," Edgar said. "This reminds me of Mum's house. I've put it with an agent, by the way, got a lawyer to get the probate started."

"All right," Frank said.

"I decided to come up and tell you. You should get a phone. Most people in the States have a phone."

"I don't need one."

Edgar looked at two dusty framed photographs on a little table. "You've got one of Dad, I see. God, he did look like you."

Frank looked at the sepia portrait of his father in uniform, staring fixedly and uncomfortably at the camera. Frank sometimes wondered if he was seeing the trenches, anticipating them.

"What's the other one?" Edgar asked.

"My year at Oxford." *Why has he come?* Frank thought. *What does he want?*

Edgar crossed to the bookcase, looking at the well-thumbed science-fiction novels. "Hey, I remember some of these from when you were a kid. You were always reading them during the holidays." He turned and gave Frank a rubbery half-drunk smile. "I'm flying back tomorrow evening, I thought I'd come up and tell you about the house." He hesitated, and then said, "I didn't want to part on bad terms."

"Oh."

"Mebbe I could stay over, perhaps come and see your labs tomorrow."

"I'm sorry," Frank babbled. "It's not convenient. I've only got the one bed here, you see."

Edgar looked hurt, then angry and somehow baffled.

"I don't really get visitors," Frank added.

Edgar's face set. "No. I don't suppose you do. Mind if I sit down?" He weaved his way to an armchair. "Oh God, Frank, don't put on that monkey grin."

Frank remembered something horrible that had happened when he was twelve. He and Edgar had come home from Strangmans for the summer holidays. Edgar was sixteen then, tall and blond, and was developing a strutting arrogance. Their mother had suggested, unusually, that they all go out together to the zoo. "We don't think enough about the animals," she had said. "Mrs. Baker says they have souls just like us." She had given them one of her sad, serious looks.

They went to Whipsnade, and walked around the enclosures. As they passed the monkey house Edgar said, "Let's go in here." He led the way, Frank following reluctantly with their mother, who had retreated into one of her dreamy, distant states. Inside it was horrible, a long concrete corridor with barred enclosures along the sides, a rank, filthy smell, clumps of straw the monkeys had thrown out of their cages littering the floor. A few people walked along, laughing at the antics of the small monkeys. A big orange orangutan glared at them from the dimness of its pen. Edgar looked at Frank, then turned to their mother. "Look at the chimp, Mum!" There was only one chimpanzee, sitting alone in its cage on a pile of dirty straw, staring at them. Edgar waved a hand and the chimpanzee leaned back, baring its teeth in a grin that Frank somehow knew meant fear and terror.

"What an ugly thing," Mrs. Muncaster said.

Edgar laughed. "Doesn't that grin remind you of Frank?"

Mrs. Muncaster looked at Frank forlornly. "Yes, I suppose it does in a way."

"The boys at school call him Monkey because of that grin. Monkey Muncaster."

"I wish you wouldn't do it, Frank," Mrs. Muncaster said.

Frank had felt so hot he thought he might faint. Edgar smirked at him. Mrs. Muncaster said, "It's awfully smelly in here. I can't imagine these things in the spirit gardens, I must say. Let's go and see the birds."

And now Edgar was in his house. Sitting in the moth-eaten armchair, he looked around the room again. "I thought you'd have something better by now."

"It does me."

Edgar gave him that baffled stare again. "I never understood why you did science at university. Was it to try and compete with me, show me you could do it?"

"No." Frank heard the tremble of anger in his voice. "I did it because I like it. It's what I'm good at."

Edgar looked disappointed. Then he sneered, just as he had at the zoo. "Studying meteorites?"

"Yes."

Edgar shifted in his chair. "Got anything to drink?"

"Only tea and coffee." They stared at each other. "I don't think you should drink any more. You—you've had enough."

Edgar reddened. He set his lips, then leaned forward. "Do you know what I do, what my work is?"

"No. Look, Edgar, perhaps you should go. There's nothing to drink here..."

Edgar stood up, swaying slightly, his expression threatening now. Frank stood too, suddenly afraid. Edgar walked across the dusty carpet, right up to him, then said, his breath stinking of alcohol, in Frank's face, "I'll tell you what I bloody do."

Edgar told him: told him what his work was and, as one scientist to another, how they had managed it. The explanation made total, horrible sense. "So you see, we cracked it," he crowed, his voice full of beery satisfaction.

Frank staggered back, face full of horror. Now he realized why Edgar's people had been reluctant to let him come to the funeral. All he had ever wanted was to be left in peace and now there would be no peace, no safety, for the rest of his life. Horrors as bad as any in science fiction had been created and Edgar had told him how. He stared at Edgar, suddenly understanding that his brother—a lonely, broken man—wanted Frank to know his power. "You shouldn't have told me," he said in a sort of desperate whisper. "Dear God. Have you told anyone else?" He grabbed at his hair, found himself shouting. "Jesus, the Germans mustn't find out..."

Edgar frowned, the seriousness of what he had just done beginning to penetrate his fuddled brain. "Of course I haven't told anyone," he answered sharply. "Calm down."

"You're drunk. You've been drunk half the time since you came here." Frank reached out and grabbed his brother's arm. "You must go home, you mustn't tell anybody else. If anyone found out what you'd told me—"

"All right!" Edgar was looking anxious now. "All right. Forget I said it—"

"Forget!" Frank howled. "How—can—I—forget!"

"For God's sake shut up, stop shouting!" Edgar was sweating now, his face beetroot. He stared at his brother for a long moment. Then he said quietly, as much to himself as to Frank, "Even if you did talk, no one would believe you. They'd think you were mad, they probably do already—look at you, grinning little cripple—"

And then, for only the second time in his life, Frank lost control. He ran at his brother, all flailing arms and legs. Edgar was much bigger than Frank but he was very drunk and he stepped backwards, raising his arms ineffectually to try and defend himself. Frank came on, hitting him again and again, and Edgar tripped and fell over, against the window. His weight broke the rotten sash and he fell through it in a shower of glass, arms windmilling, wildly crying out as he disappeared.

Frank stared blankly at the smashed window. The October breeze blew into the room. There was a groan from the garden below. He stepped forward, hesitantly, and looked out of the window. Edgar was lying on his back on the stone flags below, clutching his right arm and writhing in pain. Frank thought, that's it, I've done it, the police will come and they'll find out everything. He screamed at the top of his voice, "It'll be the end of the world!" Rage and terror filled his whole being. He turned and, pushing the table over, ran into the kitchen and opened cupboards and pulled out plates, sending them crashing to the floor. The insane notion had come into his head that if he smashed and broke everything in sight somehow he could drive the terrible knowledge of what Edgar had told him from his head, along with all the rage that filled it. He was still running around the flat, breaking furniture, bleeding from several cuts, when the police arrived.

Dr. Wilson was a small round man with a bald head, wearing a white coat over a brown three-piece suit. He sat at a big cluttered desk. The eyes behind his tortoiseshell glasses were keen but weary. As Frank entered he put down a document stamped with the government crest: shield and lion and unicorn. Frank saw the title, *Sterilization of the Unfit; Consultative Document*. Wilson gave a quick, tired flicker of a smile. "How are you today, Frank?"

"All right."

"What have you been doing?"

"Just sitting on the ward. They didn't take us for our walk around the airing courts today, because of the rain."

"No," Dr. Wilson said, smiling. "We're organizing a special day out for some suitable patients in a couple of weeks. To Coventry Cathedral. The Dean has offered to take a dozen patients on a tour, with some attendants, of course. I wondered if you might like to go. It's a beautiful medieval building. Fifteenth century, I believe. I'm looking for some—educated—patients to take. Might you be interested?"

"No, thank you," Frank answered, his face twisting into its monkey grin. He wasn't interested in churches, had never been to one—Mrs. Baker hadn't approved—and to go in his shapeless hospital clothes, part of a group of lunatics, would be shaming.

Dr. Wilson considered his response, then said quietly, "The charge nurse on the ward says you avoid the other patients."

"I just like sitting on my own."

"Do they frighten you?" Dr. Wilson asked.

"Sometimes. I want to go home," Frank said pleadingly.

Dr. Wilson shook his head. "It does pain me, Frank, that someone of your education, your class, should end up on a public ward. You're actually Dr. Muncaster, aren't you? A PhD?"

"Yes."

"You shouldn't really be with the pauper lunatics. Some of those poor people—they barely have minds anymore. But I can't just let you leave, Frank. You pushed your brother through a second-floor window. It's a miracle he got off with a broken arm. To say nothing of screaming about the end of the world. Someone heard that out in the street. There's still a police case open: causing grievous bodily harm is an imprisonable offense. Fortunately your brother didn't want to prosecute. As it is, you've been certified as insane and you must stay here till you're cured. How are you getting on with the reduced Largactil dose?"

"All right. It makes me feel calm."

A self-satisfied smile crossed Wilson's face. "Good. This is one of the first British hospitals to use Largactil. My idea. It's French, you know, so it's more expensive with the import duty. But I persuaded the Board. My cousin working in the Ministry of Health gives me a certain influence." He gave a superior little smile.

"It makes my mouth dry. And I feel tired."

"It keeps you calm. That's the main thing, in the circumstances."

"I'll never do anything like that again."

The doctor made a steeple of his hands. They were small and surprisingly delicate. "The question is, why did you do it in the first place?"

"I don't know."

"If we're going to help you, you have to talk about it." He pursed his small mouth. "Do you believe the end of the world is coming? Some religious people do."

Frank shook his head. The end could come, but religion would have nothing to do with it.

Dr. Wilson persisted. "When you arrived you were asked what your religion was. You said your mother was a spiritualist but you didn't believe in God."

"Yes."

"Did your mother take you to spiritualist churches?"

"No. She had séances at her house with a woman who said she could contact the dead."

"Do you think she could, this woman?"

"No," Frank answered flatly.

"So you didn't believe in any of it?"

"No."

"You have no relatives apart from your brother."

"No."

"No one's been to visit."

"They never did like me in the labs. I didn't fit in." Frank felt tears coming now.

"Well, there's a stigma, people are frightened of asylums. Even relatives usually stop coming after a time." The doctor shifted in his seat. "But if we're to get you into the Private Villa, which I think would be more suitable for you, the board will need funds."

"I've got money. Surely your administration can sort it out."

Dr. Wilson smiled wryly. "You can be clear and direct when you wish, can't you? The problem, Frank, is that as a lunatic your money has to be held by a trustee. That's the law. For that we need a relative."

"There's only my brother. They said he's gone back to America."

"We know. We've been trying to get in touch with him." Dr. Wilson raised his eyebrows. "I even went to the trouble of telephoning him at his university in California. But they said he's away on government business and can't be contacted."

"He won't reply," Frank said bitterly.

"You sound angry with him. You must have been, to do what you did."

Frank said nothing.

"Why did you become a scientist like your brother?" Dr. Wilson asked, his tone conversational again. "Did you want to compete with him?"

"No," Frank replied wearily. "I was just interested in science, in geology, how old the Earth is, what a little speck in space we live on. I did it for *myself*." He spoke with a sudden vehemence.

"Nothing to do with Edgar?"

"Nothing."

"Frank, if I'm to help you must tell me more. I wonder if a course of electric shock treatment might help, jolt you out of this withdrawn state. We shall have to start thinking about it."

Afterwards the Scottish attendant, Ben, took Frank back to the ward. The rain had stopped. The light was beginning to fade. "How did it go?" Ben asked.

Frank looked at Ben again. The thought crossed his mind that Dr. Wilson might have asked him to report back on what Frank said. So he fell back on his staple answer. "I don't know."

"Lucky youse is middle-class and educated, Wilson's no' interested in the chronic cases, the poor sods wi' no money that have been on the wards for years. He thinks he's too good for this place anyway. His father was a doctor, his cousin's a civil servant at the Ministry of Health. Aul' snob. Class is everything." Ben spoke quietly, but with an undertone of bitterness.

"He talked about shock treatment," Frank said hesitantly. He swallowed. "I've overheard other patients discussing that."

Ben grimaced. "It's not nice. They tie you down with leather straps and put electric shocks through your brain. They say it cures depression. I think it does, sometimes. But they're a bit free and easy with it. And they should use anesthetic."

"It hurts?"

Ben nodded.

"Have you seen it done?"

"Aye."

Frank's heart began to pound. He took deep breaths. His bad hand hurt and he massaged the two atrophied fingers. Their footsteps slapped along the wet path.

Ben said, "There are worse things. Lobotomies—a surgeon comes up from London every few months to do those. Cuts part of your brain out. Jesus, the state of some patients afterwards. Don't worry, they won't do that to you." Ben gave Frank a sudden guilty look. "Sorry I mentioned it."

Frank asked, cautiously, "What part of Scotland do you come from?"

"Glasgow." Ben smiled. "Glesca. D'ye know Scotland?"

"I went to school near Edinburgh."

"I thought I heard a trace of Morningside. One of those Edinburgh private schools?"

"Yes."

"Which one?"

"Strangmans," Frank answered quickly. He wanted to change the subject.

"I've heard those places can be hard. Harder than Glesca schools even."

"Yes."

"Still, I hear there's public schools just as tough in England."

"Yes, perhaps," Frank said, his voice catching. "Before I came in, I heard on the news about this new law they're planning, the compulsory sterilizations. Dr. Wilson was reading something about it."

"That's just for the mentally deficient, and what they call the moral degenerates. Wilson'll be quite happy to see them sterilized. Dregs of society, that's how he sees them, the auld scunner." That bitter note in Ben's voice again. He looked at Frank's bad hand. "What happened there?"

"An accident. At school." Frank turned to him. "I want to get out of here."

"Ye canna, no' unless Wilson says you're sane again." Ben considered, then added, "Unless someone can bring influence, maybe get you transferred, maybe tae a private clinic away from here. What about your brother?"

Frank shook his head despairingly. "Edgar won't even take their calls."

"What about the people where you work?"

"Dr. Wilson asked me that. They wouldn't be interested. They don't really want me in the department. I've known that for a while." Frank's face spasmed into his smiling rictus.

They had reached the door of the main building. "I'm going to be working on your ward for a while," Ben said. "Maybe I could help with finding someone to help ye."

"There's nobody."

"What about people you knew at school? Or at university? You must have gone to university."

An image of David Fitzgerald came into Frank's head; an autumn evening sitting with him in their rooms at Oxford, talking about Hitler and appeasement. His astonished realization that for the first time in his life someone was actually interested in what he was saying. As this attendant Ben seemed to be, for some reason Frank couldn't fathom. He hadn't been in touch with David properly for years, but at one time he had been closer to him than anyone. "There might be someone," he said, cautiously.

CHAPTER SIX

T he following Thursday David left for work at eight as usual, walking up the street to Kenton Station in his bowler, black jacket, and pinstripe trousers. Opposite the house was a little park, no more than a small lawned area with flowerbeds; at the far end there still stood one of the square concrete shelters that had been built in 1939 in anticipation of the air raids that never came, squat and ugly and abandoned now. Children went in there to smoke sometimes; there had been a petition to the Council. He nodded to neighbors, other men dressed in similar uniform, also heading for the station. The weather was bright and clear, cold for mid-November. His breath formed a cloud in front of him, like the exhaust of an old Austin Seven sputtering by.

The Tube was crowded, the air thick with cigarette smoke. Hanging on to the strap he read the *Times*. There was a bold headline: "*Beaverbrook and Butler fly to Berlin today for economic talks.*" That was sudden — there had been nothing on the news last night. "*Optimism on new German trade links,*" the article continued. He wondered what the Germans would want in return.

Victoria Station was heaving, thousands of commuters walking through the great vestibule, steam and smoke from the trains belching up to the high ceiling. A group of gray-uniformed German soldiers stood by a platform gate, probably on their way to the base on the Isle of Wight. They were very young, laughing and joking. They had probably been on leave in London. Those with an Isle of Wight posting were the lucky ones; the endless mincing machine of the Russian front had been killing boys like these for eleven years, would probably take these ones too in the end. David felt an unexpected stab of pity for them.

He walked down Victoria Street to Parliament Square, then up

Whitehall to the Dominions Office. Sykes was on duty again behind the desk. "Morning, Mr. Fitzgerald. Another cold day, sir."

The lift was full, clanking painfully as it rose. David stood next to Daniel Brightman from the Economic Department, who had joined the service at the same time. Like David he was a grammar-school boy, but over the years Brightman had adopted an upper-class drawl. "Another day in the salt mines," he said.

"Yes. Keeping busy?"

"Meeting with the Aussies on wheat tariffs today." He sighed. "I expect they'll be shouting as usual. The trials of Empire."

David got out on the second floor and passed the Registry. The clerks were all in. From behind the counter Carol, at her desk, gave him a quick smile and a wave. He smiled back, guiltily remembering what he had done on Sunday.

Old Dabb, checking a card index at the counter, looked up. "Mr. Fitzgerald," he said. "A brief word, if I may."

"Of course." David noticed dandruff on the old man's collar.

"I was concerned, sir," the Registrar said in his slow sad voice, "to observe you left the High Commissioners' meeting file on the counter last night, without getting a clerk to sign it back in." He shook his head sadly. "A moment of time now can spare much confusion later."

"I'm sorry, Dabb, we've been so busy. It won't happen again."

It was a quiet morning; David telephoned South Africa House and discussed who might attend the meeting the SS officials were asking for. He had spoken several times that week with an eager young Afrikaner, stressing the need for secrecy. "Teach the Russians who's boss, hey?" the South African had chuckled. "The Germans aren't settling the Congo, are they, got enough on their hands trying to settle Russia."

No, David thought, they're just looting the Congo, like the Belgians did. David hated these apartheid people and their friendship with the Nazis, but he was formally, coolly polite as he discussed which SS officials would go — out of uniform, of course — to South Africa House. Then he studied a report on the forthcoming Birmingham Empire

Week, who would be manning stalls from the various High Commissions, the important businesses taking part, like Unilever and Lonrho. He thought he might go for a swim at lunchtime, to the pool at a club he belonged to nearby. He still loved diving down into the empty, peaceful silence.

Late in the morning there was a brusque knock on the door and Hubbold came in, frowning.

"Word's come down from the Permanent Secretary. We've to stall on the Coronation arrangements at the High Commissioners' meeting."

"*The Times* said they might tie it in with Hitler's twentieth anniversary celebrations."

Hubbold laughed softly. "Ah, *The Times*. Forever planting the right seeds in our minds. Anyway, instructions from on high are for everyone to stonewall. It's a nuisance, you know how potty the High Commissioners are over royalty. They'll want to know if it'll be the spring or summer, whether Hartnell will design the dress. Pity we'll have to say nothing's decided, leaves more time for awkward subjects under Any Other Business. I've had word the Canadians may bring up the Jew laws again."

"Has that come from Canada House, sir?" David asked, antennae alert.

"Not officially," Hubbold smiled. "*Arcana imperii*, you know. Secrets of authority." He liked it to be known he had his own sources; it was another mark of seniority for him. Some of David's colleagues were on first-name terms with their superiors, but Hubbold had never even suggested David drop the "sir." Hubbold continued, "The minister does get rather embarrassed when that one comes up. Anyway, useful for you to know what the nuances will be."

Shortly after eleven one of the interdepartmental messengers knocked at David's door. He gave him a letter inside a Colonial Office envelope: *Can you meet for lunch at the club at 1.15 not 1.30? Geoff.*

When the messenger had gone David sat frowning. The words were a code that meant there was something they needed to talk about; they would meet at the Oxford and Cambridge Club at one fifteen. They never spoke on the telephone if possible, as there were rumors Civil Service phones were routinely tapped by Special Branch now. David lit a cigarette and stared anxiously through the window at Whitehall. This had only happened once before, when Jackson had advance notice of a raid on the Soho brothels, and called off a regular meeting at the flat. But at least it wasn't an emergency, there was a separate code for that.

David left the Office at one and walked up to Trafalgar Square. A huge poster had been placed on the plinth of Nelson's Column. *We Need Exports. We Work or Want. A Challenge to British Grit.* David wondered what the trade talks with Germany would bring; Volkswagens to replace the Hillmans and Morrises chugging around Trafalgar Square?

He turned into Pall Mall. Two Auxiliary policemen in their blue uniforms and caps walked slowly along, guns at their waists, watching the passers-by. Two more patrolled in parallel on the other side of the road. Something was up. He thought, Sarah's coming into town today for one of her meetings. On Sunday, after the talk about Charlie, they had made love, an increasingly rare occurrence. He had felt detached, the brief moment of warmth quickly gone.

David entered the club. A hum of conversation came from the dining room but he went directly to the library. Few people ever came in at lunchtime and only Geoff was there now, in an armchair with a view of the door. David sat opposite him.

"Got your message," he said quietly.

"Thanks for coming." Geoff leaned forward. "Message from Jackson. He wants a scratch meeting tomorrow."

"Do we know why?"

"No. I only heard just before I contacted you. Just that we've got to be there. Seven o'clock."

"Sarah's expecting me home. I can't say we've fixed up a special tennis match, not at this notice." David thought, *my wife has become someone to lie to.* He sighed. "I'll think of something."

"I'm sorry. I know it's hard. Easier for me, living alone."

David looked at his friend. He seemed tired, more nervy than usual. "How are your parents?" he asked.

"Oh, rolling along in their groove." Geoff, like David, was an only child, his father a retired businessman. His parents lived a peaceful life in Hertfordshire, revolved around bowls matches, roses, and golf. "Keep asking whether I've met any nice girls," Geoff added. "I'm tempted to say, the only ones I know these days aren't very nice." He gave his jerky laugh, then changed the subject. "How's your dad?"

"Fine. Had a letter last week. It's spring in Auckland, he went with his brother's family to look at Rotorua last week. It wasn't raining for once."

"Still hasn't met a nice Kiwi widow?"

"He'll never marry again. He was too devoted to Mum."

A shadow crossed Geoff's face; David guessed he was thinking of the woman in Kenya. He changed the subject. "Heard about Beaverbrook flying out to Berlin?"

"Yes. According to the club tickertape, Hitler isn't going to be able to meet him."

"Maybe it's true Hitler's dead, he hasn't been seen in public for what — two years?"

Geoff shook his head firmly. "He's not dead. The Nazi leaders would be fighting for his crown; they fought like rats over Göring's economic empire when he died."

"I wish Hitler were dead."

"Amen to that," Geoff replied with feeling.

When he was growing up in Barnet David did not think much about being Irish. He knew bad things had happened in Ireland and that his parents had brought him to England when he was very small. His father's parents still lived in Dublin and visited them occasionally when David was young; they died within six months of each other when he was ten. His mother never spoke of her family; over the years David gathered there had been some sort of quarrel.

There was always a burden of expectation from his mother. His father was a solid, unruffled, easy-going man, but Rachel Fitzgerald was small and thin and excitable, always busy, always chatting in her loud sing-song voice to her husband or David, the daily woman or her female friends from the Conservative Club. When not talking she was usually listening to the radio, humming along to the tunes and sometimes playing them, surprisingly well, on the piano in the dining room. She was forever telling David to work hard at school; with all the unemployment in the country since the War it was important to get qualifications. She spoke anxiously, as though their safe, secure life might suddenly be snatched away.

David was quiet and self-contained like his father. He looked like him, too, although his hair was curly like his mother's, but black not red. "You and your da," his mother would say, "you're alike as two peas in a pod. You'll break all the girls' hearts when you grow up." David would redden and frown. He loved his mother but sometimes she drove him crazy.

David went to a private day-school, then got a grammar-school place when he was eleven, passing the entrance exam easily. When they got the results his father said he was a clever lad, regarding him with pink-faced satisfaction across the dining table, but his mother looked at him fiercely. "This is your chance in life, Davy boy," she said. "They'll expect you to work hard, so make sure you do now. Make your mammy proud."

"Please call me David, Mum, not Davy."

"You're turning into a right formal English boy." She leaned across and ruffled his hair. "Wee curly top. Oh, that's a scowl to give your ma."

David did well at grammar school. He was taken aback at first by the severe formality of the masters in their black gowns, the obedience and quiet they demanded, and the amount of homework, but he soon adjusted. He made friends easily though he was never a leader, always held himself a little apart. In his first term the class bully started calling him Paddy and bog-trotter. David ignored him for a while, not wanting to make trouble, but one day the boy said his mother was an Irish peasant, and out of the blue David flew at him, knocking him down. A master saw the fight and both boys got the cane, but the bully left David alone after that.

He was near the top of the class. He was good at sport, too, in the junior rugby team though he didn't much like the game. David was a very good swimmer and loved diving—climbing the ladder to the top board and jumping off, breaking the still surface of the water and going down and down into that silent world of pastel blue. Later he entered inter-school competitions. There would be a little crowd watching and cheering, but the best thing was still hitting the water, then that fall into silence.

He won cups, which his mother insisted go on the mantelpiece. Once or twice David came home from school when his mother had her friends around for tea, and she would call him into the dining room, saying, "Here's my Davy that won all these cups. See what a handsome boy he's getting. Oh, there, Davy, don't look at me like that. See, he's blushing." The ladies would smile indulgently and David would escape to his room. He hated the attention. He wanted to be just another boy, to be ordinary.

When he was eighteen he took his entrance exam for Oxford. He had extra tuition for it, and for the first time in his life he felt tired, not sure he could succeed in the task ahead. His mother didn't help, pressing him about the exam, telling him he shouldn't go out in the evening, give all his time to his studies. She had started to look strained and ill lately. The news in the papers sometimes upset her; it was 1935, the Nazis were in power in Germany and Italy had invaded Abyssinia. Unlike some of her Conservative Club friends Mrs. Fitzgerald thought Hitler and Mussolini were monsters who would bring the world to ruin and never tired of saying so. But it was more than that, she was starting to lose weight and her endless supply of talk had dried up, like a tap turned off. David found he missed it. He wondered if it was because of worry over his exam and felt angry and helpless and guilty. He was doing his best as he always had. Why was it never enough? He became curt and rude with her.

One evening at dinner she started complaining about David wasting his time on swimming practice. He lost his temper, called her a shrieking colleen. Rachel burst into tears and went up to her bedroom, slamming the door. David's father, who hardly ever got angry, shouted at him to show his mother proper respect and threatened to give him the back of his hand if he spoke to her like that again, though David was as big as him now.

The day the news came that David had got into Oxford, his father said quietly that there was something he must tell him. He took him into the dining room. They sat down and his father looked at him in a way he never had before, serious and sad. "Your mother's very ill," he said softly. "I'm afraid she's got the cancer." There was a tremble in his voice. "She didn't want to tell you till after your exam, she didn't want to worry you. But now—well, she's feeling very poorly and she's going to have to have a nurse in. She should have done before, really."

David sat quite still for a moment. He said, his voice cracking, "I've been terrible to her."

"You weren't to know, son." His father looked at him seriously. "But now you've got to be good to her. She won't be with us long."

David did something he hadn't done since he was a small child; he put his head in his hands and burst into loud, sobbing tears. His body shook and trembled. His father came across and put a hand awkwardly on his shoulder. "There, son," he said. "I know."

David spent the summer doing all he could for his mother. He helped the daily and the nurse, busied himself with jobs around the house and taking his mother's meals up. He was consumed with guilt, all the more because her fierce, possessive love had faded to an exhausted dependent helplessness. He sometimes helped her in and out of bed; she was skin and bone now. She would smile bravely and touch his cheek with a shaking finger and say breathlessly that he was a good boy, she had always known that.

He was with her when she died, his father on the other side of the bed. It was a warm Saturday in September; he would be going up to Oxford in a few weeks. Rachel drifted in and out of consciousness, listlessly watching the sun drift across the sky. Then suddenly she looked straight at David. She spoke to him, in a voice full of sadness, some words he couldn't understand. It was little more than a whisper. "*Ich hob dich lieb.*"

David turned to his father. He leaned forward and squeezed his wife's hand. "We didn't understand you, darling," he said.

She frowned and tried to concentrate, but then her head fell back and the life went out of her.

Afterwards his father told him the truth. "Your mother's family were Jewish. They came from somewhere in Russia. In the Tsar's time, during the pogroms, a lot left for America. Your mother's parents—your grandparents—left Russia with your mother and her three sisters. She was eight."

David shook his head, trying to make sense of it. "But how did she come to be Irish?"

"There were a lot of crooked people involved in the emigrations. Your mother's poor parents didn't speak a word of English. A boat brought them to Dublin and they thought they were going to meet a boat for America but they were just left there, stuck in Ireland. Your grandfather was a cabinetmaker, very good at it, and through some other Jews he managed to set up a shop. He ran a successful business. The children grew up speaking English. They were encouraged to, so as not to be thought too different. But I suppose deep down they never forgot their first language."

"Was Mum speaking Russian?"

"No. The Jews in Eastern Europe have their own language, Yiddish. It's like German, but different. Feldman, that was the family name." He smiled uneasily. "Pretty Jewish-sounding, eh?" He was silent a long time. "Years later your mother became a music teacher. This was just before I met her. The Easter Rising was coming and things were getting rough. Mr. Feldman decided to sell the shop and go to America. They had relatives there. Better late than never, eh?" He smiled again, sadly. "He insisted the whole family go. Your mother didn't want to, though, she wanted to stay in Ireland. There were other problems, too; the family was very religious but she thought it was all hokum, just as I do. So there was a quarrel, her parents and sisters sailed off, and she never saw any of them again. They never wrote, her father ruled the roost and he cut her off. I think Mr. Feldman was a bit of an old brute, actually. I don't know where her sisters are now. I can't even let them know she's dead," he added bleakly.

"Why did you never tell me?"

"Ah, son, we thought it better if everyone just assumed your mother was Irish. She wanted you to get on so much, and she knew that here"— his eyes narrowed—"oh, it's not like Russia was, or Germany is now, but there's prejudice. There always has been. Unofficial quotas for Jews. Even the grammar school has a quota, you know." He looked at David seriously. "Your mother wanted her background forgotten, for your sake. Her immigration records were destroyed during the Troubles, I found that out. Our marriage certificate gives our nationalities as British—Ireland was British then, of course." He burst out in sudden anger, "People dividing each other up according to nationality and religion, it's the worst thing, it causes nothing but misery and bloodshed. Look at Germany."

David sat, thinking. There were a couple of Jewish boys at school who went out of assembly during morning prayers. Sometimes in the playground they got things called after them, Sheeny or Jewboy. He felt sorry for them. There was enough prejudice against the Irish; he knew it was worse for Jews.

He said, "So I'm a Jew."

"According to their rules you are, since your mother was. But as far as we were concerned you weren't Jewish and you weren't Christian either. You're not circumcised and you're not confirmed and"—his father reached forward and took his hand—"you're just your ma's Davy, and you can be anything you want to be."

"I don't feel Jewish," David said quietly. "But what is feeling Jewish?" He frowned. "But, if Mum didn't want me to know, why—why did she talk to me in Yiddish? What did she say, Dad?"

His father shook his head. "I'm sorry, son, I don't know. She never spoke it with me. I thought she'd forgotten it all. Perhaps at the end her poor mind was just going back."

David was crying, a steady flow of tears. He and his father sat in silence in the quiet lounge. When David's crying lessened his father leaned forward, clutching his arm. "No need ever to tell anyone else, David. There's no point, it'll only hold you back, and you'd be going against your mother's wishes. It can just be our secret."

David looked up at him and nodded. "I understand," he said heavily. "I understand. You're right. And I'll do it for her. I owe her, I owe her."

"It'll be better for you, too."

And it had been. In the years after the Berlin Treaty his silence had saved his job, his career. But always a part of him felt he didn't deserve what he had; he felt guilt and fear, but also a strange sense of kinship when he passed those wearing the yellow badge in the street, looking shabbier and more forlorn every year.

CHAPTER SEVEN

On Thursday morning Sarah took the Tube into London to attend a meeting of the London Unemployed Aid Committee, at Friends House in Euston Road. On the journey she read her library book, Daphne du Maurier's *Rebecca*. She reached the scene where the mad housekeeper, Mrs. Danvers, urges the second Mrs. de Winter to jump out from a window: *"It's you that's the shadow and the ghost. It's you that is forgotten and not wanted and pushed aside. Well, why don't you leave Manderley to her? Why don't you go?"* Sarah didn't like the book; it was compelling, certainly, but sinister. Apart from romances and detective stories the library shelves were so thin these days. So many writers she had liked were hard to get hold of—Priestley, Forster, Auden—people who had opposed the government, over the Treaty and afterwards, and who, like their works, had quietly disappeared from public view.

She sat back in her seat. David had not made love to her again after Sunday. He did less and less now. For most of their married life his love-making had been slow and gentle but lately, when it happened, there was a restless urgency about it, and when he came inside her he groaned, as though she were giving him not love but pain. *It's you that's the shadow and the ghost.* She passed a hand over her face. How had it come to this? She remembered their first meeting, at the dance at the tennis club, in 1942.

She had been standing with a friend and her eyes were drawn to David, talking to another man in a corner. He was classically handsome, trimly muscular, but there was a beauty, a gentleness, even then a sad-ness to him, that drew her. He caught her eye, excused himself to his friend, and came over and asked her to dance, with confidence but an odd sort of humility, too. Sarah wore her hair shingled then—how long that fashion had lasted—and as they circled the floor to the music from the dance band she made one of her bold remarks, saying she wished she had his natural curls. He smiled and said, with that quiet humor that seemed to have quite gone now, "You haven't seen me in my curlers."

They had married the following year, 1943, and shortly afterwards David got his two-year posting to the British High Commission Office in Auckland. David's father was already in New Zealand, an older, plumper version of David but with a broad Irish accent. The three of them had often discussed the darkening political situation at home; they were on the same side, they feared the German alliance and the slow, creeping authoritarianism in England. But that was before the 1950 election; Churchill was still growling from the Opposition benches in Parliament, Attlee at his side, and there was hope the situation might change at the next election. David's father had wanted them to stay, New Zealand was determined to remain a democracy; there was a freedom of thought and life there which was vanishing from England. Over the weeks Sarah had begun to be persuaded, though her heart ached at the thought of abandoning her family; it was David who in the end said, "What's going on can't last, not in England. As long as we're there we've got a voice and a vote. We should go back. It's our country." They hadn't known yet that she was pregnant with Charlie; if they had, perhaps they would have stayed.

Sarah looked out of the window of the Tube. It was a bright day, but London seemed as bleak and grimy as ever. She had a sudden memory of a trip she and David had taken to the far west of New Zealand's South Island, camping in a big old army tent they'd bought in Auckland. Their days were spent among the huge, remote mountains covered in great tree ferns. At night they heard the sound of silvery mountain streams and little flightless birds snuffling in the undergrowth as the two of them huddled together, laughing at how dirty and untidy and ragged they had become, like pioneers in the wilderness or Adam and Eve in the Garden of Eden.

She jumped as the Tube juddered to a halt at Euston. She got up, putting her book in her briefcase. A shop outside the station was already selling holly. It was little more than a month to Christmas, and soon the usual false bonhomie would begin. It was hard to bear when you had lost a child.

Sarah walked across the road to Friends House. As usual the Quaker headquarters had a policeman posted outside. The Quakers opposed the violence in the Empire, the war in Russia, and still occasionally dared to hold sit-down demonstrations. Sarah remembered how when she was a girl she had thought of policemen as amiable, solid, protective. Now they were powerful, feared. In the cinemas they were no longer portrayed as bumbling foils to private detectives but as heroes, tough men fighting Communists, American spies, Jewish-looking crooks. She showed her identity card and her invitation to the meeting to the policeman, and he nodded her past.

The London Unemployed Aid Committee had been founded in the early forties to provide food parcels, clothes, and holidays for the children of the four million unemployed. Sarah was on the sub-committee that organized Christmas presents for needy children in the North. Sometimes she wondered how the parents must feel, passing on presents from unknown do-gooders; but otherwise the children might get nothing. Sarah was good on committees, and occasionally she deputized for the Chairwoman, Mrs. Templeman, a redoubtable businessman's wife. Mrs. Templeman was firmly in charge today, though, a little round hat perched on her permed gray hair, a roll of thick pearls on her stout bosom. She nodded approvingly as Sarah reported on her correspondence with the big toy stores about discounts for bulk orders. Sarah said it was important to try to ensure the children got a variety of toys — they didn't want every child in a Yorkshire pit village to end up with the same teddy bear or toy train. She explained that ensuring variety was a bit more expensive, but would make a difference to the families. She smiled at Mr. Hamilton, a plump little man with a carnation in his buttonhole who was Charity Officer of a large toy store. He nodded thoughtfully, and Mrs. Templeman watched her with approval.

After the meeting Mrs. Templeman came over to Sarah, thanked her in her fulsome, patronizing way for all she had done, and asked if she would like to come to lunch. She was wearing a heavy coat and, around her neck, a fox-fur stole, a horrible thing with glass eyes that stared at Sarah, tail in its mouth. Mrs. Templeman looked disappointed when she declined; Sarah knew that like her she was bored and lonely, but when she had lunched with her before Mrs. Templeman talked endlessly, about her husband and her committees and her church activities—she was a committed Christian and Sarah always felt she looked at her as a possible convert. She didn't feel she could put up with it today.

She didn't want to go home, though. She had lunch on her own in a Corner House, then went for a walk; the weather was cold and clear, an icy tang in the air. Quite often, since Charlie died, Sarah had gone into central London, to escape the loneliness of the house; usually she walked around the old streets of the city, with its warehouses and offices and the tiny narrow streets Dickens had written about, the lovely Wren churches like St. Dunstan's and St. Swithin's where she would sit in quiet, if secular, contemplation. Today, though, she decided to walk to Westminster Abbey; she hadn't been there in years. She turned down Gower Street, past the great white tower of Senate House, the second-tallest building in London. The former London University headquarters now housed the largest German embassy in the world, two giant swastika flags hanging halfway down the building from poles on the roof. Grim-faced Special Branch policemen with submachine guns stood on guard all along the high railings with their covering of barbed wire in case of a Resistance attack; inside, an official in brown Nazi Party uniform stepped from a limousine. He was being welcomed by a group of men, some in suits, a couple in military field-gray, one in the glistening black beetle's carapace of the SS uniform. Sarah hurried past. When uniformed German officials had started arriving in England in 1940 Sarah had been astonished by the bright slashing colors, the black swastika armbands with the bright red hooked cross worn in its white circle; before, of course, she had only seen the Nazis on film, in black and white and gray. They knew how to use color.

Walking along she thought, by contrast, how tired and cold and gray most people looked. A one-legged man sat on the pavement playing a violin, a cap at his feet, 1940 *Veteran Please Help* scrawled on a piece of cardboard. The police would move him on presently; beggars had been a growing problem in London until a few years ago, when after a *Daily Mail* campaign they had been forcefully removed to the "Back to the Land" agricultural settlements Lloyd George had set up to grow food on wasteland in the countryside. She dropped half a crown in the man's cap. She noticed the depressing signs of poverty and oppression more and more these days. For years she had shut her eyes. When she had met David her days of political activism were already over, it was too dangerous. She and David both thought, after they returned from New Zealand, that there was nothing to do but wait until things changed, as surely, eventually, they must.

She walked on toward Westminster, noticing again that there were a lot of Auxiliary Police around. Several times she saw a new poster advertising Mosley's Fascists; it was garish and horrible, a woman in the foreground shielding a baby from a gigantic, King Kong–like ape with the long nose of a cartoon Jew, a helmet with a red star on his head. *Fight Bolshevik Terror! Join the BUF Now!* She passed down Whitehall, looking up at the windows of the Dominions Office where David would be working. She had been growing more and more angry with him in recent weeks, but her talk with Irene had made her realize the depth of her love, how much she feared losing him.

She went past the Palace of Westminster, down to the abbey. Inside it was cool and dark, her footsteps echoing. There were few people around. The Tomb of the Unknown Soldier was still piled high with wreaths from Remembrance Day. She looked around the vast spaces. They would hold the Coronation here, sometime next year. She pitied the Queen, young and alone in the middle of this mess. She had a sudden memory of the Christmas broadcast by her father, George VI, in 1939, that one wartime Christmas. The family had been sitting around the radio, wearing paper hats but in somber silence. The King, struggling as usual with his crippling stammer, quoted from a poem:

"I said to the man who stood at the gate of the year,
'Give me a light that I may tread safely into the unknown.'
And he replied, 'Go out into the darkness and put your hand into the
*   hand of God.*
That shall be to you better than light and safer than a known way.' "

The poor King, she thought, who had never wanted the throne, had had to take it after his brother, the irresponsible Nazi sympathizer Edward VIII, had abdicated. Edward and Wallis Simpson still lived an easy life in the Bahamas, where he was governor. King George, over the years since 1940, had seemed, like so many figures from the thirties, to fade away, seldom appearing in public, looking sad and strained when he did.

Some chairs had been set out for a service and Sarah sat down. In the cold half-light, she found herself praying for the first time in years. "God, if you do exist, give us another child. It would be such a little thing for You but it would be everything to us." She began, silently, to cry.

Sarah had had a happy childhood. She was the baby of the family, a pretty, blond girl adored by her mother and elder sister, though she knew that for all of them her father came first: Jim, whose disfigured face had sometimes frightened her when she was small.

Jim was an accounts clerk at the Town Hall, and spent much of his spare time working for pacifist causes, the League of Nations Union and later the Peace Pledge Union. He was devoted to preventing another war, convinced humanity could not survive a next time.

What she learned at home was different from what they taught at school. She would argue it out with her sister. "Irene, Mrs. Briggs at school says the Kaiser started the war, he had to be stopped."

"Well, she's wrong. It's not fair to blame Germany for everything. And the Versailles Treaty was unfair, ceding parts of Germany to other countries and making them pay reparations. They can't afford them and that's why their economy's in such a mess. Daddy was in the war, a lot of his friends were killed, and it was all for nothing in the end. We have to stop it happening again."

"But don't we have to have an army to defend ourselves, in case someone attacks us?"

"Nobody'll be able to defend themselves if there's another war. All countries will get bombed, the planes will drop gas. Don't cry, Sarah, it won't happen, good people like Daddy will stop it."

As Sarah grew older she became as passionate a peace campaigner as her father and sister. In her teens she signed the Peace Pledge and joined the meetings that often took place around the table in their home, though if she were honest she found many of the Peace Pledge folk argumentative and boring. Sarah's mother always played the part of the busy hostess, boiling kettles and bringing plates of cakes and sandwiches. Her father didn't speak much during their meetings, but sat smoking his pipe, his ravaged face somber.

There was one evening, though, when he did speak and Sarah never forgot it; if ever she doubted the pacifist cause it always came back to her mind. It was just before her eighteenth birthday, a sticky summer evening in 1936. There was a campaign on to get more signatures for the Peace Pledge, and people sat around the table busily putting leaflets into envelopes. Sarah was tired and irritable, wondering what teacher-training college would be like — she had just left school — and was feeling flustered over a boy who wanted to take her out but whom she didn't really like.

The Spanish Civil War had just broken out, and people who had opposed war for years were finding it hard not to take sides. A young man, a Labour Party member, said, "How can we blame the Spanish people for fighting back against these militarists who are trying to overthrow an elected government?"

Irene spoke up hotly. "Well, the Spanish army say they're trying to stop chaos and bring order. Anyway, we can't support violence on either side. We have to hold to our principles."

"I know," the young man said. "But — it's hard, seeing these Fascists trampling down ordinary people."

"So what do you want us to do, build up armaments against Hitler, like that beastly warmonger Churchill does?"

He shook his head. "I don't know. It's so hard, but—it's terrible, these Fascist and nationalist parties taking power all over Europe. Nineteen fourteen was an orgy of nationalism and flag-waving and you'd think people would have learned from that, what it led to. But now..." His voice trailed away, full of sorrow.

Jim spoke then: "In the trenches, at night, sometimes it could get really quiet. People don't realize that. Then the big guns would start up over on the German side, somewhere down the line. And I used to sit there, wondering if the sound would get closer, if the shells would maybe land on us. I used to think, there's some young fellow just like me over there, sweating to load one big shell after another. Just a young chap like me. It was nights like that which made me understand war is totally wrong. Not in the heat of battle, but during the quiet moments when you had a chance to think."

There was silence in the room. The young man looked away.

Things were never the same for the peace movement, though, after the Spanish war began. Sarah, like most pacifists, had always thought of herself as progressive, but now some people were accusing pacifists of being blind fools, reactionaries, even. War was coming, fascism was on the march and you had to choose sides. She and Irene went to see H. G. Wells's film *Things to Come* and the images of rows of bombers filling the sky, the clouds of gas, the ragged groups of people living afterwards in an endless bombed-out wasteland, haunted her. She remembered, when Germany annexed Austria, trying to explain Mr. Chamberlain's policy of appeasement to a class of thirteen-year-olds at the girls' school where she worked, now a student teacher. "I'm not saying Herr Hitler is a good man, but Germany has some right to feel aggrieved. Why shouldn't she join with Austria if both countries want it? Appeasement means trying to settle grievances, calm things down, not stir them up. Isn't that the sensible way?" Yet looking at the newsreels of Austrian Jews being thrown out of their homes and made to scrub the streets while soldiers kicked them, she felt, not doubt yet, but anguish.

It was easier for Irene; she had always been one to go wholeheartedly one way or the other and now she had joined the League for Anglo-German

Understanding. She had met Steve there and become, like him, a Hitler enthusiast. Sarah asked how anyone who believed in peace could possibly see anything good in fascism. Irene answered, "Hitler's a man of peace and vision, darling, you mustn't believe the propaganda. All he wants is justice for Germany and friendship with Britain."

Sarah turned to her father for advice. "You're right, darling," he said. "Hitler's an evil militarist. But if we go to war with him we're just using the same methods as his. Mr. Chamberlain is right." He spoke quietly, sadly. There were fewer meetings now and often Jim would sit in the lounge staring into space, his misery palpable.

Then came autumn 1938 and the Munich crisis. Men were digging up parks and lawns, making trenches where people could hide when the bombs fell, crosses of tape were stuck on the school windows so that splinters of glass would not slice into the children. Sarah thought, this time the civilians are in the trenches too. The school took a delivery of gas masks, horrible things of rubber and glass, large ones for the adults and small ones with Mickey Mouse faces for the children. When she went into school and saw the table piled with those blank, staring goggles, Sarah had to grip a chair to keep from fainting. The other teachers were staring at the masks in horror. The headmistress said they would have to show the children how to fit them. One teacher asked, tears streaming down her face, "How do we tell those little tots what those things are for, that people in airplanes will drop gas bombs on them? How do we do it?"

"Because we bloody must!" the headmistress shouted back, her voice breaking for a second. "Because if we don't they'll be dead. You think these are bad, you should see the maternity ward where my sister works! They've got bloody gas suits for babies there!"

But it didn't happen. There was a miracle, Chamberlain came back with the Munich agreement giving Germany part of Czechoslovakia. "Only where Germans live, not Czechs," Irene said triumphantly. Steve said that if a war had come it would have ruined the country financially; all the businessmen and bankers had been terrified by the prospect. "One in the eye for that warmonger Churchill!" When she heard the news Sarah felt relief course through her body like a drug. But then, a year later, in August 1939 it all happened again over Poland, trenches and gas masks and evacuation plans, and this time war was declared, Chamberlain's heartbroken voice announcing it on the radio. The horrible wail of the air-raid siren sounded for the first time, only in practice but the next time it might be real. All over London you saw people, grim or tearful, taking their dogs and cats to be put to sleep because they would be defenseless against the bombs. In the first week of September Sarah led a sad crocodile of children, carrying gas masks and little suitcases and accompanied by mothers with haunted faces, down to Victoria Station for evacuation.

The switchback of hope and horror took another turn. For months after the evacuation nothing happened, no air raids, no fighting after Poland fell to Germany. Parents began bringing their children home. The phony war, people began calling it. Some asked what point there was in continuing the war; it had been fought to help Poland but Poland was defeated, gone, divided between Germany and Russia. During the cold winter of 1939–40, watching the children throwing snowballs in the playground, Sarah began to hope again. But in April Germany suddenly invaded Denmark and Norway and British forces were thrown effortlessly back.

Chamberlain resigned and was replaced by Lord Halifax, just before the Germans attacked the Low Countries and France. Again the Germans swept all before them, shattering the French armies and sending the British army home, minus their equipment, from Dunkirk. The newscasters' voices on the BBC became increasingly serious, and people once more began looking fearfully up at the skies above London, now dotted with barrage balloons. The French army retreated further and further. Then, in the middle of June, news came that France and Britain had sued for an armistice. A month later the Treaty of Berlin was signed, a peace which the newspapers and the BBC said was surprisingly generous on Hitler's part; no occupation, no reparations, Britain and the Empire and the navy left intact, no colonies surrendered; the Belgian Congo the only European colony lost to Germany. And there was to be no German occupation apart from the large military base on the Isle of Wight. German Jews who had fled to Britain since the Nazis took over were to be repatriated, but nothing was said about British Jews. Sarah remembered seeing on a cinema newsreel, Lord Halifax returning from Berlin, Butler and Douglas-Home beside him on the airport tarmac, and the emotion in the aristocratic voice as Halifax declared, "The peace we have signed with Germany will last, God willing, forever." Clapping and shouts of "Hurrah!" broke out all over the cinema. Sarah had gone with her family; Irene cheered louder than anyone and their mother cried with relief. Sarah glanced at her father, but the good side of his face was turned away from her, and she could not see his expression.

A year later, just after the Russian war began, Halifax resigned—for health reasons they said, although his emaciated face was a mask of sorrow as he left Downing Street, and it was rumored he had been against the German "crusade." He was replaced by the ancient but cheerfully aggressive Lloyd George, who had called Hitler the greatest German of the age. People said he was little more than a stooge. He looked like a living relic on television, his false teeth clattering noisily during his broadcasts, his white hair wild. After his death in 1945 the newspaper proprietor and Cabinet Minister Beaverbrook took over, callously dismissive of the atrocity stories from Europe, his lifelong dreams of Empire free trade finally realized.

When Sarah left Westminster Abbey she was surprised to see how late it was. The sun was already beginning to set and the hundreds of windows in the Palace of Westminster sparkled with reflected light, making her blink. The sky to the west was like a Turner painting, a haze of reds and purples. She felt better for her prayer and the tears, though she did not believe any God was really there to listen.

She crossed the road to the Underground. It was busy outside the Tube station; a costermonger, wrapped in a thick muffler, was selling vegetables from a stall. A newsvendor called out "*Evening Standard!* Beaverbrook meets Laval!" She decided to buy a paper. Beaverbrook had stopped in Paris on his way to Berlin and there was a photograph of him with President Laval; like Britain, France was governed now by a right-wing newspaper proprietor.

Suddenly, she was aware of a commotion. Four boys of about twenty, in raincoats and carrying satchels, were racing down the street toward her, weaving through the crowds and pulling leaflets from their satchels, thrusting them into the hands of surprised passersby and tossing handfuls into the air. Someone shouted, "Hey!" Sarah wondered if it was a student prank, but the boys' faces were serious. They ran past, tossing a shower of leaflets at the costermonger's stall. The newsvendor shouted, "Bastards!" after them as they ran past the entrance to the Tube station. A rush of hot air from inside sent the leaflets swirling like confetti. One blew against Sarah's coat and she grasped it.

We have
NO FREE PARLIAMENT!
NO FREE PRESS!
NO FREE UNIONS!
The Germans occupy the Isle of Wight!
Strikers are executed!
The Germans make us persecute the Jews!
WHO WILL BE NEXT?
FIGHT GERMAN CONTROL!
JOIN THE RESISTANCE MOVEMENT!
W. S. Churchill

She looked up. The four boys were just turning the corner. Then, as though from nowhere, a dozen Auxiliary Police appeared, running at the boys and throwing them to the pavement. One fell into the gutter and a taxi swerved wildly, honking its horn. The policemen hauled the boys to their feet, thrusting them against the wall, heedlessly pushing several people aside. An old woman, carrying a shopping bag, was sent flying, packages in greaseproof paper spilling onto the street. A man with an umbrella and bowler hat was knocked over. Sarah watched as the bowler rolled under a bus, the wheels crushing it. The passengers inside turned to look at the scene, mouths open. Most looked quickly away again.

The police had pulled out their truncheons and were beating the boys mercilessly now. Sarah heard the crack of wood on a head, then heard a cry. The Auxiliaries, mostly young men themselves, laid in mercilessly. Sarah glimpsed a boy's mouth shining red with blood. One of the policemen was repeatedly punching another boy, his face white with fury, punctuating the blows with insults. "Fucking—Yid-loving—Commie—bugger."

Most people hurried by, faces averted, but a few stopped to look and someone in the crowd shouted out, "Shame!" The policeman who had been punching the boy turned around, reaching to his hip. He pulled out a gun. The watchers gasped, stepped back. "Who said that?" the Auxie yelled. "Who was it?"

Then, with a loud ringing of its klaxon, a police van pulled up to the curb. Four more policemen ran out and opened the double doors at the back. The boys were thrown in like sacks, the door slammed, and the van pulled away, klaxon shrieking again. The Auxies adjusted their uniforms, looking threateningly at the crowd as though daring anyone else to call out. Nobody did. The policemen shoved confidently through. Sarah looked at the pavement by the wall, now spotted with blood.

Next to her an old man in a cap and muffler stood trembling. Perhaps it was him who had shouted out. "The bastards," he muttered, "the bastards."

Sarah said, "It was so sudden. Where will they take them?"

"Scotland Yard, I expect." The old man looked Sarah in the face. "Down to the interrogation rooms. Poor little devils, they're only kids. They'll probably bring the black witches in from Senate House to them. They'll tear them to pieces."

"Black witches?"

The old man gave her a look of contempt. "The Gestapo. The SS. Don't you know who's really in charge of everything now?"

CHAPTER EIGHT

Gunther Hoth arrived in London early on Friday afternoon. He had taken the daily Lufthansa shuttle from Berlin. A large black Mercedes with embassy plates was waiting for him at Croydon; the driver, a sharply dressed young man, greeted him. *"Heil Hitler!"*

"Heil Hitler!"

"Good flight, Herr Sturmbannführer?"

"Fairly smooth."

"I am Ludwig. I will be assisting you today." The young man spoke formally, like a tour guide, but his eyes were keen. He was probably SS. Gunther sank gratefully into the comfortable upholstery of the car. He felt tired and the sore place in the middle of his back hurt. Last night he had gone straight from the meeting with Karlson to pack and get some sleep, then risen early to get the plane. He looked out of the window as the car drove smoothly through the gray London suburbs. England was just as he remembered it, cold and damp. Everyone looked pale, preoccupied, the clothes of working people worn and shabby. Many of the grimy buildings seemed in poor condition. There were lumps of dog dirt everywhere in the gutters and on the pavements too. Things had barely changed since he was last here seven years ago; in fact they looked much the same as when he first came to England as a student, back in 1929.

He was glad, though, for this assignment. He was weary of his Gestapo job, tired of interviewing informers whose eyes shone with malice or greed, tired of searching through the endless file cards. Even the payoff when, through one of his intuitive leaps, he found one of the few remaining hidden Jews, was less rewarding these days.

For over twenty years he had been full of anger at the Jews, at the terrible things they had done to Germany. He knew they were still a threat, with their power in America and what was left of Russia, but in recent years it was as though his rage, his strength, was wearing out as he got older—he would be forty-five soon. Yesterday he had arrived at a home in a prosperous Berlin suburb at daybreak with four policemen, banging on the door and shouting for entry. They had found a family of Jews, a mother and father and a boy of eleven, in a damp cellar. Bunks and armchairs and even a little sink had been installed there. They hauled the three upstairs, the mother yelling and screaming, and took them into the kitchen where their hosts, Mr. and Mrs. Muller, waited with their children, two little blond girls in identical blue nightshirts, the younger one clutching a rag doll.

Gunther's men shoved the three Jews against the kitchen wall. The woman stopped screaming and stood weeping quietly, head in hands. Then the little boy, crazily, attempted a run for it. One of Gunther's men grabbed his arm, banged him back against the wall, and gave him a punch that sent blood trickling from his mouth. Gunther frowned. "That's enough, Peter," he said. He turned to the German family. He knew Mr. Muller was a railway official with no political record. "Why have you done this?" he asked sadly. "You know it will be the end of you."

Muller, a little balding stick of a man, inclined his head to a small wooden cross on the wall. Gunther nodded. "I see. Lutherans? Confessing Church?"

"Yes," the man said. He looked at the captive Jews, and added, with sudden anger, "They have souls, just like us."

Gunther had heard that stupid argument many times before. He sighed. "All you have done is bring trouble on yourselves." He nodded to the Jews. "Them too. They should have gone for resettlement like all the others. Instead they've probably spent years running from house to house." People like Mr. and Mrs. Muller were so stupid; they could have lived normal quiet lives but now they would suffer SS interrogation and then they would be hanged.

Mrs. Muller took a deep breath. "Please do not hurt our little girls," she pleaded, her voice trembling.

"Shouldn't you have thought of them before you did this?" Gunther sighed again. "It's all right, your girls won't be harmed, they'll be sent for adoption by good German families—who've probably lost sons fighting in the East," he added bitterly, looking the woman in the eye.

Her husband said, "Do I have your word on that?"

Gunther nodded. The woman said, "Thank you," then lowered her head and began to cry. Gunther frowned; no one he had arrested had ever thanked him before. He looked at the little cross on the wall. He had been brought up a Lutheran himself, and was aware the cross was supposed to be a symbol of sacrifice. Gunther knew about real sacrifice. Hans, his twin brother, had been killed eight years ago by partisans in the Ukraine. Sitting in the comfortable car crossing London he remembered his brother's first leave, after the invasion of Russia in 1941. Hans had gone into Russia as part of an SS Einsatzgruppe, liquidating Bolsheviks and Jews. Hans was thirty-three when he came back that December, but he looked older. He had sat in Gunther's house, after Gunther's wife had gone to bed, his face pale and drawn against the black of his SS uniform. He said, "I've killed hundreds of people, Gunther. Women and old people." Suddenly he was talking fast. "A whole Jewish village once, a *shtetl*, we got them to dig a huge pit, then kneel naked on the edge while we shot them. It was so cold, they began shivering as soon as we got them undressed; it was fear as well, of course." Hans took a deep, shuddering breath, then braced himself, squaring his shoulders. "But Himmler says we have to be utterly hard and ruthless. He addressed us before we went into Russia. He said we must do this for the future of the Reich. For the generations unborn." He looked at his brother, a desperate fierce stare. "No matter what it costs us."

After the arrests Gunther had spent the rest of the day back at Gestapo headquarters in Prince Albrechtstrasse, dealing with the paperwork. He signed the documents transferring the Jewish family to Heydrich's Jewish Evacuation Department, the Mullers to interrogation. Then he went wearily down the wide central staircase, past the busts of German heroes, and walked home to his flat. His route took him through the vast, endless works being carried out in the city center to build Germania, Speer's new

Berlin, in time for the 1960 Olympics. The buildings they planned were so huge the sandy soil on which they would be built could never support them without concrete foundations hundreds of feet deep. A special railway line had been laid to take away the sand. On a cold, clear day like this the air was full of dust; sometimes the pall hung so heavy that Gunther, like other people susceptible to it, wore one of the new little white facemasks from America. Thousands of Polish and Russian forced laborers swarmed around the giant pits that made up the largest building site on earth. A few always died during the day and Gunther saw the hands and feet of corpses sticking out from underneath a tarpaulin to one side. Police patrolled with their rifles; they were vastly outnumbered by the laborers but one man with a gun can command many without.

He noticed that fewer passersby wore their Nazi Party badges these days. The streets that weren't being rebuilt looked increasingly shabby. Cheap imports from France and the occupied east had kept German living standards up until a couple of years ago, but they were falling now as the Russian war ground on; five million Germans dead and more announced each week. It was daily talk in Police Intelligence that morale was falling; many citizens didn't even give the German greeting "Heil Hitler" to each other anymore.

Back home in his flat he ate his usual lonely dinner at the kitchen table, then sat and listened to the radio. He opened a beer and began thinking of his wife and son. Four years ago Klara had left him for a fellow police officer; they had taken his son, Michael, and gone to live as subsidized settlers in Krimea, the only part of Russia that had been completely cleared of the original population and, an easily defensible peninsula, it was deemed safe for Germans. Gunther knew, though, that the thousand-mile-long railway the Germans had built to it was under constant partisan attack.

He switched off the radio—Mozart was playing and he found his music effete and irritating—and put on Tchaikovsky's 1812 Overture. He liked the confident, crashing beat, even though Tchaikovsky was Russian and disapproved of. The music stirred him but when it was over the sad empty bleakness that came over him sometimes crept back. He told himself it was the times; those who believed in Germany had to pay a hard price for the future.

The telephone's ring made him jump. The call was from Gestapo headquarters. He was to come in at once, to see Superintendent Karlson.

Karlson had a large office on the top floor of the building on Prince Albrechtstrasse. There were thick carpets and pictures of eighteenth-century Berlin on the walls, little figurines on the desk and tables. They had probably been taken from Jews; Karlson had been in the Party since the twenties and enjoyed all the privileges. He was one of the "golden peasants." He was large, with an air of cheerful bonhomie, and like many old Party men he was coarse but clever. Another man sat beside the big desk, under the portraits of Himmler and the Führer. The stranger was tall and slim, in his forties, with black hair and sharp blue eyes, immaculate in his SS uniform, the swastika in its white circle on his armband standing out against the black uniform. Karlson, too, wore his uniform today, though usually he wore a suit; as did Gunther, whose work involved moving in the shadows, unnoticed. Gunther saw the stranger had a file open on the knees of his immaculately creased trousers.

Karlson greeted Gunther warmly and waved him to a chair in front of the desk. He said, "Thank you for coming at such short notice."

"I wasn't doing anything particular, sir."

Karlson then turned to the stranger, a deferential note in his voice. "Allow me to introduce Obersturmbannführer Renner, from Division E7." Gunther thought, an SS Brigadier from the section of the Reich Security Office responsible for Britain; they're after someone important. Karlson continued, "Sturmbannführer Hoth is one of my most prized officers. He is in charge of ferreting out the Jews still left in Berlin. He caught three today."

The dark-haired man nodded. "Congratulations. Are there many left, do you think?"

"Not many in Berlin. We're near the end now. Though I hear that Hamburg still has a few."

"Maybe more than we know," Karlson said. "They're like rats; you think you've got rid of them, and then back they come, gnawing at your toes with their little sharp teeth, right?" He's playing to the gallery, Gunther thought.

"No," Renner answered quietly. "I think Sturmbannführer Hoth is right, there are not many left here now." He looked at Gunther with interest. "I believe you have met Deputy Reichsführer Heydrich."

"A few times only. When I first joined the Hitler Youth."

Renner nodded thoughtfully. He still seemed to be weighing Gunther up. He asked, "What do you think you will do, Sturmbannführer Hoth, when the Jews are all gone from Germany?"

"I don't know, sir. I've some years before I retire. I thought I might go to Poland, I hear there is still work to be done there." He had thought, maybe if he did that the spark of energy would return; if not, perhaps the partisans would get him, as they had Hans, and the family sacrifice would be complete.

Renner said, "You have an interesting history, Hoth. A university degree in English, a year spent living there, then when you returned Party membership and five years serving in the Criminal Police Department."

"Yes, sir. My father was a policeman, too."

Renner nodded, the silver skull-and-crossbones badge on his black SS cap glinting as it caught the light. "I know. In 1936 you were recruited to Gestapo Counter-Intelligence, under Brigadeführer Schellenberg as he then was, and worked on intelligence matters involving England, including the blueprint for its occupation, although fortunately as it turned out that was not needed." He smiled coldly. "Then five years in England after 1940, working from our embassy with the British Special Branch, helping build up their counter-subversion programs." As he spoke he glanced at the folder on his knees and Gunther realized he was referring to his own personnel file. Renner looked up at him with a puzzled expression. "And yet in 1945 you applied to return to Berlin, to join Department III. And here you have remained ever since, working on ethnic matters and, for the past few years, tracing hidden Jews. Never seeking promotion."

Gunther said, "I had had enough of England, sir. My wife more so. And my current rank is enough for me."

"Your wife left you, I see."

"Yes, sir."

Renner's expression softened. "I am sorry, I sympathize. Your work record is exemplary, you have done a great deal for the Reich. It says here you have a great gift for analysis, for noticing patterns other officers miss." Renner looked at Gunther again for a long moment, weighing him up, then turned to Karlson.

"Yes," Karlson said. He sat back in his chair, examining Gunther with his large, red-veined eyes. "Obersturmbannführer Renner's section has had a request from some very senior people at the London embassy. They need someone there for a"—he smiled—"a task, of some importance. You speak English, you went to university there, and you worked in Police Liaison at Senate House for five years. They would like you to go over for a week, perhaps two."

Gunther hesitated, then said, "Of course. If I can be of use."

"Though you are not fond of England?" Renner asked.

Gunther answered, "I know Britain is our ally but I don't like or trust the British. I've always thought them—decadent." Renner nodded. "And Beaverbrook is a joke," Gunther added.

Renner nodded again. "I agree. But Mosley's not strong enough to take over yet. Though being Home Secretary in England gives him great power. The English are Aryans, yet despite their achievements they do not really think racially. And yes, they are decadent, they cannot even keep control of their Empire anymore. And Churchill's people are making more and more trouble."

"So I have heard."

"Beaverbrook's in France now, talking to Laval." Renner gave a wintry smile. "Then he comes to Berlin. He wants closer economic links with Germany and to recruit more troops for India. The British cannot make their Empire pay so now they seek crumbs from our table. They will have to pay a price for that." He looked at Karlson, who linked his pudgy hands together on the desk and leaned forward.

"The operation we wish you to assist with is SS. We know you are loyal to us. You will work with our Intelligence man in London. You will say nothing to Ambassador Rommel's staff, nor to any of the people you used to know, nor any of the army people the embassy is crawling with."

So it's part of the SS–army secret war, Gunther thought, a war that has been going on for years. The army saw themselves as the historic guardians of Germany while the SS believed they were the men of the future, the ones who would police the lesser races of Greater Germany until they died off, and who would guard and preserve the future of the race. Hitler had favored the SS, had raised them up from nothing, but now he was ill, some said seriously, and neither the army nor the SS seemed able to bring victory in Russia. The rumors in the Gestapo were that the army wanted to end the Russian war, keep Ukraine and western Russia and the Caucasus and let the Russians set up a ragtag corrupt country of their own to the east. But Himmler knew that for Germany to be secure, the war had to be fought to the end. With Göring dead, most of his economic power had passed to Speer, whom the army favored but whom Himmler and the SS regarded as little better than a Bolshevik with his great state enterprises and contempt for free markets. Goebbels, Hitler's chosen successor after Göring's death, held the balance between them, but no one was quite sure where Goebbels stood these days.

"So Rommel's people aren't involved?" Gunther said carefully.

"Rommel knows nothing about it. This operation is entirely SS." Renner added, "If that creates a problem for you, Hoth, you must say so now and then this interview will never have taken place."

"It's not a problem, sir."

"Good." Renner sat back.

"You will take a flight from Templehof to London at nine tomorrow morning," Karlson said. "You will be driven to the embassy where you will be told more about your assignment. In the meantime, tell no one."

"Yes, sir." Gunther thought, *I've nobody left to tell.*

Karlson said, "Bring me back some English tea, will you? Earl Grey." He laughed and looked at Renner. "An old woman's drink. My wife likes to serve it when she gets together with her aunts."

*   *   *

As the car approached central London the traffic increased. The big Mercedes halted at a set of lights, surrounded by little snub-nosed English cars. Gunther saw a shadowy reflection of his face in the window. His features were beginning to sag; he was starting to look jowly, though his mouth and chin were still firm. He should take more exercise; Hans had always kept himself fit. A light drizzle began spotting the windscreen as they drove down the wide Euston Road.

Gunther had first come to England as a student at Oxford for a year, in 1929. Even then he had found the English effete. He had returned to London to work though, after the Treaty of Berlin, and spent five years liaising with the British police, helping train them in how to deal with riots, civil unrest, terrorism. The British had already learned a good deal themselves, from Ireland, but had grown complacent in the peaceful forties.

They turned left, past large old buildings and green squares, the trees bare. The car drove to the back of Senate House, where the embassy area was protected by twenty-foot-high concrete walls patrolled by British police. A German soldier opened the steel gates that led into the car park at the back. Gunther got out stiffly. He looked up at the nineteen-story building, stepped like a tall, narrow pyramid, the huge swastika flags hanging limp in the cold, heavy air. He had always admired its proportions, its functionality.

The driver led Gunther into the building, through the familiar stone corridors to the wide central vestibule where a marble bust of the Führer, ten feet high, stood on a great plinth. It was as busy as he remembered, the wide space echoing with footsteps and voices: men in uniforms, women typists in smart suits, files under their arms, clacking along in their high heels. He was led to the lifts. The driver showed a pass to the attendant, another soldier. They were the only ones inside as the lift rose smoothly to the twelfth floor. Ludwig said, "How does it feel to be back, sir?"

"Depressingly familiar. At least the air isn't full of dust like Berlin."

"Yes. Though the British fogs can be bad."

"I remember them well."

The doors opened. Ludwig's manner became formal again. "Your appointment, sir, is with Standartenführer Gessler. Afterwards I will show you to your flat. It is in Russell Square, very comfortable."

"Thank you." An Intelligence colonel, Gunther thought, one of the senior SS officers at the embassy. He felt a twitch of excitement, such as he hadn't had in a long time.

The office Gunther entered was small, painted white, with a panoramic view from the window of London under its pall of gray cloud. There was a globe of the world on a table under the window, the German Empire shown extending to the Urals, obligatory photographs of Hitler and Himmler behind the desk. The Hitler photo was the last one, taken in 1950, showing him gray-haired, cheeks fallen in, shoulders stooped. He glared out miserably at Gunther, a striking contrast to Himmler's cold confidence.

The man who rose to greet him wore full SS uniform. Gessler was in his early fifties, small and neat, thinning dark hair combed across his head to hide a bald spot. Round pince-nez and a severe face with stern lines around the mouth reminded Gunther of his old headmaster in Königsberg. He was one of the stiff, colorless technocrats Himmler and Heydrich favored for senior office. Yet, as Gunther knew, such people could be brutal too; like his old headmaster, they often had a temper. Gessler raised his arm in the National Salute and said, *"Heil Hitler."* Gunther followed. He was invited to sit down. Gessler looked at him. He laid his hands flat on the desk; they were short and stubby. The desk was very neat, pens and pencils pointing the same way in a little tray, papers lined up precisely.

Gessler spoke sharply, without any pleasantries. "Inspector Hoth, I am told your absolute discretion can be trusted. That you know the British, their ways, their police. That you can be diplomatic when needed. That you are a Gestapo officer to your bones." For the first time he smiled, suddenly confiding. "And that you are a good hunter of men."

"I hope all that is true, sir."

"Repeat that in English."

Gunther did so. Gessler nodded briefly. "Good. They said you spoke almost without accent." He paused. "I understand your brother joined the SS when he was quite young. Died heroically in Russia."

"He did." Gunther wanted a cigarette, but saw no ashtray in the room.

Gessler continued quietly, "And I understand you believe, like him, that Germany must be committed to the uttermost to destroying our enemies, so that future generations of Germans may live at peace and be secure."

"I have done for over twenty years, sir."

"You and your brother joined the party in 1930."

"Yes, sir. During the Weimar chaos."

Gessler crossed his legs. "And yet, unlike your brother, you never applied to join the SS. You are automatically subject to Deputy Reichs-führer Heydrich, of course, as a member of the Gestapo. But you are not SS. That did not seem to concern my colleagues in Berlin, but I think it requires—some explanation." He smiled again, but without warmth now.

Gunther took a breath. "My brother Hans was always drawn to—to an idealist's life. Whereas I was drawn to police work, like my father. It is where my skills lie. It is how I serve Germany."

Gessler gave a sharp little grunt. "I can see a life of physical fitness has not appealed to you." He himself was trim and fit in his spotless black uniform. "It is strange. I thought identical twins always behaved alike."

Gunther suspected Gessler was trying to provoke him. He answered quietly, "Not in every way."

Gessler considered a moment. Then he stood abruptly and crossed to the globe. He laid a hand on Europe. "This globe, as we both know, is a fiction. Much territory west of the Volga remains in Russian hands. They still have the Volga oilfields and new ones they've found in Siberia, while most of the territory we do hold is crawling with partisans. Poland, too. Our settlements there are increasingly unsafe. There are those who say we should end the war, settle with Khrushchev and Zhukov or some of the little capitalists sprouting up behind the Volga now the Communist Party shares power with them. What is your opinion?"

Gunther knew the answer Gessler wanted, which was the answer he believed. "If we did a deal with the Russians, left any large Russian state that might threaten us again, that would be a poor reward for the lives of five million German soldiers. And our weapons technology is advancing all the time."

Gessler swung the globe around, pointing at the United States. "But not as fast as America's. And in a few weeks President Taft will be gone, and this liberal Adlai Stevenson will be in charge. They say he's cautious, he'll be careful, but he's not our friend."

"The Americans have always been unpredictable."

"Yes. And have coupled a policy of isolationism with the development of fearful weapons. Look at their claims to have an atomic bomb, a wonder weapon that dwarfs any we possess."

"We're told it's a fake, those films are a Hollywood trick," Gunther said, though he had never been quite sure about that.

"No, it exists," Gessler countered in a matter-of-fact tone. "Those films of the mushroom clouds in the desert were not faked. The sand turned to glass." He raised his heavy dark eyebrows. "We have agents, sympathizers, in America. We have done since Roosevelt's day. And at the U.S. embassy in London too, I will tell you a little more about that. But to return to us. We have our nuclear program, that is no secret. Yet it hasn't progressed well. We believe the Americans are ahead of us in all sorts of weapons research. Biological weapons. Even in rocketry it seems they may be catching up." He laughed, with unexpected nervousness. "Maybe the science-fiction writers are correct, and we will have a war on the moon one day."

He came and sat behind his desk again. "We have found it impossible to get any real intelligence about the American weapons program because their security there, as you might imagine, is watertight." He smiled again and his eyes widened a little. "But now a chink may have opened. Just maybe."

Gunther felt the excitement again, a slight inner trembling. "Is this to do with my mission?"

Gessler leaned back in his chair. He suddenly looked tired. "Things are not good. I wish the Führer would broadcast again, speak to us as he once did. Another winter has started in Russia, the supply trains we need to keep our armies up to strength are being attacked again. The Russians know how to live off the land, what grasses to eat, what to wear to keep out the cold, and how to survive in temperatures of minus 40. We're sure they are about to launch another winter offensive, supplied from those factories they've built in deep forests far behind the Urals. Our rockets are little more than useless, we don't know where to aim them. And these Resistance movements in Spain and Italy, Britain and France..." He shook his head, then looked hard at Gunther. "To win the Russian war we need to know what the American scientists know."

Gunther shifted uneasily in his seat. If even an SS Intelligence colonel could talk with this sort of pessimism, what were Speer and the army people saying? Gessler saw his look and sat up straight, frowning, formal again. "Have you ever heard of the Tyler Kent affair?" he asked sharply.

"Kent was a sympathizer of ours in the American embassy just before victory in 1940."

"Yes. He passed on useful information about Churchill's contacts with Roosevelt before he was arrested. He knew some of the British Fascists, like Maule Ramsay, the present Scottish Secretary. The British secret services found out about him. Ambassador Kennedy—he's been there a long time, he's got lax, he's sympathetic to us. We have agents in the embassy, new Tyler Kents, and a few weeks ago one of them told us something very interesting." Gessler sat forward, lacing his fingers together. "An American scientist—there are reasons why I can't tell you what area he was working in, except that it was at the edge of their weapons research—came over to England for his mother's funeral. His name is Edgar Muncaster. He's British by birth, though he's been an American citizen for nearly twenty years. A man we have in the U.S. embassy found out the security people at Grosvenor Square were worried about him going around London on his own."

"Does he have Resistance sympathies?"

Gessler shook his head. "Far from it. Committed to an isolationist and powerful America. That's not the problem. But after a recent divorce, he has become an unpredictable drunk. He stayed in London for a while, as he wanted to sell his mother's house. He seemed more or less in control of himself. Then one day he went AWOL. He was watched, but he didn't register at the embassy in the evening as he was supposed to do. Then there was a phone call from him; he was in a hospital in Birmingham, with a broken arm."

"How?"

"He went to visit his brother. A geologist who works at Birmingham University. There was an argument, which ended in the brother pushing our American friend out of a window."

"Was he badly hurt?"

"Just the broken arm. But the Americans hauled him out of the hospital, smashed arm and all, arrested him, and put him on a plane back to the States. Destination, according to what our man at the embassy saw, Folsom Prison in California; isolation, maximum security."

Gunther said, "So he did something."

Gessler nodded vigorously. "Or said something. We don't know what. Our spy doesn't have that level of clearance."

"Were the British involved?"

"No. This is something the Americans don't want them to know about. They were told the Americans were just taking an injured citizen home."

Gunther considered. "Who does our man at the U.S. embassy answer to?"

Gessler smiled. "Not to Rommel's people. He works for us, for the SS. And we've kept hold of this information. We've made inquiries with some of our friends in the British Special Branch, though—we have some good people there. We asked them to look into the brother's background. I think you know the present commissioner."

"Yes," Gunther agreed. "From when I was here before. A strong believer in Britain and Germany working together. A good anti-Semite, too."

Gessler nodded. "We can work with some of them on this, if we're careful. Not the British secret services, what's left of them since we found out about all their Communist moles when we took over the Kremlin. It's just a few death-or-glory patriots left there now."

"Yes," Gunther agreed again. While posted in England he had watched the Special Branch grow from a specialist section of the Metropolitan Police dealing with spies and subversives to a whole Auxiliary Police force supplemented with informers and agents in anti-government organizations.

"What did Special Branch find?" he asked.

"That the brother, Frank Muncaster, was arrested for attempted murder. He smashed up his own flat and when he was arrested he was raving about the end of the world. Screaming at his brother that he shouldn't have told him what he did."

Gunther laughed, but uneasily. "The end of the world?"

"Yes. Helpfully, the charge was reduced to causing serious bodily harm. His behavior was so bizarre that he wasn't put in prison, but committed to a local mental hospital. Where he sits now. This we know from local police files in Birmingham. We've told the Special Branch people we think brother Frank may have undesirable political connections in Europe. When they told us he didn't, we said thank you very much and went away."

Gunther considered. "The Americans will be interested in this man, if the brother has told them what happened."

"Yes. Certainly they were very keen to get Edgar Muncaster back to the States. They could try to kill the brother. But they can't go through official channels, they don't want the British finding out their weapons secrets. If that's what Edgar told Frank about."

Gunther thought for a moment. "So, forgive me, sir, but we don't know whether this — lunatic — actually has any secrets."

"No, we don't. But it is very much worthwhile finding out."

"Has he said any more while he's been in hospital?"

"We simply don't know. They may have just drugged him up to keep him quiet. They usually do, with the violent ones. Unfortunately getting to him in the mental hospital will need a certain amount of delicacy and local knowledge." He shrugged. "You know the British, all sorts of bureaucratic complications, different parts of the system sealed off from each other. The Medical Superintendent, a Dr. Wilson, is related to a civil servant in the British Health Department."

"They're putting through a sterilization bill, aren't they?"

Gessler waved his hand in a gesture of contempt. "Pussyfooting, trivial. They should just gas the lot, as we did. But they won't."

"Yes," Gunther reflected. "It's even taken them over ten years to establish a sort of authoritarian government."

"Well, they're on the right path now." He smiled. "The British will have another matter to preoccupy them very shortly."

"Will they?"

Gessler smiled again, the smirk of a man with secret knowledge. It made him look suddenly childish. "They will." Suddenly he was all business again. "I want you to go to Birmingham. Get into the flat where Muncaster lived, see if there is anything of interest there. Visit Muncaster. Later we may ask you to lift Muncaster, bring him back here. But first I want you to try and find out what state he's in, whether he's talked. You'll have Special Branch help."

Gunther nodded. The excitement in him was steady now, focused.

"Of course," Gessler said, "this may well be a mare's nest. But the instruction to undertake the investigation comes from very high up, from Deputy Reichsführer Heydrich himself." Gunther saw a little gleam of ambition in Gessler's eyes.

"I'll do all I can, sir."

"You'll have an office here, and you'll be assisted by a British Special Branch police inspector called Syme. He's a good friend; he's spent time in Germany. He's young but he's clever and ambitious. Recommended by your successor here, in fact. Use him to get through the hoops." Gessler jabbed a finger at Gunther, reminding him again of his old headmaster. "But so far as Syme is concerned, and anyone else who asks, we still want Muncaster because of suspected political links. I wish we could have gone straight to the top and asked Beaverbrook for him, but in the circumstances we must fly beneath the radar, as the Luftwaffe people say. For now at least."

"Do *you* think there's anything in this, sir?"

"I know a little more than you." Gessler couldn't stop that annoying smirk appearing again. "About what Edgar Muncaster might have been working on. Enough to realize this could be important. I can't tell you, Hoth, because to be blunt what you don't know you can't tell anyone else. The point is, Himmler and Heydrich want this done."

Gunther was already thinking about how to navigate his way through the British authorities, the bureaucracy, without them learning what he was doing. He thought, if Heydrich's hunch was right — and it was only a hunch — he might do something important with his life after all.

CHAPTER NINE

At the hospital on Wednesday, two days before, the rain had been succeeded by days of fog and mist. Frank sat in his usual place in the quiet room. The previous day he had told Ben, the Scottish attendant, a little about his university friend David, and Ben suggested Frank telephone him, see if he might be able to help get him transferred to a private clinic. "After all, if he's a civil servant, they ken how to get things done. You can use the telephone in the nurses' office when I'm on duty."

But Frank wasn't sure. The fewer people he spoke to the better, because of his secret, because of what Edgar had told him. And he was suspicious of Ben; why had the attendant singled Frank out to help, particularly when he had spoken bitterly about Dr. Wilson giving Frank more attention because he was middle class? Ben seemed direct and friendly enough but still there was something in him that did not quite ring true. He noticed that sometimes his Glasgow accent was stronger, as though for effect.

Earlier that morning Ben had come up to him and asked if he had thought any more about phoning his friend. Frank asked suddenly, "Why are you doing this? Why are you helping me?"

Ben raised his hands in a gesture of surrender. "You're a suspicious wee fella. It's just I don't think you belong here, you should try'n get out. But it's up to you, pal; if you're happy to trust Dr. Wilson, that's fine." He'd walked away then, Frank staring after him anxiously. He knew it was true, he was suspicious of everybody, had been since childhood. He hadn't heard any more from Dr. Wilson about electric shock therapy, but feared he might and that it might make him blurt out what he knew. He thought again about David Fitzgerald. He had been one of the few people Frank had ever really trusted and liked. He hadn't seen him, though, for some years. After they graduated from Oxford they had kept in touch by letter, and Frank had been invited to David's wedding in 1943 but he had never been to a wedding and felt he would be unable to cope with all the people. After that the gaps between David's letters had grown longer and for the last couple of years they had only exchanged Christmas cards.

Frank preferred to stay in the quiet room but the attendants often chivvied him out, saying he must come to the day room, mix with the other patients. He didn't want to; the others reminded him of the awful position he was in. Some passed their time staring at the wall, others would suddenly erupt with fury over nothing. Some of their faces had been twisted and warped into strange expressions by years of madness. But Frank knew he had his own peculiarity, his habitual grin; and he had attacked his own brother. Was he mad too? It was all right when the drugged effect was strong in him, but as it weakened and wore off at the end of the period between his three daily doses, his heart often pounded with fear now and he wanted to scream. And though he had never dreamed about school since leaving Strangmans, he did dream about it now. This place reminded him of it in so many ways. He had even had a couple of frightening dreams about Mrs. Baker.

Mrs. Baker had been a spiritualist. Frank's mother claimed she was able to contact his father, who had been killed at Passchendaele in 1917; Frank had been born, prematurely, two weeks later. His mother had never recovered from his father's death. George Muncaster had been a doctor, he hadn't needed to volunteer, and Frank's mother had begged him not to go but he believed joining the Army Medical Corps was his duty. Then, as his wife had feared, he had been killed, leaving her alone in the big house with just two boys and Lizzie, the daily woman.

Frank knew his mother didn't love him, though she did love Edgar. But Edgar, who was nearly four years older than Frank, had been born when she was young and happy, before the world went mad in 1914. She was always saying Edgar was a good boy, clever and obedient, while Frank with his childhood illnesses and, even then, oddities, was a trial.

But it was Frank who most resembled his father. The photograph of him, draped in black, on the mantelpiece had shown the same long nose, full, feminine mouth, and large, puzzled dark eyes. Like Frank, he looked as though he might have been afraid of the world. Edgar, though, was big, stocky, and confident. Before he went on his war orphan's scholarship to their father's old school in Scotland, he would often call Frank names like "runt" and "weed" and a word he had found in a Grimm's fairytale: "You're weazened, Frankie," he would say, "a weazened creature."

Thousands of women turned to spiritualism in the 1920s, women who had lost sons and husbands and brothers in the trenches. Mrs. Baker first came to the house in Esher late in 1926, when Frank was nine. Edgar had already gone to Scotland, and Frank was at a small local day school, a quiet, fearful child with few friends.

It was because the house, which had also been his father's surgery, was so large that Mrs. Baker's séances were held there. The group came on Tuesday evenings, half a dozen women, middle-aged before their time. Lizzie, the maid, who was always nice to Frank, told him she did not hold with spiritualism and he should stay away from it all.

The women would arrive just before Frank's bedtime, greeting his mother with friendly formality. Lizzie would have prepared sandwiches and soft drinks beforehand—Mrs. Baker said alcohol interfered with her channel to the spirits—and they would chat to each other about normal things, their gardens and servants or those wretched miners still on strike. When Mrs. Baker arrived, though, they fell into a reverent silence. She was a very tall, stout woman of around fifty, her big, square face with its little blue eyes framed by short, bobbed curls. She wore fashionable dresses, though the straight lines of the day did not suit her large frame, and a long rope of pearls reached to her waist. She always carried a large bag, decorated in a paisley pattern, draped over her arm.

Frank was allowed to take the sandwiches around. The women always asked politely how he was, and Mrs. Baker would look down at him from her great height, saying she hoped he was being a good boy, a helper to his mother. One of the other women once commented that he was a poor fatherless lamb but Mrs. Baker gave her a reproving look and said earnestly, in her rich contralto, that Frank's father was with him in spirit. After twenty minutes' conversation Mrs. Baker would clap her hands. "Time to begin, ladies. I feel Meng Foo approaching." Meng Foo was her spirit guide, a princess of ancient China. "She is ready," Mrs. Baker would say. "I see her walking toward me, so delicately on her little bound feet." The women would drop their eyes respectfully, and his mother would tell Frank to go to bed. Then, the other ladies following, she would open the double doors to the dining room with its big table.

Lizzie had said, as Frank sat in the kitchen watching her cook, that it was strange how Mrs. Baker had told her ladies to avoid the new spiritualist church a mile away. "All very well for your mummy to say other spiritualists have driven Mrs. Baker away because of jealousy over her being on a higher plane. I know she gets paid for these sessions; I don't know how much but I bet it's a lot."

Frank's mother told him Mrs. Baker made a connection with his father almost every week. She had heard him speaking through her; it had been his man's voice, his Scottish accent. When she told Frank about the séances her habitual sad expression would change to a happy, wondering smile. Frank's father, she said, was in a place of sunlit gardens and beautiful palaces. Sometimes, in the distance, he glimpsed Jesus walking there, all haloed in white. She told Frank his father was sorry for going and leaving them; he knew now that he had done wrong. He was always watching over Frank lovingly.

The idea of his father watching over him meant little to Frank, for he had never met him. And inside him was a seed of doubt, nurtured by Lizzie, about Mrs. Baker and all her works.

On Tuesday evenings Frank, driven by curiosity, began creeping out of bed after the women had gone into the dining room. He would go halfway down the stairs and peer through the banisters at the closed door, listening. There would be bangs and thuds sometimes, exclamations from the women, now and then the sound of one of them weeping. The thuds frightened Frank and the weeping made him feel like crying himself, but he always stayed where he was.

One late spring evening he was at his usual post on the staircase.

From the dining room he thought he heard, briefly, a man's voice, then one of the women sobbing: a dreadful, desperate sound. It went on a long time. Frank's eyes watered. Then, suddenly, the dining-room door opened and Mrs. Baker came out. She closed the door, leaned against the wall, and shut her eyes.

Frank crouched perfectly still. The hallway was dim; if he didn't move she might not see him. Mrs. Baker was, as ever, carrying her big paisley patterned bag. As Frank watched she laid it down and opened it. To his astonishment she pulled out a half-bottle of whiskey. She glanced quickly and furtively at the closed door, then raised the bottle and took a large swig. She sighed, then took another, glancing at the door again as she wiped her mouth. The weeping was still going on. She muttered something, and Frank caught the words "silly bitches." Mrs. Baker's expression had changed; it was hard and contemptuous as she replaced the bottle in her bag, took out a packet of mints and popped one in her mouth. Then she looked up and saw Frank staring at her.

Her eyes narrowed. She glanced quickly at the dining room door, then lumbered to the stairs, the long rope of pearls swinging against her big body. Frank was frightened now, but he couldn't move. Mrs. Baker mounted the stairs and leaned over him. The pearls brushed his face and he flinched. She grasped his arm, thick, strong fingers digging in. "You're a nasty, nosy little boy," she said in a vicious whisper. "What we do is private, not for children to see. The spirits will be angry. Don't you say a word about what you saw just now, or I'll send bad spirits, really wicked, cruel ones, and they'll make you suffer." She shook him, hard. "Do you understand?"

"Yes, Mrs. Baker."

The grip tightened further. "Are you sure? Don't think I can't summon up bad spirits, because I can."

"I understand."

"You'd better. Now get to bed. Nasty spying little boy."

She watched him as he stumbled to his room. He lay on his bed in the dark, shaking. He was frightened, though not of bad spirits. He knew now that Lizzie was right; Mrs. Baker was a heartless fraud. He knew too that what he had always feared was true, the world was a bad place, full of people who would harm him if they could.

Afterwards the séances went on. Mrs. Baker was as nice as ever to Frank, although there was a new glint in her eyes when she looked at him. A few weeks later, he was summoned by his mother, who told him his father had sent a message from the Other Side that it was time he went away to school, to join his brother. She looked at him, not just with her usual anxiety but, he saw, real concern. "I've not been sure Strangmans College is right for you, you're delicate, but your father told me through Mrs. Baker that you'll learn discipline, it'll be the making of you. She says you must go, and the spirit world knows better than we do. Oh, Frank, don't stand there wearing that silly grin, please."

So a few weeks later, just after his eleventh birthday, Frank went away to school. Lizzie had tears in her eyes as she helped his mother pack his trunk. Frank thought, on the train to Edinburgh, maybe things will be better now. But he soon found out he was wrong; Mrs. Baker had indeed called down on him a whole horde of terrible spirits.

The hospital was keen on exercise. The patients, if they were well enough, took an hour's exercise every day in the airing courts. These were large courtyards in the center of the hospital building complex, open to the air but with a covered walkway beside the walls. The patients would walk endlessly around and around for an hour, the attendants in charge calling on laggards to keep up. Some patients were allowed to walk alone in the grounds, up to the signs marked *Limit of Parole*, but not Frank.

He was in his usual armchair in the quiet room, facing the window. There was another patient in the room, a big, elderly man called Mr. Martindale, who believed Communists and Jews were beaming messages into his head and who habitually sat with his hands over his ears, muttering to drown out the sound. He had been at the hospital for many years; he had been a foundry worker before that. Frank knew he didn't like being disturbed, but was all right if you left him alone.

It was late morning, getting on for exercise time. Frank heard the door behind him open, a firm military tread approaching. Ben wasn't on duty today, it was Sam, a middle-aged ex-soldier, trim in his neatly pressed uniform. He came around the chair. "Frank," he said in his Brummie accent. "Hiding in here again, eh? Come on, airing courts time. Look sharp." Frank rose reluctantly. Sam turned to Mr. Martindale. "You too, come on."

Mr. Martindale looked piteously at Sam. "Please. I'm not well enough. The voices are loud. Leave me alone!"

"We'll give you some extra pills later," Sam said. "But you need your exercise! Chop! Chop!"

The patients began making their circuits of the courtyard. Frank had had a haircut a few days ago; it was the attendants' jobs to do this and the one on duty hadn't made a good job of it, cutting Frank's untidy brown hair into a military crew cut, little more than a fuzz. He felt the cold, wet air on his scalp. Something about the mindless nature of what they were doing brought Strangmans to Frank's mind and also reminded him once again of what he was now: a mental patient. He longed to get back to the quiet room.

He was next to Mr. Martindale, who was still muttering to himself as he stumbled, hands over his ears. Sam called out impatiently, "Martindale! Hands down! You'll fall if you're not careful!"

The other attendant, a young man who was new, looked anxious but Sam, wanting to show his authority, shouted out again, "Martindale! Hands down!"

Frank saw something happen to Mr. Martindale's eyes; they had been cast down but now he looked up and stared at Sam and they were wild. He glanced around at Frank, a terrifying stare that made him step backwards. Then he looked back at the attendants, before plunging across the little piece of lawn in the center of the airing court toward them with unexpected speed and force. "Yo' fookin' bugger!" he shouted at Sam. "Can't you fookin' leave me alone!" He threw himself, fists flying, not at Sam but at the young attendant. Frank saw blood spurt from the young man's nose. His cap flew off and he crashed against the wall. Sam took out a whistle and sounded a long blast. Frank stood there petrified as Sam grappled with Mr. Martindale, trying to pin his arms behind him. All the patients stood watching; some stared at the scene, one or two laughed, one young man started jumping up and down, weeping.

Half a dozen attendants appeared, running. Mr. Martindale was pushed to the ground; Sam kicked him in the back. The other patients were shepherded quickly inside. On the ward, Frank managed to sidle off to the quiet room again. He sat in his chair. His hands were trembling and his bad hand hurt. He had seen patients cursing and shouting before, had seen people forcefully put to bed, but never open violence like that. He wasn't safe here, anything could happen. He thought again of the shock treatment, what he might find himself saying. He whispered to himself, "I'll do it. I'll phone him. David, please help me."

CHAPTER TEN

On Friday David left work at five and took the Tube to Piccadilly. Carol had asked if he would like to go to another recital the following week and he had agreed; he had been instructed to keep the saucepan simmering, as Jackson had put it, so they still went to concerts about once a month.

He walked into Soho. It was a damp, raw evening, wet, slippery pavements reflecting the neon signs in the shops—Bovril, England's Glory matches, Emu Australian Wines for Christmas. The narrow streets were crowded, city gents and sharp-suited pimps, theatrical-looking types and soldiers in heavy greatcoats on leave from India or Africa. Prostitutes in the doorways wore their hair in the fashionable German style, blond pigtails looped behind their ears. A drunk in Blackshirt uniform staggered by.

David turned into the damp alley beside the coffee shop, stepping over squashed cigarette packets and a little heap of dog's dirt. A group of teenage boys sat in the coffee shop, leering at women passersby over their cups of frothy coffee. One had an oiled quiff that stuck out inches above his forehead. One Saturday night a few weeks ago some Blackshirts had come into Soho, grabbed all the Jive Boys they could find, and shaved their heads with cutthroat razors. But nothing could keep people out.

The green door was unlocked. A single bulb provided the staircase with a dim light. Damp paint was peeling from the walls. A large middleaged man, a Homburg hat in his hand, came out of the prostitute's flat. David, going up, stood aside to let him pass. The man's sweaty face wore a contented expression. "Lovely bit of cunt," he said dreamily. "Lovely."

David knocked on the door of the flat opposite. Natalia let him in.

As usual, she wore an old shirt spotted with paint, no makeup, her hair untidy as ever. Normally she gave him her warm, knowing smile, but tonight she looked serious. "Come in," she said.

The big room was cold, smelling of paint. Another painting stood on the easel; tumbledown houses on a steep street, a big square castle in the distance. As in all Natalia's townscapes, the people on the street mostly had their faces cast down or turned away.

Jackson was standing by the fire. The big man looked anxious, his lips pressed tightly together. "Thanks for coming at such short notice," he said.

"Please, sit down." Natalia gestured to the threadbare armchairs around the fire. Often her tone was like that, formally polite. Then her slight accent sounded German, but when she spoke with emotion it deepened and sounded different, the vowels flattening and lengthening. "Something's come up," Jackson said, a little uneasily. "Something really rather important."

David asked, "Are Geoff and Boardman not coming?"

"Not tonight." His eyes were fixed on David's.

David took a deep breath. "Have we been found out?"

Jackson shook his head. "No, no, don't worry. This is nothing to do with the work of our cell. It's something else, some information that has come down from people at the very top." David glanced at Natalia. She nodded seriously. "It concerns someone you knew at Oxford, actually," Jackson continued. "A man called Frank Muncaster. Does the name ring any bells?"

David frowned, puzzled. "Yes. Geoff knew him, too."

Jackson looked surprised, then said to Natalia, "Of course, they were at the same college."

She said, "They didn't think of that."

"It could help us," Jackson said.

David had a memory of Frank, sitting with him and Geoff in an Oxford pub; his dark hair long and untidy as usual, his thin face anxious and strained, afraid of almost everyone. "What's happened to him?" he asked quietly.

Jackson said, "I understand you and Muncaster shared rooms at Oxford. You were his best friend."

"I suppose so."

"What was he like?"

"Odd, shy. Afraid of people. I think he had a pretty rotten childhood. But he was a good chap, never did anyone any harm. And he used to think about things, he had interesting opinions if you let him talk."

"You were his protector, perhaps," Natalia prompted.

"Why do you say that?"

"We know he looked up to you."

"Did he?"

"We think so."

"He hung around with Geoff and me, our group of friends. When we went into the Civil Service Frank stayed on at Oxford and did a PhD. He's very bright." Jackson and Natalia were both listening intently. "We've rather lost touch in recent years. We used to exchange letters, but now it's just Christmas cards." He looked at Natalia. "Is he dead?" David asked suddenly.

"No," she answered simply. "But he is in deep trouble."

"How?"

Jackson said, "Muncaster became a geologist, yes? Some sort of research job at Birmingham University."

"Yes. He could never have held down a teaching job."

Jackson nodded. "His father died in the Great War, I understand, and he was brought up by his mother near London, with his elder brother. Both went to a boarding school in Scotland."

"You know a lot," David said.

"We need to know more," Natalia said. "He needs our help."

David took a deep breath. "Frank didn't talk much about his childhood. But I know his mother was under the thumb of some spiritualist con artist."

"What about the older brother?" Natalia asked.

"I don't think he and Frank got on. He went off to America sometime in the thirties. He was a scientist, too." David frowned. "Frank avoided talking about himself. There was some accident at his school, his hand got badly smashed up, but he never said how. I think he had a bad time there. I think he was bullied."

Jackson looked puzzled. "Lots of boys get bullied at public school."

Natalia interrupted quietly, "One who could not fit. Poor boy."

Jackson continued, "Frank Muncaster's brother is also a scientist, a physicist. He became a U.S. citizen and for the last ten years he's held a senior position at a top California university. He does work connected with the American weapons programs. I don't know what, but something important." Jackson paused to let that sink in, then added, "Back in October, old Mrs. Muncaster died, and brother Edgar came over for the funeral. Mrs. Muncaster's house is being sold, we know that. Edgar may have wanted the money. He's recently divorced, in need of money for the—what do they call it there—alimony, and it seems he's developed a serious drinking habit."

"Has this information come from America?" David asked. "Are they involved?"

"Contacts in their secret services are," Natalia answered. "Though we also have information from certain sources here."

Jackson stood up, slowly began pacing the threadbare carpet. Through the wall came an ecstatic laugh from the prostitute's latest customer. David wondered what it was like for Natalia, alone here at night, listening to that. Jackson made a moue of distaste, then said, "The Resistance has links with the Americans. Not that they like us, most of them, though we may find them more sympathetic under Adlai Stevenson. But they don't like Nazi Europe, either, and we're a useful channel. Sometimes we help them get people over to the States—like a couple of Jewish scientists they wanted recently." He took a deep breath. "A fortnight ago somebody very senior in their Secret Services contacted us. Apparently Edgar Muncaster was brought back to America last month with a broken arm. He had something to confess to them."

"Confess?"

"Yes. While in England he'd visited his brother Frank in Birmingham. There was a heated argument."

David shook his head. "I can't imagine Frank getting into an argument with anyone."

"Perhaps he was afraid of what he might do if he ever lost control," Natalia said sadly.

Jackson shot her an irritated glance. "We don't know what the argument was about," he continued, "and the Americans won't say. Nor will Frank Muncaster. But the Americans think Edgar may have spilled some beans connected with their weapons research. Whatever it was, it was enough to send Frank Muncaster into such a state that he ended up putting his brother through a second-floor window."

The idea of Frank attacking anyone still seemed extraordinary to David. All his life he had held himself under rigid control. What could have made Frank snap? And what was he getting into?

"An accident we think, the window was rotten, but Edgar was lucky to get away with a broken arm. Frank, meanwhile, started smashing up his own flat and raving about the end of the world. The upshot was that he was taken away to a mental hospital outside Birmingham, which is where he is now." Jackson shook his head, as though such behavior were beyond him.

Natalia said quietly, "The Americans consider it important that no one here gets hold of information about Edgar's work. Not in our government, nor the Germans. We believe Frank hasn't talked, yet."

"How do you know that?"

"We have a man in the mental hospital, on the staff."

"Good God."

Jackson smiled. "Like all these places it's very large, over a thousand patients. This man is one of our many sleepers, quietly doing a normal job until, one day, he can be used. A male nurse, an attendant as they call them. A good man, experienced."

"He is looking after Frank," Natalia added. "Taking care of him."

"What happened to Edgar?"

Jackson said, "So far as we know, he is now locked up somewhere very safe in the States."

"Then they'll know if he told Frank anything."

"Yes," Jackson agreed. "They will. They're not telling us, but the obvious implication is that he did."

"My God. It could be about the Bomb."

"Or rocketry, or biological warfare," Natalia said. "The Americans call themselves the last guardians of democracy, but some of the things they have been working on are — terrible."

"The Americans want Frank Muncaster," Jackson said baldly. "Our man has managed, to a limited degree, to gain his confidence. Muncaster has of course never seen the inside of a place like that before and apparently he's terrified of what they might do to him."

"What sort of thing?"

"Electric shock treatment, or worse."

David shook his head.

Natalia said, "We may be able to get him out."

Jackson sat down again, looking at her. "Possibly. But we have to be careful just now, not draw attention to him. Of course if he does tell them whatever secrets Edgar may have blurted out they may just dismiss it all as lunatic ravings, but if he then disappears it might put a different complexion on things." He raised his eyebrows. "The doctor in charge of the hospital, Wilson, fortunately isn't the brightest spark in the medical profession but he seems to have taken some interest in Frank. He's also related to a senior civil servant under Church, the junior health minister."

David looked up. "Isn't Church the one who's pushing through the bill to sterilize the unfit?"

"Yes, he's an old eugenicist. Introduced a bill back in 1930. But not a great pro-German, apparently, a believer in the independence of British institutions." Jackson gave a hollow laugh. "Still doesn't realize that battle is long lost. Now, our man says Muncaster is very withdrawn. Wilson hasn't been able to get him to talk. He needs a friend to take an interest in him." He raised his eyebrows. "And it seems, from his conversations with our nurse, that the only person he might trust is you."

David felt a weight descending on him. "Doesn't he have friends in Birmingham?"

"He seems to have been very isolated. I don't think his department considered him much of an asset. And the Americans want his brother Edgar kept out of it."

"I always thought Frank might go off the rails in the end," David said quietly. "But not like this. And weapons research..." He looked at Jackson. "Does our government know anything about what happened?"

Jackson looked at him. "Do you think Muncaster would be sitting peacefully in a mental hospital if they did?"

David ran a hand through his short curls. "Jesus."

Natalia leaned forward. "Will you help him now? Go up there, see him, reestablish yourself as a friend."

David looked between them. "Then what? What happens to him?" His eyes fixed on Jackson's. "Surely the Americans will want him dead."

Jackson shook his head. "No. Actually they say they want him alive, so they can question him. And this operation is under our control." He smiled wryly. "And if we wanted him dead, he'd be dead already. Our man is a nurse, with access to drugs."

David leaned back in his chair. Even if Frank was safe—for now—Jackson's words still chilled him.

Natalia looked at him. "We will not let him be killed. Not unless there is an immediate risk of the Germans getting him. And if they get him, then—"

David finished the sentence. "He'd be better off dead."

"Our man at the hospital has been trying to persuade Muncaster to contact you," Jackson said. If we give him the word, tomorrow night you will get a telephone call from Frank, asking for help to get him out of the hospital. Then we want you and Natalia—and I think Geoff Drax, too, if he was a friend—to drive up and visit him. On Sunday. That's visiting day. Get his confidence, give us some assessment of the state he's in. You'd give false names to people who let you in, and pretend to have known Frank at school. Our man is making sure the hospital authorities don't know you're coming. You'll be given false ID cards, you may be asked to show those at the asylum gates."

David took a deep breath. "This is something big, isn't it?"

Jackson nodded. "Potentially. Our instructions come from the very top. It's not dangerous, not in the early stages." He smiled, a crinkly, confiding smile. "They're showing a lot of confidence in you."

David laughed mirthlessly. "The man on the spot."

"It happens. Once you join us. Do you think you can do this?" Jackson asked.

"What about my wife?"

"She doesn't need to know anything, any more than she does about what you do for us at work. You'll just have to make something up to explain your absence on Sunday."

David thought of Frank facing some SS interrogator. In the last two years he had sometimes thought of facing that himself. "Yes," he said. "I'll visit Frank."

"Thank you." Jackson stood up. "I must make some calls. And I'll speak to Drax tomorrow. I'll meet you both at the club tomorrow morning." He smiled, genuine gratitude in his eyes, as he pulled on his gloves.

"Geoff didn't know Frank nearly as well as me. He might be surprised to see us both."

"You could say Geoff offered to drive you, say your car is broken down." He turned to Natalia. "You could pretend to be Drax's girlfriend. Good cover. It would help to have a second view about how he is."

Jackson turned back to David. "Don't ask Muncaster about what happened with his brother, just encourage him to talk and see where he goes. That's important. Assess his state of mind. Natalia, by the way, is in operational charge on Sunday. If anything unexpected happens, you take orders from her. She will have a gun, just in case of trouble." He smiled. "And she's a crack shot."

David looked at Natalia; she nodded quietly.

"Everyone all right, then?" Jackson spoke with forced cheerfulness. "See Muncaster, then take a look at his flat, our man will get hold of the key. Then phone me from a call box."

"All right," David said. "Poor old Frank," he added.

"Indeed." Jackson nodded. "It's up to us to help him, sort this out." He paused, then spoke again, changing the subject. "I see Beaverbrook met with Speer and Goebbels in Berlin today."

"But not Hitler," Natalia said.

"No." Jackson smiled grimly. "Last year, I went with an FO delegation to Germany, visiting the opening of the Führer's new art gallery at Linz. All this wonderful stuff, art treasures looted from all over Eastern Europe. Someone told me Hitler had been for a private view the day before, they saw him trundled along in his wheelchair, shaking so much from his Parkinson's disease he could hardly focus on the pictures properly, let alone give the Nazi salute." His face clouded. "I met him once, you know."

"Hitler?" David asked.

"Yes. I was with the Foreign Secretary, Lord Halifax, when he visited him in 1937. He had terrible bad breath, and kept breaking wind. Loathsome man. Big mad eyes. Could see him using them to work a crowd, though."

"Maybe he was ill even then."

"Yes." Jackson smiled tightly. "And badly ill now. And we have Stevenson elected in America. Perhaps things are starting to change at last." He walked to the door, got ready to leave; they always left separately. "It's very cold again. I do hope we don't get bad fog this year. Well, goodnight." He went out and moments later David heard his heavy footsteps descending the stairs.

David stood up. He had never been alone with Natalia before. She said, "Mr. Jackson is so English. Always a comment about the weather."

"Yes. He is. Very public school, as we say."

"His life is extremely dangerous." She must have caught the note of dislike in David's voice.

"Yes."

"I am sorry for your friend. I knew someone who was ill in that way. He lived in great pain."

David sighed. "Frank wasn't always unhappy. He just didn't—"

"Quite belong in this world?"

"Yes. But he has a right to be in it. All of us do. That's what we're fighting for."

"Yes, it is." He saw a tear form in the corner of her eye and he had a sudden urge to go over to her, take hold of her. Then he thought of Sarah, waiting at home; he had told her there was a flap on at the office and he had to work late. Now he would have to tell her yet more lies. He looked away from Natalia, to the picture she was working on. "Where is that?"

"Bratislava, in Eastern Europe. Once the city was ruled by Hungary, then it was part of Czechoslovakia, now it is the capital of Slovakia. One of Hitler's puppet states." She looked at the painting, the people trudging along the narrow streets. "When I was growing up there the city was cosmopolitan, like most of Eastern Europe. Slovaks, Hungarians, Germans. Many people were some mixture of all three, like me." She smiled her sad, cynical smile again. "I am a cosmopolitan. But then the gods of nationalism rose up."

"Were there many Jews there?"

"Yes. I had many Jewish friends. They are all gone now."

Then David said abruptly, "I must get back to my wife." Natalia nodded her head slowly. He turned and walked out.

CHAPTER ELEVEN

On Wednesday afternoon, Frank had had another meeting with Dr. Wilson. Ben walked him over to the Admissions Block again. He had come to like the young Scotsman more, he was kind to him, and Frank had seen enough of him to realize there was nothing of the world of Strangmans in his makeup. Yet there was still something about Ben, something he couldn't put his finger on, that Frank didn't trust.

In his office the doctor was working on some files. He motioned to Frank to sit down. "How are you?"

"All right, thank you."

"The police have been in touch." Frank's heart lurched with fear. "There's still no decision about whether to prosecute. They can't get hold of your brother, either. The case seems to be in limbo. If it does come to court," he added reassuringly, "we can make a defense of insanity. But I wish your brother would contact us. We can't think about transferring you to the Private Villa until we have a trustee appointed to deal with your money. In the meantime you'll have to stay on the ward."

"I understand," Frank said bleakly.

Wilson looked at him curiously. "I hear you're still very withdrawn. Not interacting with staff or patients."

Frank didn't reply. Wilson sat back in his chair, picked up a pen, and started fiddling with it. "Did you and your brother play together as children?" he asked suddenly. "Perhaps together with your mother?"

Frank looked at him. He mustn't be drawn into talk about Edgar. "Our mother wasn't one for — playing."

"Did she prefer Edgar?"

"I don't know."

"Did you feel she did?"

"I don't know."

Wilson sighed. "I'm going to put you down for electric shock treatment, Frank. They're booked up next week, but the week after. We must get you out of this depressive state."

Ben took Frank back to the ward. The weather had turned colder, and there was frost in the air. Frank was terrified by the thought of shock treatment. He wished he could get away. He had been sent a get well card, of all things, from his colleagues at Birmingham but apart from that had heard nothing from anyone. And Edgar had probably decided to have nothing more to do with him. He was probably drunk somewhere in a bar in San Francisco, trying to forget it all, slugging whiskey like Mrs. Baker. Frank hated drink, it loosened people's inhibitions and inhibitions were the only things that kept them from savagery. "Drunks," he muttered aloud.

"What was that?" Ben asked.

"Nothing."

"You want to stop that, mac, muttering to yirsel'. It's a bad habit in here."

Frank wanted to ask Ben more about the shock treatment but he couldn't face it. A desperate weariness had come over him.

"What did Wilson have to say?" Ben asked.

"Just that they haven't found my brother yet."

"Did you think any more about calling that old pal of yours?"

Frank didn't answer, just looked down at his feet. He still wasn't quite sure it was safe.

Ben left Frank in the day room. Patients were sitting around the television watching Fanny Cradock demonstrating how to make sauerkraut. Some were sitting around the table cutting up strips of paper with blunt children's scissors; although it was still over a month to Christmas patients had already been set to making decorations. Mr. Martindale wasn't on the ward anymore; after his outburst he had been sent to one of the padded cells.

Frank slunk off to the quiet room, taking his habitual position in the easy chair, facing the window. He thought of his flat in Birmingham; would anyone have tidied it up? He had liked his flat, dingy though it was. Only Birmingham was so far from the sea. He had always loved the sea, ever since he and his mother had gone to visit a cousin of his father in Skegness, when he was ten. Edgar hadn't come; he was on a school trip to France. Frank had spent days wandering the sands on his own; the beach was full of holidaymakers but the sea was so vast and blank, yet always moving. It was too cold to swim; he had paddled in the surf but even that had made his feet ache, and yet he would have loved to disappear into the water. His mother, back at his father's cousin's, would be trying to persuade them of the spirit world just beyond and Mrs. Baker's unique contact with it. They were never invited again.

Over the past few days Frank had thought about killing himself, taking his secret away with him forever, rather than risking anyone finding out, even David. But he knew he didn't have the courage. And they were always on the watch in here. The blunt knives and forks the patients used were counted after each meal, and there were no strong light fittings in the rooms to hang a rope from. There was a big picture, though, on the nicotine-yellow wall in the quiet room, a Victorian painting of a stag at bay in the Highlands; there must be a strong nail or hook holding it to the wall. Frank closed his eyes, his body shuddering involuntarily. He didn't want to die, though he had sometimes yearned to do so at school. He wished he could stop thinking about that place.

Strangmans College was a long square block of a building set on a bleak, windy hillside just outside Edinburgh. One of the city's many private schools. A Victorian headmaster had moved the institution to a new site, where the bracing air would be good for the boys.

It had been bracing all right, when Frank got off the school coach which had met him at Waverley Station, that Sunday afternoon in 1928. A gale was blowing off the Forth, full of freezing rain. It almost knocked him off his feet. There were three other new boarders on the coach — most Strangmans pupils were day boys but there was a minority of boarders—and the four eleven-year-olds in their new red uniforms stood there frightened and apprehensive, each clutching his red cap against the wind.

Frank stared down the drive at the sandstone building. It seemed huge, still a reddish yellow though all the buildings he had passed in Edinburgh were black with soot, worse than London. The day boys would not arrive for the start of term until next day and the place seemed deserted. Frank had hoped that Edgar, who had traveled up the day before, might be there to welcome him, but there was only a master with a clipboard, a tall, spare man in hat and raincoat with glasses and a severe expression.

Frank was still looking around in the hope of seeing Edgar when a sharp poke in the ribs made him jump. "Hey," the teacher said in a sharp voice. "You're in a dream, laddie!" The long "R" made it sound like "drrream." "Whit's yer name? Are you Muncaster?"

"Yes. I'm Frank."

The man frowned. "Yes, what?"

Frank stared at him blankly.

"Yes, *sir*. You call the masters 'sir' here. And you're Muncaster minor, the boys get called by their last names." He frowned again. "Take that silly grin off yer face. What are ye grinning at me like that for?" One of the other boys tittered. Frank held himself rigid, fighting a frantic urge to run away.

The master led the boys to an annex behind the main building, where he took them into a bleak room with four iron beds, a locker beside each. Rain lashed and spat at the windows. "This is your dormitory," the master said. "Number 8, remember that. I'm Mr. Ritner and your form number is 4B. Remember, 4B. There'll be tea at four, the dining room's on the second floor. Get yourselves unpacked now, go on." He walked off, footsteps clumping on the bare boards. Frank stood gawping, the rapped instructions swirling in his head.

At tea, served in a corner of a huge dining room filled with long benches, Edgar appeared along with a dozen other boarders of various ages. Edgar was fifteen now, tall and broad, a junior prefect with a tassel on his cap. He sat beside Frank and spoke to him quietly. "So you're here."

"Hullo, Edgar. Gosh, it's good to see you."

His brother's look was stony. "Listen, Frank, just cos you're my brother disnae mean we see each other at school. Understand?" His voice had taken on the local accent. "You're just another wee tiddler. You don't bother me, right? I'm in the seniors' bug hut so you won't see much of me anyway."

"Bug hut?"

"It's what we call the boarding houses," Edgar answered impatiently, as though Frank should have known. He got up. "You have to stand on your own two feet here. That's the Strangmans way. You'll need to toughen up."

In the days that followed Frank was in a constant panic; he couldn't find his way around the enormous building where huge crowds of boys now milled or walked along in lines. Several times, lost, he asked other boys the way but they only laughed. One said threateningly, "Whit're you grinning at me like that for? Ye look like a fuckin' spastic." Frank blinked back tears. "Are you crying, ye wee sissy?" Other boys looked at him with disgusted contempt. Very quickly, word went around the school that there was a new kid in the bug huts who was a softy, who'd been seen crying. To make it worse he was Edgar Muncaster's brother. How could someone like Ed Muncaster have a wee runt like that for a brother? It was letting the school down.

Frank's life became a misery. Boys would surround him in the playground and start shouting and jeering at him, poking fun at his thinness, his large ears, his strange spastic grin, and his tears. At first, terrified, he would stand in the middle of the circle and scream and shout at them to leave him alone. That only made things worse and after a while Frank realized he must keep quiet, not weep, show no emotion at all.

Once, and only once, Frank lost his temper. There was a day boy called Lumsden in his form. He was large and fat and wore glasses, and could have been bullied himself had he not been smart enough to adopt a confident swagger and make an asset of his size. He soon became the leader of Frank's tormentors. One cold autumn day, the first frosts already whitening the tough grass on the treeless hillside, a gang of boys had gathered around Frank at morning break, trying to make him cry. He stood in the middle of them, unmoving. Then Lumsden stepped forward and dropped into a sort of crouch, swinging his arms to and fro, a grin on his face that Frank realized was an imitation of his own habitual grimace. "Wooo wooo wooo," Lumsden went, making monkey noises. "Muncaster's like a chimp I saw at the zoo in the holidays, they grin like that all the time. Monkey Muncaster, Monkey Muncaster."

The boys cackled; Lumsden had scored a hit. Something broke inside Frank and he leapt at the big boy, swinging his fists and lashing out. He wanted to knock his teeth out, kill him, but his wild fury made him clumsy. Lumsden kicked a leg from under Frank and he crashed down on the asphalt playground. Lumsden leaned over him. "You've done it now, Monkey," he said, his face twisted with anger.

"Don't mark him, Hector," one of the others warned.

Lumsden straddled Frank and punched him in the stomach, again and again so every last vestige of breath was driven from his body and he almost blacked out. "That's enough, Hector," someone called out. "You'll kill the wee squirt."

Lumsden stood up, his face red. He gave Frank a satisfied leer. "That'll learn ye to remember who ye are."

Frank knew now that there was nothing he could do; he was quite helpless here. He couldn't appeal to his brother about the bullies—Edgar would go the other way if he saw Frank coming—or to the masters. They knew—they would have had to be blind and deaf not to—how he was treated, but as Edgar had said, the Strangmans philosophy was that boys must learn to fend for themselves. The masters would do nothing unless they saw a boy with a visible mark. They disliked Frank anyway; in class he couldn't concentrate, seemed to live in a dream, and was often called to account for staring out of the window. Sometimes he got the tawse for it, struck on the hand with the narrow leather belt, a long slit at the end to make it sting more.

So Frank learned to hide, and he became an expert at it. During break and at lunchtimes he would conceal himself in the toilets or in empty classrooms. Best of all, in a corner of the big assembly hall where the boys met for prayers every morning he found an enormous stack of wooden chairs which were only brought out for prize-giving days and other ceremonies. They were covered by a thick old fire curtain. Squeezing in among the stacked-up chairs, Frank found a space in the middle big enough for a little boy to crouch in. He knew it wasn't very safe but he didn't care, he had a refuge.

The bullies couldn't be bothered to come and find him. There were, after all, other fish to fry in such a big school and Frank ignored everyone as much as possible. Although his silent unresponsiveness meant that for most of the time he was left alone, he was often accompanied, as he walked along, by calls of "Monkey! Spastic! Gie' us a grin, Monkey!"

So things went on, because there was nothing to stop them. The boys were allowed to go out on the hills after school and Frank spent long hours walking alone among the gorse and granite outcrops, over the long grass blown flat by the endless keening winds, always watching the horizon and dodging behind a gorse bush if he saw any other Strangmans boys.

Frank turned twelve, then thirteen and fourteen, and still he had never had a single friend. Edgar turned eighteen in 1931 and left Strangmans, going up to Oxford to read Physics. By now Frank didn't really live in the real world. The only place he liked was the library. The most popular books — Henty and Bulldog Drummond — didn't appeal to him much, but he loved science fiction, Jules Verne and H. G. Wells especially. He marveled at their stories of worlds under the earth and the sea, journeys to the moon and invaders from Mars, visits to the future. During the holidays he had read in a magazine about a German scientist, who predicted that one day rockets would carry men to the moon. When the boys began to learn physics, and about how the solar system worked, Frank's ears pricked up. The science teacher, who had been told that Muncaster was a problem pupil, found him quick and attentive, able to pick up complex calculations easily. For the first time Frank started getting good marks in a subject. The other masters frowned and tutted; they had always said Muncaster had a brain but was too damn dreamy and lazy to use it. Now he used it to understand Newton and Kepler and Rutherford. He imagined himself traveling to other worlds, where advanced beings treated him with kindness and respect. Sometimes too, asleep on his hard iron bed in the dormitory, he dreamed of Martians invading Earth, one of Wells's giant tripods aiming a ray gun at Strangmans and shattering it to pieces like a gigantic ruined dolls' house.

He jerked awake. He had fallen asleep in his chair. The quiet room was cold. Outside the trees and grass were rimed with hoarfrost, the dampness turned to ice. He wondered what time it was; it was starting to get dark so probably it was around four. Ben came back on duty then. He would probably chivvy him about contacting David again. Frank began thinking back to his university days; at least, there were no horrors there.

His school science teacher, Mr. McKendrick, the only one at Strangmans who had tried to help him, had supervised his coaching for the Oxford entrance exam. "I think you'll pass," he had told him. He hesitated, then said, "I think you'll find life better at Oxford, Muncaster. You'll have to work very hard to excel but you'll be able to study independently in a way you can't as a schoolboy. And I think you'll find life—well—easier. But you'll have to make an effort if you want to make friends. A real effort, I'm thinkin'."

Frank arrived at Oxford in 1935 to read Chemistry. Edgar had already graduated and gone on to do postgraduate work in America; good riddance to bad rubbish so far as Frank was concerned. He had walked around Oxford, astonished by the beauty of the colleges. He had hoped for a room on his own, and was worried when they told him he would be sharing. But Frank had learned to judge people on whether or not they were likely to be a threat, and as soon as he saw David Fitzgerald he felt safe. The tall, athletic-looking Londoner was self-contained, but perfectly amiable.

"What are you studying?" David asked.

"Chemistry."

"I'm doing Modern History. Listen, which bedroom do you want? One's a bit bigger but the other's got a view of the quad."

"Oh—I don't mind."

"Take the one with the view if you like."

"Thanks."

Frank was too shy and suspicious to make real friends; he worked with other students in the laboratories but avoided their conversations. He could not help fearing they might suddenly turn on him, calling out "Monkey." But he managed to tag on to the fringes of David's group, who tended, like David, to be serious, thoughtful, not prone to larking. David had status among the other students, as he had taken up rowing and was in the university team.

Frank always remembered one evening toward the end of his first term. Italy had invaded Abyssinia, and a pact between Britain and France allowing Italy to annex much of the country was raising fierce political opposition. Frank and David were sitting in their rooms discussing the situation with David's best friend, Geoff Drax.

"We have to accept Italy's won the war," Geoff said. "I wish there had been a different outcome but it's better to make a settlement now and stop the fighting."

"But it'll be the end of the League of Nations." David's normally quiet voice betrayed unusual emotion. "It's a license to any country to start an aggressive war."

"The League of Nations is finished. It didn't stop Japan invading Manchuria."

"All the more reason to make a stand now."

Frank had seen, on sixth-form visits to the cinema, what was happening in Europe: the sinister Stalin; the strutting dictators Hitler and Mussolini. Newsreels of Jewish shop windows in Germany being smashed by jeering Brownshirts, the owners cowering inside, aroused an instinctive sympathy in him for the victims. He had begun following the news. He said now, "If Mussolini's allowed to get away with this, it'll encourage Hitler. He's already brought back conscription, and Churchill says he's building an air force. He wants to go to war in Europe again; God knows what he'll do to the Jews then."

Frank realized he had been speaking passionately, vehemently even. He stopped himself suddenly. David's eyes were fixed on his and it dawned on Frank that, for the first time he could remember, someone was actually interested in what he was saying. Geoff, too, though he said, "If Churchill's right and Hitler's a danger, all the more reason to try and get friendly with Mussolini."

"Hitler and Mussolini are cut from the same cloth," Frank countered. "They'll come together sooner or later."

"Yes, they will," David said. "And you're right, what will happen to the Jews then?"

Someone came into the quiet room, disturbing his reverie. Ben looked down at him keenly. "Are ye all right? You look awful worried."

"I'm fine." Frank thought again, *why does he care?* Then he remembered his terrible thoughts of suicide earlier, Wilson and the shock therapy. He saw now, there was only one possible alternative. He took a deep breath. "I've been thinking. Perhaps I should contact my friend, David, who I knew at university."

Ben nodded quickly in agreement. "All right. You could phone at the weekend when I'm on the nurses' station. Don't tell the other staff, you dinnae want Wilson stickin' his nose in."

Frank thought again about the shame of telling David where he was. When he'd been with him and his friends at university, sometimes then he had felt almost normal, human. But that was all gone now.

Ben raised his eyebrows, inclined his head interrogatively. "Deal?" he asked.

"All right," Frank said. He essayed a smile; a real one this time.

CHAPTER TWELVE

S arah returned home from her meeting shortly after five on Friday. As she walked down the road she looked across the little park to the old air-raid shelter; she had often thought, thank God we never had to use the shelter, but now she wondered, would fighting on in 1940 really have brought something worse than this? She shook her head in helpless perplexity.

There was a handwritten note on the doormat. It was an estimate from the builders she had contacted, offering to come and re-wallpaper the staircase. She sat down wearily in an armchair, the note in her hand. She thought of the boys who had been beaten up outside the Tube, all the blood. She wished her father had a telephone; despite the cost she would have phoned him in Clacton. She could have phoned Irene but knew what her sister would say: there had to be law enforcement, even if the Auxiliary Police did go over the top sometimes.

She remembered her father's arrest, back in 1941. The pacifists who had supported the 1940 Treaty—the pacifist Labour MPs, the Peace Pledge activists, the Quakers—all those people had had qualms early on when anti-Nazi refugees, mostly Jewish, were sent back to Germany under the Treaty. But it was the start of the German war against Russia the following spring that had stirred them into mass protest when the ancient warhorse, Lloyd George, delighting in being back as Prime Minister after almost twenty years, urged British volunteers to join Germany's campaign against communism.

A new campaigning organization, For Peace in Europe, had sprung up, and Sarah's father had joined. There were marches, leafleting campaigns, a boycott of German produce. The newspapers, like Beaverbrook's *Express*, had mocked the sandal-wearing vegetarian brigade who had turned their coats, as the Communists had, now Hitler had broken the Nazi-Soviet pact and invaded the homeland of communism.

In October 1941, just after the fall of Moscow, there had been a huge demonstration in Trafalgar Square and Sarah's father had decided to go. It was the only time Sarah and Irene had had a major row; Irene was married to Steve and no longer a strict pacifist, but Sarah still planned to go on the march with her father. It was Jim who had refused to let her; even the BBC was calling the antiwar campaigners dangerous Communist stooges and though Jim was retired now, Sarah had her teaching job to lose. So she wasn't there; she only heard on the news that the demonstration had collapsed into violent anarchism. She heard later, from her father, what had really happened, about the thousands sitting peacefully under Nelson's Column: Bertrand Russell and Vera Brittain and A. J. P. Taylor, clerics by the hundred, London dockers, housewives, the unemployed, and peers of the realm. The authorities had ringed the square with armored cars, then sent in the police with batons. Many of the leaders had ended up in the Isle of Man detention camp with a ten-year sentence, and some were rumored to have been shipped over to the Germans on the Isle of Wight. Further demonstrations were prohibited under the old wartime regulations that had remained in force after 1940. Lloyd George spoke of crushing subversion with a firm hand. Some famous pacifists, like Vera Brittain and Fenner Brockway, went on hunger strike on the Isle of Man but were left to die. It was, Lloyd George said, their choice. There were other, smaller demonstrations, that Jim heard from old friends, but they were never publicized and ruthlessly suppressed. Jim said he was too old to be of use in illegal political activity, and told Sarah she should keep quiet, wait for better times. That had been David's view too, when Sarah met him. But things had got steadily worse; people groused and muttered but they were powerless now.

Standing in her hall, Sarah wondered if she would even tell David what had happened this afternoon; he wouldn't be back for hours and she didn't know whether his story of working late was true. She walked into the lounge and stood there for a moment, arms wrapped around herself. She sighed. It was so easy to forget the things that went on now; perhaps it was good to have them thrust in your face. She lit the fire, which the daily woman had made up, then went back into the hall. She looked at the torn wallpaper. On a table in the hall stood the large, colorful Regency vase, decorated with bright flowers, which had been one of David's mother's proudest possessions. When his father moved to New Zealand he had left it with David. Sarah remembered another afternoon, a lifetime ago. Charlie, crawling now, had gone over to the table and slowly, steadily, tried to stand, clutching at the table edge. The vase had wobbled. David stepped toward his son, big, silent steps so as not to startle him, and grabbed Charlie under the arms and pulled him away. The little boy turned and stared at his father with an expression of such astonishment it made his parents laugh and Charlie joined in too. David raised him above his head. "We'll have to move Grandma's vase, or little Charlie rascal will get it." They had put the vase in a cupboard; but after Charlie died David had wanted to put it back. "It was always in the hall at our house."

Sarah looked at the vase now. Then she doubled over, and began weeping helplessly.

David arrived home at eight. Sarah had composed herself by then and made dinner. She was knitting a pullover, a Christmas present for Irene's elder son. She spent more and more time knitting these days; it was one way of passing her time alone in the house. She put the pullover down and looked at her husband. He seemed tired and pale, not like someone who had been in bed with a lover. She kissed him as usual. There was no smell of perfume on him, just the stale, cold tang of the London streets. He said, "I'm sorry, I wanted to get home at a decent time." He *has* been working late, she thought, he's tired out. Unless the strain was from trying to act a part. She pulled away. David looked at her. "Are you all right?" he asked. And then, when she did not reply, he took her gently by the arms. "Sarah, has something happened?"

She must look more rattled than she had thought. "Yes," she said. "In town, this afternoon. I saw something horrible."

They sat down and she told him about the attack. "Those boys were just distributing leaflets. Those Auxiliaries are barbarians, they beat them within an inch of their lives then took them away in a van. An old man told me they were taking them to the Gestapo."

David looked into the fire. He said, "Didn't Gandhi say peaceful protest only works if those you're protesting against are capable of being shamed?"

Sarah looked up. "They were taking a stand. They were brave. All this violence that the Resistance has started, it's just making things worse. That's why the government's recruiting more and more Auxiliaries. It's a vicious circle."

David gave her a strange, intent look. "What are people supposed to do? We've let it all go. Democracy, independence, freedom."

"Just go on waiting." She laughed bitterly. "Isn't that what we've been doing for the last twelve years? Well, I suppose it's how ordinary people have coped with bad times through the ages. Hitler hasn't appeared in public to meet Beaverbrook, has he? His most important ally. Maybe Hitler *is* dying."

"If he dies, Himmler could succeed."

Sarah looked at David. He was as much against the regime as she was these days, and she had thought he would shout and rage about what had happened to the boys. At length he said, "It's all unbearable, what's happening in the world."

"You're tired," she said. "Go upstairs and change out of your work clothes. I'll lay the table."

She put the decorators' note beside his plate. As David sat down to eat, and Sarah set out the lamb chops, she said, "That came this afternoon, while I was out. He can come next week."

David looked across the table. "Has that upset you, too? As well as those boys being attacked?"

"A little, yes." She hesitated. "I don't think we've always helped each other as we might."

"I know," he said quietly. "I'm sorry."

She smiled ruefully. "It's been a tough couple of years, hasn't it, one way and another?"

"Tough as hell."

"I've got another committee meeting on Sunday."

"Will you be all right to go?"

"Yes. Yes, I'll go."

Afterwards they watched the news on television, in their separate arm-chairs. Beaverbrook was broadcasting from Berlin; he stood on the steps of the Reich chancellery smiling cheerfully at the reporters, bright as buttons as always. He spoke in his sharp voice with its Canadian twang: "I am happy to report, gentlemen, that my talks with Herr Goebbels have gone very well. I also had an audience with Herr Hitler this morning. He sends his warm greetings to the British people and the Empire. A new era of economic and military cooperation with Germany is dawning, which can only help our country in these difficult times. Tariffs on trade between Britain and Europe are to be reduced, easing trade conditions and helping our industries. The size of the British army is to be increased by a hundred thousand men, amending the Treaty of Berlin, to strengthen our Imperial forces. I shall bring back the keys to a new prosperity and strength for our country and Empire. Thank you."

David laughed emptily. "If the Germans are going to let us trade more with Europe and recruit more soldiers they'll want something in return. Trade — I expect that'll mean contracts for our arms industry; they've been trying to get in on the Russian war for years."

"Oh, God." Sarah shook her head. "Remember in the thirties, how people used to laugh at Mosley and his Blackshirts strutting along. We used to think British people could never become Fascists, or Fascist collaborators. But they can. I suppose anybody can, given the right set of circumstances."

"I know."

The television was now showing a giant fir being cut down in Norway, the annual gift that in a few weeks would be erected in Trafalgar Square. Prime Minister Quisling clapped as the huge tree fell, sending up clouds of snow. Sarah knew the sight of him would bring back memories for David of the 1940 Norway campaign. He said, "I've got to go into the office tomorrow, early. Just for a meeting. It's a bore. I'll be back by lunchtime."

"All right," she said with a sigh.

"I'm tired. I'm going to bed," he said. "No need for you to come up yet. Stay downstairs if you want."

Late on Saturday morning David returned from his meeting with Jackson with a hard, tense feeling inside him. Sarah must not know about Frank's call, and when he went to Birmingham tomorrow to visit him, she must think he was going somewhere else.

David had a great-uncle in Northampton, who had helped his parents when they first came to England. He had owned a small building firm but was in his eighties now, a childless widower. David's father had asked him to keep an eye on Uncle Ted, and David visited the old Irishman a couple of times a year, usually on his own for Ted's grumpiness was legendary. The story, he had decided, would be that Ted had had a fall and was in hospital. Frank's telephone call, which Jackson said would come between four and five that afternoon, would supposedly be from him. David had asked at the meeting, "How can I stop Sarah taking the call? We've a phone in the bedroom but why would I be up there at four on a Saturday?"

"An illness," Jackson had suggested. "Not something that would stop you traveling the next day."

After lunch he went out into the garden and tidied up the leaves. It was another cold, raw day. Sarah came out in a headscarf and old coat and helped him rake the wet leaves into a pile. They lit a fire, and a thin column of smoke rose into the still air. Sarah's cheeks had reddened with the cold; it was a long time since they had done something like this together. She looked pretty, relaxed by the work. She was so honest, so good. David felt a dreadful stab of mingled affection and guilt.

At half past twelve Sarah went in to prepare lunch. As he worked on alone, digging out dead plants from the flowerbeds, David wondered what on earth it was that Frank knew. Or did he know nothing? Had that fragile mind just snapped at last? No, that couldn't be it, the

Americans wanted him. He hated the thought of Frank in danger, hunted. He had felt in danger himself for so long.

He remembered standing with his father on the wharf in Auckland, in 1946, waiting to get the ship back to England, at the end of his posting to New Zealand. Sarah had gone to the ladies. David's father said, "They say they're having a bad winter in England. Still, it should be over by the time you get back."

"Yes, we'll go from late summer straight into spring."

Suddenly his father said, "Stay here, David. Things are getting worse in England."

"Dad, we've been through this. Sarah and I feel—it's our country, we belong there."

His father said quietly, "There's one way you don't belong there, son, not now. And that hardly matters here."

"Nobody knows. There's no way anybody can."

His father sighed. "I've often wondered what it was your mother was trying to say to you. Just before she died. Perhaps it was a warning."

David remembered the last sight of his father, waving from the quayside as the ship pulled away, his graying black curls flying in the wind. He put down his spade and went in. He said to Sarah, "I think I've done too much bending, my back hurts. I think after lunch I might lie down."

Over the meal Sarah looked at him sympathetically. "You did too much," she said. "Go on up and I'll bring you a cup of tea. Lie flat on your back with your knees bent, that's the best way." She believed him and that made David unreasonably angry with her again—he wanted to shout that there was nothing wrong with his bloody back. But he went up and lay down on the bed in the position she had suggested. On the table beside him stood the telephone extension he had installed last year; in case there was a nighttime emergency at work, he had told her.

She brought up the tea and he drank it. After a while the posture made him uncomfortable so he sat on the side of the bed, looking through the net curtains at the bare trees and gray sky.

At ten past four, just as the light was starting to go, the phone rang.

Though he had been waiting for it the shrill sound made David jump. He snatched up the receiver. "Kenton 4815."

For several moments he heard only silence, then a voice, thin and tremulous. "Is that David Fitzgerald?"

"Yes. Who's that?"

"It's—it's Frank, David. Frank Muncaster. You remember?"

"Of course. Frank? Long time no see. How are you?" David spoke quietly.

"Oh..." There was a despairing note in the voice. "I'm—having a few problems. I've not been well."

"I'm sorry to hear that, Frank. Really sorry."

"I'm—well, I'm in a mental hospital." Frank's voice was louder now, full of anxiety. "David, I'm really, really sorry to trouble you like this out of the blue, but I need someone to help me. I'm in the hospital and there's a problem with the fees—it's not the money, I've plenty of money, but I can't get at it." Frank stopped suddenly, as though he couldn't go on.

"Listen, Frank, I'll do anything I can to help. Just tell me."

The voice became tremulous again, speaking rapidly now. "I've been certified as a lunatic, David. I can't get out. They need a relative to be my trustee. But Mum's died and Edgar's in America and they can't get hold of him. David, is there any way you could help me get things organized somehow? There's no one else. No one."

"Where are you?"

"Bartley Green Hospital, just outside Birmingham."

David took a deep breath. "Listen, Frank, I could come up tomorrow." He spoke quickly, he could hear Sarah's footsteps on the stairs.

"Could you? Oh, it's so much to ask..."

Sarah came in, stood in the doorway looking down at him inquiringly. David said carefully into the telephone, "I'll come. It's easy on the train. What are the visiting hours?"

"If you could come in the afternoon. There's a nurse, he's called Ben. They have male nurses here, attendants—"

David cut in. "I'll come tomorrow, say about—oh—three o'clock?"

"Yes. Yes, that would be so good. Oh, thank you." Frank's voice trembled again. "It'll be good to see you. But I'm sorry — it's your weekend, I never asked how you are, and your wife —"

"Sarah's fine. Listen, I'll see you tomorrow, I'll do anything I can to help —"

"Thank you. David, I have to go, this is the hospital line and it's a trunk call."

"All right. Good-bye."

"Good-bye, David." Frank sounded tremendously relieved. "Thank you, thank you." There was a click. David waited a second, then said into the dead line, "All right, Uncle. Don't worry, I'll see you tomorrow. Good-bye." He put the receiver down slowly, and turned to Sarah. "It's Uncle Ted. He had a fall at home, he's in hospital."

CHAPTER THIRTEEN

Gunther looked around the lounge of the big flat in Russell Square. It was Friday evening. I might be here for weeks, he thought. The flat was in a Victorian building but the interior had been modernized, all clean lines, rectangular furniture, the lights around the walls shaped like inverted shells. In contrast the pictures were German scenes, standard diplomatic issue. His eye was caught by a seascape, a view across windswept marram grass to the Baltic, gray-blue under a wide pale sky. A lone sailing boat was visible near the horizon. It reminded Gunther of visits to the coast during his childhood.

There was a double bedroom, and a study with a large desk, where a notebook and pencil were laid neatly on the blotter. In a corner was a photograph of Reichsführer Himmler, his face in half profile, the keen eyes behind the spectacles staring at something just off camera. It was a reminder that Gunther's loyalties were to the SS now, not Ambassador Rommel.

He went into the kitchen. A tall refrigerator contained rye bread, spiced sausage, and cheese as well as several bottles of beer. Good, the English policeman would probably expect a drink when he came. He went into the bedroom, took off his jacket and shoes, and padded back to the lounge in his socks. A little clock on the mantelpiece showed a quarter to seven. The policeman, Syme, was not due until eight thirty. Gunther wondered what he would be like. On his walk to the flat from Senate House he had noticed how shabby and tawdry London looked; dog dirt and litter on the pavements, tired-looking people shuffling home after work, no zest or sense of purpose in their step. A newspaper hoarding spoke of more strikes in Scotland, a Special Conference of the Scottish National Party resolving to assist the authorities all they could in return for a convention to consider Home Rule as a first stage toward possible independence. Gunther's own vision of the future, the German vision, was clear and logical and bright; a total contrast to this confused, dirty mess of a country. He switched on the television that sat in a corner. A cowboy drama was showing, cheap American nonsense, not allowed on German television. He turned off the set, lit a cigarette, and sat staring at the seascape, remembering his childhood.

Gunther had been born in 1908, six years before the Great War. His father was a police sergeant in a small town not far from Königsberg in East Prussia, Imperial Germany's easternmost province. He was ten minutes older than his twin brother Hans. They looked identical, the same square faces and light blond hair, but their personalities were different; Hans was quicker, funnier, with a quicksilver energy Gunther lacked. Gunther was more like his father, solid and steady. He was a clumsy, untidy boy, though, always creasing his clothes, while Hans was as neat as a new pin.

Both did well at school though Gunther was a plodder while Hans was quick and imaginative, too much sometimes for the disciplinarian teachers. Gunther always felt protective of Hans, yet at the same time jealous, envying him for the qualities that made him the more popular twin among the other boys and later, with girls. It was Hans, though, who always wanted Gunther's company, while often Gunther preferred to be alone.

Their mother was a small, tired, self-effacing woman. Their father was a big man, with a craggy face and a mustache with upturned waxed points like the Kaiser's. In his uniform with its tall helmet he could look intimidating. He believed in order and authority above all. When the Great War came he spoke proudly of bringing German order to all Europe. But Germany lost the war. The decadence and disorder of the Weimar Republic that followed horrified the ageing policeman. Once at the dinner table, not long after the war, he told them with tears in his eyes, "There were students demonstrating in the town today. Anarchists or Communists. We came and stood on the side of the square, to make sure it didn't get out of hand. And they stood there *laughing* at us, mocking us, calling us pigs and lickspittles. What will become of us?" Gunther was horrified to realize then that his father, his strong father, was frightened.

At secondary school, Gunther developed an interest in English; he was good at the language and became fascinated by British history and how Britain had built a gigantic worldwide empire. Germany had overtaken Britain in industry, but had been too late to create an empire to provide the raw materials it needed. His teacher, a strong German nationalist, taught how England was in decline now, a great people gone to seed through democratic decadence despite their magnificent past. Gunther wished Germany had an empire, instead of being what the teacher called a cowed nation, provinces hacked away at Versailles, the economy ruined by reparations. Gunther would tell Hans about his thoughts of Empire and his brother, who had much more imagination, conjured up stories for him of great battles on sweltering Indian plains, settlers in Africa and Australia struggling against hostile natives. Gunther was in awe of his brother's ability to picture another world.

The twins often went out cycling at weekends, along the straight dusty roads between the plantations of tall firs, the forest stretching away into shadowy darkness on each side. One hot summer Sunday when they were thirteen they went further than before. They passed carts lumbering by, little villages, a massive redbrick Junker country house surrounded by wide lawns. At lunchtime they stopped to eat their sandwiches by the side of the road. It was very quiet and still, insects buzzing lazily in the heat. Hans had been thoughtful all morning. He said now, "What shall we do when we grow up?"

Gunther nudged a stone with his foot. "I want to study languages."

Hans looked disappointed. "Oh," he said. "I couldn't do that."

"What do you want to be?"

"I want to be a policeman, like father." Hans smiled, his blue eyes alight. "We could both join. Catch all the bad people." He pointed a finger down the empty road. "Bang, bang."

*   *   *

In 1926, when the twins were eighteen, Gunther won a place to study English at Berlin University. Hans, bored with school, had already left and taken a clerk's job in Königsberg. He seemed to have forgotten his dream of following their father into the police. Gunther had not; he had thought about it many times but the prospect of going to university was exciting. He had never left East Prussia before and longed to see Berlin. His parents, delighted with his success, encouraged him.

The evening before Gunther left he sat with his father by the fire. The old man was nearing retirement; he was happier these days, life was easier. A degree of prosperity was returning to Germany under Stresemann after the nightmare of the Great Inflation. His father gave Gunther a beer and offered him a cigarette, smiling through the thick mustache, drooping now, that had turned from blond to white, stained yellow-brown with nicotine.

"A son of mine, going to university. The train will take you across the Polish Corridor, the part of Germany that was stolen from us in 1918. They'll pull the blinds down over the windows while you cross Polish territory. At least, I think they still do that. I hope so." His heavy face became serious. "You take care now, don't get into bad company, nightclubs and places like that. A lot of bad things go on in Berlin."

"I'll be careful, Father."

"I know you will. You're a steady lad." The old man smiled again, sadly. "If it were Hans I would be worried. I don't know what he gets up to in Königsberg." He shook his head.

Gunther said nothing. He had always known he was the one his father preferred, though he felt Hans was better than him in so many ways.

Gunther spent three happy years in Berlin. He seldom visited the fleshpots; his friends were mostly quiet, studious people who, like him, despised the avant-garde Berlin crowd, the artists and hack writers and queers. One day during his first week, he was walking along a street far from the city center with some fellow students, watching the scenes around them. Looking down an alley, Gunther saw an extraordinary-looking old man staring at him. He wore a long dark coat, and his black hair, surmounted by a skullcap, curled around his cheeks in long side locks. He stared back at Gunther with fearful, hostile eyes. Gunther said, half laughing, "Who the hell was that?"

One of the others said, in a voice full of contempt, "A Jew."

"They don't look like that. What about Steiner and Rabinovich in our class, they look and dress just like us."

His fellow student turned on him angrily. "Those Jews, they pretend. That old man is what they really look like, but most of them dress and talk like us, pretend to be Germans, so we won't recognize them as they steal from us. Don't you understand anything?"

The encounter made Gunther feel queasy, gave him for the first time a sense of the strange, half visible threat in their midst.

In the summer of 1929 he left for England for a year at Oxford; he felt alone and out of place the whole time there, surrounded by people who mostly seemed either to be decadent aristocrats or pretending to be. Gunther wasn't political, but like his father he supported the conservative German Nationalists who wanted Germany to be great again, stable and ordered. He longed for East Prussia's clean, bracing air as he endured the endless, dirty English drizzle. He had no money to socialize or travel and sometimes went for days without talking to anyone; he studied and studied, English history especially. He had letters from his parents, and less frequently, from Hans, who was bored in his clerk's job but couldn't think what else to do.

That autumn the American stock market collapsed. In Britain businesses closed and unemployment mushroomed. Gunther learned that things were terrible in Germany too, the brief prosperity of the late twenties gone, unemployment rising to millions, homeless workers in Berlin paying to sit on stools in drafty halls, with elbows balanced on ropes strung across the room on which they leaned to sleep. The politicians seemed helpless, running about like headless chickens. Hans wrote that he had lost his job in Königsberg and gone back to live with their parents. Nobody knew what was going to happen next.

In the summer of 1930 Gunther returned to Germany, glad to shake the grime of England from his feet. Arriving in Berlin he saw homeless beggars, women and children selling themselves on street corners. On the tram from the station to his university lodgings he passed a Communist demonstration, men in mufflers and caps marching under a red banner with the hammer and sickle, carrying placards demanding work, singing "The Internationale."

The term had not yet started, so Gunther went back home, the blinds on the train lowered again as they crossed the Polish Corridor. He arrived back at the house; behind its little fence the garden his mother tended was as neat as ever but in the warm sunlight the cottage looked dowdy, in need of a coat of paint. His mother opened the door and embraced him. "Thank God you're back," she said. His father was sitting in his usual chair by the fire, a jug of beer by his side. "Hello, son," he said. The big man looked shrunken somehow, huddled. Gunther and his mother sat down at the table. He asked, "How are things?"

His mother answered, "Not good. Your father's pension has been cut. It's hard to manage."

Gunther asked, "Where's Hans?"

"He should have been back by now." She smiled. "He is so excited you're coming."

"Does he have a job?"

His father made a sound like a snarl. "Oh, yes," he said bitterly. "Hans has a job all right."

Gunther looked at his parents, puzzled. His mother lowered her head.

He heard the kitchen door open. Hans came into the room. He smiled at Gunther, white teeth in a tanned face. He wore a uniform that Gunther had glimpsed on the Berlin streets: brown shirt and black trousers, beautifully ironed with sharp creases, a brown cap and dark tie, solid black boots. Gunther's first thought was how fine Hans looked, what a contrast to his own pallid rumpledness. His twin's shirt sported a bright swastika armband.

That night Hans took Gunther to a meeting. He had joined the Nazi Party that spring and for the last two months had been working for them as a youth organizer. The party was taking on more people with the Reichstag elections due in a few weeks.

Gunther knew little about the Nazis, just that they were a fringe party with a few seats in the Reichstag; he remembered hearing about a comic-opera putsch in Munich when he was a boy, newspaper pictures of a man with a fierce frown and a toothbrush mustache. Upstairs, in their old room, Hans now told Gunther all about the Movement, his eyes alight and happy. "We're on the march now, we're hoping for a hundred deputies in the Reichstag elections in September."

"A hundred?" Gunther asked scoffingly.

"Yes. People are joining us in hordes. The bourgeois parties have failed Germany."

"Bourgeois? You sound like a Communist."

"In Berlin we're chasing the Communists off the streets," Hans said seriously. "We're a German party, a racial party, we're for Germans of all classes."

"Father doesn't seem to approve. I'm not surprised if your party's into street fighting."

Hans shook his head vigorously. "Only to stop the Reds handing us over to the Russians. When we take over, we'll bring order back. Real order. It won't be easy, though, we know that. We're realists. Father thinks that somehow you can wave a magic wand and go back to the Kaiser's time but it's not like that. And then..." Hans's eyes lit up. "We'll make Germany the master of Europe." He laid a hand on a thick volume on his table, reverently, like a pastor touching the Bible. "It's all set out here, in the Leader's book *Mein Kampf*." The gleam in his eyes, mirrors of Gunther's own, was frightening but compelling too. "Come on, Gunther," Hans said, spreading his arms wide. "You know Germany's been done down and crushed, that this isn't how it's meant to be."

"I know, but..."

Hans leaned forward. He asked his brother, "What do you believe in?"

"Getting away from English rain."

"What are you going to do now?"

Gunther shifted uneasily. This was a new Hans, jabbing these questions at him. But Hans had always thought about things more than he had. "I don't know," he answered. "While I've been away—I've decided, this academic stuff isn't for me, I thought of giving it all up, maybe even joining the police after all. Doing something real, something honest."

"Come with me tonight," Hans said quietly. "I'll show you something truly real and honest."

They cycled out to the forest, their front lamps piercing the darkness. Gunther was tired and his head was full of jumbled impressions of the last few days—leaving England, the long train ride to Berlin, the beggars and demonstrators, Hans in this uniform. Moths danced in the thin pencils of light cast by their lamps. Other cyclists in Brownshirt uniforms appeared, many of them teenagers in black shorts, and they exchanged happy shouted greetings with Hans.

They came to the entrance of a forest path that led to one of the many little East Prussian lakes. Families went walking there on Sundays. Hans and Gunther had gone with their parents as children. Tonight a group of older Brownshirts, big men, stood on the forest verge where the path began, oil lamps on the ground beside a neat stack of bicycles. Hans walked over to them, extending his arm and shouting out, "Heil Hitler!" It was the first time Gunther had heard the Nazi greeting. A big Brownshirt put a hand on Gunther's chest. "Who are you?" he asked threateningly. "Where's your uniform? You look like a fucking tramp." It hurt Gunther that the man didn't realize they were twins.

"He's my brother," Hans said. "He's just traveled back from England."

The man shone a torch in Gunther's face. "All right, Hoth. But he's your responsibility."

Gunther and Hans joined a trail of men and boys walking down the path, talking excitedly, lighting the way with their bicycle lamps. They came to the little lake. Tall torches in braziers had been lit on the shore, a boy watching each to make sure the flames stayed under control in the dry forest. There were about two hundred people there. Hans said, "I've got to get my lads lined up. There's a speaker coming from Berlin. Just stand somewhere on the side and watch. Don't sit down," he added. "That would be disrespectful."

Gunther watched as Hans organized two dozen boys efficiently into straight lines. They stood to attention on the shore. At a command everyone fell completely silent. Gunther could hear the wood crackling in the branches. The scene was beautiful and dramatic: the torchlight, the uniformed men still in their silent lines before the calm moonlit lake, the forest behind. Gunther felt a shiver of excitement. Then four Brownshirts walked out of the trees, accompanied by a tall, slim young man in black uniform. He had light blond hair and an extraordinary, long face, ascetic with a proud beak of a nose and a wide, full mouth that somehow spoke of strength and immense firmness. He stood beside a torch, back to the forest, facing the assembly. He was introduced as National Comrade Heydrich from Berlin, recently appointed to the Leader's personal guard.

Heydrich began speaking, in a confident, penetrating voice. He said, "Sixteen years ago, in 1914, in a forest not far from here, Germany fought and won a great battle. Russia had invaded us, they were set to conquer and destroy us. But at the Battle of Tannenberg we threw them back. We destroyed their army. The few Russian survivors ran away. Germany suffered 20,000 casualties; brave men many of whose bones lie in these forests, in the German soil they defended. *This* is what brave Germans can do! So how, comrades, have we fallen so far?"

Heydrich spoke of the surrender by Socialist German politicians at the end of the War, the destruction of the German economy by the Allies, the Depression, the dithering bourgeois parties, and the growing Marxist threat. He spoke of a new Germany to be built on the ruins. He had taken a military stance, hands behind his back, his voice growing more insistent. "We shall prevail, because greatness is Germany's destiny; that is the lesson of history, clear to all who read it. A legacy handed down by our ancestors who first settled these forests, the heroic Teutonic Knights." Gunther suddenly thought, I've spent years studying English history. But what about my history, Germany's history? Have I wasted all this time?

Heydrich raised a slim hand, pointing at the ranks before him. "But if we are to fulfill our mission we must be alert, aware of the enemies within and outside the Reich! It will take years to beat them down but we shall do it. The French, the Socialists, the Catholics with their masters in Rome, the Communists with their masters in Russia. And the masters of them all, the controlling hand, the enemy within and without. The Jews."

Gunther hadn't thought about the old Jew he had seen in the alley for years but he remembered now.

Heydrich fell silent. Gunther glanced over at Hans to see him looking back at him. His twin smiled and nodded. At a signal, the Brownshirts began singing, their clear young voices echoing across the lake:

"The flags held high! The ranks are tightly closed!
SA men march with firm courageous tread . . ."

As he listened, Gunther thought, Now I can be proud to be German again.

He woke with a grunt. Sitting there, thinking back, he had fallen asleep. He looked at the clock; the Englishman would be here in half an hour. He was hungry. He walked into the kitchen and, sitting at the little table, ate some bread and sausage. Then he went back to the bedroom and took some fresh clothes from his case. He looked at himself in the mirror, the sagging features and protruding belly. He was letting himself go, had been ever since his marriage broke up. His wife came from a police family, too, but even so she had never been able to adjust to Gunther's irregular hours. She had loathed England during his posting there. Back in Germany she hadn't liked his new work either, finding the remaining Jews and the networks that harbored them. "I know they must be resettled," she had said, "but I don't like the idea of you hunting people out, hounding them."

"If you accept they should all be resettled in the East, what would you have us do?"

"I don't know. But I don't want you talking about it in front of our son."

It was then that he had realized she disapproved of him. As though she could understand the things he had to do. Even in his early days in the police, hunting down ordinary thieves and murderers, you had to be hard—especially in those last disordered days of Weimar. And it was the same with the Jews, you couldn't eliminate the threat with softness. He had visited the ghettos in the East on training courses, seen what the Jews were like when they were forced to live together—filthy and stinking, fawning around the Germans in charge. Vermin that had to go. It was hard and unpleasant but necessary, as Hans had said.

He remembered when an informer had put him onto someone he said was Jewish. He had picked up the suspect, and later heard he had died under interrogation. Then he learned it was all a mistake, the dead man hadn't been Jewish at all, the informer was carrying out a personal vendetta. It had saddened and angered him, but in war sometimes the innocent died too.

He didn't miss his wife anymore, but he missed his son every day. Michael was eleven now. He hadn't seen him for a year. He turned away from the mirror. He felt, as so often, that somewhere deep inside he didn't measure up. Least of all to his dead brother. He remembered Hans's enthusiasm, his energy, his purity.

Syme was ten minutes late, which annoyed Gunther. When he answered the doorbell he saw a tall, thin man in his mid-thirties, wearing a heavy overcoat and a fedora. He had a lean, clever face full of cheerful, eager malice, and keen brown eyes.

"Herr Hoth?" The man extended a long, thin hand, with a friendly, confident smile. "William Syme, London Special Branch." Gunther shook his hand and ushered him in. He took his coat. Underneath Syme wore a sharp, expensive suit, a white shirt, and a silk tie. It was secured with a gold tiepin, in the middle a black circle with a single pointed white flash, the emblem of the British Fascists. "I hear you flew over from Berlin today," Syme said, in a cheerful friendly voice.

"Yes. Please, sit down. May I offer you tea or coffee?"

"Not for me, thanks. I'll have a beer if you've got one." Gunther noticed an undertone of a Cockney twang and guessed that Syme, like many ambitious Englishmen on the way up, was trying to develop a "received" English accent.

Gunther brought out two beers and offered Syme a cigarette. Syme looked around the room. "Nice flat," he said appreciatively.

"A little modernist for my taste."

Syme smiled. He said, "I've been to Berlin a couple of times. Jollies with the Party. Great buildings there. We went to the Nuremberg rally two years ago, we were sorry the Führer couldn't attend. I'd have liked to have seen him. I hear he's been ill." Syme's eyes flashed with curiosity.

"The Führer has many responsibilities," Gunther said coolly.

Syme inclined his head. "Beaverbrook's there now. Wonder what they've agreed?"

Gunther wondered too, remembering what Gessler had said about the English police soon having their hands full. Whatever it was, Syme didn't know. He realized he disliked this man. Then he thought, that won't do, we're going to have to work closely together. He smiled disarmingly. "So, Mr. Syme, have you been in the police long? You're young to reach an inspector's rank."

"Joined when I was eighteen. Promoted two years ago, when I went to Special Branch."

Gunther smiled. "I was working in Britain when the Auxiliary Branches were formed. I remember your then commissioner's words to the first intake—'You should not be too squeamish in departing from the niceties of established procedures which are appropriate for normal times.' I thought, a very English way of putting things."

Syme said, "Yes. Nowadays our essential job's fighting the Resistance. Any way we can."

Gunther nodded at the tiepin. "I see you are a member of the Fascist party?"

Syme nodded proudly. "I certainly am."

"Good." Gunther waved a hand to the chair. "Please sit down. We are grateful to your people for assisting us in this case."

"We're all good pro-Germans in my section of Special Branch."

Gunther nodded. He said neutrally, "I believe there has been some unease among British Fascists about joining the coalition with the old parties, Conservative and Labour."

Syme shrugged. "It's a way in. It's how Herr Hitler began, isn't it? And having Mosley in charge of the police is a big step to power."

Gunther nodded seriously. "Yes. You are right."

"Though the commissioner is a bit puzzled over why you want this loony Muncaster so badly." Syme's eyes narrowed. "According to our records he hasn't any political past or Resistance links."

Gunther leaned forward. This man was cocky, but clever too. He said, "No police or intelligence service is infallible." He smiled self-deprecatingly. "Not even ours. But we do think this Muncaster may have political associations in Germany. Concerns have been raised. At a high level."

"I thought the anti-Nazis had all been dealt with."

Gunther raised a hand. "Mr. Syme, I may not say. It is an internal matter. I would have thought you would have been told this," he added.

Syme smiled. "You can't blame me for trying."

Gunther frowned. The young man was going too far. "The terms of reference for cooperation were, as I said, set at a very senior level."

Syme looked discomfited. His mobile face was expressive, too expressive perhaps for a detective. He said, a slight edge in his voice, "Well, the commissioner says I'm at your disposal."

"Thank you."

"What is it you want done?"

Gunther drew on his cigarette. "We wish to find out all we can about Frank Muncaster. What his mental state is, whether he is lucid and if so, what he says. Our problem is that we, the Gestapo, cannot just go into this hospital demanding to see him."

"No." Syme frowned. "The British police force can do more or less what it wants these days, especially Special Branch. But lunatic asylums remain under the authority of the Health Department."

Gunther nodded agreement. "Quite so. And we do not want our interest in Muncaster known."

"I understand. I think."

"Has anyone outside the hospital shown any interest in him?"

"Who? The Resistance?"

"We've no evidence they know anything about him. But we need to be careful."

Syme pulled out a packet of cigarettes, unfiltered Woodbines, and Gunther took one, though he preferred milder brands. Syme said, "No one's shown a peep of interest in Muncaster. I've seen the local police reports. Frank Muncaster has no record, but in October he suddenly went potty, pushed his brother out of a second-floor window in some family quarrel then started screaming about the end of the world. He was put in the bin and that's all we know. He's a geologist, an academic. All these types are loopy."

Gunther smiled again. "I am sorry we can't confide in you fully. But we will work together, find out what is at the bottom of this. If there is something, we will both get considerable credit."

That struck a chord. Syme nodded slowly. He said, "And if you decide you want him, would you take him back to Germany? Extradite him?"

"Perhaps. For now, what I would like is for both of us to go up there this weekend, take a look at his flat, and interview him. If that is convenient," he added politely.

"It's already arranged. We sent a letter to the hospital saying we want to talk to Muncaster about the police case over the assault. Sunday's their visiting day. The doctor in charge, Wilson, phoned us wanting to know what it was all about, angling to be at the interview. Protective of his charges," Syme added contemptuously. "Said Muncaster was a Doctor of Science, a man of some status was how he put it. I know what I'd do with the loonies, the same as you Germans have. I spoke to Wilson, quoting the Defense of the Realm Act. That shut him up."

"Good."

"Might have to watch him, though, his cousin's a civil servant, close to the junior Minister of Health. That could give him some clout if we piss him off."

"Yes." Gunther smiled. "I know. Kid gloves. Now, when we talk to Dr. Muncaster, please say I am your sergeant. I will say nothing. I lived in England for five years but my German accent might be picked up."

"Yours is hardly noticeable."

"Thank you. I was at university here and for a few years after the Treaty I worked as an adviser with Special Branch. I knew the present commissioner." He paused. "He approved this operation."

Syme nodded slowly, impressed; his hands twitched slightly in his lap. He lit another cigarette.

"What do you want me to ask him?"

"I have a list of questions we could go over now. Can you arrange a car, by the way?"

"We can go in mine. Afterwards we can go to where Muncaster lives. It's a flat. His keys will be held by the hospital. The local boys will provide a locksmith, I've already been onto them."

Gunther nodded appreciatively. "Thank you. You have been very efficient."

"Yeah, well, we English aren't completely useless, you know."

They spent the rest of the evening going over the plans, the questions Gunther wanted asked of Muncaster. He stressed several times how the Gestapo appreciated Syme's cooperation. They finished at about ten.

"Time I got home." Syme stood up and stretched his long arms.

"You have a wife waiting?"

Syme shook his head. "No, I live in my parents' old house. Inherited it when my mother died last year."

"Where is that?"

Syme hesitated, then said, "Wapping. My dad owned it himself, though," he added proudly.

Gunther nodded. "What did he do?"

Syme paused. "He was a docker. Got squashed flat when a crate slipped off a crane and fell on him."

"I'm sorry."

"It happens in the docks. I'm well out of that." As he spoke, the underlying Cockney twang was gone again. He looked Gunther challengingly in the eye.

"My father was a policeman," Gunther said. "Dead too now, sadly."

As they moved toward the door Syme said, "We thought we had a lead on Churchill last week, living as a guest of some distant Marlborough relative at a big house in Yorkshire. But if he was there, he was gone by the time we arrived. He moves around all over the place."

"He must be nearly eighty now."

"Yeah, the old bastard can't last much longer. And we caught and shot his sidekick Ernie Bevin last year." At the door Syme turned to Gunther and said, "Lot of Jews down our way. At least they're kept in their place now. Used to be a cocky lot."

"Yes. They are an alien element."

A look of ferrety curiosity appeared on Syme's face. "People here often ask, what have you done with them? There were millions in parts of Europe, weren't there, milling around like beetles? I know you say they've all been resettled in the East, but we hear things sometimes, in the Branch. Big gassing plants."

Gunther smiled and shook his head. "So far as I know, Inspector, they are all in camps in Poland and Russia. Safely secured, taken care of, made to work hard."

Syme smiled and winked.

When he had gone Gunther sighed deeply. He hadn't liked Syme. But he had been very efficient, prepared everything well. He remembered what he had said about the Jews. Like everyone in his section of the Gestapo, Gunther knew exactly what had happened to those Jews deported to the East; they were all dead, gassed and cremated in the huge extermination camps of Russia and Poland. Some of the smaller camps had closed now, though others remained open for any Jews and social misfits who had not yet been swept up, and for Russian prisoners of war. Some of the senior camp personnel had come back to staff jobs at Gestapo HQ; they tended to be reliable, efficient men, though a lot were prone to drink. But what else could Germany have done, with the war in Russia raging? They couldn't be burdened by millions of hostile, dangerous Jews in the ghettos of the East. By express order of Himmler himself, though, the subject was never mentioned outside Gestapo offices.

He thought again about his hostile reaction to Syme. He knew himself well enough to wonder whether his dislike might be linked to his unease at what Gessler had told him at the end of their interview earlier: "If the English policeman finds out anything about the secrets Muncaster may hold, he is to be disposed of. There and then. We will deal with the Home Office afterwards." What Gessler said had been in the back of Gunther's mind all night. He had been shocked. Policemen didn't kill their own.

CHAPTER FOURTEEN

Next morning, Sunday, David left the house shortly before nine. He was to take the Tube to Watford, meet Geoff and Natalia there and drive to Birmingham. Sarah was still asleep when he got up; he dressed in a sober suit. Downstairs, he ate some cereal and toast, several slices. It would be a long day. He remembered Sarah was going into town again, for another meeting. He hoped she would be all right.

He had a little time before his train, so he went into the garden and stood smoking a cigarette. It was cold, a light rime of frost on the grass, the sky milky white. His eyes felt sore and gritty. He had lain awake most of the night. David admitted to himself that he was frightened. He knew he was not a physical coward, his service in Norway had shown him that, and it had needed courage to spy at the Office. Yet in a curious way, although what he did there was treasonable, he had still somehow felt enfolded, even protected, by the Civil Service. What he was about to do now was utterly different and he felt exposed. He looked at his watch. Time to go.

Natalia and Geoff were already in the car park when David arrived at Watford, waiting in the front of a big black Austin. Church bells sounded somewhere nearby as he went up to the car. Natalia wore a white trench coat with a scarf, a jumper underneath. For the first time since David had met her, her face was carefully made up; she looked like an ordinary middle-class woman driving her boyfriend and his friend on a weekend mission of mercy.

"Is everything all right?" Her manner was even more practical and direct than usual.

David answered a brusque yes. "Sarah believed the story about my great-uncle. I left her asleep."

"Remember both your identity cards?" Geoff asked, with heavy-handed humor. He, too, was dressed quietly and formally.

"Yes, the false one for the hospital and the real one for anything else. Though no one's likely to stop us, are they?"

"You never know," Natalia said. David saw now that she, too, was tense, perhaps even afraid.

"There's going to be fog in the Midlands later," Geoff said. "According to the forecast."

Natalia said, "After we visit your friend remember that we are going on to Birmingham to look at his flat, see if there is anything of interest to us there, any papers. Our man at the hospital is getting the key."

David didn't answer. He felt uncomfortable at the thought of breaking into Frank's flat.

They pulled out onto the new M1 motorway to the north, modeled on the German autobahns. Natalia drove smoothly, maintaining a steady pace. There was little traffic, a few family cars and some lorries. Outside Welwyn Garden City an army truck passed them. The tarpaulin flaps at the rear were open, a row of khaki-clad soldiers looking back. Seeing a woman driving the Austin they made obscene gestures, then the truck, moving fast, sped away.

"I wonder where they are going," Natalia said.

"Up to one of the army camps in the North, I expect," David answered. "They say there's another miners' strike coming."

She looked at him in the mirror. "You were in the army yourself in 1939–40, I think?"

"Yes. In Norway."

"What was it like?" She smiled but her eyes were sharp.

"For the first few months nothing happened, and I spent the winter in a camp in Kent." He turned to Geoff and said jokingly, "You were all right, nice and warm out in Africa."

"They wouldn't let District Officers like me join up. I wanted to."

David continued, "Then the Germans invaded Denmark and Norway out of the blue. My regiment got sent to Namsos, up in the north."

"I heard it was a chaotic campaign," Natalia said.

"All the 1940 campaigns were." David remembered after they finally set sail, the troopship plowing through massive, heaving seas, all the soldiers seasick, then blizzards that turned the decks white. Their first sight of Norway, giant white peaks rising from the water. "When we arrived we disembarked and marched out immediately to meet the Germans. We had on thick army greatcoats, you'd get covered with sweat inside and then during the night it would freeze. Our boots just sank into the snow as soon as you stepped off the roads. But I heard at other landing points the soldiers didn't even have winter clothing."

"The Germans must have had the same disadvantages, yet they just smashed their way through," Geoff said.

"They'd planned for it. We hadn't. It was the same in France." David remembered marching down a Norwegian road, mountains and forests and snow on a scale he could never have imagined. He saw again German bombers and fighters roaring down on them, the fighters coming so low he could see the pilots' set faces; gunfire smashing into the column, fallen men lying on snow that turned red. The picture in Natalia's flat had reminded him of that. "The Germans seemed invincible," he said quietly. "I got frostbite, I was back home recovering when they served up the same medicine in France. I didn't see how we could fight on after that."

"Nor me," Geoff agreed. "I remember thinking, if we don't surrender London will just be bombed to annihilation, like Rotterdam or Warsaw was." He frowned, a guilty look.

"They are not invincible," Natalia said, her tone certain. "Russia has shown us that. In many places there they do not even have a front line, the Germans control one village and the partisans the next, and it all changes from season to season. They are completely bogged down."

"But Russia hasn't beaten the Germans either," David replied. "It's a stalemate. I think it's going to boil down to who runs out of men first," he added bitterly.

"Not just through the fighting," Geoff added, "if what we hear about the cholera and typhus epidemics on both sides of the line is true."

Natalia shook her head. "There are more Russians than Germans. And they have General Winter on their side, Russians deal with the climate better than the Germans. They know what to wear, how to survive in the forests, what seeds and mushrooms you can eat."

David thought the remark cold. "I expect you have hard winters too where you come from."

Natalia nodded. "Yes, long winters with a lot of snow."

They passed an ancient country church where the service had just ended, the warmly dressed congregation talking in groups beside the porch. A red-faced vicar in his white surplice was shaking people's hands. David said, "They look a contented bunch."

"Yes," Geoff agreed. "They'll be with Headlam's lot." The Church of England had split two years ago—a large minority opposed to the government forming their own church as the German Confessing Church had—but this prosperous-looking congregation was more likely to have stayed with the pro-German Archbishop Headlam.

"Were you brought up an Anglican, Geoff?" Natalia asked.

"My uncle was a vicar. I believed for a long time, that's partly why I joined the Colonial Service, going out to help the poor benighted natives." He gave his sharp little bark of laughter and ran a finger quickly over his fair mustache in an oddly cross, peremptory gesture. "David and I used to argue about religion at university. He won the argument in the end, so far as I'm concerned."

"You would have been brought up a Catholic, David, with your Irish family."

"My parents had had enough of religion in Ireland." He turned to Natalia. "What about you?"

"I was brought up a Lutheran, though most people in Slovakia are Catholics. But I also became disillusioned with religion. Did you know that our little dictator, Tiso, is a Catholic priest? His Slovak nationalists were glad to help Hitler break up Czechoslovakia, and now we have our own little Catholic Fascist state, just like Croatia and Spain. Our Hlinka guard, the equivalent of your Blackshirts, loaded the Jews onto trains when the Germans wanted them deported in 1942."

There was an anger in her voice David had never heard before. Geoff said, "I thought all Czechoslovakia had been occupied by Germany."

"No. We are a satellite state with our own government, like Britain and France." She looked away, concentrating on the road as a little sports car passed them, a young couple out on a Sunday drive.

Geoff asked, "Are your paintings of your home town?"

"Mostly of Bratislava, the Slovak capital where I lived before I came here."

"And the battle scenes?" David asked.

"Slovakia sent soldiers into Russia with the Germans when Hitler invaded. We were the only Slav country to join the invasion. Only a token force." She hesitated, then added, "My brother was with them on the Caucasus front. He was badly wounded. Later he died."

"I'm sorry," David said.

"It was ironic, because in the thirties he was a Communist. He went to Russia for a while, full of hope, but came back disillusioned. Russia was the graveyard of his hopes and then it took his life, too."

"And then you came to England?"

"A few years later, yes. And here I am," she added, a note of finality in her voice.

Beside the motorway they passed one of the agricultural settlements for the unemployed. The government's propaganda preached that the countryside represented the British soul, that the people needed to be brought back in touch with it. David saw shabby prefabricated huts set in mud, plots all around marked off with chicken wire and sagging little fences, like a city allotment on a larger scale.

"Recreating our glorious medieval past," Geoff said with angry sarcasm.

People were working there, bent double, planting spindly trees. A tired-looking woman in coat and headscarf carried a muddy toddler between the shacks.

"It is the same all over Europe," Natalia said. "Countryside worship. The heart of the nationalist dream. Look at it."

Geoff suggested they put the radio on, and for a little while they listened to *Two-Way Family Favorites*, records requested by soldiers' families for their loved ones serving in India and Aden, Malaya and Africa. After a request from a mother for her boy in Kenya, Geoff asked Natalia to turn it off, the program was depressing him.

The place where they stopped for lunch was an old coaching house, but the interior had been modernized, all black-painted oak beams and whitewashed walls gleaming with horse brasses, a shield and crossed swords nailed above the fireplace. There was a television set at one end of the bar, showing a display of morris dancing. During the week it would have been full of traveling salesmen but today there were only a few elderly people at the tables, a couple of retired military types propping up the bar. David went to get drinks and order lunch.

"The problem with the British working man," one of the old men at the bar was saying, "is that frankly he just doesn't like work, he's too bloody *lazy*." He jabbed a finger at his friend. "The answer's to put them under military discipline, give the slackers a damn good flogging in front of the others. And shoot some more of these demonstrating trade unionists, like they did in Bradford in the summer."

"I don't know if they'll go in for *public* floggings, Ralph. Beaverbrook's still a bit soft for that."

"Mosley's calling the shots now. He'll get the shirkers working properly, then our industry can maybe match the Germans and the bloody Yanks." He laughed. "Same again?"

As he walked back to the table David remembered that talk of shooting trade unionists had once been a joke among some of his father's lawyer friends; but now it was actually being done and people like those old barflies were happy about it. They had taken a table by the window with a view out over brown frosty fields. Geoff had lit his pipe. He said with a self-deprecating bark of laughter, "I've been talking about life out in Kenya again. Boring poor Natalia."

She smiled at Geoff; David felt an odd pang of jealousy. "It is not boring," she said. "It sounds like another world, Africa. Like the Garden of Eden."

"It's hot and full of disease."

"The White Man's grave."

"That's West Africa. But it's hard work. Out where I was in the tribal areas there were just a few of us running an area half the size of Wales. Well, the chiefs ran it really, but they had to defer to us. We pushed a road through while I was there. I thought it was a good thing, would help them develop some commerce, but it was just used to ferry black labor to the white settler areas." His mouth set hard.

Natalia said, "It must have been very lonely if you were the only white man."

"Yes, their way of life's so different. They don't really trust us. Can't blame them, I suppose, we just arrived and took things over." He gave his bitter laugh. "Sometimes among them I felt like a man stumbling about in the dark with a dim lantern."

David said, "We used to have black visitors at the Dominions Office sometimes. I remember not long after I started, I had to meet a South African student who was stranded here without any money, and didn't want to go home. I thought I had liberal ideas about race but when he came in all I could do was sit and stare at him because he looked so different. He must've thought I was mad. Spoke to me in perfect Oxford English." He shook his head. "Of course, Africans and Indians aren't allowed to come to England to study any more."

Geoff pulled at his pipe. "If I was honest I was always happy to see other white officers, veterinarians and forestry people. And I'd go down to Nairobi often." A shadow crossed his face and he fell silent. David thought, he still hasn't got over that woman he knew out there, though it was years ago. It was a strange sort of fidelity, admirable but somehow frightening. He wondered if Natalia knew Geoff's story. She probably did, she probably knew everything about them.

She met his eye briefly, then glanced out of the window. "Winter has come early this year. It reminds me of my country." She smiled sadly, in her self-contained way.

The men at the bar were becoming drunk and loud-voiced. "During the Great War, if a man wouldn't go over the top and fight you gave him a quick court-martial, then took him out and shot him. I've seen it done. Why should it be any different with people who won't bloody work?" David remembered something Sarah had said once, that the Great War had made mass slaughter ordinary, that was why Stalin and Hitler could commit murder on a scale inconceivable before 1914. It was why these old men could talk like Soviet Commissars or SS men.

The barman had turned the television up. Everyone looked around. The background of a turning globe, the BBC initials underneath, was showing; they heard the announcer say, "...special broadcast from the Minister for India, the Right Honourable Enoch Powell MP." Powell's ascetic face with the black mustache and fierce, passionate eyes appeared. Everyone was looking. He began to speak, in his ringing voice with its Birmingham accent; unsmiling—Powell never smiled. "I wish to broadcast to you today about our most important Imperial possession, India. You will all be aware of the seditious rebellion and terrorism there. It has even infected native regiments within the Indian army. But I want to tell you today that we shall not, will never, give in. We know that the majority of the Indian people support us; the ordinary people to whom we have brought railways and irrigation and a measure of prosperity, the rulers of the princely states, our loyal allies. The Muslim League, who fear Hindu domination. For two hundred years we have governed India, firmly and fairly. Ruling it is our destiny."

He leaned forward, those blazing eyes on the screen seeming to fix on each of them individually. "That is why, with the agreement of our German allies, we are recruiting a hundred thousand soldiers to strengthen our presence there. Firm and quiet rule will soon descend on India once more. We shall not withdraw, or compromise, ever. A nation that showed such weakness would be heaping up its own funeral pyre. So be reassured, British rule and British authority in India will be established ever more firmly."

The old men at the bar cheered and clapped.

"We knew something like that was coming," Geoff muttered.

Natalia said, "India. Churchill was determined to hold on to it too, wasn't he, before the war?"

"He knows he's lost that one," Geoff said.

A waitress came with shepherd's pie, stodgy but filling. Afterwards Natalia said she would like to stretch her legs, just for ten minutes, as there was still a long way to go. Geoff said it was too cold for him and he would wait in the car. There was nowhere to walk except around the edge of the almost-empty car park behind the roadhouse so David and Natalia began to circle it, going slowly, smoking. She kept one hand in her pocket. David thought, *perhaps her gun is in there.* Jackson had called her a crack shot. *Who had she shot?* he wondered. Across the fields he saw a village. Like others they had passed recently it was built of red brick; they were well into the Midlands now.

Natalia said to him, "Soon you will see your friend Frank. He sounds like a man with many difficulties." Her expression was sympathetic.

"I wonder how Frank made it through, sometimes."

She said, "My brother had difficulties as well. All his life. Though that did not stop our government sending him to fight in Russia."

"I'm sorry. I didn't know."

She gave a sad smile and looked away, to where a farmer was working a field, two big carthorses pulling an ancient plow. She turned back to him. "There seem to be certain people who have some quirk in them, something they cannot surmount."

"I think a lot of things went wrong in Frank's early life."

She stopped, watched the carthorses. "With my brother something inside him was different from the start. But he had a right to live." She looked at David with sudden fierceness. "A right to live, like everybody."

David hesitated, then said, "You told me your government helped load the Jews onto trains."

"Yes, they did."

The fate of the Jews was a subject David avoided. But Natalia knew, something at least, of what had happened to them in Europe. He asked, "Do you know where they went?"

"Nobody knows for sure. But I think somewhere bad."

"We don't really know anything about it over here. We've been told about comfortable labor camps."

She began walking again. "We had many Jews in Bratislava before the war. I had several Jewish friends." David nodded and smiled, encouraging her to continue. "It happened in steps; restricting where the Jews could work, then taking away their businesses, turning the screw, bit by bit."

"As is happening here."

"In 1941 they were all expelled from Bratislava." Her voice was flat and unemotional again, and David began to realize what it cost her to keep it so. "There was a family in our street, the man was a baker. One morning I was woken by the sound of breaking glass. I looked out of the window and saw men from the Hlinka Guard—our Fascist paramilitaries—pulling them out of the house, kicking and hitting them. They threw them in a van and drove them away. Some of the Hlinka men stayed behind, and I heard them in the house, breaking things and coming out with armfuls of clothes and ornaments. Later we learned the same thing was happening all over town. One of the Hlinka people and his family moved into the bakery and started it going again, as though it had always been theirs. That is what most of these Fascists are, thieves waiting for loot."

David shivered. "Did nobody protest?"

She gave him a sudden fierce look. "What should I have done that day, gone and told the Hlinka Guard to stop? What do you think they would have done to me?"

"No, of course you couldn't have done anything."

"And it was all done so quickly. Some people did protest after it started, even some priests, which embarrassed Tiso. They stopped the deportations for a while. Though I heard they resumed later." She sighed. "I wish I could have done something."

"You couldn't. I'm sorry; I know you couldn't."

She smiled, looking suddenly vulnerable. "No. People should know though. It is good you are interested."

"And they were put on trains?"

"That was a year later. We'd been told the Jews were in work camps somewhere in the remote countryside, we didn't know where. People were starting to forget them. Then one day, it was a beautiful summer day, my fiancé and I went for a long drive. He had a car, not many do in Slovakia. We drove a long way. A long way." She looked into the middle distance. "We had a picnic on a hillside, I remember some deer came out of the woods nearby and drank at a stream. We sat watching them. Afterwards we went for a hike. We went over fields and meadows, saw the mountains in the distance." So she had a fiancé, David thought. What had happened to him?

"We crossed a big hill. On the other side was the railway line that goes over the mountains into Poland. We hadn't realized we had come so far." Her voice had slowed. "And there was a train standing there, in the middle of nowhere, there must have been an obstruction on the line somewhere. A huge goods train, wagon after wagon, just standing there in the sunshine. We wouldn't have thought anything of it, but we heard noises." She shook her head slightly, closing her eyes. "All the wagons had small ventilation windows and barbed wire across them. We heard voices, calling to us in Yiddish. We didn't understand what we were see-ing, Gustav and I, so we walked down a little, toward the train, and then we caught this terrible smell—I don't know how long those people had been traveling but it must have been a long time in the heat."

"How many were on the train?"

"I don't know. Hundreds. One woman was calling to us over and over, begging for water. Then two men in the black Hlinka uniform, with rifles, came around the end of the train—they must have been patrolling the other side—and waved and shouted at us to go away. So we walked back. I was frightened we might get a bullet in the back for what we had seen. But I think they would not have hurt us, because of Gustav's uniform."

"Was he a soldier?"

She answered, quiet defiance in her voice, "Yes. He was German."

David glanced at her in surprise. She said, suddenly defensive, "He was with German Army Intelligence, the Abwehr. He hadn't known what was going on, he was very junior, it shook him. We both knew that if people were transported in that state, by the time they reached their destination many would be dead." She turned and stared at him. "The British, like the French, say they are proud of protecting their own Jews, only deporting foreign ones. But that is what happened to those they did deport."

"My God, it's terrible."

"I know." She smiled wryly. "I have not told many people this story."

"It must be hard to tell."

"It is."

"What happened to your fiancé?"

"I married him. And now he is dead." Her tone changed, that flat finality again. She turned away, stubbing her cigarette on the tarmac. "And now we should get back on the road. Focus on your friend Frank."

CHAPTER FIFTEEN

F rank sat in his usual armchair, staring out at the grounds. There was a slight mist this morning. It was Sunday and some of the patients had gone to the church service, so it was quiet on the ward.

David was coming today. After Frank had telephoned him yesterday he had felt agitated; talking to his friend had got all his feelings jangled up, about how he had ended up in here and about what he knew. He was frightened that somehow he might let his secret slip. Sitting in his chair he found his mind wandering back to school. Maybe because he had only just had his Largactil dose, for once he found himself thinking of his time there in a detached way, almost as though it had all happened to someone else.

By Frank's second and third year at Strangmans things had settled into a strange routine. Everyone pretty much shunned him, although the boys still shouted "Monkey" after him in the corridors, "Give us yer grin, chimp," and other things, too; names like Spastic and Weed and, occasionally, "English Cunt." There were several other boys from England at the school but it was another stick to beat Frank with — metaphorically, for the school believed firmly that though sticks and stones could break your bones, names could never hurt you. In the bug hut sometimes the sheets would be stolen from his bed, or someone would piss in his bedside glass of water, but he had his books and most of the time he lived, or existed, in a world of his own. Yet the knowledge that the other boys and most of the masters despised him left him with a deep, heartbroken sorrow.

At the beginning of his fourth year, when he was fourteen, things got worse again. Edgar had just gone to university and the boys in his year were changing. It was not just their bodies, which were getting larger and sprouting hair, as Frank's was. Their personalities were changing too, some becoming withdrawn while others seemed to fizz with angry energy. Frank would overhear them, in class before the teacher came, talking about girls and sex, sticking their cocks up women. Frank had his own sexual imaginings but they were different, oddly romantic and untroubling. During the school holidays in Esher he often went to the cinema on his own. It was 1931, the talkies had come in. The romantic elements in the films Frank saw there, usually pure and chaste, stirred him; it was a strange window into a world of happiness.

Lumsden, the boy who had caused Frank trouble in his first year, now came back into his life. He was big now, nearly six foot, his fat turning to heavy muscle. He was loud and swaggering and he led, as always, a little bunch of cronies. One day, as Frank passed his group in the corridor, Lumsden leaned forward and, without a word, punched him hard in the stomach, as he had that day long ago when Frank let fly at him. Frank doubled up, gasping desperately for breath. Lumsden and his friends laughed and walked away.

Lumsden wouldn't let him alone after that. He and his friends would come up to Frank and swing their arms low, do the monkey routine. Then one day Lumsden placed himself in front of Frank in the corridor, and asked why he was such a fuckin' useless grinning spastic chimp, why didn't he bloody say something for himself? He wanted a response; he wouldn't be satisfied with Frank's usual silence. Frank looked up into the bully's eyes; they were large and bright blue behind his glasses, they seemed to spark and flash with rage.

"Please," Frank said. "I haven't *done* anything!" He heard the plaintive anger rising in his voice.

"Why the fuck should we leave you alone?" The big boy frowned, genuinely angry. "Ye silly, grinning wee idjit, ye're a disgrace to the school, crawling around the place like a daft monkey. Are ye not?"

"No! Just leave me alone." And then, losing control, Frank shouted out, "You're evil!"

Lumsden grabbed Frank's arm with a damp, meaty hand, swiveled him around and twisted the arm behind his back. "Ye're a fuckin' grinning wee chimp! Aren't ye?" He twisted harder, making Frank cry out with pain. "Go on, say it!"

Frank looked desperately around at Lumsden's friends; they were smiling, eyes bright as their leader's. He said, gasping out the words, "I'm — a grinning — wee chimp!" There was laughter. One of Lumsden's friends said eagerly, "The wee spastic's going t'cry!"

One of the other boys whispered, "Teacher!" A black-gowned figure could be seen, approaching from the other end of the corridor. Lumsden let Frank go. As he staggered away he spat a threat. "Evil, eh? We'll show you fuckin' evil, Monkey, don't you worry about that."

He came to himself with a jump; the door to the main ward was half closed and from outside he heard the crash of glass, then cries and running feet and a scuffle. Frank was scared.

Moments later the door opened and Ben came in. He had been frowning but when he saw Frank his face relaxed into a smile. "Och," he said. "You're in here again."

Frank shrank into his chair. "What's happening in the ward?"

"Nothing to worry about. The new patient, Copthorne, put his fist through the glass. Tried to slash his wrist." Ben spoke casually; suicide attempts often happened in the asylum despite all the precautions against them.

"Why?" Frank asked.

Ben shrugged. "No' sure. He'd been to the church service; maybe something in the sermon upset him. Anyway, listen, your pal will be here in a few hours. You can see him in here if you like, I'll keep other folk out."

"Thanks."

Ben looked at him closely. "You seem a bit woozy. Not quite with us."

"I'm okay."

Frank was conscious that the room was cold, the central heating radiator in the corner giving out only its usual low heat. His bad hand ached. He rubbed it.

Voices sounded from outside. Frank thought he heard Dr. Wilson's. "I'll have tae go," Ben said. "The big brass will want to know all about Copthorne. You'll be going around the airing courts after lunch, try and get your head clear for your friend coming, eh?" Frank looked up into Ben's sharp brown eyes and thought again, *why are you doing this?*

During that terrible autumn term at Strangmans Frank felt in danger all the time. If Lumsden's group passed him in the corridor or sat anywhere nearby in the dining room, they would give him deadly looks. Once, from a couple of tables away, Lumsden drew a finger menacingly across his throat. Frank felt safer when the day boys had left and he was in the bug hut. They had a quiet study room there, usually with a master on duty, and it was the safest place to spend the evenings. It was in the afternoons, when many of the day boys stayed behind to play rugby or train with the school cadet force, that Frank was most afraid of running into danger.

A red-and-white bus from Edinburgh ran past the school gates, bringing the day boys out from the city in the mornings and back in the afternoons. Its terminus was some way to the south, in the foothills of the Pentland Hills. In the afternoons, once classes were over, Frank took to going out of the gates and catching the near-empty bus, riding to the terminus and back again. It took half an hour or so each way. He would take a book and read. Sometimes he would make the return journey twice in one afternoon. The conductors gave him curious looks and once or twice asked why he kept traveling to and fro. He said he just liked the ride. He always had his penny ready for the fare.

The terminus was a little lay-by, the hills all around. The bus waited for twenty minutes before turning back, the driver and conductor sitting in a little wooden shelter drinking tea from Thermos flasks and smoking. Sometimes Frank would go for a little walk down a footpath, toward the hills. If it was one of those windy days when clouds scudded across the sky, the alternating light and dark on the hills was beautiful. Sometimes he thought of just continuing to walk, on and on into the Pentlands, until eventually, sometime in the night, he would drop from exhaustion.

But as autumn turned to the early Scottish winter, and there were days of cold rain and sometimes streaks of snow high in the hills, he thought defiantly, why should I let the bastards make me go and die out there in the cold?

At the last assembly before the Christmas holidays, the headmaster announced that cross-country runs would take place on Wednesday afternoons next term, unless there was heavy snow. Over Christmas Frank's mother had to buy him running shoes, complaining at the cost.

Frank hoped that snow might prevent the runs but when he returned to school in January the weather was mild and damp. And so, on the first Wednesday of term, Frank found himself in the big changing room next to the gym that reeked of sweat and old socks. As he had feared, Lumsden was there with a couple of his friends; as he changed into his singlet and shorts Frank avoided their eyes. He would try to stay near the teacher who was going with them.

They set off, a hundred boys trotting out of the school gates and into the hills. The gym teacher, an enormous former Scotland rugby player called Fraser, shouted to the boys to keep moving to stay warm, set a good steady pace and they'd be fine.

Frank did his best to keep up with Fraser, but a life sitting in classrooms, on buses, and hiding under the chairs meant he was unfit. The new running shoes were tight and soon began to pinch his feet. The long line of boys became more strung out, the bigger and fitter ones at the front, laggards like Frank at the back. Mr. Fraser ran near the front, looking behind him only occasionally, and Frank fell further and further to the rear, though he was relieved to see that Lumsden and his two friends were well ahead.

As they ran up the first hill more and more boys fell behind. Mr. Fraser didn't realize, or didn't care, that many of them couldn't keep up the pace he set. By the time a panting Frank reached the top of the first hill Mr. Fraser and the leading boys at the front were out of sight over the crest of the next one. One boy just ahead collapsed onto the wet grass with a groan, clutching a stitch in his side. A little afterwards two others, realizing the teacher was well out of sight, stopped running and sat down, too.

Frank pressed on, toward a clump of bushes and rowan trees nestling in the dip between the two hills. He was the last one now. He thought, I can hide in there. He felt a little dizzy, his heart was racing, and his feet were very sore. There was a narrow path through the trees and here, out of sight, he sat down with a gasp on a carpet of damp leaves, his back against the trunk of a rowan. He pulled off the running shoes with relief, his feet throbbing, and closed his eyes. His breathing gradually returned to normal. He became conscious of the leaves under his bare legs, cold sweat drying on his body. Then he smelled something, a familiar smell, rich but sharp. He sat up suddenly, heart pounding. Lumsden and his friends, each smoking a cigarette, were standing looking at him from a few yards away, their arms and legs red and blotchy from the cold. Lumsden was smirking. His eyes, fixed on Frank's, were coldly predatory, like a cat's.

"Look at this," he said. His voice was very sharp and clear. "The babe in the woods. The monkey, anyway." The three boys walked toward him. Frank scrambled up but Lumsden gave him a heavy push that sent him staggering back against the tree.

"We've no' seen ye for a wee while, Monkey," said McTaggart, a tall, rangy boy with black hair. His tone was friendly, but with an edge of menace to it.

"Uh-huh," the third boy agreed. "It's as though he was avoiding us, ye'd think he didn't like us."

"He does not, too," Lumsden said. "He wis fuckin' rude last time he spoke to us. And now he's dropped out of the race, hiding in the bushes." His voice rose with fake self-righteousness.

Frank said desperately, "So have you, and you're smoking."

Lumsden leaned forward threateningly. "Are you trying to tell us off, you wee spastic?"

"Sheer insolence," McTaggart said.

"He's a most cheeky wee lad." Lumsden folded hefty arms across his chest. He sounded like a teacher. He glanced down at Frank's running shoes. A slow smile spread across his big round face. "I think he needs a few strokes of the tawse. This'll do." He bent and picked up one of Frank's shoes, running a big hand across the spikes.

McTaggart chuckled, but the third boy, a small stocky lad called Vine, looked worried. "What're ye goin' to do, Hector? We don't want to get into trouble just over Monkey."

"We won't," Lumsden said.

Frank scrambled up and tried to make a run for it, but it was hopeless; McTaggart and Vine grabbed him by the arms. He kicked out frantically but they threw him on the ground again. Lumsden leaned over him and grasped his chin, staring into his eyes. He said, quietly, "We're going to give you the tawse, wee monkey man, just to teach you manners." There was a catch of pleasurable excitement in his voice. "When you get back, ye're going to say you took your shoes off here, and when you got up again you fell onto one of them. See? If you don't," he added, very slowly, "it'll be your word against three of us, and next time, you wee cunt, we'll kill you."

Vine said, "Ye're no going to hit him with the spikes, Hector?"

Lumsden turned on him threateningly. "Do you want some?" Vine glanced at McTaggart. The dark-haired boy hesitated for a moment, then gave a quick, strange smile. "All right. It'll just be a wee bit blood, won't it?"

Frank screamed, "Please don't, Lumsden, I just want to be left alone, please, don't—"

"Ye called me evil, you wee bastard!" Lumsden pulled a dirty handkerchief from the pocket of his shorts and shoved it in Frank's mouth. His cries turned to muffled squeals as Vine and McTaggart dragged him to his feet. Lumsden seized his right arm and yanked it forward. Instinctively Frank clenched his hand into a fist.

"Open your hand," Lumsden snapped. "It'll hurt more on the knuckles." He spoke sternly like a teacher, he was pretending to be a teacher.

McTaggart laughed. "Look at him with that snot rag in his mouth."

"Hold him!" Lumsden snapped. Vine held Frank around the waist and McTaggart held his arm out straight. Frank stared at Lumsden in horror as the big boy raised the running shoe, spikes down, shifting his balance to get the best aim. Frank closed his eyes as the shoe came down with all the force of Lumsden's arm. The pain was terrible, sharp spikes cutting into his palm, and Frank gagged, almost choked. He opened his eyes. The blow had made several deep cuts, which were all bleeding heavily, but one spike had penetrated his wrist, and blood was spouting out of it like water from a pump.

"Fuckin' hell, Hector," McTaggart said quietly, dropping Frank's arm. Pulling the handkerchief from his mouth, he pressed it to the pumping wrist. It turned bright red almost instantly. A stream of blood was running down Frank's arm now. He began to moan.

"Shit, Hector," Vine said. "How do we stop it bleeding?"

Lumsden had gone pale. "I don't know. We've got to somehow, it's a mile to the fuckin' school."

Frank slumped against the tree, clutching his arm as more blood flowed down onto his vest.

McTaggart said urgently, "We have to make a tourniquet."

"A what?" .

"My sister fell out a tree once and gashed her leg. My dad tied a hanky around it and told her to hold the leg up. Said it was what they did with injured men in the trenches."

"Well, do it!" Lumsden shouted. "Do it, or we're fucked."

McTaggart went over to Frank, pulled away the bloodstained handkerchief and lifted his arm up. He tied the handkerchief tight, halfway down his skinny forearm. "Ye'll be all right, wee man," he said. His voice was suddenly, astonishingly, gentle. There was a sudden gush of blood from Frank's wrist, making him cry out, but then the stream slowed to a trickle. His arm began to go white.

"You have to keep your arm up," McTaggart said. Frank just stared at him blankly so McTaggart lifted his arm and held it pointing upwards. The trickle of blood slowed further, though it was still coming.

Lumsden stepped forward. "We'll get you back to school," he said quietly. "We'll say we found you here and brought you back. Ye'll tell them you fell on the spikes, right?" Frank just stared at him, his face blank. His teeth began to chatter. Lumsden said, louder, panic in his voice, "Say ye'll tell them that, Muncaster, or we'll bloody leave you here!"

Frank's eyes focused on Lumsden's red, frightened face. He nodded.

"Swear on the Bible?"

Frank nodded again.

"Say it! I swear on the Bible!"

"I swear," Frank whispered. "On the Bible."

"Come on then, keep that arm up. Here, I'll hold it."

They took Frank and helped him get his shoes back on, helped him out of the dell, telling him to watch his feet as he stumbled over a fallen branch. It was strange how they were aiding him now, as though they were his rescuers.

Halfway to the school, Frank fainted dead away.

He woke in a hospital bed. All around him men, mostly old, lay sleeping or reading. His right arm lay on the counterpane, swathed in bandages almost to the elbow. He tried to move his fingers and pain coursed through his arm. A nurse appeared, a stout woman in a blue uniform and large white cap. She leaned over him. "Hello, you're awake then?"

"Where am I?" Frank croaked.

"Edinburgh Royal Infirmary. The school brought you in earlier. We did an operation on your hand, you'll be a bit groggy for a while from the anesthetic." She put cool fingers on his uninjured hand and took his pulse.

"Will—will my hand be all right?"

The nurse smiled at him. "We'll see," she said evasively.

After that Frank slept again for a while. He was gently shaken awake by another nurse. There was a doctor with her, a thin, gray-haired man in glasses and a white coat, a stethoscope around his neck. He smiled at Frank. "How are you feeling now, son?"

"My hand. If I move it, it hurts. But I can't feel it properly." Tears came to Frank's eyes. The doctor pulled up a chair and sat beside him. He said, quietly, "I'm afraid we think you've damaged the nerves in your wrist. We'll see how it goes, but you may have problems with some of the fingers." He smiled. "But your thumb and forefinger should be all right, you should be able to write." He paused. "The school said there was a cross-country run, and you took your shoes off, then fell over on the spikes. Is that right, son?"

Frank hesitated, then said, "Yes."

"Only you must've landed on that shoe with all the weight of your body."

"Yes. Yes, I did."

"Odd way to land."

"Is it?"

"Lucky those boys were just behind you, lucky they found you."

The doctor looked at him quizzically. Frank thought, if I tell the truth, maybe I'll never have to go back. But then the doctor smiled and said, "Strangmans was my old school. It's a fine place. Those boys who found you showed real presence of mind making a tourniquet like that. Otherwise, you could have bled to death, you know."

Frank closed his eyes.

Next day his mother came to visit. She wept at the sight of his bandaged hand, shook her head, and asked how Frank could have been so careless, so stupid. He asked if he could come back home but she said she couldn't cope; after what had happened she was sure he needed to stay at the school, be properly taken care of. She told him this was what his father had told her from the other side, through Mrs. Baker.

Back at school, the other boys left him strictly alone now. Lumsden and his friends kept well out of his way. Teachers treated him more gently. From the way they looked at him sometimes Frank guessed the authorities knew or suspected what had really happened, but it was always spoken of as a dreadful, careless accident. Lumsden left at the end of the term, to go to another school. Frank, relieved, wondered if Strangmans had asked him to go. His English teacher, who had formerly mocked him for his lack of interest in anything but science fiction, was now patient and careful in helping him learn to write again. He continued to work and work, hardly speaking to the other boys at all. He would listen to their conversations though, and had a dim awareness that life was passing him by, leaving him behind. He didn't even understand some of the slang they used nowadays.

One day in the spring the science teacher, Mr. McKendrick, asked him to stay behind after class. He was a large, middle-aged man, the suit under his black gown always shabby. He had a gentle, enthusiastic air, unusual among the crusty Strangmans masters. He sat at his desk on its dais, looking down at Frank.

"How's the hand?" he asked in a friendly way.

"All right, sir." It wasn't, it tingled and hurt a lot of the time, but the doctor said there was nothing more to be done.

"You're a clever boy, Frank, you know that."

"Am I, sir?"

"Yes. You can grasp scientific ideas as well as any boy I've taught. You could go to university, spend your life doing real scientific work."

Frank felt a glow of pride, and something else new: hope. Mr. McKendrick continued, "But you'd have to work harder in your other classes. Your English isn't bad, but your marks in other subjects aren't great."

"No, sir."

Mr. McKendrick seemed thoughtful. He leaned forward and said, "You don't appear to have any friends, do you, Muncaster?"

"No sir." Frank wriggled a little, the pleasure replaced by shame.

"You should make an effort to join in." McKendrick looked at him appealingly. "Why don't you try harder at sport, perhaps, once your hand's better."

"Yes, sir," Frank answered woodenly. He had hated rugger, was glad the doctors said he mustn't play that term. Nobody ever wanted him in their team and they would kick or barge him out the way if he came anywhere near the ball.

"Oh, Muncaster, please do take that grin off your face." McKendrick sighed. "I just don't want you to waste your talents, that's all." He paused. "Waste is a terrible thing," he said quietly. "I remember during the Great War, the casualty lists, those boys whose names are on the memorial in the Assembly Hall. For me they weren't just names. I look over the desks and think, this boy sat here, that one there. I pray to the Good Lord another war never comes."

Frank stared at him. He understood what McKendrick was saying about the War, he had lost his own father, but as for the rest, he was talking nonsense. As though the other boys would ever let him join in. But he thought, yes, he would work in class. The idea of spending his time somewhere studying science gave him, for the first time, a sense of purpose. A life somewhere far, far away from Strangmans.

"Frank!" It was Sam, the older attendant, shouting from the doorway.

He stood up wearily; it must be time for his walk around the airing courts. But Sam said, "You've to come to Dr. Wilson's office. People to see you."

Frank frowned, puzzled. It was too early for David, and he had thought he was seeing him in here. His heart pounded. But he had come. David might rescue him.

But then Sam said, "It's the police. Probably something to do with what happened to your brother."

CHAPTER SIXTEEN

Gunther was picked up from his flat by Syme, driving an old Wolseley, at ten o'clock. They set off an hour after David's party, through quiet suburban streets empty save for a few early churchgoers. It was a cold, cloudy day.

When Gunther had got up he had found a letter pushed under his door. It was addressed to his flat in Berlin, and he recognized his wife's handwriting. The postmark, stamped over the Führer's gray head, was Krimea. The Gestapo must have collected it from his flat and forwarded it to the embassy, who had then brought it around here for him. He was certainly getting first-class treatment.

There was a brief, formal note from his ex-wife, dated a week before. She said his son was doing well at school, that she hoped the security situation would allow Michael to visit his father in Berlin next spring. She hoped he was in good health.

He opened the letter from his son and read it eagerly.

Dear Father,

I hope you are well and that your work in trapping bad people who work against Germany is going well. Here it has become cold, but not so cold as Berlin, and I am wearing a new coat Mummy got me for school. I am doing quite well in German, not so well in mathematics. I am second top of the class in gymnastics. A new settler family from Brandenburg has moved in next door. They have a little boy called Wilhelm who comes to school with me and I am helping him find his way around. There was a terrorist attack on the railway line to Berlin last week and a freight train was derailed. It was out near Kherson. I hope there is a bad winter in Russia and the terrorists all starve.

*Thank you for saying you are sending me a train set for Christmas.
I look forward to getting it so much. We will be putting the Christmas
tree up next week and I will think of you on Christmas Day.*

*Mummy says I may come to Berlin to visit you next year. I would
love to come.*

Kisses,
Michael.

Gunther folded the letter and laid it on the coffee table. He kept his
hand on it. His son, the only family he had left, so far away.

Syme said little as he drove but there was a hint of a smirk in his expression that puzzled Gunther. The inspector was restless, too, lighting one
cigarette after another. Then, as they reached the outer suburbs, he said,
"I thought we might've seen something interesting on the way, but it
looks like the fun hasn't started yet."

"What do you mean?" Gunther tried to keep the irritation from his
voice.

"I heard about it when I went to collect the car. They're moving all
the Jews in the country this morning, taking them to special camps.
Everyone's involved, Special Branch, Auxiliaries, regular police, even
the army."

Gunther stared at him, annoyed at his smug tone.

"We've had the plans ready for years, of course, we thought the government would give in to German pressure eventually. About bloody
time so far as I'm concerned."

Gunther frowned. "I did not know this." So that was what Gessler
had meant about the police having something else on their minds.

"Nor did anyone else." Syme smiled, obviously happy to be in the
know when the German wasn't. "Apparently Beaverbrook and Himmler
agreed the final details in Berlin. Mosley going to broadcast about it on
TV later on."

"What sort of camps are they being sent to?"

"First to army barracks, closed factories, football grounds. Sounds like they're going to shift them somewhere else afterwards." He looked across at Gunther, smiling. "Maybe we're giving them to you."

Gunther nodded slowly. This was a big political step, a move closer to Germany. The price, he guessed, for economic advantages and the right to raise more troops for the Empire. And of course with Mosley's people in the government, there were more at the top who wanted rid of the Jews. "Do you think there will be any opposition from the public?" he asked.

Syme tapped his foot on the floor of the car. "If there is we'll deal with it. But the idea was to do it out of the blue on a Sunday morning, when nobody's around apart from the churchy types. If they make any trouble we can easily deal with them."

"I congratulate you," Gunther said. "It has worried us, this alien element in Britain, our most important ally. Maybe the French will get rid of their Jews now," he added thoughtfully, remembering Beaverbrook had stopped in Paris on his way to Berlin.

Syme said, "Dockland's always been crawling with Jews and foreigners. I've always hated the lot of them. So did my dad." His eyes were shining. He was excited now, worked up.

"Is that why you joined the Fascists?"

"Yes. I joined in '34, when I was a police cadet. Quite a few of us East End police supported Mosley. Having a Party card helped with advancement after the Berlin treaty. Even more now, with Mosley Home Secretary."

"It is the same in Germany. Being an Old Fighter, an *alte kämpfer*, it helps you get on."

Syme looked at him. "Are you in the Nazi Party?"

"I joined in 1930. I, too, was young."

"It helped me get into Special Branch, then up to inspector. I've led a couple of investigations now, winkling Resistance people out of the woodwork."

"I am sure your own talents helped as well."

"Trouble is, so many idiots sympathize with them these days, with the depression going on forever. I wish we could find Churchill."

Gunther looked at the near-empty motorway, the still, cold country-side. "I think in England you have left things too long, taken too many half measures. We rounded up all our enemies at the beginning, took firm control. To make a revolution you must act hard and fast."

Syme frowned and took another drag on his cigarette. "We couldn't do that. Remember, you let us keep our so-called democratic traditions at the Treaty negotiations."

Gunther nodded agreement. "Yes. It seemed the easiest way to end the war, then."

"It's taken twelve years to get shot of all that. We still allowed an Opposition till 1950. Now we're getting tough, they're fighting back. We don't have your German respect for authority, you see," he added with heavy humor. "But we'll beat them. This is the last campaign."

Gunther wondered if they could. Britain had grown weak and corrupt after so long. Syme continued, "I've thought of getting a transfer up North. There's a lot of London boys up there now. Good overtime, and I could do with a bit of excitement. Scotland, maybe. You know we're arming some of the Scottish Nationalists to take on the strikers in Glasgow. They've always had a pro-Fascist wing, they opposed conscription of Scots in 1939 and we managed to split the party, get rid of the woolly-minded liberals and lefties." He smiled at Gunther. "We learned that from you, recruiting local nationalists against the Reds. Promise them some goodies in return." He laughed. "Beaverbrook's promised to return the Stone of Scone to Scotland—it's some slab of rock the Scottish kings used to put under their throne. And road signs in Gaelic and vague promises about Home Rule at some time."

"Yes. We have used the Flemings and the Bretons. Offered them baubles in return for fighting the Reds. And the Croats—setting them against the Serbs; they have been a big asset. It is a useful tactic. But this Stone of Scone, do not underestimate the importance of ancient symbols to a nation. Reichsfuhrer Himmler has a whole organization, the Ahnenerbe, dedicated to uncovering the origins of the Aryan race." Gunther's voice took on an enthusiastic note; it was a subject that interested him. "Recently we found what were definitely swastikas in some caves in Poland, proving the Aryan race was there first. It is part of our ancient heritage."

"Yeah?" Syme wasn't interested. "Fighting the Reds up North, that's what I'd like, I could do with a bit of excitement. The Irish have offered to help us, you know, De Valera's people. Put spies in the Irish community here—lots of Reds there. But he wanted a stake in Northern Ireland in return, so we turned them down. The Ulster Unionists would go berserk."

"Yes," Gunther agreed. "He offered Germany help too, on similar terms. But Ireland is one nationalist conflict we do not want to get bogged down in." A bit of excitement, he thought with distaste, there were so many in the Nazi Party who spoke of the things they had to do like that. He was always uneasy around such men, they tended to be wild, unfocused. But Syme seemed focused enough.

"What's your job in Germany now, if there aren't any troublemakers left?"

"Oh, there are always some. I look for Jews, William, and the people who shelter them. There are very few left now. Some in Poland."

"So there's still some action?"

"Action is not what I am looking for," Gunther replied seriously. "We are trying to make Europe safe for future generations, William, cut out the Jewish-Bolshevik cancer. We have to be serious, totally serious." Syme didn't answer, and Gunther realized he was sounding pompous. There was silence for a few moments, then he asked, "Have you family in London?"

"Nobody that matters. I was engaged a few years ago, but the girl broke it off. Said between the job and the Blackshirts she never saw me."

Gunther smiled sadly. "My wife left me for similar reasons. She took my son to Krimea."

Syme gave him a sympathetic look. "I'm sorry. That's tough."

"Women do not understand the pressure men must live under in these times."

"You've got that right. The heroic generation, eh?"

"The generation that must sacrifice everything." Gunther looked out of the window. A wet, sleety snow had begun to fall.

Dr. Wilson sat behind his desk, fingers laced together, looking disapprovingly at the two policemen. Driving up to the mental hospital, through the wet snow, Gunther had been impressed by the neat gardens, the building's grand facade, but once inside he was appalled by what he saw: glimpses of crowded wards, patients with vacant or desperate faces. He was glad there was no more of this in Germany.

They were taken to Dr. Wilson's office, where Syme introduced himself as a Special Branch inspector and Gunther as his sergeant. The little fat mad doctor had waved them to a couple of chairs then sat behind his desk, looking self-important, but worried too. He said, "I find it inconceivable that Dr. Muncaster could be involved in political activities."

Syme answered with a wry smile, "It's often the last person you'd think of who is, sir."

Wilson's frown intensified. "You don't understand. He is frightened of everything, he finds safety in quiet and routine. I don't like that routine being disrupted." All Wilson's attention was directed at Syme; he barely glanced at Gunther, no doubt thinking him just a middle-aged sergeant, which was exactly what Gunther wanted. "I would ask you to be careful with Dr. Muncaster," Wilson went on. "If you provoke another outburst I'm not responsible. Last time, as you will know, someone was badly hurt."

Syme's voice took on a soothing tone. "I'll treat him gently, I promise. I just want to get an impression of him for now. I'll tell him I'm new to the district, picked up his case and I'd like to go over it with him. You may be right about him not being political, it may not even be necessary to raise that directly. We just want to tie up a loose end."

Wilson shook his head. "It's not usual to have someone like Dr. Muncaster, a graduate, on a common ward. We'd move him to the Private Villa if we could sort his money out. He's my responsibility. I want to sit in on the interview."

Syme shook his head. "That won't be possible, sir. I promise you, I'll try not to upset him. Just a bit of questioning." He added, "If you're not happy, you can always phone London."

Wilson set his lips tight, but did not reply. Syme, Gunther thought, was doing well. Like most people, Wilson was frightened of getting into trouble with the Home Office.

There was a knock at the door, and a middle-aged attendant entered. He held the arm of a thin man, with a closely shaved head in a baggy gray hospital uniform. Apart from his protuberant ears, Muncaster's face, with its large eyes and full mouth, might have been handsome were he not so obviously consumed with fear as he stared between Wilson, Gunther, and Syme. Syme stood up and smiled reassuringly. "Frank," Dr. Wilson said gently. "These men are from the police. Inspector Syme here has taken over the case of your brother."

Muncaster jerked back. The attendant grasped his arm more firmly. "Easy, Muncaster, easy." He guided him to a chair and sat him down.

Dr. Wilson went on, "We're going to leave you with these officers for a few minutes, Frank. It's all right, they just want to ask a few questions." He looked at the attendant. "Wait outside, Edwards." With a last sharp look at Syme, Wilson left the room, the attendant following.

Muncaster sat on his chair, gripping its wooden arms hard, chest rising and falling rapidly. It was, Gunther thought, as though he were in Gestapo headquarters already. He noticed Muncaster's right hand was deformed. He nodded to him, and Muncaster smiled back, a horrible grimace. Syme took a notebook from his pocket, looked at it, then said in a disarming, friendly tone, "Like the doctor said, I've just been transferred up here from London and I've taken over the case of your brother's fall. I see he didn't want to prosecute. But the files are still open, you see. I just want to go over a few things. It was quite a serious assault, Frank, wasn't it? Is it all right if I call you Frank?"

Muncaster nodded. "I — I know it was serious, but it was an accident really." Gunther noticed that the large brown eyes were watchful; there was something more than fear, something calculating in them as he looked between Gunther and Syme.

"Well, it's down as an assault, you see. You did push him out of that window. If you were charged it could mean prison. We don't want that, of course," Syme added reassuringly, then he smiled. "Now if he provoked you, that would be a defense. We might even decide not to bring the case." Syme had folded one leg over the other and was jiggling his foot. Gunther wished he could keep still.

"Come on now," Syme said. "Tell us what happened that night. I know you weren't in any condition to give a proper statement then but you're better now, eh?"

Muncaster looked at the floor. "Our mother died," he said quietly. "Edgar came over for the funeral. He and I never got on very well and Edgar—he was, well, hitting the bottle. We had a row, he started it, and I pushed him. He stumbled and went through the window. It was an accident. He was drunk, he couldn't keep his balance, the window frame was rotten."

It's like a recital, Gunther thought.

Syme leaned forward. "But what did your brother do to make you lose your rag with him? Must've been something serious, you don't look an aggressive chap and you've no police record, I know that."

"It was a family matter," Muncaster answered quickly. "Personal." He gave that strange grin again.

Syme looked at his notebook. "Your brother lives in California, doesn't he? Ever been there to see him?"

"No." Muncaster glanced down at his bad hand.

"What happened there, with your hand?" Syme asked.

"It was an accident, at school. I fell onto the spikes of my running shoes." He looked away as he spoke and Gunther thought, that's a lie.

Syme said, "Do you think it's because you don't get on that your brother won't reply to Dr. Wilson? I hear he can't get hold of him. Maybe it's because he knows he provoked you?"

Muncaster picked up the point eagerly. "Yes, yes, I think that must be it."

"I understand your brother's a scientist, like you."

Muncaster clenched his good hand into a fist. "No. He's not like me."

"A physics professor. That sounds impressive. Not that I know any-thing about it."

"I don't know what Edgar does," Muncaster said quickly. "I hadn't seen him for years till Mother died."

Syme pressed him. "I would've thought you spoke about your work, two scientists."

"I'm only a research associate." That strange grin again. "He didn't think I was worth talking to."

Syme considered Frank's reply, then looked at Gunther. "It seems there must have been an element of provocation here, Sergeant."

"Yes," Gunther agreed. He saw hope flash in Muncaster's eyes. He had seen that look often during interrogations; desperate people would jump at any prospect you held out that they might not, after all, be pros-ecuted. He felt sorry for this pathetic little man, as he had for the family in Berlin who'd sheltered those Jews. He asked Syme, careful to make his accent imperceptible, "Will Mr. Muncaster be released if he is cured?"

"Perhaps." Syme looked at Muncaster. "What would you do if you were let out, Frank?"

Muncaster shrugged his thin shoulders. "I don't know. I don't know if they'd have me back at the university."

"Any other family, anyone who could take you in?"

"No." There was a momentary hesitation, then Muncaster said, "I don't know if anything can be done for me."

"Well, we'll have to have another look at this case. You'll be staying here for now," Syme said casually. "With so much trouble in the world, all this industrial unrest and everything, you're probably better off in here, eh?"

"I don't know."

"Apparently, after what happened with your brother, you were shout-ing about the end of the world. So your police file says."

"I can't remember what I said." Muncaster's large eyes narrowed. Syme glanced at Gunther, who nodded, and the two of them stood up. Syme said, sympathetically, "Well, I can see you've been having a bad time." He looked at Gunther. "I think we should get on, Sergeant. We've put this poor man under enough strain." Gunther nodded agreement. He turned back to Muncaster. "We might want to talk to you again, but don't worry, it'll all get sorted out."

Syme went to the door and called the attendant. He waited as Muncaster was taken away. Then in the doorway Frank turned and met Gunther's gaze for a second. Again Gunther noted how watchful his look was; as though someone intelligent and calculating was looking out through the crippling fear. The attendant said Dr. Wilson would be back shortly. Gunther sat in the chair, thinking.

"Seen enough?" Syme asked.

"Enough to see that man was hiding something."

"I thought so, too. But he doesn't look like he's got it in him to be anything to do with the Resistance. Wilson was right there, he acted like he'd be afraid of his own shadow."

"He may not be political, but he could be protecting people who are."

"What about the brother? He wasn't telling the whole story there, was he?" Gunther didn't answer directly. "His flat in Birmingham. Has anyone been around there since the police were called?"

"Not according to the file. The freeholder was going to make the window secure."

Gunther rested his chin on his hands. "I think I would like to take a look at the flat now. Can we get that locksmith you mentioned?"

Syme said, "The Birmingham Special Branch has a list of locksmiths ready to get doors open with no questions asked." He tapped the file. "We'll go and see the superintendent at local HQ who's been liaising with me. He's a good Fascist. Though he'll have a lot on today, with the Jews."

Gunther nodded. "Thank you. Let's do that. Cast our net upon the waters."

"Our what?"

"It's from the Bible. I was brought up a Lutheran."

"My dad never had any time for religion."

Gunther shrugged. "The Bible is good literature, at least."

Syme gave him a keen look. "What next? After you've been to the flat?"

"I think we need to force Muncaster to tell us the things he is keeping back. And that will be easier done away from here. I will recommend we get him moved to Senate House."

"You're going to give him the full Gestapo works?"

Gunther inclined his head. "I think just being taken there would be enough."

"That Dr. Wilson won't like you treading on his turf. And he's got the law on his side."

Gunther gave him a serious look. "Dr. Wilson will not know of any German involvement. If my people agree with me the embassy will talk to the Home Office again, and they can put pressure on him."

Syme looked at him hard. "Just what's going on here?"

Gunther smiled. "I can only tell you again that we are very grateful for your help. You are showing yourself to be a true friend." He looked at Syme meaningfully. "Our gratitude might smooth your path to this transfer you want." He became brisk. "Now, Dr. Wilson will be back soon. Please ask him to tell his patient we were quite happy with what he said." He looked out of the window. The snow had stopped but a gray fog had descended, obscuring the grounds. "Look at that," he said. "We must get on to Birmingham."

Syme laughed. "You should see the fogs we get in London. This is nothing."

CHAPTER SEVENTEEN

S arah left the house an hour after David. There was a special meeting of the Christmas Toys Committee at twelve. It was a nuisance having to go into town on a Sunday, but an important committee member, who was on the board of a major toy manufacturer, was unable to attend during the week. She walked briskly up to Kenton Tube station. She thought of David, driving north. She couldn't prevent the niggling thought that perhaps it hadn't been Uncle Ted phoning, but that woman from his office. She told herself she was being stupid, she had heard the tail end of his conversation and he had looked worried and anxious for the rest of the day.

On the way into the station she saw a poster by the newspaper kiosk: *Mosley to Address Nation on TV Tonight*. She bought a copy of the *Sunday Times*, another Beaverbrook paper now. It told her the Prime Minister was back from Germany, and the Home Secretary was to broadcast at seven; there was no further detail. A color supplement inside the newspaper advertised the latest Paris fashion for men, tight-fitting dark suits with short lapels, like military uniforms. "SS kitsch," she had heard people call it.

There were fewer trains on Sundays but Sarah had to wait an unusually long time, over half an hour in the open. She was cold, she was glad she had put on a thick jumper and her new gray winter coat, though the fashionably wide sleeves left her wrists bare. The few other people on the platform looked at their watches and tutted. Sometimes on these journeys to committee meetings Mrs. Templeman got on at Wembley. At least, Sarah thought, if there were problems with the trains she might be less likely to run into her and have to listen to her talking nineteen to the dozen all the way to Euston. When the train arrived at last she got into the nearest carriage, even though it was a smoker. An old man in cap and muffler sat across from her, a laborer in heavy hobnailed boots. He was smoking a pipe, surrounded by a cloud of aromatic blue smoke. Sarah's father had always enjoyed his pipe, and she didn't mind the smell.

Her luck was out; when the train came into Wembley she saw Mrs. Templeman's tall, stout figure on the platform, swathed in her heavy coat, a round fur hat over her permed curls and the fox-fur stole around her neck. She saw Sarah, waved a plump hand, and headed for her carriage. She sat down heavily opposite her. "Hello, dear. Goodness, I had to wait ages."

"So did I. It was jolly cold on the platform."

"They say it's the coldest November for years. Let's hope we don't get another winter like '47. All our pipes froze." As ever Mrs. Templeman spoke loudly, in a rush. She adjusted her stole, the fox's eyes staring glassily at Sarah. "All shipshape for the committee, dear?"

"Yes. I've got the costings here." Sarah tapped her bag. "If everything gets approved today I can start placing the orders tomorrow."

"I do wish we hadn't had to come in on Sunday. It's all such a rush, after church."

"It's a nuisance, but I suppose we have to keep Mr. Hamilton sweet."

"He is generous. Goodness, it's a bit of a fug in here, isn't it?" Mrs. Templeman looked disapprovingly at the man with the pipe. He gave a little smile and turned to face the window, blowing out a fresh cloud of smoke.

"It's a smoking carriage," Sarah said mildly.

"Yes, of course. I do like a cigarette myself in the evening, but my husband—" She broke off as the train juddered to a halt, jerking them violently in their seats. "Oh, dear, what now? We shall be late—"

"There must be a problem on the line." Sarah looked out of the window, thinking that no trains had passed them on the "up" line. They hadn't entered the tunnels yet, they were on a stone bridge looking down on rows of back-to-back houses of soot-stained yellow London brick. Gray smoke rose from chimneys, washing was hung out to dry in the backyards. A big poster had been put on a wall: *Buy National Bonds.*

Save For All Our Futures. Being Sunday the streets were almost empty. A rag-and-bone man led a thin brown horse along the cobbles, discarded furniture and a pile of rags in his cart. Sarah remembered the man who had visited their street when she was little; her mother would give her a penny to take to him in return for letting her stroke his horse. Nowadays it was salesmen in suits who called at the house in Kenton, selling vacuum cleaners and refrigerators on the new hire-purchase schemes, raising their hats with cheerful, sometimes slightly desperate smiles. She remembered the jingling bells on the horse's harness of her childhood, and thought, Charlie would have loved that.

"In a brown study, dear?" Mrs. Templeman smiled at her inquiringly.

"Sorry. I was just thinking about my little boy."

"Left him at home with hubby, have you?"

"No. He died in an accident at home, two years ago."

"I'm so sorry, dear." Mrs. Templeman looked shocked, genuinely concerned. She spoke softly: "That must have been terrible for you."

"He fell down the stairs."

"I still think of my Fred," Mrs. Templeman said quietly. "He died in the war, at Dunkirk. He would have been forty this year." She paused, then added, "I find my faith a great help. I don't know how I'd cope without it." Sarah didn't answer. "I believe He leads us all, though often we can't see the path clearly. But we know He wants us to help those in need. That's why I'm on the committee."

"I sometimes wonder if it's any use," Sarah answered bleakly. "Whether anything is."

Mrs. Templeman changed the subject, talking about her brother who had just retired from the Indian Civil Service and was living with them till he found a house; he had had a bad time, in the thick of the Calcutta riots last year. Sarah asked if Mrs. Templeman had heard the news about Mosley's address but she shook her head, saying she avoided reading the papers these days, it was all so depressing.

The meeting at Friends House went well. Nobody could deny Mrs. Templeman was a good chairwoman, moving business quickly along.

Afterwards coffee was served. Sarah had a headache and couldn't face the thought of the long journey back in Mrs. Templeman's company. She decided to tell a white lie. "I'm not going back to Euston," she said. "My husband's meeting me at Tottenham Court Road Tube."

"I'll walk that way with you, dear, if I may. I need a breath of air after the meeting. It's a nice walk through the squares. I can get the Tube at Tottenham Court Road and then change."

"Oh, all right. Yes." Sarah supposed that when they got there she would have to pretend her husband hadn't arrived, that she would have to wait for him. Well, that was where lies got you.

"I'll go and put my face on." Mrs. Templeman walked off to the ladies, and Sarah went over to stand by the door. A couple of committee members called good-byes as they passed her, huddling into their coats as they stepped outside. Sarah noticed there wasn't a policeman at the entrance today. Probably off having a cigarette somewhere.

Mrs. Templeman returned, face freshly powdered. "Right, dear," she said, adjusting the hideous fox fur. "Let's face the cold."

They turned into the network of Georgian squares behind Euston Road, wide streets with gardens in the middle, full of expensive flats, little hotels, and university departments displaced when the German embassy took over Senate House. They walked along quickly; it really was cold, the sky a leaden gray. There was hardly anyone around.

"Thank you for all your work, Mrs. Fitzgerald." Mrs. Templeman smiled. "I know phoning around shops isn't the most exciting job in the world."

"It's all right. It gives me something to do during the day."

"Your husband works in the Civil Service, doesn't he?"

"Yes. The Dominions Office."

"My sister lives in the Dominions. In Canada. Vancouver." She laughed. "Family scattered all over the Empire, you see. I keep pestering my husband to go out and visit—" She broke off. "Good God, what's going on?"

They were turning into Tottenham Court Road. It was almost as quiet as the squares had been. The shops were closed, although behind a plate-glass window in one department store opposite an assistant could be seen putting up Christmas decorations. The few pedestrians, though, had all stopped in their tracks, watching the extraordinary procession coming down the road toward them. Perhaps a hundred frightened-looking people were trudging along, men and women and children, some in coats and hats and carrying suitcases, others wearing only jackets and cardigans. They were escorted by a dozen greatcoated Auxiliary Police in their black caps, pistols at their hips. At the front two regular police-men in blue helmets were mounted on big brown horses. For a second Sarah was reminded of the crocodile of children she had helped escort to the station for evacuation in 1939. Unlike them, though, this proces-sion was silent. Apart from the clop of the horses' hooves and the tramp of feet the only sound was a shrill, persistent squeak from the wheels of a pram a young woman was pushing along. As they drew close Sarah saw flashes of yellow in people's lapels.

"They're Jews," Mrs. Templeman said quietly. "Something's happen-ing to the Jews."

Most of the passersby walked quickly on or disappeared into side streets. Others, though, stood watching. The two mounted policemen at the head of the group rode past. One was an older man with a sergeant's stripes on his sleeve; the other was young, with a wispy pencil mustache. He seemed to be having trouble keeping his horse steady. One of the passersby, a young woman holding the hand of a little girl, nodded with satisfaction and spat into the gutter. Someone else called out, "Shame!" One of the Auxiliary Police, a tall, thin man with a Mosley mustache, smiled at the watchers, then looked back to the marching prisoners—for that was what they must be—and said, with mocking cheerfulness, "Come on, pick those feet up. Let's have a song, give us 'A Long Way to Tipperary.'"

Mrs. Templeman clutched her handbag to her chest with her gloved hands. "Oh no," she said. "They can't do this. Not here, not in England."

"They're doing it," Sarah answered bleakly.

"Where are they taking them?" Mrs. Templeman's face was anguished now, white beneath her powder, all her brisk confidence gone. A big Vauxhall passed by slowly on the other side of the road, a middle-aged woman looking out from the passenger side in astonishment. An Auxie waved it briskly on. Sarah looked at the Jews shuffling past. An old man in a bowler hat marched stiffly by, like the old soldier he had probably once been, marching as though to the front. Behind him a middle-aged woman, still wearing a flowered pinny and headscarf, held a skinny little boy in shorts and school pullover tightly to her. A young couple in fashionable duffel coats and bright university scarves held hands; the boy, tall and squarely built, had a defiant expression; the girl, slight with long dark hair, looked terrified. The squeaking pram passed; Sarah glimpsed a baby bundled up inside.

Then there was a shout, a yell, from the other side of the road. Everyone, Jews and policemen and the people on the pavement, turned to look. The door of a shabby building between two department stores had opened and a group of a dozen men in Sunday-best clothes had come out. They were carrying, of all things, musical instrument cases of various sizes. Sarah saw a notice board on the wall, *University of London Department of Music*. They must have been at some sort of practice. As Sarah watched a big, elderly man with untidy silver hair, wearing a rumpled suit, marched straight out into the road, shouting out in a deep voice, "Stop! What's happening here?" He halted right in front of the two mounted policemen. They had to halt or knock him down. The younger officer's horse whickered in alarm. The other men who had come out with him stood on the pavement, uncertain and frightened, staring at the old man. One called out, "Sir! Be careful!"

The old man's face was red with fury, fierce little eyes under white brows fixed on the mounted sergeant. "What are you doing?" he shouted in anger. "What's happening to these people?"

The older policeman's back was to Sarah but his voice carried back, deep and firm. "Move along, sir. All the London Jews are being moved out of the city."

The Auxie nearest Sarah, a middle-aged man with the white flash of a Blackshirt badge on his coat, laughed scoffingly. "Bloody academics."

He turned to the Jews, putting a hand to the pistol at his belt and said threateningly, "You lot stay put. This show won't last long."

Sarah felt shocked, frozen to the spot. Beside her Mrs. Templeman was breathing hard, a strange expression on her face, her fingers digging into Sarah's arm. The old musician didn't move. He gestured wildly at the group of Jews. "You can't do this! These are British citizens!" The young policeman's horse, frightened, tried to step back. The sergeant turned, snapping, "Keep that bloody animal steady."

Someone shouted from the pavement, "They're Yids, you old nosy parker!" One of the men outside the music department turned up his coat collar and began walking quickly away. Another followed, then another.

The mounted policeman's voice was loud and clear, still steady. "We're following official orders. You're causing a breach of the peace, sir. Move on or you'll be taken into custody."

Then, letting go Sarah's arm, Mrs. Templeman stepped out into the road. She walked up to the old musician and stood beside him. Sarah could see she was trembling, gray curls shaking beneath the fur hat.

"Fuck this," the policeman nearest Sarah said, fingering his holster. The Jews were shifting uneasily, looking frightened.

"Right, that's it," the sergeant said. "You two are both under arrest." The musician looked appealingly across to those of his people who remained standing on the pavement. They looked at each other. Three more men walked away. One young man carrying a violin case stood where he was with an agonized expression on his face, but the four remaining others stepped hesitantly into the road, walked across and stood beside the old man and Mrs. Templeman. The sergeant called over his shoulder, waving an arm. "Get these people out of the road!"

"You turn this world into hell!" the old musician shouted. He was beside himself, spittle at the corner of his mouth. Along the line, some of the Auxies began to move forward, reaching for the batons at their belts. Sarah's heart began to pound, thumping in her chest. Mrs. Templeman looked at the approaching Auxies and then suddenly sat down on the cold tarmac, the skirts of her coat billowing out, fat stockinged thighs exposed. Her white face was determined now. The old man stared at her for a moment, then sat down as well, stiffly putting a hand on her shoulder as he got down. The four other men, all younger, hesitated for a moment then sat down too. On the pavement, the one who hadn't been able to make up his mind turned and walked away.

Four of the Auxies ran forward, past the horses. The one ridden by the young policeman bucked and reared. The rider cried out, trying to bring the animal under control. It jolted forward and Sarah watched in horror as a big flailing hoof struck Mrs. Templeman on the forehead. She gave a little moan and fell backwards, her hat and the fox-fur stole falling off onto the road. She lay quite still, her arms flung out backwards, blood spilling from a huge gash on her forehead and dripping, shockingly red, onto the gray tarmac. Her eyes were as still and glassy as Charlie's had been that terrible day, and Sarah realized with horror that she was dead. The demonstrators and the Auxies both looked at the bucking horse; somehow amid the mayhem, the young policeman managed to bring it under control.

On the curb Sarah froze. All the instincts of self-preservation made her want to do what the young man with the violin case had done, turn and walk away. An image of David flashed into her mind, of home and safety. Then something firm and cold rose up in her and she gripped her handbag tightly and strode into the road. As soon as she stepped off the pavement she thought, quite coolly, there, that's it, everything's over. Two Auxies had grabbed the white-haired musician under the arms and were hauling him to the pavement. He was shouting and struggling furiously. Sarah went over to where Mrs. Templeman lay sprawled on the street in that awful indignity, and sat down beside her body. She looked over at the pavement, hoping desperately that others would follow her example. A thin young man in a muffler stepped out and sat down with them, sweating with fear. Four more Auxies ran forward. Sarah stared at them, her heart pounding so fast it made her gasp.

The Jews stood huddled together, terrified, though some of the younger ones were looking around them now, perhaps wondering if they could run. The remaining Auxies pulled out their pistols, covering the prisoners. The old musician had been pushed roughly down onto the pavement but was still struggling, shouting and swearing. The other Auxies began hauling the demonstrators to their feet. Sarah felt hard, strong hands grip her under the arms and pull her up. One of the musicians tried to resist and was hit over the head with a truncheon, slumping forward unconscious. As Sarah was lifted up she realized she might never see David again and thought, how I love him.

Then she heard more shouts. Glancing around, she saw half a dozen Jive Boys rushing down the street toward them, quiffs bouncing absurdly, the tails of their long coats flapping behind. They looked the worse for wear, unshaven. One had a black eye, another carried a near-empty whiskey bottle. They were probably on their way home from a long night out, drawn by the noise. One shouted, "It's a ruck! Pig down! Get the fuckers!" The whiskey bottle sailed up and out, just missing the sergeant, as the Jivers pitched into the Auxies who were moving the demonstrators. The one who was lifting Sarah said, "Shit!" as one of the boys went for him. Sarah saw the flash of a blade in the Jiver's hand. The Auxie let her go and she fell sideways into the road. The sergeant pulled out his pistol and fired into the air. It was too much for the nervous horse. It reared right up on its hind legs, throwing the young policeman into the road. He lay there, screaming and clutching his leg, as the horse turned and ran off down the empty road, hooves clattering. The sergeant's horse was uneasy now too, trying to turn in a circle. It was pandemonium. Sarah looked wildly around, and saw a glimpse of Mrs. Templeman's dead face, her bloodied head.

Then the group of Jewish prisoners seemed to surge outwards, like a wave, as some began to run. Others, the older ones mostly, huddled closer together. The woman with the pram leaned protectively over her baby. Half a dozen of the younger Jews ran into the fight. A shot was fired and one of the Jive Boys pitched forward, his chest gushing blood. There were screams, another shot.

Sarah felt herself being picked up again and hauled to the pavement. She lunged out and an angry Yorkshire voice shouted in her ear, "We're trying to get you out of here, you stupid cow!" She turned and saw it was the boy with the university scarf and duffel coat she had noticed earlier, the girl beside him. Sarah scrambled to her feet and joined them, running for the pavement. Other Jews were fleeing all around them now, making for a little alleyway that ran down the side of a pub. There were more shots, loud cracks. Beside her Sarah saw the old Jew in the bowler hat tumble over. On the other side of the road the shop assistant who had been putting up Christmas decorations could be seen cowering behind a counter. A long piece of tinsel hung forlornly in the window.

Sarah followed the young couple into another alley. Then the boy ran into the open door of some flats, leading them into a dark, smelly hallway. They stopped, taking long whooping breaths. Other people ran past, feet pounding on the paving stones. In the distance Sarah heard more shots, then the sound of a police whistle being blown, over and over again.

"Joe," the girl said breathlessly. "We've got to run!" She had a middle-class accent like Sarah's.

The boy shook his head impatiently. "No. There'll be dozens of them here in a minute. Hide under here." He pushed his way into a dank alcove under the stairs. The girl followed. "Come on, lady," he said impatiently to Sarah. She squeezed in beside them, feeling the warmth of their bodies. There was a big metal dustbin there, stinking of rotten vegetables. Sarah felt cold and clammy, though strangely calm.

"Bloody hell," Joe said. "I thought we were stuffed."

The long wail of a police siren sounded in the distance. The girl began to cry. "They shot people, they've killed people." Her voice was rising hysterically. Sarah grasped her shoulders. "Please, please," she said. "We have to keep quiet."

The girl took a couple of heaving sobs, then looked past Sarah at the boy. "What are we going to do, Joe? Where can we go?"

"Wait till dark, then we'll head out to Mark's friend in Watford." He raised a hand to the yellow badge on the front of his coat. "I'm getting rid of this fookin' thing. The identity cards can go too." He pulled at the badge but his fingers were shaking and he couldn't get it off. The girl, calmer now, laid a hand on his. "No Joe, unpin it. If they see you with a tear on your coat they'll realize you've pulled something off."

"Okay. Can you do it, Ruth? I — I can't seem to manage."

They worked together to remove their badges, then pulled out their identity cards, yellow stars prominent on the front, tore them up, and dropped the pieces into the fetid bin. Sarah listened, frightened someone might come out of one of the flats and find them. But the people who lived there had probably heard the shots and were cowering indoors. She turned to the young man. "Thank you," she said breathlessly. "Thank you for rescuing me."

Joe smiled, a flash of white teeth in the dark space. "That's all right." Though it was hard to tell in the dimness Sarah sensed he blushed. They're just children, she thought with a desperate ache.

Ruth said, "You helped us. You and your friend."

Sarah felt a catch at her throat. "My friend's dead."

"I know. I saw." The girl began to cry again.

Joe peered cautiously out of the alcove. "There's a good few dead out there now." His voice was trembling.

"What happened to you?" Sarah asked Ruth. "Where were they taking you?"

"They're taking every registered Jew in London out of the city. We don't know where. I live at the university halls of residence, they came for us at seven this morning." She put her head in her hands.

"I thought Jews weren't allowed in the universities anymore."

Joe said, "We started just before the law came into force. There's still a few of us third years left." He looked at his girlfriend. "You were right, you said they'd come for us one day." He turned back to Sarah, his face working with emotion. "I thought we were safe, I thought our government wouldn't let us be shipped off. Offense to national pride, against British fair play," he added bitterly. "Though they might kick us out of our jobs and businesses, I thought they'd stop short of handing us over to the Germans. But that's what they're doing now, it has to be."

Ruth spoke quietly. "Beaverbrook must have agreed this with the Nazis in Berlin."

Joe shook his head. "This must have been planned for some time."

"Maybe there was a contingency plan," Sarah said. "And now the

Germans have forced them to implement it. The Civil Service are always making contingency plans, my husband's a civil servant—"

Joe's look became instantly hostile. "Is he?"

"He's in the Dominions Office, they're not involved in anything like this—"

"They're all involved, everyone who works for Beaverbrook and Mosley."

"Keep your voice down," Ruth urged him.

Joe went on, quietly now, but his voice was still savage. "Well, now we know what British fair play's worth when the chips are down. From the moment we were picked up people just stood watching, drove past in their cars. Kept their heads down."

"Except that old man," Ruth said. She looked at Sarah. "And your friend."

"What really turned it was those Jive Boys." Joe smiled sadly. "Not that they'd care what happened to us, I've heard plenty of stories of them beating Jews up. They just saw a fight and joined in."

Sarah found thoughts rushing through her head. It was because of her that Mrs. Templeman came that way. She'd thought her just a bossy old woman. Then she did that incredible act of bravery. Sarah shivered as she realized she could have been killed too. She had feared David might abandon her but it was she who would have abandoned him had she been shot.

The boy took her arm, jolting her back to reality. He said, "It's quiet out there now. It won't stay that way for long. I'd get out of here while you can. You've got your ID card?"

"Yes."

"Where do you live?"

"Kenton. Out toward Pinner."

Ruth said, "You shouldn't wear that coat, it stands out. You sat down in the street, they'll be looking for a fair-haired woman your age in a gray coat."

Sarah said, "Swap coats with me. Lots of people wear duffel coats."

They stepped out of the alcove, and while Joe watched the entrance the two women switched coats. Ruth's duffel coat was tight on Sarah. She picked up her handbag and took out her purse. "Here, take my money." She held out two ten-shilling notes, a handful of silver. "Please. I've got a return ticket, I don't need money for anything else."

Joe looked reluctant but Ruth took the money. "Thank you."

Sarah asked, "Where do your families live?"

Ruth said, "Mine live in Highgate, they'll have been picked up too." She blushed. "I was spending the night with Joe."

"Mine are in Bradford. They're probably rounding up Jews there too." Joe's voice cracked, and Sarah could see he was at the end of his tether. "Go now, lady," he said roughly. "Go on."

Ruth took her arm. Sarah's gray coat looked big on her. She said, "We'll never forget what you and your friend did."

Sarah smiled. "Good luck," she said, then took a deep breath and stepped outside. Everything was quiet now, nobody in sight. She adjusted her bag on her arm and walked away, in the opposite direction to Tottenham Court Road. More sirens sounded in the distance. Her legs shook like jelly but she made herself walk on, toward the Tube station and home.

CHAPTER EIGHTEEN

I t took longer than David had expected to find the hospital. Although they were so near Birmingham, they were on narrow country roads shaded by trees, with few signposts, and after a brief period of wet snow it had begun to get foggy. They discussed, again, how he should tackle Frank Muncaster: with sympathy, caution. Afterwards they drove on in silence and David thought about what Natalia had told him about the Slovak Jews. He knew she could have done nothing to help those people and it frightened him. He wondered how Sarah would react if she found out he was half Jewish. She hated what had been done to the Jews in England but that was different from being married to one. He knew prejudices ran very deep, had done even before anti-Jewish propaganda began in the 1940s.

His thoughts were interrupted by Geoff. "We're here," he said quietly. They had come to a fork in the road, and a wooden signpost pointed to Bartley Green Asylum. They passed through a little copse and then saw an immense redbrick Victorian building a little way ahead, on top of a low hill, with a big water tower and well-tended grounds surrounded by a high wooden fence, lights shining through the mist. David hadn't expected it to be so big and imposing.

The road followed the side of the fence to high, iron-barred gates. Beside them was a porter's lodge with a window overlooking the road. They drove up to it, passing a woman in a dark nurse's cloak walking toward the gates, and an elderly couple, heads down. David looked through the bars of the gates, down a long straight drive to the big building. Natalia stopped the car. "You two go and talk to the porter," she said.

Geoff and David got out. It was slightly warmer, but a clammy mist clung to them. They walked up to the window, where the nurse was talking to a porter through a panel. Ahead of them, the old couple stood, silent. The porter was small, elderly, his black uniform reminding David of old Sykes on the Dominions Office front desk. There was even a similar large rack of keys on the wall behind him. Another younger porter was working at a desk beside the plugs and sockets of a switchboard.

"Been a bit busy with visiting time, but the rush is over now." The porter gave the nurse a key and turned to the old couple ahead of David and Geoff. The old man said in a Black Country accent, "We're here to visit our daughter. Amy Lascelles, on Domville Ward."

The porter shook his head reprovingly. "Visiting time's nearly over."

"It takes a long time to get over from Walsall."

The porter sighed. "Identity cards?"

The old couple produced them and the porter made an entry in a ledger. "Okay," he said. "Just wait to the side a minute." He turned to David and Geoff. "Yes, sirs?"

"We've come to visit a patient too, Frank Muncaster," David answered. "I'm sorry we're a bit late, we've driven up from London."

The porter's manner became deferential on hearing David's accent. "Does the ward know you're coming, sir?"

He took a deep breath. "No. This gentleman and I are old school friends of his. We heard from a friend of Dr. Muncaster's at the university that he was here—it was a bit of a shock. We decided to come up and see him."

The porter looked over at Natalia, sitting in the car. "And the lady?"

Geoff said, "She's a friend of mine. She drove us up."

"Well, I dare say it'll be all right. Can I just see your identity cards?"

David handed over the fakes. The porter wrote down the false names, then turned to the young man at the switchboard. "Give Ironbridge Ward a ring, Dan, tell them Muncaster's got visitors. Send someone out to the front steps to meet them. Muncaster's popular today," he added.

David looked at Geoff. "What do you mean?" he asked noncommittally.

"A couple of policemen came earlier, more questions about the incident I imagine." The porter leaned comfortably on the ledge. "You know he attacked his brother, threw him out of a window? I saw him when he came, he didn't look violent but you can't ever tell. I remember a man who were as quiet as a mouse for years, then one day he laid out two attendants and a doctor before you could say Jack Robinson." The porter shook his head with gloomy relish.

The younger man turned around from the telephone. "Mr. Hall will wait for the visitors at the entrance."

"Open the gates for them, would you?"

The young porter went out, jangling a large bundle of keys. The nurse had already let herself in. David and Geoff got back into the car. The porter opened the gates and they drove through, the old couple walking in behind them. As Natalia started the engine David told her about the police visit. They heard the gates clang shut behind them.

"What was it about?"

"He didn't know. He guessed it was about the attack on Frank's brother."

"We'll have to ask this Ben Hall. It can't be anything too worrying or he'd have warned us off. We know there's a police file open."

Just beyond the gate a concrete bridge passed over a wide ditch with steep sides, muddy water at the bottom. Beyond it thick, tall privet hedges had been planted. David looked up the drive at the big house. As they approached the main doors a stocky young man in a brown, short-jacketed uniform came out and stood at the top of the steps. He was in his thirties, with a pleasantly ugly, prematurely lined face and a broken nose. He had a whistle on a chain at his belt, and a bunch of keys. Natalia parked the car to one side of the door. "All right," she said quietly. "That's our man, I've seen a photograph. I'll stay here. Good luck." David and Geoff got out again. The young man smiled and extended a hand, looking at them with sharp eyes.

"Mr. Ladyman and Mr. Hedges?" He had a strong Glasgow accent.

"Yes," David replied. "I'm Hedges. Good afternoon."

"Hi. Thanks for coming. Frank'll be pleased to see youse."

David glanced back. The old couple were approaching the steps, their heads cast down in shame as they neared the asylum.

Inside the walls were painted an institutional green, the floors scuffed wooden blocks. Ben unlocked a heavy inner door leading into a long corridor. Two men in gray woolen uniforms stood watching them listlessly. They had comically bad pudding-basin haircuts, their ears sticking out below.

"The porter said some police came to visit Frank earlier," David said quietly.

"Aye." The attendant lowered his voice too. "We can talk about that when we get to the office."

"Security seems pretty tight here," Geoff said.

"It is. Ye cannae get in without a key from the lodge and all the inner doors are locked." Ben turned to David, his tone still conversational. "So, you an' Frank used to be good pals?"

"Yes, at university. But I haven't seen him for years."

"He seems to think a lot of you," Ben said. "He remembers your friend, but it was you he was attached to. I've got him in a separate wee room."

"Are there other visitors around?"

"A few. Most have gone already, they don't stay long. Most o' the poor sods here don't get visitors. Relatives come for a year or two, then stop. Out of shame, or seeing what their folk have come to."

David said uneasily. "You said Frank was attached to me? You make him sound like a dog."

Ben nodded. "Aye, it's what he's like. A whipped dog, looking for a good master."

"He's very clever, in his way," David answered, a note of reproof in his voice.

Ben nodded again. "He keeps that hidden. Disnae talk much. He may say more to you. Drop in the idea ye might be able to take him away if you can." He opened another door, with thick glass panels, and they entered a large room where a couple of dozen men, all in the same gray suits, stood around or sat watching television. Some were seated at a big table making Christmas paper chains, supervised by an older man in a brown uniform like Ben's. There was a smell of tobacco smoke and disinfectant. A young man sat in a corner talking to a middle-aged couple, who looked anxious and afraid. Parents, perhaps, visiting their son. People in the ward looked at the two well-dressed men with interest.

"Visitors for Muncaster," Ben said to an older nurse.

"He's popular today."

Ben answered lightly, "Aye. Where is he?"

The other nurse nodded to one of the inner doors leading from the main room. "Skulking in the quiet room as usual." There was bored contempt in his voice.

"I'll just have a word with these guys in the office first." Ben led David and Geoff into a small room with a desk, a couple of battered easy chairs, and a big locked cupboard on the wall. He closed the door.

"What's this about the police?" David asked at once.

Ben's friendly expression was gone; he looked alert and serious. "Two o' them came to see Frank late this morning. I wasn't on the ward, but I spoke to Frank later. From what he said it was some new inspector in charge of his brother's case, wanted to have a general word with him. That wis what he said. The police haven't made up their mind whether to prosecute. I think it's all right. I hope so. But it scared Frank rigid."

David asked sharply, "Did he tell the police we were coming?"

"He says not. I'd asked him no' to tell anyone, I said it wis in case the bureaucrats wanted to get you involved."

"Would they?"

Ben shrugged. "Possibly. Frank's a bit of a problem for them, no' having any relatives or friends to act for him. Anyway, I said I wanted to keep this meeting quiet."

Geoff asked, "How much do you know? About why we're here?"

Ben gave him a direct look. "Only that our people are very interested in Frank." He smiled sardonically. "Not that they're goin' to provide any details to the likes of me. I know you report to the high-ups in London.

Posh fellas like yourselves, I've nae doot. Now," he added briskly, looking at David, "I'm told the high-ups want you to talk to Frank on his own to begin with."

"That's what was suggested." David thought how wide the Resistance network reached, yet how little the members knew of each other. From the little dig at his class David guessed the Scottish nurse was left-wing, maybe even a Communist. He probably resented people like him.

"Frank does want to get out of here, doesn't he?" David asked abruptly.

"Aye." Ben met his gaze. "I've been warning him about some of the things they do to people here. Electric shocks and these lobotomies, brain surgery."

David frowned. "To frighten him?"

"To warn him," Ben answered evenly. "Listen, pal, the superintendent's already talking about shock therapy for him." He looked David in the eye. "But yes, Frank's needed a load of pushing to make the effort to get himself out o' here. He's kept quiet on drugs but he's still feart of his own shadow. Just sits in the quiet room all day, staring out of the window. It wasn't easy persuading him to contact you."

"Just don't forget I'm his friend."

"We're all his friends, pal."

Geoff asked, "What's the superintendent like?"

"Bampot," Ben answered contemptuously. "Frank doesn't trust him, he hasn't told him anything about what happened wi' his brother." He looked keenly between them. "And I've been told by our people not to press on that one. I just know what everyone knows, there was a bad quarrel and the brother ended up goin' out a window. And that's when the police were called to Frank's place. A passerby said he'd been ranting on about the end of the world. That's why they sent him here. I've been wondering what he meant by that."

"Who knows!" Geoff answered, shaking his head.

Ben said briskly to David, "Okay, fella. Let's go and see him. He looked at Geoff. You wait here for now, please."

They walked back into the day room. David looked at the men

watching *Children's Hour* on television; there was something sad and lost in the way they slouched. The middle-aged couple were still sitting with the young man. He sat turned away from them, his face red with anger. The woman was crying.

Ben led them into another, smaller room, furnished with heavy old leather armchairs, an enormous Victorian painting of a stag at bay on one wall. A gray-haired man stood in a corner, trembling from head to foot. Ben went up to him and said, very quietly, "Could you go back to the day room, Harris, we need a wee word with Muncaster." The man nodded and went out. David stared after him. Ben said, "Shell shock from the Great War, poor auld fucker."

At first David thought there was no one else in the room, but then a thin, gray-suited figure rose from a high-backed armchair facing the window. Frank Muncaster stared at him and then smiled, not the embarrassing rictus David remembered but a shy, sad, almost wondering smile. "David?" he said quietly, as though he wasn't sure that he was real.

"Hello, Frank." Awkwardly, David went over and extended a hand. "Sorry we're a bit late."

Frank walked toward him, with an old man's slow shuffle. His face had a white pallor and his thick brown hair had been badly cut into a short untidy fuzz that made his prominent ears stick out; his uniform was shapeless and too short for him. He extended his hand and David shook it, gently as always because of the damaged fingers; it felt limp and damp. The look in Frank's eyes was unutterably weary.

"How little you've changed," Frank said. "I can't believe you're here," he added, his voice shaking.

There was a moment's awkward silence, then Frank pulled himself together. "Take off your coat. Sit down. Thank you for coming."

"That's all right."

They sat opposite each other. Ben went and stood by the door, just in earshot. Frank looked over at him, a little uneasily, David thought. "Can I talk to him alone?" he asked.

Ben said, the Glasgow accent prominent, "I wis telt tae stay."

David offered Frank a cigarette.

"No thanks. I don't."

"Of course. I forgot. Mind if I do?"

"No." David lit up. Frank glanced out of the window. "I've been sitting looking at the mist," he said quietly. "It was snowing earlier. I'm sorry to drag you away at the weekend."

David leaned forward. "I wanted to see if I could help, old chap."

"How's your wife, by the way?" Frank puckered his brows. "Lizzie, isn't it?"

"Sarah. She's fine."

"Of course." Frank shook his head. "Lizzie was our daily, when I was a boy." He frowned. "I get things a bit mixed up these days. The drugs make me tired. I was sorry to hear about your little boy," he added, looking at the floor.

"Thanks." David smiled. "Thanks for the letter you sent."

"How long is it now?"

"Over two years."

Frank nodded sadly.

"How are they treating you?" David asked after a pause.

"Not too bad."

"Ben said you spend a lot of time in here alone."

"Yes. It's quiet." Frank looked over at Ben. "It was Ben persuaded me to phone you. He's taken a bit of interest in—in my case. I'm not sure why," he added quietly.

There was another short silence. Then Frank said, laughing awkwardly, "The other nurses try to get me to sit in the lounge, socialize with the other patients. Not that they say much, and they can be a bit— scary." He looked away. "Though maybe they think I'm scary too, after what I did."

"Ben told us a little about that," David said.

Frank's eyes were suddenly alert, suspicious. "Us? I thought you came alone. Who else—"

David raised his hands in a soothing gesture. "Geoff's with me. He works in the Colonial Office now. I told him you'd phoned. My car's in dock and his—his girlfriend offered to drive me. He's outside, but I thought I'd see you on my own first." The lies were coming smoothly; but David had had so much practice.

Frank looked relieved. He gave another sigh that shook his thin body. "I'm sorry," he said. "Only the police came today. It—upset me a bit."

"Aye," Ben called from the door, his voice artificially casual now. "About whether there's to be a prosecution. Frank thought it was youse arriving early."

"What did they want, Frank?"

"The inspector said they may drop the case. I don't know. There was a sergeant, a big, quiet man. I didn't like him."

"Why?"

"I don't know. There was something about him." Frank frowned, then said softly, "You never met my brother, did you?"

"No. He'd gone to America just before we went up to Oxford."

"He came over for the funeral after Mother died. Only a few weeks ago, but it feels like years. That's when it all started." He shook his head.

"I'm sorry," David said.

"She had a stroke. My mother. She didn't suffer." Frank spoke almost indifferently. David remembered his terrible sense of loss and inadequacy when his own mother had died. But he knew Frank and his mother had never been close.

"Edgar's divorced," Frank went on. "He wanted Mother's house sold quickly. He drinks, and he could always get nasty. Anyway, one day he was at my flat and I lost my temper and I pushed him and he fell out of the window. It was an accident, the frame was rotten. And it was all about nothing really," he added, giving that old rictus of a smile. He had told the story quickly, but carefully, as if it were rehearsed or memorized.

"Not like you, to lose your rag, Frank," David said gently.

"No. And if I hadn't, I wouldn't be in here." He gave a sad little laugh. "Actually I've always been frightened I might end up somewhere like this one day. I know they always thought I was pretty odd at work." He hesitated again. "Maybe you thought so too."

"No. You were shy, that's all."

Frank looked at him. "It was just an accident. What happened."

David thought, but didn't say, *and the shouting about the end of the world?*

"The trouble is," Frank went on, "the hospital's been trying to get in touch with Edgar but he won't return their calls. I can't blame him, I suppose, but he's the only relative I've got now and that leaves me in a bit of a hole." He rubbed his hands nervously down his thighs, the two wasted fingers on the right one pale as chalk, then started picking at the fabric of the chair arm with his good hand. "I've got the money to go somewhere private, and the sale of Mother's house will bring in more though it's all held up for now. But I can't touch it, you see, I've been certified as a—a lunatic, and a trustee has to be appointed to deal with my money. Maybe you know, David, do I have to have a trustee? With your father being a lawyer, maybe you could ask?"

"I'm sorry, my dad's in New Zealand. He emigrated years ago—"

"Yes. Of course, you told me in a letter." Frank hesitated, then said in a rush, "They're bringing in a law to sterilize some lunatics, did you know that? And they give people electric shocks here, and there are worse things, brain operations. I want to get out of here. If I could get to some private institution somewhere, it might be better. I might be safer."

"Safer?"

"I mean, somewhere they'd leave me to be quiet. Give me a room on my own and just leave me. I wouldn't do anything like—what I did—again."

"I'll see what can be done."

"I'm so tired, David," Frank said suddenly.

"I can see that, old chap." David smiled kindly while Frank collected himself.

"University seems like a hundred years ago now. I was grateful to you, you know, the way you used to take me out with your friends. I know I was strange, it must've been embarrassing sometimes."

The brutal honesty was unexpected. David didn't know what to say. Frank shook his head. "I used to enjoy our talks, about politics and things. It's a different world now, everything seems to be getting worse, all the violence everywhere. Here, in Europe, the war in Russia. We never thought it would get as bad as this, did we?"

"No. I often wonder how we've let it happen."

"You must see things up close, in the Civil Service."

David looked away. "Not really."

"I used to try not to think about it, just live quietly. Most people do that, don't they?"

David looked over at Ben, then back at Frank. "Ben said that when you were admitted you were shouting about the end of the world. Is that what you meant, the world situation?"

"Yes. Yes, that's what I meant." Frank spoke quickly and David sensed he was lying. "David, I'm so sorry about your son," he said again. "That must have been dreadful."

"We miss him." There was silence again. "Look here," David said, "would you like to say hello to Geoff? He's just outside."

Frank thought for a moment, then sighed. "Yes, why not?" David realized Frank didn't want anyone else to see him in this state, understood how much it had cost to appeal even to him, the shame he must feel. But the Resistance people had wanted to get Geoff's views, too, if possible.

"Let's go get him," Ben said. He inclined his head for David to follow him. David had hoped Ben might go and fetch Geoff, leave him alone with Frank for a minute, but he wasn't going to. David got up and went to the door, pressing Frank's shoulder as he passed. He and Ben went through the day room, aware of more curious glances. Geoff was sitting in the office, looking out at the mist.

"He'll see you," Ben told Geoff.

The three of them went back to the quiet room. Geoff went over to Frank and shook his hand firmly. "Hello, Frank," he said.

"Thanks for coming. Sorry to drag you here."

"That's all right," Geoff said, with a too-brisk heartiness. "We'll have to see what we can do to help you."

"David wrote saying you'd lived in Africa."

"Yes. Kenya. Been back a few years. I work at the Colonial Office in London now, just around the corner from David."

"Are you married, too?"

"No. Not yet." Geoff gave his sharp little bark of laughter.

"Not met the right girl yet, eh? Like me." Frank gave his new sad smile.

"Oh, I met her all right, but she didn't think I was the right man." Geoff bit his lip, then said, quietly, "I'm sorry to see you in here."

"You know what I did to my brother?" Frank asked suddenly.

"Yes. It was a surprise. You must've been provoked."

Frank blinked. "Yes, you're right," he said eagerly. "I was. That's what I told the police."

David said, "Apparently Frank's brother got pretty drunk and offensive."

"There you are, then." David looked at Geoff. He had made Frank brighten up a little.

"Your brother's some sort of scientist, isn't he?" Geoff continued.

"Yes."

"He won't help?"

"No. He won't even reply to telephone calls."

Geoff glanced at Ben in the doorway. He shook his head slightly.

"Listen, Frank," David said. "I'll get in touch with my father's old firm, see if I can find someone who deals with—well, this area of law. See what we can do." As he said it he thought, our people probably won't let me do that. To make it worse Frank's eyes suddenly filled with tears. He leaned forward, cradling his head on his good hand, and began to cry, a desperate, lost sound. "I'm sorry," he sobbed. "I'm sorry. I can't seem to— to control myself this afternoon."

Geoff said gently, "It's all right."

Frank pulled a dirty handkerchief from his pocket and wiped his eyes. He looked up, his face red now. "I just want to get out of here. I can't trust anyone, I can't tell what's real and what isn't anymore. Oh, if only Edgar hadn't come."

David put a hand on his shoulder once more. "We'll help you, Frank, we'll do all we can." He hesitated, then added, "You can trust us. But don't tell anyone else we've been here, not yet." He looked at Geoff. "Let's find out what we can do first."

Afterwards Ben took them back to his office. They lit cigarettes. Ben said, "You two look fair puddled."

"What?" David frowned. He wished the nurse would talk properly.

"Done in. Knackered."

"Well, we've done our job," David answered shortly. "He wants to get out of here."

Ben said, "Would you two agree he's holding something back? About his brother?"

David looked at Geoff, who nodded slowly. "Yes."

"He's at the end of his tether," David said.

"So," Ben asked. "Where do things go now?"

"I don't know," David answered. "We have to report back."

"That woman with you, she's in charge of this op, isn't she?"

"Natalia? Yes."

"I've heard she's good."

David looked at Ben. "Frank trusts me to get him out of here. But not enough to tell me about his brother. And I don't think he trusts you completely, he doesn't understand why you're helping him."

Ben laughed dryly. "No' such a heidcase as he looks then, is he?"

David said angrily, "You scared him into phoning me."

Ben's face reddened. "Don't you get all moral with me," he snapped. "Mister fuckin' la-di-da. You've been given a job to do, just like me."

"David," Geoff said, putting out a hand. "He's right."

David brushed it off, glaring back at Ben. "I care about Frank, and don't you bloody forget it."

"Dae ye?" Ben leaned forward and spoke with a quiet, angry intensity. "Then you ought tae be thinking about how to get him out of here, pal, before he tells whatever it is that's so bloody secret to the wrong people. Because if that happens, Mosley's guys will take him and they won't fanny around. I got done over in '41, when the Communist Party was banned, that's how I got this nose. But that's nothing to what they'll dae to him. They'll squeeze him like a bloody orange. And none of us wants to see that." He stood up. "Now come on, do you want people to hear us arguing, you silly prick?"

"Look here—"

"We all want him safe," Geoff said firmly, looking Ben in the eye.

David took a deep breath. "All right. But don't forget what I said."

"And dinnae you forget I'm the one keeping him safe, day after every fuckin' day. Now come on."

Ben took them outside, locking and unlocking door after door. There was rain in the mist now. Natalia was still sitting in the car. She had turned the engine off; David thought she must be cold. The three men stood on the steps. Ben looked around, then handed an envelope to David. "I've lifted the key to Frank's flat from the stores," he said curtly. "You're going over there now, yes?"

"That's right. Natalia has the address."

"And the place in town to drop the keys off afterwards? Natalia knows where?"

"I think so."

"Good. I have tae get the keys back to the stores, or I'll be in the shit."

"We'll make sure they're returned."

Ben said, "Right then." He took a deep breath. "I've been told it might become necessary to spring Frank, get him out of here. If he knows something important and he's keeping mum, that's maybe just what the big bosses will decide to do. Try and get him out of this country."

"But how could he be got out," David asked, "with the security this place has? And if anyone tried to take him by force, he'd yell the place down."

Ben spoke quietly: "There's only one person who'd be able to inject him with something to keep him quiet, then persuade the other staff they was authorized to take Frank outside. Me. Then I'd have a price on my head, pal, and my job gone too. I'd be well and truly fucked. But you can tell them in London I'll do it if I'm told to."

David saw Ben's utter determination. He nodded. "All right," he said quickly.

"Now fuckin' hook it."

They all looked around as the main door behind them opened and a patient was led out by an attendant, holding him by the arm. Ben nodded to him as he led the man down a side path. The attendant wore a peaked cap but the patient was bareheaded; he didn't react as the cold rain fell on him. Ben looked at David again. He said, more calmly, "Dinnae worry. I'll keep him safe."

CHAPTER NINETEEN

David took the backseat again; he could think better there.

They told Natalia about what had happened at the hospital: Frank's quiet desperation, his unwillingness to talk about his brother, the visit from the police. She thought for a moment, then said, "So you think he may have some secret."

"Maybe. Or perhaps it was just something personal."

"My sense was it was more than that," Geoff said quietly.

"And the police," Natalia said. "It is worrying they are still interested."

"That chap Ben said he didn't tell them any more than he had already."

"They may come back," Natalia replied.

David looked at her face in the mirror. "So what happens now?"

"It will be for Mr. Jackson and the people above him to decide."

"If Frank were to be got out of England," Geoff asked, "how would that be done? It would have to be by sea."

"I don't know."

David saw Natalia give Geoff a quick, sharp look. He thought, is that what the people at the top are planning? He wondered, too, if Frank had some big military secret, the Resistance might want it for themselves. He realized suddenly that although he had been active among them for more than two years he still thought of the Resistance as an entity separate from him. He said, "How could you get Frank to the coast? It's well over a hundred miles in any direction."

"And he'd probably try to get away," Geoff added.

Natalia looked at David in the mirror. "Unless he was traveling with someone he trusted."

"You mean me?" David frowned. "I doubt he'd trust me that far. Especially if I've said I'll help him, and then I kidnap him."

"And what will happen to him if he knows something important and lets it slip in that place?" It was more or less what Ben had said. Natalia went on, "I am not being unfeeling. I am sorry for your friend. But nothing good can happen to him in that asylum."

"I know," David said. Natalia was still studying him, the slightly angled Tartar eyes hard again, calculating.

As they approached the southern outskirts of the city the weather was still foggy, a wet mist through which light rain fell. They came onto a main road, driving past a complex of low factory buildings from which they heard a continual mechanical crashing. They passed a vast space where hundreds of identical cars stood, end to end. A sign by the gates was marked *Longbridge Works.*

"That must be the big Austin Morris factory," Geoff said. David saw there had been a fire in a tall building beside the road; it was a black skeleton. Geoff continued: "I heard an office block got burned down last month. The workers rioted over not being allowed to join a union. It's not just happening in the North anymore."

Natalia said, "Remember that lorryload of soldiers we saw on the way up? Things are getting rough in Yorkshire."

"There'll be a lot of bloodshed," David said.

"What else are people to do?" she demanded.

"What are you hoping for?" David asked her. "The workers' revolution? I think that's what that nurse Ben's after. I doubt Churchill would agree."

"The Resistance is an alliance of anti-Fascist forces, like every resistance movement in Europe. When we win, there will be elections and people can choose their own government. And, no, I am not looking for the revolution."

Geoff said, "I wish we could go back to where we were before the war."

"That is a dream," Natalia answered flatly. "Things will get worse before they get better. Whatever comes in the end, it won't be like the world before 1939. We must get used to that."

Following directions Natalia had memorized, they passed the university and drove into a district of terraced houses, shabby front doors giving straight out onto the streets. As they continued east, though, the houses became bigger, with little gardens in the front. They neared a park, then found themselves among streets of big, detached Victorian villas, three or four stories high. Lights were already on in the murky afternoon, the windows yellow squares in the mist. In one house David glimpsed a high-ceilinged lounge, mirrors and pictures on the walls, a man with a little girl on his knee. In the top flat of the next house he saw a middle-aged woman stirring a pan on a cooker. They drove slowly along, peering at the houses to try to make out their numbers. Then Geoff said, "Stop here. See, a second-floor window's been boarded up."

They got out and approached the house. Compared to its neighbors the building was shabby, streaks of moss on the red bricks. Mizzly rain dampened their faces. The first and second floors were in darkness, though a light was visible at a third-floor window. They walked up the little path. David looked at the boarded-up window, then at the paved area below, where weeds sprouted between stone flags. "Frank's brother was lucky he didn't break his back."

"It would have been a murder charge then," Geoff agreed.

The front door was big and solid, three doorbells beside it. David took out the two keys Ben had given him, tied together with string. He inserted the larger one in the lock and the door opened smoothly. A damp, cold smell came from inside. Natalia was looking up and down the street, checking. Nobody was about on this unpleasant Sunday; it was getting dark, streetlights would be coming on soon. David stepped inside, pressed a light switch. A bare bulb revealed a dusty tiled floor, walls with blistered paint.

"What a dump," Geoff said.

"Keep your voice low," Natalia cautioned.

They climbed the stairs. There was a landing with a door, marked Flat 2. David unlocked the door. He noticed a musty, unwashed smell. He switched on the light and they entered a little hall with a threadbare carpet. There were several closed doors; they opened each tentatively. There was a small, rather dirty bathroom, mildew on the tiles, and a kitchen with a blackened old cooker. All the kitchen cupboards were open, cans and broken crockery strewn over the floor. The large bedroom with its single bed and ancient wardrobe seemed to have escaped destruction. The last room was a cavernous lounge, the big window boarded up. The room had been wrecked; pictures hung askew; chairs lay on their sides. Books and magazines, science fiction from what David could see, had been pulled from the big bookcase and left on the carpet. The television had a crack in the screen. The only undamaged piece of furniture was a large rolltop desk. A couple of photographs lay face down on the floor beside it.

Geoff said, "Good God, did Frank do this?"

"He must have." David looked at the blocked-up window, heavy chipboard nailed to the frame. "I wonder who organized this; the landlord perhaps." He turned to the photographs. Like everything else they were dusty. One was their college photograph, from 1936. He picked it up; his younger self looked out at him, along with Geoff and Frank, with his strange grin. The other, smaller photograph was of a man in uniform, looking out with an apprehensive stare.

Geoff whistled. "It's Frank's spitting image. It must be his father."

Natalia studied it. "I have a photograph of my brother, just before he was sent to fight in Russia." Her voice softened. "His expression was like that."

"Frank's father was a doctor," David said. "What did your brother do?"

She smiled sadly. "He painted, much better than me. He had an exhibition in Prague once." She turned away and opened the desk, rolling up the wooden slats with a clatter. "We must search this flat. You two, please search the other rooms. Look for letters, any papers or notebooks." She began removing papers from the dockets inside the desk, riffling through them expertly. "Please, we should work quickly. Pull the curtains before switching on any lights."

Geoff said bleakly, "She's right. If there's anything here the authorities shouldn't see, Frank would thank us for taking it."

David went into the kitchen. His feet crunched on broken plates; there were dents in the plasterboard wall where cans had been thrown. It was hard to reconcile the pale, shrunken figure in the hospital with this manic destruction. All the cupboards were empty, bar some battered cutlery in the drawers. Geoff appeared at his elbow. "Nothing in the bathroom," he said. "I thought I'd leave the bedroom to you."

"Okay."

David went into the bedroom. He searched the bed—the sheets needed washing—riffled through the socks and underwear in the chest of drawers, then the pockets of the few jackets and trousers hanging in the wardrobe. He found nothing apart from a farthing and screwed-up bus tickets. He bent to look under the bed and saw a big brown suitcase there. He pulled it out and slipped the clasps. Inside was a packet of some sort, wrapped in brown paper. He lifted it. Papers. His heart quickened as he undid the parcel, but it was just a collection of pornographic magazines, naked women lying on beds or sitting astride chairs. There was a collection of film magazines from the early thirties too: Jean Harlow and Katharine Hepburn and Fay Wray in soulful romantic poses. He made himself look through the magazines in case anything was hidden inside them but there was nothing. He rewrapped the packet and shoved the suitcase back under the bed, stirring up a cloud of dust.

In the lounge Geoff had righted an armchair and was sitting riffling through the books and periodicals. Natalia was still poring over the papers at Frank's desk. She looked up.

"Anything in the bedroom?"

"Nothing."

"I'm seeing if there are any papers hidden in these," Geoff said. "Nothing so far." He held up a copy of an American magazine, *Amazing Science Fiction*. "Just Frank's cup of tea."

David took up a magazine. "Better than the stuff my nephews read, war comics about the fighting in Russia."

"Nothing in the desk," Natalia said. "Just bills and some letters from a lawyer about his mother's estate. Oh, and these." She handed David a bundle of envelopes, neatly tied in a rubber band. David was surprised to see his own handwriting. It was the letters he had sent Frank over the years. He opened one.

21 August 1940

Dear Frank,

Sorry I haven't written earlier in reply to your last, but it's all been a bit hectic. They discharged me from the nursing home last week (so no more pretty nurses, sad to say) and the old feet seem to be okay now. It's felt so silly, recovering from frostbite in summer! I'm staying with my dad for the moment, starting back at the Office next week.

Well, what d'you think of the Berlin Treaty? I must say we've come off pretty lightly, given the way Adolf trounced our army. Pity we've got to give up the air force . . .

Natalia was looking at him curiously. "He kept your letters," she said. "Almost like a lover."

"There was never anything pansy about Frank," David answered sharply. He thought of the pornography, but he wasn't going to tell her about that.

"Did you keep his letters to you?"

"No. But then I had other friends." David looked around the dismal room. "Exactly what happened here? What was it all about? Edgar came to visit. He was drunk; he said something that pushed Frank over the edge. After all these years of holding everything in."

"It could have been something personal," Geoff suggested. "Some family thing."

"Possibly," Natalia agreed. She replaced the papers in the desk.

David picked up the letters. "I think we should take these with us."

She nodded. "Yes. That might be best." David stuffed the packet into his overcoat pocket. Natalia wiped her dusty fingers on a handkerchief. She smiled at David, her wry smile. "You English hold your feelings inside yourselves; it is not surprising sometimes you crack up."

"Sometimes there's a lot to hold in."

They all jumped and turned quickly at the sound of a key in the door. Natalia's hand went to the pocket of her coat; now David knew she had a gun in there. She stood in front of the desk as the hall door opened, and a little old man with white hair, in an old cardigan and carpet slippers, came in and stared at them. He shuffled into the lounge.

"Thought I 'eard someone in 'ere." He had a high-pitched voice with a Birmingham accent. He peered at them shortsightedly, quite unafraid. "Who are you?"

David said, "We're friends of Dr. Muncaster, we've been to visit him in hospital."

"Do you live in one of the other flats?" Geoff asked.

"The one above. I'm Bill Brown." The old man looked around the room. "It were me called the coppers, last month. You'll know all about it, if you're friends of Dr. Muncaster."

"Yes."

The old man shook his head. "I've never heard anything like it, screaming and shouting then that window going. I looked out and there was that poor man lying on the ground, I thought he were a goner." He stared at them, bright-eyed. "And Dr. Muncaster yelling and raving, smashing things up. Thank God me daughter got me to have the phone put in, I dialed 999 straight off. I can do without things like that at my age. I'm eighty, y'know," he added proudly.

"Who boarded the window up?" David asked.

"I got the freeholder to do it. He's a spare key to all the flats. He left one with me." Bill stared at him with watery eyes that still had a sharpness to them. "A house with a broken window's a magnet for burglars. How is Dr. Muncaster? Is he coming back?"

"Not in the near future."

The old man nodded. "Are you family?" He looked around at them.

"My friend and I were at school with him." David didn't give their names. "We've come up from London to see him. We heard what happened through someone at the university. We came over to check everything was all right here."

" 'Ow's Dr. Muncaster's brother?"

"He's safely back in America," Natalia said.

"Broken arm, the police said." Bill looked around the chaos again.

" 'E were always very quiet, Dr. Muncaster. Polite. Never thought he'd go off his head like that."

"No," David said. He added conversationally, "Apparently he was shouting about the end of the world."

"He were that. Never 'eard anything like it. This has always been a quiet house, I've lived here since my wife died. Fifteen years. Gor, the way he was raving, yelling. How the world was ending." Bill looked at Natalia. "Are you German, miss?" he asked suddenly.

"No."

He held her gaze for a moment, then asked, "What are they saying at the hospital?"

David answered. "They don't seem to know much. When we saw Frank he was very quiet."

"Bartley Green loony bin, isn't it? A man I worked with had a sister in there once. Said it was a miserable place. Of course once you're in somewhere like that often you're there till they bring you out in a box." Nobody replied. "Like I said, I'd nothing against him. Though that funny grin of his used to give me the willies." Bill looked at the photograph of Frank's father. "That his dad?"

"Yes."

"Doesn't half look like him. I lost me son at Passchendaele."

"I'm sorry," Geoff said.

Bill turned to him. "We were fighting the wrong enemy then." His eyes brightened. "Have you 'eard about the Jews?"

"What about them?" David asked.

The old man smiled. "They're being rounded up, all over the country. It was on the news: Mosley's to broadcast on TV about it later. They were all taken away this morning."

"Where to?" David asked.

"No idea. Isle of Man, Isle of Wight? I think it's best to turn 'em over to the Germans."

"Are you sure about this?" Geoff asked.

" 'Course I am. I told you, it was on the news. Surprise, innit? I never realized how many Jews there were in Brum till they made 'em wear those yellow badges. Good riddance. Glad I won't be seeing them badges anymore, they gave me the creeps." Bill looked between the three of them, then said sarcastically, "Still, you sound like educated people, mebbe you don't see it that way. Well, I'll leave you to it." He glanced around the flat again. "If 'e's not coming back, maybe this place should go on the market." He nodded at them, smiled maliciously, then shuffled out, shutting the door behind him.

David turned to Natalia. He said, trying to keep the shock from his voice, "Looks like you were right. About the Jews having no future."

She didn't answer. Geoff said, "It'll be part of some deal with the Germans, Beaverbrook will have got something in return."

Natalia said, "I think we should leave. There's nothing here." She frowned. "The end of the world. What did he mean by that?" She looked around the room again, took a deep breath. "Come on, we should find a telephone box, ring Mr. Jackson."

CHAPTER TWENTY

Gunther and Syme drove on to Birmingham, the windscreen wipers working against the misty rain. Syme looked preoccupied, lighting cigarettes one-handed. He was suspicious, Gunther guessed; having seen Muncaster he couldn't believe he could be a man with dangerous political contacts. He knew something else was going on.

"How long since you visited Berlin?" Gunther asked, to begin a conversation.

"Five years. I bet it's changed a lot. They hope to have all those huge new buildings ready for the 1960 Olympics, don't they?"

"Yes. But there are problems with building such huge structures on sandy soil. They are still digging the foundations. They will be finished in time, they hope." He smiled at Syme. "The center of Berlin is always so dusty. Lots of people have chest problems these days."

"Do you have a house there?"

"Just a flat. My wife and I had a house but it was sold in the divorce."

"Maybe if I do a spell in the North I can earn enough for a mortgage on a decent-sized house. Then I might look around for a nice girl who doesn't mind the hours."

"Yes. There is nothing like a house and family." Gunther spoke regretfully. "I hope to visit my son in the spring. In Krimea."

"Any problems with Russian terrorists there?"

"Not in Krimea. We cleared the natives out of the peninsula ten years ago. There are only German settlers there now. So it is safe, though there have been attacks on the trains coming from Germany. Fewer now, we're concentrating more on protecting the lines." He paused. "Russia is vast; I think it will be another generation before we control it completely. This is the greatest war of conquest in history."

Syme turned to look at him. "They say Speer and the army would like to do a deal with the Russians, let them keep the country east of Moscow. Goebbels too, I've heard."

"No," Gunther said firmly. "What we have started we will finish. Squash Jewish Bolshevism forever."

Syme laughed, his good humor restored. "Well, we're doing our bit here now, with what's happening today. What times to live in. Bleedin' exciting, eh?" He slipped back into Cockney for a moment.

Gunther thought, yes, I know, you like your bit of excitement, while I am starting to feel old and tired before my time.

As they drove through the countryside there was little sign that this was anything other than a normal Sunday. Once, though, they passed near a railway line where a freight train of closed boxcars was moving slowly south. For a moment Gunther thought he heard faint cries coming from inside, but he wasn't sure and Syme didn't seem to notice anything.

It was mainly quiet on the outskirts of Birmingham, too, although Black Marias, their klaxons shrilling, occasionally sped past. Once, looking down a suburban street, Gunther saw two parked outside a house where some sort of struggle seemed to be going on. But he couldn't see clearly; it was too misty.

They drove into the city center, full of big Victorian Gothic buildings dark with soot. There weren't many people around but quite a few Auxiliaries were on patrol; Gunther noticed several outside the closed doors of a church, arguing with a little group of people, one in a white clerical collar.

"I told you the churchy types would be a nuisance," Syme observed. "Not far now, Birmingham Special Branch HQ's just around the corner, in Corporation Street."

They turned into a wide commercial street and pulled up beside a door with a blue lamp above it. Several other cars were parked there. Gunther saw a queue of people straggling down the steps of the building and along the street. Two Auxiliaries stood by the door and two more walked up and down keeping an eye on the queue. As Gunther and

Syme got out one of the Auxies in the doorway came over. He was very large, but young, a rash of pimples around his mouth. His expression was hostile until Syme showed his warrant card.

"Is Inspector Blake in?" he asked.

"I think so, sir. He's very busy, though, you know what's been happening today?"

"We heard."

Gunther looked along the waiting queue. No one seemed to be wearing the yellow badge, though many looked anxious and some angry. One young man had grabbed the arm of an Auxiliary and was pleading with him, almost in tears. "It's my wife's brother. I need to know where they've taken him."

"Just wait your turn, sir," the policeman replied, his voice bored. "They'll tell you at the desk." An elderly couple, faces rigid with grief, came through the swing doors of the police station and walked down the steps, holding each other tightly.

"These are friends of the Jews?" Gunther asked the Auxiliary.

Catching his accent, the man looked at him with interest. "Are you from Germany, sir? An observer?"

"Just a visitor. I am in the Gestapo, though." He nodded toward the young man in the queue who had asked about his wife's brother. "You are exempting Jews who have married Gentiles?"

"I'm not sure quite what the rules are, sir." The boy looked embarrassed. "We were just given the names and addresses of those to be picked up."

Gunther looked at the sad queue, the rain pattering down on them. "We made some exemptions at the beginning. Too many: it just causes trouble for everyone later."

The young man said uneasily, "I feel a bit sorry for them, to be honest."

Gunther nodded. "Yes. It affects us, it's hard on us. But it needs to be done nevertheless."

The Auxiliary took them into the building. More people were standing at a counter, behind which policemen riffled through typed lists many pages long. "I'll see if Inspector Blake is available," the young policeman said, opening a flap on the counter. Gunther heard snatches of conversation, familiar from police stations in Germany long ago.

"They'll be held outside the town for a while, till new accommodation is ready for them —"

"Winter clothes will be provided. They'll be quite comfortable —"

"No, we can't tell you where they are. National security —"

"No visits —"

"Well, can't you take their dog into your own house —"

Gunther looked at Syme, who grimaced, a half-amused, half-contemptuous look. The young policeman came back. "The inspector is free now, sir, but only for a few minutes. You can see what it's like here." He opened the flap for them and they went through, passing plainclothesmen working at desks, and down a dark little corridor to a small room with a half-glassed door.

Inside a plump, tired-looking middle-aged man in a rumpled suit was sitting at a desk working on papers, smoking a pipe. The air was blue with the smoke. He leaned forward and shook hands with them unsmilingly, introducing himself as Inspector Blake. Syme introduced himself and Gunther. "Nice to meet you, sir," Syme said smoothly. "We've spoken on the phone."

Blake was looking at Gunther. "I didn't know the Gestapo actually had a man over here on this case. That loony of mine must be important."

Gunther responded politely. "We are concerned he may have certain political contacts in Germany."

"He's British. We can handle him," Blake grunted. He gave Syme an unfriendly look. "Even we provincials."

Syme spread his hands. "It's what the commissioner wants. We've been up here today visiting Muncaster."

"Find anything?" Blake looked curious now.

"Nothing definite," Gunther answered. "But enough to make us want to investigate further."

"As we're here," Syme explained, "we thought we'd like to take a look at his flat. We understood you might lend us a locksmith to get in."

"We would be very grateful," Gunther added.

Blake laughed. "You've picked the worst possible day. We've got locksmiths out all over the city securing the Jews' houses. We've already had some trouble with looters trying to get in and take stuff, even some of our own people have been trying to lift things." He looked at Syme. "Can't you just bash the door in?"

"We don't want to attract attention," Gunther said. "And we would like to leave the place secure."

Blake frowned. "Just what is it you're looking for?"

Syme said, "Evidence of foreign affiliations. I'm sorry we came today, I didn't know about the Jews until this morning. The Gestapo would be very grateful if you could help us."

Blake shook his head wearily, but picked up the telephone and asked someone if they could find him a locksmith. "Well," he said, "the work's starting to wind down now, but it may be an hour or two before someone's free. Can you wait?"

"Of course," Gunther said.

"How's it gone today?" Syme asked.

Blake leaned back in his chair, folding his hands over a large stomach. "Not too bad. Most came quietly, though there was a bit of a ruck with some students at the university, and one or two made a fuss elsewhere when they were picked up. From what I hear it's much the same story all over the country." He smiled wearily. "Take everyone by surprise, that's the way." He looked at Syme, his attitude more friendly now. "I know you're an old Blackshirt like me. We should have done this years ago."

"You can say that again. Where are they all being taken?"

"I can't tell you." Blake shook his head. "That one's embargoed. We don't want people turning up and making trouble. We're getting some stick from the church people; the Bishop's threatening to hold a demonstration on the Town Hall steps tomorrow. We didn't expect that, we thought he was with us. We're going to have to get roadblocks ready in the town center tonight."

"Arrest the bugger," Syme said.

Blake shrugged. "I agree. But the high-ups haven't made up their minds yet. They're still bloody soft about arresting bishops." He looked at Gunther. "Have you any idea why the Jews are being rounded up now? We've had contingency plans for years but the green light came through while Beaverbrook was in Germany."

"I don't know," Gunther said.

Blake's eyes narrowed. "Looks to me like it's the price for closer alignment with Germany. Now Stevenson's won the presidential elections we can expect a cooler relationship with America. Well, suits me, America's run by Jewish capital."

"I suppose they make some good films," Syme said.

"Propaganda. Hollywood's run by the Jews, too."

"It is," Gunther agreed.

"Well, I can give you an interview room to wait in, until the locksmith comes. Though we may have to turf you out if there are problems in the city and someone needs a going-over. I'm sure we could have handled your loony for you," Blake added, the resentful note back in his voice, "but the commissioner knows best."

It was dark by the time they left the police station to drive to Muncaster's house. The locksmith was to meet them there. The misty city was quiet. They drove out to the suburbs, parked outside the house and walked up the path. Gunther looked up at the boarded window. There was no sign of the locksmith. Then, to his surprise, the front door opened and a little old man in a cardigan came out. He looked at them with keen interest. "Inspector Syme?" he asked.

"Yes," Syme answered abruptly. "Who are you?"

"I'm Bill. I live on the third floor. I saw your locksmith waiting about outside and let him into Dr. Muncaster's place. What about the Jews, eh?" he asked excitedly.

"Yeah," Syme answered noncommittally.

The old man led them upstairs and into a shabby flat. Through the open door of the kitchen Gunther could see smashed crockery and dented tins. In the lounge a gray-haired man in a long brown coat sat in an armchair, nursing a cup of tea the old man must have brought him. Gunther surveyed the chaos. Strange to think of that frightened-looking man, Muncaster, doing this.

"Looks like you won't be needed," Syme said curtly to the locksmith. "You can get off."

The man rose. "Right-oh. But I'll still charge for the callout."

"He's been telling me he's been securing some of the Jews' houses," the old man said. "Gor, I bet there's some valuable stuff in there." He accompanied the locksmith to the door, chattering away happily. "You still see a few blackies around. Get them next."

"Britain for the British," the locksmith agreed. He left, but the old man, Bill, stayed, hovering. "Where've you taken 'em?" he asked Syme. "The Yids?"

"Watch the TV later. Mosley's broadcasting."

"What do the police want here, eh?" Bill pressed; he seemed unembarrassable. "Dr. Muncaster wasn't a Jew, was he?"

"None of your business, mate."

"Suit yourselves. Only it's funny, nobody comes to this flat for weeks and then two lots of visitors in one day."

Gunther turned, giving Bill a look that made him step back a pace. "Two lots? Who were the others?" he asked sharply.

Bill happily told them about the earlier visitors, the two men who had known Dr. Muncaster at school and the foreign woman. Syme became suddenly friendly, complimenting the old fellow on his memory and his patriotism in helping them. Gunther added a few questions. Realizing he was German, Bill looked at him with a fascinated, half-fearful awe. He told him how he'd heard Muncaster shout out, "Why did you tell me?" at his brother, and something about the Germans. He looked at Gunther with narrowed eyes and said, "It sounded like 'they mustn't know.'"

"Know what exactly?"

"I don't know, sir," Bill replied. He had become respectful. "I didn't tell those other visitors that."

"Why not?"

"Didn't like them. Hoity-toity, they were. Posh voices. You could see they weren't pleased when I told 'em about the Jews."

Gunther smiled. "That was wise."

"Don't tell secrets to people you don't trust," Bill said. "It's a good rule."

At the end Gunther thanked him courteously for his help, and asked him to contact Syme at once if anyone else called. Syme nodded agreement.

Bill asked, "Is this about the brother? Was he injured worse than I were told? He hasn't died, has he?"

"Let's just say he's not very well. Now, I'd like you to let me have the key to the flat."

Bill looked disappointed. "It's the freeholder's." Gunther wondered if Bill was planning to have a nose around when they were gone. Syme held out a hand and, reluctantly, the old man retrieved the key from his cardigan pocket and handed it over.

Syme led Bill out; the old man turned in the doorway for a last curious look, then left. Gunther went over to examine the photographs of Muncaster's father and the university group. He looked up at Syme. "We'd probably have bumped into them if we hadn't been waiting at the HQ." He smiled grimly. "And I wonder what might have happened then. Some excitement, perhaps. So, these visitors had a key. Now where did they get that?" He studied the college photograph. "I spent a year at Oxford, you know. Over twenty years ago."

"Yeah?"

"I hated it." Gunther looked at the row of faces. "Born to rule." Then he frowned. "Someone's picked this up and looked at it. See those fingerprints?"

"The old man?"

"Why would he do that?" Gunther considered. "School friends coming to visit. Nearly twenty years after they all left." He shook his head. "University friends, though, whose picture you kept..."

"You think that's who they might have been?"

"Possibly. The old man said they were the same age as Muncaster."

"But why lie?" Syme asked. "If they're Resistance, Special Branch need to be involved."

"I don't know who and what they are yet." Gunther studied the photograph carefully. "There he is, that's Muncaster. Look at that grin. Easy enough to contact the college and find the names of all these other people."

"Then what?"

"I don't know. I'm sorry. I'll have to talk to my superior and he'll get in touch with yours."

"Why am I getting uneasy about this?" Syme asked. "The brother is an American scientist. What did he tell his brother that the Germans shouldn't know about?"

"I don't know. I promise you, if there is a Resistance angle to this your people won't be kept in the dark. Now, I am going to have a look around this flat and then we're going to see the old man again and ask if he handled the picture, or recognizes either of the men who came here in it."

"Want some help?"

Gunther hesitated, then said, "Yes. Yes, thank you."

They did a methodical search together. They found nothing except the dirty magazines under the bed, but Gunther soon saw that the flat had already been searched; there were finger marks in the dust everywhere, the signs of busy hands looking for something. When they had finished they stood in the lounge together. Syme looked up at a cobweb. "Miserable place, ain't it?"

"Let's talk to the old man, show him the photograph. Then get back to London, see what they make of all this at the embassy."

He went over and took the two photographs, Muncaster's father as well as the university group, slipping them under his arm as they left the flat. Then Gunther switched off the light, plunging the room with its blocked window into total darkness again.

The old man's flat was almost as messy and decrepit as Frank's. However, he had a large new television set, which was showing a police serial, square-jawed officers trapped by American spies in a cellar filling with water. Gunther showed him the photograph and asked if he had touched it.

He shook his head. "No, why would I?"

"No reason," he answered reassuringly. "Perhaps it was these visitors. I know they said they were old school friends, but could you look at the photograph, see if you recognize either of the men here?"

"All right." The old man answered cheerfully, clearly pleased at the prospect of helping. He fetched a pair of glasses and peered at the photo. "Gor, it's a grainy old thing, innit? And they're all much younger." He pointed at one of the students. "That one, the fair one, that could have been one of them. Yes, yes, I think it was." He scanned the photographs again, then pointed at a dark-haired, good-looking boy in the back row. "The other one could've been him. But I'm not sure." He looked up apologetically. "I'm sorry, I didn't have my specs on when I saw them."

"That's all right. You've been very helpful," Gunther said, and smiled.

CHAPTER TWENTY-ONE

Sarah made the journey home in a state of numb shock. Alone in the Tube carriage, huddled in Ruth's duffel coat, she began shivering uncontrollably. She thought, *I must get home, I mustn't draw attention to myself.* She hugged her bag close and looked out of the window. It was the same quiet, unremarkable Sunday scene as it had been on the way in with Mrs. Templeman, what seemed like an age ago.

A young couple got into the carriage and began arguing irritably about whose family they would be spending Christmas with. Sarah carried on staring out of the window, trying to control her trembling. When the train stopped at Wembley she thought of Mrs. Templeman's husband, at home probably, awaiting her return, and had to put a clenched fist to her mouth to prevent herself crying out.

When Sarah got back to the house she took off Ruth's duffel coat, laid it on the sofa, and stood looking at it. David wouldn't be back for hours. She thought in sudden panic, *I should get rid of it, if they come after me it could incriminate me.* She tried to remember if anyone at Friends House had seen her leave with Mrs. Templeman. She didn't think so, but she wasn't sure. She was in danger, they might be looking for her, David and her family could be caught up in it all. Her heart started pounding wildly and she took deep breaths to try to calm herself. Then the image of Mrs. Templeman falling back onto the road returned to her and she cried out, "She's dead, she's dead!" She put her hands over her face and sobbed convulsively in a way she hadn't since Charlie died.

After a while the telephone rang, the shrill sound making her jump. She went into the hall; it could be the police. Hesitantly, she picked up the receiver.

"Hello."

"Hello, dear." It was Irene. "Have you both been out? I tried phoning earlier."

Sarah gasped with relief. "David's had to go to Northampton, his uncle's in hospital. I've been — I've been out at a committee meeting —"

"Are you all right, dear?" Irene's voice was suddenly anxious. "You sound odd."

"No — no. I think I've a cold coming, that's all."

"It's not to do with David, is it? Have you spoken to him about that woman at his office yet?"

"No. No, I haven't."

"Did you see anything happening in town today?"

"No." A jump of the heart. "What do you mean?"

"Haven't you heard the news? Apparently they moved all the Jews out of the cities today. To some sort of camps. Mosley's going to broadcast this evening."

"I — I hadn't heard." So it had been publicly announced now.

"Steve thinks it's about time. But I hope they're not being mistreated. We wouldn't do that, would we?" Irene's voice was for once uncertain.

"I don't know. Irene, darling, I have to go, David'll be back soon, I've got something cooking —"

"Oh, all right, dear." Irene sounded surprised by her abruptness. "Tell David I hope his uncle's better soon."

"Yes. Yes, I will." Sarah put down the receiver and stood in the hall. It was starting to get dark; she switched on the light. She would have liked to telephone her father, but she mustn't tell any of the family. *But what about David?* She thought, *when I stepped out on that pavement I was abandoning him, abandoning them all.* She looked through the frosted glass of the front door at the darkening afternoon, thought of uniformed men standing there, and felt a desperate need to see David, hear his voice.

She went back into the lounge and sat down. She picked up Ruth's duffel coat, holding it to her tightly. She wondered where she was, whether she and Joe had made it. She heard the crack of shots in her head again and flinched. She began crying again, not anguished sobbing anymore but with a slow, relentless misery.

It was nearly seven when she heard David's key in the front door. She had been sitting for hours, holding the duffel coat; she hadn't bothered to light the fire or put the lights on, she was too shocked and exhausted. When David turned the lights on she blinked. At once he came across the room to her, grasping her by the arms.

"What's happened?" he asked urgently, "Sarah, what's happened?"

She said, "They've taken the Jews away."

"I know. I heard."

She saw that his own face was pale, bleak with anxiety. "I saw it. In the Tottenham Court Road. There was a protest, people were shot. Mrs. Templeman's dead, she's dead…" Sarah gasped and began crying again. He sat beside her and held her close in a way he hadn't for ages. His strength gave her a feeling of safety, refuge. She told him the whole story. At the end he said, "It's part of some new deal with Germany. It has to be. The bastards."

"Where did you hear? At the hospital?"

"Yes—yes, they were talking about it there. Just that people were being moved."

"How's Uncle Ted?"

"Better now, they're going to discharge him next week. He's grumpy as ever." He gave a brief, twitchy smile and looked away from her and something in his tone told her he was lying. Her heart sank again and she thought, *I can't cope, I can't cope with that, too.*

David said, quietly, "Do you think they'll be looking for you?"

"I don't know. They never found out who I was, but they saw me. They'll have found Mrs. Templeman's identity card, they'll be inquiring at Friends House, questioning her poor husband. She lost a son too, you know, in 1940." She frowned. "I keep calling her Mrs. Templeman but her first name was Jane, I should call her Jane."

David shook her shoulders, made her turn and look at him. "Sarah," he said urgently. "That duffel coat, it's evidence. We should get rid of it. I'll put it in the bin, the dustmen are coming tomorrow."

"Yes." She sighed. "Yes, all right."

"I'll light the fire. Look, darling, you're frozen. Have you been sitting in the dark all this time?"

"Yes. I—I couldn't think what to do."

"Sit here and get warm."

She said, "I'm sorry, David, I'm sorry, I've put you all in danger—"

His mouth worked, and she could see he was close to tears himself. He said, "You did a brave thing, a good thing."

"What should we do?"

"If we get rid of that duffel coat there's no evidence it was you. We just have to sit tight."

She could see from his face, though, that he was worried. "What if they pick up Joe and Ruth and question them?"

"Did you tell them your name?"

"No. Will you stand by me?" she added quietly.

He grasped her hands, looking at her with pain and, she thought, guilt. He said, "Of course I will." He glanced at the clock on the mantelpiece. "It's ten to seven. We ought to watch the news."

She nodded wearily.

When David turned on the television *Songs of Praise* was on, people standing in a big church, singing lustily, all the women in large hats, a normal Sunday evening service. Then the credits rolled and a voice announced, in serious tones, that a broadcast from the Home Secretary, Sir Oswald Mosley, would follow. And there he was, sitting in a big office, hands folded on his desk. He looked firm and avuncular, beautifully dressed as usual, his Blackshirt badge prominent on his lapel. He began, in his deep, rich voice:

"*Tonight I want to tell you that, after much consideration, the government has decided to move all British Jews into special areas which have been set aside for them outside our major cities. For the present they are being housed in temporary camps, warm and comfortable. More permanent arrangements will be made later. Most were moved earlier today. We believe this step to be necessary because of evidence that terrorists from the so-called Resistance movement have been receiving support from subversive elements within the Jewish population. Keeping them in separate areas will protect us, and also protect the Jews themselves, from trouble and disturbance from these outsiders.*" Mosley smiled reassuringly. "*Today's exercise was carried out with typical British efficiency and good nature, proceeding smoothly and qui-etly throughout the country. Any Jews who have not yet been transferred are required to attend immediately at their nearest police station, bringing what-ever hand luggage they wish to take and, of course, their identity cards."*

His voice became stern. *"This measure is necessary for Britain's security. The threat from Resistance terrorism is, alas, ever present. Everyone must be vigilant, for their own sakes and for the country's. These are trying times, at home and in the Empire."* He smiled in a fatherly way, his gray mustache twitching. He went on, his tone lighter, *"However, I can also tell you that following the discussions the Prime Minister had with our German allies last week, as well as the new increase in British forces available for India, which Mr. Powell announced earlier today, new economic agreements have also been reached which will allow British firms to trade much more fully with Europe—"*

He went on for several more minutes, talking of new joint ventures between British arms firms and Krupps to supply heavy artillery for the war in Russia, and joint commercial projects between ICI and IG Far-ben. He concluded his broadcast gravely. *"Together the British people can defeat anarchy and communism. God Save the Queen."* As the National Anthem sounded Mosley stood, chest held out proudly. David switched off the television. He and Sarah sat looking at the blank screen.

"Nothing about the people that were killed today," Sarah said qui-etly. "Nothing. What else has been happening up and down the country?"

"I suppose they chose a Sunday morning because there'd only be a few people around, and not much traffic." He looked at her intently, his blue eyes hard. "They must be going to hush up what happened in Tot-tenham Court Road, maybe in other places too. To avoid any sort of big official inquiry."

She stood up suddenly, still clutching the duffel coat.

David said, "What is it?"

"Do you have to be so—so clinical? So like a bloody civil servant? I saw people shot this morning, young students running for their lives, a woman I know killed..."

He stood too, took her by the shoulders. "I'm not clinical about it,

Sarah. Dear God, I'm not." He took a deep breath. "This is how I cope." She sat down again. He put his hand over hers. He said, "I feel it all as much as you. More, perhaps."

"More?"

"I'm sorry, I didn't mean…" He shook his head. "It's not easy, always, at work. I see those people, Mosley and the other Fascists and their friends going in and out of Downing Street. I hate it as much as you do. I'm sorry, darling."

She thought, maybe I've been wrong, maybe it's because of every-thing that's happening around us that he's become so cold and distant. She said, "How can people believe such rubbish, that the Jews are a threat to national life?"

"There's always been prejudice, and they've been stoking it up since 1940. If a government keeps telling people the same simple message year after year, most end up believing it. Goebbels called it the big lie." He picked up the duffel coat. "Let me get rid of this; take it out to the bin now, I'll empty the wastepaper baskets on top of it."

"There are some potato peelings in the kitchen bin," Sarah said wea-rily, "and those chops in the fridge are off. Put them in too, then nobody'll go poking about in there." She surrendered the coat with an odd feeling of reluctance.

David ripped the sleeve of the duffel coat in case some dustman won-dered why they were throwing it out. He filled the bin and carried it through the house to the front garden. Their neighbor, a middle-aged man he acknowledged at the station, was taking out his own rubbish. He nodded to David. "Cold evening again, isn't it?"

David answered with forced cheerfulness, "Yes, winter's here by the look of it."

"Forecast said there'll be fog tomorrow." The man nodded again and went back into his house, closing the door. Neighbors didn't talk much in this street; people generally seemed to talk to strangers less and less these days. David stood by the gate, looking across the road. The old air-raid shelter was a ghostly glimmer at the other end of the little park. He thought of Sarah's courage. When he'd seen her sitting there in the dark he had thought for a second the authorities had found out about him, had been to question her. For a moment he had actually been glad to think all the secrecy and lies were over, and had felt a sudden rush of his old love for her, the feeling he had started to think was twisted and broken beyond repair. But there was no telling her the truth now. Not after today. It was too dangerous.

When they had left Frank's flat he and Geoff and Natalia had driven around the dark, foggy streets, looking for a telephone box. When they found one Natalia went inside, leaving David and Geoff in the car. They watched as she dropped shilling pieces one after the other into the box. She must have carried them ready in her pockets, like the gun. She was in the box a long time, gesturing with her arms, her face animated. David wondered if she was talking to Jackson but he thought not; she would have been more controlled speaking to him. When she came out and rejoined them in the car she spoke quietly. "There's going to be a meeting tomorrow, some of the top people." She paused. "I think we're going to have to move Dr. Muncaster. Probably soon."

David asked, "Did you tell them he seemed to trust me?"

"Yes. We will probably need you again. Perhaps both of you."

"I'll do it. But my wife's got to be kept safe."

"They'll take care of that," Geoff said.

"What about the Jews?"

"It's true," Natalia said flatly. "They've been moved. We didn't know anything about it, Mosley organized everything from the Home Office."

They said little on the journey back to London. David's mind was whirling, going over the meeting with Frank, wondering what the hell exactly was happening to the Jews. Everything was quiet in the cold streets. They drove out to Pinner and dropped Geoff off at his house. Natalia said she would take David on to the bottom of his street. They didn't speak, but when they arrived he got out and stood beside the car, looking at the rows of mock-Tudor semis, suddenly reluctant to move. She rolled down the window. "Are you all right?" she asked.

"Yes." He took a deep breath. "How could the Resistance not know what they were planning for the Jews?"

"We don't have anyone in the Home Office or in the higher levels of the police. Not anymore."

"You did have people?"

"We had a network. There was a betrayal, three years ago. The man we thought was ours was working for them. A lot of good people died."

"You carry a gun in your pocket, don't you?" David said. "I saw, when that old man came into Frank's flat."

"There are circumstances where we have to defend ourselves. You understand that."

He asked, "Would you ever use the gun on Frank?"

"Only if he were about to fall into their hands." She met his gaze. "Then it would be best for him, trust me."

"Have you ever killed anybody?"

She nodded slowly. "Yes. Not in England, though. I wish it were never necessary. But sometimes it is."

He sighed. "Yes. Yes, I know."

"What is it, David?" she asked quietly. "Ever since we saw the old man in the flat you have looked—desperate. It's more than just seeing your friend in that state."

He smiled sadly. "Perhaps we English aren't so good at keeping our feelings hidden after all." He shrugged. "It was hearing about what's happening to the Jews. It's upset me."

She nodded, then gave him a long, searching look. She said, very quietly and carefully, "I remember my Jewish friends in Slovakia. I saw how they reacted when things began to get bad."

David took half a step back, nearly tripped on the curb. He thought, she's guessed.

She reached through the window and took his hand, holding it in a tight grip. "Who else knows?" she asked.

"Nobody." David's heart was throbbing violently. "Only my father. It was my mother who was Jewish, an Irish Jew. Her records were destroyed, during the Troubles in Ireland. My father is sure. He's a lawyer. I've lied on my census returns, said my parents were both Catholic."

"And he is in New Zealand now?"

"Yes."

"Your wife doesn't know?" She sounded surprised.

"No. How did you guess?"

"Like I said, I have seen how people react. Some are pleased when the Jews are taken away. Some don't care, or don't want to get into trouble. Some hate it. But I think only those who are themselves at risk show the fear, the sorrow I saw on your face today. And"—she smiled, an unusually hesitant smile—"I often watch your face. Your expression."

He asked, "Will you tell them? Jackson, his people?"

"Our people." She hesitated. "No, I will not tell them, though I should. You should tell them yourself."

He looked at her hard. "You said you married a German. In your country."

"There was more to the story than that." Her mouth twitched suddenly. Then she pressed his hand with surprising strength. "Be careful."

"I've been careful for years."

"I know." Natalia bit her lip, then rolled up the window again and drove slowly away.

CHAPTER TWENTY-TWO

Gunther called Senate House from a telephone box just outside Birmingham, leaving Syme in the car. Gessler had been waiting for the call, and told him to report for a full debriefing immediately when he returned to London. A little over two hours later, Syme dropped him off at the embassy and Gunther went straight up to Gessler's office. The senior man listened while Gunther gave his impressions of Muncaster, as a man consumed by fear but evasive and secretive. He told him, too, about Muncaster's other visitors, who had been at the flat before them and, he believed, had searched it.

Gessler frowned, his black eyebrows almost meeting in the middle. He was worried. "Were they Resistance?"

"I think they could be. Why else carry out a search of the flat?" Gunther laid the photographs he had removed on the table and pointed. "If they were university friends, they're in there."

"Damn it!" Gessler burst out. Gunther was surprised; on Friday he had seemed like a man who kept his emotions in check. He told Gunther to write his report, then go home and return early the following morning. Gessler himself would talk to Berlin overnight.

Gunther sat in the little office he had been given along the corridor and wrote quietly and steadily in his small, neat hand. The office was bare apart from the obligatory desk, chairs, and filing cabinets, and a wardrobe where he kept his Gestapo uniform. He wore it seldom, thought he looked fat in it, the puffy shapelessness of his face emphasized by the uniform's clean, hard lines. He resented that Gessler looked trim in his SS uniform, though he was ten years older. There were pictures of Hitler and Himmler on the walls, photographs of his brother and his son on his desk. The window behind the desk had a panoramic view of London, the same as Gessler's office. After an hour he walked back to the flat, dead tired.

He had something to eat and watched the news, followed by a repeat of Mosley's broadcast. It was good the British had done this at last, but Gunther wondered why now. Before going to bed he read his son's letter again. Gunther had been to Krimea to visit Michael last summer, two days on the train clacking through the Belorussian forests and swamps then across the Ukrainian plains, manned concrete guard posts at every mile on the track. Michael had been happy to see his father again, and they had gone to the beach almost every day. His son was energetic and enthusiastic, blond and athletic. He had Hans's undisciplined enthusiasm too and, perhaps, the beginnings of his dead twin's physical grace. Michael had turned eleven in October; all he had been able to do was send a present and a card. He went to bed and slept uneasily, tossing and turning. He had a confused dream of being with his brother again in the forest, the night Heydrich had addressed them by the lake. Hans was looking away from him, over the water, infinite sadness in his handsome face.

He returned to the embassy at eight the next morning. When he entered Gessler's office the SS man was staring out of his window, down over the city. His eyes were bloodshot and, remarkably for such a neat man, he was unshaven. He must have been up all night. There was a cold, leaden sky again today, a touch of fog in the air. Gessler waved him to a chair. He was frowning, tense with anxiety and excitement, quite different from Friday.

Gunther still felt the flat sadness of the evening before in himself. He didn't try to fight it; it helped him stay distanced, objective. He noticed that the report he had prepared last night was lying on Gessler's desk, alongside the photograph of Muncaster's university group.

To break the silence, he said, "The papers this morning are full of the Jews being moved. The government are congratulating themselves on a smooth operation."

Gessler turned and gave him a nod and a thin smile, like a stern schoolteacher acknowledging a pupil whose work was good. "That is your line of business at home, isn't it? From what I understand the British operation wasn't entirely without problems. And of course," he added contemptuously, "some of the preachers are making a fuss, trying to organize protests. If only England were Catholic; the Pope knows the Communists are his real enemy."

"But they've all been gathered in?"

"Nearly all. Almost 150,000. I knew it was going to happen, of course, but unfortunately I couldn't tell you." The old self-importance was back in Gessler's voice. "The operation had to be kept very secret for it to succeed."

"Of course, sir."

"It was part of a larger deal between the governments. Up to now the British have always resisted our pressure. But now"—he gave a wintry smile—"we may be able to get a Jew-free Europe at last. We're talking with the French, too, about a final clear-up over there."

Gunther nodded. "What's going to happen to the British Jews now?"

"They'll be sent to the Isle of Wight, then out East. Hopefully soon. Arrangements are being made for their reception in Poland. Getting the Auschwitz ovens up to full capacity." He smiled again. "Beaverbrook's never been that much of an anti-Semite, but he knows what side his bread's buttered on."

"He's effete and corrupt. Like Laval, like Quisling. We'll need better men to build the new Europe."

Gessler nodded agreement. "Yes. General Franco's the only one with any real spine. He shot all his enemies at the first chance." He sighed and scratched the bald crown of his head. Then he said quietly, "I spent a lot of time talking to Berlin last night. The Führer is very ill indeed. I was told he could die at any time." He leaned forward. "I'm authorized to tell you this because when he does die there will be a struggle for control. Those loyal to the SS must be ready."

Gunther suddenly felt cold. "Ready for what, sir?" he asked.

"A power struggle between us and the army. Things aren't good in Russia, and we think the Russian winter offensive this year will be a big one. And there's been an outbreak of bubonic plague among our troops in the Caucasus. The army want a settlement, the Russians keeping everywhere east of Moscow and north of the Caucasus."

"What? With the Communists? Zhukov and Khrushchev?" Gunther answered bitterly. "Because that's what they are, however they fudge it and talk about their Great Patriotic War."

"No. SS Intelligence think the army are already lining up other factions in Russia. The criminal element that's always existed under the Communist state—some of them have made money now the Russians have brought limited markets back. And some in the Russian Security Police, old NKVD people who made friends in our army during the Nazi-Soviet Pact. It'll be a criminal state, ruling the old Russian ethnic areas."

"We'll be in eternal danger." He thought of his brother Hans. "Is that what five million Germans have died for?"

"That's why we have to be ready. In case, God forbid, the SS has to fight the army."

"What about the Party?"

Gessler shook his head. "Divided. Speer is with the army. Reichsführer Goebbels is the biggest Party figure now Göring's dead and poor Rudolf Hess is in a madhouse: he's the Führer's nominated successor. He could make things go one way or the other. He's strengthening his position. That's what this deal with Beaverbrook is all about. Strengthening his ties with Britain, giving them economic support we can't afford in exchange for getting rid of the Jews."

"Goebbels has always been totally sound on the Jews."

"He's wobbly on Russia, though. This could be a maneuver to link Germany to England and through them to the U.S. There's talk that Stevenson might embargo trade relations with Europe; if he does it would hit us hard. Goebbels is loyal to the Führer but with the Führer gone—"

Gunther considered. "With the British Jews actually deported, the Americans would have no choice but to accept that reality. They would no longer be a possible bargaining issue for them."

Gessler said, "If there is a battle for control of Germany it could ripple through this embassy." He shook his head. "After all our victories, I thought, we can't lose, we're omnipotent. But now—"

"We still can be, if we keep our courage," Gunther countered. "SS power has been growing for twenty years."

Gessler said, more to himself than Gunther, "If there is a struggle and the SS lose, I suppose they can't shoot all of us. I expect we'll all be demoted and redeployed." His manner softened unexpectedly, became confidential. He took off his pince-nez and rubbed the bridge of his nose. "I wonder where. I was in Leningrad in 1942, you know. After the Army cut the city off completely and starved them all to death over the winter. The Wehrmacht has never hesitated at what has to be done in Russia, some of them will pretend to scruples if they argue for peace but I've seen the Army lads in action out there, seen how they deal with the Russians. But more and more of the senior officers have lost the spine for it. Weakness in the face of the enemy." He sat still, reflecting. "I was with the first SS group into Leningrad, in April, to question some of the few survivors— mostly Communist Party officials, they had what few supplies were left by then, though even they were like walking skeletons. God, the city stank, what our artillery and bombing had left of it. Three million bodies, rotting in that rubble. The corpses could be dangerous, you know, especially if there was a pile of them—they decomposed fast when the snow went. The gases would build up inside and they'd explode. You'd hear them banging off, at night. Wolves had come in to forage, and there were rats everywhere. No water, no sewage—we all had to clear out again after a month, the troops were coming down with typhoid—it's all still cordoned off. At least in Moscow we took the city without a long siege; kicked the population out and put them in camps to starve quietly. The Führer wants to demolish the buildings and build a lake there when we win. But I never want to go east again; it was disgusting." He wrinkled his face with distaste, sighed, then focused on Gunther again. "I see from your file you're divorced, Hoth."

"Yes, sir. But I have a son in Krimea."

"I have a wife, two daughters, in Hanover. I taught physical education in a school there, when I came back from the Great War. Then I joined the Party, then the SS. I did well."

A little golden peasant, Gunther thought, not wanting hard times back again. "We'll win through, sir," he said quietly.

Gessler slammed his hand on the desk, his mood turning in a moment. "Of course we will! None of us must doubt it!" He took a couple of deep breaths, replaced his pince-nez, then spoke calmly again. "Don't repeat anything of what I said to anyone."

"Of course not, sir."

"Besides, it may be mostly rumors. You know what HQ's like."

"Yes, sir." But Gunther still felt cold.

"Now, these visitors Muncaster had," Gessler said, businesslike again. "Do you still think they could have been Resistance? After sleeping on it?"

"Yes, sir. It's not certain but it is possible."

"Why didn't Dr. Wilson tell you other visitors were coming?"

"I think he didn't know, sir."

"He'll be phoned this morning." Gessler shook his head. "If they were Resistance, how would they know about Muncaster?"

"The obvious answer is through the Americans. The brother will have told them all about what happened." Gessler nodded. Gunther thought, *all about what? What exactly did Muncaster know? And how much did Gessler know of it?*

"And the old man definitely reported Muncaster as saying 'The Germans mustn't know.'"

"Yes, sir."

"Given how important this could be, Berlin agrees Muncaster should be brought here and questioned. He would fold quickly, I am sure; we would soon find out whether he actually knows anything important."

Gunther said, "I think locking him in the basement and telling him a few details about what we can do should be enough."

"Good. Actual interrogation of a British citizen is politically tricky. They like to keep things in their own hands."

"I know."

Gessler frowned again, tapping his fingers on the desk. "And that is our problem. What I would like to do is send an SS squad into that hospital and just take him. But the orders from Berlin are that we must avoid doing anything that would cause a stir. If the British authorities realize Muncaster's importance they may want to keep him. We don't want the British secret services anywhere near this; they're unreliable, full of wild adventurers. And if the Resistance people are onto Muncaster, too, it is vital they know nothing of our involvement; they might try to snatch or kill him first."

"They've had access to him already. If he has a secret the Americans don't want to get out then why haven't they killed him yet?"

"Maybe the Americans want him alive. Maybe the British Resistance want his secret for themselves."

"What if these visitors come again?"

"Dr. Wilson will be told very firmly to ring a good friend of ours in the British Home Office. He'll do it, he'll huff and puff but he knows he could lose his job if things go wrong."

"Don't forget he has a relative in the Health Ministry."

"It's the Home Office that counts. Meanwhile we need to look into the people in that university photograph, two of whom the old man thought he recognized, which brings me to the next issue. How did Syme do yesterday?"

Gunther had considered how to answer this. "Very well. Took the lead in questioning Muncaster, but took cues from me. I don't think Muncaster even realized I'm foreign. Then Syme helped me get into the flat."

"How far do you trust him?"

Gunther considered. "He's not an easy colleague. Bit of a chip on his shoulder about us being in charge. He's clever, he's guessed there's more to this than meets the eye. But he's fond of money and the good life, and I've told him he'll be rewarded for helping us."

Gessler tapped the photograph of the group at Oxford. "Would you trust him to look into this, find out the identities of the people in this picture? The names the visitors gave at the asylum were fake, of course."

"Yes. But I'd watch him; if it came to a conflict between British and German interests, I'm not sure which way he'd jump. He's a good Fascist, but, as I say, with a chip on his shoulder. The question of reward would be important."

"You don't like him, do you?" Gessler asked.

"No. But that doesn't matter. I think he can be very useful."

"Then let's play on his greed." Gessler smiled. "It works often enough." He was his old confident self again, as though the conversation about Hitler's illness had not taken place. "I'll speak to his superintendent. Ask for him to contact Oxford, find out who was in that photograph. Take Syme to a top restaurant tonight, say the Cafe de Paris; we can arrange the booking. Thank him for his help, talk about a grateful German government opening a Reichsmark account for him." He looked at the clock on the wall. "And now, I have a call from Berlin due shortly. Go back to your flat, contact Syme, butter him up. Apart from that, wait in for the telephone." He looked at Gunther sharply again. "But be ready now, for anything. And remember this, Heydrich himself wants Muncaster in our hands. And if it comes to it, Syme is dispensable."

That night Gunther took Syme to dinner at the Cafe de Paris as arranged. When he got back to the flat he had telephoned Syme's office, put on an artificially jovial voice. Then, as he was not supposed to go out, he phoned the embassy to ask if they could get him a dinner suit. They delivered one an hour later, just the right size, with a crisply ironed shirt. They had booked places for them at the restaurant, too, which couldn't have been easy at a few hours' notice.

He turned what Gessler had said over and over in his mind. He had known, objectively, that Hitler was ill and might die, and that the politics then could become difficult, but being told it was a strong possibility now was different. For over twenty years Gunther had believed the Führer was something more than human, delivered to a broken Germany by Fate. He remembered the posters on the streets in the thirties, *All This We Owe to the Führer*. He knew Martin Bormann was Hitler's right-hand man, but also that he was a nonentity. Gessler was right, Goebbels was the key figure. Which way would he jump, toward the SS, or the army? Gunther sat and calculated, but underneath it all was cold fear at the thought that Hitler, the keystone of everything, could soon be gone.

Eventually, worn out with thinking, he went and lay down on the bed. He fell into an uneasy doze, and had a dream about his young son. Michael was walking through a field of stubble, and Gunther knew there were mines in the field but somehow he was powerless to call out to the boy. Then he saw someone else crossing the field, walking toward Michael. It was his brother Hans. He knew that Hans and Michael were both about to be blown up, but though he tried to shout to them he couldn't speak, could only utter a little croak. He woke up gasping for breath.

There were no calls from the embassy and at seven he phoned Gessler's office where his coldly efficient secretary confirmed they would contact him at the Cafe de Paris if need be. He walked up to Euston Square Tube; there was fog in the air, a sulfurous tang that made him cough as London fogs always did. If it persisted he would have to get one of those facemasks. He remembered his nightmare. He felt full of emptiness and fear. He must show Syme no trace of it.

On the Tube platform he saw a huge garish poster: a man in a clown's outfit with a painted face holding up a big flaming hoop through which a lion jumped. *Billy Smart's Circus Christmas Spectacular.* He wondered if there were any circuses in Krimea.

The Cafe de Paris was a huge basement room. Gunther had been there when he was posted in England before, usually for boring embassy functions. He had heard that in 1939–40, when the British were terrified of German bombs, it had been advertised as the safest restaurant in London. The lighting was low, little shaded lamps on the tables. Gunther had hoped for a place in the balcony area that surrounded the ballroom—somehow he always felt safer watching things from above—but he was led to a table near the dance floor, with a view of the band. They were playing loud, discordant jazz music.

Gunther looked at his watch; he was early. He glanced over at the people at the other tables. Some older women wore ball gowns but most of the younger women had short dresses, some wide and flouncy, others daringly tight. Many had expensive mink stoles over their bare shoulders. Four Wehrmacht colonels sat together, probably military advisers from the embassy, Rommel's people, part of the clique who wanted to cut a deal with the enemy. They looked cheerful and confident. At a big table nearby a group of middle-aged Englishmen accompanied by younger women who looked like prostitutes were getting cheerily, noisily drunk. From their shouted conversation he gathered they were from ICI, celebrating a possible new contract with Siemens. A waitress came and he ordered an orange juice. He didn't want to drink too much alcohol tonight.

Syme arrived a quarter of an hour later, in a dinner suit that was too big for him. Gunther sighed inwardly, then rose to shake his hand. They took their seats. Syme looked around, his expression appreciative. "Quite a place, eh? I've heard of it, but never been."

"We wanted to show our appreciation." A waitress appeared. "What will you have to drink?"

"A brandy if that's all right. Push the boat out. What's that you've got?"

"Orange juice. But I'll have a brandy now."

Syme said, quietly, "I got called in by the superintendent today."

"Did you?"

He smiled conspiratorially. "They want me to carry on helping you."

"And what do you think about that, William?"

"I'll be glad to." A serious expression came over his thin face. "Sounds like you put in a good word for me. I'm grateful."

"Whatever we can do." The drinks came. Gunther raised his glass. Syme shifted in his chair; Gunther wished again that he wouldn't twitch about all the time.

"Let me know what you need." Syme laughed. "We'll be like Sherlock Holmes and Dr. Watson, solving the great crimes."

Gunther smiled, though he had always thought the Sherlock Holmes stories contrived and moralistic, not like the real world. The band finished their number, to Gunther's relief, but then an exaggeratedly handsome, Latin-looking man in a suit with sparkly lapels walked onto the stage. Everyone clapped, and Syme gave a little whistle. "Wow, that's Guy Mitchell."

"Who?"

"American singer. He's big, not like Crosby or Sinatra but pretty good. They're always playing him on the radio." He laughed with pleasure. The man sang a couple of numbers; he had a good voice but the lyrics were nonsensical. Syme had turned to watch, foot jigging in time to the music. Gunther was relieved when the singer bowed and left the stage; his stomach was grumbling and he wanted to order. Syme, who was on his third brandy now, turned back to him.

"Good stuff, eh?" He looked speculatively at the girls with the businessmen's party. "There'll be dancing later. Those tarts look taken but there might be others who aren't." He raised his eyebrows. Gunther noticed his Cockney accent had returned as the drink loosened his tongue. How foolish, this English obsession with class. As a Fascist Syme should know it was race and nationality, not class, that mattered. He said, straight-faced, "Your voice has changed."

Syme smiled sardonically. "You need to try to talk a bit posh if you're aiming to reach the top of the Service. Don't drop yer bleedin' aitches. Now, what about lookin' for some nice juicy tarts?"

Gunther shook his head. "I don't seem to have the energy these days. And I must get up early tomorrow."

A waiter came and they ordered. The food was good but the band started again and they had to raise their voices to talk. Syme said, "Don't you like the music?"

"No. It is like all the American influences I see over here. Loud and brash, tuneless."

Syme looked at him with amusement. "What do you prefer, German classical stuff?"

Gunther shrugged. "Anything but this."

"Our Arts Ministry's trying to encourage traditional folk music, morris dancers waving silly twigs around village greens, blowing penny whistles." He laughed. "I prefer something with a bit of a swing."

"Negro music. I thought you didn't like blacks."

Syme leaned across the table. He said seriously, "You know, mate, I like you, but you should take the chance to enjoy life a bit. Let the old juices flow."

Gunther smiled ironically. "I have given my life to duty."

"The generation that has sacrificed everything to save Europe?"

"And you for your Empire, too."

Syme leaned further forward. "Listen, I know the Russkies aren't completely sorted out yet, but they will be. And everywhere else, we're top dogs. We've got everything. All the Jew money, like you got when you carved up Switzerland with the Frogs and the Wops in 1940." He laughed. "That was a masterstroke. You got all the Swiss banks, confiscated all the assets the German Jews put there after you came to power. Russian assets too. Germany and us together, we call the shots, so we get the goodies. We should take advantage of it."

Gunther smiled and inclined his head. "If things go well with this," he said, "grateful people in Germany might open an account in Basel for you."

Syme's eyes sparkled. "That would be—great." He grinned, "I've already been promised that if things go well there's a four-bedroomed house in Golders Green earmarked for me, a Jew's house, full of expensive furniture." He took a drink of the fine wine he had ordered. "Live a little, mate," he said, a half-friendly contempt in his voice. "I plan to."

CHAPTER TWENTY-THREE

F rank stayed in the quiet room after David and Geoff left with Ben. He turned his chair around to the window again, so he couldn't be seen from the half-open door to the ward.

David had promised to help, look into the legal position, and Frank told himself he should cling on to that. It had been so strange to see him and Geoff after all this time; David didn't look much older although his face had been full of uncomfortable anxiety, as had Geoff's. Geoff had aged all right; his face looked strange with that fair mustache. Frank realized he must have looked terrible to them; he was used to his baggy, ill-fitting clothes and clumsily shaven head, he didn't think about his appearance anymore, but had been aware of how alien he must look to his old friends.

There was something that had worried him, though, about the interview, something in a look David had exchanged with Ben, as though they shared some secret. And Ben hadn't wanted David to talk to him on his own. Why was that? And they had asked him about his brother, just like those wretched policemen earlier. He told himself he was getting paranoid—a term often used in the asylum—David was bound to ask about the event that had brought him here. But there had been something that didn't fit about both visits. He hadn't liked the policemen— the tall one's friendliness was false, Frank had seen it in his eyes, and the fat, silent sergeant had had something frightening about him. The inspector had glanced at the sergeant once or twice as though he were the more important one in the partnership. They weren't like the policemen who had interviewed him before.

"How're ye daen, wee man?" Frank jumped violently. Ben had come in and was standing beside him, looking down. "I've seen yer friends off, back doon tae London."

"Good."

"I think that went okay, didn't it? Looks like they'll dae what they can to help."

"Yes. Yes, I think they will."

Ben looked at him with those hard, sharp eyes. "Must've been a bit strange, seeing them after all this time. Just after the police came, too."

"It's—it's been a bit of a day."

"Ye seem jumpy, Frank. It's gettin' toward time for yer next pill. I'll get it for you. I'm away off duty soon."

"Yes. All right."

"I think it might be best not tae tell Dr. Wilson or the other staff about your friends helping you to get out of here," Ben said, his voice elaborately casual.

"Why not?"

"Just for the now. Let your pals find out the legal position first. So that when they talk to Dr. Wilson they've got all their ammo ready."

Although he nodded, Frank was suddenly, horribly certain that something secret was going on, something involving Ben and David and Geoff, and maybe the police, too. He thought, surely David wouldn't betray me; but then why shouldn't he, what did Frank really mean to him?

"Good lad," Ben said. "I'll get yer pill."

He went out again. Frank thought, I won't take it, I'll pretend to but I won't. I need to think hard, I must think. He felt a stab of pain in his bad hand. He had been clutching the chair arm so tightly he had hurt it; the damaged fingers were tingling.

Later the older attendant, Sam, the one who had taken Frank to see the policemen, came to fetch him to dinner. Ben had come back and given him his pill with a glass of water. It was easy to slip it under his tongue and then as soon as the attendant turned to put it in his pocket. He needed to be awake, alert, not let himself be taken by surprise.

"C'mon, Muncaster," Sam said impatiently. "Time for dinner. Along to the dining hall."

"All right."

Sam led him down the corridor to the dining room. "You've had a busy day."

"Yes."

"What did them coppers want?"

"Just a new inspector wanting to go over the case."

"That older one, fair-haired, was he English?"

Frank looked at Sam, alert. "I don't know. He hardly spoke."

Sam said, "I saw him in the corridor and wondered if he was German. They hold themselves stiffly, even a fat man like that. If they're soldiers, or officials. I was in a German prisoner-of-war camp in the Great War, y'know. Hard lot. Still, them's what's been needed to sort out the mess Europe was in, I suppose." He looked at Frank curiously. "He didn't speak, you say?"

"Hardly at all." Frank feigned disinterest.

His mind was in a whirl, though, as Sam led him into the dining room with its smell of overcooked vegetables, crowded with long tables. The patients queued along the wall by the serving hatch, watched by Sam and two other attendants. Frank joined them, still desperately trying to fathom what might be going on. Had Edgar confessed to the American authorities about what he had let slip to Frank? But surely the Americans wouldn't involve the British, still less the Germans.

"Wake up, Muncaster," Sam said. "Join the queue or the food'll be gone."

Frank felt trapped, like a rat in a cage. He took a tray to the hatch and received a plate of grayish liver and soggy vegetables, with lumpy mashed potatoes served from an ice-cream scoop. As he turned toward the tables a loud crash made him jump. A middle-aged, gray-haired man had turned and thrown his plate of food to the floor. The other patients looked on with mild interest; such things often happened. A burly attendant ran across, grabbing the man's arm roughly. "Jack, what the fuck d'you think you're doing!"

"I won't eat this food!" the patient shouted. "There's things in it, chemicals to sterilize us! I won't!"

"Shut up, you silly bastard! There's nothing in the food! If you don't want your dinner, you can damn well do without. Come on, back to the ward." The attendant hauled the man away, who was wailing like a child now.

Frank sat opposite Patrick, a fat little man in his thirties with a dirty black beard. He was one of those who hardly spoke, spending most of his time in the day room staring at the television. The senior attendant said Grace, gabbling quick thanks to God for the food He had provided. It was one of the hospital rules. The patients picked up their knives and forks; the knife blades were kept so blunt, and the forks had such short tines, that Frank had found them hard to use at first. He forced himself to pick at the watery mess on his plate. He thought, surely David couldn't be working with the Germans. But he was a civil servant, he worked for the government.

"People are getting the wind up," Patrick said suddenly. "This new Act of Parliament."

Frank looked at him in surprise. Patrick's eyes were clear and alert. It sometimes happened like that, someone who spent weeks shuffling around in silence would suddenly say something sensible and you realized there was a real person hidden in there.

"Poor old Jack," Patrick continued. "He's got the wind up about the sterilizations. Got put in here when he was seventeen for fiddling about with his sister. Did you know that?"

"No. He's been here ever since?"

"Oh yes." And then Patrick abruptly seemed to lose interest, bending to chase a piece of rubbery liver about his plate.

Frank overheard some other patients talking about the Jews being deported from the cities. Apparently there was going to be some announcement on the television and afterwards they went to watch Mosley's broadcast in the day room. The Fascist leader's calm explanation of the latest and worst thing they had done only intensified Frank's growing sense of fear. Afterwards people sat talking listlessly about the deportations, some saying it was overdue, others that it was cruel, many not seeming really to register it. Frank crept back to the quiet room. He paced up and down. He felt worse than ever, as though ants were crawling over his skin. He thought of taking his pill after all but he didn't. He had to be able to think. He breathed fast, on the edge of panic, his mind whirling. Was that policeman a German? Were he and Ben and David in league? If so, what were they planning to do?

That night, on the ward, he was, like all the patients, given the usual double dose of Largactil to get him to sleep. Nonetheless he woke up in the small hours: sleeping patients all around him, the night attendant reading at his lamplit desk. Frank thought again of suicide. If he was dead there was no way for his secret to come out, he would not be responsible for the terrible things that might follow. He thought, I'd have defeated them, all this pain and fear will be over, I've no future anyway apart from existing in a place like this. And if the Germans got hold of me . . .

Another day began: getting out of bed, dressing, being taken to breakfast. Sam was on duty again. After breakfast the patients went back to the day room for their pills. Frank took his from Sam and again only pretended to swallow them. Sam said to him, "Dr. Wilson wants to see you at ten, Muncaster. You're to stay on the ward."

In his panic Frank nearly swallowed the pill. He managed to mumble, "What about?"

"Don't know. You'll have to ask him."

The patients clustered around the television in the day room; there was a keep-fit program on at nine, people in the world outside were crazy about keep-fit these days. Frank had heard the patients talking about it in anticipation; there had been a preview, it was about the Butlins holiday camps' exercise classes, there would be half-bare women stretching and bending. The men, many of whom had barely seen a woman in years, smiled with anticipation as they sat down.

Frank went back into the quiet room. He pushed the door almost shut. The weather was foggy again, only gray misty shapes visible outside the windows. What did Wilson want? Was it to begin the electric shocks? Was it to tell him the police would be taking him away? He stood looking at the big picture on the opposite wall, *The Stag at Bay*. Out of desperation an idea came to him. With trembling steps he walked over to it. It was very heavy and with the limited power in his right hand it was difficult to unhook the picture, even standing on a hard chair which he dragged across, but he managed it. His arms trembling with the effort, he carefully lowered it to the floor. He was bathed in sweat. He glanced nervously at the door to the day room, heard a cheerful female announcer's voice from the television. He saw that behind the picture, driven deep into the brickwork, was a large metal hook.

Frank stared at it. Again he thought, *I don't want to die.* But he wouldn't be doing it for himself, it would be to make sure he took his terrible secret with him. He reached up and grasped the hook with both hands, letting his full weight rest on it. It didn't move. He walked away, looked out of the window again. He took long, deep breaths, wondering once more if he could have been mistaken about yesterday's events. He thought, David and Geoff never liked the Nazis any more than I did. But he hadn't seen David for over ten years. In that time everything had changed. He thought, they and the policemen could be working together, trying to grind him down. And if they put real pressure on him he knew he would crack. He thought of the things they said the Germans did to make people talk. He squeezed his eyes shut. He thought suddenly of his father, his death in action. If he did this it would be a heroic act like his. Outside, he heard ribald laughter. He walked back to the hook. Blood thundered in his ears. There wasn't much time before they came and took him to Dr. Wilson. Quickly he took off his jacket, then his crumpled shirt. He wound the shirt into a long strip of thick cloth. It was difficult but he made a clumsy noose. He stood on the chair in his vest and tied one end of the shirt tightly around the hook. He was completely determined now, like a soldier going over the top in the trenches. He stood on the chair and put the home-made noose around his neck. He bent his legs so it drew tight, taking all his weight. It held. Then he jumped.

CHAPTER TWENTY-FOUR

The following day David left for work as usual. The weather was still cold, the sky a leaden gray; fog was forecast for later. It felt strange, after all that had happened since Friday, to be walking to the station, catching the Monday morning Tube with the other commuters.

On Sunday night, after the broadcast about the Jews, David and Sarah had sat in the lounge in dismal, heavy silence. Sarah had had an urge to telephone Mrs. Templeman's husband, but knew she mustn't — she wasn't even supposed to know her friend was dead. They both started when the telephone rang; it was Irene again, phoning to ask how Uncle Ted was and asking about family arrangements for Christmas. Sarah sat on the hard chair by the telephone table, looking exhausted by the effort of trying to sound normal, lighting one cigarette from the butt of another. They had both been smoking like chimneys since the broadcast; the air reeked. From her end of the conversation David gathered Irene had started talking about the Jews. Sarah began to sound impatient. "How can you possibly say they'll be kept comfortable — hauled out of their homes and marched off under guard, they'll be terrified..." Eventually Sarah said wearily, "I don't think there's any point discussing it further, Irene." She banged the receiver back on the hook. "If she wants reassurance over that one, she's come to the wrong bloody shop!"

"Careful what you say. Remember Steve's Blackshirt chums."

"Oh, to hell with the lot of them," she snapped. In a way David was glad she had become angry; her strength of character was reasserting itself even if she obviously thought he was being cold, overcautious. She came over to the settee again and they both sat staring at the blank television screen, chain-smoking, fearing the telephone ringing again, or worse, a knock at the door.

*　　*　　*

Next day they were both red-eyed from sleeplessness, but they got up wearily and started the morning routine as usual. Over breakfast David asked Sarah if she was all right to be left alone. She was in her dressing gown, pale and washed out.

"I'm supposed to phone around the toyshops this morning. I'll find an excuse to phone Friends House as well, see if anything's being said about poor Jane."

"Watch what you say."

"Of course I will."

"I'll phone you from a call box at lunchtime, see how you are."

"Why can't you ring from the office?"

"I'm just being careful."

"If you use that word again, I'll scream."

Traveling in on the crowded Tube, strap-hanging, the previous day's events kept crowding into David's mind. Natalia had guessed his secret, the only person who ever had. She had said she wouldn't tell anyone but her loyalties were to the Resistance, not him. And what would happen now with Frank? And Sarah, he was placing her in more and more danger.

People were reading the newspapers with unusual concentration. An elderly couple was talking in fierce undertones as they read. "Bastards. It's wicked, evil. Makes you ashamed to be British." They didn't seem to care about being overheard. One or two people frowned at them, but most buried themselves deeper in their papers. The train went into a tunnel and David caught a glimpse of his reflection in the window. He looked ravaged, exhausted. He must try and pull himself together.

For the first time, entering the Office, he didn't feel it was a place of refuge. He had known for years that the service supported an evil government, had been irreparably contaminated by it, but it was the first time he had actually felt it, deep in his bones.

In the lift two of his colleagues were discussing the effect the deportations would have on Dominion relations in the cool, detached Civil Service way, as though it were a more abstract problem.

"Of course our counterargument will be that they've all closed doors to further Jewish immigration themselves, apart from New Zealand. They feel they've taken enough."

"Yes. The pot calling the kettle black argument."

"Quite."

"They may raise the Palestine option again."

"Not going to happen, old boy. There's just too many imponderables."

"Did you see there's a new Resistance leaflet?"

"No."

"Someone had scattered them on the floor of the Tube on my line. Usual Churchill stuff—destroying our liberties, dividing the British people, who will be next? Plastered with 'V's and 'R's. I thought, can you call the Jews British people?"

"Well indeed? There you do have an interesting question of definition."

"I suppose there'll be more strikes and riots with this one."

"It just gets worse all the time. I know Mosley wants reprisals, taking captured Resistance people's families hostage, shooting one for every soldier and policeman killed."

"The German way, eh? That's going a bit far."

"Perhaps."

David stared fixedly ahead as the lift clanked upwards. He wanted to punch them, break their faces.

That morning it was hard to concentrate; fortunately there was only routine deskwork to attend to. He thought of Natalia, her almond-shaped eyes looking at him from the car. *You should tell them.*

Outside, fog settled slowly over the city. Toward noon David got up and put the light on. At lunchtime he went out for a swim, but first he phoned Sarah. She answered at once, her voice level, normal.

"It's me, darling," he said. "Any news?"

There was a tired, ragged edge to her voice. "Yes, they told me at Friends House that Mr. Templeman had phoned to say his wife had died of a heart attack. I rang him, to give my condolences. Poor man, he was trying to be brave but you could hear his voice was about to break."

"A heart attack?" David repeated incredulously.

"Yes. The police called around to say she'd dropped dead outside the station at Wembley. They told him it was a heart attack. He said there'll be a postmortem. They'll fake the result, won't they? I saw the blood..." Sarah's own voice was close to breaking now.

"It'll be a Home Office pathologist, it won't be the first time they've faked something."

"Mr. Templeman said the funeral's next week. I want to go."

"Yes, yes, of course. Would you like me to come too?" he asked.

"Why? You never met her. To make sure I don't say anything stupid?"

David closed his eyes. "No. To support you."

Sarah sighed. "I'm sorry; I just—yes, please come."

"Listen, this means they're going to cover it up, but they'll still be looking into what happened. We have to go on taking care."

"I know. When will you be home?"

"I'll try to get away a bit early."

"Do." She paused, then said, "It's hard, isn't it?"

"Yes. Yes, it's hard."

He walked back to the office, huddled in his coat. Carol was in the lift, along with other people returning from lunch, the tip of her thin nose red with cold. She smiled brightly, "Hello, David. Putrid weather, isn't it?"

It was hard to speak cheerily, conversationally. "Dreadful. Hope this fog doesn't last."

"They say it won't."

They got out on the second floor. Carol looked at him with concern. "Are you all right?"

"Bit of a cold, I think."

She smiled. "You look a bit peaky, if you don't mind me saying."

He wondered what Carol thought about the deportations. She was a kind woman, but you never knew; perfectly decent people could turn out to condone terrible things.

"I hope you're better in time for Friday," she said.

"Friday?"

"The concert. Bartok, at St. Mary's."

"Ah, yes, of course, I'm sure I'll be better by then." He had forgotten.

"There's one at the Queen's Hall, on the ninth of December. Beethoven's Fifth. I know it's a bit of a trek over there, but if we asked for an extra half-hour at lunchtime..."

"I'll see." He turned away, aware of her hurt look at his curtness.

A little after three there was a peremptory knock on his door, and Hubbold came in. He sat down, took out his little silver snuff box. "I've just been with the Permanent Secretary," he said abruptly. "This business with the Jews will put the cat among the pigeons. The Canadians and Aussies will be up in arms at this week's High Commissioners' meeting. Our line will be that this is for their own protection as well as ours. Handle the issue with kid gloves, that's the word from on high. Thank God the agenda's gone out, they'll have to bring it up under Any Other Business." He stared at David, the eyes behind those thick lenses impossible to read as usual, but there was a note of challenge in his voice, as though to emphasize this was just a piece of business like any other.

"Yes, sir. I see." David kept his voice neutral.

"Thanks for fixing up that meeting between the SS and the South Africans, by the way."

"I think the South Africans are going across to Senate House on Wednesday."

Hubbold nodded. "Good. I expect they'll tell the Germans their problem is that they were never able to disarm the Russians. They never let the blacks anywhere near a gun."

"Yes," David agreed. "It's all about who has the guns."

Hubbold nodded slowly. All at once he looked uneasy, embarrassed. David wondered whether he, too, had been shocked by yesterday's events, was going to say something unplanned. But instead he said, "There's a problem with one of our files. One of the secret files I'm cleared for. The Canadian one. I found a document that didn't belong there, to do with South African military assistance to Kenya. It was in the wrong file."

David thought, I put it there, the Sunday before last, when Hubbold came down to Registry. He stared at his superior. Hubbold said, "You had that file for last week's meeting. Did you notice whether the Kenya paper was there?"

"No. It wasn't one I needed to consult." He managed to speak steadily. "I remember it though, it's a few weeks old, isn't it?" To his relief, Hubbold just nodded his white head thoughtfully.

"Yes, it would have passed through a number of hands. I'm checking with the people in this department who had it. But I haven't come up with anything. Ten to one that girl of Dabb's misfiled it." He frowned. "But I don't see how the Kenya file would have got into her possession. It's restricted, but not top secret. You're friendly with her, aren't you?" he added.

"Quite friendly." David's heart thudded in his chest so hard he feared Hubbold might hear it.

"D'you think she's up to the job? You know how scatty women can be."

"I've no reason to think not."

Hubbold seemed to slump a little in his chair. "I'll have to tell the Permanent Secretary. There'll be an investigation. He'll keep it internal, he won't want those MI5 clowns clumping around in here." He shook his head. David thought, he's frightened this will be a black mark before he retires. Hubbold stood up, smiled ruefully. "Well, thank you. Obviously, keep this between ourselves." He went out.

David sat staring at the door for a moment, then reached for a cigarette. This could get serious. For the first time he had been careless. He felt danger closing all around. And Carol, what about Carol? Was he going to end up taking her to the bottom, too?

He got an interdepartmental messenger to take a note to Geoff. Could he meet him after work for a drink, outside the office at five? A reply came back, yes, certainly.

When he left the building the fog was quite thick, cars and buses moving at a crawl, the office workers crowding out of their buildings, then quickly disappearing into the murk. He waited on the steps of the

Dominions Office, and after a minute Geoff appeared, pipe in mouth, dressed like David in dark coat and bowler hat, looking tired and, as he always did, somehow rumpled. "Let's take a turn around Trafalgar Square," David said. "I've got some news."

Geoff looked at him. "So have I."

They walked up Whitehall, moving slowly along with the crowd. David thought of the Jews, all those trapped, frightened people, crammed together somewhere while London commuters went home as usual. In the distance the chimes of Big Ben sounded.

In Trafalgar Square the traffic was almost at a standstill. A newsvendor on the corner called out, "*Evening Standard!* Railwaymen threaten new strike."

Geoff said, "Let's see if we can get across into the square. It's a bit quieter there." An old man passed them, hunched over, coughing in the sharp tang of the fog: a dreadful hacking noise.

They crossed the road with care, choosing a point where the traffic had come to a halt. They passed in front of a stationary bus, the engine rattling. Passengers stared wearily out of the condensation-smeared windows. A small boy in a school cap stuck his tongue out at them cheekily.

There were few people on the big concrete island in the center of Trafalgar Square. Nelson's Column was virtually invisible. They began walking around the broad circle of pavement, beside the crawling traffic. Geoff said, "There's some bad news from Ben Hall at the mental hospital."

"About Frank?"

"Yes. We had word this afternoon that—well, he's tried to hang himself."

David stopped. "Oh, God."

"He didn't succeed. He tried to use a picture hook in a wall, but it wouldn't take his weight." Geoff sighed. "Let's keep walking. Frank's been taken to a room where he can't harm himself. A padded cell and a straitjacket, I'm afraid." Geoff's face twisted with distaste.

"Poor bloody Frank." David took a deep breath. "What happens now?"

"Frank's going to have to be got out. They want us both involved. They're looking at the practicalities. It could mean another trip to Birmingham, David, at very short notice."

"Jesus." David looked at his friend. "Listen, I've a problem." He told Geoff about the paper he had misfiled. "Hubbold's going to have to set an investigation in train."

"Is there anything to lead them directly to you?"

"No. Several people have had the file. But we'll all be questioned. When they don't get an answer they'll bring the security people in. Hubbold doesn't want that, but they're bound to do it before too long."

Geoff halted. His pipe had gone out. He chewed on the stem. They were beside the plinth where one of the colossal bronze lions stood guarding Nelson's Column. It reared up, a wall of sooty wet granite. On the other side of the pavement the traffic was moving slowly again. Geoff said, with a tight smile, "It's getting pretty difficult, isn't it?"

David nodded.

"Well, we always knew it might."

"That's not all. Sarah found herself in the middle of a riot yesterday. The police were leading a group of Jews away, and a few people sat down in the street in front of them. Sarah did, too. Some Jive Boys joined in and it got out of control."

Geoff nodded. "Our people have heard the deportations hadn't gone smoothly everywhere."

"It was worse than that. People were killed. Including a woman Sarah knew."

"Good God! Was she arrested?"

"No. Some of the Jews escaped, and a couple of them helped her get away. Students. But she's pretty shaken up. Her friend who was killed— her husband's been told she had a heart attack in the street, they're hushing it up. But they won't let it drop. The trail might lead to Sarah." He paused, then said, "I'm a risk now, Geoff." The wild thought had come to David, maybe the Resistance could help Sarah and him to disappear, maybe get them out of the country with Frank. Before his deepest secret, that he was a half-Jew, was discovered.

"It's not your fault," Geoff said.

"Some of it is," he answered bleakly. "Misfiling that paper."

Geoff stopped and took his arm. "Stop blaming yourself for every-thing. That's your biggest weakness, you know that, it always has been."

"What the hell are we going to do?"

Geoff's face set doggedly. "Find a telephone box. And tell Jackson."

CHAPTER TWENTY-FIVE

Early on Tuesday morning Gunther was woken by a telephone call from Gessler's office, ordering him to present himself there in person at eight. As he dressed he hoped they could move forward now, get Muncaster safely to Senate House.

He had a few minutes to spare, and he switched on the television for the news. There had been no further announcements about the Jews since Sunday. An item about the Russian war was showing; a British reporter broadcasting from a V3 base somewhere on the North Volga; one of the enormous rockets stood on a launching pad a little way off. There was a countdown in German and then the V3, belching fire from its base, shot into the sky with a low, deep rumbling. The camera followed the rocket, as it became a dot and vanished. The reporter said, *"This rocket is headed for a Russian town somewhere in Western Siberia. Faced with such a sight, one has to ask, how can a race even as obstinate and fanatical as the Russians survive such a continual onslaught?"*

Gunther grimaced. He knew that however much damage the rocket might do to some Siberian city, the Russians had dispersed their war production over dozens of sites scattered across the immensity of the Siberian forests, many beyond even V3 range. He crossed to the window and looked out. The fog had cleared overnight. On the opposite side of the street was a newsagent. Outside the door there stood a wooden figure of a little beggar boy with polio, both legs in calipers, his painted face sad. He held up a sign saying, *Please Give.* There was a slot in the top of his head for people's donations. Gunther had seen polio victims, dragging themselves painfully along the London streets. Far better, he thought, to end such a child's suffering with a quick, painless injection.

*   *   *

At Senate House Gessler was in his office. He looked angry today, spots of red in his cheeks. He glared at Gunther, then said brusquely, "That lunatic Muncaster tried to hang himself last night."

"Why would he try to kill himself now? I thought he had been very quiet all the time he was there. Was it because we came? Or the other visitors perhaps?"

"Who knows why lunatics do anything?" Gessler's brow creased with fury. "Apparently he's refusing to talk at all now. Not a word. Won't even confirm the names of his visitors. I'd get it out of him soon enough. But we've got a problem with that Dr. Wilson. He's become obstinate; our friends at the Home Office have asked him to turn Muncaster over to us but he won't, says he can't just transfer someone so ill for interrogation. If he is to be questioned he wants it to be under hospital supervision."

Gunther frowned. "Why is he doing this?"

"British obstinacy and self-assertion, I think."

"Yes. That still rears its head from time to time."

"The problem is that Wilson has gone to this cousin who works for the junior Minister of Health, Church. He spoke to him yesterday and he's backing Wilson."

"I thought the Health Department was full of eugenicists now. Isn't Marie Stopes advising them on sterilizing lunatics?"

"Yes, and the Duke of Westminster's in charge of the Ministry. Beaverbrook put him in to show social issues aren't a priority for this government, but though he's one of us, he's stupid and old. And that Department's still full of pre-war do-gooding types. Berlin are working on it, but they've told me they're going to have to be careful. It may take some days. If what we want gets Mosley's Home Office and the Health Department involved in a Whitehall turf war, the British government are going to get curious about why we want Muncaster."

"And time is something we don't have."

Gessler banged his fist on the desk in temper, making the pens and inkstand jump. Gunther noticed the papers on his desk were piled untidily now. Gessler was losing control of himself. "I know that, damn it! But they won't listen. And they won't *tell* me why Muncaster is so important, they won't say what this damned secret is that he has. Can't I be trusted after all these years?" He glared at Gunther as though it were his fault. Gunther wondered if it was the frustrations of the case that were making his superior so anxious, or whether it was the worrying news from Germany he had spoken of yesterday.

Gessler leaned back, bringing himself back under control. He waved a hand impatiently. "We must just carry on as best we can."

"Have we learned any more about Muncaster's other visitors?"

"We've got identities and descriptions, but the names are false. The nurse who took them in to Muncaster says he was given the same false names. He just took them to Muncaster and left them. Apparently he told Wilson, 'You don't question that class of people.' The porter confirmed they had what he called 'posh' accents."

Gunther shook his head wearily. He felt a spasm of contempt for Gessler's inability to keep his temper like an adult.

"Wilson says Muncaster is to stay locked up securely under his personal supervision. He doesn't realize what we could do to him if he goes on fooling about with us," Gessler added viciously.

But Gunther also knew how the British jealously guarded what was left of their independence. This wasn't Poland. Gessler had turned to stare out of the window, his face full of surly anger. He changed the subject abruptly. "Goebbels is to make a big speech today, thanking Britain for taking the steps it has with the Jewish problem. He'll say he hopes for closer links with Britain, new developments in foreign policy."

"He's getting Britain on his side for the succession."

"I know. New developments on foreign policy, what can that mean? Talks with the Americans? The Russians?"

"I don't know, sir," Gunther said worriedly. "I wish I did."

Gessler was silent for a moment. Then he asked. "How did it go with Syme last night?"

"Oh, I think he is in our pocket."

"Good."

"He said his superintendent has told him to go on working with us. He knows there will be rewards."

"That inducement came from me." Gessler squared his shoulders, back in control again. "Right, I want you to send Syme to Oxford today, get the names of the people in that photograph. We've got a car ready for him. He'll have to go alone, it has to be a wholly Special Branch inquiry. He's waiting downstairs, brief him before he leaves."

"Yes, sir. And afterwards," Gunther added, "it might be a good idea to have Muncaster's colleagues at Birmingham University questioned again. I know the police didn't come up with anything when they were interviewed after the accident, but perhaps Syme could dig deeper, see what he can turn up. Perhaps his Birmingham Special Branch colleagues could help."

"I'd want you to be in on that, keep an eye on it. Oh, and Muncaster's mother's house in Esher. The local paper says it is on the market."

"Then perhaps I could go and look at it. Pretend to be a buyer."

Gessler looked doubtful. "A German buyer?"

Gunther smiled. "I can pretend to be Swedish. Useful that we left them unoccupied."

Syme was waiting on a leather-covered bench in the Senate House vestibule, tapping a foot on the marble floor, watching the busy comings and goings with a keen, happy interest. He had on another new suit and wore a plain tiepin, not the one with the BUF flash. As Gunther approached he stood up, extending a hand.

"What's happening?"

Gunther handed him Muncaster's university photograph and told him he wanted him to get the names of the students in it. Syme seemed pleased at the prospect. "I'll enjoy questioning some of those snobby academic types."

"Soft-soap them if you can. Tell them you're looking for Muncaster's friends to see if someone can act as his trustee."

"All right." Syme looked at the giant bust of Hitler, the huge swastika flag hanging from the high ceiling. "So this is where it all happens. I always wondered what it was like in here. It's like a different world. Clean, light, modern."

"Yes," Gunther agreed, though he thought of the faction fights, the endless power struggles between the SS and the army.

"I hear there are going to be some big celebrations at Senate House in January, for the Führer's twenty years."

"Only two months away now."

Syme smiled and raised his eyebrows. "I'm told there's also going to be a reception for the BUF. Sir Oswald will be here."

"Yes." Gunther smiled softly. "Would you like to see if I can get you an invitation?"

"That would be good."

"I am sure something can be arranged. Now, you should go, you have a driver waiting."

Six hours later Gunther walked up a long street of detached Victorian villas in Esher, the key to Mrs. Muncaster's house in his pocket. Yesterday's fog had gone but it was a cold, dank afternoon. He had phoned the estate agent that morning, saying he represented a Swedish company interested in entering the English property market, renovating old houses. The agent had been very keen, and when Gunther arrived in his office had been delighted to give him the keys so he could go and look around for himself. "You're wise to get into the housing market now," the agent had said with a sort of cheerful desperation. "Everyone says it will go up next year. The house does need a lot of work, an old lady lived there alone for years. It's ideal for a developer. The solicitor for her estate hasn't got probate yet, so I'm afraid we haven't been able to clear out the house." Good, Gunther thought. "The beneficiary who instructed the solicitor and us lives in America," the agent continued. "It's holding things up. But if we got an offer in I'm sure we could move things along."

When he reached it Gunther saw the agent was right; the house was noticeably run down, paint flaking off the windowsills and door, the gate half-rotten and the front garden rank with weeds. It was big for an old woman living alone. When he opened the front door his nostrils were filled with a smell of damp and old dust. The house was dim and gloomy and the electricity had been switched off. Something in the atmosphere reminded Gunther of Muncaster's flat.

He wandered from room to room, looking into drawers and desks. The house hadn't been painted inside for years. In the kitchen he saw some plates and cups left to dry on the draining board. Two people had been here, not that long ago; Muncaster and the brother probably. A big room at the front was a doctor's consulting room, with equipment that looked forty years old. Mrs. Muncaster must have left it as it was after her husband died. Stupid woman, Gunther thought, she should have sold up and moved somewhere smaller. He opened the drawers of the doctor's desk but they were empty. In a bureau in the lounge he found a drawerful of household accounts and some old photographs, which again looked as though they came from before the Great War. This was disappointing. He coughed; the dust and damp were getting to his nose and throat.

Gunther fared no better upstairs; there were a couple of bedrooms with single beds, maps and pictures of trains on the walls, small boys' rooms. A large bedroom must have been Mrs. Muncaster's; there was a wardrobe full of dark clothes, already starting to smell musty. On the wall was a photograph of a solidly built, good-looking young man in academic cap and gown; it must be Edgar, the brother. Gunther had seen no photographs of Frank anywhere.

Gunther felt thwarted now; there was nothing here, no information about either brother. Another brick wall. It was getting dark, becoming hard to see properly. He opened another door, the last. It was another small bedroom. Another single bed, a Victorian chest of drawers. But there was a table by the window as well, and on it he saw something unexpected and strange: a large photograph of a woman, in a big silver frame covered in black crêpe. In front of the photograph a candle stood in a silver candleholder; there were spent matches in the bowl. Gunther went over and picked up the photograph, the crêpe falling off it. The woman was middle-aged, with short, tight curls, a rope of pearls around her neck. Her face was striking: big fleshy features and sharp-looking eyes. Not a trustworthy face, his policeman's instinct told him. In the right-hand corner of the photograph was a signature: *Ethel Baker, 1928,* and the words *"The spirits are with us."*

Gunther put the photograph back on the desk. The room looked like some sort of shrine; it made him feel uneasy. Gunther believed in reason, order, the clear light of historical destiny. He had no truck with fancies and imaginings, but standing in the room the sadness of the house appeared to thicken and a horrible, seeping darkness seemed to gather. He had a strange mental picture of desperate broken-backed creatures crawling toward him over the dusty carpet. Suddenly he felt the whole world was full of them and soon there would be nothing and nobody else left. He shook himself angrily, went out and left the house, slamming the door shut. He had found nothing there, nothing at all.

CHAPTER TWENTY-SIX

That evening, after work, David went to Soho again. He had had a message from Geoff; Jackson wanted to meet them tonight. David had telephoned Sarah, saying he had to work late once more. She had asked, angrily, whether he really had to. He knew she was still shocked by what had happened on Sunday. He was apologetic, reassuring and promised to be back as soon as he could.

A day had passed since Hubbold had spoken to him about the missing file. Nobody had mentioned it further, but he guessed Hubbold was speaking to others and that he had told them, like David, to keep the matter confidential. When he went up the corridor to the lift to go to lunch he had seen Carol sitting smoking at her desk, a blank, vacant look in her eyes. For once, she did not even see him. She must have been questioned, too.

It was a cold, raw evening. The exotic Soho grocery shops were closing, assistants in brown overalls packing away stock and pulling down shutters. A couple of young men in trilby hats and coats with wide shoulders passed him, talking Italian. Under one of the tall, glass-paneled streetlamps a man in his forties, dressed like David in a dark coat and bowler hat, stood looking around him nervously. David guessed he had come to find a prostitute. The street girls wouldn't be out until later. The man met his eye and looked away quickly. David turned into the alley beside the coffee bar.

He was about to ring the bell when the door opened and a tall, attractive young woman appeared. She wore a green coat and had striking red hair under a fashionable saucer-shaped hat. She looked at him with bright green eyes, then smiled. "You're one of Natalia's friends, aren't you? I'm Dilys from the other flat. I'm just going out to the shops, I thought you was an early client. It's all right, I was given pictures of all of you, to memorize. I watch out for you all, you know. Go on up," she added, a little reproachfully. David realized he was blushing.

"I — thank you."

She smiled at his embarrassment, then walked away down the alley. David went upstairs and knocked on Natalia's door. She opened it a little, peering out at him anxiously for a second before she recognized him and her face cleared. She let him in.

"I'm sorry," he said. "I didn't ring the bell. The — Dilys let me in, she was on her way out. She knew me, she said she had pictures of us."

Natalia nodded. "Yes, Dilys is important. We would not have this place but for her. She is a good friend."

Natalia wasn't wearing her painter's smock tonight but a thick gray sweater that set off the paleness of her skin. "How are you?" she asked, looking at him with concern.

"There's been a bit of a problem at work."

"So I understand. Don't tell me about it, wait until Mr. Jackson gets here." She gave her sad, wry smile. "That's the way he likes to do things."

"I know."

There was a charcoal sketch on her easel, a narrow cobbled street with tumbledown houses on each side, figures walking along. She came and stood beside him. "I started that yesterday. After our talk. It is the old Jewish Quarter in Bratislava."

"It looks a run-down sort of place."

"It was where the poorer Jews lived, shopkeepers and boot menders, laborers."

David said, "My father told me after my mother died that my Jewish grandfather was a furniture maker, a carpenter. It's not the sort of job you associate with a Jew somehow."

Her wry smile again. "Jesus Christ was a Jewish carpenter."

"I suppose he was."

"Where did they come from? Your mother's family?"

"Somewhere in the old Russian Empire, I'm not sure where. Poland perhaps, Lithuania. Slovakia was part of the old Austro-Hungarian Empire, wasn't it? Before the Great War?" He laughed self-consciously.

"My father had an old school atlas from before 1914, I looked at it again the other night."

"Yes. Some called the Empire the prison house of nations. But after the war it was worse in many ways, everyone splitting off to claim their own nationality, creating new minorities, each hating the other more and more. And all the nationalists hating the Jews as an alien people, of course. Czechoslovakia was not so bad as most, though, till Hitler destroyed it." She put out a hand and touched his arm quickly. "I'm sorry, I'm not giving you much comfort."

He offered her a cigarette. "You haven't told anyone, have you? About me?"

"I said I would not." She looked at him. "But I still think you should."

David laughed bitterly. "I really don't feel this is the best time."

She inclined her head and stepped away. He was making her keep a secret for him. If only she hadn't spoken on Sunday. He asked suddenly, "Did the Jews in Bratislava speak Yiddish?"

"Yes, they did. The Jews spoke Yiddish all over Eastern Europe." She smiled. "Our countries, they were such a babel of languages, everyone speaking at least a bit of three or four." She asked softly, "Did your mother speak Yiddish?"

"She put all that behind her, became Anglo-Irish. She said something though, just before she died. Neither my father nor I understood it."

"Do you remember it?"

David gave an embarrassed laugh. "It was seventeen years ago. I don't know, it was something like, 'Ik hobdik leeb.'" He turned away, suddenly full of emotion. He heard her repeat the words, with a different emphasis. "*Ich hob dich lieb.*" He turned around. "That sounds like it. What does it mean?"

"I don't know," she said, looking away. "I only knew a few phrases."

The doorbell rang, making them both jump. Natalia went out, and David heard her light footsteps descending the stairs. She came back with Geoff. "Hello, old man," Geoff said with forced cheerfulness. "How are things?"

"I think Hubbold's questioning people."

Geoff took off his coat and hat, gave David a tight smile though his blue eyes were anxious. "It'll be all right."

The bell rang again. Minutes later David heard Jackson's heavy footsteps accompanying Natalia back up the stairs. He came in, grim-faced, nodding to David and Geoff without smiling. He took off his coat and hat, sat down heavily, then said to David, "You seem to have set some hares running, one way and another."

David told him again what had happened to Sarah on Sunday, and about the missing file. Jackson listened, expressionless, putting in the occasional sharp question. When David had finished he sat thinking for some moments.

"I think your wife is safe," he said at length. "We've managed to trace that student couple. Most of those who got away — not that there were that many, anywhere — have ended up with our people. Those Gentiles who're willing to help them usually have some contact with us."

"What will happen to them?"

"They'll get new identities. The Jews won't be the first people we've done that for, not by a long chalk. Now, is your wife quite sure nobody on this committee of hers knew that she went off with this woman who was killed?"

"She's certain."

"You've put us to a lot of work, tracing those two students." He sighed. "And the other matter, putting secret papers in an open file, that's worrying." His hard, sharp eyes were angry now.

Geoff said, "David thought he was about to be caught, he had to act in a hurry."

Jackson glanced at Geoff briefly, but did not reply. He turned back to David. "You say you think Carol Bennett's been questioned?"

"Yes, from the way she looked at lunchtime."

"How do you think she'll have reacted?"

"She won't be pressured. She'll say it wasn't her, she doesn't know how it happened. Which is true."

"Do you think she might make any connection between the missing papers and you?"

"No. She's no reason to. And her picture of me is — distorted."

"Try to behave normally with her. Don't tell her about being questioned yourself, she might smell a rat if you do."

"I'm supposed to be going to a concert with her on Friday."

"I should cancel. Probably best if you and Miss Bennett aren't seen around together."

"I'll do it tomorrow." He sighed. "I'll think of some excuse."

"What should David do? If he is questioned again about the papers?" Natalia asked.

Jackson stared hard at David again. "Say you know nothing about it. I've been in the Service nearly forty years, it's not the first time something like this has happened. They'll go around in circles for a little while, asking everybody, then when nobody accepts responsibility for the mistake, eventually they'll have to approach MI5 to deal with it, what's left of them these days. Unless they can find a scapegoat, someone they don't like who could plausibly be responsible. Possibly Miss Bennett." He thought for a moment. "We're safe for the time being. Enough time to deal with the immediate issue, which is Frank Muncaster. Can you hold your nerve, Fitzgerald, if you're questioned again?"

"Yes," David said. "I just deny everything, don't I? But sooner or later they're going to connect it to the fact I come in at weekends."

"You're not the only one. And you've a twelve-year record of unblemished service, being loyal and unambitious, a happy family man." Jackson smiled, coldly. "Don't forget the importance of that. It's why we took you on."

"Yes. I'm used to lying," David answered quietly. He looked at Natalia, who glanced away.

Jackson stood, paced up and down the room as he sometimes did, while the others stayed seated. Geoff lit his pipe. They heard two pairs of footsteps ascending the staircase outside, and the door of the prostitute's flat door slammed shut. David heard a woman's laugh. Jackson sat down again. He said, "Our friend Ben Hall at the asylum has been very nifty. They questioned him about your visit on Sunday and he said so far as he's concerned you were strangers, old chums he'd allowed Muncaster to contact by telephone. His descriptions of you are mildly misleading." He shook his head, smiled coldly again. "They do have some steel, those Reds. Now, the danger, as it always has been, is that Muncaster spills the beans, but apparently he's on some sort of strike, won't talk. Well, that suits us."

"I don't imagine it suits Frank much," David said.

Jackson frowned. "Fortunately Hall can keep an eye on him."

"The suicide attempt," Geoff asked. "Was it serious, or just a cry for help?"

"Oh, it was very serious, according to Hall. But we can't rely on Muncaster staying quiet." Jackson took a deep breath. "The people at the top have said he is to be lifted, and soon." He looked around the room. "They want the three of you involved. You've been to the asylum before, and Drax and Fitzgerald know him. You may be able to get his cooperation."

"How would it be done?" Natalia asked.

Jackson got up, began pacing the room once more. "Ben Hall will get himself on night duty. He can't do it for a few days unfortunately, he doesn't want to put in an urgent special request in case it arouses suspicion. Apparently all the patients are drugged at night to get them to sleep and there's only a skeleton staff. It will be down to him to get Muncaster out, and you'll be waiting in a car outside. You'll take him down to the coast, short rides via a series of safe houses over two or three days. We're fixing that up now. And an American submarine will be waiting, at a point we're arranging with the Yanks, to pick him up. Ben Hall will go with you. You'll have to take leave—some sort of family emergency." He stopped and looked between them, his tone suddenly gentle. "I won't pretend there won't be danger. But you'll have false papers, cover stories, and so far as we're aware nobody knows that Muncaster is any more than just an escaped lunatic."

"We're kidnapping him," David said. "That's what it boils down to. Kidnapping Frank."

"For his own good," Natalia said. "His own safety."

"I know," David said, looking at her and then Jackson. "I know we have to do it."

Jackson nodded. "Good. Ben Hall will keep him drugged, sleepy. He'll be given new clothes. To other people he may just seem a bit subnormal." Jackson raised his eyebrows. "It'll be several more days before we can get all the pieces on the chessboard, I'm afraid."

David said, "And he'll be taken to America. Then what?"

Jackson shrugged his broad shoulders. "Questioned. Afterwards, perhaps given some scientific work, a new life. Ben Hall will go with him, his cover will be completely blown at the asylum."

"Could Frank be locked up like his brother?"

"His brother broke the law. Frank Muncaster's circumstances are quite different."

"We've no way of knowing what they'll do to him," Geoff said.

Jackson spread his hands. "What else can we do?" He spoke angrily. "What other chance does he have?"

"None." David thought a moment. He took a deep breath, then said, "What if I went on the submarine as well? With Sarah. Then we wouldn't be a risk anymore."

Jackson stared at him. "What do think your wife would say to that?"

"I think, now, she'd take any chance to get out of England."

"We can't just do that, Fitzgerald," Jackson said impatiently. "If you go on the run, disappear from your job, there really will be a big inquiry, our whole network in the Civil Service would be in danger. That's a very last resort."

"I'm a danger," David said. "I'm a risk."

Jackson said, "So far as getting Frank Muncaster out is concerned, you're one of our biggest assets."

"What will you tell Sarah?" Geoff asked.

"I've got an old uncle out of town, I pretended he was ill when we went to visit Frank; I can say he's died. I'll say I have to go to Northampton to make arrangements."

Jackson said, "Good."

David asked him suddenly, "What the hell is it that Frank knows?"

Jackson reflected a moment, then spoke quietly. "The world is at a tipping point. Hitler's illness, the Germans losing the war in Russia, resistance growing everywhere, the new American president. And what Muncaster knows, if the other side get hold of it"—he held out a big, manicured hand, tipping it gently from side to side—"it could just tip that balance the wrong way."

CHAPTER TWENTY-SEVEN

On Thursday afternoon, Sarah drove with David to Mrs. Templeman's funeral. It was held at an ugly modern church in Wembley, not far from the stadium. On a wall nearby someone had painted a Resistance "R"; it made Sarah's heart rise a tiny bit. A hearse was waiting at the churchyard gate, a flower-covered coffin in the back. Sarah's stomach clenched as she thought, the lid must have been nailed down after the autopsy, nobody would be allowed to see that ruined head. It was cold for late November; as she walked up the path arm in arm with David she noticed frost on the grass around the graves. She remembered Mrs. Templeman, on the train last Sunday, saying brightly, *They say it's the coldest November for years.* A little way off, two men in overalls stood by a newly dug grave, spades on the ground beside them, holding their caps as a mark of respect. Sarah clutched David's arm tightly, grateful to him for coming.

People in black were gathering in the doorway of the church. She recognized some from Friends House committees; others must be family and friends. She was introduced to Mr. Templeman, a small, thin man, his face white as paper under his Homburg hat. He seemed to have collapsed into himself with grief, leaning heavily on the arm of a woman who, from their resemblance, must be a sister. Sarah thought, thank God the poor man has family; she remembered Mrs. Templeman saying their son had died in the 1940 war. Mr. Templeman shook her hand and smiled without recognition when she offered her condolences; he must have forgotten speaking to her on the telephone. A top-hatted undertaker came and murmured quietly to the sister. She said, "Yes, we should go in now."

Sarah glanced back down the path. The coffin was being unloaded from the back of the hearse. She looked at the houses opposite the church, wondering if there might be a Special Branch policeman at one of those windows, watching who went in and out. David said, "Come on, darling." She turned and went into the church.

Sarah had been dreading the funeral, and that morning had occupied herself by doing some mending, then preparing lunch for David, who was coming home to pick her up. She put the radio on, hoping the Light Program might relax her a little, but when the doorbell rang she jumped.

On the doorstep was a man in his sixties, in cap and brown overalls. He touched his cap. "Mrs. Fitzgerald?"

"Yes?"

"I'm Mr. Weaver. Weaver and Son. You asked us to estimate for some redecoration. Your staircase." Sarah had forgotten they were coming this morning. She asked him in and showed him the torn, discolored wallpaper where the gates had been. "We'll need to change the wallpaper all the way up if it's to look right," he said. "I won't be able to find an exact match."

The man took measurements, then asked what sort of wallpaper she wanted. Sarah realized she had no idea. He produced a book of patterns and she chose something more or less at random.

"Can I leave it with you now?" she asked the man. "Only I'm getting my husband's lunch."

"All right. I'll send you an estimate." The decorator smiled. "What was it you had there, a child's gate?"

"Yes."

"Old enough to get up and down stairs now, is he?"

"Yes," Sarah said quickly, "that's right." Only a short time ago the man's words would have brought her close to tears.

"Well, I'll get on," the man said. "I'll let you have a full quote in a couple of days. Would you like it done before Christmas?"

"As soon as possible, really."

The cheerful dance music from the kitchen had stopped for the twelve o'clock news. At the end of the broadcast, as after every bulletin that week, the announcer asked any Jews not yet relocated to attend at the nearest police station. Mr. Weaver said, "Looks like some are still at large." He spoke neutrally, the way people did nowadays to someone whose political views they didn't know.

"Yes," Sarah agreed. After closing the door she looked up the staircase. She felt somehow that Charlie had really gone now, disappeared into whatever place the dead went to.

The vicar at the funeral was dull, uninspired. He told the mourners he had known Mrs. Templeman for years, praised her faith and good works and kindness. He said that she had had a quick and painless end, for which all should be thankful. He promised she was safe now, in the arms of Christ Jesus. Sarah saw Mr. Templeman wasn't listening; he looked as though he didn't really know where he was. It had been like that for her and David at Charlie's funeral. She glanced at her husband; he was looking at the minister with a sort of uncomprehending anger. They sang a hymn, "Onward, Christian Soldiers." Her voice was shaky. David sang tunelessly in his heavy, flat baritone. Neither had ever been good singers, they used to joke about it.

After the burial they walked back to the gate; the reception was for family and close friends only. Sarah said, "Thanks for coming, David."

"Everybody seems to believe the story about the heart attack," he said quietly.

"Nobody knows otherwise, except us. Those poor people."

He said gently, "Let's go home."

In the car she told him about the decorator's visit. "We should have done it ages ago," he said, but when they got home he suddenly said, "I'm afraid I may have another funeral soon. Uncle Ted's not doing so well."

"I thought he was getting better."

"So did I. But he's back in hospital. You know how it is with old people and hips."

"How did you hear?"

"I gave the hospital my work number. He could go at any time, they said." He smiled awkwardly. "If it happens I'll have to go up and sort everything out. No need for you to come."

She frowned. "That doesn't seem fair to you. I'll come with you. You came today."

"I'll have to take several days off to arrange things. I'm his executor, you see."

She thought of blank-faced Mr. Templeman. "Poor Uncle Ted," she said quietly. "No one to really mourn him."

David looked uncomfortable. "No one left suffering, you could say. As we have with Charlie."

She sighed. "I suppose we'd better get some wine to take to Steve and Irene's tonight."

"I wish they hadn't invited us." Irene had phoned with the invitation the day before.

"Well, they did. I'll go up to the shops. I saw they had some Belgian chocolates in. We can taken them to Irene's. A box will cost the earth with the import duty, but still—"

"All right."

The telephone rang. It didn't make them jump this time, but they both tensed. Sarah was closer and picked it up. "Hello."

For a moment there was silence at the other end, then a woman's voice, cultivated and a little breathless, said, "I wonder if I could speak to Mr. Fitzgerald, please."

Sarah turned and looked at David. "Who is it calling?" she asked.

"My name is Bennett, Miss Bennett. I work with Mr. Fitzgerald. Is that Mrs. Fitzgerald?"

"Yes, it is. How can we help you, Miss Bennett?" Sarah asked, quietly and evenly, looking at David as she spoke. His eyes widened but the rest of his face seemed to constrict slightly, go deliberately blank.

The voice at the other end was anxious. "It's about a problem at work, something that's come up. I really would be grateful if I could speak to him."

"Hold on a moment, please." She put her hand over the mouthpiece and looked at David.

"What does she want?" he asked.

"She says there's a problem at work, and she wants to talk to you about it."

"Hell." David reached out for the telephone. Sarah stayed standing next to him, so she could hear. She remembered Carol Bennett's face from office functions: thin, intense, predatory.

"Hello, Carol," David said, in a puzzled tone. "What happened, why are you ringing me at home?"

"Why did you leave that message canceling tomorrow's concert? Did Mr. Hubbold ask you to?" Sarah could hear her; the woman's voice had risen in volume, sounding panicky.

"No," David answered. "I said in the message, I had to go to a funeral today and I'll have to catch up on work tomorrow. We've just come back."

"Only — have they been asking you questions about a missing file?"

David hesitated, then said, "I've no idea what you're talking about."

"Only they've been asking me, and I'm afraid I'm in trouble. I'm sorry to ring you at home, I looked your number up in the book. Can we meet for lunch tomorrow? I need someone in the office I can talk to."

"Is it about a confidential file? Only if it is —"

"Please meet me tomorrow, for lunch. At the British Corner House. One o'clock. Please." And then she must have put the phone down, because David stared at the receiver blankly for a moment before replacing it on its rest.

Sarah's legs were shaking. She went into the lounge and sat down. David came in after her. Sarah took what felt like the longest breath of her life, then said, "Are you having an affair with that woman? A lost file, was that your cover story in case I answered the phone?"

He stared at her blankly. "Of course not. What on earth would make you think such a thing?"

"She said you canceled a concert. You've been going to concerts with her. I know, I found a ticket with her name on it, weeks ago!" She heard herself beginning to shout.

David stood looking down at her, his face suddenly red with anger. "You've been going through my pockets?"

"Of course I bloody haven't! I found it when I was getting your coat ready for the cleaners. And don't you think anyone would get suspicious, the number of evenings you ring saying you have to work late? The number of weekends you go into the office? Tennis evenings with Geoff that are arranged all of a sudden? You must think me a fool!"

"I don't —"

"I phoned the tennis club the week before last, when you were supposed to be there, and you weren't!" The words came tumbling out. She felt frightened but it was a huge relief as well. "Why would she phone you at home about some missing bloody papers?"

David stood there, breathing hard. "Sarah," he said. "For God's sake. I am not having an affair with Carol Bennett. I've been to lunchtime concerts with her, but apart from that I've never seen her outside the office. Never, not once."

"You've been to office functions with her —"

"Only when you were there as well —"

"I've seen the way she looks at you —"

He shouted, "I can't help that! I've been to concerts with her to get a break from the bloody Office. It's only once every few weeks!"

"What about that time you weren't at the tennis club?"

She saw he needed a second to think before he answered. "There must've been some mix-up at reception. I was there. You can ask Geoff."

"Oh yes, Geoff. Your best friend, he'd cover for you!" It was flying out of her now, all the anger.

"Now you're being stupid. Geoff wouldn't do anything like that."

"I'm not bloody stupid!"

David closed his eyes, sighed deeply. When he opened them again he spoke coldly and evenly. "I'm not having an affair with Carol Bennett. Or anyone else. If she's got herself into some sort of trouble at work, I'll tell her to speak to — to the authorities." Then his face softened, and he said, "Don't be too hard on her."

"Why not?"

"She's just a silly, lonely woman."

"You feel sorry for her, don't you?" Sarah pressed. "That's what women like her do. Get men like you to feel sorry for them. That's how it starts."

"I'm not having an affair." David went on, quietly, "I've tried to protect you. God knows what I've done to try to protect you."

"From what? From this affair?"

"There is no affair!" He too, was shouting, now. "From the world, from everything that's happening outside this house."

She stared at him. "I don't need protecting. Tell me the truth."

"I'm not having an affair with Carol Bennett; I have no interest in her. That's the truth. If you won't believe me, I can't make you." And then, as though he couldn't trust himself to say more, David left the room.

CHAPTER TWENTY-EIGHT

Gunther had sent Syme to Oxford on Tuesday. Late on Thursday, 27 November, they still hadn't found out who had visited Muncaster the previous Sunday. In his office, Gessler was getting increasingly frantic. The Ministry of Health had dug their feet in, protecting their turf—they wouldn't let the Gestapo take Muncaster. Gunther, though, was calmer after his odd panicky moment at Mrs. Muncaster's house. He knew from long experience how difficult it could be to identify people who wanted to stay hidden. It was steady, painstaking work, waiting for the crucial piece of data, the flash of inspiration. Syme was doing his best; he and his superintendent had people steadily working on the students in the photograph, cross-referencing the information the university had reluctantly given to Syme with the vast Special Branch records in London.

Syme had gone back to Birmingham too, and questioned Muncaster's old workmates again. There was nothing new there, though. Muncaster had been a loner, good enough at his work but with no social contact with anyone. They had told Syme they used to play practical jokes on Muncaster sometimes, which he didn't like. "What was the matter with the twerp?" Syme said impatiently to Gunther. "You've got to put up with a bit of joshing in this world, you have to stand up for yourself." He had found a similar picture when he spoke to Muncaster's old lecturers; Muncaster kept very much to himself, nobody could recall him having any particular friends. Quite a few people remembered only his strange monkeylike smile. His old personal tutor was still at the college, but was currently traveling home by ship from an academic conference in Denmark, and would be back late on Wednesday.

On Thursday Gunther reviewed the information which Special

Branch had sent to Senate House about Muncaster's former fellow students at Oxford. He was interested to see what had happened to these people in the last eighteen years. Some had become academics, other had gone into business or the Civil Service. Several had served in the 1939–40 war, and one had died. Some had emigrated to the Empire. A few had gone down in the world; one was in prison for fraud. None of them had any links with the Resistance although that didn't prove there weren't supporters among them. One was a Jew but his file confirmed that he had been picked up on Sunday. Gunther had considered whether the people who visited Muncaster might have had some separate connection with him. But Muncaster had no other connections who might have visited him, and according to Muncaster's neighbor, the old man, the people who came were the right class and age. Gunther's instinct was that they were there in the photograph.

With the legwork in the hands of Syme and the Special Branch, Gunther was left with hours of free time. He wrote to his son in Krimea, told him he had come back to England on a case, that the country was cold and damp as always. After a page he found he had run out of things to say. He couldn't divulge more about his work, he didn't want to write about England, and there was nothing else in his life now. He got up and flexed his stiff shoulders, telling himself he'd become prone to gloom and fantasy since going to that miserable empty house.

Earlier that day Gunther had gone to visit the officer in charge of the interrogation center in the basement of Senate House, in his little ground-floor office. The man, Hauser, welcomed him as another Gestapo man. He was a little older than Gunther; solid and strong, he hadn't gone to fat as Gunther had. He said he had worked in Poland and Russia for years, but had begun to suffer from arthritis in his feet, brought on he was sure by too many winters in the East. He was fit again in England, despite the damp. "I was in Britain before, in the midforties," Gunther said. "We set your basement outfit up while I was here."

"I was out in Russia then. Hard days. Not that they're easier now. Their General Rossokovsky's in charge of this winter offensive they say has started. He's good. Him and Zhukov, they must have German blood."

He looked at Gunther meaningfully. "But we have to go on till the job's done."

"We do. I lost a brother out there. It's amazing how they just keep coming at us, keep living. We know Stalin killed millions before we invaded, and we've killed about thirty million. But they keep on coming, out of the East."

"So many good Germans lost." Hauser clenched his big fists. "But we'll go on, we'll finish them and then it'll be as the Führer planned; everything west of Archangel to Astrakhan for German settlement. We'll let the Russians starve, keep some of them to work as slaves. None of them allowed within a mile of a gun. When the war's over we'll settle the whole country with our veterans."

Gunther nodded. "And other Aryans, Dutch and Scandinavians and East Europeans who meet the racial criteria. We have to. It's Germany's destiny."

"German farms to the Caspian, eh?"

"Yes," Gunther agreed quietly. "And the giant memorials to our German fallen, like my brother. I've heard them speak of them, in Berlin; great war memorials, hundreds of feet high, topped with eternal flames that will light the countryside at night."

They looked at each other in silence for a moment. Then Hauser asked, "What are you working on here?"

"Confidential, I'm afraid." Gunther smiled. "But if it goes well, we may have a new customer for you."

"We can always make room for another. We've got quite a few German Jews in from the roundups this week, ones that came here as refugees in the thirties and hid out with the British Jews when the German refugees were sent back in '40."

Gunther shook his head. "The Jews always look out for each other."

"That's why we've got to see things through in Russia, get the ones behind the Russian lines."

"Any news from Berlin?"

"I don't think the Führer's getting any better." Hauser looked at him meaningfully again. "We have to make sure the right people take over if he goes."

"We do."

"I saw Rommel striding across the lobby the other day in his uniform, stiff and frowning and full of piss as usual." Hauser laughed. "Did you hear he got paint thrown at him at the Remembrance Day ceremony?"

"Yes, everyone has been talking about it."

"Some little freelance British group. We dealt with them down here. If it had been the Resistance they'd have shot his head off. Done us a favor, perhaps," he added quietly.

"Yes. If the Führer dies and the army tries to take over, Rommel will be with them."

"And we'll be with Reichsführer Himmler. He'll have a million Waffen SS forces ready to move, don't you worry."

"I hope so."

Hauser was belligerently confident, but Gunther felt that trickle of fear again, fear at the unimaginable prospect of German forces turning on each other.

Syme was due to come to see Gunther at four. It was half past two now. Gunther had a copy of Muncaster's university photograph on his desk, propped up by books. He looked at it again; if you studied all those grainy little faces for too long, your eyes stopped focusing. He stood up. There was an exhibition on at the headquarters of the Anglo-German Fellowship nearby, *Ashes to Glory, Twenty Years of National Socialist Germany*, and he decided to go for a quick look, to clear his head. The exhibition was well organized; moving through successive rooms he followed the story of how Germany had gone from defeat and ruin in 1918, through the horrors of inflation, the Depression, the triumph of the Jews. Then the coming of the Führer, the rebuilding of the state, the conquests in Central Europe and the defeat of the West, the great epic in Russia. Gunther felt uplifted again. He thought, I've lived through all this, been part of the greatest adventure in history.

He returned to Senate House. As he went through the main door he saw Syme sitting on the same bench he had occupied a few days before, watching as a delegation of German businessmen were welcomed by embassy staff. There was a thoughtful smile on his thin face, one foot jigging up and down as usual. Gunther went over to him. Syme looked up and said, in a quiet voice, "I think we've identified one of Muncaster's friends."

Muncaster's old tutor, just back from Denmark, had provided the crucial information. "He remembered this David Fitzgerald better than he did Muncaster. He taught him." Syme imitated, very well, an effete upper-class English drawl: *"Fitzgerald was a very personable young fellow; could have been quite charismatic if he'd bothered. But he was one of those serious grammar-school boys, he mixed with a rather dull crowd. Muncaster shared rooms with him and Fitzgerald took him under his wing. Personally, Muncaster gave me the shivers."* Syme resumed his normal voice. "Got the impression the old poof might have fancied Fitzgerald." His eyes narrowed. "Fitzgerald's crowd was anti-appeasement, he remembers."

"What about the other man? The fair-haired one?"

"He doesn't remember him."

"And we still don't know about the woman. Still..." Gunther looked at the notes he had made on the students, turned to David Fitzgerald's. "A civil servant," he mused. "Dominions Office."

"Yes," Syme repeated. "A civil servant." He gave Gunther an odd, calculating look. He seemed even more tense and jittery today. "I got this," Syme added, laying a photograph on the desk. It was one of the boys in the picture taken from the flat, the image blown up to full size, grainy. A handsome face, serious-looking as the tutor had said. Dark, curly hair. Irish-looking. Syme said, "I got a courier to drive that photograph up to the old man at Muncaster's flat this morning. The message is that he is definite Fitzgerald was one of the visitors."

"Thank you," Gunther said sincerely.

"We Brits can be efficient too."

"I know."

"Of course there's still the possibility Muncaster did just telephone Fitzgerald, as an old friend, to ask him to help him out of the hole he's in.

Fitzgerald has no Resistance links we know of. Nor the other man, if he was the other one at the flat."

"Then why search his flat? That's what I keep coming back to." Gunther looked at his notes again. "I see his wife comes from a pacifist family."

"But the pacifists don't like the Resistance. Too much violence. Did you hear an armored car was blown up in Liverpool yesterday, by the way? The bastards," Syme added. "And Fitzgerald's been in the Civil Service since 1938, apart from war service."

"Yes. In Norway."

Syme took a deep breath. He said, "If Fitzgerald is Resistance, and he's working in the Civil Service, then he's a security risk for Britain. We don't know what information he could have access to in his job, which he might be passing on to them. My superintendent says we have to question him about that. Us, Special Branch. We can't just let you have him." Syme gave a quick smile, half nervous, half challenging.

Gunther said, "I understand your point. I think I should speak with Standartenführer Gessler."

"All right." Syme smiled again, meanly now. "But I believe the Special Branch Commissioner may already have spoken to him."

When Gunther went up to Gessler's office the Standartenführer looked drawn and exhausted, too tired to shout and curse. The Special Branch Commissioner had indeed spoken to him on the telephone about Fitzgerald, and they had reached a compromise: Fitzgerald as a civil servant should be jointly questioned by Gunther and Syme. Serious issues of domestic security could be involved. "And the Health Department is still making problems over Muncaster," Gessler said. "Someone from Berlin is going to have to speak to the minister, but there's a holdup there. I don't know what's happening to everyone in Berlin. If this goes wrong you know who'll get the blame." He looked at Gunther with a touch of his old fierceness. "Well, the deal with the commissioner is that you and Syme go to Whitehall, ask this man Fitzgerald's superior about him. Alerting the Dominions Office to the fact they may have a Resistance man in their ranks would be a feather in the Special Branch cap."

"Help them in their turf war with MI5?"

"Exactly." Gessler smiled sourly. "And we in the embassy know all about turf wars, don't we? After that, if you still feel he's the man you want, the two of you can arrest him for questioning."

"Where?" Gunther asked quietly.

"Here, in Senate House. But by both of you. That's as far as I could get the Special Branch Commissioner to go."

Gunther said, "If Fitzgerald knows whatever secret it is that Muncaster is carrying, then Syme will get to know, too."

"Then, as I told you before, Syme will have to be dealt with. If you bring Fitzgerald back here take a gun to the interview," he concluded brutally.

"But how would we explain shooting Syme?"

"That'll be Berlin's problem," Gessler answered brusquely. "They've been quite definite. Any information Muncaster has is for us alone."

Back in his office, Gunther told Syme about the joint questioning. There was a new cockiness about the inspector; the relationship between them had changed, or at least Syme thought it had. Gunther accepted that it might, now, be necessary to dispose of him. Well, the man was trying to play off German and British agencies against each other; he had told his commissioner about the Civil Service angle without mentioning it first to Gunther. He should have realized where that might lead. He's blinded by arrogance, Gunther thought.

"So we're off to Whitehall," Syme said. "They all go home at five, so I'll get the Branch to make an appointment with Fitzgerald's boss first thing tomorrow morning."

Gunther gave him a long, hard look. "Tell him to keep it strictly confidential. Don't mention Fitzgerald's name."

Syme grinned. "We'll see to that."

"What will my role be? A silent sergeant again?" Careful, he thought, don't show too much annoyance.

"No. We thought it might be useful to say the German police are helping us on overseas aspects of the case." Syme smiled, provokingly.

CHAPTER TWENTY-NINE

Early on Friday morning Syme drove Gunther to Whitehall, along the busy central London streets. It was another cold day, the sky blanketed with gray cloud. Gunther asked, "Have you worked on investigations involving government departments before?"

"No. It's MI5 territory still. Though there haven't been any spy cases in Whitehall since that Resistance group in the Home Office a few years ago; and they were double agents. The Whitehall bosses weeded out anyone potentially unreliable years ago. Or thought they had."

"Who is it we're meeting?"

"Fitzgerald's Head of Department. Hubbold. Time-serving old fart heading for retirement, my boss said. Hubbold sounded apprehensive when he got the call. I don't think he'll give us any problems."

"What's he been told?"

"Just that there's some suspicion about one of his department's staff. It's all right, we didn't give Fitzgerald's name."

They drove down Whitehall, past the Cenotaph, stopping on the corner of Downing Street. Going up the steps of the Dominions Office, Gunther looked up at the frieze outside, the Africans and Indians and Imperial figures, all covered now in soot. Syme gave his name to the old janitor at the reception desk, saying they had an appointment with Mr. Hubbold. The old man telephoned his office and told them a clerk would be down in a minute to take them up. He asked them to sign a visitor's book; Gunther made an incomprehensible squiggle. They stood watching the brown-overalled messengers, civil servants in their black jackets and pinstriped trousers. Syme said quietly, "What a crew. Look at those fusty clothes."

Gunther smiled. "Some government servants still look like that in Germany. Though not so many now."

A young clerk appeared and took them upstairs in an ancient, creaking lift. Looking through the grille Gunther saw partitioned rooms, cubbyholes, long, dark passages. They were led to a door with the name Mr. A. *Hubbold* picked out in gold letters. The clerk knocked, and a deep voice called, "Enter."

Syme introduced himself and showed Hubbold his warrant card. Then he introduced Gunther as a German colleague. Hubbold started visibly.

"I didn't know the German authorities were involved here."

Syme said, "Our information on this matter comes from Germany. We are working with our German colleagues."

Hubbold swallowed. "Has the Permanent Secretary been informed?"

"All in good time," Syme replied firmly. Gunther had to admire the way he took control. "For now, sir, you are to keep this matter entirely confidential. As the commissioner told you last night, under the Special Powers Act the security organizations have power to direct any citizen—"

"Yes, I know," Hubbold said quietly. "I cannot believe one of my staff could be involved in—treachery." He drew a deep breath. "Who is it? Who are you investigating?"

"His name is David Fitzgerald."

Hubbold stared at them, eyes still with shock behind his glasses. "Mr. Fitzgerald has an exemplary record," he spluttered.

"How long has he worked for you, sir?" Syme asked.

"Three years. He has always been hardworking, diligent, quiet. A settled family man."

"Do I detect a 'but' in there, sir?" Syme asked, with a little smile.

Hubbold looked down at his hands, which were small and delicate. His jaw worked slightly, then he looked up. "There has been a question raised recently, a problem. Mr. Fitzgerald is—well, potentially involved. But only potentially, it's a problem in Registry, which isn't under my control."

Hubbold told them then about the memorandum that had unaccountably appeared in the secret file. He spoke to Syme but the eyes behind the thick glasses kept wandering to Gunther's impassive face. "It's been my duty to help make inquiries. But it's a Registry issue as I said, the Head of Registry is speaking to the woman officer"—a momentary distaste entered his voice—"in charge of the restricted files room. But the open file, from which the extraneous document came, has been through several hands."

Gunther said, "And Mr. Fitzgerald has clearance for that file, but not the confidential files in Registry."

Hubbold turned and looked at him with his wide, blank gaze. "Correct."

"What was the secret file about?"

Hubbold sat up, clenching his slim-fingered hands together. "I can't say. Not without clearance from the Permanent Secretary—"

"Could we have the Head of Registry up here, and the woman officer, see what they have to say?" Gunther spoke quietly and politely, playing soft policeman to Syme's hard one. "Then perhaps we might talk to Mr. Fitzgerald."

"Now?" Hubbold asked.

"Yes, please," Syme said. "And perhaps you could have Mr. Fitzgerald's personnel file brought up, too."

Gunther added, "I take it, by the way, he is at work today?"

"Yes. I came up in the lift with him this morning."

Gunther turned to Syme, and said mildly, "Perhaps the janitor on the desk could be asked to detain Fitzgerald if he sees him going out."

Syme nodded, and gave Hubbold his nasty smile. "Could you do that, sir? Make those phone calls, now?"

"This is some mistake. Fitzgerald—"

"The phone calls, sir." Syme spoke sharply; he was enjoying bullying the old civil servant. Hubbold picked up the telephone and spoke first to the porter's desk, then the personnel office. Finally he asked Dabb to come up and bring Miss Bennett. A slight tremble had appeared in his deep, even voice.

They waited. Hubbold stared at his hands, clutched together now on his blotter. Faintly, from outside, came the sound of workaday voices. Hubbold reached into his pocket, took out a little silver case, and to

Gunther's surprise emptied two little pyramids of brown powder onto the back of one hand. Syme leaned forward. "What are you doing, sir?"

Hubbold stared back at him. "Taking some snuff. Do you object, officer?"

Syme shrugged, laughing. "I thought that went out with the ark."

"Not at all. Much better for you than cigarettes." Hubbold sniffed up the powder with a snort. He frowned for a moment, then said, "Dabb, the registrar, will tell you that Fitzgerald is rather friendly with this woman officer, Carol Bennett. Just friends, I'm sure, but—well, I should mention it."

There was a knock at the door and a clerk appeared with the personnel file. Hubbold took it and, after a moment's hesitation, passed it across the desk to Syme. He opened it. Gunther bent forward to read. *Works well with colleagues but displays a certain reserve. Rather a lack of ambition.* As well as the wife, Gunther saw, there had been a child, too, but he had died. Fitzgerald's mother was also dead, and his father was in New Zealand. There was a photograph of a young man in military uniform, the same erect pose as in the university photograph. It was typical of the British not to have updated Fitzgerald's photograph since 1940.

Gunther memorized Fitzgerald's home address and looked up to see Hubbold staring at him. "All this is"—Hubbold struggled for a word—"distasteful."

"Treachery is pretty distasteful, sir," Syme said. Hubbold winced.

There was another knock and two people came in, a thin-faced, intelligent-looking woman in her thirties and a stooped old man in an old-fashioned wing collar. Hubbold invited them to sit and they drew up chairs. He introduced Gunther and Syme as being from Special Branch. The old man's mouth set in a firm line, and he gave the woman a quick, angry look. Her eyes widened with fear.

Hubbold spoke first. "This is about the—ah—extraneous paper in that secret file."

Dabb looked aghast. He said, sharply, "How has this become a police matter? The internal investigation hasn't finished yet."

Hubbold shook his head wearily. "I can't say. Only that full cooperation is required of us."

All at once the fight went out of Dabb. He slumped in his chair, then said, with quiet, angry intensity, "All these years, nothing like this has ever happened in my Registry. People don't follow procedures as they should, reprimands have to be issued. But a secret file under my control mishandled. Never!" He shook his head in disbelief.

"You're in overall charge of the confidential files, then?" Syme asked brusquely. "This separate room?"

"I have supervision of the Registry," Dabb replied hesitantly. "But I have to trust my staff to be competent, not to make—gross errors." As he spoke he looked accusingly at the woman. She stared back at him, breathing hard. They're trying to shift the blame onto her, Gunther thought.

"Have you any comments, Miss Bennett?" Syme asked.

"I don't know how the Kenya document came to be in the secret file. I'd never seen it before." She spoke clearly and levelly. She wasn't a particularly attractive woman, Gunther thought, but she was striking, obviously bright.

"So how do you think it got in there?" Dabb asked wearily. "I suppose it decided to go for a little walk."

"I don't know. I swear to that."

Gunther thought, that's true, but there's more to it.

"Can't be many women doing your sort of work," Syme observed. "Wouldn't have thought it was a woman's job, not like teaching or nursing."

He was trying to provoke her but she answered evenly. "I've worked in the service for thirteen years. I have full security clearance. I don't think Mr. Dabb has ever had cause to complain before." She flashed her superior a spirited look.

Dabb made a quick, angry pout. "You're compromised," he said bitterly. "Compromised." He looked at Syme. "I can't believe it's just coincidence that the file this document came from was handled by an officer

Miss Bennett is known to be very friendly with." He looked accusingly at Hubbold. "Your subordinate. Mr. Fitzgerald."

So Dabb had made that connection too, Gunther thought.

"Several others had the file," Hubbold replied, suddenly tetchy.

Carol looked at Syme. "Mr. Fitzgerald has been a friend of mine for years. But only a friend."

"Men and women can't be just friends," Dabb snapped. "It's not in the nature of things."

"Something in that," Syme agreed, raising an eyebrow at Carol. Her face was reddening now. He asked her bluntly, "Do you have an improper relationship with David Fitzgerald?"

She answered firmly. "No."

"They sometimes go to concerts," Dabb said. "It's been department gossip for ages."

Syme's smile became a leer. "Where do you go, eh? Little hotel somewhere?"

"We go to lunchtime concerts, that's all we've ever done," Carol answered. Her voice was trembling. "Inquire as much as you like, ask David—Mr. Fitzgerald. You'll find nothing improper. Nothing. Ever. He's a married man."

Gunther heard the undertone of bitterness and thought, *you wish he wasn't.* He said, "A friendship. Just so. But would Mr. Fitzgerald have had the opportunity, through this friendship, to gain access to secret material?"

Carol looked at him, swallowed, then took a deep breath. "You're German, aren't you? Please, how are you involved in this?"

"That's none of your business," Syme said, harshly. "He's working with me, that's what matters. Answer the question."

"I can't think of any way David could have got access to the file room," she said. "I never discussed my confidential work with him, I wouldn't ever. And he didn't ask me to."

Gunther asked, "What about the keys to the room where the files are kept? You never gave him access to those?"

"Of course not," she answered, her voice desperately sincere. "I always have the keys with me in the office, and if I go out I leave them at the front desk." She looked at them steadily. "It's not fair, you wouldn't be asking these questions if it was a friendship between two men."

Syme laughed. "I could tell you some stories on that subject." Hubbold and Dabb glanced at him with distaste.

Gunther thought, *the keys, people find many ways of making copies of keys.* He said to Carol, "So, the fact one of the few people who had access to this file is a friend of yours — that is just a coincidence?"

"I don't know what it is," she answered vehemently. "I don't understand it."

"Did you and Mr. Fitzgerald ever discuss political matters?"

"No," she answered heavily.

"What would you say his politics were?" Syme asked.

"I don't know."

"And yours?"

"I don't have any." Her voice sounded weary now. "I've a sick mother to look after, my job to do. I don't poke my nose into politics."

There was silence for a moment. Gunther looked at Syme, then said, "I think that's all we need from Miss Bennett for now." He stood up, and the others followed. Gunther smiled at Carol. "Thank you, Miss Bennett."

She looked at him uncertainly, then went out. When the door had closed, Dabb said to Syme, "I've taken her off her usual duties. I'm looking after the secret files myself for now. Is that in order?"

"I think so. For now."

"The Permanent Secretary should be told. At once. Police in the office."

"We'll deal with that." Syme looked at Gunther. "I think he can go too, now?" Gunther nodded agreement again. Syme grinned at Dabb. "Off you go then, matey."

Dabb made a sort of choking sound, then went out quickly. They were left with Hubbold. "Well?" he asked quietly.

"Do people here ever work outside normal hours?" Gunther asked. "At weekends?"

"When necessary." Hubbold hesitated, then added, "Mr. Fitzgerald deals with the Commonwealth High Commissioners' meetings. There's been a lot to do these last few months. He does come in at weekends. I've twitted him about it occasionally, said he shouldn't be leaving his wife alone at home so much."

Gunther said, "I think we'd like to see Mr. Fitzgerald now. On his own. Could you leave us for a while?"

"This is my office," Hubbold answered with unexpected stubbornness.

Syme said. "Tell you what, why don't you go down and get Fitzgerald for us? Fetch him from his desk?"

Hubbold set his lips, then stood up. He clenched his hands, as though he would have liked to strike them, then said, "Very well," stiffly, and left the room.

When the door shut Syme said, "There's something fishy between Fitzgerald and that woman. I can smell it."

Gunther said, "I don't think she gave him access to that room. But I think he got access through her, got hold of her keys though I can't work out how."

"He was with the secret files at the weekend and got some papers mixed up?"

"That would make sense."

"What do we do when they come back? Get rid of that old fool and then arrest Fitzgerald?"

"Yes, I think so."

"What about arresting the woman, too?"

"No. Not yet." Gunther looked at Syme. "Let's not make too many waves. Just Fitzgerald. We'll take him back to Senate House, interview him."

"Interrogation German-style?" Syme asked.

"Just ordinary questioning to start with," Gunther answered wearily. "Then we'll see."

Syme shrugged, then looked seriously at Gunther. "Resistance spies going through secret government files. This could be big."

"I know."

The door opened. Hubbold stood framed in the doorway, his face red, his white hair wild, eyes more enormous than ever behind his glasses. He spoke in a rush. "He's gone. Fitzgerald's gone. I went to his office and he wasn't there. I phoned the porter. He said Fitzgerald came down in his hat and coat, the porter told him I wanted him to stay in the Office but he just walked out. He ignored my order. He's gone." Then, with sudden emotion he hit the side of the door and wailed, "He's betrayed me."

CHAPTER THIRTY

That morning David was preparing the agenda for the next High Commissioners' meeting. When he came into the office Carol was not yet at her desk. He had been very worried by the telephone call last night; he didn't know whether she was looking for a shoulder to cry on after being questioned about the missing file, or had somehow guessed at his own involvement. He had been horrified to realize Sarah thought he was having an affair.

Last night they had gone out to Steve and Irene's house. David and Sarah had both been anxious and preoccupied. Over dinner Irene had rattled on about Christmas arrangements, how the children were doing at school, the cold weather, all the while looking sharply between David and Sarah, sensing something was wrong. Steve had been put on his best behavior and neither politics nor the deportations were mentioned, though Irene spoke about some trouble at Wandsworth; a crowd of Jive Boys had torn up the seats of a concert hall where one of the new rock 'n' roll bands from America were performing. "They're talking about banning any more of those records coming in from America."

"So they should," Steve agreed. "The Jive Boys are always fighting. Bunch of louts. They look like queers in those long frock-coat things, but they behave like thugs."

"And the Blackshirts don't?" David asked.

"Now," said Irene quickly, to stop the discussion getting out of hand. "Everyone agrees the Jive Boys aren't political, they just like making trouble with anyone."

After eating they watched a television comedy program with Frankie Howerd, which made David want to scream with boredom. As they got their coats to leave Steve told them he was going on a business trip to

Germany after Christmas. "Linz," he said. "The Führer's home town. Another new building project."

David didn't rise to the bait. He and Sarah drove home in chilly silence. As they turned into their street David said, "I'm not having an affair with that woman. I wish you'd believe me."

"I wish that too," Sarah answered sadly. "But I can't."

It was hard to give any attention to work that morning. Just before ten his telephone rang. "Fitzgerald," he answered abruptly.

"David?" He recognized Carol's voice. It sounded strained, breathless.

"Yes?"

"David, I'll have to be quick. Something's happened."

"What—"

"I'm phoning from an office along the corridor. It's empty, but someone may come in. Please listen, there isn't time." She spoke urgently. "I've just left a meeting with Dabb and your boss, Mr. Hubbold. There were"—David heard her take a deep breath—"there were two policemen present as well. They said they were from Special Branch but one was a German. There was a document in one of the restricted files that shouldn't have been there, it came from a file you'd been handling." Her voice quickened. "Hubbold reported it to Dabb and he was trying to blame me—"

David's heart was beating fast. He said, "Was this what you wanted to talk about last night?"

"Yes. David, please listen. The policemen, they wanted to know about our—friendship. They think I might have given you access to the secret room. I told them we were just friends, you hadn't asked me for anything. But there was a file open on Hubbold's desk, I saw your name. I think it's your personnel file. I'm ringing to warn you, they might call you up."

David forced himself to speak calmly. "How are Special Branch involved in this? And the German?" He thought, this has to be because of Frank, somehow he's led them to me.

"I don't know. But I had to warn you. I don't know what's going to happen." Carol's voice faltered again. "Don't tell me, if you've been doing something you shouldn't, I don't want to know—"

He said, "Carol, I'm sorry—"

"Don't tell me anything." Her voice was a sudden urgent hiss. "I can't tell them what I don't know. You're a good man, David." She spoke in a softer tone. "Whatever you did would be for good motives, I know that." Then she said sadly, "You know what I've always felt about you. You do, don't you? I could tell."

He didn't answer. He couldn't.

There was a moment's silence. Then Carol said, very quietly, "They won't be able to find evidence against me, because there isn't any. Even if you go away." He didn't answer. "You're going to go away, aren't you? No, don't answer that, don't."

"Carol—"

"You have to do what you think is right. You're a *good* man, David." The line went dead.

He put the phone down, shocked. Then his mind clicked into the routine he had learned, what to do if there was an emergency at work, if it looked as though he had been discovered. Leave the office at once, go to a public telephone and ring a number he had memorized a long time ago. He stood abruptly. If he left, he knew, Carol would be in deeper trouble. She had loved him and he had used her and still she was trying to save him.

Sarah. She was in danger too; everyone was if they caught him. He looked at the door. Now the moment had come; Hubbold, everyone he knew in the Office, was an enemy, a potential captor. And two policemen here, one a German. He grabbed his coat and hat from behind the door, picked up his briefcase and umbrella. Rapidly, he walked the two floors down to the vestibule; he wanted to run but knew that would attract attention. As he crossed the lobby he heard Sykes, the porter, call out, urgently: "Mr. Fitzgerald! Mr. Hubbold said you were to wait." David didn't stop or turn, just walked steadily to the exit. An elderly cleaner in flowered housecoat and headscarf stared at him over her mop.

"Mr. Fitzgerald!" Sykes was shouting now. "Please, wait!"

He went through the doors, down the steps to the street, then ran all the way down Whitehall.

*   *   *

He found a telephone box on the corner of Trafalgar Square. It smelled of urine. He found some pennies in his pocket and dialed the number he had memorized. He stood, waiting to press Button A. The phone rang and rang but nobody answered.

He felt panic clawing at him. Had the police already got the people on the other end, was this part of a general sweep? It couldn't be, surely, or they would just have come and taken him, not involved Hubbold and Dabb first. The number cut out suddenly. He dialed again. He was holding the heavy black receiver so tightly his hand hurt. Again nobody answered. He slammed the phone down and stood staring through the dirty windows of the telephone box at the people walking by in the gray morning, the dirty pigeons fluttering around the foot of Nelson's Column. Absurdly, he felt afraid to leave the box, as though it were some sort of refuge. Then he thought, *I have to get to Sarah. They'll know where I live, they'll go there, but I have to try.* That was against orders but something must have happened; he was on his own now. He dialed his home number. He remembered the daily woman did not come on Fridays; Sarah would be alone. He would tell her to leave at once and meet him in town. Again, though, the number just rang and rang. At the thought she might have already been arrested his legs trembled and David had to lean against the cold, damp wall of the box. He told himself she could just have gone to the shops, she usually did once a day. He had to go to her. He knew it could be dangerous, there could be police watching the house, but he had to. He dialed the number again but there was still no reply. He pressed Button B to get his pennies back—he might need them—and stepped out of the telephone box. He noticed for the first time how cold it was. He walked toward the Tube station, only feeling relief when he disappeared into the anonymity of the Underground.

Although he took the Tube to work every day, it was years since he had used it in the middle of a weekday. The last time had been when Charlie died. That had been wintertime too; it had snowed heavily and the trains had been delayed. He had felt sick on the journey and when he got home he had slipped on the path and fallen and then somehow he couldn't get up, his limbs wouldn't move. Sarah had seen him and come to help him, letting go of Charlie's body at last.

Someone had left a copy of *The Times* on a neighboring seat. He picked it up. On the front page was a report of a meeting between Himmler and his East European allies, a picture of him with the leaders of Slovakia, Romania, Croatia, Bulgaria. One of the leaders was a large fat man with a slab of a face and a downturned mouth, wearing a clerical collar. That must be Tiso, the Slovak Prime Minister Natalia had told him about. Natalia, who attracted him. Carol, who stirred nothing in him. Sarah, his wife. What would happen to them all now? He put his head in his hands. *Don't think,* he told himself. *Try to stay cold and clear.* He looked down at the briefcase between his legs. He had picked it up by instinct. He would probably never use it again, never see the Office again, never again be part of an ordinary crowd of bowler-hatted commuters.

He got out at Kenton Station. Walking home he looked around for anything unusual, fearing the sound of quickening footsteps coming behind him, tensed, ready to run. He remembered his father saying once, after a big criminal trial, that he could never understand why anyone took to a life of crime, living in constant fear of a policeman's hand on their shoulder. Now David understood: he was a criminal himself.

The house, the whole street, was quiet in the winter morning. He let himself in carefully, leaving the front door ajar in case the police were here and he had to turn and run. But the house was silent, the only sound the clock ticking steadily in the kitchen. Had Sarah been in she would have heard him and come out, but she didn't. David walked from room to room, frightened of what he might see each time he opened a door, but the house was neat and still. He noticed that the telephone book had been taken out of its basket and lay on the telephone table, beside his mother's vase. He closed the front door and sat in the lounge, waiting for Sarah to return, watching the street from the window. He thought, this is crazy, the police could come at any time. But he couldn't leave Sarah, not now. It was utterly quiet in the house. He thought, this is what it must be like for Sarah all the time when she's at home alone; silence, and the memory of Charlie. If she had gone to the shops she should be back in half an hour at most. He opened the back door, then returned to the lounge; if he saw anyone coming in at the gate he would run out the back, try getting over the fence. Or would it be best to let them take him? Would that stop them being interested in Sarah? But what about the others in his cell, Geoff and Jackson and Natalia and the man from the India Office? He didn't think he could hold out if they tortured him.

Half an hour passed. He had been pacing the room impatiently and now he went into the hall and dialed Irene's number. She answered almost at once. He tried to make his voice casual. "It's David here. I've had to come home, I'm not very well. Sarah isn't here. Any idea where she might be?"

"Goodness," Irene said. "Is it something serious? Can I help at all?"

"A bad stomach, I've been sick. I'm just a bit puzzled Sarah isn't home."

"I'm sorry, David, I've no idea where she is. She hasn't got one of her meetings, has she?"

"No. Not today."

He ended the call and stood irresolutely in the hall. He thought of ringing the contact number again but he mustn't do that from home, since this number was probably already tapped. He shouldn't even have rung Irene. He remembered the miniature camera and the copy of the key to the secret room were upstairs. He went and got them, then put on his hat and went out again. There was a telephone box outside Kenton Station. He would try the contact number again from there. He might even meet Sarah coming back.

But he didn't see her. He went into the phone box, rang the number again and this time a male voice answered at once. The pips went and he pressed the button, relief flooding through him. He said quickly, "This is Fitzgerald, David Fitzgerald. The police have come to the office, about a document I misfiled. Two of them, one's a German—"

The man seemed to know who David was and asked sharply, "Where are you?" It was a young voice, with a strong Cockney accent.

"In a phone box near my home. In Kenton. A colleague told me the police were with my boss, so I left the office at once. The janitor tried to stop me but I got out."

"Shit."

"I tried to phone you from near the Office over an hour ago, but there was no answer."

"I had to go out, I was only ten minutes. I shouldn't have—hell! Why did you go home?" The voice was loud, suddenly accusing.

"I was worried about my wife. She's not home, I don't know where she is."

"Is your house all right? Any sign anyone's been there?"

"No. I waited, I thought she'd gone to the shops." David took a deep breath. "What do I do? I was told if anything happened you'd protect my wife."

The voice became quieter, almost soothing. "Okay. We need to get you somewhere safe. Go to the safe house, now. We'll send someone up to Kenton, to watch the house and pick up your wife when she gets back."

"And Geoff. Geoff Drax—"

"We'll phone him, and the others in your cell. I'll arrange it all now. But you have to get yourself to your safe house. At once."

David took a deep breath. "All right. I'm at the Tube station now."

"Good. The Underground's the safest way to travel. We've got your home address, we'll send someone in a car to wait at your house for your wife."

"I'm on my way."

David left the telephone box and stood uncertainly in the station entrance. A woman looked at him curiously. He tried to pull himself together. He thought, how do I know they're telling the truth, that they'll really send someone for Sarah? But he had to trust them now, there was no one and nothing else. He understood suddenly how much of him, all this time, had remained anchored to the world he had been brought up in and longed, deep inside, to believe still existed: Britain, his country, dull and self-absorbed, ironic even about its own prejudices. But that Britain was gone, had instead turned into a place where an authoritarian government in league with Fascist thugs thrived on nationalist dreams of Empire, on scapegoats and enemies. And he was now, irrevocably, an enemy.

CHAPTER THIRTY-ONE

After David left for work on Friday, Sarah, alone in the house, couldn't settle. She still didn't believe his denials about Carol; surely if he had nothing to hide he would have explained, been open, but instead he had drawn himself in even more and so, in response, had she. That morning she was due to begin chasing up the toyshops, ensuring they were making up the toy parcels for the unemployed, but she couldn't face it. She hadn't opened her case with the files in it since Tottenham Court Road.

She went and sat in the lounge, trying to read her *Woman's Own* which had been delivered that morning. It was cold but she couldn't be bothered to lay the fire. She felt restless all over, she couldn't settle. She had a desperate urge to do something, anything. She went into the hall and took the telephone directory from its rack. She remembered, from meeting Carol at the last office social, that she lived with her mother somewhere in North London. She found the entry almost at once: *Bennett, Mrs. D and Miss C, 17 Lovelock Road, Highgate.* That had to be her. She thought, she'll be at work now. I'll go around there, I'll go this evening, I'll deal with this once and for all. And in the meantime she had to get out of the house.

She fetched her hat and coat and went to the door. Opening it, she stopped dead for a second, thinking, if I do this, it really could be the end for me and David. She stood still, clutching the door handle. She considered telephoning Irene, but she knew her sister would try to talk her around. *I can't go on like this*, she thought, *I'll go mad.*

Sarah went out, closing the door firmly, and walked up the road, deciding to catch the Tube into town, try to find something that might distract her. It was very cold under the leaden sky. She had a vague idea of going to visit the Tower of London, but when the Tube reached Tottenham Court Road, on an impulse she got out. She had to see the scene of those deaths and shootings again, as though somehow that might help her understand the horrible madness she felt was all around her.

But at the scene of the riot it was as though nothing had happened. Cars and buses drove down the street as usual, over the spot where Mrs. Templeman had died. The streets were full of women Christmas shopping—all the shop windows were full of colored paper chains and little Christmas trees in pots. She stopped in front of one of the big stores, realizing it was one that was helping with the toy appeal. A big wooden dummy in a Santa Claus outfit stood in the window, with painted red cheeks and a white false beard. A woman in a fake-fur coat, a grizzling child holding each hand, almost barged into her, and snapped, "Would you please look where you're going?"

"I'm sorry," Sarah said, but the woman ignored her and passed on. Sarah thought how the shoppers all looked cross and anxious. It was what Christmas did to people, perhaps it always had but she had never really noticed before. Charlie had loved the tree they had bought for his last Christmas, decorated with tiny colored bulbs. They said Christmas was for children but really it was supposed to be about celebrating the birth of Jesus, who would later sacrifice himself. She remembered her desperate prayer in Westminster Abbey. Since then things had only got worse.

Sarah went into the shop, to get out of the cold as much as anything. The big vestibule was filled with toys. They were much more expensive than when she had last bought presents for Charlie three years before. She passed a display of dolls' houses. On the opposite side of the aisle were boxes of tin soldiers, *A treat for every boy*. There was a display of the soldiers arranged as for battle on a papier-mâché field. There were German soldiers in smart gray painted uniforms and coal-scuttle helmets, with minute swastika armbands. On the other side of the hill stood a small group of Russians in dull green, little rips and tears painted on their uniforms.

"Mrs. Fitzgerald?" The voice at her elbow made her jump, as any little thing seemed to these days. She turned and saw a small, thin man in his late fifties, with sparse gray hair and kindly eyes; she recognized the manager of the store, who had attended a couple of committee meetings at Friends House.

"Mr. Fielding, hello." She extended a gloved hand.

"I'm sorry if I startled you."

"I was in a bit of a brown study."

"Looking for Christmas presents?"

"I might get something for my nephews. Everything seems terribly expensive these days."

He nodded sadly. "It's a shame. I often see people going around the store then walking out again empty-handed, looking disappointed."

"It's very good of your shop to help with our work."

"We like to do what we can for those who can't afford anything. It's all on track with your order, by the way, it will be delivered to Friends House on time." He sighed. "If only there weren't all these terrorist attacks and strikes, that's what's stopping the country getting back on its feet. I hear the railwaymen are coming out now."

Sarah could have argued but she didn't have the heart. And Mr. Fielding was a decent, generous man. She said, "It's very cold out, isn't it?"

"Yes. If it goes on like this we might get a white Christmas." He paused a moment, then said, "I was sorry to hear about poor Mrs. Templeman. I couldn't get to the funeral, but we sent some flowers."

"I saw them. That was kind."

"A sudden heart attack, I believe. Well, there are worse ways to go." He looked sad for a moment, and Sarah wondered if he was a Great War veteran, like her father. He smiled. "She was a character, wasn't she?"

"She was a very selfless woman."

"Well, I must carry on with my rounds. Good morning, Mrs. Fitzgerald."

Sarah watched as he went off down the store, nodding at the assistants as he passed the tills. His gentle touch had brought tears to her eyes. She went back out, into the cold.

*   *   *

She had lunch in a cafe, then went to the National Portrait Gallery and spent an hour with the pictures of kings and queens and statesmen. The gallery was almost empty, uniformed janitors dozing in dim corners. She came to the section where portraits of modern leaders were displayed. Although the gallery was dedicated to English portraits, a picture of Adolf Hitler was prominent. It had been painted about five years ago, before the Führer became so ill. He wore a brown double-breasted jacket, standing with one hand on a globe of the world, the blue eyes under the gray forelock gazing into the distance, contemplating destiny. He had spent twenty years building a world of blood and fear and there seemed no end to it, ever.

She walked the streets for an age, thinking again how normal everything looked, as though nothing had happened the week before. She looked at her watch. Half past three. Her resolve was weakening; it would be so easy just to go home. She thought, I'll go to Highgate now, wait in a cafe or something. She walked to Embankment Tube, stopping at a newsagent to buy a London A–Z. She found Carol's street and saw it was close to Highgate Station.

She stood on the platform, waiting for the train. Workmen were altering the Underground maps. There were black circles around several east London Tube stations, Bethnal Green and Whitechapel and Stepney Green, and the men were painting on the words *Closed to the General Public*. She thought, those were Jewish areas, maybe the Blackshirts are looting their houses and don't want people to see.

The train came and rattled slowly up to Highgate. When she came out into the street the gloomy winter's day was already starting to fade toward dusk. She took a deep breath and then, A–Z in hand, went to find Lovelock Road.

It was a street of Victorian terraced houses, tall lime trees on the edge of the pavement, small front gardens behind dusty privet hedges. She walked up the even-numbered side of the street until she was opposite Number 17, then stopped and looked across. The privet hedge was neatly clipped, net curtains over the windows. She walked further up the street,

then slowly back down again. There was little traffic. A milk-float put-
tered along behind her, crates rattling on the back.

She stopped again in front of the house. She felt as she had in Tottenham Court Road, that she needed to see the place, but it was just an
ordinary suburban home. She realized again how cold it was. She was
wearing her old brown coat, and hoped the Jewish girl, Ruth, was still
wearing her new one, somewhere safe.

The front door of the house opened suddenly and a little old woman
stood in the doorway, glaring at Sarah. She wore a grubby housecoat and
had a wrinkled face and angry eyes. Her bushy white hair was unbrushed.
She advanced down the path with quick, jerky steps, keeping those wild
eyes fixed on Sarah's. She thought with horror, it's Carol's mother. She
knows who I am, she knows everything.

The old woman threw open the gate and walked across the road
without looking to see if there were any cars. She planted herself a few
feet from Sarah, staring up at her. "I've been watching you," she shouted
furiously in a fluting upper-class voice. "I'm not as stupid as you think I
am. You want to take me away, don't you?"

"No. I was—"

"Anyone can get taken away these days, I know! Well, my daughter
won't let you. She steals things, I know that, but she won't let you take
me away! Do you understand?"

Sarah realized the woman was senile, half mad. She looked into her
blazing eyes. "It's all right," she said calmly. "I'll go." She stepped away.
The old woman remained where she was, arms folded across her thin
chest. Sarah turned and walked a few paces before turning to look back.
The woman was still standing in the road. Sarah called, "Be careful! A
car might come!"

"You mind your own fucking business, damned snooping cow." The
sudden tirade of abuse sounded even more deranged in that cultivated
voice. Sarah walked on a few more steps and when she turned back again
the old woman was stumbling back across the road to her house. Sarah
realized her legs were shaking.

*   *   *

She went back to the station. She was exhausted, freezing cold. It was starting to get properly dark, the streetlights coming on. Next to the station she saw a cafe, yellow light visible through the steamed-up window. She walked in, desperate to get warm. It was what they called a greasy spoon, tired-looking old men in caps sitting at tables covered with black-and-white oilcloth reading the *Mail* or *Express*, a couple of bored-looking boys in their teens with quiffed greasy hair. The air was thick with steam and cigarette smoke. A big old-fashioned radio played music from the Light Program. She went to the counter where a fat man in an apron stood under a framed portrait of the Queen, and ordered a cup of tea and a bun. The man looked at her curiously, as this wasn't the sort of place a woman of her class came to; but Sarah didn't care, it was any port in a storm. She took her tea and found an empty table. The boys stared rudely at her. She looked away.

She sat for nearly two hours, drinking several cups of the strong, sweet tea. Nobody spoke to her, and the boys went after a time. She felt oddly relieved to be in a place where no one knew her. She thought about the mad old woman and found herself actually pitying Carol, who must have to deal with her day in, day out. On the other side of the steamed-up window it was quite dark now, passersby vague shadows in the gloom. She looked at her watch. It was a quarter to seven; David would be on his way home now, he would return to an empty house. It was a strange thought. She could telephone and say she had gone into town, been held up somewhere. But the obstinacy that had come over her that morning still gripped her.

She left the cafe. It was even colder and there was a faint sulfurous tang in the air now, though no fog. She walked slowly back to Lovelock Road: Carol might be home by now. She stood in front of the house; the curtains were drawn but she could see several lights on. She shrank from the thought of going and ringing the doorbell, maybe finding herself face to face with the mad old woman again. But she made herself walk up the path and, with a deep breath, pulled the old-fashioned bell cord.

It was Carol who came to the door. Sarah recognized her at once. She wore a roll-neck sweater and baggy slacks. She looked red-eyed, as though she had been crying. She stared blankly at Sarah for a second, then a look of alarm crossed her face. "Mrs. Fitzgerald?"

Sarah felt the blood pounding in her ears, but forced herself to speak firmly and calmly. "Yes. Miss Bennett, I'm very sorry, but I need to speak to you urgently."

She thought there might be some sort of argument on the doorstep but Carol just quietly said, "Come in," and stood aside to let her enter. Sarah saw her look quickly up and down the road before she closed the door. Inside, the hallway was full of heavy old-fashioned furniture. A voice called out from behind a closed door, "Who is it, Carol? What do they want?"

"It's all right, Mother. Stay there, I'll bring your dinner in a minute."

"What's happening?" The elderly voice quavered. "Something's happened, Carol, I saw from your face when you came in!"

Carol shouted, "Mother! Just wait!" Sarah was frightened the door would open and the old woman would come out raving again but she didn't. Red-faced now, Carol opened another door and ushered Sarah into a cold front room.

"Please, have a seat," Carol said quietly. "Can I offer you a sherry?"

Sarah sat in a big armchair with white crocheted antimacassars. She said, with cold formality, "No, thank you." On a big table in the window, next to an aspidistra, stood several framed photographs, the largest showing a young officer in naval uniform.

Carol sat on a settee opposite her. "What's happened?" Her voice was sharp with anxiety.

"I beg your pardon?" Sarah stared at her.

"To David—Mr. Fitzgerald—please, what happened to him?"

Sarah frowned. "Nothing, so far as I know he's home by now. What on earth do you mean?" Her own voice was rising now. She began to feel uneasy. Something was going on here she didn't understand.

Carol asked abruptly, "Then why have you come?"

"Why did you telephone my house last night? I was by the phone, I heard what you said. Why did you want to meet my husband today?"

Carol looked down. Sarah could see the woman was fighting for control. She took a deep breath. "I need to know what is going on between you and my husband."

Carol raised her head. She looked embarrassed, her face flushed. "What do you mean?"

"I've known something was going on for a while. I found a concert ticket with your name in his pocket. Then you rang last night. Was it because I answered that you said there was a problem at work?"

Carol clasped her hands in her lap, looked down at the floor for a long moment. Then she looked at Sarah and said, slowly, "Mrs. Fitzgerald, there is nothing going on between me and David. I'll be honest, I do have—feelings—for him, I have for a long time. He doesn't return them, but I've been fooling myself for quite a while." She gave a quick whinny of a laugh. "Isn't it strange, here we are sitting talking about it. I've often wished you didn't exist, you know, or even that you'd die." Her look was so intense Sarah wondered if Carol might be a little unhinged, too, like her mother.

"At least that's honest," she said flatly.

"David's a good man. Believe me, I've met plenty who aren't." She frowned. "Did you come around here earlier this afternoon? My mother said a woman was watching the house."

"Yes. Yes, that was me."

Carol said, "When she told me that, I was frightened. So it was because of the phone call you decided to come around. Was that the only reason?"

"Yes. What other reason could there be? Miss Bennett, why did you ask whether something had happened to David?"

Carol stood and walked over to the table. She ran her hand along the top of the naval officer's photograph and Sarah wondered if he was her father; there was a resemblance. Carol turned and looked at Sarah. "Something happened at the office today. I'm in charge of the room where the confidential files are kept, secret files. A few days ago a document turned up in one of our files that shouldn't have been there. Today I was questioned about it by the police." She looked away. "You see, they all know David and I are friends at the office, they laugh about it. And today I was called in to be interviewed by these two policemen. They asked whether we"—her voice stumbled—"whether David and I—well, I told them I hadn't, which is true."

"Policemen?" Sarah asked, aghast.

"They said they were from Special Branch. But one of them was German. They asked whether I'd given David access to my files, though I didn't do that, I wouldn't. I may be—what do they call it—a lovelorn old spinster but I'm not that lovelorn." A thought seemed to strike Carol and she frowned. "But maybe David thought I was, maybe that's why he became friendly with me."

Fear washed through Sarah then, from her head to her feet, like cold water. A German. "Are you saying that you—that they—think he's some sort of spy?"

"They had his personnel file on the desk. After they let me go I phoned David, I had to warn him. They don't send Germans along just for nothing, do they? I didn't ask him if he'd done anything, I didn't want to know. But he didn't deny it." She shook her head sadly. "He didn't really say anything."

Sarah asked, quietly, "Did you and my husband ever meet in the evening?"

"No. Never. I swear."

"He's been going somewhere. For over a year. He said he went to play tennis and I've been getting—suspicious." Her voice tailed away.

Carol leaned forward. "You have to help him now."

"Good God." Sarah closed her eyes. "Did they call David in for questioning?"

"I don't know. I said he should leave but I don't know what happened after that."

"So they could have arrested him?"

"I don't know. All I know is that Mr. Dabb, my boss, said the police would want to speak to me again tomorrow; they'll contact me."

"So David might be under arrest?"

"I tell you, I don't know. But if he got out—wouldn't he come home?"

"I've been out all day." Sarah didn't add, *because of you.* "I should go home, he may be there."

"Yes," Carol agreed quickly. "Even if he's not there, he may telephone you."

Sarah looked at her. It was strange, now they were on the same side. She asked, "Why did you help him today? You're putting yourself at risk."

"I know he's a good man. If he does something it's because he believes it's right."

"Would you believe it's right? For a civil servant to spy against the government?"

Carol smiled sadly. "I don't know anything about politics. And David and I never discussed it. You don't, in the Service, unless you know someone well. I don't like a lot of the things that are happening now, some of them I hate. But I have to get by. Isn't that how it is for most people, they just want—need—to get by? My mother—well, you've seen what she's like. And if the alternative to Beaverbrook and Mosley's a revolution I'm not sure I'd want that either. I'm not brave, not like David."

Sarah said, "I've always been a pacifist. I don't like the Resistance violence. But things lately—"

"Yes. The Jews, the deportations and violence, it's awful." Carol paused and then asked, "Do you think David could be a spy?"

"It might explain a lot." Sarah stood up suddenly. "I should go now."

Carol took a step toward her, then stopped. She rubbed a hand across her forehead. "I don't know if I should have told you. But I had to. Will you tell him I've spoken to you?"

"I think I must, now." It was Sarah's turn to laugh. "I made myself come here, I was determined to get the truth, but you often get more than you bargain for if you do that, don't you?"

Carol smiled sadly. "Yes. But you—you have to help him now."

"Yes, I do." Sarah looked at Carol. She didn't feel anger now. She realized that in different circumstances she and this woman might have been friends. But when Carol impulsively extended a hand Sarah shook her head quickly. She knew Carol would have taken David from her if she could.

Carol showed her out. On the doorstep she said, "Good luck. To both of you."

Sarah nodded. She turned away, then looked back and said, "Thank you."

Sarah went home. The rush hour was over, the carriages only half full. She stared unseeingly at the tunnel walls. The idea that David was working for the Resistance fitted with the facts. She felt rage toward him, fury at all he had kept from her if this was true, the danger he had placed them both in. Then she thought of him lying in a police station somewhere, maybe even in Senate House where they said the SS tortured people, and the thought of him in a cell, bruised and broken, made her want to scream out loud.

She arrived at Kenton Station and walked home. Now, for the first time, she began to observe, to calculate. She thought, the house might be watched. If it was there would be someone in a car outside or very close. What would she do if there was? She realized there would be no point in running, they'd soon catch her and running would be a sign of guilt. No, she would go back to the house. But what if David wasn't there? He might have come while she was out. She would look and see if he had taken any clothes. Then what? She would have to throw herself on Irene's mercy. Then she thought of Geoff, steady, reliable Geoff. If David wasn't there she would go to Pinner.

There were a few cars parked at the roadside but none close to the house and none seemed occupied, though it was hard to be sure in the dim yellow streetlight. No lights were on in the house, none of the curtains drawn. She unlocked the door and went in. All was silent and still. The London telephone directory lay on the hall table where she had left it that morning. She went into the kitchen and switched on the light. Then she screamed.

Two men were sitting at the kitchen table; they had been waiting for her in the dark. She saw that the back door had been broken open. One of the men was in his thirties, tall and thin, with a mean, hard face. The other was older, plump, with sad, pouchy features and untidy fair hair. He looked at her with cold, light blue eyes: a horribly penetrating stare. Then he spoke, in what Sarah recognized at once was a German accent; not angrily but somehow sadly. "Good evening, Mrs. Fitzgerald."

CHAPTER THIRTY-TWO

At Kenton Station David found himself reluctant to go in; he knew the Resistance people would have a far better chance of rescuing Sarah, but he felt that leaving now would be his final betrayal of her, as well as a final departure from his old life.

He had never been to Soho during the day before. It seemed grayer, more ordinary—narrow streets, now filled with markets selling fruit and vegetables. The coffee bar beside the alley was closed; the alley itself looked even dingier in daylight. The door with the two bells beside it had, he saw, once been green but most of the paint had flaked away long ago, revealing strong old planks. He pressed Natalia's bell.

There was no answer. He waited and rang again but still no footsteps sounded on the stairs. He tried the door but it was locked. An old man in a threadbare overcoat, bent with age, shuffled down the alley and gave David a look of dislike as he passed; he must have thought him a client for the prostitute. David felt panic rising again, wondering whether something had happened here, too. He wished he didn't look so conspicuous in his overcoat, pinstripe trousers, and bowler hat.

Eventually footsteps clattered down the stairs inside. The door half opened and the prostitute peered around the frame at him. She wore an expensive-looking silk dressing gown, her red hair curling around her face. "You've woken me, ringing the bell like that." She spoke crossly, then she recognized him and her face became suddenly alert.

"Dilys, I need to speak to Natalia—"

"She's just gone to the shops. Is something the matter?"

"I need to see her urgently."

The girl thought a moment, then said, "Come up."

David followed her up the creaking stairs, into a poky little bedroom dominated by a large, unmade double bed and a dressing table covered with pots and powders. The room was separated from the rest of the flat by a flimsy-looking door. It stank of cheap scent and cigarette smoke and was stiflingly hot, a gas fire hissing away in the corner. The girl sat on a hard chair at the dressing table and waved David to the bed. "Sit down." She turned to the partition, and to David's surprise, shouted "Helen!" A middle-aged woman in an apron came through the inner door. Dilys said, "We're out of tea, love. Go and get some, will you? Get some groceries as well, take your time."

The woman gave David a stony look. "Be all right, will you?"

" 'Course I will. This one's a shy boy, aren't you?"

With a doubtful look at David, the old woman left. Dilys smiled archly. "First time you've been in a place like this?"

"Yes — yes, it is."

She nodded at the door. "Helen, she's my maid. We girls always have an older woman working with us, to help us, keep us safe. Helen doesn't know about next door." Dilys took a deep breath. "Something's up, isn't it? I can see by your face."

"I'm afraid so."

"Am I going to have to go?"

"I don't know. I'm afraid they're on to me."

Dilys looked sad. "Luck always runs out in the end, doesn't it?" She spoke quietly. "Just give me fair warning when I have to go, will you ask them that? I'm okay for money, but I'll have to look after Helen till we find somewhere else. I don't want her in the clutches of the bloody Blackshirts."

"I'll tell them."

"Thanks. Don't say any more," Dilys added quickly. "It's best I know as little as possible."

"Yes," he agreed. It was just what Carol had said to him over the telephone.

"You can only tell what you know. Would you like a cup of tea?" Her tone was suddenly cheerful again. Poor girl, David thought, she must have to put on a cheery face all the time.

"No—no, thank you."

She glanced at him wistfully. "Nice-looking chap like you, bet you can get it whenever you want, eh? Don't need the likes of me." David felt himself blush. "I see you've a wedding ring. Bet you're the faithful sort." Her manner was bantering now, trying to keep her spirits up. "You got any Maltese blood in you?" she asked suddenly.

"Not that I know of."

"You remind me a bit of my Guido. The bastards deported him two years ago. England for the English, as they say. And for the Germans and Italians, of course," she added bitterly. "That's when I joined up with you people. They put me here, to keep an eye out for you."

"Thank you," David said.

Dilys opened a drawer of the dressing table and pulled out a bottle of gin and two smeared glasses. "Want one?"

"I'd better keep a clear head." David realized he hadn't eaten since breakfast. "You haven't any food, have you?"

"I'll see what there is."

She went through the inner door, returning with some cold ham and bread and butter. David took it eagerly. Dilys sat at the dressing table, watching him eat while she swigged back her gin, the hand holding the glass trembling slightly. When he had finished she said, "Should I get ready to open up today?" He looked at her blankly and she laughed. "For business. I usually open up at five, and it's nearly four now."

"I think—maybe better not. There may be more of us coming."

She took a deep breath. "I'll put a note on the door, say I'm ill. I've a couple of Friday regulars, they'll be disappointed but it can't be helped. Oh well, it'll save me the trouble of getting ready, won't it?"

David looked at her curiously. "How did you get into—into this?"

She frowned. "Shock you, does it?"

"No. It's just—I never—"

She smiled again. "You're quite an innocent thing, aren't you? My dad died at Dunkirk, he wasn't one of the ones that got away. My mum went to pieces, turned to drink. We hadn't any money. A friend got me into this game."

He looked around the room. "Isn't it—well—dangerous?"

She laughed suddenly. "You're asking, is what *I* do dangerous? That's the pot calling the kettle black if ever I heard it."

It was fifteen minutes before footsteps sounded again on the stairs. Dilys sat up, looking relieved. "That's Natalia." She went out and David heard the two women talking quietly. They came back into the flat together. Natalia wore an old gray coat and hat and carried a shopping bag; she looked dowdy and ordinary beside Dilys's colorful femininity. David thought it was probably a look she cultivated deliberately, so as not to be noticed. It was sad she had to. His heart had leapt at the sight of her but then sank again as he thought of Sarah, out there somewhere, in grave danger.

Natalia looked at him, then said quietly, "Come through. Dilys, I'll tell you what's happening as soon as I know."

They went back to Natalia's flat. It smelled of paint as usual, but she had taken most of the pictures down, stacking them against the walls. Only the striking battle scene remained, the dead soldiers lying in the snow with the high white mountains in the distance. The room was cold. Natalia followed David's gaze. "Yes," she said in a low voice. "I'm packing up, I'll have to leave too. This is very serious."

He turned to her. "I'm sorry."

She smiled wanly. "It happens. We always have a fallback place ready."

They stood looking at each other for a long moment. Then Natalia said, "Sit down." David took a seat and watched as she switched on the gas fire, bending to slot pennies into the meter. She said, over her shoulder, "I am sorry I was out. One of our people came to tell me you'd had to run, and I had to make some telephone calls. Mr. Jackson will be coming soon, Geoff Drax too."

"Geoff? Oh no."

She stood up and spoke sadly, almost apologetically. "If they're making inquiries about you they will soon find out you and he are friends. I had to phone Mr. Jackson at work. We don't usually do that, we don't know which Civil Service phones are tapped, but it was an emergency."

"What about the other man in the cell? Boardman, from the India Office."

"He'll be warned. But there's nothing to lead them to him that we know of." She sat down opposite him, a fixed expression in those clear, almond-shaped eyes. "Please, tell me everything that happened today."

She sat still and quiet as David explained, nodding occasionally. When he had finished she asked, "The woman Carol, you're sure she knows nothing of what you have been doing?"

"Yes. But—they'll question her again. She was the one who warned me. They'll make her talk."

"With luck she will only lose her job. If she knows nothing."

David took a deep breath. "The man I spoke to on the telephone said they'd send someone to fetch Sarah. That was always part of the deal: if anything happened you'd help her."

"We will."

"If only she'd been at home—"

"You shouldn't have gone back there, you know," Natalia said, her tone quietly reproving.

"I didn't know what else to do. If that man had answered the phone the first time—"

"Yes. If he had to go out he should have got someone to cover him. That was a mistake."

"I didn't know what to think when I didn't get an answer." He smiled at her ruefully. "Somehow I'd thought you were all infallible."

"Nobody is infallible. Not us, and not them, either. They should have realized this woman Carol might go and warn you. Just occasionally, you see, they overestimate the power of fear." She gave him one of her long, steady looks. "This woman must be very fond of you."

"And now I've landed her in it. I've landed everyone in it, haven't I? All because I misfiled that bloody document."

"As I said, nobody is infallible. But the question is, what led them to you in the first place?"

"It all points to Frank Muncaster, doesn't it? They've got him to talk."

"That seems possible, I'm afraid."

"Then it's all been for nothing." David put his head in his hands. "Poor bloody Frank."

Natalia didn't get up, but said, gently, "I'm sorry. It's hard when you have personal loyalties."

He glanced up at her. "Don't you have any?"

She lit a cigarette from the pack on the table. "Not anymore." She looked him in the eye. "Everyone I cared about is gone. That's another thing the enemy don't consider, that they might leave people with nothing else in their lives but to fight them. That's what they're doing in Russia."

David pointed at the painting of the battle scene. "You've left that one on the wall."

She said, "When my brother came back from Russia he told me about the last battle he was in. His leg was badly injured, that's why he was sent home. He didn't talk about it much, he couldn't bear to, but one night he was in a bad state and he did." Her voice had become monotonous, holding in God knew what feelings. "It was in 1942, the Caucasus offensive, the Russians were defending a strong position and Peter saw a lot of his friends killed. Those are the Caucasus mountains in the distance. All in German hands now."

"I didn't know that your brother came back. I thought he'd been killed."

"No. His leg was shattered, he didn't get good treatment at the field hospital and he was never able to walk properly again. But it was his mind that really suffered. Some people can survive a war with their minds intact but not Peter."

David shook his head. "Yes, it always stays with you. It was because of what I saw in Norway that I felt the peace with Germany was right. Like all the other fools, I needed peace."

"Although you are half Jewish."

"I told you," he replied bitterly, "we kept that well hidden. I pretty much hid it from myself for long enough." He paused. "Since we spoke I've wondered whether I might have family—second and third cousins, perhaps—who were on trains like the one you described. It makes me ashamed."

"Why? Because you have been able to escape the trains and these new British camps? You shouldn't be." She spoke emphatically. "It's not your fault you happen to be different in a way that gets you singled out. And you *are* fighting them, fighting the Fascists."

David smiled bleakly. "Making restitution, eh? When the anti-Semitic laws got really serious, that's when I first began to feel ashamed. I suppose that was why I decided to join the Resistance. Everyone probably thinks I'm just another old-fashioned Englishman outraged by what's being done. But I'm not, for me it's personal."

"It is personal for all of us, one way or another," Natalia said quietly.

"You mean your brother?" They were talking intimately now, leaning forward slightly. The gas fire hissed gently in the background.

"Partly. When he came back I nursed him at home. My father helped but he died later that year. Then it was just me and Peter. He wouldn't go out, the only place he felt safe was in the house and even then he feared someone would come—Russians or Germans—and kill him. Not for any particular reason, but just because killing had become what people did. The strange thing was, Peter was so afraid of dying but in the end he killed himself, he jumped out of the window of our flat. We were on the third floor. He did what your friend Frank tried to do."

"I'm sorry." They were silent for a moment, then David asked, "What's happened to Frank?"

"Mr. Jackson may know more."

He looked at her, then said, "You hate the Fascists, yet you had a German fiancé."

Natalia's mouth set firmly. "He wasn't a Nazi. And I wasn't just his fiancé, I married him. I am actually a German citizen by law. I'm not sure I meet the race criteria, but we managed to fudge that—that's the word, isn't it? Fudge." She pointed at her eyes. "The Mongols reached the edges of my country, and it was part of the Turkish empire for centuries. I have some Asian blood from long ago." She smiled. "I have seen you notice."

Her expression changed, became hard. "The most precious things in life can just be snatched away from you in a moment. But your wife, we will save her if we can. And she—well, she is your precious thing. Or you would not care so much about leaving her."

He looked down. "I…" Slowly, he stretched out a hand. He needed the contact, he needed it.

They both jumped as the doorbell rang violently. Natalia's face worked for a moment, then she nodded quickly at David, got up and went out.

David heard two more pairs of footsteps returning with her: Jackson and Geoff. Jackson seemed angry; there were red spots on his plump cheeks. He was carrying a briefcase which he put on the table. He looked at David and said heavily, "Your chickens have come home to roost, I'm afraid, Fitzgerald." He walked over to the fire and stood with his back to it.

"It's not David's fault," Geoff protested but Jackson gave him an annoyed glance, took a deep breath, then turned to David. "Full story, please."

David told him, leaving nothing out.

"The woman, Carol, she was sure one of the policemen was a German?" Jackson asked.

"I don't think she would make a mistake."

Jackson put his hands behind his back, rocked on his heels, thinking. "It's the Gestapo, working from the embassy with Mosley's people at Special Branch. It has to be." He stared out of the window; it was dark now. He said, in a gentler tone, "We've sent someone to your house, to pick your wife up. You're quite sure she knows nothing?"

"I've never given her even the vaguest hint."

Jackson looked at Natalia. "Well, it's the end of this cell," he said heavily. "We close everything up here tonight."

"What about Dilys?" Natalia asked.

"She has to go, too. Tomorrow if she can. I suppose someone in her profession is at an advantage in a way, she can soon find somewhere else, continue working. I almost envy her." Jackson looked at David and Geoff. "I'm afraid you two are finished as agents. Done. Exposed. On the run. It's better you both realize that now."

David turned to Geoff. "You, too?"

"I left this afternoon, when they rang. Besides, I think they were beginning to have doubts about me. Lack of enthusiasm for the settlement program in Africa; I've never been a brilliant actor. Of course, I didn't have to act at first, I really did come back because of a broken heart"—Geoff gave his little bark of laughter—"but that was a few years ago. Anyway, they'll make the connection between you and me soon enough, it's no secret we've been friends for years." He looked at Jackson. "I can stick it, sir, but what about my parents? Is there any chance you could get them away somewhere?"

Jackson shook his head. "That's not the best idea. If they disappear they'll be hunted, and at their age—well, life with us isn't easy. They know nothing?"

"They wouldn't approve if they did. My dad's a Rotarian, they're both members of the Coalition Conservative Party, even now."

"All that will protect them," Jackson said. "Fortunately the Germans are constrained—still—by the fact we're not an occupied country. They can't just spirit people away if they haven't done anything. The British authorities like the notion that they're still in charge. That's why Muncaster is still at the asylum."

"Is the whole Civil Service spy network under threat?" David asked quietly.

"I don't bloody know!" Jackson burst out. He began pacing the room. He frowned, turned to David. "I'm sorry," he said. "We're all under stress."

Natalia said, "David and I think the Germans must have been investigating him because of some lead from Muncaster."

Jackson shook his head. "I don't think so. We've been in touch with our man at the asylum this afternoon. Muncaster's still not speaking, and nobody's tried to interrogate him. Our man thinks Dr. Wilson may be trying to protect him. Muncaster's become a sort of pet patient."

Geoff asked, "Your man? You mean Ben, that Scottish attendant we met?"

"That's the name you know him by. We've always made contact via shortwave radio. He too is more at risk now." Jackson looked at the anxious faces around him, then gave his sudden disarming smile. "I must stop this habit of pacing around, mustn't I? Bad for everyone's nerves.

Come on, Drax, let's sit down. I have to tell you all what's been decided, what's going to happen next. And we don't have much time."

Jackson took the armchair by the gas fire. He took a deep breath. "I've spent today having conversations with people at the highest level. The *very* highest level." David wondered if he meant Churchill. "And it's been decided Muncaster is to be taken from the hospital. We're going to turn this into an opportunity. You three will go, Natalia will lead you again."

"How do we do it?" she asked.

"At eleven on Sunday night the attendant, Ben Hall, will fetch Muncaster and bring him to the gates. We'd have liked to go sooner but Hall couldn't swap a night shift till the day after tomorrow. The hospital give the patients a sedative to get them to sleep and there's only the night staff on the wards. Ben has swapped with the nurse on Muncaster's ward. He has enough authority within the place to take Muncaster out of his room. Then he brings him out of the building and down to the gate. The problem will be getting Muncaster past the porter's lodge, where the keys are. There's usually only one person on duty there at night, and Ben will have to put him out of action temporarily."

David said, "If Ben's acting alone, how will he cope with Frank? He could be in a state."

"He will give him extra sedation that evening to make sure he's quiet. Muncaster should just about be able to stagger along if Hall gets the dose right. Let's hope he does, a great deal rides on that."

"Poor bloody Frank," David said again.

"Poor bloody Frank will be a lot more bloody if the Germans get him." A touch of asperity had returned to Jackson's voice. "Hall will bring him out and a car with you three in it will be waiting by the gates."

"It makes sense," Geoff said. "We're on the run anyway. We've nothing to lose." He took his pipe from his pocket, began filling it with tobacco.

"Exactly," Jackson agreed. "Afterwards you'll all go to another safe house some way from the asylum. Hall, too; when the authorities find out what happened they'll be after him as well." He looked hard at David and Geoff. "As Drax says, you're the ideal people to do this, you've been there before and you've got to disappear anyway. But also, it's easy to foresee possible problems with Muncaster when the drugs wear off. God knows how he'll react when he finds himself out of the asylum, in a strange place, guarded by people with guns." Jackson looked at David. "That's why it's important you're there. If anyone can convince him we're acting in his best interests, you can."

"And if we get Frank out, what happens then?" David asked.

"In a few days an American submarine will enter the English Channel. Muncaster, and you and Drax and Hall, will be picked up. The plan is to get Mrs. Fitzgerald there too. Next stop—if all goes well—New York."

"My God," David said.

"We always do our best to get our people out." Jackson pointed to his briefcase. "I've got your false identity cards in there."

"Do I stay in England?" Natalia asked.

"Yes, if all goes well," Jackson answered. "Your identity isn't compromised, and we have other work planned for you." He gave her a searching look. "Unless, of course, you'd rather leave, too."

Natalia glanced at David, then said, "No. No, I should stay here."

"Good." Jackson turned to David and Geoff. "Any questions? Comments?"

"I'll do it," David said. He had done all he could for Sarah now, and Jackson was right, they must try to get Frank out.

Geoff spoke next. "Okay. I suppose my parents will never know what's happened to me," he added slowly.

"I know it's hard," Jackson said. "But we all knew that one day we might have to go on the run, never see our loved ones again. It's the same for all of us. Me, too." He smiled sadly, seeming momentarily as vulnerable as the rest of them.

David thought of Irene, Sarah's parents. Sarah would probably never see her family again either. Would they be all right? Steve's Blackshirt connections will help, he thought.

Jackson got up, crossed to the table and opened his briefcase. He pulled out two brown identity cards and handed one each to David and

Geoff. David opened his; a couple of years ago he had gone to a photographer's to have his picture taken in case he ever needed a fake identity, and here was the photo, impressed with what looked like the Home Office stamp, on a card which named him as Henry Bertram, of Bushey, Hertfordshire. Married. A civil servant in the Department of Transport.

Jackson said, "You're both down as civil servants, close enough to what you actually do to let you talk convincingly about your work if need be. There are still a lot of police around in the cities, and some of the roads that lead to the new Jewish camps have roadblocks. It's possible you might be asked to show your IDs, and a lie is always more convincing the closer it is to the truth." He put his hand on the briefcase again and pulled out a bulky white envelope. "There's one more thing." He looked between them, his eyes hard now. "If you get caught by the Germans, it'll be the full works, I'm afraid, from the Gestapo in the Senate House basement."

David glanced at Geoff, who took a deep breath as Jackson opened the envelope and carefully tipped two small, circular rubber pellets into his hand. "These are cyanide capsules," he said. "Natalia knows what they are, she has one. Carry them in your trouser pockets, loose. For God's sake don't lose them. If you're captured, if they're coming for you and you know you can't get away, put the pellet in your mouth. Don't swallow it, crunch down. There's a glass phial inside. It's very quick." He held out his hand and David and Geoff each took a capsule. As he put the thing in his pocket, David thought, *death weighs almost nothing.*

"We've all faced dying, I suppose," Jackson said. "I was in the trenches in the Great War, Fitzgerald was in the 1940 war, and you, Drax, you must have faced some tricky situations in Africa. It's a funny thing, I found that in action you always have to be prepared for death; you must keep it in a separate compartment, but you have to be ready to open that compartment at a moment's notice, look death squarely in the face knowing it might be the last thing you see." He smiled with unexpected awkwardness. "I guess every human being knows they're going to die one day; everyone has that compartment locked away somewhere. It's easier if you've got religious faith, I suppose."

David touched the pill in his pocket. He looked across at Natalia but she was staring into the middle distance, her face stony. She had probably had a capsule already for a long time.

Jackson clapped his hands together, making David jump slightly. "Well," he said, "looking on the bright side, the mission has every chance of success; you could all be heroes. And if we get you to the States, we've an arrangement with our sympathizers there. They'll get you to Canada, give you new papers as British immigrants."

David thought, it won't matter if I'm a half-Jew there. Or not much. I could maybe even get to New Zealand, be with Dad. He wondered if Sarah would come with him, or whether, as he feared inside, that was all over now. Then he realized something else, and looked up sharply at Jackson. "There isn't a pill for Frank," he said.

Jackson shook his head. "There's no guarantee he'd take it. Or he might take it the moment it was given him. If it comes to it, Natalia will be armed and we'd rely on her to stop Muncaster from being taken."

David looked at her. She said, "David, I have to be the one with the gun. They don't expect a woman to carry arms. I am experienced and it gives me that little extra element of surprise."

"Which can be useful if you have to act quickly," Jackson agreed. He closed his briefcase. "Natalia, I'm afraid I've got to ask you to prepare to leave within the half hour. Just take what personal things you need, and make sure there's nothing here that could be of use, or lead them to us. I've got an address for the three of you to stay the next couple of nights. Go through and see Dilys first. Tell her to make arrangements to move."

"I suppose I have to leave my paintings," Natalia said.

"Yes, I'm afraid so." Jackson gave his apologetic smile again. David thought, he respects her, he trusts her. But Geoff and I are underlings and I've already failed once.

Natalia went out, shutting the door quietly behind her. Jackson raised his eyebrows. "Well," he said. "This is it."

Geoff said, "It'll be strange if Frank Muncaster turns out to know nothing important."

"Oh, no," Jackson said heavily. "We're pretty sure he does."

CHAPTER THIRTY-THREE

Gunther took the woman back to Senate House. In the car she had said nothing although sitting in the back with her, Gunther could feel the trembling of her body through the leather seat. In her kitchen, when she'd come in and found them, she had stood rigid with shock. Syme had told her she was being arrested on suspicion of being a member of an illegal organization, that this was a matter of national security. Gunther asked where her husband was and she replied she didn't know, she would have expected him home from work by now. Looking at her face Gunther thought, *there's more to it than that,* and he asked her to give him her handbag and empty her pockets. Then she said, firmly, that she wasn't going to say anything else until she had a lawyer present. She added primly that she was sorry if that seemed discourteous, which made Syme laugh. After that she didn't say another word.

At Gunther's direction, once they were through the Senate House gates, Syme parked the car beside a side door. A Wehrmacht guard stood to attention outside. They got out, Gunther taking Sarah's arm. He saw her eyes widen. Perhaps the penny had dropped that she was on German territory now. He thanked Syme and told him he would take matters from here. "I'll telephone you later."

Syme's face flushed. He leaned in close to Gunther and whispered, "I should be in on the interrogation. That's what was agreed."

"That was agreed about the man. You need to find him, it's urgent. You can talk to her later."

Syme's eyes narrowed. "This is a joint project."

"I know, but we need to find the man. It's you that has the resources for that."

Syme still looked suspicious. When they had broken into the house in Kenton, earlier that afternoon, he had insisted on searching the place with Gunther. They had found nothing. Gunther now wondered whether the time was coming for Syme to be dealt with, too.

"All right," Syme said. He turned back to the woman, who was looking up at the immense floodlit wall of Senate House. Her eyes followed Syme as he got back into the car, leaving her in German hands. Gunther said, gently, "It's all right, we just want to ask you some questions." He smiled reassuringly. She gave him a look of fear and hate.

The guard let them in and Gunther led Sarah along an echoing marble corridor. At the end was a metal door with another soldier on guard, this time wearing the black uniform of the SS. Gunther nodded and the guard opened the heavy door. Gunther took the woman down the stone staircase to the basement. As he had told Hauser, when the Germans took over Senate House as their embassy in 1940 they had converted the basement into interrogation rooms. The busiest time had been in 1943 when the Abwehr, German Army Intelligence, had been found to include elements plotting to kill Hitler and been purged, the loyal elements incorporated into the SS. Gunther had still been in England then; it had been a difficult time. A couple of officers he had known had been brought down here before being shipped back to Germany.

There were, he knew, cells equipped for carrying out severe physical interrogations, but also rooms which looked like the places where police questioned suspects in British television programs like *Sergeant Dixon*. He took Sarah into one of these. There was a table bolted to the floor, a few hard chairs and a telephone fixed to a bracket on the green-painted wall. He said he would have to leave her for a short time, and asked if she would like some tea. Sarah shook her head. She hadn't spoken since they left her house. Gunther closed the door on her and walked up to the far end of the corridor, past other closed cell doors, to where a stocky young Gestapo man in his twenties sat reading the German army magazine *Signal*. The cover showed a group of German soldiers sitting on the edge of an ornate fountain, talking to some girls. *The Pleasures of Service in Rome*. Gunther nodded at the telephone. "Get me Standartenführer Gessler, please."

Gunther watched as the soldier dialed. Gessler had been furious, wild with rage, when Gunther telephoned him earlier to say Fitzgerald had escaped. Gessler had told him that they still hadn't got clearance to take Muncaster. "This is turning into the biggest fucking balls-up in history," he had screamed impotently down the phone.

The soldier passed the telephone to Gunther and he told Gessler he had Fitzgerald's wife in custody. Gunther replaced the receiver. "He's on his way," he told the soldier, who quickly put *Signal* in a drawer of his desk and brought out a sheaf of forms.

"How are things at the moment?" Gunther asked. "I hear a few German Jews have been picked up."

The boy wrinkled his nose. "Pieces of shit who thought they could hide in the bigger cesspool."

Gunther shook his head. "They never learn."

Gessler arrived a few minutes later. He carried a thin file. Gunther thought how tired he looked, ill, red-faced and unshaven, a complete contrast to his confident schoolmasterly manner when Gunther had arrived. Yet he was still managing it all, just keeping control. The Gestapo boy stood to attention and saluted. Gessler turned to Gunther. "Where is she?"

Gunther led him to Sarah's cell, pushing aside the cover of the little spy hole in the outside of the metal door. Gessler bent and looked, then straightened up. "Have you started questioning her?"

"She wouldn't say anything in the car, said she wanted a lawyer." Gessler laughed. Gunther smiled. "I thought I'd leave her here for a few minutes, let reality sink in."

"She's just sitting, staring into space." Gessler considered. "You know, Dr. Zander's in tonight. You could show her some of his handiwork. That would soon open her mouth."

"With respect, sir, I'd like to try a bit of question-and-answer first. I can soon work out whether she's had any training in dealing with interrogation. If she hasn't, that would indicate she hasn't been working with her husband. If she has—"

"We hand her over to Zander straightaway." Gessler tapped his wristwatch. "Time is short."

"Interrogation is an art," Gunther said.

"It's a science as well," Gessler answered bluntly. "A branch of *medical* science."

Gunther knew torture was necessary sometimes, had seen it applied in training films and in interrogations, but he could never enjoy it. In the future, once Germany's enemies were defeated, it wouldn't be needed; but, he knew, they were still a long way from that.

Gessler handed over the slim file. "That's what we've been able to find on her. Not much. Most of it comes from a Special Branch file on her father. An active pacifist before the war, one of the ones who didn't like us. This woman and her sister were both pacifists, too. But no record of political activities since 1940. Her sister's husband's got connections in the BUF."

As Gunther flicked quickly through the file, Gessler said, "A civil servant in the Colonial Office also went AWOL from his desk this afternoon. Geoffrey Drax. It's pretty certain now that he was the other man who visited Muncaster's house. It does look like we've uncovered a spy ring in the Civil Service now. Special Branch will be keen to move in. And we haven't caught anybody apart from this woman yet."

Gunther tapped the file with his fingers. "Who warned Fitzgerald we were in the Dominions Office? I'd like to get that Carol Bennett woman in here, too."

"Later," Gessler said. He pointed at the door of the cell. "Get this one to talk first, Hoth."

"Is someone watching the Fitzgeralds' house?"

"Yes. In a car a little further up the road. Our people. That won't be so easy in daylight, people sitting in cars on suburban streets get noticed. Net curtains twitch."

Gunther nodded. He had had a thought about that.

Gunther went back into the bare windowless cell. The woman was sitting in a chair. She hadn't taken off her coat although it was hot down here and she looked at him with that same mixture of fear and defiance. She had a strong face, she had probably been quite attractive once but she was beginning to age. She wasn't trembling now, she was holding her fear in. He laid the file on the desk and sat opposite her, smiling again. "I haven't introduced myself. My name is Hoth, I'm from the German security police. I'm not a soldier, just a detective."

"Gestapo," she said suddenly, with an utter bleakness.

He inclined his head. "That's a very broad term."

"I want to speak to a lawyer."

Gunther shook his head. "You don't have that right." He continued, in the same mild tone, "You see, you're at the embassy, you're on German territory now. I want to ask you some questions. That's all, just some questions. Now, your name is Sarah Fitzgerald, yes?" She just stared at him. "Come on now," Gunther laughed. "It can't do any harm to answer that one."

She hesitated. "Yes."

Gunther guessed that she knew nothing about interrogation techniques or it wouldn't have been so easy to get her to answer. "Good, good," he said. "And you were born on 17 May 1918." She looked startled. He smiled again. "It's on your identity card. Remember, when we took your handbag and got you to empty your pockets, at your house? I'm sorry we frightened you then, by the way. But we couldn't leave the lights on."

"You wanted me to walk into your hands. And I did."

"Yes."

She stared at him, uncertainty now as well as fear and anger in her face; she obviously hadn't expected to be treated so gently. Gunther tapped the file. "I see your father was a pacifist in the thirties. Along with you and your sister. Well, I wish your people had won the day then, we'd never have had the 1939–40 war."

"Where did you get all this information?" she asked.

"The Home Office have records of people who were active in politics before the war." He spoke almost apologetically. "But according to the records your family seems to have accepted the status quo after 1940, certainly your sister. And, after 1941, your father."

"The government must have files on thousands and thousands of people, then," she said quietly, almost to herself.

Gunther spread his hands. "With all the trouble from the Resistance, you can see why they think it's necessary. The violent demonstrations, the bombings, the assassinations. It's as bad here now as in France. Though I know as a pacifist you wouldn't be involved in any of that."

She did not reply. Gunther smiled. "I want peace as well, you know. Germany's sick of war. I long for the day when the world is at peace."

"With everyone under your thumb," she said bitterly.

"I wish you could understand." Gunther couldn't keep a touch of irritation from his voice. He did wish for peace; this woman, a nice educated woman, pure Aryan by the look of her, should be happily at home caring for her husband and children. He said, "Where were you this afternoon, Mrs. Fitzgerald?"

"I went out for the day. I went into town, to Blakeleys Stores, to the toy section, I spoke to the manager there. You can check that with him if you like."

"How do you know the Blakeleys man?"

"I do voluntary work for a charity that sends toys to the children of poor people. Mr. Fielding has been helping us."

"Ah. Something like our Winter Relief in Germany."

"No," she said. "Not like that." Then she thought a moment and said quietly, "Or maybe it is."

"You and your husband have no children?"

She looked at him. "We had a son, but he died in an accident."

"I'm sorry," Gunther said.

She was clearly surprised by the catch of real sympathy in his voice. "Have you children?" she asked.

"A son, Michael. He is with his mother, out in Krimea. I miss him."

"Why have you arrested me?" she asked suddenly. "What have I done?"

"In a moment. Now, where did you go after visiting the shop?"

"To the National Portrait Gallery. I had lunch before."

"It was after eight when you got home, Mrs. Fitzgerald. The gallery closes at five. What did you do after your visit?"

She hesitated. Gunther saw that. "I walked."

"On a cold, dark winter's day?" She was starting to lie now, he felt it.

"I sat in a cafe for a while."

"Where?"

"Somewhere near Victoria Station."

"Now why would you do that? Wouldn't your husband expect you to be home when he returned from work?"

"Sometimes he works late." He caught a little bite of anger in her voice. He thought, things aren't so good at home. She asked, "Do you know where he is?"

"No."

"Look at me." Gunther spoke quietly. "Look at me. I know you're keeping something back."

She was silent a long moment. He could see she was thinking. Then she said, almost in a whisper, "I've been afraid my husband was having an affair. I noticed little things, changes in his manner, the way he behaved to me. Our son dying was a bad blow."

"Who did you think he was having an affair with?"

"I—I don't know. Women have always found him very attractive."

Gunther saw it now. He said, "Was the woman concerned named Carol Bennett?"

Sarah drew in her breath sharply. Her eyes widened.

"It was, wasn't it?"

"How do you know?"

"We had information that your husband might be involved in illegal activities. We questioned some people at his work today, those who knew him well. Miss Bennett's name came up."

Sarah said, "She wasn't having an affair with him. She'd have liked to, but he—didn't. I spoke to her this evening, you see. I went around to see her, that's where I went. I wanted to confront her."

Gunther smiled. "I believe you. Tell me," he asked, "how long have you been married?"

"Nine years."

"My wife left me after seven. She didn't like the hours I work."

She looked at him curiously. "Where did you learn to speak such good English?"

"I studied in Oxford. Then I worked here at the embassy for several years."

She shook her head. "You're one of those who believes it all, aren't you? All the Nazi poison."

"Remember where you are, Mrs. Fitzgerald," he said, an edge to his voice.

She gave a little humorless laugh. "I'm not likely to forget, am I?"

"Were you expecting your husband to be at home when you returned? From Miss Bennett's?"

"Yes. I've no idea where he is. Nor why you want him." She paused. "He always told me political action was useless, we had to get along with the system. All these years he's said that."

"He was protecting you, perhaps." She didn't answer. "The evidence is pretty conclusive, I'm afraid. It seems your husband was part of a larger ring of spies inside the Civil Service. You'll know his friend, of course, the one he went to university with. Geoff Drax."

"Geoff?" There was real surprise in her face.

"Yes. They both disappeared from their offices this afternoon. They were going to be arrested, but somebody warned them." Carol Bennett, he guessed, but he didn't say.

"Why should I believe anything you tell me?" she asked.

"Why else would we have broken into your house?"

"You're saying I may never see David again." She said it bleakly, a statement.

"You really never knew?"

"No. No, I swear he told me nothing."

"You swear. Are you a Christian?" He thought suddenly of the woman he'd caught sheltering Jews in the Berlin flat.

"No. I've stopped believing in God." She looked him in the face again. "After all, how could He allow the world to be like this?"

"Maybe this is the world that destiny intends for us. A safe, clean world. And it is the forces of evil and violence that prevent us from building it." Gunther smiled wryly. "Did you ever think of that?"

"No," she answered vehemently. "What's just been done to the Jews, that order came from Germany, didn't it? What's going to happen to them now?"

"With respect, Mrs. Fitzgerald, you are here to answer my questions, not I yours. Does the name Frank Muncaster mean anything to you?"

She seemed puzzled. "He's an old university friend of my husband's. They write occasionally. I've never met him."

She had a very readable face. He wasn't sure she had told him the entire truth about this afternoon, though she had told most of it, but he was certain her husband had never taken her into his confidence, and that she knew nothing about Frank Muncaster.

He left her and went up to Gessler's office. Gessler was on the telephone, his face angry but his tone deferential. He waved a hand for Gunther to sit while he finished his call. "The Home Office can't just order a Health Department civil servant to release a mental patient. The civil servant would take it to the minister, if we're involved it would go to the Prime Minister. And you know how unpredictable Beaverbrook is—"

Gessler broke off and listened to the voice at the other end. Whoever it was seemed to be shouting. "With respect, sir," Gessler said eventually, "it's only one section of Special Branch who are cooperating with us, and even they've no idea what it's about—"

More shouting from the other end, a harsh, tinny sound. At length Gessler said, "My man who's been questioning the woman has just come in. Let me talk to him and I'll call you again—yes, in ten minutes—yes. Heil Hitler." He put the phone down. "Heydrich's people," he snapped. "I've told them about the Civil Service spy ring. Will Syme keep his mouth shut?"

"For the present."

"His superintendent's attitude is that they need to act soon on the spy ring. They'll want to do a proper clear-out. We can't keep the lid on this for long. What's the woman told you?"

"I'm pretty sure she didn't know what her husband was up to. She suspected him of having an affair. I asked if the name Muncaster meant anything to her, and she said only as an old friend of her husband whom she never met. I believe her."

Gessler frowned. "The fewer people know we're interested in him, the better."

"I asked very casually."

"So you're saying she's a dead end?" Gessler looked at him accusingly, as though the dead end were Gunther's fault.

"I wonder, sir, could I make a suggestion?"

Gessler nodded.

"When we were waiting for Mrs. Fitzgerald tonight, I noticed a big lawned area opposite her house, a little park. There's one of the old concrete air-raid shelters at the other end, two or three hundred yards away. It looks pretty run-down but if we could get a man in there with a radio and powerful enough binoculars, he could watch the house. We could let her go, order her to stay at home, and see who comes to visit. It's a point of honor for the Resistance people to get agents' families out. They won't telephone her, they'll know the phone will be tapped. If they come for her in a car someone in that shelter could take the number and have them picked up. But if we keep her here they won't do anything, they can't *get* at her. And I don't think she can be of any more material help at the moment."

Gessler looked at him, eyes narrowed. "You really don't want her to get rough handling, do you? It's all very well to be sentimental about women but spies, well, they're not normal women."

"I don't think she's a spy, sir. But I think the way I suggest would give us a better chance of getting hold of those who are."

Gessler thought again, then nodded. "You've had a lot of experience with this sort of thing, haven't you? Picking up Jews and their friends." He shook his head. "Forgive me, I was wrong to call you sentimental. Your work in Germany certainly wasn't that, I know."

"Thank you, sir," Gunther replied humbly. He hadn't thought Gessler a man capable of apology.

"If we do this we'll have to provide the manpower from the embassy."

"I think we should do it, sir," Gunther pressed, his voice quiet but determined. "I think we could get them."

CHAPTER THIRTY-FOUR

Frank was in a padded cell now, somewhere deep inside the asylum. The walls, and the floor too, were covered in a coarse, thick material; it was like being inside a huge, stifling mattress. There were nasty-looking stains on the padding, and the whole room smelled faintly of disinfectant and vomit.

Frank had blacked out after jumping off the chair. When he came around he was lying on the floor of the quiet room with a terrible pain in his throat, attendants gripping his arms and legs. *I'm still here*, he thought sorrowfully, offering no resistance as they put him in a straitjacket and hauled him away, his feet dragging on the floor, people turning to look. They had taken off the straitjacket when they put him in the padded room, but told him he would be here for a while and if there was any trouble he'd be restrained again.

Dr. Wilson had come to see him a couple of times. He seemed disappointed, as though Frank had let him down; annoyed, too. "I thought you were settling in," he said reproachfully. "What was so bad you wanted to end your life?" Frank saw something calculating in Dr. Wilson's look, at variance with his manner. He also seemed, in an odd way, afraid. He guessed Wilson had put two and two together, connected his suicide attempt with the visits from his old friends and the police. Frank had already decided the only protection he had left was not to talk at all, maintain complete silence. He looked away. Dr. Wilson was probably involved in the conspiracy too.

Wilson said, "You'll have to stay in here if you won't talk, Frank." Frank was tempted to cooperate for a moment, doing whatever was necessary to get out of this room. But he knew that even if they let him out of the padded cell they would be watching him, he wouldn't have an easy chance to kill himself again. But he would do it; he would take the first opportunity that came. Wilson looked at the plastic beaker of iced water on a tray on the floor. He said, "Drink as much as you can. It'll help your dry throat." Frank just looked at him blankly, feeling a strange perverse satisfaction in defying him. He was on a double dose of Largactil all the time now.

That had been days ago. They brought in all his meals on a tray and Frank had to knock on the door and wait whenever he wanted to go to the toilet.

The staff who brought his meals made sure that he took his pills. But as with the lower dose he found there was a period just before his next dose was due when the effects wore off and his mind was clear; too clear, because his head filled with images of jangling terror. But it was better, safer, to have a clear mind for part of the time. Along with silence it was the only weapon he had left, and he would use it as long as he could.

Ben brought his supper that night. Frank had been lying on the floor of the padded cell, dozing, his head on the pillow they had given him, when the door opened with its metallic creak. Ben came in with a tray balanced on one hand. There was something different in the way he looked at Frank, sharp and calculating. He smiled his usual cheerful smile, though, and said, "Wakey wakey, Frank, dinnertime."

Frank sat up. He wanted to ask the time but he wouldn't, he wouldn't speak. Ben was part of whatever conspiracy was going on, he must be; it was he who had brought David here. His watch been taken away and there were no windows in the cell, only a light in the ceiling protected by an iron grille, which dimmed during the night; apart from that meals were the only way Frank had of knowing the time of day. If it was dinnertime it must be around six.

"Another cauld night, at least you're warm in here," Ben said. He laid the tray on the floor. Plastic tray, plastic plates and utensils, a chunk of gray fish among soggy vegetables, a bowl containing a bright yellow jelly, and, in a plastic cup, next to another containing water, his pills. Frank noticed they were different, the same white color but bigger.

Ben bent down on his haunches. "Come on, pal," he said encouragingly. "It's me. Talk to me, Frankie."

Frank looked at the pills again. They were definitely different. He remembered the stories among the patients about been given something to drink that would make them sterile. Or was it something else Ben was giving him? He couldn't ask, he mustn't speak. He stared up at Ben. The attendant sighed and shook his head. "Jesus, Frank," he said. "That's some nasty look. It was better when you grinned." Frank reached over and picked up the glass of water. He put the pills in his mouth and swallowed them, then opened his mouth for Ben to inspect as usual. Ben frowned. "Okay, if that's the way it is." Ben nodded at the tray. "Go on, get your dinner."

Frank didn't want it. He went and sat against the rear wall. Ben sighed heavily. "Look, Frank," he said, "you've got to eat. Wilson'll get worried if you won't eat on top of everything else." His look and words were gentle, but there was still something else in his face, too. Frank closed his eyes. After a moment he heard Ben leave. The smell of the fish on the tray made him feel sick. Soon he began to feel sleepy, and his head nodded.

He woke once and found the main light was off, only a faint glow in the padded cell. It must be nighttime. The tray was gone, Ben must have come back and taken it away. How strange he had seemed tonight. Frank remembered David and Geoff coming, how pleased he had been to see David. But he was with the enemy now. He remembered that conversation about appeasement at university, how wonderful it had been to realize that David, that anyone, was actually interested in what he had to say. He felt tears at the corner of his eyes but he was too tired even to cry.

He slept again, deeply this time. He was jarred into sudden wakefulness by the sound of the door opening. The light was switched on. Frank blinked, disoriented.

He felt himself hauled to his feet. "What's—"

Strong arms twirled him around and Frank found himself looking into Ben's face. The attendant's expression was hard, the mouth below the broken nose a thin line. Ben spoke very quietly, but in a deadly serious tone. "You've tae to come with me, Frank, right now. I'm taking you somewhere safe. Come on. But don't say anything, don't pick now to start talkin', please. Or I'll have to knock ye oot. I don't want tae, but I will."

Frank blinked at him, still in a stupor. Ben took him firmly by the arm and led him out of the room, into the corridor. He blinked again, his mind swimming. The corridor was dark, only the nightlights on. He let Ben lead him away. He thought, *this is it, he's taking me to the Germans.* But there was nothing he could do and nothing that could shift the muzziness in his head. It was the big pills, it must be, they had knocked him out. He let himself be led through the dim corridors, stumbling once or twice. They passed another attendant and he felt Ben's grip on his arm tighten. The attendant, a young man, looked bored and tired. He gave Ben a curious glance.

"Where are you taking him at this time of night?"

"He's no' well. I'm taking him to the duty doctor."

"Good luck. Blackstone's on duty tonight."

"Aye, he'll be stocious by now." They passed by.

Ben led him on, past wards where rows of drugged men slept, each with an attendant sitting at his table, reading by the dim light of a lamp. Then Ben opened a side door and freezing cold air hit Frank, who was dressed only in a hospital pullover. He gasped.

"It's all right, we've just tae walk tae the gate." Ben started taking Frank down the path, quickening his pace. Frank stared muzzily around him. It was a clear, cold, moonlit night; frost sparkled on the grass. He began to shiver. They walked right down to the porter's lodge, by the closed gates. Frank glanced through the little window of the lodge, which was open on the inner side. He caught a glimpse of a man lying sprawled on the floor, unmoving, and saw with horror that his arms were tied behind him with rope, and that there was a streak of blood on the man's face. He jerked back, terrified. Ben said, "He's okay, Frank. Honest, he's okay. I'm getting you out of here, Frank, I'm helpin' ye escape. For fuck's sake, come on."

Frank groaned, but let Ben lead him to the gate. His legs were shaking badly. He thought he might fall as Ben reached into his pocket and pulled out a key, a big one, not one of those he carried on his chain. Still holding Frank with one arm, Ben opened the gate. Frank looked back at the dark, blank windows of the asylum.

Ben hauled him through the gate, into the roadway. Their breath steamed in front of them. It was very dark; the road seemed deserted.

Then, a few yards away, headlights came on and Frank saw a car, a big car. A door opened and a tall man in a hat and coat got out and started walking rapidly toward them. Another followed, then a woman. Frank thought, *it's the Germans, they've come to take me, I won't be able to keep quiet.* Then his legs did give way and he would have fallen to the ground if Ben hadn't grabbed him and held him up.

The man halted a couple of feet away. Frank didn't want to raise his head and look at him. It would be one of the policemen, the German perhaps. Then he felt a hand on his shoulder and a familiar voice said, "It's all right, Frank, it's me. Geoff's here too, we've come to help you."

He looked up. "David?"

David smiled. His look was full of concern, as it had been when he came to visit. But there was something different about him. In the light lancing from the headlights his face looked years older.

CHAPTER THIRTY-FIVE

David and Geoff had spent two nights in a flat above a grocer's shop in Brixton. Natalia had left them there, saying she would come and fetch them on Sunday, when they would drive to Birmingham. Sunday the thirtieth, David thought, the last day of November. It seemed a long time since the demonstration on Remembrance Sunday.

The grocer, Mr. Tate, was a middle-aged man with sandy hair and a brusque, cheerful manner. He warned them to keep quiet during the hours the shop was open and David and Geoff spent much of their time in the bedroom assigned to them, reading and playing cards. The room was cold with a sharp smell, a mixture of cheese and bacon, wafting up from below. The grocer brought them food. On the second day he told them how his son had been killed fighting nationalist guerrillas in Burma, and his wife had died from a stroke shortly after. He had joined the Resistance then. "We have to stop it, all the killing," he said. "Make some sort of settlement with those people out East. You can't even always get good Indian tea anymore, because of the strikes on the plantations." David asked if there were any news of Sarah but there was nothing yet.

On the first evening, when the shop was shut, David and Geoff sat and talked quietly. Geoff spoke about the woman he had known in Kenya. "Her husband was a doctor. He'd come out to work for charity, do good work among the natives. He was a decent enough chap, except he took his work too seriously, he didn't really consider Elaine. She was left—well—adrift. Local white society looked down on her as a do-gooder's wife. The irony was she hated the blacks, was really frightened of them, she'd been brought up to that like most people. I think I educated her a bit on that one. A bit." He smiled crookedly. "I suppose we were drawn to each other because neither of us quite fitted in. I asked

374

Elaine to come back to England with me, divorce her husband. But she wouldn't; she was a Catholic, she didn't believe in divorce." He sighed. "So we agreed to chuck it, and I applied for a transfer home. You know what the strange thing was? After we broke up, heaven knows why, she told her husband about us. Why do it then, when it was finished?" Geoff shook his head wearily. "It was all over the town, during my last weeks."

"Didn't she ever tell you why?"

"I never spoke to either of them again. They avoided coming into town after the news got out. I think Ron—the husband—must have told his colleagues. I saw Elaine, once. I was at one end of the street and she was at the other. She saw me and turned and went into a shop. I thought, well, that's that." He laughed sardonically again. "Still, coming home with a broken heart made good cover for me when I started spying for the Resistance."

"Have you got over her?" David asked.

Geoff shook his head. "You know, I never believed in that romantic stuff about everyone having just one person specially for them—"

"I don't either—"

"But I haven't met anyone else since." He frowned, his face suddenly severe. "I suppose it's made me bitter. I think that's why I was ready to join the Resistance."

David said, "I was angry after Charlie died. That was part of it for me." He looked at Geoff. "Did you see it, back then? How angry I was?"

"I saw you getting slowly angrier after the 1950 election. Talking more about politics. I didn't connect it to Charlie. Do you regret it?" he asked. "What we've done?"

"I regret deceiving Sarah. And now where is she? God knows what will happen to her."

Geoff leaned forward and touched his friend's arm. "They'll find her. They're good at that."

"And Carol, you know what I did to her. Strung her along. Yet she saved me in the end."

"There's loyalty for you."

David looked at his friend. "Maybe she feels for me what you felt with Elaine. It can be a bit frightening sometimes, I tell you."

"Yes," Geoff said slowly. "I suppose it can. So, what about Natalia?"

David shifted uncomfortably. "What do you mean?"

"I've just wondered—if there's something there? Between you two?"

David said sharply. "This is hardly the time for something, is it?"

"No. No, it isn't."

On their second day, Sunday, the shop was closed. It was raining, hard, steady rain. David watched as an elderly couple in their best clothes walked up the street, huddled under their umbrellas. They looked as though they were going to church. David thought, it's just a week since the Jews were taken.

The grocer, Mr. Tate, came in with some lunch. There was still no news about Sarah. Mr. Tate seemed a little more relaxed now the shop was closed. He said, "The Chinese have launched a new offensive against the Japs. Place called Zhijang. The news says the Japanese are rallying for a counteroffensive but it's like the Germans in Russia, in a lot of areas they only hold the towns and the roads between them. It's getting like that in parts of India, too, from what I hear. Like the strands and knots in a net. Break enough strands and the whole thing falls apart. The German army knows that, that's why they'll make peace with Russia if Hitler dies."

"Any more word from America, about what Adlai Stevenson will do when he takes over as President?" Geoff asked.

Mr. Tate shook his head. "No. Not on the BBC, anyway. They've been very quiet about the Jews, as well. I think they're hoping we'll all forget about them."

David thought, in time, if the government encourages us, perhaps everyone will.

Natalia arrived shortly after three that afternoon. She had brought a change of clothes for Geoff and David: cheap suits, trilby hats, and dark overcoats. David was still wearing his dark jacket and pinstripe trousers from the office, a little creased and crumpled now.

She was in a brisk, businesslike mood, telling them they needed a shave, they must look respectable. Geoff went to the bathroom first. Left alone with David, Natalia said, "I'm sorry, there's still no news of your wife. But one of our radios is down, it's very possible she is safe, that whoever has her can't get through." She gave him a quick, uncertain smile. "Quite likely, in fact."

"So much for modern technology."

"We will get her to safety. We'll get you all to America."

David said, "I don't think she'll want to be with me. Why should she, now? She always thought I was safe, stable, honest. She didn't know about all these layers of deceit."

Natalia looked him straight in the eye. "From what you have told me of her, she will understand what you have done." She smiled, sadly. "I know it's been hard for you to do the things you have. It's easier for me. In an odd way, I'm free. Where I come from people never had the sort of secure identity you British middle classes have. My part of the world was always mixed, people shifting their roots. Perhaps that makes things easier for those of us who have got out. We're not so tied down."

"Easier? Despite everyone you've lost?"

"Yes. Even so. Easier than for you with your ties," she said, with sudden tenderness. "When we get you away you will have the chance to rebuild those again." She hesitated, then asked, "Do you want that chance?"

"I don't know."

"You should try."

He looked at her. "And you?"

"I go where the struggle takes me. That is my life now." She looked at him tenderly again. "You must understand that. And now, get ready. We have an important job to do."

CHAPTER THIRTY-SIX

Geoff offered to drive this time. Natalia sat in the front with him, David in the back again. As Geoff put the car into gear David looked at his watch. Past six already. They must arrive at the asylum by eleven; Ben would come out at a quarter past. The porter's lodge should be lit; Ben would have dealt with the porter. Jackson had told them that once they collected Ben and Frank they were to drive at once to a safe house in the countryside, fifteen miles from the hospital, in case the alarm was raised quickly. Once they arrived there, they would be sent further instructions about getting back to London; they would stay in London at least one night before driving on to the south coast. If Ben and Frank did not appear by midnight they were to drive to the safe house anyway.

They said little in the car. Geoff put the radio on and they listened to the Light Program, cheerful music and, every hour, the news. The announcer said in his clipped, even voice that the threatened rail strike had been called off. Ben Greene, the Minister of Labour as well as Coalition Labour Leader, had reached agreement with the railwaymen's unions.

"Didn't think that would happen," Geoff said.

Natalia agreed. "They were talking yesterday about using troops to run the railways, arresting men who didn't turn up for work."

David said, "Maybe they think they've got enough on their plate just now, without taking on the railwaymen as well."

They drove on through the dark, along almost empty roads. Near Stratford they saw that one of the exits from the motorway was blocked off; armed Auxiliary Police standing beside a hastily erected wooden guard post. David wondered if one of the new camps for the Jews was down there. He put his hand in his pocket where the tiny rubber pellet was. He knew he shouldn't fiddle with it, but his hand was drawn to it like a tongue to a bad tooth. He thought of the gun Natalia was carrying, somewhere under the big trench coat she wore. He was very conscious of her presence, as well as his terrible anxiety about what might be happening to Sarah. But he knew he didn't feel her loss, her absence, in his heart as a lover should.

The journey went without a hitch. There was no sign they were being followed and the narrow wooded lanes leading to the hospital were deserted, lights from farmhouses the only sign of life, everyone indoors on the cold, frosty evening. The rain had stopped outside London and it had got steadily colder as they drove north. They came in sight of the hospital, its big dark shape outlined against the top of the hill, only a few pinpoints of light visible within. It was well past ten o'clock now; the patients would be in bed, in their sad drugged sleep, with only a few night staff on duty.

They waited in a lay-by until almost eleven, then drove slowly along the asylum fence, toward the porter's lodge. There was a dim light within, but no sign of any occupant. On Natalia's instructions they drove past, drawing up a little way beyond and turning off the headlights. Natalia, briskly professional, said, "I'll have a look. Geoff, if there is any trouble, drive away."

She got out and walked steadily down the road. She had a hand in her pocket, holding on to the gun no doubt. David shifted to the middle of the back seat so he could see more clearly through the windscreen. He thought, *how many missions like this has she done?*

She approached the lit window of the lodge. She stood on tiptoe to get a good look inside, then turned and walked quickly back to the car, looking relieved as she got back in. "The porter's tied up under his desk," she said. "He seems to be out cold. That means Ben is in the hospital now, fetching Frank." Unlike Jackson, she used his first name. "Put the headlights out for now, please."

Geoff switched them off. "Will the porter be all right?" he asked.

"He should be. He's gagged, if he wakes up he can't move or shout."

"If someone's gagged and unconscious there's the risk of them being sick when they wake up, choking to death. There was a case in Kenya when I was there, a robbery that went wrong."

"Ben is a professional," Natalia replied steadily. "He knows how to do these things."

"I'm just saying—"

"You know what's at stake here," she answered sharply, her accent stronger. "There are risks we have to take—" She broke off. Something was happening at the gates. David saw one of them was slightly open. He leaned forward to look more closely. "Someone's coming out—no, two people." As he watched a short, stocky figure slipped through, leading someone else, slight and stumbling, by the arm.

Natalia leaned over and switched the headlights on. Frank and Ben stared at the car, blinking. David opened his door and got out, Natalia and Geoff following as he walked over to them. He saw Frank sag suddenly, almost falling, but Ben held him. His head had flopped forward onto his chest. David touched him gently on the shoulder. "It's all right, Frank," he said. "It's me. Geoff's here too, we've come to help you."

Natalia took the wheel. They drove through a sleeping village. Just beyond it she slowed the car. Frank seemed to have fallen asleep, his head lolling on his chest. David gave him a little nudge; he grunted but did not wake. The country road was very dark. Natalia said, "We're looking for a long brick wall, with the name *Rose Grange* on a plaque by the gate."

"Who lives there?" David asked.

"A retired military man. Colonel Brock. He spent most of his life serving in India."

"One o' thae types," Ben said disapprovingly.

"He's been with the movement since 1940. He's too old for action now, but he has sheltered many of us before. Look, there it is, the plaque."

She stopped the car. Geoff got out and opened a pair of creaky iron gates, and they drove up a short gravel drive with shrubbery on either side. They passed a palm tree, the leaves looking shriveled and dead, and drew up outside a Victorian detached house, probably once a country vicarage. There were no lights. Inside, a dog began to bark. Natalia got out and opened the rear door. "Bring him out," she said gently.

Ben and David eased Frank out of the car. He muttered a little, shivering as the cold air hit him. He couldn't stand unaided but between them Ben and David got him to his feet. They stood supporting Frank on the gravel, while Natalia went up to the front door and rang the bell. It was very cold; you could smell the frost in the air.

A light came on in the hall. The barking grew louder. A man's voice shouted, "Nigger, shut *up!*" David and Ben walked Frank up to the front door. It opened and a man stood looking at them. He was tall, with thin gray hair and a lined, stern face.

"Colonel Brock?" Natalia asked.

"Yes."

"Aztec." It was the code word for their party.

The old man nodded. "Mission accomplished?" he asked quietly.

"Yes. We got him out safe."

"Hiya, pal," Ben said cheerfully.

The colonel nodded stiffly, then looked at Frank. "That him? He looks pretty groggy."

"He's drugged," Ben said. "He needs putting to bed."

"Come inside."

They took Frank into the house. The cold had woken him up a little and he gazed fearfully around the hall, blinking in the light. The furniture was an odd mixture of shabby English fittings and exotic mementos of India—a little stone sculpture of an ox pulling a cart, a portrait of a royal-looking Indian in a turban. A big black Labrador stood beside Colonel Brock, looking uncertainly at the visitors. An inner door opened and a short, plump woman came out. "My wife," the colonel said, nodding at her. "Elsie, my dear, could you help our visitors to some food?"

"Of course." The woman looked at them nervously, her gaze lingering on Frank.

"He's all right," the colonel said firmly. "We're going to put him to bed. Come on now, darling, food. Chop! Chop!" Colonel Brock led them to the stairs. David and Ben helped Frank, the old man walking ahead, a gnarled hand on the banister. David saw that though he tried to keep his back straight he had a stoop.

He led them to a little bedroom with a single bed: a boy's bedroom, a map of the world with pictures of the peoples of the Empire around the edges, schoolbooks on shelves, old copies of the *Magnet* piled in a corner. On the front of the topmost comic Billy Bunter, trying to skate on an icy pond, was falling over, other boys laughing as he went up in the air. They eased Frank onto the bed, where he turned over and fell asleep at once. Ben checked his pulse, then eased off Frank's shoes and put a blanket over him. "He'll sleep till morning, I should think. But someone should stay with him." He looked at David. "I'll sit wi' him till say four, then can you take over? If he wakes he should see someone he knows."

"Of course."

The colonel looked down at Frank. "What's he on?" he asked bluntly.

"Largactil. It's a sedative. I gave him a heavy dose to quiet him while I got him oot."

"Looks done in, poor bugger."

They left Ben with Frank and went back downstairs. The colonel showed David and Geoff into a big dining room. The television was on with the sound turned down, a quiz show, Isobel Barnett in an evening dress. A statue of the four-armed god Shiva stood incongruously on a Welsh dresser. David looked at it. "Pagan stuff, I know," Colonel Brock said, "but it's very well done." He turned to Natalia. "I'd better get to the radio, let them know you've arrived. Elsie's got it in the kitchen."

"Thank you."

David asked, "Is there any news of my wife? Someone was being sent to pick her up."

"I haven't heard anything." The colonel looked at him sympathetically. "I'll ask." He went out. David and Natalia and Geoff sat down at the dining table.

"Maybe no news is good news, old chap," Geoff said.

"If they've got her safe, you'd think they'd have let us know by now."

The colonel's wife came in with a large tray containing bowls of vegetable soup, a loaf of bread, some butter. Geoff got up and helped her lay it on the table. "Short commons tonight, I'm afraid," she said. "We've sent our housekeeper on holiday for a few days, since we heard you were coming."

The colonel returned and sat at the head of the table. "Thank you, my dear," he said to Elsie. "You'd better get back to the radio." He looked at David. "No news about your wife yet, Fitzgerald," he said gently, "but London might not have been able to get through. There's been a lot going on with this Jew business. Elsie will come and tell us if anything changes."

"Thanks," David said.

"I'm told the chap upstairs is pretty important?" Colonel Brock said.

"He could be, sir," Geoff answered.

The old man raised a hand. "Don't need to know the details. I gather Churchill's been personally involved with this one, though." He looked at Natalia, a little uneasily David thought. There was another silence while they ate the thick, flavorless soup. David suddenly felt very tired. He thought, about forty-eight hours ago I was sitting in my office, at work. How fragile our lives are, how a day can turn them inside out.

Geoff said, to break the silence, "You have a lot of Indian mementos, sir."

"Yes. Served there thirty years. My son's out there now, God help him. Rioters broke his bloody arm with a brick in Delhi last year."

"I worked in the Colonial Office. I was in Kenya for quite a while."

The colonel smiled. "Wondered if you'd been out in the Empire. Your tan hasn't quite faded." He grunted. "Quieter out in Africa. The blacks know their place. God knows how it'll all end in India." Geoff set his lips, but didn't reply. The colonel continued, "Lefties in the Resistance say we should pull out, and even Churchill seems to have accepted that now. I suppose I must, too, though it's not what I joined the Resistance for."

"Why did you join, sir?" David asked.

Colonel Brock pulled himself upright. "Because it was cowardly to surrender the way we did in 1940. I always knew it'd end with these Nazi thugs dictating to us. Winston was right, we should have let them try to invade and fought them off." He looked at them fiercely. "I know I'm an old relic of Empire, my views aren't popular in the Resistance anymore. But it's hard, when you see your life's work falling apart. God knows what sort of mess the Indians will make of independence if they get it."

He got up abruptly. "Let's have something stronger." He crossed to a tray of drinks beside the statue of Shiva. He poured whiskey for them and, quaintly, a sherry for Natalia. As he passed the glasses around the door opened. David looked up sharply, hoping it might be the colonel's wife with news of Sarah, but it was Ben, carrying a tray. He laid it on the table. "Yer wife said tae bring this doon when I'd done," he told the colonel. He was deliberately exaggerating his Glasgow accent.

"Your chap still sleeping?"

"Frank? Aye, like a wee bairn. No' bad soup, mate," Ben said to the colonel with a grin. "Compliments to the wife." The old man answered, "Thank you," stiffly, as Ben went back out. The colonel looked at the door and grunted, "He's a Communist, you know, that chap. Outranks me in the movement, likes to remind me of it."

"He's done brave work tonight," Natalia said quietly.

"Oh, I don't question his courage. Just worry that one day his lot will put me up against a wall." Brock gave a humorless laugh, then took a long slug of whiskey and stood up. "I'd better take that dog for his evening walk, or he'll be restless tonight."

David was deeply asleep when Ben woke him at four. For a second he thought he was in bed at home and it was Sarah shaking him awake, then he remembered everything and his stomach went as cold as the dark little room.

"Ready to take over?" Ben whispered.

David nodded and got up. Geoff was still asleep, breathing regularly. David asked quietly, "Is there any news? About Sarah?"

Ben shook his head. "I'm sorry, pal, no' yet."

David dressed quickly, then followed Ben across the corridor to

Frank's room. Inside Frank lay curled up, his hands one on top of the other by his head, like a child praying. "Not a peep out of him," Ben whispered. "Here, the colonel's left a cardigan out for you, it's cold. He's no' such a bad old sod, I suppose," he added grudgingly. "For one of his sort."

David nodded; he didn't want to wake Frank. He thought, let him sleep through, wake in daylight. He looked at him, deeply asleep. He thought of the hell Frank must have been living through, his attempted suicide. He wondered if he had been trying to take his secret with him. He wished he had written to him more often these past few years. Even back at Oxford, Frank's hopeless, desperate vulnerability had made David fear that one day something bad would happen to him.

He looked at the orange-and-blue covers of the *Magnet* in the corner. He remembered reading it himself as a boy. Colonel Brock's son would have lain on the bed reading the same public-school stories. He was out in India now, on the wrong side so far as the Resistance was concerned. David remembered his mother telling him off sometimes for reading comics, such nonsense she called them, so common. He realized now how lucky he had been, the only child of devoted parents, top of the class and good at sport, like the heroes in the Greyfriars stories. Yet he had always resented the demands people made. He didn't want to be special, just ordinary. But had people really asked that much of him? He looked down at Frank's thin, unhappy face, and felt a renewed sense of purpose; Frank knew something that could help the Germans and they had to stop them getting it, whatever it took.

He had meant to stay awake, he had been on night watch plenty of times during the Norway campaign, but the armchair was comfortable and he must have fallen asleep because suddenly he was being shaken again, and it was full day. He blinked in the sunlight, then stared at Natalia. She was looking down at him, smiling a little ironically. She wore a white roll-neck pullover, like someone in the navy; it suited her. "Oh God," David said. "I fell asleep—" He turned around quickly. "Frank—"

"He's fine." Frank was still asleep; he hadn't even changed position.

"I'm sorry—"

"You had a hard day yesterday. It's all right, Ben and I have been up all night manning the radio, and watching to make sure nobody came near the house. We looked in on you from time to time. We sent the old people to bed."

"The radio—is there any news—"

"Of your wife? No, I'm sorry, not yet."

David rubbed a hand over his stubbly face. Natalia stared at him hard with those green, slightly slanted eyes. "Your wife is safe, I'm sure. We'll get her out, you will all get to America."

David laughed hollowly. "It sounds like a dream, a fantasy."

He looked at her. He wanted her, he knew she wanted him, but she had been right to say he must put Sarah first. And she was staying behind, in England. David sighed, and turned to Frank again. "I suppose we need to wake him."

"Yes. I'll get Ben. It will be good if he sees you both when he wakes up."

David said, "The colonel says Ben's a Communist. Like your brother was."

She smiled. "You remember me telling you that?"

"Yes."

"Peter was not a Communist after he went to Russia." She looked down at him. "Maybe I will tell you all about it one day."

"On the way to the submarine, eh?"

She smiled and left the room. David wondered where Natalia stood on politics. Where did he stand himself, for that matter? He wanted democracy, an end to authoritarianism and fear, and to the persecution of the Jews. Beyond that he didn't know. He leaned over and shook Frank's hand gently, feeling the thinness of his wrist under his sleeve. He didn't move at his touch, just lay there breathing heavily.

The door opened and Ben came in. He too looked tired, unshaven, but his eyes were sharp and keen as usual. David said, "I've tried to wake Frank, I shook his arm, but he didn't move . . ."

Ben walked over to the bed. "He's just in a deep sleep, poor wee man. It's all right, I'll wake him." He pinched Frank's arm. He stirred and groaned. His hands shifted, revealing the right one with its withered fingers and scarred palm.

"Come on, Frankie boy," Ben said encouragingly. He gave him another, harder pinch. Frank's eyes opened and he blinked. He stared at them in terror, then sat up and screamed.

CHAPTER THIRTY-SEVEN

Sarah had sat on her own in the cell for an hour after the German left her. She was still in shock at being there, at what David had done. Where was he? After a while, through sheer tiredness, the cogs of her brain stopped turning and she just sat staring around the bleak room. But fear soon grew again; she thought of the weight of the great building above her, all the power of the Third Reich it represented, the terrible rumors about what they did to people here. She felt faint and had to grip the edge of the table.

Shortly before midnight, there was a rattle of keys in the door. Heart beating fast she looked up, expecting to see the big fair man again. She feared him; for all his civility earlier, there was something implacable about him. But it was a young man who entered, in the black uniform of the SS, with a pudgy face and heavily oiled brown hair. He carried a leather bag, which for a horrible moment Sarah thought might contain instruments of torture. But when he emptied it on the table her own possessions tumbled out, handbag and identity card, purse and keys.

"You can go, Mrs. Fitzgerald," the SS man said in a strong German accent. His tone was formal, polite. "I will escort you out. You are to go straight home and to remain there until further notice. The British police may wish to speak further with you."

"My husband—"

"You must tell the police if he tries to contact you. And now..." He looked at the items on the table, then waved an arm toward the door.

Sarah gathered up her things and followed him out of the room, and down the corridor. Two more SS men approached, half carrying an elderly man in a rumpled suit with a yellow badge. He was unshaven, his face bruised, gray hair standing up in tufts, eyes wide with fear. They walked past Sarah and her escort; behind her she heard a door slam. She looked at her guard. He took her back up the same flight of steps Gunther had escorted her down, along empty corridors then through a side door and out into the cold night air. He led her around to the front of Senate House, the building and its immense swastika flags floodlit. The guard walked Sarah to a gate in the side of the high wall, bars of thick iron with barbed wire on top, and unlocked it for her. He actually bowed slightly as she passed him and stepped out into Gower Street. A British policeman standing on duty outside the embassy with a submachine gun turned and glanced at her without interest. The gate closed behind her with a little clang, and she stood staring blankly down the dark street. Then she began walking away, fast.

She caught the last Tube back home. There were not many people on it at that time of night. There was a man, though, a small man in a heavy overcoat, who got into the carriage with her at Euston Square who also got off at Kenton. But he turned in the opposite direction as she left the station. By the time she arrived home she was so frightened and exhausted that when she tried to put her key into the lock her hands shook and it took several tries to open the door. She entered the cold, empty house and went into the kitchen. She stood looking at the table where the men had sat waiting for her. The door to the garden hung open. She closed it—the lock was smashed—and went upstairs, kicked off her shoes, and lay on the bed. She fell asleep in an instant, still in her coat. Alone.

She was woken by the sound of the doorbell ringing loudly and insistently. Her body shuddered. She had been having a terrible dream; she was back in the cell with the German but this time David was there, too, a prisoner. His face was turned away and when she called out his name he wouldn't look around and she knew it was because they had done something terrible to his face. She sat up with a groan. It was daylight, she had slept through the night. She heaved herself up and walked shakily downstairs, in coat and stockinged feet, terrified they had come to take her away again.

But it was Irene standing on the doorstep, smart in her coat and her little circular hat with the red feather. Her eyes widened. "Darling, what's happened to you?"

Sarah swallowed, her throat dry. Irene reached out and took her arm. "I rang and rang last night! How's David, is he better, how ill is he..."

Sarah stared blankly at her sister. "Ill?"

"He telephoned me yesterday. He said he was ill, he'd been sent home from the office, he was trying to get hold of you—"

"David was here? Yesterday?"

"Yes. In the morning—Sarah, what's happening—"

"Come in."

"Why are you in your coat? Have you been out—"

"Come into the lounge, let me get the heating on. My feet are bloody frozen."

Irene took charge, lighting the fire and going to make a cup of tea. Sarah stretched her numb feet to the warmth. The clock on the mantelpiece showed ten o'clock. Irene came back with a tray and set it on the coffee table. Sarah saw that her sister was forcing herself to be calm. She thought, I have to tell her what happened, they might question her and Steve. She took a cigarette, passed one to Irene, and had a sip of the hot, sweet tea. It tasted wonderful. She took a deep breath, then said, "David wasn't having an affair, Irene. He was spying for the Resistance, passing them files from his work. His friend Geoff Drax was, too. They're both on the run. I spent last night being questioned at the German embassy."

Irene stared, her blue eyes wide. "David was working for the Resistance?"

"I'd no idea, I couldn't tell them anything because I didn't know. They let me go. I've been told to stay at home. I think I was followed home on the Tube, though I'm not sure."

"Did they—did they do anything to you..."

Sarah shook her head. "They were very polite. Though as I was being taken out I saw another prisoner who looked—bad." She told Irene everything that had happened. Then she said, in a low voice, "I'm scared."

"The swine!" Irene exclaimed. For a moment Sarah thought she meant the Germans, but then she continued. "Bombings and riots and killing policemen! They're murderers! I knew David had gone anti-German the last few years, but this—"

"What other choice have they left people who oppose them?"

"We've always believed in peace!" Irene's voice rose in indignation. "He's placed you in terrible danger! All of us, the whole family! Spying for those Resistance thugs!"

Sarah put her head in her hands. Irene, suddenly apologetic, reached out. "I'm sorry," she said, "It's just such a shock..."

Sarah looked up. "I know. Thank God Charlie was spared this. But then I think, if he hadn't died David wouldn't have done this. I wasn't enough, you see. All these times he's not come home till late, disappeared at weekends—God, his uncle Ted, that must have been a lie, too."

"He knew what you'd think of what he was doing," Irene said bitterly.

Sarah looked at her sister. "I wonder if he cared." She frowned. "You said he phoned you from here, he must have come back to look for me." She took a deep breath. "He must have wanted me to go with him."

"On the run? You're not saying you would have gone?"

"I don't know." But even as Sarah said the words she knew that she would have followed David.

Irene said, "He always looked down on Steve and me, always seemed to think he was better—"

"I don't think it was like that," Sarah said quietly. "I think the anger just grew in him these last few years, anger at what Britain's become."

"Are you saying you agree with him? After what he's done?" Irene's voice took on its familiar self-righteous tone.

"Maybe I do." Sarah thought of Mrs. Templeman. "I've seen some things I haven't told you about. What Mosley and his people are doing." She spoke with sudden fury. "Helping the Germans build their empire of sadism."

"Oh, Sarah," Irene answered impatiently. "What would the

Resistance bring if they won? More violence, more scapegoats, maybe even communism? And how can they think they could ever defeat the Germans?"

"Are the Germans really so invincible? Maybe that's the mistake we've been making for the last twelve years. They're being beaten in Russia, people say the regime would fall apart if Hitler died."

"But—"

"They're having trouble in France now they're trying to force French men to work in Germany. And in Spain. And we're not exactly doing a brilliant job of keeping the Empire together, are we?" Sarah shook her head. "Dear God, here we are arguing bloody politics again!"

Irene's face softened. "I'm sorry, dear. I just—I don't know. I don't think it's right what's happening to the Jews, putting them into camps like this, but—" Her eyes filled with tears. "I fear for my children, you see, the boys. If—if order breaks down, I'm so frightened for their future."

"This isn't the world any of us wanted, is it?"

Irene shook her head. "No."

"Do you remember when we were young, all the peace work we did with Daddy?"

"It seems so long ago."

"Poor Mummy and Daddy," Sarah said. "I should think this'll just about finish Daddy off. I wonder if David ever thought of that," she added bleakly.

Irene stood up. "I'm going to stay with you for a while," she said decisively. "Steve's at home, I'll ring and tell him he can jolly well look after the boys today. Now come on, let's get you washed and dressed. When did you last eat?" She took Sarah's arm and helped her to her feet.

"I had some tea and buns yesterday afternoon." Sarah realized how hungry she was. She remembered the cafe in Highgate, her encounter with Carol and thought, *what will happen to her?* She groaned. Irene held her close. "Come on, dear, let's get some food inside you."

Irene looked after her as though she were a child again, running a bath and cooking a meal, then sitting talking to her about their childhood, not their peace activities but ordinary family memories, life at home and at school. The morning was cold and clear. Sarah said gratefully, "You've always taken care of me, haven't you?"

"It's what a big sister has to do."

"Remember when I was little and used to be frightened by Daddy's facemask? Mummy would get cross but you'd comfort me. I always felt guilty about that, how it must've hurt Daddy."

"Those masks people wore just after the Great War were terrible things. It was easier for me, I was older. Any little girl would have been frightened." Irene led Sarah upstairs and saw her safely into bed again. She drifted off to sleep once more, to the reassuring sound of Irene washing up downstairs.

She slept another couple of hours. When she woke again she felt properly awake. It was nearly three. Irene was sitting in the lounge, drinking tea. She looked tired herself. There were streaks of gray in her sister's hair, Sarah saw; she was starting to look middle-aged. Irene turned to Sarah with a weary smile.

"How are you, dear?"

"Oh—all right. I've a bit of a headache."

Irene stood. "Now you're awake, why don't I go home and get an overnight bag, then come and spend the night here?"

"What will Steve say?"

"It'll be all right, I'll tell him you're not well. I'll just go to the loo, then get my coat."

She went upstairs, touching Sarah's arm as she passed her. Sarah sat looking out of the window. Across the road there was frost on the lawn of the little park with the old air-raid shelter at the end. She thought of David: looking dapper in his suit and bowler hat; dancing with her the night they met; collapsing in the snow after Charlie died. His cold withdrawal recently. Why had he come back for her? Was it just his sense of duty, a reluctance to throw her to the wolves, or something more? If I'd known what he was doing, she thought, would I have supported him? That's the pity of it, he didn't trust me enough to ask. A cold anger began to grow inside her.

A ring at the doorbell brought her back to reality with a jump. Fear clutched at her again as she walked to the front door. She called out, tremulously, "Who is it?"

"Police."

She opened the door a crack. A tall, middle-aged man with a bushy mustache stood on the doorstep, a sergeant's stripes on the blue sleeve of his coat. He looked like the traditional image of a British policeman but he wore the flat cap of an Auxiliary and there was the bulge of a gun at his waist.

"May I come in, madam?" His tone was polite but very firm. Sarah stepped back and he entered, looking around the hall as he wiped his boots carefully on the doormat. He took off his cap, revealing a head as bald as his mustache was luxuriant.

"Mrs. Sarah Fitzgerald?"

"Yes."

"I'm afraid we're going to have to take you in for questioning, madam."

"Senate House again?" Her voice rose.

"I've to take you to the local station for now. There's a Special Branch officer there wants to talk to you."

Sarah asked, "Is there — is there news of my husband?"

He shook his head. "I don't know anything about that, madam." The sound of the toilet flushing came from the floor above. The sergeant looked up the stairs. "Who's that?" he asked abruptly.

"My sister."

Then, looking past him into the kitchen, Sarah saw the back door slowly open. To her astonishment a middle-aged woman in a gray coat came in; she was short and stocky and had a round face, hard, sharp eyes behind steel spectacles and a tight mouth. She was carrying, of all things, a shopping bag. She put a finger to her lips, indicating Sarah should be quiet. Then, as Sarah watched frozen to the spot, she walked quietly but very quickly through the kitchen into the hall, up behind the policeman. She drew something from her pocket, raised it and hit the policeman sharply on the back of the head just as, becoming aware of something, he'd begun to turn toward her. He let out a cry and stumbled sideways into the banisters, blood seeping from the base of his skull. Sarah saw the woman had a small lead pipe in her hand, the sort of weapon the Jive Boys used.

"I'm from the Resistance," the woman said, quickly and sharply. "Your husband is with us, we've come to get you." All the time she had one eye on the dazed policeman. He groaned and to Sarah's horror began to stagger upright, blinking as he looked at the two women. "You fucking bitches," he said groggily, "You've had it now..."

He reached inside his coat. The woman was holding up her piece of pipe threateningly, ready to lunge forward, but the policeman was pulling a gun from his pocket. Sarah heard a click as he cocked it. Then he turned at the sound of a shriek from the top of the stairs. Irene stood there, her coat over one arm, staring at the man in horror.

Sarah reached out and picked up the heavy Regency vase from the telephone table. She lifted it above her head with both arms and brought it down with all her strength on the top of the policeman's head. He made a little moan and fell down in a heap.

Irene put her hands to her face. "Oh my God, oh my God," she moaned, over and over again. The stranger reached down and picked up the gun. Then she put a hand to the policeman's neck. All her movements were swift and professional.

"He's alive," the woman said in a sharp voice. "You did well there." She stood up, then went into the lounge and, twitching the net curtain aside, looked out. Irene came down the stairs and stood at the bottom, staring. Sarah put her arm around her. The woman came back. "Mrs. Fitzgerald," she said sharply, "we must go now." She looked at Irene. "Are you her sister?"

"Yes. Are you from—"

"The Resistance. Does anyone else know you're here?"

"No—"

"Then you get out of here, now. Get into your car and drive away. We'll go out the back way. Go on. We won't have much time; they'll soon start wondering what happened to him." She looked down at the unconscious policeman. "I'll deal with him."

"What do you mean, deal with him?" Irene asked, her voice horrified.

The woman looked meaningfully at the gun, then back at Irene.

"No!" Sarah shouted. "You're not going to kill a man in my house."

"He saw me," the woman answered levelly. "And worse, he saw your sister. Do you want her identified, her family arrested and questioned?"

"Oh God, the children..." Irene sat on the bottom stair, on the point of collapse.

The woman looked fixedly at Sarah. "This is a war, and you're in it now. You're not on the sidelines anymore."

Sarah said, "How did you know to come in when you did?"

The woman snapped, "Because I've been watching this house for hours. Watching you two through the window. I was just about to come and get you this morning when"—she inclined her head at Irene—"you drove up. I've been walking up and down the road, waiting for you to leave, pretending to be a woman shopping. I saw the police car come and thought it was now or never. All right?" Her voice rose angrily.

"Go now," Sarah said to Irene. "Now." She went to her and gave her sister an immense hug. "I'm sorry, I'm so sorry."

Irene pulled away. She looked at the body by the stairs, the brightly colored pieces of the broken vase. She said to Sarah, "I love you."

"I love you, too. Now go, think of the children."

For an unbearable moment Irene stood irresolute, then she put on her coat, walked slowly to the door, and went out.

The woman turned to Sarah. "You'd better get your coat too, it's cold. Go on."

"What's your name?"

"Meg. Now hurry."

Sarah fetched her coat and handbag. Outside, she heard Irene's car engine start and the vehicle pull away. She wondered if she would ever see her again. Meg said, "Go and wait in the back garden. I'll join you in a moment."

Standing in the cold garden, looking at the brown flowerbeds she and David had worked on not much more than a week ago, Sarah heard a muffled bang from inside the house. She closed her eyes.

Meg came out. Her prim little mouth was set hard. She met Sarah's look challengingly. "We have to climb over the fence, get to the lane that runs along the back. That's how I got in. Be careful not to tear your clothes. We're going on public transport, you don't want to draw any attention to yourself."

"Where are we going?"

Meg smiled encouragingly then, the first touch of humanity Sarah had seen in her face. "Somewhere safe," she said.

CHAPTER THIRTY-EIGHT

F rank felt Ben's pinch and when he woke he thought he was back at school, in the dormitory, and they were doing something to him. He screamed. Then he saw he was in a strange room, with David and Ben and it all came back; he hadn't managed to kill himself and now they had him.

David leaned forward and put a hand on his shoulder, making him flinch. He said, "It's all right, Frank, we've got you away from the hospital, we're going to take you somewhere safe." Frank stared back at him. Last night, when David came up to him in the road, he had felt a surge of relief for a second and then renewed fear, because his friend had to be part of the conspiracy. He couldn't remember anything since then. David's expression now was the same as last night's, a sort of desperate compassion.

"Where am I?" Frank said. His head was thumping, his voice hoarse.

"In a house some way from the hospital. We're safe." Frank became aware of sounds outside the room, footsteps. David gave him a sickly smile. "You've startled everybody, yelling like that."

The door opened and Geoff came in. "What happened?"

"Frank woke up; he shouted, he's confused. It's all right."

Ben asked Frank, "How're ye feeling?"

"I've a headache." There were other people in the doorway now; he saw a tall, pretty woman who Frank thought had been there the night before, and a stern-looking old man.

"What's going on?" the old man asked sharply. "That yell gave Elsie a shock. What's the matter with him?"

He gave Frank a worried stare. Frank had seen that look before, on the faces of visitors coming to the asylum, people who were scared of the mad. Ben said, briskly, "Leave David and me wi' him, will you? Everything's all right."

The others went out, the old man giving Frank that look again over his shoulder. Ben asked him some more about his headache, which was fading now, held fingers up in front of his face for him to count, took his pulse. "You'll do," he said, looking relieved. "Sorry I had tae give you such a big dose last night, but we had to get you out." He looked genuinely apologetic.

"Why have you done this?"

"We're all working for the Resistance, pal. We're gonna get ye oot the country."

Frank turned to David, his voice catching. "Why?"

"You remember why you got put in the hospital?" David hesitated. "Because your brother"—he hesitated—"fell out of the window."

"I pushed him," Frank said bleakly.

"Well, we know your brother told you something important." Frank's eyes widened with fear, and David raised his hands in a soothing gesture. "That's all we know. Your brother told people in America what he had done, and they asked us to get you out. We don't know what it is that you know, we don't want you to tell us. We probably wouldn't understand anyway," he added in an attempt at humor.

"Where is Edgar?"

"Still in America. He's being held somewhere safe. That's all we've been told. You see, the American security services got in touch with us, they asked us to free you."

"We're going across country to the south coast," Ben continued. "The Americans plan to pick us up in a submarine. What aboot that, eh?"

Frank tried to think. He said, "But two policemen came, just before you did. One of them was German. I thought you were all working together."

"No." David looked hurt. "How could you think that?"

"How would I know any different?" Frank asked with sudden anger.

Ben said, "We think the Germans also know you have important information. That's why we had to get you out straightaway."

Frank looked between them. It was hard to take in. Ben said, "Did you tell the police anything when they came to see you that day?"

"No! And I'm not saying any more to anyone. Maybe I don't know anything," he added defiantly.

"All right, Frank," David said soothingly. "But please, you have to trust us."

Ben asked, "Is that why you tried to kill yourself? Because you were scared someone wid force you to tell what you knew?"

Frank nodded dumbly. His head still ached but he had to concentrate. He still couldn't quite believe what David and Ben were saying was true, but he was starting to feel flickers of something he hadn't known in a long time: hope. He said, "They'll be after us."

"Yes," David agreed heavily. "We have to hide out here till our people tell us it's safe to continue to London."

A thought struck Frank. "What about your wife, David? Your job?"

"My job's finished. I'm on the run like you now." His eyes were bleak. "My wife didn't know I was working for the Resistance. Our people are trying to get her out, too."

Ben said, "Why don't we gi' you a shave, then you can get dressed in some nice new clothes we've got for you, and get something to eat." He reached out and grasped Frank's shoulder, making him cringe again. "It's okay, you don't have to tell us anything, just go along with us. That's how we'll stay safe. Will ye dae that, Frank?"

"They'll be after us," Frank said again. "When they find we've gone."

"They won't get us, we're smart."

"I don't want to be drugged again like last night."

"All right. I'll just give you your normal dose. Just to keep you calm."

"I'll behave," Frank said bitterly. He hated the way Ben spoke to him sometimes, as though he were a child. He was beginning to believe their story, but even if what they said was true the police and the Germans would be searching already. If the Germans had any inkling of what he knew they would be desperate to find him. He thought, *I'll wait, I'll find a chance, I'll still finish it.* Then he glanced at David's serious, unhappy face and something in his look, the memory of their old friendship, made him want to cling to life. He clenched his good hand into a tight fist. He mustn't allow himself to think like that. There was still only one certain way to keep his secret safe.

Ben took him to the bathroom and shaved him, Frank guessed because they didn't trust him with an open razor. Afterwards he changed his clothes under Ben's eye. When he had finished dressing he went over and looked out of the bedroom window. He saw a gravel drive, some shrubbery, a dead-looking palm tree, everything covered in frost. Directly below him was the car they had arrived in, the roof glittering with ice crystals. They were only on the second floor. If he jumped out he would land on the car and might break a leg or an arm but that was all. The enormity and horror of what he was thinking, what he had already tried to do, suddenly overwhelmed him and he leaned his head forward, resting it on the cold glass.

Ben came over. "What are you doing?" he asked sharply.

"Nothing."

"Come on. Let's get some breakfast." He took Frank's arm and led him to the door.

Downstairs, the others had already eaten and were sitting around the table smoking, the old woman he had seen the night before bustling about with plates. Geoff stood up. "Morning, Frank. Feeling better?"

"A bit woozy." I'll pretend to be more dopey than I am, he thought.

The woman brought him a plentiful breakfast, bacon and eggs and porridge, toast and butter. Frank found he was very hungry. As he ate the others all watched him. The foreign woman was there. He saw there was a touch of a slant to her eyes. Her expression as she looked at him was kind but there was a hardness in her face. David had shaved, too, but still looked washed out, though Geoff seemed like his old self, puffing away on his pipe.

Afterwards Ben gave him his pill—just one small pill, his usual dose—and the foreign woman brought him an identity card with the name Michael Hadleigh on the front. She leaned over him, those slightly slanted eyes staring into his, and said in accented English, "Just in case we get asked for identity cards for any reason, this is your name. Look at it and remember it. Do you think you can do that, Frank?"

"Yes, yes, I can." He wondered where she came from. The accent didn't sound German, thank God.

"I've a doctor's letter as well, not a real one but it looks authentic enough. It says you've got TB and we're friends taking you to a sanatorium in London. If anyone asks us to show them our ID cards they're likely to let us past quickly, people are frightened of TB. There's more of it around every winter now."

"Pretty clever, eh?" Geoff said.

Frank said, "Yes, it is."

Natalia turned to him, a little apologetically. "Before we go we'd like to wash your hair and tidy it up. Would you mind?"

"No," Frank said, touching his uneven fuzz. It sounded a good idea. "Are we likely to get stopped?"

"No," Geoff said reassuringly. "But you never know these days."

"Especially with what's happening with the Jews," Natalia agreed.

"What have they done with them?" Frank asked. "I heard they'd all been taken away."

"We don't know," David answered bleakly. "They've put them in resettlement camps outside the towns. But we don't know what's going to happen from there."

"Maybe they're going to take them by train to the Isle of Wight. Maybe the Germans will kill them there," Geoff said. "Perhaps Beaverbrook will keep them where they are for now, dangle them in front of the Germans as a bargaining chip."

"They'll hand them over to the Germans, all right," David said bitterly. "They'll take them to Eastern Europe and finish them off."

"Barbarians!" Colonel Brock burst out suddenly, standing up. "Never had too much time for the Israelites myself, but this—it's barbarism, barbarism!"

The door opened and his wife came in, excitement glowing in her face. She looked at David. "I've just had news over the radio," she said. "From our people in London. Your wife's safe, our people have got her!"

David's whole body flooded with relief. Colonel Brock came over and shook his hand vigorously. "Thank God! Congratulations, old chap!" Geoff clapped him on the shoulder. Frank saw David look over at Natalia. She gave him a tight little smile, and a nod.

Mrs. Brock continued, "You've all to stay here a few days." She had seemed nervous last night but the news seemed to have energized her. "There are roadblocks around Birmingham. That's good, though, because they must think Dr. Muncaster's been taken there." She gave Frank a quick look; like her husband she seemed a little frightened of him. "The submarine will be off the south coast to pick you up at the weekend. In the meantime, when it looks quieter, you'll all go down to London."

Her husband asked, "Do we know where on the south coast?"

"No, they're not telling us yet."

Colonel Brock nodded. "That's wise." He looked around the group. "Well, looks like you'll be here for a while. Please don't go out, and stay away from the second-floor windows. Passersby can see up there from over the wall."

"We're safe here?" Geoff asked.

"Yes. So far as the neighbors are concerned we're just a couple of retired local worthies." He nodded at his wife. "Mrs. Brock's the producer of the village Christmas panto."

Natalia said, "We ought to hide the car. Just in case."

Colonel Brock nodded. "Quite right. I'll put it in the garage, under a dust sheet. So," he said emphatically. "We all know where we are then, eh?"

They stayed there four days, not leaving the house. The weather remained cold and dry, with frosts each night. Frank spent most of the time in his bedroom. There was always someone with him, usually David or Ben. He said as little as possible and to his relief they kept their word and didn't ask him about what had happened with his brother.

Sometimes they played chess, a game for which Frank had always had a gift. Ben gave him his drugs regularly, and always watched carefully to make sure he swallowed the pill. At night, as at the hospital, he had a double dose to make him sleep. He wondered how much Ben had given him on the night of their escape. He saw little of Natalia or the Brocks, though from his window he would see Mrs. Brock going out from time to time, presumably to the village, and twice a day Colonel Brock took the black Labrador, like its master stiff and elderly, for a walk. When they met for meals Ben would sometimes try to provoke the colonel into an argument. One evening the colonel showed them a gold-gilt carving of the Hindu elephant-headed god Ganesha, a beautiful thing. "Picked it up in Bombay for a song," he said proudly.

"Looted it from the subject peoples, eh?" Ben said.

The colonel reddened and Frank thought he would explode, but he only snapped, "I paid the fair market price." Frank wished Ben wouldn't do things like that.

He still intended to do away with himself if he got the chance, but they watched him constantly. Meanwhile he tried to find out as much as possible about what was going on. In their room he asked Ben about his past, how he came to be working in the asylum.

"I was already there when you came," Ben said. "There's a lot of people in the Resistance now, we're everywhere. There's sympathizers, and activists, in most of the bigger asylums."

"How did you come to be in that job?"

Ben smiled, showing crooked teeth. "A few years ago I'd been in trouble up in Glasgow. Fighting the Fascists. They decided I needed a new identity and a new job. I'd got into trouble when I was a lad, too. So I got a new name and applied to train as a mental health nurse. It's easy to get into, even these days, the job disnae exactly attract thousands of applicants. And I can handle myself, that's important in the job."

"So Ben's not your real name?"

He shook his head. "No. Mind, I've been Ben Hall for so long I've near forgotten my old one."

"What sort of trouble did you get into when you were young?"

Ben shrugged. "I got put in a Borstal when I was seventeen, I got radicalized in there. Afterwards I was a union organizer in Glasgow, for the Party, trying to get people to stand up for themselves. A few fights, too, when they sent the Auxies in."

"The party—you mean the Communist Party?"

"That's right." He looked at Frank. "We've never been frightened of getting our hands dirty."

"Killing people, you mean," Frank said.

"Ye cannae make an omelet without breaking eggs."

Frank thought of Russia, all the prison camps the Germans had discovered. "Poor eggs," he said.

"Ye've nae idea what life's like for poor people." Ben glowered. "Prices going up, wages going down, locked up if you protest or strike. That last strike I organized, in the shipyards. We marched into Glasgow, a peaceful demonstration, plenty of Labour and nonpolitical people wi' us, but as soon as we got near the city center the Auxies came out with batons, just hitting out at anybody, and when we tried to run they had a crowd of SNP thugs waiting for us in the side streets. They laid into us with knives and knuckledusters while some cunt in a kilt stood on some steps playin' the bloody bagpipes. One of them hit me on the head. I'd've been a goner if some of my pals hadnae got me away. That's when it was decided I needed a change of identity. They'd had me marked out."

Frank looked at him. "We had a teacher at Strangmans who was a Scottish Nationalist. History teacher, always going on about the English landlords and the Highland clearances."

"He wasnae much good then. It was mostly Scottish landowners who cleared the Highlanders out of their crofts for sheep. The SNP." His face wrinkled with distaste. "There were some Fascist sympathizers among them that founded the SNP. Everything for the glorious nation. Some romantic-minded left-wingers too, but they got kicked out after 1940. You know, the Nats opposed conscription in 1939, sayin' it wis against the Act of Union for Scots to be conscripted into the British army. That was more important to them than fighting the Nazis." Ben laughed bitterly. "Whenever a party tells you national identity matters more than anything else in politics, that nationalism can sort out all the other problems, then watch out, because you're on a road that can end with fascism. Even if it doesn't, the idea that nationality's some sort of magic that can make other problems disappear, it's like believin' in fairies. And of course nationalists always have to have an enemy, the English or the French or the Jews, there always has tae be some other bugger that's caused all the problems."

Frank didn't answer. He was a little scared by Ben's passion.

"That Edinburgh school you were at, did you get bullied for being English?" Ben asked.

"Not really. Though sometimes they'd shout English — well, and a rude word. But I'm half Scottish, my dad was Scottish."

Ben looked at him curiously. "How d'yae feel about Scotland?"

Frank shrugged. "As you said once, I'm sure there are places just as bad in England. I don't care about whether people are Scottish or English, all this stupid nationalism. I agree with you there. But I'm not a Communist either."

Ben nodded, smiled sadly. "Ye're a good man, Frank, ye've nae malice in ye."

Frank hesitated, then said, "You remember you told me it was in my hospital notes that I got my bad hand through an accident at school?"

"Aye."

"Well, it wasn't an accident."

"You mean someone did it deliberately?" Ben looked shocked, though Frank wouldn't have thought anything could shock him.

Frank shook his head. His head felt a little odd suddenly. He had said too much.

Frank found it easier talking to David and Geoff. They would reminisce about their time at Oxford. Still trying to find out as much as he could, Frank asked them how they had come to join the Resistance.

"For me it was seeing the blacks cleared off their lands in Kenya, to make way for settlers." Geoff took his pipe from his mouth, pointed the stem at David. "Then I recruited this chap."

"What did you do to help?" Frank asked.

David looked him in the eye. "Passed government secrets on to the Resistance."

"Did you get found out because of me?"

"No. No, that was because of a mistake I made."

"And your wife didn't know?"

"I couldn't involve her. She's a pacifist, you see."

"I suppose I am too," Frank said. "But these days—it can be just an excuse not to get involved, I suppose."

David frowned. "Sarah's no coward."

"I'm sorry. I didn't mean—I meant, I'm the coward. I always have been."

"I don't think so, old chap." Geoff looked at Frank squarely. "Not after what you tried to do in the hospital."

Frank changed the subject. He turned to David. "Well, if we get away, you and your wife will be reunited."

"Yes. Yes, I suppose we will." He sighed.

"It's odd being here, isn't it?" Geoff said. "Being on the run makes you feel—isolated." He frowned. *I've been isolated all my life*, Frank thought. Yet he felt less alone here than he had anywhere, ever.

On the third day at the Brocks' house, when he was sitting playing chess with Ben, Natalia, the European woman, knocked at the door and came in. Frank thought she seemed to be avoiding the men. She hardly spoke to David, she seemed to avoid his eyes. Maybe she didn't like David, though Frank couldn't see why. He knew that Natalia was the leader.

She sat down at the table opposite Frank. "Well," she said, "we're off tomorrow. We've just heard over the radio. We are to drive down to London, there's a place for us to stay south of the river until things are ready for us on the south coast."

"Great," Ben said. "I'm fed up sitting roond here. What d'you think of that, Frank?"

"All right." Frank thought, *when will I get a chance to do it, to kill myself?* His heart began to pound as he realized he didn't want to go through with it now. But he must. Natalia was looking at him keenly.

"Do you feel up to traveling, Frank?"

"Yes."

"Do you trust us?" she asked, in her disconcertingly direct way. "Do you believe we're trying to get you out?"

"Yes," he answered. "I do now."

"Good. You have to be ready to do just as we tell you."

"Because the Germans will be after us?" He met her look.

"Yes. But the heat's died down now. And we've got our new identities, a cover story."

"They could still catch us."

"There's always a risk. But we're confident, or we wouldn't be taking you away from here now."

Ben said, "That's right." He turned to Natalia. "He's talkin' a lot more now. Quite chatty sometimes, aren't ye, Frank?"

Natalia looked at Frank. "If by any chance we were captured," she said seriously, "they wouldn't take us alive. We've made plans to make sure of that."

"What plans?"

"We've decided to tell you, we think it's better you know. If we're taken, we have pills to take. Poison."

"What about me?"

She shook her head. "No, I'm sorry." Frank thought, *they're frightened I'd take my pill the first chance I got.* She said, "I'd take care of it, Frank, I promise." She looked into his eyes. "If it comes. Do you trust me?"

He didn't answer. He believed Natalia, but he desperately feared she might fail; the whole mission might fail. The forces ranged against them were so strong. He thought of the German policeman who had visited him in the asylum. Whatever happened, he couldn't fall into that man's hands again.

CHAPTER THIRTY-NINE

They left on the morning of Friday, the fifth of December. The weather was still cold and frosty; it felt strange to Frank to be out in the open air again. The car they had arrived in was brought out of the garage; the previous evening Geoff and Colonel Brock had fixed on new number plates. David was to drive, Natalia sitting beside him in the front passenger seat, a map on her knees. Colonel Brock and his wife came out to see them off. Frank was about get into the car, Ben's hand on his arm, when the colonel unexpectedly leaned forward and shook his hand, very gently. "Good luck, old chap," he said awkwardly.

A weak sun was starting to melt the frost covering the trees and hedgerows. Geoff had told Frank they planned to take quiet country roads for the first part of the journey, then join the motorway near Northampton. Frank stared out of the window at the empty countryside. He found himself thinking about what had happened to the Jews. He wasn't surprised by what the government had done; he'd always known those in charge were capable of anything now. He remembered there had been a Jewish boy at Strangmans, Golding. There was actually less anti-Semitism at the Presbyterian school than in other places Frank had been; their religious prejudices were directed at Catholics, not Jews. All the same Golding had stood out as different, not attending assembly or religious knowledge classes, but otherwise he had always conformed, been good in class and always part of a crowd of boys. He had sometimes shouted "Monkey!" and "Spastic!" after Frank like the others. Frank had asked himself how Golding, an outsider, had been able to belong while he couldn't. What was it about him? They had gone for him since the first day; it had been like a snowball that rolled on, getting bigger and bigger, nothing and no one to stop it. Well, he thought with heavy desperation, it doesn't matter now.

Following the circuitous route Natalia had traced on the map they passed through a village called Sawley and then came to a fork in the road. To his horror Frank saw a Black Maria turned sideways to block the entrance of the right-hand turning, the one they were going to take. Two young Auxiliaries in heavy blue greatcoats, rifles slung over their shoulders, stood blocking it, stamping their boots in the cold. Frank felt everyone in the car tense.

David turned the wheel to take the left-hand turning, but one of the Auxies waved them to stop. He approached the car, slouching across the road, the barrel of his rifle gleaming in the winter sun. David slowly wound down the window and the Auxie leaned in, nodding to him. He didn't examine their faces closely, he didn't seem that interested. His chubby face was red with cold.

"Where are you headed for, sir?"

"Northampton," David answered, emphasizing the upper-class drawl in his voice. "We've come from Sawley. Is there a problem, Constable?"

"No, sir, only this road's shut off now. We're guarding the new residential camp for the Birmingham Jews."

Frank stared up the closed-off road. It was fringed by trees, their bare branches a skeletal latticework, brown plowed fields on either side. In the distance he thought he made out a row of high poles, what might have been wire strung between them.

"Is it?" Something in David's tone made the policeman look at him sharply.

Ben leaned forward. "Sae long as we get the Yids out of the towns, eh?" he said cheerfully. "It's all right, we can take the longer route." The constable looked at David again, then nodded and stepped away. David steered the car left and they drove in silence till they had crested a hill.

Geoff let out a long breath. "Jesus Christ," he said.

"I'm sorry," David said. "I couldn't help my tone."

"You need tae be able to act in this job, pal," Ben spat angrily. "Our fucking lives could depend on it."

That policemen could have asked for our papers, Frank thought, taken us back to his post, and then—"I need to wee, I'm desperate," he said. "Can we stop?"

"How desperate?" Ben asked. "Can't you wait a bit? When we find a cafe or somethin' ye can go to the cludgie there."

"I need to go now. I'm sorry, please—"

"We should get on," Ben replied. "I want to get as far away from thae Auxies as possible."

"If Frank needs to go, he needs to go," Geoff answered irritably. He leaned over and spoke in a whisper to David. Frank caught his words. "What if he pisses himself? The car'll stink."

They turned down another lane, high laurel hedges beside the road. David stopped the car beside a little gap, just big enough for someone to squeeze through. Ben got out and held the door open for Frank. It was strange to be out in the empty, undulating countryside. It made his head swim after his weeks confined in the hospital. He was glad of the winter coat they had given him before they left the house. He really did need to urinate but he was also thinking, this was a chance to get away. The effects of his morning pill were wearing off, he thought he would be able to run. There was a brown plowed field beyond the hedge, the furrows still white with frost, and what looked like a thick wood beyond. He would head there, if he could get in among the trees all he needed was to find one with a large branch, then use his belt...

"Come on, Frank, wake up," Ben said, not unkindly. He pointed at the gap in the hedge. "We can just aboot squeeze through there."

"I can go on my own."

Ben hesitated. Natalia had wound her window down. She said with unexpected sharpness, "Let him go. Stop treating him like a child."

Ben frowned, and Frank wondered if he was going to argue. He started walking across the verge, frosty grass crunching under his feet, and bent to get through the gap. Ben didn't follow. Little thorny twigs clutched at his clothing, making him wince.

On the other side of the hedge Frank quickly opened his coat, unzipped his flies, and urinated copiously onto the plowed earth. As he did so he looked around quickly, heart thudding fast. He took a deep breath. Then he began running, fast as he could, across the field.

It was much more difficult than he had thought. The frost had made the ground hard but he had to jump from ridge to ridge, earth cracking and flaking under his shoes. He hadn't run for a long time and his legs began shaking; there was a pounding in his ears.

Then he felt something irresistibly strong clutch his legs and he tumbled over, face forward, his chest landing on top of a plowed ridge. He lay there winded, gasping for breath. Hands grabbed his shoulder, pulling him roughly around. David was kneeling over him, his own face red with effort. "For God's sake, Frank," he shouted. "What in hell d'you think you're doing?"

Frank sat up, wheezing. Geoff and Ben and Natalia had got through the hedge and were running toward him. David raised his hand and they halted a little way off, standing like scarecrows in the empty field. He shouted angrily, "Why did you run away from us, Frank? Why?" His voice, echoing across the fields, startled some crows at the edge of the wood. They rose into the air, cawing.

"I'm sorry."

"Don't you trust us?"

Frank looked into David's eyes. "It's not that. I just don't think you can do it," he said. "I'm frightened they'll catch us, they'll get what I know out of me."

"Did you think you could get away on your own?" David asked furiously. "Where the hell would you go?" He grasped Frank's shoulder and shook him roughly. "Where were you planning to run? If you've got someone who might help you around here, Frank, you've got to tell us about it. We're risking our lives to get you out."

Frank looked into the woods again. The crows had circled and were settling back in the trees. "There's nobody, David," he said quietly. "I was going to kill myself. That's what I've got to do. It's the only way I can be sure they don't win. Can't you see that?"

David knelt beside him. "You shouldn't hold your life so cheap, Frank."

"You don't know what it is that I know. I'm so tired, David." He whispered, "It's the Bomb. Edgar was working on the atom bomb, and he told me something about how they built it. If the Germans find out it would let them build atomic weapons, too."

David stared at him, openmouthed. "For God's sake," he breathed. "Don't tell me any more. Not another word."

"Wouldn't it be easier if you just killed me? Wouldn't it be safer? I haven't spoken to anybody else about what Edgar told me, nobody."

"You really mean this, don't you?"

Frank nodded slowly.

David said, "You know that if it comes to it, we won't let them take any of us alive." He sighed. "There's no turning back. We all depend on each other now, we have to trust each other. We've got a good chance if we stick together and keep our heads. There's a whole network of people helping us, Frank. Please promise me you won't do anything like that again. If you try it again you could risk everyone's lives."

He hesitated, looking into David's eyes, then nodded.

David helped him up. They began trudging back to join the others. David held his arm. "You always hated the Nazis, didn't you?" Frank said.

"So did you."

"That's why I'd die rather than help them."

"Better to confound them and live," David answered fiercely.

Frank said, "All those years ago, at university, I must've been a bloody nuisance, hanging around you and Geoff."

"You were our friend."

"All I ever wanted was to be ordinary, to blend in. But I can't."

David smiled wryly. "It's been the same for me. Always." He laughed. "Even more so now, after what you just told me."

"For God's sake," Frank whispered. "Don't tell the others—"

David looked at him. "All right, I won't. But you've got to stay alive for all our sakes, Frank."

David got him back in the car, then stood outside for a few minutes talking with the others. Frank wondered if they might be angry with him now, especially the woman, but she caught him staring at her and smiled. Frank thought, *she understands.*

As they started off again, Ben said, "You've had a hard time, Frank, I know that. You did bloody well holding out against the police in the asylum. But you're with us now, and we'll see ye through. We will. Ye've got tae see that."

"All right," Frank replied. He was too weary to say anything else. They continued on through the countryside, then onto the Great North Road, now driving fast. They're all willing to die to get me out, Frank thought. Though he was still full of dread about what might happen, he felt a rush of warmth toward his companions.

Around one o'clock, after Geoff had passed around some sandwiches the colonel's wife had prepared, and Ben had given him another pill, Frank dozed off, dimly aware of the steady hum of the wheels beneath him.

He woke up at the sound of voices. It was getting dark.

"That's the second train we've seen stopped on the line," Ben was saying.

"Maybe there's a problem with the signals or something," Geoff said. "It always seems to happen on a Friday evening," he added lightly, as though they were ordinary people off for a weekend drive. Frank looked out of the window. On an embankment beside the motorway, he could see a stationary train and, through its lighted, steamed-up windows, passengers in their hats and coats. "Where are we?"

"Another twenty miles to London." Natalia smiled at him as she turned to answer.

They drove on. Frank dozed again. He was woken by the car slowing down. He became conscious of a strange, unpleasant, sulfurous smell. He sat up. It was dark outside. They were in a long queue of traffic, moving very slowly. He realized he couldn't see any lights from streetlamps or houses, and looking ahead he saw a thick, greasy, swirling vapor in the beam of the headlights. Fog, as thick as he had ever seen it.

He sat up. "What's happening?"

"We're stuck," David answered. "That's the last bloody thing we need tonight. It started half an hour ago and it's getting thicker the closer we get to town."

Geoff whistled. "This is some bloody fog," he said.

CHAPTER FORTY

I t was the densest fog David had ever seen, and he had lived in London all his life. Not ordinary fog but a sulfurous chemical smog, with a greenish-yellow tinge. Swirling in the headlights it looked almost liquid, flowing in little waves and eddies. Through it the traffic crawled along, inch by painful inch. The sharp, sulfuric smell in the car grew stronger, and David felt a stinging at the back of his throat. Behind him, Geoff coughed and David remembered his friend was affected by smog, that he sometimes wore one of the little white face masks you could buy from the chemists now.

"Where are we?" David asked Natalia.

She looked at the map, holding it up to her face. "Just outside Watford, I think."

David pulled down the car window. He could see almost nothing outside; even the streetlights were just hazy yellow smudges, distance impossible to judge. He wound the window up. The car in front juddered forward and David followed, but he could only drive a few yards before halting again. Now he could make out a red glow ahead, and peering through the windscreen he saw, in a brief gap in the eddies of fog, a glowing brazier with the hazy figure of a policeman beside it directing the traffic, his arms made visible only by long white gloves.

David looked in the mirror. Frank, sitting between Geoff and Ben, was staring fixedly ahead, an anxious look on his thin face. "You all right there, Frank?" he asked.

"What are we going to do? We're not safe, sitting here. They could get us."

Natalia leaned back and spoke reassuringly. "Nobody knows we're here. The fog helps us, it must be throwing everything into confusion."

"Where are we going?"

"South of the river. New Cross. To a safe house there."

"It'll take fuckin' hours in this," Ben said impatiently.

"He's right," Geoff agreed. "It's going to get worse the further we get into the city." He coughed again.

David thought a moment, looked at Frank's scared face in the mirror, then said, "We could leave the car at Watford and get the Tube to town. At least we'd be moving."

"Yes," Frank agreed insistently. "We should move, we must move. It's not safe stuck in one place."

Ben looked at him dubiously. "You'd have to stay with us, no more running off."

"I will, I promise."

The car in front jerked forward again. Slowly, painfully, they approached the roundabout. The policeman raised a gloved hand for them to halt. The light from his charcoal brazier cast a strange, dim red glow inside the car. Frank shrank back in his seat. The policeman waved them on and they passed into Watford High Street, moving at a snail's pace. There was less traffic here but the cars still crawled along; you couldn't see the taillights of the car in front until you were almost on top of it.

All the shops were shut, but eventually they saw the station entrance, indistinct figures moving to and fro in its light. "This is it," David said. "We have to decide."

"What about the car?" Geoff asked.

"We'll just leave it," Natalia said. "There's nothing to identify us. The number plates are fake. I think there are going to be a lot of abandoned cars tonight."

They left the car and walked into the station entrance, following the signs for the underground. Frank was in the middle, Ben's hand on his arm. To David's relief he showed no sign of wanting to run; rather he seemed happy to have them between him and the anonymous crowds of people milling about. Everyone, it seemed, had decided to take the Tube rather than struggle with cars and buses. The fog had even penetrated the station entrance; David could see it swirling around the lights in the tiled ceiling, a dirty yellow-green. He had seen smog several times before, but never this thick.

"I'll get the tickets," he said to Natalia. "What station?"

"New Cross Gate."

David pushed his way to the ticket booth, leaving the others standing by the wall, Frank shrinking back against it. David thought, he's been shut away for weeks, and now he's in the middle of all this. He bought five single tickets, realizing as he handed over a pound note that he had little money left. He put his wallet back, feeling the hard little pellet of the cyanide pill in his pocket.

They went down the escalator and stood at the back of the platform, which was heaving with people. A train came, but those like them at the back of the crowd were unable to get on. As it pulled out the remaining passengers moved up to the edge of the platform. Next to him David saw Frank looking down at the rails with a sort of horrified fascination. He gripped his arm. It felt painfully thin. "All right?" he asked.

"All these people," Frank muttered. On David's other side, Geoff coughed again.

Another train rattled in. The doors opened, disgorging a crowd of passengers. They were tired and grumpy and one or two looked ill, coughing or gasping. David, still holding Frank's arm, guided him quickly to a double seat and sat down beside him.

The journey into London was horrible. The train was packed, more and more people squeezing into the carriage at every stop. People were complaining about the smog, saying they had never seen anything like it. Some parts of the city were worse than others, they said; you could have a patch that was almost clear and then suddenly you couldn't see a hand in front of your face. It was as though the fog moved about, like a living thing.

Frank sat staring down to where someone had dropped an empty bottle of cream soda, which rattled to and fro on the dusty wooden carriage floor. He watched it intently.

"Bearing up all right?" David asked.

"Yes." He did not look up. "That bottle."

"What about it?"

"You'd think you could predict how long it would take to roll from one side to the other, where it's going to end up, but you can't. Just little variations in the way the train moves change its trajectory." He looked at David seriously. "People can't predict things the way they believe they can. Too many variables."

David knew he was thinking of their journey, the hope of reaching safety. "Well, don't you go rolling away anywhere."

Frank glanced up. "I won't. I promised you."

David smiled at him uncertainly. He wished Frank hadn't told him in the field that his secret involved nuclear weapons. He wondered if those in charge of the abduction knew, or just the Americans. He supposed that if Frank's knowledge might help the Germans to build an atom bomb, it might help the British as well. And the Russians. Did the Russians have the knowledge or resources to do something like that? Nobody knew; they could have been experimenting for years. The Anglo-German treaty forbade nuclear research in Britain, but who knew what went on in secret?

They changed trains twice. The crowds were a nightmare, the smog creating a haze inside the station concourses, which were jammed with people. It took well over an hour to get to the end of the line. When they got out into the street again the smog was thicker than ever; they could see each other but little more. As they stood on the pavement a bus suddenly loomed up, invisible a second before though every window was lit, then vanishing again just as suddenly.

"Where to now?" Geoff asked.

"It's close," Natalia said. "I memorized the directions."

She led them to the left, walking at a snail's pace into an area of small terraced houses with low, walled front yards. David hoped to God Frank wouldn't make a run for it because if that happened, they would lose him in this. Ben was holding his arm. There were few people about, most edging their way along, clutching at hedges and fences; without anything to fix on you lost your sense of direction immediately. They could see smudgy yellow lights from streetlamps and vague muzzy glows from the curtained windows of the houses they passed, but nothing else. Distance was impossible to judge. It was very quiet, sound muffled by the swirling fog.

They almost collided with three young women walking slowly along, one behind the other, holding hands. They held scarves over the lower halves of their faces to keep out the stinking smog. Natalia asked if they were going the right way for Kitchener Street, and was told it was the next turning. When they had gone Natalia said, "We should do that, hold hands. Then we won't lose each other."

"Good idea," Ben agreed quickly. He still held Frank's arm, and David reached out to take his other hand. Frank said quickly, "That's my bad hand. Take the wrist, not the hand, or it'll hurt."

"Okay."

Natalia took David's other hand. Hers felt warm and dry. It struck him that he had never touched her before. All the time at the Brocks' she had avoided him; he knew she didn't want to make him feel worse when he was reunited with Sarah. But her touch made him realize he still wanted her.

They walked on, still at a snail's pace, brushing against the privet hedges. The leaves felt damp and greasy. Twice more they almost collided with people, but everyone seemed good-natured. David was reminded of the air-raid warnings of 1939–40, when he was home on leave that winter, people's forced cheerfulness as they hurried to the shelters in the blackout, hiding their fear of the destruction from the air that in the end never came.

They found the right turning, peering up to read the street sign. Natalia bent to look at the number on a gate. "This is Number 4," she said. "We want Number 42. Count the houses."

They reached what they thought was the right house. David opened the gate, went up the little path and knocked at the door. A thin, harassed-looking woman in curlers answered, children's voices sounding behind her. She stared at him. "Yes?"

The code word was the same as they'd used at the Brocks', Aztec, but David sensed it was the wrong house. "I'm looking for Number 42," he said instead.

The woman frowned. "Two doors along."

David touched his hat. "Thank you."

"This bloody stuff," she said. "You're letting it in." She closed the door on him with a snap. As he walked away, David saw a curtain had been pulled back from the front window. A little boy was staring out at him, eyes hostile and unblinking.

They went to the next house but one. This time the door was answered by a big dark-haired man in his forties, in a vest and braces. He looked at David inquiringly.

"Mr. O'Shea?"

"That's me." His Irish accent made David think of his father.

"Aztec," David said, feeling oddly foolish.

"You all safe?" the man asked quietly.

"Yes. Yes, we are."

He took them along a narrow hall, into a crowded living room at the back of the house. A coal fire blazed in a grate. An old-fashioned television with a tiny screen was on in a corner, showing a program about a new dam the Italians were building in Ethiopia. A small, squarely built woman in a flowered pinny, with graying black hair, sat working a sewing machine on a large table that dominated the room. She stood up as they crowded in. The man spoke quietly. "They're here safely. Five of them, like they said."

The woman smiled. Her face was lined, kindly, but strong. "Everything go all right?" She too, was Irish.

"Like a dream," Ben answered. "Apart from that fog."

The woman's eyes went to Frank. "Are you the scientist?"

Frank had been staring with that wide-eyed, fearful look again but something about Mrs. O'Shea seemed to reassure him. "Yes," he answered calmly.

She looked to the others. "Now, which of you is Mr. Fitzgerald?"

David stepped forward. "I am."

She came up and took his hand. For a terrible second he thought it was bad news, but then she said softly, "Your wife is still safe, dear. Just to let you know, all's well there."

David took a long, shuddering breath. "Thank you, thank you. Is she—is she coming here?" He realized suddenly that he feared the prospect.

"No, we felt it safer to get her out of London straightaway. You'll meet up later. It's all taken care of. Now, where's my manners? Sit down, all of you."

They gathered around the big table. Mr. O'Shea switched off the television and sat in a sagging armchair beside it. He took up a pipe and lit it, his eyes darting between them. Natalia said, "What is to happen next?"

"You're to stay here a couple of days," Mrs. O'Shea answered. "Then you'll go south to the coast, by train probably. We'll have to wait till this fog clears, it's too thick for anyone to move about safely, and there's something up with the railway timetables just now."

"I work in the goods yards," her husband said. "They were arranging some big transports to Portsmouth this weekend. We think that's why they settled the strike. But whatever they were going to do, they've had to call it off because of the fog."

"We think they were planning to move the Jews across to the Isle of Wight. Into German hands." Mrs. O'Shea smoothed down her pinny with work-roughened hands. "It's a terrible thing."

David was appalled. "As soon as this?"

Mr. O'Shea nodded through a haze of pipe smoke. "I think so. We should've seen this coming. We know the army have been ordering vast quantities of barbed wire for months. To build the detention camps, of course."

"And when they were all lifted from their homes, the Sunday before last, it was done so quietly and smoothly most people didn't even notice. We've heard today the same thing's happened to the French Jews. Oh, they've been planning this a long time, the devils."

There was a moment's silence, then she continued, "Anyway, moving you all is going to be a bit more complicated than we thought. And while you're with us you'll have to stay indoors, I'm afraid. There's too many of you to be visitors. People notice things around here."

"We're gettin' used tae it," Ben said. "Eh, Frank?"

"We went to another house by mistake before this one," Natalia said. "Two doors down, it would have been Number 38."

Mr. and Mrs. O'Shea exchanged a sharp glance. Mr. O'Shea asked, "Who did you speak to?"

David said, "A woman. And there was a little boy peering out of the window. I didn't give her the code word, just asked for Number 42. She shut the door on me, saying I'd let the fog in."

"That's the Sperrins," Mrs. O'Shea said. "He's active in Coalition Labour, he's got Blackshirt friends." She thought a moment. "Did she see all of you?"

"I don't think so. The fog's so thick, I think they just saw me."

"She'll be at the shops tomorrow. I'll tell her you got the wrong street in the fog, you were after 42 Majuba Street." She stood up. "Now, I'll get you something to eat."

"Can I help?" Natalia asked and followed Mrs. O'Shea out to the kitchen.

Her husband caught David's glance. "Bert Sperrin was in the old Labour Party with me. When it split in 1940 I stayed with Attlee but he went with the other lot. He was always a big Empire man." He pursed his lips sadly. "We used to be friends, would you believe it? He knows where I stand, so we have to watch him."

"I'm sorry."

He didn't answer for a moment, puffing at his pipe. Then he looked at David. "Fitzgerald, that's an Irish name."

"Yes, my father was from Dublin."

"You were brought up in England, though?"

"Yes. Dad has the accent. He's in New Zealand now."

Mr. O'Shea sighed. "Well, there's nothing good for the Irish left in

De Valera's republic, unless you're a pro-German Catholic like him and his friends."

"I've never been that," David said.

"No," Mr. O'Shea said. "You sound like you went to some English public school."

"Grammar school, actually."

"Yes. Well."

"You've got children?" Geoff nodded at a box of comics under the table.

"Eamonn and Lucy. Eleven and twelve." Mr. O'Shea's voice softened. "We've sent them to their auntie's. Little pigs have big ears and even at their age the school goes on at them to beware of terrorists everywhere. That and teaching them about the endless glories of English history," he added bitterly. "Bringing civilization everywhere, even to Ireland. The history teaching's got even more nationalistic and imperialistic since that Fascist fellow traveler Sir Arthur Bryant got made Education Minister." He looked curiously at Frank. "Well, so you're the man everybody wants."

Frank shrank back in his chair. "I can't say anything about it. I mustn't."

"You wouldn't believe the effort that's been put into getting you out the country."

"Leave 'im, pal," Ben said firmly.

"Is he safe?" Mr. O'Shea asked brutally. "I know he's been in a loony bin."

"He's safe."

Frank said, "I don't feel good, Ben. My mouth's dry, my heart's started jumping."

"I think you need your pill, Frank. I'll get you a glass of water."

Frank looked at Mr. O'Shea. "I don't want to take it in front of everyone," he said with a touch of defiance.

Mrs. O'Shea came in from the kitchen. "Got a cludgie I can take him to, missus?" Ben asked.

"Yes. I might as well show you where you're sleeping, while I'm at it."
She smiled at Frank. "Poor lamb."

There were three small bedrooms upstairs. Mr. and Mrs. O'Shea had one
and mattresses had been laid on the floors of the other two, little children's beds pushed into a corner. Frank and Ben would have one room,
David and Geoff the other. Natalia would sleep downstairs. As they had
at the Brocks' they would each take turns to stay awake during the night,
though, as Mrs. O'Shea said, there would be little enough to see in the
fog. The television news, which they watched when they went back
downstairs, showed buses crawling along London streets led by policemen carrying lanterns; people queuing to buy facemasks at London
chemists; theaters and cinemas being closed. Two women had been
attacked and robbed in the smog. There was no sign of it lifting, and
people with chest problems were being urged to stay indoors.

Natalia and Mrs. O'Shea brought in the food and they all crowded
around the table. Frank was quiet, half asleep. Natalia began by thanking the O'Sheas on behalf of them all. "We know what we are asking of
you," she said.

"Call me Eileen," Mrs. O'Shea said. "This is Sean." Her husband nodded briefly. "I'll go out tomorrow and get some supplies, then I'm meeting
my contact to get some news." She looked at David. "I'll get them to tell
your wife you're safe."

"Thank you."

"Sean'll be leaving early in the morning for his shift. I may be out a
good while, it won't be easy getting around even in daylight by the look
of this. Remember you mustn't go out, any of you." There was steel in her
clear blue eyes as she looked at each of them in turn.

"We'll stay in," Natalia answered firmly.

Geoff coughed again. "If you're near a chemist, could you get me one
of those facemasks? Sorry, it sounds silly."

"It's not silly at all. I'll be sure I do."

"Even in here my throat's rasping." David looked at his friend. He did look
uncomfortable. The bitter smell of the fog was starting to seep into the house.

Mr. O'Shea asked, "What's the phrase the Germans use, when they make people disappear?"

"Night and fog," Geoff answered. "*Nacht und nebel*. It comes from Wagner."

"It would. We hear enough of that bastard on the radio."

"It'll be all rock 'n' roll when you get to America, I expect," Eileen said, resolutely cheerful. David shook his head; it was hard to imagine.

"The archbastion of capitalism," Ben said ironically. "Still, needs must when the devil drives." He turned to Sean. "You work on the railways, then?"

"Have done since I came over here in '23. After the Irish War of Independence."

"Did you fight?" David asked.

Sean nodded. "In the Civil War, too. I was a Michael Collins man. My people are dirt-poor farmers. From Wexford."

"What d'ye think about the railwaymen's pay claim gettin' settled?" Ben asked. "I didnae think the government would give way."

"Ah, they got the union leaders in and offered them just enough to buy the men off. They'll need them if they're going to transport the Jews. The so-called union," he added bitterly, "full of right-wing Coalition Labour people."

Ben nodded agreement. "They're crafty. They know the minimum the men will accept. Real unions would have the men out, like the Liverpool dockers. But the workers will win in the end, they must."

Sean looked at him askance. "That sounds like the Communist line."

"It's the truth, mac."

Sean shook his head. "No, it isn't. The railwaymen have always been right-wing. Have you forgotten Jimmy Thomas, that betrayed the miners in the General Strike?" He pointed the stem of his pipe at Ben. "You'd be surprised how many union people supported the peace in 1940, and have ever since. Even now it's low wages that brought the threat of the railway strike, not politics."

"The shop stewards should've held out for more. The railwaymen could bring the whole country to a stop."

"Then they'd bring the army in."

"My husband's been a shop steward over twenty years." Eileen raised her voice. "It's getting more dangerous all the time, all it needs is for him to make some pro-Resistance comment to the wrong fella and he'd be charged with sedition." She stabbed an angry finger at Ben. "So don't tell him all he needs to do is snap his fingers to bring the revolution."

"But they're fighting up North," Ben countered fiercely. "Demonstrating, facing down the police, fightin' back. What about the Liverpool dock strike, the Yorkshire miners, the Scottish printers—"

Geoff said, "They're desperate in the North, with wages driven down to nothing by unemployment—"

"And there are special circumstances there," David said. "Everyone knows the mine owners are hopeless, all those little inefficient companies, and they keep going by driving wages down—"

"Wages are bad down here, too," Ben responded. "Though on a civil servant's pay I dare say you widnae notice," he added sarcastically. "The tide's turning, and that's what it is, the tide of history. The pro-German newspaper magnates have controlled the press since before the war— we've got one as bloody Prime Minister—and the BBC, and the radio, but they cannae keep us down forever, the ordinary people—"

"The proletariat, you mean," Natalia said, sounding weary.

"Aye, the proletariat. The working class. We'll win in the end, like Lenin did in Russia—"

"So, Ben, you'd like Europe to be as Russia was?" Natalia said. "With those huge prison camps the Germans found there?"

"The Germans built those camps, got German actors to pretend to be Russian prisoners—"

Natalia shook her head. "No, you're wrong. I understand enough Russian to know what the survivors were saying. And you saw their faces on the newsreels, they were starving, dying—"

"All right. Mebbe Stalin went too far, but people exaggerate that. Khrushchev and Zhukov want a different Russia—"

Sean said, "Opposition may be growing here. But this government's still got plenty of supporters, including working-class people like our bloody neighbor. Beaverbrook's got his newspapers behind him. And the police and the army and the Germans. It'll be a long bloody battle and I hope to God we get something new and better at the end of it. Not what the Russians had."

"Probably we'd end up like America," Geoff said. "Not sure that'd be a good thing entirely."

Frank sat up. "Don't fight among yourselves like this," he said pleadingly. "Please, don't."

Ben said, "We're just having a wee chat—"

"It's because of me you're all here." There was a sudden silence around the table. "You're the brave ones, the ones who decided to fight. You need to stand together."

They went to bed after the meal, tired out. In their room Geoff undressed and got under the covers.

"Are you all right?" David asked.

"I'll survive." Geoff nodded at the mug full of water he had brought up. "My throat's so damn dry, I keep drinking. I'll be getting up to piss in the night, I'm afraid. Funny how this damned fog affects some people more than others." He smiled. "Good news about Sarah, eh?"

"Yes."

"I can't help worrying about Mum and Dad. But like Jackson said, they don't know anything, and they've got contacts."

"They'll be okay."

"How d'you think Frank is?"

"He's in a state still, you could tell from what he said at dinner. But I don't think he'll try to run again. He promised me. I think I'll just drop in on him now, before bed."

David knocked at the door of the next room. Ben had stripped to his underwear and was folding his clothes neatly beside his mattress. David saw a big round scar on the side of his stocky torso, a row of long scars on the backs of his thighs. The round scar looked like a bullet wound. He realized how little he knew about Ben, what he had been through. Frank was just taking off his shirt, his white body painfully thin.

"Everything all right?" David asked.

"Aye," Ben answered cheerfully. "Just settlin' doon for the night, aren't we?"

"I'm very sleepy," Frank said. "I've had my nighttime pills."

"We all are," Ben said. "Still, we can rest up tomorrow. That's war, isn't it? All action one day, then sitting around doing nothing the next." David realized Ben was happy, he was enjoying the danger. "We can have another game of chess tomorrow, if you like," he said to Frank. "You can beat me again."

David said goodnight. He wanted a cigarette. In case it made Geoff's throat worse—his friend hadn't had his pipe out all evening—he went downstairs to the kitchen. Natalia was standing there, quietly smoking. He felt the sudden rush of physical attraction again.

She nodded at him, smiled. "I just had a look outside," she said. "You can't see a thing."

David lit a cigarette and leaned on the edge of the cooker. "Safer for us all if we can't be seen."

"Yes."

"I think you got the better of that argument with Ben earlier. About the Soviets."

"Ben is a good man, he cares more about Frank than he shows. But he is naive about Russia." She sighed heavily. "He needs something to cling on to, I suppose, like all of us do who have turned our backs on normal life."

"What do you cling on to?"

She blew out a cloud of smoke. "Beating the Fascists."

David said, "I hope this smog goes on. If it stops them moving the Jews to the Isle of Wight. The Germans would take them east then, wouldn't they?"

"Yes." Natalia cast her eyes down. "I'm afraid the fog can't go on forever."

He hesitated, then said, "Natalia, you haven't told anyone, have you? About me being half Jewish? Only there was something in the way Mrs. O'Shea looked at me earlier..."

She frowned. "No, I have said nothing. I promised." She looked at him seriously. "You should tell our people about yourself," she added. "We are all against what is being done, you know that."

"Perhaps. Only—I've kept it secret so long."

"Are you ashamed?" she asked. "That you are a half-Jew?"

"There are no half-Jews left in Europe, Natalia. You know that. You're either a Jew or you're not. No, I'm not ashamed of being Jewish, though I've no idea what it's like to be a Jew; and why should it matter what your parents were, why should it mean anything? But nationality and race— that's all that matters now."

"I know. All over Europe."

"What I'm ashamed of is secrets. Even though my parents kept mine to help me get on." He smiled sadly. "It was good practice for being a spy, I suppose."

She nodded, sympathetic now.

"You know," David said suddenly, "I'm afraid of seeing her again. My wife."

"Don't you want to?"

"All the secrets I kept from her." He shook his head. "So many. You know, this is the first time I've been away from Sarah since we were married. But in other ways we've been apart for years. I really don't know if we can come together again. I've taken away her house, her safety, any reason for her to trust me again. I don't know if she'll even want to try." He bit his lip, then said, "Or if I do." He looked down. He felt Natalia step closer, put a hand on his arm. He glanced up at her in surprise. She smiled softly. She was giving in to him, she had wanted to all along. And he wanted to cling to her, to cling to a woman but especially to her, more than he ever had in his life. But then, abruptly, he shook his head. "No. You were right. Not now."

She smiled sadly, and stepped away.

"I'm sorry," he said, turning away to the stairs.

CHAPTER FORTY-ONE

After shooting the policeman Meg had led the way rapidly up the road to Kenton Station. Sarah could hardly believe what she had done; she kept seeing the vase shatter against the policeman's head, the blood and the porcelain shards flying out. But he'd had a gun and would have killed them all.

She stumbled; Meg turned and gave her an angry glare. "Come on," she snapped. "Before that man's missed and a hundred of them come down on us. Don't draw attention, try and look normal. But hurry." Sarah tried to compose herself. She thought of what it must have been like for Meg, walking up and down her street, waiting for Irene to go, then seeing the policeman enter the house. She seemed quite unaffected by cold-bloodedly shooting a man. Were they all like this in the Resistance, this brutal? Was this what David was like, underneath?

They reached Kenton Station. Meg bought a couple of tickets. A Tube came quickly and soon they were clattering down to London. They got off at Piccadilly Circus. "This is it," Meg said briskly. A queue of excited children and their parents, wrapped against the cold, waited outside a shop where a large poster over the door proclaimed, *Santa Claus is here this afternoon!* Meg looked at it, disapproval glinting in her eyes behind their steel spectacles. "Christmas is supposed to be a time to remember the birth of our Savior," she said.

They crossed the road. The traffic was heavy, it was starting to get dark. Sarah thought of her house, the dead man lying there. Meg led her into a maze of streets full of coffee bars, shops selling exotic foods, rundown pubs, and shop fronts with black-painted windows.

"Godless place," Meg muttered angrily.

"What?"

"Den of Satan. Nobody cares about morality anymore. It's all because of the Catholics."

"What is?" Sarah began to wonder if Meg was a little mad.

"The Blackshirts. The Nazis. They're all tools of the Pope. It all started in Rome with Mussolini, didn't it? Look at Italy, or Spain, or France. The Catholics are hand in glove with the Fascists. They run everything really."

"I know the Catholic Church collaborates, but they're not in charge —"

"Undermining Protestant morality, that's what they're doing. I used to teach in a secondary school, I've seen it, boys swaggering around in Blackshirt uniforms, making obscene comments to teachers and getting away with it, that's why I left..." She stopped, so suddenly that Sarah almost walked into her, and turned into a dirty alleyway. She rang a bell beside a door with worn green paint, turned to Sarah and smiled grimly. "I hope you're not easily shockable."

There was the sound of footsteps and a young woman opened the door. She was tall, with striking red hair, wearing a green polo-neck sweater. She looked at Meg, who gave her a prim nod.

"Oh, it's you," the woman said without enthusiasm.

Meg nodded brusquely toward Sarah. "I've brought her."

The woman gave Sarah a friendly smile. "Hello. I'm Dilys. Come on in."

She led them into a tatty hallway, up a flight of stairs and through a door into some sort of waiting room, hard chairs around the walls. A man was sitting on one of the chairs, a big man in his fifties in a dark coat with a velvet collar, a bowler hat and umbrella on the chair beside him. He stood up and extended a hand to Sarah. He smiled but his eyes were cold and hard.

"I'm Mr. Jackson," he said. "Mrs. Fitzgerald?"

"Yes."

"There was trouble," Meg said bluntly. "She had her sister with her and I had to walk up and down the street for ages. Then a copper came. We had to get rid of him." She looked at Sarah. "She knocked him on the nut. I shot him."

Jackson frowned. "They won't like that. One of their own, they'll be redoubling their efforts."

"He could have identified me. And her sister."

Sarah staggered; suddenly she thought she was going to faint. She said, "I'm sorry. I just can't believe—what I did," as Dilys helped her to a seat.

"This is war, dear, better get used to it," Meg said implacably.

Jackson frowned at her. He said over his shoulder to Dilys, "Get us a cup of tea, will you, there's a good girl?" Dilys, who had been glaring at Meg, went away.

"What is this place?" Sarah asked.

"It's a brothel," Jackson answered, his voice quite matter-of-fact. "Meg here doesn't approve but there we are, it takes all sorts." Jackson smiled again, condescendingly, Sarah thought. "I expect all this has been a bit of a shock for you."

"Please, do you know where my husband is? I'm desperately anxious—"

"He's safe. With us. Geoff Drax, too. They'll rejoin you later."

"Please, you must tell me—"

Jackson's tone hardened. "There's no must about it, Mrs. Fitzgerald. We've gone out of our way to rescue you, and as Meg said she put herself in no little danger."

"How long has David been working for you? Can you tell me that at least?"

"Quite some time. He's good man, your husband. Tenacious, trustworthy. He's been helping us, getting information from his department. Unfortunately something went wrong and he risked exposure. We're lucky he got out."

"I didn't know," Sarah said. "The Germans questioned me. At Senate House. But I had nothing to tell them."

Jackson and Meg exchanged a sharp look. He leaned forward. "They asked you about your husband?"

"Yes. But I didn't know anything."

"Did they mention the name Frank Muncaster to you?"

"Frank?" She frowned. "Yes, they did. They didn't say why, though."

"What did you tell them?"

"That I've never met him. David gets Christmas cards and the odd letter from him. I just know he was a friend of David's at Oxford, had problems, mental problems I think. David used to sort of protect him. Is he one of your people, too? They told me Geoff Drax was."

Jackson looked relieved. He gave her a gentle smile. "Drax is, yes. I'm sorry you've been caught up in all this. But we take pride in getting our agents' families to safety. I understand you are a pacifist," he said, still smiling. "Perhaps you don't approve of us."

"I've never believed in violence. But now, everything that's happening, some of the things I've seen..." She shook her head.

"Well, events are moving our way. Adlai Stevenson's just made a speech saying the United States is to start trading with Russia. And the new Russian offensive seems to be pushing the Germans back all along the front. They may take a couple of cities this winter."

"All this blood," Sarah said.

"It will end one day. Your husband is part of a network of Civil Service people I hope will take over running the country, stop the Reds running wild. And the Catholics, too, eh, Meg?"

Meg bristled. "I know you think it's a joke..."

Jackson gave a wintry smile. Sarah didn't like him. And Meg was some sort of Protestant fanatic.

Dilys returned with a tray. Jackson rubbed his hands together. "Ah, tea. No bickies, well, never mind." He took a cup and handed it to Sarah. "Now, Mrs. Fitzgerald," he said, slowly and seriously. "This is the plan. Dilys is going to dye your hair, cut it in a different style. Give you some new clothes. People will be looking for you, you see. Then we're going to send you down to the south coast."

"The south coast? Why?"

"That's where your husband will be going, quite soon. We'll be able to send you tomorrow, I hope, though the trains are a bit erratic this week. We're shutting up shop here, Dilys is leaving tomorrow. We'll give you a new identity card, and a cover story —you're a widow, going to the south coast for a bit of a break. You'll be staying with some of our people. Now, is all that clear?"

"Yes."

"Are you reasonably good at memorizing things?"

"Yes. But when will my husband arrive?"

"In a few days we hope. Then we have a plan to get you all away. I can't say more than that for now, Mrs. Fitzgerald." He smiled again, that patronizing smile. "You have to trust us."

Jackson and Meg left shortly after. Dilys took Sarah into an adjoining room, with peeling wallpaper and a big, dirty unmade bed, and sat her down at a dressing table. Sarah had flinched a little as she realized she was in a prostitute's bedroom, but Dilys was friendly, a relief after Meg. She put a hairdresser's cape around Sarah's shoulders.

"I'll cut it short first, then dye it. You're going to be a redhead, dear."

Sarah smiled bravely at her in the mirror. "Well, my life's been turned upside down already; I suppose a different hair color won't make much difference."

She sat still as Dilys cut her hair, quickly and efficiently. Sarah wondered if she had been a hairdresser once. "I've met your husband, you know," the woman said. "Careful, dear, don't jerk your head. Mr. Jackson used to meet his civil servants in the flat next door. And your husband came yesterday, after he went on the run. He's a nice chap, isn't he, good-looking, too. I like dark men. I asked him if he had any Maltese blood."

"He's Irish. I know you wouldn't think it to hear him talk."

"He's got a nice voice. Like Mr. Jackson, but not so pompous." They both laughed.

"So you have to move," Sarah said.

"We have to change houses quickly sometimes. I'll miss the woman who used to stay at the old flat. East European, very smart. She's a painter, she was a bit upset at having to leave her pictures behind. I saved a couple, in case I ever saw her again. There's one over by the wall there. I knew it was her favorite."

Looking in the mirror Sarah saw the painting, snow and mountains and what seemed to be fallen soldiers in the foreground: gray figures with red splotches of blood.

"So this woman knew David, too," Sarah said. A whole world of people she had had no idea about.

"Yes." Dilys smiled reassuringly. "But don't worry; I could see your husband's the loyal type."

Loyal, Sarah thought. And Jackson had called him trustworthy. They didn't see the irony, though they must all have known that he had lied and lied to her, for years.

CHAPTER FORTY-TWO

Dressed in a bathrobe, Gunther stood looking through the window of his flat, into the smog. It was horrible, poisonous, greasy stuff; it had appeared in the middle of the day and got steadily worse. Walking home from Senate House he had had to feel his way, one of thousands of shadowy figures groping along the dark streets, his throat smarting painfully. He had just watched the weather forecast on television and it was going to continue; some expert had appeared and talked about high streams of warm air trapping cold air underneath, the effect of millions of coal fires in the Thames valley. This will make our task even harder, Gunther thought.

He turned away, tiredness and a sense of failure in his very bones. At the embassy, Gessler was a pale shadow of his old self; Gunther often found him sitting staring blankly into space, helpless. After the events of the past week it was an easy state to fall into. Five days, five days since the lunatic Muncaster was lifted from the asylum, and they still had nothing. Every inquiry had drawn a blank.

Gessler had been very different on Monday, when the news came through that Muncaster had been taken. He had raved and shouted, full of angry panic. Gunther, though, had stayed calm, the remote calm that often came upon him in a crisis, though inside he felt a sinking in his stomach, as though he were in a lift whose descent went on and on.

"This is a hunt now, not an inquiry," Gessler had said when he calmed down a little. "If only we'd got Muncaster out before! It's not my fault, I won't be blamed!"

"The important thing now, sir, is to find him."

Gessler flicked him an angry glance. "I *will* be blamed, you know, and so will you. If he gets away—we'll be shot. Scapegoats for Berlin's failure to get him."

More likely we'll both be sent to some dangerous posting out East, Gunther thought. That was what he had craved anyway, an honorable end to his lonely life, though something in him resisted the idea now. He wanted, very much, to find Muncaster, to complete his mission. He said, "If we're to find him, and those who took him, we'll need to bring Special Branch in fully now. We'll have to let them have everyone involved in the Civil Service spy ring. I know. I've spoken to Berlin." A note of self-pity, then a sharp glance. "I've had to tell them about the mess-up at the Fitzgerald house."

"Yes," Gessler replied. On Saturday afternoon, Gunther had learned how the SS man, in plain clothes, had got to the old air-raid shelter, broken in, and then spent hours watching the house through binoculars. As nobody entered or left, and no lights came on as it got dark, the man realized there was nobody there. Then a police car came and some men went up to the house, then around the back. The SS man ran across the little park to the house and knocked on the door. An angry policeman answered. Behind him another uniformed officer was lying dead in the hall. Sarah Fitzgerald was gone, had been before their man arrived.

Gessler said, "I was hours on the phone yesterday. I couldn't get hold of the right people, nobody was available, the senior people are all in meetings. Something big's happening over there. But there's nothing we can do about it. More hours wasted." He drew himself upright in his chair. "They confirm that from now on it's full cooperation with the British Special Branch. I don't know what the information is that Muncaster has, only little hints, but if the British police find out—" He shrugged. "It'll be up to Berlin to sort it out with Beaverbrook. And forget what I told you about eliminating Syme if he got hold of anything from Muncaster. As I say, full cooperation. The Branch are being asked to devote major resources to finding Muncaster. A nationwide manhunt. You and Syme will work on the Fitzgerald angle. Dabb and Hubbold and the Bennett woman are being arrested tonight and brought here. You and Syme are to question them, then chase up everyone connected with Fitzgerald and Drax. Everyone.

"They're clever, our enemies. The Bolsheviks and Jews," Gessler continued, with quiet anger. "We always knew that, we knew how hard the fight would be." He shook his head. "The Jews were going to be moved to the Isle of Wight today, but this damned smog's put paid to that."

"It won't last, sir. And we will win," Gunther said. But, along with relief that he would not have to kill Syme, doubt was flickering inside him now, about the possibilities of success for the mission and what was happening in Germany; it was eating him up, exhausting him.

When he met Syme in his office, late on Sunday, Gunther expected the Special Branch inspector to be full of himself, triumphant that the Branch were taking the lead. But he wasn't. Syme was angry that Muncaster had escaped, that, as he put it, "the bloody bastard Resistance had scored." And killed a policeman, one of their own. Gunther could understand that.

"We'll get that fucking loony," Syme said viciously.

"I'm glad you feel like that."

Syme gave him a hard look. "You should have taken Muncaster earlier."

"I know. We met with all sorts of political difficulties."

"We think we've found the identity of the attendant, the one who left with Muncaster. A Scottish Communist, we've been after him for years. We think they gave him a new identity and a new trade when things got too hot for him up North. He was already working at the mental hospital so they used him with Muncaster. Some of the things that Scottish bastard's done"—he shook his head—"even before he got involved in politics—you wouldn't believe the sort of scum they recruit." Syme continued, "It seems likely Fitzgerald and Drax were already working as spies and then were brought into this because they knew Muncaster."

"That makes sense."

"According to Fitzgerald's personnel file there's some old uncle in

Northampton. I wish we could get hold of his father, too, but he's beyond our reach. I'm told the Dominions Office people we spoke to last week are being brought in here for joint interviews with us tomorrow. Let's scare them a bit."

Gunther said mildly, "Will you let me take the lead on the interviews?" He thought, Syme might go at them too hard, especially the woman.

Syme smiled grimly. "All right."

The old Dominions Office Registrar, Dabb, was first. He was fetched into the interview room where Gunther had interrogated Sarah, by one of the young SS jailers. He was terrified, sweating so profusely Gunther feared he might have a seizure.

"Please." Dabb stared at them with desperate appeal. "I'm just a clerk. I'm nobody. I don't know anything, I don't have any politics—you shouldn't have politics in the Civil Service. That Fitzgerald, he's nothing to do with me. He's one of Archie Hubbold's protégés," he added with sudden viciousness.

Gunther asked, "And Miss Bennett?"

Dabb lost control completely now, shouting out a string of obscenities: "Fucking traitorous whore! Eyeing Fitzgerald like a bitch in heat—don't think I encouraged it, I didn't, I was always watching them—"

"It seems you did not watch carefully enough, if Fitzgerald got access to the room with the secret files."

At that Dabb collapsed. "I did my best. All my life, I just tried to do my best at my job. Just my best, my best..."

Soon Gunther realized there was nothing more to be got out of the ridiculous old man; he had never even heard the name Muncaster. He was taken back to his cell and Archibald Hubbold was brought in. In contrast to his colleague, Hubbold stepped into the room quite coolly, took a seat, and stared at Gunther and Syme with an air of injured innocence. Gunther thought, he's got courage, the limited courage of the stupid. He didn't realize what they could do to him if they wanted. Behind his thick glasses Hubbold's eyes moved like slow, heavy fish.

"Have you ever heard the name Francis Muncaster?" Gunther asked, mildly.

Hubbold frowned, thought a minute, then shook his head. "He's not Dominions Office Establishment." He set his lips. "Is he another traitor, in some other department?"

"Fitzgerald never mentioned the name to you?"

Hubbold thought again. "Never."

Syme said, with a grin, "Old Dabb told us Fitzgerald was one of your protégés."

"I liked Fitzgerald, yes," Hubbold said, his tone pompously sorrowful. "I brought him along, gave him more responsibility. He seemed conscientious, loyal. Clever, too. He lacked ambition, but clever people don't always have that."

"It sounds like an almost filial relationship."

Hubbold's face darkened a little. "I thought it was, almost. I trusted him."

"Did you know about his friendship with Carol Bennett?"

"There was some gossip within the office. I don't take notice of petty gossip. I valued Fitzgerald's work," he added heavily.

Syme said, "Took some of the load off you, did he?"

"He was a hard worker."

"And you never had any inkling he might be a spy?" Gunther asked.

"No. Why should I?" Hubbold set his lips hard, smoothed a hand over his white hair. He leaned forward, and then said in a voice trembling with anger, "A civil servant betraying his minister, it's the worst treachery. I will help you any way I can."

Hubbold told them everything about David's work then, his routines, the occasional social meetings with the wives. It was all quite useless: Fitzgerald had taken Hubbold in completely. Gunther wondered, does he realize his career is over, early retirement's his best hope now? We could make things much nastier for him than that, in here, right now; Gessler probably would have, just from frustration, but what was the point? When he was sure Hubbold had told them all he knew Gunther said, "I think that's enough for now. Do you agree, William?"

Syme nodded wearily.

Hubbold frowned, turned to Gunther. "I wish to help you all I can."

"I know."

"Fitzgerald didn't just betray his department, he betrayed me personally. That's what hurts most," he added. "I'll be frank. I don't always approve of the things my government is doing. But they're my government. What Fitzgerald did—his betrayal of a post of responsibility—I find it unspeakable." He clenched his hands in anger.

He wanted vengeance; Gunther wasn't interested. "Thank you, Mr. Hubbold. Good morning," he said, dismissively.

Hubbold rose, suddenly uncertain.

"Do I—can I go to the office tomorrow?"

Syme gave him a wolfish grin. "No, mate. Doubt you'll be going there anymore. You stay at home. The Branch will be wanting to talk to you again."

Hubbold looked stricken. He'd realized, at last.

The SS man who showed Hubbold out gave Syme a telephone message. He showed it to Gunther. A Special Branch man had driven up to Northampton to speak to Fitzgerald's uncle. He turned out to be a crotchety old man in his eighties who couldn't tell them anything about his great-nephew. The old man had said David Fitzgerald and his wife had airs and graces, David had forgotten his Irish roots. Then he had started insulting the English. The note ended with the words, "Reprimand issued." Syme laughed. "That means our man gave him a bit of a smack. It doesn't matter, does it?"

"We don't want any unnecessary attention, so be careful in future, please. Now, let's have Miss Bennett in."

Carol Bennett came into the interview room looking disheveled and frightened, her big eyes staring. Gunther had decided to be direct and sharp. He leaned back, folded his hands over his stomach, and said, "Your foolishness has landed you in a mess, Miss Bennett. That is, if it was indeed just foolishness. If you've actually been helping the Resistance you'd be better off confessing everything now, and appealing to your government for mercy."

"I haven't." She looked terrified. "Dear God, I haven't." She took a deep breath, tried to collect herself. "Please, when I was arrested this morning I had to leave my mother. She's ill, she might go wandering the streets. Can't you at least let me arrange someone to look after her?"

"Your mother will have to fend for herself for now. Your friend David Fitzgerald ran away from the Dominions Office on Friday. The question is, how did he know we were there? I've been thinking, you were the only one in a position to tell him."

Syme joined in. "If you don't tell us, there are people down here who'll get it out of you. Afterwards your poor old mother won't recognize you."

It was brutal but it worked. Carol said, "It was me. I warned him."

"Why?"

She put her head down. "I love him."

Gunther said, "Did you give him access to secret files? Look at me, please."

She looked up, her large eyes full of tears. "No. I didn't know anything about all this until you came to the office. I didn't help David. I never gave him any access to my files, I wouldn't have if he'd asked but he didn't, ever."

"You never gave him your keys?"

"No. I swear. I always used to keep my key in my handbag. And I had to hand it in whenever I went out."

Gunther thought a minute, picked up a pencil and tapped it on the table. "Is the key numbered?"

She looked puzzled. "Yes, there's a number on the tag."

"And who makes the keys?"

"I've no idea. The Ministry of Works, I suppose."

Gunther remembered a case his father had been involved with long ago, a locksmith who made keys for safety deposit boxes at a bank and who, given a number, could make a duplicate. "Could he have seen the number on the key?"

She looked stricken. That was it, Gunther thought, that was why Fitzgerald had befriended her, in the hope he could get a look at the key. He saw that she realized it, too. Syme looked puzzled, then very interested. "There's someone who makes locks for the government involved in this?"

"Possibly."

"He looked at the number somehow while she was looking between his legs?" Carol flinched as though she had been hit.

"Maybe." Gunther turned to Carol, who had flushed a deep red. "Did Mr. Fitzgerald ever mention the name Muncaster?"

"Who?"

"A friend of his. Frank Muncaster."

"No. The only friend of his I knew of was a Mr. Drax."

"Are you sure?"

"I swear. In God's name."

Gunther saw she was telling the truth. The disappointment must have shown in his face, because Syme said, "I want her when you've finished, I want to find out more about how Fitzgerald got hold of that key. We'll take her to Special Branch HQ."

"Agreed."

"Please," Carol said. "Can I make arrangements for my mother?"

"Fuck your mother," Syme replied.

Carol looked at Gunther, desperation flashing in her eyes. "There's something else I can tell you," she said. "It's all I know, it's the last thing I've kept to myself."

Gunther raised his eyebrows.

"It's about Mrs. Fitzgerald. I've thought about it, if I tell you it can't hurt her, because it shows she wasn't working with David." She spoke in a rush, about Sarah's visit to her, her belief that David had been having an affair with her. "I told her about warning him that day. I told her it looked as though he could be a spy. She was shocked, she didn't know. So you see, now I've told you everything."

"You warned her, and before that you warned him," Gunther said levelly. "If it wasn't for you we would have got him. The British authorities will deal with your treason." Gunther couldn't feel sorry for her; this was the sort of woman who wrecked marriages, ruined other people's lives. "How well did you know Geoffrey Drax?" he asked.

"Not well," she answered, her voice shaking. "I met him a few times. But he's a reserved man, not easy to know."

"Did you discuss politics with any of these people?"

"No. You don't in the Civil Service, unless you know someone well. David and I never—never crossed that barrier."

He asked bluntly, "So you and Fitzgerald never slept together?"

She shook her head. Tears had begun to roll down her cheeks.

"He was almost certainly using you, you know."

She looked at him with a sudden fierceness. "I loved him. I kept hoping he'd—it's hard for a woman, you know, you can't make the first move the way a man can." She gave a fractured laugh. "Just seeing him, just going to concerts with him, and lunch, it was—almost like a drug. A little makes you want more, doesn't it?"

"Fucking tart," Syme said.

She looked down again, spent.

"Well, Miss Bennett," Gunther said heavily, "now the scales have fallen from your eyes." He thought of his wife. He had loved her, too, right up to his discovery of her betrayal.

She looked at him. "I still love him. Think of me how you like. I can't help it." It was pathetic, yet said with an odd dignity. Gunther felt a twinge. He looked at Syme. "Perhaps you could get the local police to visit her mother, see if they can arrange something. After all, we don't want the old woman making a public scene."

Syme shrugged. "I suppose so. But I want this one taken to Special Branch HQ."

"I'll get our people to arrange a car."

Carol cringed back in her chair. "I advise you to talk as freely, Miss Bennett," Gunther said severely, "as you have here."

Syme smiled. "We'll make sure of that."

Afterwards he and Syme went up to his office to talk. So far as Muncaster was concerned they had found out nothing. They found nothing the next day either, or the next. Muncaster and Drax and the Fitzgeralds were gone, vanished, no doubt hiding somewhere in the network of

Resistance safe houses. Muncaster's fellow workers were questioned again, and some of his old fellow students at university. Drax's parents, too. None of them knew anything. Gunther learned from Syme that all sorts of inquiries were going on in the Civil Service; MI5 had been brought in now. Gunther said he was glad, but he wasn't really interested in the spy ring.

On Friday afternoon, a week after Fitzgerald's flight, a thick fog came down, in the afternoon, smothering London. Gunther's office was at the top of Senate House and from the window he saw an odd thing; the smog did not quite reach the top of the building, so from his office he could look down on it. He had an extraordinary view of a grayish-yellow sea, stretching to the horizon. It was like the poisonous atmosphere of some alien planet, with only the very tops of the tallest buildings visible. It was one of the strangest things he had ever seen. Above the smog the air was milky-white, the winter sun just visible as a pale red orb.

Syme came in; he walked across and joined Gunther at the window. "Jesus Christ," he said.

"I hope it doesn't last." Gunther looked at him. "Any news?"

"Nothing. We've plenty of agents in the Resistance, but nobody's seen or heard anything of these people. And trawling the whole country, it's going to take a hell of a time."

"Any progress on the Civil Service spies?"

"A few leads. They haven't come to anything yet, but they will. I'm not allowed to talk to you about it," Syme added, "only if something comes up that is relevant to Muncaster."

"I understand," Gunther said. "We'll get there, you know. We will." He smiled encouragingly. "You will get your promotion, your exciting job in the North, a big house there to go with your new Jew's one."

"And you?"

Gunther shrugged. They both looked down at the fog. It swirled and eddied below them, the top lit by a reddish tinge now as the sun began to set. Gunther smiled. "This view reminds me of a story I learned at school." He began to quote from the Bible. "*He took Jesus to a high place, and showed him all the kingdoms of the world, and the glory of them; and* said, 'All these things I will give thee, to have dominion over, if you will fall down and worship me.'" He frowned. "That is not quite right. Was it 'dominion' or 'power'? Anyway, it was something like that."

"Jesus was a Jew, wasn't he? Who was it who took Jesus to the high place?"

Gunther shrugged. Then he remembered, with a superstitious shiver, that it had been the Devil.

"My parents never took me to church," Syme said.

"You were lucky." Gunther smiled again, sadly. "It was very dull."

When Gunther left Senate House that evening he had to navigate the streets by memory, walking right next to the buildings, a hand touching the walls, bumping into people who were doing the same. The walls were damp, the fog thick and stinking of sulfur. The fumes made his nose and throat sore. He was relieved when he got back to the flat. He knew that he needed to think, to try to find some way forward. He had a bath and a meal. After looking out he drew the curtains against the horrible night and sat at the table in his bathrobe, a strong cup of coffee beside him.

The interrogations, the telephone calls, all the frantic activity had taken them nowhere. They had to find a new way of thinking.

He got up, pacing the thick carpet. He was starting a headache; the fog had brought it on just as the dust gave him headaches in Berlin. He thought, what would the Resistance people do with Muncaster now they had him? What would *he* do if he were them, had hold of someone with a big secret, who was mentally ill, and unstable? Kill him, surely, to prevent him being captured and telling all he knew. Muncaster had wanted to kill himself anyway.

But the man calling himself Ben Hall could easily have killed him at the hospital. No, they wanted him alive. Why? It had to be because of the Americans. It had all started with them. They must have put the British Resistance up to this. He thought, they're going to try and get Muncaster to America.

He went to the window and pulled aside the curtain again. Outside, thick, gluey darkness, the faintest fuzzy glow from a streetlight below the flat, car horns breaking the silence — distant, muted, like sounds from a ship out at sea. Was that how they would try to get Muncaster away, on a merchant ship going to America? Descriptions and photographs had already been circulated to the ports. He thought, in his mental state, and with his damaged hand, Muncaster would be easy to spot. No, they wouldn't risk a ship.

An aircraft? He dismissed that, too. Security at the airports would be even tighter than at the ports. A submarine, that was surely the most likely option. An American military submarine. It was known they sometimes came into the Channel.

He crossed to the bookcase. He pulled out an atlas and looked at the map of England. Birmingham, where they had started from, was right in the center of the country. They would have to get Muncaster to the coast, but probably have to hole up somewhere for a while first. If a submarine were picking them up it would have to be from a southern or western port. The Welsh coast? Devon or Cornwall? Certainly nowhere too near the Isle of Wight, under German control. Sussex or Kent? He thought, if it were me I'd set it up so they could go due south, the shortest way via London. He ran his finger down the long straight line of the motorway from Birmingham to London. They could hide up in the city. They would have to wait for the right weather, a calm sea and a moonlit night — then travel from there to the Sussex or Kent coast.

He thought, if it was a submarine it would communicate with the coast by radio. But how to find the wavelength, the code? He took a slug of coffee. He thought of Muncaster, that piteous little man, led down a beach somewhere. A picture of his own son, playing on the sand in Krimea, came unexpectedly into his mind. He thought it all through again, looking for holes in his theory. Then he went to the telephone. He would call the embassy, tell Gessler the Germans should be told to watch for a submarine, authorities on the Isle of Wight listen for radio signals. First, though, he telephoned Syme, at home. He took a little while to answer, and he sounded sleepy. It was past one o'clock; Gunther had lost track of time.

"I have been thinking, William. I believe Muncaster and his people may be in London. How many agents inside the Resistance do you have in the city?"

"A good few."

"I think you should concentrate here. Try to sweep up as much of the London Resistance as you can. Do you think that would be possible?"

Syme said, "Usually we only do that if we've hopes of netting some big fish."

"Muncaster is a very big fish. And his people have killed one of yours in the city."

"This weather won't make it easier."

"It won't help them either. It'll make it harder for them to move around. Can we meet early tomorrow? First thing? I'm at home now, but I'm going to the embassy straightaway."

"In this fog? It's the middle of the night."

"Justice never sleeps," Gunther said.

CHAPTER FORTY-THREE

David woke next morning to the sound of voices downstairs and the smell of frying bacon. He heard the quick murmur of Eileen's voice, Sean's slow one. Only a dim gray half-light penetrated the thin curtains of the room. Geoff was still asleep. He didn't look well; several times in the night David had woken to hear him coughing.

He got up and dressed in the change of clothes he had been given the day before. Geoff sat up, coughed again, and took a drink. David pulled aside the curtains. In daylight the smog was a dense grayish-yellow, pressing against the windows, which were dotted with greasy smuts of soot. He could make out, dimly, a brick wall surrounding a little yard. "It's as bad as ever out there," he said to Geoff. "How are you?"

There was a sheen of sweat on Geoff's forehead. "Not brilliant. My throat's still sore. I've a headache. God, how that filthy stuff seeps in, I can smell it. Sorry if I woke you last night."

"You couldn't help it."

"Funny, I had a dream I was back in Africa. I was going to see Elaine. Her husband was away and I was walking up the steps to her bungalow but it was my parents who opened the door, Mum and Dad. They looked young, like they were when I was a child." He lay staring pensively up at the ceiling. David had never before heard him talk with such lack of reserve.

"They'll be all right," he said.

"It's just the thought I'll probably never see them again."

"Unless we kick out the Germans, eh?"

Geoff smiled weakly. Sarah must feel the same, David thought, about her family. It was all right for him, he just had his father now and he was safe in New Zealand. He might even go and join him.

* * *

Downstairs they found Ben and Natalia already eating breakfast, Eileen bustling around with plates. A radio in the kitchen played *Housewives' Choice*. Sean was pulling on a pair of hobnailed boots. "Bacon and eggs?" Eileen asked David. She looked at Geoff. "How are you feeling?"

"A bit groggy."

"I'll get some headache pills. I'm afraid this pea-souper looks set to go on all day, according to the radio, maybe longer. They're worried about the Smithfield cattle show; some of the animals are getting ill. Filthy stuff. Here now, sit down."

As they sat David met Natalia's eye. She smiled sadly, half conspiratorially. She had washed her hair; it was brown and lustrous. David saw that Geoff had caught the look between him and Natalia, and quickly glanced away. "Where's Frank?" he asked Ben.

"He's no' feeling too good either. I'm going to take his breakfast up in a minute."

Sean stood. "I'm off to work. Back about six." He nodded at his guests, then kissed Eileen tenderly on the brow. "You be careful, you hear? Keep everyone safe."

"Get off now." She touched his cheek briefly, then hurried back out to the kitchen. The front door shut behind Sean. "Frank thinks Sean's got it in for him," Ben said quietly. "That's why he wanted to stay upstairs."

"People are afraid of mental illness." Natalia shook her head. "Frank could see it in Mr. O'Shea."

David said, "I'll take him up his breakfast. Has he had his pill?"

"I gave it him when he got up."

"He is addicted to those pills, isn't he?" Natalia said.

"No," Ben answered. "He isnae. They're no' addictive, but people get used tae feelin' calmer with them, so ye have to take them off them gradually. We'll wean him off them when we're safe." Ben looked at her seriously. "But for now he needs to be kept quiet, not just for his safety but ours, too."

David took a tray upstairs. Frank was sitting on the bed, wearing one of Colonel Brock's old cardigans, staring out at the fog. A single-bar electric fire took the edge off the cold. He gave David a sad little smile, quite different from that horrible rictus grin.

"I brought you up some breakfast. Hungry?"

"Yes. I could do with something."

"Ben said you didn't want to come downstairs."

"No. That Mr. O'Shea…" He shrugged wearily.

"Sean's all right. It's just a worry for him, having us here." David put the tray on the bed.

Frank gave a long, despairing sigh. "He sees."

"Sees what, Frank?"

"I've always felt I was under some sort of curse." Frank spoke so low David had to bend to hear. "There's something in me—I don't even know what"—he waved his bad hand in a helpless gesture—"that makes people want to hurt me. It's always been like that." He looked at David and gave one of his harsh little laughs. "You think it's my madness talking, I can see."

"Frank, some people are just, well, afraid of people who've been—where you have. And you're not mad," he added firmly.

"No, it's always been the same." Frank shook his head decisively. "Since I was a little boy, before I went away to school. Mother had her life controlled by this fake spiritualist, Mrs. Baker. She got me sent to that school. I dreamed about her last night, she was sitting in a garden. There were angels in the sky, I suppose it was heaven. She was drinking whiskey from a bottle and laughing at me."

David touched him on the arm. "Eat your breakfast, eh? It's getting cold."

Obediently Frank took the tray on his knees and began to eat. Despite not having full use of his right hand he could use his fork dexterously. Experience, David supposed. When he had finished Frank said abruptly, "Did you notice it when you met me?"

"What? Your hand?"

"No. Everyone notices that. I mean this thing about me, this—aura. My mother used to talk a lot about auras."

"No, Frank. I just thought you were—afraid. I thought maybe because of that school; you didn't say much about it but it sounded bad."

"It was." Frank looked out of the window at the fog again. "But most people survived it. I just couldn't, somehow." He shook his head. "Unless you were exactly like them and did what they wanted—well, they'd do anything to you. They were like the Nazis in lots of ways. You know," he added, "I always had a feeling my life would end with something really bad, it was bound to somehow." He glanced at David and said, curiously, "You remember yesterday, in that field, I said I'd always wanted to be normal and you said you'd always felt the same. Why? You're not like me, you're the opposite of me. People respect you, they like you. They always have."

"Do they?" David shifted uneasily. "They expect things. Since I was a kid, everyone expected something special. I had advantages, you're right, but I always felt I couldn't be just normal, any more than you." He remembered school, diving into the swimming pool. Down into silence, peace. "Anyway, I brought all this on myself. I went into the Resistance, deceived my wife, everyone I worked with, because—"

"Why?"

"Because underneath it all I was so angry. I think I always have been." He turned to his old friend. "You must be too, Frank. You must be angry?"

Frank shrugged. "I don't know. Maybe. But what's the point of being angry with your fate?" His voice sank to a whisper. "Frightened, yes, because you can't change fate, you can't do anything."

"You pushed your brother out of that window."

"That was an accident. But yes, he made me lose control. I have to keep control." Frank spoke with a sudden emphasis. "If I hadn't, they'd have got it all out of me at the hospital. You—have—to—keep—control," he repeated, slowly, fiercely. "I learned that at school."

"Easy, Frank, easy. No one's threatening you here. Not Mr. O'Shea, not any of us."

"All right."

"That took some guts, not spilling what your brother told you when you were alone in that hospital, or to the police."

"I shouldn't have told you. That it was about the Bomb. I'm sorry, but it's a—it's a big thing to bear." He looked at David with sudden sharpness. "You haven't told anybody?"

"I promised you I wouldn't."

"In the field, you see—I thought if you knew how important it was, you'd realize I had to die."

"You don't. We'll get you out. And you made a promise too, remember. To stay alive."

"I know." There was silence for a few moments, then Frank said, "What will it be like, in America? I've met a few Americans, they always seem so noisy. Then there's all the gangsters in the films. But it's a big country, isn't it; maybe I could find somewhere quiet. Do you think I could, David?"

"I hope so."

"Where would you go? You and your wife?"

"I don't know about Sarah, but I'd like to go to New Zealand. It's a good place. They're decent people, they hate this Fascist shit."

Frank looked puzzled. "You'd go together, surely?"

"I don't know."

Frank said quietly, "We're not going to get there, you know, David. It's only a dream. They'll get me still."

"No, they won't. Come on, Frank, we've got this far. We have to be positive."

Frank picked at a loose thread on his mattress. "You said you had cyanide pills, if the Germans came. That Natalia would shoot me to stop them taking me. But what if you didn't get the chance? David, I want a cyanide pill as well. I won't take it unless they come, I promise, but I—I want the same chance as the rest of you."

David looked at him. Natalia and Ben would never take the risk of Frank trying to kill himself again. The Americans wanted him alive; though Ben and Natalia had also become protective of him, wanted him to live. "I'll talk to them," he said.

Frank nodded. But from his expression he knew it wasn't going to happen, David saw. That uncanny sensitivity of his, he thought, the sensitivity of an endangered animal.

After breakfast Ben persuaded Frank to come downstairs. Eileen had gone out to the shops, and to meet her Resistance contact. They sat in the lounge: Geoff still looked ill; he coughed frequently, a dry, hacking sound. Ben suggested a board game; Eileen had said there were some to be found in the next room. David went to fetch them. He switched on the light — the fog made everything so dim. The room had the faintly damp smell of a little-used "best parlor." There was a cardboard box of games under the table, chess and drafts and Monopoly.

For a couple of hours they sat around playing Monopoly, like some strange family party. Frank turned out to be an easy winner, piling up a heap of paper money beside him. Ben said jokingly, "You're a Monopoly capitalist, Frank, that's what you are. Ye've taken all my money, I've nothin' left."

Frank looked pleased. "I just try to think ahead, that's all."

Ben shook his head. "I played a bit when I was inside, I wisnae bad but you're a bloody genius, mate."

"Why were you in prison?" Geoff asked. "Was it for political reasons?"

Ben looked at him intently. "No, I wis a naughty boy at school, did some bad things. The Glasgow magistrates thought they were bad anyway. Got two years in a Borstal when I was seventeen, and a good dose of the birch." David remembered the scars he had seen on Ben last night. "Put an end tae a promising career, that did. Parents disowned me, the auld bastards. Though it was being inside taught me about politics, people in there gave me a proper education about the class system. So I don't regret it."

David smiled ruefully. "Everything's class with you, isn't it?"

"Aye, it is. I've seen you once or twice, ye don't always follow what I'm sayin', do ye, with ma accent?"

"You put it on sometimes."

"Where ah wis brought up, ye'd no've understood a word."

"That's because you've a Scottish accent."

"No." Ben looked at him intently. "It's because I'm *working-class* Scottish."

Frank said, "He's right. My school was in Scotland, but I understood the accents all right."

"Because they spoke middle-class Scots, that's why. *Morrrningsiide.*" Ben drew out the name in a way that made Frank do something David could barely ever remember him doing. He laughed.

"It's class that's the real divide, not nationality," Ben said finally. He nudged Frank. "Come on, Rockefeller, David's still got a few houses left."

They moved on to chess. David played Frank as he had promised, the others watching while Geoff went upstairs to lie down. Frank had just won his second game when, in the middle of the afternoon, Sean returned. "They've sent me home," he said. "There's problems all around London, freight's not moving. Drivers can't see the bloody signals. Everything all right here?"

"Yes."

"Eileen back?"

"Not yet," Natalia said. Sean bit his lip.

"It'll be the fog, don't worry," she reassured him.

Sean turned to Frank with a smile. "How are you, feller? Listen, I'm sorry I was a bit rude last night. It's the strain, y'see?"

Frank smiled uncertainly. "It's all right."

"Mates, eh?" Sean stretched out a hand, and Frank took it. David wondered if Eileen had told him off. Sean looked around the table. "Where's the fair-haired feller?"

"He went upstairs for a rest," David said. "He's feeling poorly. I think it's the fog."

"It's a bugger. One of my workmates is asthmatic, they had to take him to hospital this afternoon. Hope they manage to get him there, traffic's hardly moving. If they were planning to move the Jews today, that's definitely off." He sighed. "I'm going to make a sandwich." He went out to the kitchen. David cleared the table and took everything back to the front room. He switched on the light and put the box back under the table. As he stood up he saw someone standing outside the window, a little white face looking in at him. He stood stock still for a second, then stepped forward. He glimpsed a cap and child's raincoat as the figure darted away into the murk. He went quickly back to the living room.

"What's the matter?" Natalia asked sharply.

"There was a little boy, standing in the front garden, looking in. It might have been the one from two doors down."

"Shit," Ben said, half rising. Sean came out of the kitchen and ran to the front door, throwing it open. A minute later he came back, breathing hard.

"I heard the door slam at Number 38. That little fucker, he's always nosing around, he watches the TV programs telling people to keep an eye out for terrorists."

Natalia said, "He has only seen David, and he saw him yesterday."

Sean frowned. "He'll tell his dad the man with a posh accent is staying here now." He sat down, chewing anxiously on his knuckles. "I don't bloody know. We'll have to see what Eileen says."

She returned half an hour later, weighed down with shopping bags. "What weather," she said. "The bus was so slow. The smog's leaving black grease on everything, you should see the steps." Eileen looked around them, her face suddenly tense. "Has something happened?"

Sean told her about David seeing the little boy. "Ah, that's bad luck. And I didn't see his mother at the shops, I thought she'd be there. But young Philip's always peeping into people's houses, playing at spies and terrorists like all the little boys." She looked at Natalia. "What do you think?"

"I don't know. I don't know these people."

"We've had him looking in the window before when we've had visitors. He's a lonely wee lad. Used to play with our two till his parents stopped him last year. I think it's all right. He hasn't seen any of the rest of you?"

"No."

"I'll have to try and get an excuse to speak to his mother, tell her you're some sort of relation."

"With that accent?" Sean said.

"I only said a few words." David reddened.

"Well, there's nothing we can do about it now," Eileen said.

"Go and see her," Sean urged.

She shook her head. "No, she'd wonder why I was so worried about it. It'll have to be casual." Eileen frowned, obviously still uneasy. She looked at her guests. "It looks like you're staying in London another day or so. The submarine's waiting in the Channel now, but it's a question of when the weather's going to be right for you to be picked up—I can't say yet where from."

Geoff had come down and was sitting by the fire, looking pale and sweating. He shook his head. "So there actually is a submarine waiting for us?"

"There is."

David thought, it's real, it could happen. He said to Eileen, "Any word on my wife?"

"She's all right. She's out of London, near where you'll be leaving from." Eileen hesitated, then added, "Only an hour away."

Natalia gave her a warning look. David thought, she's right, the less everyone knows, the safer we are.

When dinner was over Eileen asked them to split the night watch, Ben first. After eating they all sat in the living room, except for Natalia, who went upstairs, to David and Geoff's bedroom, for a rest. Geoff coughed frequently; with six of them packed into the living room, most smoking, the room had quickly become a fug. Eileen suggested Geoff go and sit in the front room. Frank asked if he could rest upstairs for a while. Ben looked at David, who nodded; Frank had given him his promise to do nothing stupid.

They watched the news; London was at a standstill because of the fog, emergency rooms in all the hospitals full of people with weak chests. A couple more women had been attacked by assailants they hadn't been

457

able to see, hit on the head and their handbags taken. One had been knifed. Sean grunted, "The good Lord save them, as my mammy would have said. Only he doesn't."

"You were brought up a Catholic?" David had noticed that unlike other Irish homes he had visited, there was no Catholic imagery anywhere in the house.

"We both were," Eileen said. "You?"

"No, my parents weren't believers."

A look of sadness crossed her face. "How can anyone believe in the Catholic Church, after what they've done to support all the Fascist regimes — in Spain, Italy, Croatia?"

Sean nodded agreement. "Ireland too, that's no paradise. Did anyone see that film the Pope made a few years ago?"

"I did," David said. "Pius XII walking in his garden, showing the world the way of peace. As though he didn't live in this world at all."

"Live in it. Ha." Sean growled. "He helped build it. That's why they even show him on British TV now."

At the end of the news there was an extended interview with Beaverbrook about the new reduced tariffs on trade with Europe, Beaverbrook pugnacious and optimistic, the interviewer respectful as usual. The Jewish deportations were not mentioned. The Prime Minister said that on his recent visit he had formed the closest relations with Dr. Goebbels, praised all the propaganda minister had done for Germany. Sean said, "The wind's shifting further to Goebbels all the time. If Hitler dies, who will he go with, Himmler or Speer?"

Ben agreed. "Beaverbrook's, making Goebbels his insurance policy. Bet it was Goebbels who got him to promise he'd get rid of the Jews when he went to Germany. A personal favor."

David went upstairs to check on Frank, who was sitting on the mattress massaging his bad hand. He looked up at David. "It's sore tonight." He winced. "It doesn't like the damp."

"Hopefully we'll be off in a day or two."

"Where?"

"We'll know when it's safe for us to know."

Frank said, "Natalia came in to talk to me for a while. She's nice, she understands things. She told me about her brother. He had problems too. Women—they mostly don't understand, they can be even worse than men. But she's not like that, is she?"

David smiled. "No. She's pretty special."

"I told her about school." He looked at his hand. "You know, sometimes I wonder what my life might have been, if my mother had never met Mrs. Baker, if I'd never gone to Strangmans. There's a physicist in America who thinks the world we live in is only one of millions of parallel worlds, existing alongside each other, each different in tiny little ways. Maybe worlds where everyone is happy." His face clouded. "And maybe ones where everyone was killed by the atom bomb. I try not to think about that."

"We're stuck in the world as it is," David said. "It's a bad place but we have to do the best we can."

"That's what Natalia said."

"I'm going to sleep here while Ben goes on watch. Leave Natalia to rest in my room for a bit."

"I'm ready to go to bed, too."

"I'll leave you to get ready, go and have a last fag."

"Okay." Frank smiled a gentle little smile again. "Thanks, David," he said. "Thanks for everything."

David passed the room where Natalia was resting. He heard movement inside. He hesitated, then knocked quietly on the door. She called to him to come in. She was sitting on the side of the mattress, the one he had slept on last night, brushing her hair. She smiled at him.

"Couldn't you sleep?" he asked.

"No. Usually I can sleep anywhere, but not this evening."

"I've been thinking about what you said last night." David closed the door. "You're right. I will tell people I'm Jewish. But I want my wife to be the first to know."

Natalia looked at him. "Will she be unhappy about it?"

"I don't think so. I don't know. But she'll care about there being yet another secret, so I want to tell her first."

"That sounds — right."

He shook his head. "Ever since our son died — it's strange, you'd think tragedy would bring people together, but just as often it drives you apart."

She looked at him seriously. "My husband — he had a secret from me, too. I told you he was German Army Intelligence, you remember? The Abwehr?"

"Yes."

"He was posted to England, at the end of 1942; the year we had seen the Jews taken away in the summer. We married just before we left, in Berlin. My brother was not long dead. He was a cipher clerk, at Senate House."

"Hasn't the Abwehr been dissolved? There was talk of some plot to kill Hitler."

"Yes. In 1943. I don't know what sort of Germany the officers would have created" — she smiled sadly — "something old-fashioned and proper, I think, Gustav was a very old-fashioned man."

"Was he involved?"

"Yes. He never got over that time we saw the Jews, on that train. Someone betrayed the plotters, we never knew who. A lot of the Abwehr people were executed. Others who the Nazis weren't sure of, like Gustav, were sent to the East. To posts they would not return from. There were even suspicions about Rommel, you know, but nothing was proved."

"How did you find out your husband was involved?"

"When he was posted to Russia, I stayed behind. He arranged it." She sighed deeply. "Then one day, not long after he was killed at the front, in 1945, the Resistance contacted me. That was in their very early days, Churchill was still in Parliament, but he could see what was coming. They had already set up networks of supporters, people who could help with intelligence. And I was working as an interpreter; I met many of the Germans who came here. The Resistance had been in touch with my husband, you see, he was working for them, he had become what you call a double agent. He told them I might help them, if anything happened to him. But while he was alive he never told me. He wanted to protect me, as you wish to protect your wife. I think he also wanted me to know he had opposed the Nazis." She looked at David, smiling her sad smile. "So, I too know about secrets, brave people with secrets."

"And you decided to join the Resistance?" She's lived this dangerous life for seven years, he thought.

"Yes. Because I had nothing left. And I wanted to get back at them. For Gustav, for my broken country, for my brother. And to try and end Europe's nationalist frenzy. It's not just vengeance, you know, I want something better, a better world."

David looked down at the floor. "Frank said just now he thinks you understand him. I suppose that's because of your brother's problems."

She nodded, not speaking.

"I'm sorry," he said quietly. "They've taken everything from you, haven't they?"

He saw tears in her eyes, but she smiled bravely and said, "Gustav and I had happy times. My brother Peter and I had good years, too, before the war. Bratislava was a cosmopolitan city then, and we were part of it. We went to university together." She sighed. "In that pretty old city by the Danube. I am sentimentalizing, it was dirty and poor, too. But in our circles, among our friends, whether you were part Hungarian, part Jew, part Slovak, part German, part Tartar, it didn't matter. Everyone is part something, you know. In the nineteenth century not having a fixed national identity was perfectly common in Eastern Europe. But then nationalism turned that into a danger."

David hesitated again, then sat down on the bed beside her. "We English think we're special."

"It's that part of your culture you share with the Germans. The great Imperial nation part. I think in the thirties you thought fascism would never come to Britain; you had been a democracy so long, and you felt, as you said, special. But you were wrong; given the right circumstances fascism can infest any country, feeding off the hatreds and nationalisms that already exist. Nobody is safe."

"I know."

"We have our own little Fascist leaders in Slovakia. People for whom nationalism is everything."

"And your leader is a priest."

"Yes. Monsignor Tiso. The ruling party has Fascist sections and Catholic components. The Vatican and the Fascists work together in most of Europe. They both like order. Though when the Jews were taken away, some Catholic priests came out and protested." She shook her head in puzzlement. "While others said they deserved all they got. My husband Gustav was a Catholic, you know, a good Catholic." She turned to him. "A good man, like you." She hesitated, then laid a hand on his. And this time David responded. He leaned forward and kissed her.

CHAPTER FORTY-FOUR

Since coming to Sean and Eileen's house Frank had, for the first time in over a week, passed hours at a stretch without thinking of death. Sitting with the others, talking to them, he would feel a strange warmth inside, toward these people who were endangering their lives for him. He had been frightened of Sean at first but then he'd apologized for his behavior, something Frank couldn't remember anyone ever doing before. That afternoon, playing games in the lounge, he had actually forgotten the constant danger, relaxed a little. After dinner his drugs made him tired and he went upstairs to lie down, dozing off for a while.

A soft knock at the door woke him.

"Yes?"

The woman, Natalia, came in. Frank smiled at her nervously.

"How are you?" she asked.

"Not so bad."

She leaned against the wall—weighing him up, Frank thought, though in a friendly way. "Things must have been very bad for you," she said quietly. "Ever since the accident with your brother." She hesitated. "But trying to run off like you did in that field, that was not right."

"I know. It put you all in danger. But I didn't see how we could escape."

She smiled and spread her arms. "But we are here. And you heard Eileen, there is a submarine waiting to collect us. We are moving closer to safety, Frank, step by step. And already you have changed."

"What do you mean?"

"I have watched you, this past week. When we first picked you up from the hospital your walk was slouched; you slumped over. Already it is a little less so. And your speech is more"—she smiled—"direct."

"Is it?" He wanted to believe her, to hope, but it was hard. He changed the subject. "Where are you from?" he asked curiously.

"I am from Slovakia. It was part of Czechoslovakia once: you remember, the country Mr. Chamberlain gave to Hitler."

"I was always against appeasement. David and Geoff and I used to talk about it at university."

She took out a packet of cigarettes. "Do you mind if I smoke?"

"Please. Did you escape from your country?"

"I was lucky. I met a German, a good German. I came to England with him. After he died I decided to help the Resistance."

"You must have met Nazis, too. We're told they're our friends, but I never thought so."

"The Germans have fallen under the spell of a madman, much of the German army, also. Though they are realists, too, they know now that they can never conquer all of Russia. I think when Hitler dies the army and the SS will fight each other." She smiled. "And then the Resistance in Europe will have a great opportunity."

Frank said, "The Germans must never get hold of my secret. You do understand that."

"Yes." She nodded seriously. "It must be hard, carrying dangerous knowledge in your head."

"But you don't know what it is, do you?" Frank looked alarmed for a moment.

"No."

He hesitated, then asked, "Do you carry one of those poison pills David has?"

"Yes."

"I told him to ask you if I could have one."

She shook her head. "I'm afraid the answer is no. If the Germans come, I promise you they won't take any of us alive." She looked him in the eye. He admired her clear, cool directness.

"You must think about dying too, all of you," he said. "A sudden blackness, ceasing to exist. Or heaven, walking in a garden with Jesus." He laughed bitterly. "Or hell. The lives God gives to us, the awful things we can't escape from. Sometimes I think that sort of God would enjoy making hell for us after we die."

"I think we'll all just face the blackness."

"So do I, really."

"May I sit down?" Natalia asked.

"Of course."

There were no chairs in the room so she sat on the floor opposite him, leaning back against the wall. Frank asked, "Why do you want to keep me alive?"

"I've been told it's what the Americans want. For us to rescue you and get you to the coast."

"Aren't you curious? You and the Resistance people? About what I know?"

She smiled. "We've been told not to ask. And the Resistance is like an army, we're soldiers, we obey orders."

"You kill people like soldiers as well, don't you? The stories about bombs and assassinations, they're true, aren't they?"

"I wish there were another way. But all other roads have been blocked off."

"Have you killed anyone yourself?"

She didn't answer. Frank said, "My brother, he started all this, put us all in danger."

She smiled sadly. "I had a brother, too."

"Did you?"

"Yes. But he was not like yours. We were close. But he had—what they call mental problems. Difficulties in dealing with the world. When he was young he was very confident, but I think there was always fear underneath."

"Did he go to hospital like me?"

"No."

"My brother Edgar was confident. Everything came his way. Or seemed to."

She smiled encouragingly. And then, to his own surprise Frank found himself telling her about his childhood, his brother and his mother, Mrs.

Baker, and then the school. He had never talked to anyone about these things the way he talked to Natalia now. Because she listened, and believed him, and didn't judge. At the end Frank said, "I've always been afraid, like your brother."

"But you had real things to be frightened of," Natalia said. "My brother was different, he didn't have any real cause for fear. Not until the war came."

"What was he like?"

She smiled. "Peter was two years older than me. He had Tartar eyes like mine, but blond hair like our mother, who had German blood. A mixture. A beautiful mixture. A big, noisy boy, always getting into scrapes. But everyone forgave him, because he never meant harm to any living thing. And all the girls loved him."

Frank frowned slightly. He sounded too good to be real. Natalia caught his look and smiled. "It's true, everyone loved him. I worshipped him. Yet sometimes I would find him standing in a room quite still, looking so afraid. I used to ask him what the matter was and he would say, 'Nothing, I was just thinking.' Our mother died just after Peter started university, while I was still at school, and that made him worse."

"I'm sorry."

"She had a sudden heart attack. I remember one day after she died going into our sitting room and Peter was standing looking out of the window, his hands clasped together so tightly. He had that frightened look and there were tears in his eyes. I asked what the matter was. He said, 'We're all alone, Natalia. There's no meaning, no safety. Something can just come out of the blue and destroy us like it did Mother and there's nothing we can do.' He said, I remember it exactly, 'We spend all our lives walking on the thinnest of thin ice, it can break at any moment and then we fall through.' I see him now, standing there, the words rushing out of him, the blue sky outside our window." Natalia broke off and smiled. "I'm sorry, I don't mean to distress you."

"Thin ice. Yes. I've always known about that."

"Perhaps we all do. But we all have to go on hoping it won't break." She sighed. "Otherwise, like Peter, or your mother, you can go looking for salvation in some mad theory, some pattern to the world that isn't really there."

"What did he believe in?"

"Communism. He joined the Party just after our mother died. So many people in Europe turned to the Fascists and Communists in those years. Peter became a Communist and he was much happier for a while. He thought he had found the key to history. The Fascists thought they had too, of course, in nationality. Peter finished university, did some painting—he was a painter like me, though a much better one. Before he joined the Party he did some remarkable work, surreal, I think it reflected the confusion in his mind. But later he designed Party posters, square-jawed workers and beautiful maidens waving scythes..." She laughed. "Our father was a merchant, he was so angry when Peter became a Communist."

"I've never really believed in anything," Frank said sadly. "I just wanted to be left alone."

"You believed in science. You worked at a university."

"Believed in it? I was interested in it." He shook his head. "In my old life I worked. I ate. I slept. I read science-fiction magazines and books. I had a flat in Birmingham. I don't think I'll see it again."

"Peter was living in a science-fiction book called communism," Natalia said with sudden bitterness. "He thought he saw the future of humanity, its true meaning, in Russia. But then he went there. On an official tour. I had been away studying English, in London."

"That's why you speak it so well."

She lit another cigarette. "I remember when I came back Peter was getting ready for his visit to Moscow, he was full of it, he even said he might emigrate to Russia. But when he got there, being Peter, he wandered off on his own one afternoon, gave the tour guide the slip and went exploring Moscow. The Communists were destroying the old city then, putting up big blocks of flats, bright and white, accommodation for the workers' future."

"They're starting to build them here, too. The high-rises."

"There were some near where Peter was staying, they were new, they hadn't even laid the pavements yet. Peter told me how he walked over the muddy ground, opened the door of one of the blocks and went inside. He said it was indescribable, filth everywhere, people had been going to the toilet on the floor. The flats were full of families crammed into single rooms, more than one family sometimes, just a tatty curtain to divide them and give some privacy, all swearing and fighting with each other. They screamed abuse at him when he wandered in. And somehow, seeing the inside of that block of flats, seeing how people really lived in his Communist paradise—he was never the same after that."

Frank thought of Peter stumbling through the mud of that Moscow building site. "Poor man," he said.

"Yes. Poor Peter. I don't know what he expected to find there, a palace?" Her voice was angry. "He got into trouble with the tour people for that. He was lucky he had a foreign passport. That was 1937, during the worst of Stalin's Great Terror. When Peter came back to Bratislava he left the Party and spent more and more of his time indoors, alone in his room."

"A room, a home, it's a place to hide, isn't it?"

"Yes." She blew out a cloud of smoke, sighed. "Meanwhile, out in the world, things were getting worse. Next year Hitler took the Sudetenland, then in 1939 he made Slovakia an independent puppet state, and then the war broke out. Father was retired by then, but he had money and I was working as a translator so I was able to take care of Peter. I looked after him for two years. Father helped too, but he was old, he did not really understand."

"Peter was lucky. Having someone to look after him."

"I did what I could. Then in 1941, the Germans invaded Russia. The Slovak government sent soldiers to help them. My brother was conscripted, he was young and fit and they didn't care about his mental state. He fought all the way to the Caucasus. He came back with a shattered leg. It healed, but the effects on his mind"—she shook her head sorrowfully—"he was terrified people were going to come for him, terrified. Communists or Fascists or priests—I don't know who, anybody. Father had died while he was at war. In the end he jumped out of the window." She gave Frank a long, hard look. "It was a terrible thing to do to me."

"He couldn't live with his fear," Frank said simply.

"The whole world has had to learn to live with fear now." She got up, her knees creaking. It reminded Frank that she was his age, she wasn't young. "I'm sorry," she said quietly. "I did not mean to talk of all these sad things."

"It's all right."

She walked over to the window, pulled the curtain aside. The fog was as bad as ever, thick, cloying, almost liquid; there was nothing to see but darkness. "No sign of this ending," she said. Then she turned to face him, smiling. "Thank you."

"What for?" he asked, surprised.

"Because you understood about Peter."

After she had gone Frank thought, was her brother really like me? He felt a little awed that she'd talked so openly to him. Then David had come to check on him. He'd tried to doze again but he was restless now, all the conversations he had had that day coming back into his head. After a while he decided to go downstairs. As he passed the door of the next room, he was surprised to hear low voices. He wondered whether they were talking about him. He stood next to the door. He heard Natalia's voice, very quiet, "You need a woman as much as I need a man." He stepped away, suddenly filled with a betrayal and loss and jealousy. Then he felt numb.

Downstairs Ben was sitting with the O'Sheas, still playing cards. He looked up. "A' right? Thought you were asleep."

"No. No, I — I couldn't settle —"

Ben looked at him keenly. "Sure you're all right?"

"Yes."

"It's a bit early for your bedtime pill. I'll give it you in an hour, that'll get you to sleep."

"Would you like a cup of tea?" Eileen asked with a smile. "A bit of cake maybe?"

"No, no thanks. Where's Geoff?"

She nodded to the door of the front room. "He's asleep in there. Why don't you go and see how he is?"

Frank opened the door. He felt their eyes on his back. The light was on; Geoff was asleep in an armchair but he woke as Frank came in. He coughed.

"I'm sorry," Frank said. "Did I wake you?"

"I was only half asleep." Geoff sat up, coughing again, a harsh rasp. He didn't look well, there was sweat on his brow. "What time is it?"

"Nine o'clock. How are you feeling?"

"A bit rotten." He looked at Frank. "How are you? Holding up?"

"Yes. Yes, I suppose so. I've got a bit of a tickle in my throat, but it's not getting any worse."

"I think I might go up to my room and lie down."

Frank raised a hand. "No, I don't think"—he stumbled over his words—"not yet."

Geoff gave him a puzzled frown. "Why not?"

"I—I think David and Natalia are up there." Frank felt himself blush. "Together."

Geoff nodded his understanding, gave a sad little smile. "I wondered if something was going on there. Thanks for the warning." He frowned. "But I wouldn't have thought"—he looked at Frank intently—"listen, if we get to meet up with Sarah, David's wife, you mustn't say anything. He and Natalia—well, these things happen when everyone's thrown together, under such a strain—"

"I won't say anything. I promise."

Geoff sat back wearily in his chair. "I suppose I'd better stay down here for a while then."

"David and Natalia," Frank said. "His wife. They shouldn't—"

"Who are we to say?"

Frank looked down. "I don't know."

Geoff shook his head. "Only fifteen years ago you and I and David were at university. It was a different world then, wasn't it?"

"Yes, it was."

Geoff smiled. "Do you remember the day when we were all in this pub, and there was that idiot loudmouth from our college, I've forgotten his name now, arguing that Hitler only wanted to revive Germany's national spirit, just wanted territories that were historically German and he was entitled to them—"

"Carter," Frank said.

"That's right. And you said, 'They're not territories, they're places where people live and it's the people that matter.' I remember he just sat and stared at you. I think he was a bit surprised you'd answered him back."

Frank said, "You remember that, after all this time?"

"Oh, yes. I—"

Geoff broke off suddenly, at the sound of a tremendous crash from the front door. Frank turned, so fast he almost lost his balance, as another followed. Geoff looked at him, then threw open the door from the front room to the hall. Outside, in the hallway, Sean had come out of the lounge and stood, a gun in his hand, facing the front door. As they watched it splintered and flew open. Three men burst in from the fog, pistols drawn. Two were uniformed Auxiliary Police. One was carrying a sledgehammer and the other a pistol. The third was in plain clothes and to his horror Frank recognized Syme, the tall, thin policeman from the hospital. He had a gun too. Sean fired at the Auxiliary who had the pistol, a tremendous noise in the confined space. The policeman toppled back onto the other two, unbalancing them, blocking the doorway, blood gushing from his neck. The plainclothesman, though, had time to fire at Sean, and the big Irishman went down with a crash, his body hitting the floor with an impact that shook the boards.

Frank stood paralyzed. As the two intruders struggled with the body of their dead colleague in the doorway, Geoff grabbed his arm and pushed him toward the open doorway of the lounge. Ben stood there, also holding a gun. There must have been guns in the table drawers. Behind him Eileen stared through the door at her husband's body, eyes wide with horror. Frank glanced at Sean's face; the blue eyes whose gaze had scared him were still and dead now.

There was a clattering on the stairs and David and Natalia appeared, running down, David frantically buttoning up his clothes. In any other circumstances it would have looked ridiculous. Natalia, too, was holding a gun. Syme and the other Auxiliary were in the hall now and both raised their firearms but Natalia fired first, Ben following from the doorway a second after. They missed Syme but Natalia hit the other Auxiliary in the arm. He yelled and staggered. Just outside the house, they heard the sound of a police siren.

Geoff had Frank inside the lounge now. Natalia and David followed and David banged the door shut.

"Out the back!" Eileen pointed at Frank, her voice a loud scream. Geoff grabbed Frank's hand and pulled him toward the kitchen. The others heaved the heavy table in front of the door to the hall, blocking it, just before the plainclothesman threw himself against it. Other police were coming and it would not hold for long. Eileen shouted, "Go!"

Ben opened the back door, slowly and carefully. Outside, nothing but a bank of fog. There could have been a dozen more armed policemen out there, but there was nowhere else to go. Other policemen had arrived through the front now, and were throwing themselves against the lounge door. Frank looked back at Eileen. She smiled weakly, then reached into her dress, between her breasts. She pulled something out and put it in her mouth. Frank had a momentary glimpse of her body convulsing.

The back door was half open, Ben peering around it, gun in hand. He waved to the others to stand back. Frank braced himself for another rush of blue uniforms from the backyard. But there was nothing, just the fog. Ben took a deep breath and stepped outside, gun raised in both hands. David and Natalia followed, then Geoff hauled Frank out, too, slamming the back door shut to cut off the light. He had taken the key from the side of the door and turned it, locking it.

They were out in the yard, in the dark and fog. There was a flash of light from somewhere and a bang. Beside Frank, Geoff gave a cry and toppled over, letting go of Frank's hand. He lay still on the ground, blood spreading across his chest. He twitched violently once and then was still. Ben and Natalia both fired blindly back into the murk, and Frank heard the sound of someone falling, cursing and swearing. There must have been only one policeman around the back. Then Ben had Frank's hand, pulling him through the fog, across the yard. Frank cried out, "Geoff!"

"He's dead!" Ben said. He hauled Frank across the little yard; a brick wall loomed up. There was a big metal dustbin beside it. David helped Natalia onto it. She climbed over the wall. David followed. Behind them, they heard crashes at the back door.

"Come on!" Ben shouted at Frank. He climbed onto the wall, then reached down, took Frank under the arms and lifted him up. Frank grasped the wall, bracing himself to feel a bullet in his back, half hoping for it, but it didn't come. From the top of the wall Ben fired back toward the house.

"Fucking come on!" Ben screamed in Frank's ear. Then Frank was hauled bodily over the wall. He fell on wet cobbles with a crash that winded him. Ben and David pulled him up and half carried him down an alley, into a street that was just a choking yellow-gray mass of fog. More shots sounded, flashes in the gloom ahead. More police had been waiting in the street. Frank collided with the wall of the alley, grazing his arm. Ben had taken a grip on Frank's other arm but it loosened as he fired again into the street. Everyone was just firing blindly, nobody could see. Frank heard a sound from behind him; more policemen and Syme, no doubt, climbing over the O'Sheas' wall in hot pursuit.

Frank pulled away from Ben's grasp. He was gripped by utter panic — the gunshots, the images of Sean and Geoff falling, Eileen's body convulsing. They couldn't save him, they were going to be captured as he had known they would be. He turned and ran away, blindly, into the fog.

CHAPTER FORTY-FIVE

A ll Frank could hold in his mind was to get away, disappear in the fog. He ran blindly, arms out in front of him. He felt a jolt up his spine; he had stepped from the curb into the roadway without seeing it. Behind him he heard more shots, a police whistle. He half turned but already it was impossible to make out who was firing at whom; he saw vague moving shapes but a second later they disappeared. He reached the pavement on the other side, nearly tripping on the curb, and stepped up, groping in front of him. He touched a wall, stumbled along, keeping his hand on walls and damp hedges so he didn't wander back into the road. A police whistle sounded again a little further off. He reached a corner and turned, walking on until a bout of coughing brought him to a halt. The air stank. He leaned against a privet hedge, trying to get his breathing under control. More shots sounded, but further away now.

The house had been raided; the little boy from the neighboring house must have betrayed them. The others were gone, probably dead — if they hadn't been shot they would have taken their cyanide pills. At the thought a choking sob rose up in Frank's throat.

He must keep walking, all night if he had to. If only he could see. When it got light visibility would be a bit better, though that meant it would be easier for them to find him. Thank God he hadn't had his bedtime pills; at least his mind wasn't dulled by them, he wasn't sleepy. They would be hunting him all over London. He thought, there are road bridges across railway lines. All he needed to do was find one, jump off, and end it. The thought calmed him; he had his goal again. He had known they wouldn't escape, he had been stupid even to imagine they might. He remembered Geoff falling, the blood, and almost sobbed again.

There was nobody else in the street. He could make out, very dimly, the little circles of light from the nearest streetlamps—how the fog seemed to swirl and eddy about them. People weren't coming out in this weather and the shots would have been heard, which would keep people indoors. He shivered; he was clad only in one of Colonel Brock's cardigans and a thin shirt and trousers, and was very cold. He thought of David and Natalia, running down the stairs half dressed. He was glad now they had had their chance together before the end.

He heard a sound in the distance, growing closer: the shrill electric bell of a Black Maria. Quickly, he felt his way along the privet hedge beside him. He came to a garden gate; dripping wet from the fog, it felt like it was covered with thick, cold sweat. He pulled the gate open, slipped into the tiny front garden and crouched down on the inner side of the hedge, long grass soaking his trousers. He must be quiet, there was a thin pencil of hazy light a few feet away where the curtains of the front window didn't quite meet. He heard the sound of an approaching car, moving very slowly. Frank thought, they won't find me, not in this. It passed on down the street. He huddled down, shivering. After a few minutes he crept out of the gate again, carefully, crouching. His shoes and the bottom of his trousers were soaking wet. He shivered and coughed, then stood up and walked slowly on.

He reached a corner. A little way ahead he saw Belisha beacons, two orange globes flashing on and off, for some reason their light penetrating the fog better than the faint glow from the streetlamps. It was extraordinarily quiet, as though Frank was somewhere in the countryside rather than London. Carefully, he crossed the road. It was wider; this must be a main road. On the other side his outstretched hands made contact with a high brick wall. He felt over it. There was a windowsill, high up. It seemed like a big building, maybe a warehouse or office block; perhaps he could break in and hide. He groped his way along the wall. Then, from further up the street, he heard a hollow echoing shout through the fog. "Go on to the end of the road, to the roadblock!"

"There's no fucking point in this, Sarge! They could be anywhere!"

"They." He was sure he'd heard them say "they." His heart pounded,

he tried to steady his breathing. Some of the others at least must be alive. Dimly, ahead, he saw moving points of light approaching. Torches, powerful ones, fog whirling in their beams. He felt his way along the wall, away from them. He came to a corner, rounded it, and saw a tall iron gate. Peering through the gloom he made out a flight of stone steps. He heard another shout, closer now: "Fuck this! Dunno how I'm even going to find my way home, never mind find these bastards!"

Frank thought, there's a roadblock, I have to find somewhere to hide. He opened the gate — mercifully it didn't creak — and climbed the steps. At the top was a heavy wooden door. He dreaded he'd find it locked, but it opened under the pressure of his hand. He slipped inside, pushing it to behind him.

He saw he was inside an enormous Victorian Gothic church with high, stained-glass windows and an arched roof. It was empty. There was dim electric lighting along the walls. Long rows of pews stretched away to a railed-off altar where a red candle burned inside an ornate golden container. Paintings of Christ on the way to the cross lined the walls. It was as cold in here as outside, chill and dank, but though the smell of the fog was in the air the filthy muck itself seemed not to have penetrated the cavernous building.

Frank looked back at the main door. There was a big iron latch; very slowly and quietly he slid it across. Then he looked around the church again. There were several more doors along the walls. He thought, if one led to a flight of stairs, perhaps to a belfry, he could get up there and jump off. His promise to David to stay alive hardly counted now. His heart was beating wildly. His only experience of church had been the chapel at school; cold, with whitewashed walls, a lectern with a ferocious eagle carved on the front. Mrs. Baker had forbidden her acolytes from going to what she called the false temples of the old religions.

He walked slowly to the nearest door, careful to make as little noise as possible on the stone flags. Next to it was a plaster statue of Christ, white body hanging from the cross, desperate agony on the thin bearded face. According to his mother, Mrs. Baker said Christ was always waiting in a white robe, smiling in a garden, to welcome those who passed into spirit, but this figure was quite different: an agony of suffering.

Stealthily, Frank opened the door. It gave onto a long corridor. At the end was a closed pair of double doors; behind them he could hear voices. For a second he stood rooted to the spot, terrified they had found him and were gathered there, waiting to pounce. He stepped backwards, suppressing a cry, as one of the doors opened. A tall young man came out, wearing a shabby apron over a black shirt with a white clerical collar. He had a shock of untidy brown hair and a round, tired, good-natured face. The smell of cooking drifted from the room. The man saw Frank and smiled.

"Hello," he said cheerfully, in a loud upper-class voice. "Come for some grub?"

Frank stared at him; he had no idea what he was talking about. He half turned, about to run, but the man said, gently, "Wait! It's all right. You look as though you could do with some food." With an encouraging nod, he stepped back and opened the door wide. Frank saw a room filled with wooden trestle tables, where ragged-looking men and women sat eating bowls of soup. Two women stood by an enormous tureen on a table, passing out bowls and plates of bread. Frank realized it must be a soup kitchen. He knew there were more and more of them these days with all the unemployment but he had never seen one himself before. He wasn't hungry but he was desperately cold and there was a gust of warmth from a big coal fire. He stayed where he was as the man came up to him.

"Hello. I'm the vicar here. Call me Terry."

Frank knew some churches supported Beaverbrook and Mosley and others were against. He hesitated, but then walked slowly toward the warmth of the big room. Inside, it smelled of unwashed bodies and damp, fusty clothes. Most of the people at the tables were beggars, such as you saw on street corners, with matted hair and beards, tattered coats tied with string, lined, dirty worn-out faces. One or two, though, wore stained shiny suits in attempts to keep a former respectability. There were ragged women, too, one holding a tiny baby.

"What's your name, friend?" the vicar asked.

Frank hesitated. "David."

Terry looked at him curiously. He said quietly, "Never been some-where like this before, eh? Where did you hear about us?"

"I—I forget."

"Well, lots of people are down on their luck these days, it's nothing to be ashamed of. Come on, get some food. It's not a night to be out. This filthy smog, I've never seen anything like it. You haven't got a coat, you must be freezing." The vicar looked at him again, more closely, and then his eyes widened. Frank followed his gaze and saw, on the front of his gray cardigan, a dark splash of blood. He drew in a horrified breath, thinking he had been hit after all, then realized it must be Geoff's blood.

"You're hurt," Terry said, quietly.

"It's nothing, I cut myself—"

"Let me have a look."

Frank whispered, "It's not my blood." He swallowed. "It's my friend's. He's dead."

Terry hesitated, then leaned close. "Please, come with me."

Frank looked into the vicar's tired face. Something in his voice and manner made him allow the man to lead him to a side room. It was a little office, with a steel filing cabinet and a table with a telephone on it, a black jacket slung over a chair. White surplices hung from a row of pegs. The vicar shut the door. He said, "A couple of people who've just come in said they heard shots nearby, police cars. They thought it was the local Jive Boy gangs. Was it something to do with you? Don't worry," he added quickly, "I won't give you away."

Frank leaned against the table. He didn't answer but a desperate sigh escaped him. Terry looked at him. He said, "I know there's something going on today, there have been raids all over town in spite of the fog. Are you Resistance?" Frank didn't answer. "I can help you but you have to trust me. I'm taking a risk even telling you I'll help." He took a deep breath and Frank saw that Terry, too, was afraid. Everything in the vic-ar's face told Frank he was sincere, but if Ben and Natalia and David hadn't been able to save him, how could this man? Telling him anything was a desperate risk.

The vicar stepped over to a door in the wall and opened it. A wave of cold stinking air and tendrils of yellow fog came into the room. He left the door open and went and stood by the other door, the one that led to the soup kitchen. "See," he said. "If you want to leave, you can. You might be able to get away in the fog, but you might not. I'll help you but you have to tell me what happened."

"I was with some friends," Frank said. "They're from the Resistance, we're trying to get out of the country. We were at a house a couple of streets away. There was a raid. Some of my friends were killed. I ran away to stop them getting me. The Resistance don't want the Germans to take me alive. I'm important; I wish I wasn't but I am. Please—please, shut the door. Someone might see, and it's so cold."

Terry closed the door. He took the jacket from the chair behind the desk. "Sit down, go on, you look done in." Frank sat, and Terry put the jacket around his shoulders. He looked at Frank's bad hand. "How did you get that? The Germans?"

Frank shook his head. "No. Some other people, when I was a boy. I'm not with the Resistance, I'm just—someone who needs to be got out of the country."

"Why?"

Frank shook his head firmly. "I can't tell you. The Resistance people know."

"Is David your real name?"

Frank shook his head. "No. He was one of my friends." He felt tears pricking at his eyes.

"Can you tell me your real name? If you can, I can ring for help. I've a number." Terry nodded at the telephone on the desk.

Frank hesitated, but it was all or nothing now. "Muncaster, Frank Muncaster."

Terry picked up the telephone. He dialed a number. Someone answered and he spoke with unexpected crispness, "Reverend Hadley,

St. Luke's Church. I've a man here, says the police are after him. There's been a raid nearby. His name is Frank Muncaster, repeat, Muncaster. Medium height, thin, brown hair, injured right hand." Then there was silence, the vicar occasionally nodding and saying "yes" briskly. He looked at Frank again and asked quietly, "Do you know how many of your people got away?"

"Sean and Eileen, the people who were sheltering us, they were" — his voice trembled—"I saw them killed. And Geoff, one of my friends, he was killed too, it's his blood on my cardigan. The other three—I don't know. Outside, I heard a policeman say they were looking for 'them,' so I hope some got away."

The vicar relayed the information to the person at the other end. At length he said, "All right," and put the phone down. He looked at Frank. "They'll come to collect you. But it may take a while, the police are putting up roadblocks, closing off the whole district."

Frank stood up, panic searing through him. "They could be searching the streets. What if they come here—"

Terry said, "It's all right, if they do I'll deal with them, they don't know I've contacts in the Resistance." He smiled sadly, making his face look years older. "They think I'm just the local do-gooder. Our man told me you were in a mental hospital where you tried to kill yourself," he added, more gently.

"I'd do it now if I could. So they don't get me."

Terry shook his head. "That's not what God wants."

"Isn't it? Then why did he make a world where sometimes it's the only choice you have left?"

Terry closed his eyes. How exhausted he looked. "Would you like to pray with me, for your friends?"

"No." Frank's voice shook with emotion. "No."

They both jumped at the sound of a loud knocking. The vicar said, his tone suddenly one of command, "It's the back door. I'll go out and see. You stay here. If you hear me coming back with someone else, run outside. But wait for me outside the door, don't go back on the streets or they'll get you." He looked at Frank. "Will you promise? I'm your only chance. Please, do as I say. My wife's in the soup kitchen," he added, his tone suddenly pleading.

Frank nodded wearily. It was like David had said in that field, he had responsibility for other people's lives now. And all because Edgar had wanted to show him how clever he was, that evening weeks ago in Birmingham.

The vicar went outside. Frank got up and put his ear to the door. He heard voices from the church, echoing in the cavernous space, but couldn't make out the words. Then footsteps, several of them, in the soup kitchen. He stood by the vestry door, ready to jump outside.

But when he heard footsteps approaching the door there was only one set. Terry came back into the room and sat down on the chair. He let out a long breath, running his finger around the inside of his dog collar, then produced a packet of cigarettes from his pocket and lit one. He said, "They've gone. Did you put the latch on the church door when you came in from outside?"

"Yes."

"Thank God. I've convinced them I did it hours ago, and so no one could have got in from outside. Otherwise they'd have searched the whole place. The only other way in or out is through that back door, you see, that's where people come for the soup kitchen. They gave me your description, they said there were two men and a woman as well."

So David and Ben and Natalia had all got away, at least so far. Terry said, "It seems to be it's you they're keenest to find." He looked at Frank curiously. "Are you a Jew? These roundups are unspeakable."

"No. No, I'm not a Jew."

"Cigarette?"

"I don't smoke."

"We had quite a few Jews coming to the soup kitchen, till they took them all away. Poor people, not even allowed to work in their professions anymore." He sighed. "And all the others without work and homes — my predecessor started the kitchen back in the thirties, when the Depression and mass unemployment began; it's been used ever since. It's gone on for twenty years, apart from when everyone had work in the 1939–40 war. The police know me, they took my word nobody of your description came in. I hate lying, you know, even to them," he added.

Frank said, "Thank you. Thank you for what you did."

The vicar smiled. He said awkwardly, "Perhaps the Lord is watching over us, eh?"

"He didn't watch over my friend Geoff, did he?" Frank answered bleakly. "Or Mr. and Mrs. O'Shea." He looked up at Terry. "He doesn't protect anybody, not really. Don't you understand that?"

CHAPTER FORTY-SIX

David and Ben and Natalia stood, trying to quiet their rapid breathing. In the entrance to the alley they had taken refuge in, they saw two thin, weak beams of light. David thought, if it wasn't for the fog, we'd all have been caught. But Geoff was gone, both the O'Sheas too, and Frank was lost. They would catch Frank now and it would all have been for nothing.

"Where the bloody hell are they?" an angry voice asked from the road.

"We'll never find them in this. They're putting a cordon around these streets. We're going to have to pen them in, do a house-to-house." The policemen's footsteps faded away. They heard the sirens of Black Marias in the distance.

Suddenly a yard door opened right beside them in the alley. Ben and Natalia instantly turned and covered it with their guns. David saw a shape in the entrance, made out a fat old man in a cap and raincoat, his mouth falling open with shock. There was something white at his feet — a small mongrel dog on the end of a lead.

"Dinnae move, pal!" Ben said quietly but fiercely. "Dinnae say anything and ye'll no' get hurt." The dog stared at him, then at his master. It growled softly.

The old man gestured wildly at one ear. "Deaf," he said.

"Fuckin' 'ell!" Ben leaned in to him. "Do you live in that house?"

"Yes."

"Alone?"

"Yes."

The dog growled again. "Quiet, Rags," the old man said. "Don't 'urt 'im," he whispered pleadingly. " 'E's old, 'e won't hurt you. Please, 'e's all I got since my wife died."

Ben said, "We need coats." He gestured with his gun. "Go on, go back inside."

"Who are you?" the old man asked pathetically. "What's happening?"

"Never you mind. What you dinnae ken can't hurt you."

A note of anger came into the old man's voice. "You're Resistance, aren't you? Takin' advantage of the fog for some stunt. Why can't you just leave people alone?"

"We need warm clothes," Ben repeated grimly. "Fuckin' get back in."

Natalia touched David's hand briefly. "I'll go in with him. Stay here, don't move. Take this." She handed him her gun. "You know how to use it?"

"I was in the army."

"Good." She touched his arm softly, then followed Ben and the old man through the gate.

David stood in the fog. He was starting to shiver from cold; none of them had coats. He looked down the alley. It was quiet now but the streets would soon be full of policemen. A cordon, how could they get out of that? They would be captured, or shot like Geoff. He gripped the cyanide pill in his pocket. He thought, at least Sarah's safe.

He remembered the moment when the banging sounded at the front door. David had been lying naked on the mattress. Natalia was sprawled across him, a happy, slightly teasing expression on her face as she played with the hairs on his chest, making them into little bunches of curls. But she jumped up, immediately alert, at the first crash from the front door. She said, "Get dressed!," her voice fierce, already throwing on her clothes. David had learned in the army to dress in moments. A second, splintering crash told him the door had been broken in. As he pulled on his trousers he felt the cyanide capsule. She had given him a smile, fleeting, of infinite regret.

Ben and Natalia returned, slipping back through the gate. Natalia was wearing an old-fashioned fur coat that reached almost to her ankles, and Ben had on the heavy coat and muffler the old man had been wearing. He passed a blue raincoat to David. As he put it on David asked, "What have you done with him?"

"Left him tied up on his bed. The dog's wi' him." He shook his head. "Stupidest bloody mutt I ever saw. He says a neighbor's coming to do some shopping for him tomorrow. She'll find him. If the police don't first."

"Good at tying people up, aren't you?" David couldn't help saying.

"Just as well for you I am, pal. And for Chrissake, keep your voice down."

Natalia walked slowly to the end of the alley, the others following. David said, "I don't suppose there's any chance of finding Frank in this."

"No," Natalia agreed. "We must find somewhere to hide. At least we have coats now, and they'll be looking for people without them. Don't worry, there is a contingency plan."

They spent over an hour feeling their way through the dark, deserted streets, not talking above a whisper, walking slowly to avoid bumping into things and to make as little sound as possible. They didn't hear any more police cars. Twice they ducked into alleys or behind garden fences at the sound of footsteps, once they saw the weak lances of torch beams. They stood huddled by a wall until they faded away. Natalia whispered, "They'll need hundreds to search the streets properly in this fog."

"Remember one of them was talking about a roadblock," Ben said. "That's what I'd do, cordon the area off. Let's keep movin', we might be able to get out before they can set it up."

They came out into a wider street and walked slowly along, pressed against the walls. Then the brick gave way to spiked iron railings, bushes behind and the dim shapes of trees. There was a gate with a sign on it. Natalia bent down close to read it. *Hanwick Park.* She looked along the road. A little way ahead was a tall, fuzzy rectangle of light which after a moment David realized was a telephone box. Natalia whispered, "Let's go in the park, we can hide among the trees. And I can telephone our people, get someone to try and collect us."

"What about the roadblock?" David asked. "They'd never get some-one here in time, in this."

"There's a plan for something like this."

"What? Shooting their way through?"

"Maybe not." She gripped his hand. "I can't tell you. In case we get caught first. Wait and you'll see."

"Come on," Ben said. He took off his coat and laid it over the spiked railings. David did the same and he and Ben managed to climb over. Natalia walked away up the street, invisible almost at once. Inside the park, David saw the hazy light from the telephone box dim, saw a shape in there. His heart lurched; she was exposed in there, any police coming close could see her. It seemed an age before she came out again, disappearing at once into the murk. She reappeared at the side of the railings and they helped her over.

"I got through," she said, a triumphant note in her voice. "They're coming."

The three disappeared into the dripping vegetation of the park. They followed the inner side of the railings right around; it was small, an open lawned area in the middle. Then, at the far end, they saw flashing lights in the road, torch beams, the shapes of men walking to and fro. Peering through the railings, they made out a police car parked sideways to block the entrance of the road, its interior lights on. More cars were parked behind.

"We almost walked into that," Ben whispered.

Natalia said, "It's all right. We have to wait now. They'll come."

"How are they going to get through that?" David asked despairingly. He thought again of the cyanide pills. They could die here, together, he and Natalia and Ben. He felt a rush of fear.

"Trust me," Natalia whispered.

They fell silent, straining to see and hear as much as they could of what was happening ahead. They heard a hiss of static, then a man's voice, talking loudly. "It's going to have to be a bloody powerful light to do anything at all in this damn stuff! Is it on a lorry?" Other figures passed to and fro, bulky shapes revealed briefly by the car with the lit interior.

Natalia said, "Move a little further into the trees, away from the railings."

They eased their way through the bushes, holding branches aside for each other to avoid making a noise. They came to a spot surrounded by trees but with a view of the roadblock. Ben said, "If they shine a search-light on the park, will they be able to see us?"

"I don't know," David replied. "Like he said, it would have to be a pretty powerful beam." He looked at Natalia. "Should we go back to the street?"

"No, we have to stay here. This is where I told our people we would be."

They were quiet for a minute. Then David whispered, "They killed Geoff, didn't they?"

Natalia said quietly, "I think so."

"He was the best friend I ever had."

She touched his arm. There was a rustle behind them. David whirled around, but it was only a gray squirrel, sitting on a branch looking at them. It made a chittering noise and disappeared.

"Something's happening out there," Natalia whispered urgently.

They turned back to where the police were. They heard a sound, a jangling bell but much louder than a police car, approaching very quickly. "The lorry with the searchlight," David said. "Jesus, why is it moving so fast?" His hand went to the pill in his pocket. Was this it?

"No," Natalia whispered. "That's our people."

The sound grew louder. There was something familiar in the tone. Then a huge shape, red behind powerful headlights, loomed out of the fog, traveling at a dangerous, reckless speed along the side of the park, toward the roadblock. It passed the spot where they were standing and came to a screeching halt just in front of the police car blocking the road. David saw to his amazement that it was a fire engine, huge, solidly and squarely built, the turntable ladder on top. The bell stopped and the light in the cab came on, illuminating the figures of several men in tall helmets who stepped down to the street. Staring through the railings

David saw three policemen approach the firemen. He whispered to Natalia, "The Fire Brigade? Those are our people?"

Ben turned to him with a grin. "Always been the most left-wing union in Britain, the firemen. Good Socialists. Let's just say this is no' a real call."

The firemen and policemen were talking urgently now. David couldn't hear at first but then their voices rose, one of the policemen shouting, "This whole area's cordoned off. Nobody in or out."

"But the police at Priory Street let us through the other end. We're on our way to a big fire —"

"They shouldn't have! Orders are to seal these streets off!"

"Listen, it's a hospital fire! There's people trapped, they can't get out! And we've got to get another mile through this. D'you want to be responsible for kids and old folk getting burned to death? Do you?"

David saw another figure slip down from the back of the fire engine, quiet and stealthy. He walked across the pavement, slipping along the park railings, and Ben shook a bush to attract his attention. A man in fireman's uniform stood before them, a pale young face under a helmet that looked too big for him.

"Quick," the young man whispered. "Get over the fence. Climb on the back of the engine."

The police hadn't seen them through the fog, and a few yards away the argument was still raging. The fireman ran back across the pavement to the back of the engine, half crouching, the others climbing over silently and following. "Come on!" the young man breathed. "Up the back!"

It was a difficult climb — over six feet up the side of the fire engine on slippery metal steps. There David found himself in the open back of the vehicle, and they all crouched down, beside the long, coiled hose and the lower end of the turntable ladder, crowded closely together. The fireman whispered, "Hold on to something, we'll be going fast!" David grasped a rail as tightly as he could. Like everything in the smog, it felt wet and slippery. He saw the fireman was clutching a pistol.

He heard footsteps returning to the fire engine, the cab doors shutting, and the revving of a motor; the firemen must have persuaded the policemen to move their car. Then he was jolted backwards as the fire engine started up. In a blare of noise they were off, the police car and the shadowy figures around it disappearing in a blur. They sped on down the main road, at what seemed a mad, suicidal pace. They passed a car that was crawling along ahead of them, grazing it, the jolt running through their bodies. Beside David the young fireman let out a whoop. "We did it, we fucking did it!" He brandished a fist in the air. "We'll go down in fucking history for this!"

On David's other side Natalia's hair was flying in the wind. She said to the fireman, "There was another man with us, he's very important. He panicked and ran off."

The young man turned to her. "We've got him too! He turned up at the local church, they've got him safe." There was a loud hoot from a car coming in the opposite direction, only visible for a second before the fire engine managed to swerve aside. David hoped to God they didn't hit a pedestrian, or a wall. But he knew that fire engine drivers were incredibly skilled, and the huge, powerful vehicle could knock any other vehicle aside. He looked at the fireman. "He's all right? Frank?"

The young man's face was alive with excitement. "Yes. That's what I mean! We're going down in fucking history!"

It sunk in then: Frank was alive.

CHAPTER FORTY-SEVEN

Gunther sat at his desk in Senate House, four photographs laid out on his desk. There was also a blank sheet of paper, *Unknown woman* written on it in his small, neat hand. He looked at the pictures: Muncaster, his admission photograph from the hospital, the thin, beaky face wild-eyed and distorted in a monkeylike grin, showing every tooth in his head; the Civil Service personnel photos of Fitzgerald and Drax; and finally a young man holding a card with a prison number written on it, his face scowling and angry. Special Branch filing clerks had labored hard to match Ben Hall's personnel photographs from the asylum with this man. Real name Donald McCall; jailbird, member of the Communist Party since the thirties, and other things too, some very unpleasant.

Gunther looked again at Drax's photograph. The only one those Special Branch clowns had managed to catch in the raid. Shot in the chest, but still alive. Gunther looked at the long nose and chin, the fair hair and mustache. A strong face but not a happy one.

Gunther had been right; the questioning of Resistance informers in London which he had set in train had thrown up the O'Sheas, known opponents of the regime, and loyal neighbors had spoken of a visitor with an upper-class accent who matched Fitzgerald's description. But when Syme and the police raided the house there had been a firefight, and only Drax had been taken alive. Four of them had fled, including Muncaster from the descriptions. Now the police were putting up roadblocks, but the smog was delaying everything. Gessler had said, at least if the fugitives got away they could blame it squarely on the British. But Berlin still needed Muncaster, alive.

Gunther had already had one interview with Drax. He lay on a bench in a cell downstairs, a heavily bloodstained bandage around his chest. Normally, it was a good idea to leave prisoners to stew alone in their cells for a few hours, work up a panic about what might be done to them, but Drax was too ill. He was coughing when Gunther came in; he looked at the end of his physical tether. He looked up at Gunther, the expression in his blue eyes one of helpless anger. Gunther said, "They've patched you up, I see."

Drax just gave Gunther a furious glare.

"The doctor thinks you've a sinus infection as well as a chest injury. Not surprising, with this filthy smog. I get similar trouble with all the building dust in Berlin. Would you like some water?"

"No." His voice was very hoarse.

"Well, suit yourself. You had a cyanide pill on you, I'm told."

"My bad luck I didn't get the chance to use it."

"I expect your friends have them too. We know Mrs. O'Shea used hers."

"I won't tell you anything," Drax said, bleakly, without bravado. "I know what you do to people who don't talk, you might as well just get started."

"Geoffrey Simon Drax. You went to university with David Fitzgerald and Frank Muncaster, worked in Africa, then after you came back to a desk job in the Colonial Office you started supplying secrets to the Resistance. That whole Civil Service spy ring's going to unwind now."

Drax just stared at him. Gunther studied his exhausted face. A very Aryan face, probably of Saxon or Norman ancestry. The sort of Englishman, he guessed, who believed in "noblesse oblige," bringing civilization to the poor natives of the Empire, as though an empire could be built on anything but power. He admired Drax's sort in a way, though, they were tough. "I'm not planning to hurt you," he said gently. "Why did you join the Resistance?"

"I've told you, I'll say nothing."

Gunther shrugged. "It was just curiosity. We're not interested in the Civil Service spies. The British authorities can deal with that. It's Frank Muncaster we want to know about: why you took him, what you're planning to do with him. What he knows, why you're keeping him alive."

"I'll say nothing."

It was the answer Gunther had expected, though it was a pity. Well, he had his plans. He turned back to the door. "I'll get you that water," he said.

Gunther made some telephone calls, then he had a long conversation with the naval people at Portsmouth about monitoring radio activity on the south coast. Finally he spoke to Gessler, who wanted to be present at the next interrogation stage.

Half an hour afterwards there was a knock at the door and Syme came in. He looked tired and discontented and brought the sulfurous reek of the fog in with him. Gunther invited him to sit. Syme sat with one leg over the other, jiggling his foot. Gunther said, "You haven't found them, have you? Muncaster and his people?" If they had, Syme would have been cock-a-hoop.

"No. There's been another balls-up, we think they've got out of the area they were holed up in. We cordoned it off; we were starting a house-to-house search." He shook his head. "But the police allowed a fire engine right through the closed-off area. The firemen said they'd been called to a hospital fire. They waited till it had gone through before checking with the fire station and found out there was no sodding fire. We're afraid they picked up Muncaster and his people. A fire engine and its crew have gone AWOL."

Gunther leaned back in his chair. He didn't feel angry; he seemed to be past anger now with this mission. Syme continued, "The Fire Brigades Union were always fucking lefties, we made the union illegal as it's a public service but some of the bastards are still there." He shook his head again. "I suppose the Gestapo would have taken the risk of letting a hospital burn down."

"We would, if we needed to catch important people."

Syme said, unexpectedly, "You must think we're a bunch of useless fannies."

"Oh, we make mistakes too," Gunther said. They still needed Syme and his people. "Are you all right, you weren't hurt in the raid?"

"Not a scratch. Any word of the one we shot?"

"He's not cooperating. Unsurprisingly. I'm having steps taken to encourage him."

Syme gave a lubricious smile. It reminded Gunther of how much he disliked him. "Rough stuff?"

Gunther inclined his head. "In a manner of speaking."

"Good." Syme nodded at the photographs. "Is that them? The group in that house?"

"Yes."

Syme pointed at David and Ben. "I saw them. And a woman. Tall, pretty, brown hair. I've written down a description." He smiled sourly. "She was shooting at me at the time, so I remember her. And I glimpsed Muncaster again." He looked at Muncaster's photo, then shook his head. "All this for that weird-looking loony."

The telephone rang. Gunther thanked the caller, then stood up. "Well," he said. "The arrangements I wanted are in place. I'm going down to see Drax again. Standartenführer Gessler is attending too, I must ring him."

Syme said, "Can I come?"

Gunther hesitated, then nodded. "Yes, why not?"

Drax was still sitting on the bunk but this time there was a man in SS uniform beside him: Kapp, a foxy little man in his thirties, lean but fit-looking, who Gunther knew specialized in what Syme had called "the rough stuff." Gessler was there already, in a corner of the room, standing with his arms folded, glaring angrily at Drax through his pince-nez. One eyelid twitched occasionally. A gray-haired, bespectacled man in a technician's white coat was setting up a cine camera on a tripod on the other side of the room; Drax was looking at him uncomprehendingly, Kapp with keen curiosity, Gessler with a little secret smile, because he knew what was coming.

Gunther addressed Drax, inclining his head toward Syme. "You remember this man?"

"He was at the O'Sheas' house."

"That's right," Syme said with a smile. "Chest all right?"

Drax didn't answer. The technician opened a circular can and inserted a roll of film into the projector. "What's this?" Syme asked.

"We're going to have a film show," Gessler said with a nasty smile. The technician unrolled a white screen and set it up against the opposite wall. He spoke to Gunther. "We should have the lights off, sir. They're very bright."

"Yes." Gunther nodded to Kapp, who left the cell, switched out the light and returned, closing the door with a clang. The technician turned a switch and there was a whirring sound in the darkness. Then the image of another cell appeared on the screen. The film, Gunther noted with approval, was in color. The other cell in the film had a metal table and a chair, and the woman Carol Bennett sat tied to the chair with ropes. Her hands were fixed to the table by straps on each wrist. She wore a stained white smock, and her hair was pulled back. Two guards stood behind her, one holding her shoulders. She looked terrified. Gunther heard Drax say, softly, "Oh no."

"Recognize her?" Gunther asked.

"It's Miss Bennett, she's a friend of David's. She's nothing to do with us"—his voice rose—"she's nothing to do with the Resistance."

"We know."

In the film another man stepped into view. He wore a long green smock, like a surgeon's, and he held a large hacksaw with a serrated blade. Gunther glanced at Syme. He was leaning forward slightly.

The man with a hacksaw said, "Hold the right hand steady."

Carol began to scream. "Stop! No! Stop, stop!" She was struggling wildly now but one of the guards grasped her shoulders firmly while the other stepped forward and held her hand down. Without another word the man with the hacksaw leaned over and took a grip of her little finger. He brought the hacksaw down on it, just above the knuckle, and began to saw. Blood spurted over the table. Carol screamed and pleaded for them to stop but none of them took the remotest notice. They were implacable. In the dimness Gunther heard a horrified gasp from Drax, then a brief scuffle as he tried to get up. Kapp held him down. He started coughing again, a choking sound. Gunther looked back at the screen; Carol Bennett's little finger had been severed, it was lying on the table, blood still leaking from her mutilated hand. She was still screaming as the man laid down his hacksaw, unstrapped her hand and with brisk efficiency held it up, tying a tourniquet around the wrist. The film ended suddenly, the screen going blank. The projector was still on, faintly illuminating the room. Drax shouted, "You bastards, you—" His voice broke in another wild fit of coughing.

"That took place a couple of hours ago," Gunther said quietly. "Before we turned her over to the British Special Branch. She'd warned Fitzgerald to get away from his office, you see."

Gessler stepped away from the wall. "That was just what you call the B picture. The main feature is next."

Drax had stopped coughing, gone quiet again. Through the semidarkness Gunther caught the glint in his wild eyes. He nodded to the cameraman. The man clipped another reel to the projector, working with surprising agility in the near dark; Gunther supposed he must be used to it. Another cell appeared on the screen, another chair and table. A man stood, clutching a heavy carving knife, dressed in a leather apron, leather gloves. The camera panned around, showing an elderly man and woman, each held by a guard. They were naked, white, wrinkled flesh exposed, the woman's breasts long and sagging. They held each other's hands; both were shaking, faces full of fear. Drax screamed out, "Mum! Dad! No! Stop!"

The screen went blank again. Drax was still screaming, "Stop! No!"

"Lights, please." Gunther spoke quietly. Kapp went out and switched the light on again. At a nod from Gunther the technician lowered the screen with a snap and began packing his equipment away. He kept his head averted from the others in the room; he had not looked at anyone the whole time. Syme was leaning against the wall, rather pale.

"We've only made that first scene so far," Gessler said to Drax, voice full of sarcastic amusement. "It could be quite a long film if you want it to be."

Drax turned to Gunther with a desperate look on his thin face. "Don't hurt them," he pleaded. "Please don't hurt them. They know people, you'll get into trouble —"

"Not in this case," Gunther said quietly, almost sympathetically. "They're only members of a provincial Conservative Party branch, Beaverbrook won't do anything to protect little people like that. Since Muncaster escaped Berlin has been applying real pressure on your government, and he's given them to us." He added, "I'm sorry you had to see that, but we need you to talk. Heroics won't help here. Your parents are just a few doors away, we filmed what you saw ten minutes ago." He took a deep breath. "We've shown you what we're prepared to do and if you don't tell us what we want to know we'll start on them. And afterwards we'll show you the film." Gunther hoped Drax would talk now, he hadn't liked any of this and would be pleased if one woman's finger was all it cost.

Kapp turned to him cheerfully. "Otherwise, you know." He shrugged. "First the fingers, then the toes. This little piggy went to market, then this one. None of them stay at home. Then we go for the eyes."

"We don't need them alive, you see," Gunther continued. "And then, if you still don't talk, it'll be your turn, though in your case we'd probably combine the physical methods with drugs. We learned a few things from the Russians there. So you see, however brave you are personally, it won't help in the end. But we'd rather have you fully awake. You'll talk tomorrow at the latest, you should understand that." He looked intently at Drax. "There's no shame in talking to save others. Four people are on the run, four lives. They'll probably get caught but even if some of them get away the Americans will almost certainly kill them once they've got what they want out of Muncaster." Drax's head jerked up at that. Gunther didn't know what the Americans had planned for them, though he wouldn't have been surprised if they killed Muncaster, given he had a head full of dangerous knowledge. He could see, though, that the thought hadn't yet crossed Drax's mind. "Weigh that against your parents being tortured to death."

There was silence for several seconds, then Drax said, his voice desperately weary, "I don't know anything. That's how we do things, on a need-to-know basis only. I haven't a clue why the Americans want Muncaster, I've no idea."

Gunther nodded. "We know more than you think." He took a deep breath. Time for his bluff, while Drax was in a weakened, shocked state. He said, "You were planning to leave the country. A submarine, we believe, from the Sussex coast. The coasts are being watched, we'll pick them up."

Gunther saw from Drax's surprised expression that his guesswork had been right; this was what they were going to do.

"How do you know all this?" Drax looked appalled.

Gunther didn't answer, just inclined his head. The Englishman was silent for a moment, then lowered his head and began to cry, weeping like a child, his shoulders shaking, all that proud reserve gone. He had broken. Gessler smirked. Gunther closed his eyes.

"If I tell you the little I know will you let my parents go?" Drax's voice was toneless and dead. "You seem to know all of it already."

"Of course. We've no further use for them."

Drax's shoulders sagged. "I don't know where we were going to be picked up from, except that the rendezvous is only an hour from here."

Gunther considered. An hour to the coast. Central Sussex. A lot of cliffs there, which narrowed down the places they could be picked up from. He said, "Thank you." He gestured at the wall where the screen had been. "I'm sorry you had to see that, I really am."

Drax said, "All that you know—who told you?"

"I'd worked it out; the look on your face confirmed I was right. And now we can narrow the pickup point down further."

Drax's head fell hopelessly forward, the way people's often did after they broke. Gunther nodded to Gessler, who followed him and Syme out of the cell, leaving Kapp on guard. They halted a few feet along the corridor. Up ahead a young SS man was sitting at his desk, filling in forms. The telephone on his desk rang and he picked it up.

Gessler said, "Well done, Hoth. That was a masterpiece of interrogation. Admirable. We could turn this around after all."

"Thank you. I would ask you, please make sure the guards keep a careful eye on him. He'll be a suicide risk. Guilt will come now."

Syme said, "You bluffed him. About the submarine."

"Yes. We can tell our people on the Isle of Wight to look for an American submarine off the Sussex coast. He's not sophisticated. People like him are brave, but they have too narrow a focus. Since being captured he was probably thinking only about how to bear great pain himself. He would have held out a long time."

Gessler laughed. "You had him crying like a child. Like a little girl."

Gunther said sadly, "My brother used to say that for him that was the hardest thing to see. When grown men cried like children, kneeling beside the graves his men had made them dig."

Gessler frowned at the unexpected remark. He said a little stiffly, "Well, keep me closely informed." He nodded at Syme and walked away down the corridor, boots clacking on the marble. The young SS man had put the phone down and was standing up. His face was very pale. He saluted Gessler, then said something to him in a low voice.

Gunther turned to Syme. "You need to work out the best methods for each individual, you see. I learned that a long time ago." He saw that Syme's face had a film of sweat on it, he was blinking fast. He looked as though he might faint.

"Are you all right?" Gunther asked, extending an arm.

"Yes," Syme said brusquely. "I was just expecting something a bit rougher, a bit more — basic. The film — I was a bit taken aback."

"It was too much for you?" Odd, Gunther thought, what sensibilities appeared in the unlikeliest people. If they'd beaten Drax up, Syme would probably have been happy to join in.

" 'Course not," Syme answered sharply. "It's just it was so bloody hot in there, all those people. And the camera, those things generate a lot of heat. A lot of heat," he repeated fiercely.

Sudden footsteps, Gessler was walking quickly toward them, his hands raised, as though he were trying to ward off something terrible. Behind him, at the desk, the boy had put his head in his hands.

"What?" Gunther asked.

Gessler's face was stricken, his lips trembling. "It's the Führer," he said. "He's had a heart attack. Our Führer is gone."

CHAPTER FORTY-EIGHT

On Sunday, 30 November, Sarah had traveled by train to Brighton. She had been told where she was going the previous evening by Meg, who had returned to Dilys's with a suitcase of new clothes, some money, and new identity papers. Briskly, Meg went through the details of Sarah's new identity. From now on she would be Mrs. Sarah Hardcastle, widow of a London schoolteacher. She would be staying in a Brighton boarding house until David, and some others, were ready to join her. The cover story was that she had wanted to get out of London for a few days following her husband's death in a car crash earlier that year. Meg didn't know or wouldn't say where they would be going after that.

Dilys had dyed her hair — it was dark red now, the color surprisingly convincing, the style quite short. By the time Meg left it was late evening and Sarah was very tired. She spent the night on a camp bed in the room where she had met Jackson, and where, Dilys told her, her customers waited. I've gone from a suburban lounge to a prostitute's waiting room, all in a day, Sarah thought. She wanted to laugh hysterically.

Next morning Dilys walked with Sarah to Piccadilly Circus Tube station, Sarah carrying her suitcase and wearing a pair of tough, sensible shoes. In the crowded foyer Dilys hugged her tightly. "Thank you," Sarah said. She added, "Will you be all right? Where are you going to go?"

"A new flat. Good luck, love." Then Dilys hugged her again and left. Sarah forced herself to move, she shouldn't just stand there, she would draw stares. A little group of young Blackshirts, the electric flash of the BUF on their armbands, strolled along on their way to some function; she walked rapidly away to the ticket booth. She caught a Tube to Victoria and bought a ticket for the Brighton train. Waiting on the platform, her heart jumped at a glimpse of a patrolling policeman. She was glad to get on the train.

After the horrible chaos of the last few days the normality of the train journey felt surreal. Sarah stared blankly at the Southern Railway Company crest embossed on the seat opposite her. Someone had left a newspaper there. It was the *Guardian,* the old liberal newspaper which her father always took. Beaverbrook had bought it last year and now it was laden with right-wing propaganda like all the other papers. An article said there had been an incident in France: Communist agitators from the Resistance had attacked a lorry taking Jews to the internment camp at Drancy. Some gendarmes had been killed, a couple of Jews too. She wondered how much of it was true; she knew the French Resistance was said to be growing larger and to be even more violent than the British. There was an article too about a senior civil servant, working for the junior health minister, Church, being suspected of having relations with a prostitute, visiting brothels with a mental hospital superintendent, a Dr. Wilson. She was dubious; people said the government often blackened the names of people they wanted rid of by leaking such stories to the press. Either way, he would soon be gone.

There were few people on the train, and by the time it left Haywards Heath her carriage was almost deserted. Sarah had been to Brighton a few times as a child, on summer day trips with her family, the train full of eager, excited children. At the thought she might never see any of her family again she burst into tears, sat hunched over in the empty carriage sobbing quietly. She knew she should do nothing to draw attention to herself but couldn't help it.

She had been told to get a taxi to the hotel. Brighton Station smelled of smoke but when she stepped outside the air was wonderfully clean, bitterly cold with a salty tang. She hailed a taxi and it drove her through dingy streets, then came out into the broad avenue of the Steine. She saw the domed roofs of Brighton Pavilion, George IV's Indian palace. The taxi drove across the Steine and turned into a side street of narrow three-story buildings with flaking paint, hotel signs above the doors, boards with *Vacancies* in the windows. At the end of the road was the sea, startlingly close.

The hotel was called Channel View. There was no porter and she dragged her suitcase into a dark, poky vestibule. Behind the little counter sat a small, tired-looking woman in her forties. Sarah put her identity card on the desk. "Mrs. Hardcastle," the woman said, then looked at her anxiously. "Come through and meet my husband." Her voice had a gentle burr, an almost rural sound. She opened a flap and Sarah followed her into a little office where a plump, balding man in shirt sleeves and waistcoat sat working on some accounts. His wife gave him Sarah's identity card. He read it, then looked up and studied her.

"You got down here all right?"

"Yes."

"You look as though you've been crying." His tone was reproving.

"Yes. On the train. There was no one else in the carriage."

He looked at her severely. "Someone might have come in."

Sarah took a deep breath. "Two days ago I was a normal housewife. Now I'm on the run, I've learned my husband's a spy, I've no home and I don't know if my family are all right or whether I'll ever see them again. So yes, I'm sorry, but I had a cry."

"You didn't know your husband was working for us?"

"He never told me."

"Well, that's often best," the man said, his voice less hostile. "Your family are all right by the way, we know that. We've been watching their houses. Your sister and parents have had Special Branch visits, but that's all. Your brother-in-law has a lot of Blackshirt friends"—he looked at her sharply again for a moment—"that will have helped."

Sarah closed her eyes and took a deep breath. "What about my husband?"

"There are delays in London. It may be a few days before he gets here."

"Then what happens?" Sarah asked. "No one will tell me."

"The plan's to get you out of England. You and your husband, and some friends."

"How? Where to?"

The woman said, "Somewhere safe, we can't tell you any more for now. I'm sorry." She added, "I'm Jane by the way, and this is Bert."

Bert handed back her identity card. "We've got you a room here. You can go for little walks around the town if you like but don't stray too far. We don't have many residents this time of year, just a few commercial travelers who come and go. Best if you keep yourself to yourself."

"I've been told to say I wanted to get out of London after my husband died. I can say I don't like all the fuss about Christmas. It's true, I hate it."

"Good," Jane said. "Don't get into conversation with the other guests, some of them have a roaming eye."

"I won't."

"Mealtimes are on a card in your room." Jane gave her a key. "There's hot water on if you want a bath."

"Thank you," Sarah said. As she went through the door Bert said quietly, "Mrs. Hardcastle?"

She turned. "Yes?"

He smiled. "Just making sure you remember your new name."

The hotel was a strange little place, with narrow corridors, small rooms, threadbare carpets. The bed in Sarah's room sagged from the hundreds of people who had slept there before. Channel View was probably full in summer, but now the only other guests were a few middle-aged men in shabby suits who nodded to her in the dining room. She nodded back, politely but distantly. The food was awful.

For the next few days Sarah barely spoke to anyone. Several times when Jane was on her own at reception, Sarah asked if there was any word of when her husband's group was coming, and always she was told not yet. Jane was pleasant enough but Sarah sensed that Bert was uneasy about her. She wondered if it was because she wasn't in the Resistance, she was just a spy's wife, an encumbrance.

She avoided the communal lounge, only going in to see the news on the old TV. On her first night she wondered whether there might be something about the policeman Meg had killed, half expecting to see her house appear on the screen, but there was nothing. They would hush it up of course. There was only the usual news—there had been a big demonstration in Delhi, the Blackshirt mayor of Walsall had been shot and injured by Resistance terrorists, the Germans were making "temporary strategic withdrawals" on sections of the Central Volga. When the news was on some of the commercial travelers muttered and grunted about Communists and uppity wogs.

Sarah spent long hours in her room, reading dog-eared romantic novels that guests had left behind in a little bookcase, or sitting looking out of her window, with its view of a yard choked with bins and the backs of neighboring buildings. During the short December afternoons she went for walks around the almost-empty town, drinking tea in little cafes. Once or twice she saw small groups of Jive Boys on the corners in their long, colorful coats and drainpipe trousers; but they looked listless and pasty, smoking roll-ups. Probably just unemployed lads, she thought, as she steered away from them. Occasionally, on walls, she saw the Resistance logos "V" and "R" painted, just like in London. The weather was sunny but very cold; there was ice on the pond in a little park she walked around. She thought constantly about David, where he could be, what he was doing, when he would get here. She ached with worry and longing but she was also filled with fury about his lies to her, going over his absences in her head. She knew David had loved her once, but then Charlie had died and he had turned aside from their quiet home life together to become a spy. Without a thought of telling her, taking her into his confidence. Making her into what Bert thought she was, an encumbrance. She remembered her desperate jealous anxiety when she thought David was having an affair with Carol. She determined she would never put herself through anything like that again. If David didn't love her anymore they had to part. If they survived this, if they did go on to new lives, she would not cling on to something that was dead. Walking the cold streets, the seagulls making their sad cries above her, she could have cried out, too, with desperation and anger and sorrow at the thought of losing the only man she had ever loved.

On her sixth night at the boarding house, she saw a thin man in his forties with a big, untidy mustache at the next table, reading the London *Evening Standard*. The headline caught her eye. *"Fog Brings London to Standstill."* Hesitantly, she asked the man if she might see the paper when he had finished with it.

"Of course," he said. He nodded at the headline. He had friendly brown eyes, like a dog's. Sarah noticed there was dandruff on his collar. "I've just come down from the city, it's brought chaos up there. Worst ever, some say. Lot of people in hospital. Are you from London?" he added.

"Yes. Just—having a few days away." She heard the coolness in her voice.

The man smiled gently. "I'll leave you the paper when I'm finished." He nodded and returned to his meal.

Later that evening Sarah sought out Bert and Jane in their little office. She said she was worried there was still no news and asked if the smog in London was part of the problem. Jane smiled nervously. "I'm sorry, dear. We don't know any more than you've been told. It's always a worry for us too, the waiting time." From the way Jane had spoken, this wasn't the first time they had helped people get out of England.

On Sunday she went for another walk, down to the promenade. It was still sunny but very cold, the sea completely still and calm, the promenade deserted apart from a few elderly people walking dogs. The sea looked freezing cold. She walked toward the Palace Pier, past closed booths advertising their summer wares in faded paint.

She went on to the pier, her shoes clumping on the wooden boards. She passed the carousel and the shuttered freak show, and walked on toward the end of the pier. There was a little breeze out here, cold as a knife, the sound of the sea all around.

There was only one other person there, leaning over the rail, gazing toward the shore. She recognized the man whose paper she had borrowed at the hotel. There was a battered suitcase at his feet. Hearing her footsteps he looked up, tipping the brim of his bowler hat to her. "Out for some sea air?" he asked.

She approached him. "Yes. Freezing, isn't it?"

"Bitter."

"I heard on the radio that the fog is as bad as ever in London."

"Yes. So they say."

She was about to walk on, she knew she shouldn't be talking to him, but there was something appealingly pathetic about the man huddled against the railing, and she was desperately lonely. So she said, "Not working today?"

He shook his head. "Just booked out of the hotel. Off back to London now. Not having much luck this trip. I travel in toys and novelties, you know. Going around the Sussex resorts. People normally buy in for next spring at this time of year, but times are hard." He smiled ruefully. "I'm not going to be splashing out on Christmas this year, I don't think."

"Toys and novelties?" She remembered her committee, the toys for poor children in the North, Mrs. Templeman.

"Yes." He smiled. "I'm from Brighton originally, everyone knows me around here." He extended a gloved hand. "Danny Waterson."

"Sarah Hardcastle."

They were silent for a moment. He said, "I heard the Coronation's fixed for June."

"Is it?"

"Yes. I phoned the office this morning and they told me. They still haven't found anyone she'll marry. They say the Queen Mother's pressing German princes on her."

"Maybe she'll stay single, like the first Elizabeth?"

He looked across to the shore again. "I remember this place in 1940. Barbed wire all along the promenade, down on the beach too, concrete tank traps in the water. You can't believe it now."

"No."

"And the rationing, remember that?"

"Yes."

"Now you can buy what you like. So long as you can afford it." He spoke with a touch of bitterness. "I was in the Home Guard for a couple of months, remember them?"

She did: old men and boys on the newsreels, parading with wooden sticks because there weren't enough rifles. She had thought of how they would all be slaughtered in an invasion. Danny went on, "I was just too young to be called up. Then in a couple of months it was all over." He leaned on the railing again. "I wonder what would have happened if we hadn't made peace, whether the Germans would've invaded. It would have been difficult, you know, getting an army across the Channel."

"They tell us it would have been easy. We'd lost all our equipment at Dunkirk."

"Maybe. Well, we made our choice in 1940 and here we are." From his tone he was antiregime though he hadn't actually said anything incriminating.

"Yes." Sarah sighed heavily.

Danny shook his head sadly. "I worry about my kiddies' future, I do. I saw one of those places where they're holding the Jews outside Worthing yesterday. In the distance, from the train, it looked like an old army barracks. Surrounded with wire, guards patrolling. My wife says the Jews deserve it, they can't be trusted, they're not really loyal to Britain." He shook his head again. "Well, there's nothing we can do."

Sarah realized she had hardly thought about the Jews over the last few days. "There's been nothing on the news," she said.

"No. People will forget soon, they do if it's things they can't see and don't affect them."

"How old are your children?" she asked.

"Two boys. Six and eight. You?"

"No. I—I'm a widow."

"From the 1940 war?"

"No. Recently. My husband died in a car crash."

"Ah. I'm sorry."

"Maybe I should be getting back," Sarah said. "It's cold."

He looked at her. "Must be a hard time for you, Christmas."

"Yes. That's why I had to get away for a few days." She realized that lying was already coming easily to her. Had it been like that for David? She looked into Danny's sad face and felt guilty.

He said, nervously, "Perhaps you'd like to come for a drink. Lots of nice little pubs in the Lanes, warm coal fires. They'll be opening up about now."

She thought, he's trying to pick me up. But maybe not, perhaps he was just looking for companionship on this bleak morning. She hesitated a second, then smiled and said, "Thank you very much, but no. I should be getting back."

He was apologetic and a little embarrassed. "Of course, I'm sorry, I hope you don't mind—"

"Not at all. But I must go."

He tipped his hat again, an awkward little gesture, then said, "This is a sad sort of town in winter. Maybe, don't think I'm intruding, but maybe you'd be happier back in London."

She sighed. "Yes, perhaps. Well . . ." She turned away.

"I hope I didn't speak out of turn—"

"No. No, it was nice to talk to you."

She walked away, down the pier, back to the promenade, bleakly conscious of the loneliness that might now lie ahead forever.

As she reached the promenade a newsboy was shouting, from the stand outside the Old Ship Hotel. "Hitler dead!" she heard, "Führer dies!"

CHAPTER FORTY-NINE

After passing through the roadblock the fire engine continued racing dangerously fast down the road, sirens blaring. At one point the driver sounded the horn and a man in a white facemask crossing the road jumped wildly out of the way, his leaping figure momentarily visible in the headlights. Then, so suddenly that David was thrown violently sideways, the powerful machine juddered to a halt. He and the others stood, a little shakily, and looked over the side. The headlights were still on and though they barely penetrated the fog David was able to see that they had stopped in front of a large stationary truck, its canvas-covered back facing them. It's an army truck, he thought with horror. Beside him the young man who had rescued them threw off his helmet. "Go on," he said cheerfully, "get down. Your new transport's waiting."

"But it's army..."

He laughed. "We stole that, too. Now, come on. It won't take the police long to realize this engine was on a fake call."

David climbed down into the street, Ben and Natalia and their young rescuer following. The three firemen who had been in the cab stepped out too. David looked around; they were in a cobbled street, lockup garages on either side. He saw a man in military uniform standing beside the army truck, tall and burly.

"Who's that?" David asked the young fireman.

"Don't know, mate. We were just told to bring you here." He clapped the side of the truck. "Good old Merryweather engine, never lets you down." He brought out a packet of cigarettes and passed them around. David took one gratefully.

The military man came over, looming out of the fog. He was in his fifties, with a lined face, black mustache, and severe, hard eyes. He wore the uniform of a captain. He looked them over.

"Are you a real soldier?" Ben asked.

"Yes," the captain answered brusquely. "I'm with Churchill now. Right. All of you in the back of the truck. We need to get you out of here." He turned and barked, "Fowler, open up!" The canvas back was pulled aside and a stringy little man in a private's uniform jumped down, lowered the tailgate, and waved them up impatiently. David saw he was carrying a rifle.

David shook the hand of the young fireman. "Thank you." He looked at the rest of the crew. "Thank you all." They raised their hands in acknowledgment.

"Come on," the captain said impatiently. "We haven't much time."

They all climbed in. The truck smelled of sweat and machine oil. The private shone a torch into the back, showing a double row of benches. Another man in private's uniform sat at the far end, with a rifle across his knees. Next to him was a civilian in a dark jacket, hunched over. David's heart jumped when he saw it was Frank. Frank's face lit up and he cried out, "It's true! You're alive!"

"No thanks to you," the stringy man said grumpily in a Cockney accent. He waved his arm to indicate that David and Ben and Natalia should sit down on the benches. He closed the canvas flap, and the soldier next to Frank leaned over and banged on the back of the cab. There was a little window, giving a view into the front. The driver, another man in military uniform, was already sitting there; the captain got in beside him. The truck started and began moving slowly down the street.

The stringy private played the torch across their faces. "Right," he said. "We'll get into one of the side streets and then you're all going to change into uniform. We're going to be a group of soldiers traveling to guard duty at the Jew camp in Dover." He turned the beam on Natalia. "Except you, miss, they'll not take you for a soldier if we're stopped, you're going to be dropped off and debriefed about today. You'll rendezvous with the others later."

"Where?" Ben asked.

"You'll find out when we get there," the soldier next to Frank answered quietly, in a Yorkshire accent. "Can't really say anything more." He was a big man, with a wrestler's build, but his manner was friendlier than his comrade's.

"Who are you all?" David asked. "The man in front's got a captain's tabs."

"Used to be a regular soldier until Churchill left Parliament," the Yorkshireman answered. "Decided to help him 'set Britain ablaze.' Remember that speech?"

"And you two?"

"We're soldiers of the Resistance," the Cockney answered, "not forces of the Fascist state. We steal army uniforms as well as trucks. Two of the men who brought you here were real firemen, though. That's their jobs finished, because of this," he added reproachfully. "They're on the run now."

"So am I, pal," Ben said, an edge to his voice. "I had a safe job nursing in a loony bin for years till last week. That's the price of servin' the cause, eh?"

"We're all in it together," the Yorkshireman said gently.

The truck halted. They had only traveled a few streets. The thin Cockney shone his torch under the seats; David saw a number of canvas bags there. "Right," the Cockney said briskly, "everybody take a bag, get out and get changed."

"I want tae know where we're going," Ben said stubbornly.

The Cockney shone the torch full in his face. "Listen, Jock. We lost good people tonight in London, thanks to you lot. So do as you're fuck-ing told. Now out, all of you."

They were in a narrow street beside what looked like a small factory. A man was waiting there, a thin man in a bowler hat and a long coat; he looked like a rent collector. He went over to the captain, who had stepped out of the cab, and exchanged a few whispered words. Then he came over to Natalia. "You're to come with me please, miss."

Natalia glanced at David. She said to the man, "Can you give us a few moments?"

He nodded reluctantly. "All right. But just a minute."

David and Natalia stepped away from the others. He said, "We — I'm sorry that —"

She smiled. "I'm not. How could I be? We'll meet again soon."

David looked at the group of soldiers, a dim huddle in the fog. Frank and Ben were changing into army uniform. "Will we?"

"Yes. I'll see you soon." She hesitated. "Though from what Eileen said your wife will be joining us."

David took her hand. "Do you know, that was the first time I've ever been unfaithful to her?"

Natalia took a deep breath. "Then perhaps you were right, and it is over between you?" She looked uncertain.

He didn't answer. He couldn't. The captain came over. "You have to leave now, miss," he said sternly. "And you" — he gave David a look of disapproval — "you have to change into uniform. Now."

Natalia leaned up and kissed David quickly. "Till later," she said with a sad smile. She touched his hand briefly, then went over to the man who had come for her. Without another word the two walked away, their shapes instantly swallowed up in the fog.

"Come on," Ben called impatiently. David wondered what the Scotsman thought of him and Natalia; he hadn't given any sign. Geoff might have disapproved, but Geoff was dead.

They changed quickly into thick, itchy army uniforms. They were all privates now. The uniform felt familiar to David, took him back to 1940. He adjusted his cap and felt in his pocket for the cyanide capsule he had transferred there. They climbed into the back of the truck again and it set off once more, rumbling slowly through the empty streets. Through the window into the cab David looked past the heads of the driver and the captain, outlined against the weak beams of the headlights. The road ahead was full of swirling fog.

"How are you doing, old friend?" he asked Frank quietly. He was sitting next to him; he seemed in a daze.

"All right, I suppose. It's strange wearing this uniform." He took a deep breath. "I'm sorry I ran, David, I broke my promise. But I thought we were going to be captured and I was the only one who didn't have—you know, a pill."

"Where did you go?"

"A church. The police were coming. This vicar found me. He helped me, got me to the Resistance people, gave me his jacket." He was silent again, then he said, "I keep thinking about Geoff."

"I know. He was a brave friend." He glanced at Ben, sitting on his other side. He was frowning.

"You all right?" David asked quietly.

"I just wonder what they're goin' tae dae with us," Ben whispered. He looked at the Yorkshireman, then asked, "Where are we goin' now?"

"Out of town, that's all I know."

They passed through a busy area, the truck slowing to a crawl, inching along in the fog. Then they speeded up again for a while. Outside the fog seemed to be lifting a little. Then David heard the captain say from the cab, in a tense tone, "Here we go." Looking into the cab David saw a roadblock ahead, a wooden barrier across the road. The Cockney got up and pushed David aside to watch through the glass panel as the truck pulled to a halt. The Yorkshireman leaned across and tapped Frank on the knee.

"We're being stopped. But the captain will get us through okay." He spoke as though to a backward child. "You just keep quiet. All right?"

David whispered to Ben, "I suppose Frank's pills are back at the O'Sheas'?"

"The Largactil? Yes." A policeman appeared then, shining a torch into the cab. The captain wound the window down. "Evening, officer," he said confidently. The policeman saluted.

"Where are you going, sir?" he asked. His tone was respectfully polite but there was something worried, David thought, about his look.

"Taking some men to the Jew camp at Dover. Guard duty. I'm going to be assisting the Commander." He handed a document to the policeman, who studied it by the light of his torch. "Having trouble with the Yids?" he asked apprehensively.

"No. Why should we be? But the camps need guards. Why the roadblock?"

"Escaped terrorists. Three men and a woman, all in their thirties. They got away from a raid at New Cross. The Branch is pulling all the stops out on this one for some reason."

"Locking the stable door after the horse has bolted, eh?"

"That's about the size of it, sir," the policeman answered heavily.

"We haven't seen anybody. Though it's hard to see your own hand in this fog."

"I know. Never seen anything like it. Strange night for—what's happened in Germany."

"What do you mean?"

"Hitler's dead. It's official."

The men in the back of the cab looked at each other, their faces suddenly bright. Frank said, "Did he say—" The Yorkshireman leaned forward and put a hand over his mouth. "Shhhh."

"Are you sure?" David heard the captain ask.

"They're saying at the police station that it's true."

"Good God," the captain said. "What'll happen now?"

"Who knows?" the policeman answered. "I hope the Jews don't hear, that's why I wondered if there might be trouble at the detention camps. Anyway, we've got to check all vehicles going out of London. Mind if I just have a look in the back?"

"Be my guest." The captain leaned back and called out, "Open up!"

The Cockney private opened the canvas flaps. The policeman leaned in and shone his torch over the men, and under the benches. Ben said in a joking voice, "Wisnae anything to do with me, Constable, that missing crate of Spam in Aldershot!" The others laughed. The policeman grunted and closed the flap. He waved them on, saluting the captain again as they passed. Everybody let out their breath and relaxed, except Frank, who sat staring rigidly ahead.

The captain slid open the glass partition. His face was animated now, excited. "You chaps hear that? They're saying Hitler's dead!"

"That bastard, gone at last," the Yorkshireman said feelingly.

*   *   *

They weren't stopped again, and they drove slowly but steadily on. David thought they were heading east rather than south but he wasn't sure. He wondered where Natalia was, whether he would see her again. And Sarah. Was it over with Sarah? He still didn't know.

The fog thinned further, eventually vanishing to leave the starry darkness of a December night. Twisting his head to look into the cab, David saw they were traveling along country roads now, the skeletal shapes of trees appearing and vanishing again, ghostly white in the headlights. He thought, we're not going to the coast, we'd have been there by now. He glanced at Ben, who sat looking ahead of him, frowning. The roads became worse, the truck banging and clattering over them. As the journey continued, heads began to nod despite the jolting. David leaned across and whispered to Ben, "Frank's asleep. He wasn't looking too good earlier."

"He needs another dose. But I had to leave all his stuff at the O'Sheas'. Where the hell are they taking us?"

"Why are you so worried?" David whispered.

"I want tae know where we're going. Why won't they tell us? There's something in their attitude—I don't like it."

"They've lost people tonight."

"So have we."

David sat back. After a while his eyes closed from sheer weariness. He woke with a jolt as the truck came to a halt. The captain opened the cab window. "Everyone out!" he called.

They all climbed down. David helped Frank, who was shaking. They stepped into pitch darkness, onto what felt like a graveled driveway, tall trees on either side just visible as shapes outlined against the sky. It was very cold; there was a smell of wet, freezing air. No lights were visible anywhere.

"David," Frank whispered urgently. "Where are we?"

"I don't know."

"No talking," the captain snapped. "Follow me." The three soldiers had surrounded them, their rifles held at the ready. Beside David, Ben

515

took a deep breath. The thought flashed through David's head: *they're going to shoot us*. We've caused them so many problems they've decided to get rid of us, somewhere quiet out in the country. Or perhaps they'll keep Frank alive, interrogate him, find his secret. If Hitler's dead everybody's calculations will change. He looked at the dim outline of the captain, marching steadily ahead of him. He didn't like him, there was something cold and implacable about the man.

They were led down the pitch-dark driveway, footsteps crunching softly. Then the shape of what looked like a large country house loomed ahead, and David glimpsed tall chimneys against the sky. They walked slowly on toward it.

A slit of light appeared, as a door in the side of the house opened a fraction. "Aztec," the captain said, quietly. The slit widened. David's party was led up a short flight of stone steps and through the door. They found themselves in a long corridor lined with pictures, blinking in sudden light. A young man in khaki uniform with a Union Jack sewn on the breast pocket was posted at the end, a rifle over his shoulder. The corridor windows were all heavily curtained, the sort of thick material David remembered from the 1939–40 blackout. In the distance he heard voices; this place was big, probably owned by some aristocrat who had come around to supporting the Resistance. A telephone rang somewhere in the depths of the building. It was answered quickly.

The man who had opened the door was elderly, tall and thin, dressed in a white shirt and black waistcoat, like a butler. He looked them over, then stepped forward with a smile. "Welcome, gentlemen. Mr. Fitzgerald?"

David stepped forward. "Yes?"

"Could you take Dr. Muncaster upstairs please? Mr. Hall, could you come with me? Your account of what happened in London is needed."

"All right," Ben said. "See you soon, Frank." Ben followed the man away down the corridor. The captain accompanied them. The man with the Union Jack on his uniform stepped forward, addressing David and Frank in a friendly tone with a strong Welsh accent: "Come with me, please." He turned to the uniformed men. "You chaps, go outside and someone will show you where to park your truck and bunk down."

He led David and Frank down the corridor to a hallway with a wide central staircase. Through a half-open door David glimpsed furniture covered with white dustsheets. Another man in a uniform with a Union Jack and a rifle joined them. They walked upstairs. From behind a closed door nearby they heard a murmur of male voices; another telephone rang somewhere. David guessed this place was some sort of headquarters. The reports of Hitler's death would be causing a flap.

David and Frank were shown into a large bedroom, again with heavily curtained windows. There was a double bed and a pair of camp beds on the floor. "Keep the curtains closed please," the Welshman said, his tone still amicable. "There's a toilet just up the corridor. We'll have some food brought up. Mr. Hall will join you later. I'm Barry, by the way." He was the first person they had met since their rescue who had given them his name.

"Can you tell us where we are?" David asked.

"No, sorry," Barry answered apologetically. "Not now. Is there anything else you need?"

Frank said, "I'm supposed to have my—my medicine, to help me sleep. I need it. Ben knows about it."

The Welshman nodded. "I'll have a word with him." He smiled. "Have you heard the news?"

"The rumors that Hitler's dead? Yes."

"It's more than rumors. German radio say Goebbels is the new Führer. Maybe things are going to happen now, eh?"

When he left the room Frank sat down wearily on the bed.

"What d'you think of that?" David asked.

"I don't know if I believe it." Frank scratched his chest. "I feel bad. I can't stop thinking about Geoff, seeing him on the ground. And Sean and Eileen. I nodded off in the truck, but the pictures that came into my mind... He put his head in his hands.

David sat beside him. He looked at his watch; it was past one in the morning. He felt exhausted, and suddenly angry with Frank. Was it any worse for him than the rest of them? David knew that what had happened tonight would affect him for the rest of his life. Assuming he survived. He looked at the top of Frank's head, then thought, he didn't volunteer for this the way the rest of us did. He put a hand on his arm. "We're safe now."

Frank looked up. "Are we?"

There was a knock at the door and Barry returned. He had a tray with sandwiches on it, and also a glass of water and a bottle of pills. Frank's eyes lit up. "This what you need?" Barry asked.

David said, "You had this stuff here? You knew we were coming?"

"We thought you might be. We know it's important Dr. Muncaster has the—what is it—Lar-something."

"Largactil." Frank eyed the bottle with an addict's greed. Barry opened it and passed the glass and two pills to Frank, who swallowed them eagerly and lay back on the bed. "I'll feel better in a few minutes," he said. "Then I'll sleep." David thought, he may not be physically addicted, but he can't do without them.

Barry looked at David. "I'd get a bit of sleep yourself now if I were you. Will you be—er—all right with him?"

"Of course I will," David answered sharply.

Barry left. Frank lay on his side and after a minute his breathing became deep and regular. Wearily, David took off his boots, then the army tunic. He switched off the light, then walked over to the window and parted the curtains slightly. It was pitch dark outside, only the stars visible high in the sky, the suggestion of a tree line in the distance. There was a stone terrace directly below. Then a soldier with a rifle stepped into the slit of light and gestured at him angrily to close the curtains. David thought, there must be guards all around this place. He felt his way over to one of the camp beds and lay down. At least it was warm in here; the room had central heating. To the sound of Frank's regular breathing, he fell asleep.

He was woken by Ben switching on the light. He looked haggard. David sat up and, putting a finger to his lips, pointed at Frank. Ben stepped quietly over to the bed and looked down at him, then came over to David. "He's out for the count," he said quietly.

"They gave him his pills. He wasn't feeling too good before. We'll have to get him off them when we get away."

"If we get away." Ben sat down wearily on the other camp bed. He looked at his watch. "Christ, it's near four. They've been questioning me all this time, trying tae work out how those Special Branch bastards found us. There's raids going down on Resistance suspects all over London, despite the fog. A few people have been picked up but it seems it was us they were looking for."

"I think that little boy put them onto the O'Sheas."

"Aye, likely." Ben lowered his voice. "The people who questioned me were all military. They're pissed off by all the trouble this mission's caused. They don't seem too happy with us."

"All we've done is follow orders."

"They seem to think we're more trouble than we're worth."

"I was scared when we were taken off that truck," David confessed. "I thought they might shoot us. You did too, didn't you?"

"Aye. I thought they'd decided to get rid of the problem."

"Are we still going to the coast?"

"They won't say. Nor where the fuck we are."

"I took a quick look outside, could only see some sort of terrace. There was a guard outside, he made me shut the curtain again."

"There's people with rifles all over the house, and a guard posted in the corridor outside."

"Are they going to move us on?"

"Fuck knows." Ben looked across at Frank. "Poor wee bastard, he's best off out of it all for a while."

David said wearily, "I was thinking earlier, I wonder if this is any worse for him than for the rest of us?"

Ben said, "I think life *is* worse for him than for most people. In the asylum, you know, some of them were quite happy, just living there. Though others just pretended to be. But Frank hated it." He looked at David seriously. "I know you think I'm a bit hard on him sometimes, but in the loony bin you have to make it clear who's boss. It just reflects the system, keepin' people under as cheaply as possible. It'll be different after the revolution." A misty, longing look came into Ben's eyes. "I didnae like it much, reminded me too much of when I was inside."

David looked at him curiously. He realized the chippy young Communist was becoming a friend. "You said you were in prison when you were young. What was it for?" he asked.

Ben glanced at him doubtfully, then said, matter-of-factly, "When I was seventeen I got found in bed with my best mate. He wis sixteen."

"Oh." David was astonished. He thought queers were girlish, effeminate, like a man who had worked in the Dominions Office and been sacked when they'd cleared out possible security risks a few years ago. Involuntarily, he leaned away. Ben saw the movement and smiled sarcastically.

"Yeah, that's right. I'm one of those. The Glasgow magistrates threw the book at me, and ma family disowned me. They were all Presbyterian Orangemen, poor as fuck and blaming it on the Irish." He shook his head, smiling sadly. "There wis five of us kids in three rooms, the babies had to sleep in drawers at night; there wisnae anywhere else to put them. My sister accidentally shut the drawer on ma wee brother Tam one night. He near suffocated, he wis always a bit slow after. I wis the clever one, no' that it did me much good. A year in a reformatory and six strokes of the birch."

David couldn't think of what to say. He remembered the scars he had seen across Ben's back. "The birch," he said quietly. "My father had clients who were sentenced to it. He used to say it was barbaric."

"Disnae sound much when you say it, does it, the birch, but when you're strapped to a rack with nothin' on and they bring that bunch of knotted canes out, well, I fucking wet myself. Still," he added bitterly, "it toughened me up, as they say." He looked David in the eye. "And we have to be hard, if we're to fight for something better."

"I know." They fell silent. Then David asked, "Did they say when Natalia's coming back?"

"They didn't tell me nuthin'." Ben smiled sarcastically again. "So you and she got together, then? I saw you both as you came down the stairs."

"Yes," David answered quietly. "Yes, we did."

Ben shrugged. "It's all right by me, pal. I'm the last one to cast asper-sions. Natalia's a tough one. I admire her. She's been on some hard mis-sions. I wouldn't get too many romantic notions, though," he added.

David shook his head wearily. "I don't know what notions I've got anymore."

"It's like that, bein' on the run. Nae anchor, nae certainty about any-thing, nothing familiar. Sometimes you cling to people, take pleasure when you get the chance. It's no' a great way to live."

"No. That's true enough."

Ben looked at him seriously. "That's why I'm glad I'm a Marxist. I've got something bigger than me, a truth to hold on to."

"A belief, at least."

"If you like."

David said, "All I want's an end to this savagery."

"Don't we all?" Ben stood up. "Anyway, I'm away for a piss, then I'll try and get some sleep."

David couldn't get to sleep again. The terrible events of the day before kept spinning around in his mind. A few feet away, Ben had begun to snore lightly. His confession had been a total surprise. David thought, *nothing in the world is how I believed it was, none of the safe certainties were true, ever.*

After a while he padded over to the door in his stockinged feet and opened it gently. Outside, a young man in the ubiquitous khaki uniform with the Union Jack on the breast sat on a chair, rifle over his knees, half asleep. He blinked, sat up straight, and looked at David.

"I need the toilet," David said quietly.

The guard jerked his head to the right. "Second door down."

"Thanks."

This corridor looked modern, plasterboard walls, perhaps added to the house recently. David went to the door the guard had indicated. The lavatory looked as though it was a recent addition, too, just a little win-dowless cupboard room with a toilet and washbasin. As he went in he heard male voices murmuring. They seemed to be coming from low down, by his feet. He knelt and bent his ear to where the toilet pipe joined the wall and found he could make out the voices. There was some sort of conference going on, perhaps in the next room. There was a mixture of accents, arguing in loud tones. David made out the voice of the captain who had brought them. "It's got too dangerous. We have to abort the mission. We tell the Americans it's too risky."

"Then what happens to Muncaster and the others?" A Liverpudlian accent.

"I still say we could get this secret of Muncaster's out of him ourselves," said a languid upper-class drawl. "Might be useful, whatever it is; if Germany collapses and Britain becomes properly independent again, we'll be doing our own weapons research."

The captain again: "Don't be so bloody silly, Brendan. That would really piss the Yanks off. We're going to need them now more than ever."

"What do we do with them, then, shoot them?"

The captain raised his voice: "Those people have risked their lives to get Muncaster here. We can absorb them within the organization. But Muncaster—given his mental state—I don't know."

"If the decision's to get rid of him, we might as well get what he knows out of him first," the man called Brendan retorted.

"How can you even talk about it?" The Liverpudlian accent. "An innocent man?"

"A potentially dangerous man—"

The Liverpudlian: "Look, the Germans don't know anything about the pickup."

"And if we go ahead and they're caught..."

A new voice, cold and flat: "They've got suicide pills. Except for Muncaster—"

"Well, we know the options." The Captain spoke with a touch of weariness. "We're not going to agree. The ultimate decision is out of our hands. The briefing meeting's at half past six tomorrow, so I suggest we get some rest, but think over the options carefully. There'll have to be a decision first thing, there's going to be a hell of a lot to decide over the next few days, with Hitler's death announced."

David heard murmurs, chairs scraping, a laugh, a door slamming. Then nothing. He stayed crouched over by the toilet, his fist in his mouth, trying to contain his rage, his eyes full of tears. They were pawns, just pawns. But then he thought, it was war and they were soldiers, volunteers. But not Frank.

There was a sharp rap at the door. The guard's voice, loud. "You all right in there?"

David heaved himself to his feet, went and opened the door. The guard looked suspicious for a moment, then sympathetic. "Blimey, you look rough."

"Yes. Constipated. Not really eaten properly recently."

He went back to the room. Ben and Frank were still asleep. David thought of waking Ben and telling him what he had overheard, but Frank might wake as well and he didn't know how he would react. He would wait until the morning. He lay back down on his camp bed, shaking with anger. He knew he wouldn't sleep now.

At shortly before seven, by his watch, David heard people moving in the corridors outside. It was beginning to get light, though with the heavy curtains drawn the room was still dark. Frank and Ben were still asleep. David got up, stretched, then padded over to the window. The meeting to decide their fate would be going on now. He parted the heavy curtains and looked out.

The beauty of the scene outside made him catch his breath. Wide lawns stippled with frost dropped away to a reed-fringed lake with still, clear waters where ducks swam, leaving a broad wake behind them. A red sun was just clearing the trees, and there were fragments of pink-tinged cloud in the blue sky. Beyond the lake, more lawns rose toward thick woodland, a mixture of trees, some with bare branches, others evergreens. The impact of the sharp colors was almost physical after the last few days in the smog.

Behind him he heard Ben stir. Ben went to look at Frank, then came over to stand beside David. He looked at the view and whistled. "That's somethin', is it no'?"

"Where are we?"

There was a sharp knock at the door. As David and Ben turned, Barry, the Welshman they had met last night, came in. He was tired-looking, unshaven. To David's astonishment, he was followed by two young housemaids in uniform, black skirts and blouses, white pinafores and caps, each carrying a large tray loaded with food.

Barry nodded. " 'Morning." He looked at Ben. "You need to get Dr. Muncaster awake. Have some breakfast and a quick wash and shave, then we need you downstairs. Spruce yourselves up a bit, there's some shaving stuff in the toilet up the hall." He went over to Frank and looked down at him. "Will he be all right to answer some questions?"

"Leave him," Ben said sharply. "I'll get him up. He'll be fine. We'd better be with him, though, or he'll get scared."

Barry nodded. "All right."

"What d'ye want to ask him?"

The man looked at them seriously. "It won't be me, mate. Some of the bigwigs have been talking about the next step for your people. You'll be talking to them. Come on now, girls, leave those trays."

After the maids and Barry left the room there was silence for a moment, then David said, quietly, "Don't wake Frank just yet. Listen, I found something out last night. You should know."

As Ben listened his face darkened and he clenched his fists. "Bastards," he breathed. "You mean they might try to force this secret out of him for themselves, after what he was promised, or even fuckin' kill him? What, take him out and shoot him on that terrace?"

"Keep your voice down. I don't know. But there's nothing we can do, we're too closely guarded." He took a deep breath. "Except make sure we stay right by Frank, and if it looks as though they're going down that road, give him one of these." He took the cyanide pill from his pocket and held it out. "Did you transfer yours when you changed into your uniform?"

"Aye. 'Course I did." He stared at David. "If we do that, we'll really be in the shit."

"I don't care," David said. "I've had enough, I won't stand for it."

Ben nodded agreement. David couldn't help wondering, would Ben's reaction have been different if it were the Russians who wanted Frank's secret? Who knew? Everything was in flux now, with the three of them at the center.

Frank was hard to wake, a little groggy at first, but he came to himself as they ate. He asked Ben for his morning pill. Ben said he would ask the staff, exchanging a look with David and shaking his head slightly; if the worst came to the worst Frank should be fully awake. They went to the little toilet in turns to wash and shave. When they returned to the room, Ben told Frank some people wanted to talk to them.

"What about?" His eyes were instantly wary.

"We're no' sure." Ben looked at David. "Might be a committee of bigwigs, we think. To talk about what's to happen to us next. That's what we hope anyway."

Frank dropped his knife and fork with a clatter. "What do you mean by that? What else could it be? Bigwigs? You said nobody would ask about my brother, about what happened, they'd just try to get me out to America." He turned to David. "I can't tell them, I won't —"

"A promise is a promise," David said steadily. "It's all right, we'll be with you."

Ben looked into Frank's eyes. "All the way, pal," he said. "Understand? All the way."

CHAPTER FIFTY

Two soldiers with rifles led them downstairs, to a long corridor. At the far end they could hear several voices behind a closed door. They were taken into another, nearer room, a big window giving a view of the parkland outside. The room was some sort of study, crowded with paintings, dominated by a large desk with a comfortable chair behind it. It had a high, arched oak-beamed roof, medieval or Tudor; this must be the oldest part of the house. There was a bust of Napoleon on the desk, another of Nelson. A row of hard chairs stood against one wall. The three of them were told to sit there and wait.

Frank spoke in a quiet, fierce tone David had never heard from him before, almost hissing, "I won't tell them anything, I *won't.*"

"Maybe they won't ask."

"Give me one of your pills, now, please."

Ben and David exchanged a look. If they gave him one he might just take it right away. "No," Ben said. Frank sat forward, clutching his hands together.

"I *won't.* Whatever they do—"

"We'll sort it for you," Ben said.

There were sounds from outside, a muted hubbub of voices; the door at the far end of the corridor had opened. Several pairs of footsteps approached the room, and the door opened. A tall, stern-looking man in early middle age came in. He was immaculately dressed in a dark suit, the edge of a snow-white handkerchief projecting from his breast pocket. He said, "Stand up, please, gentlemen."

They stood. Two armed soldiers came in, taking their places on each side of the door. They were followed by a very old man, walking with the aid of a stick. He was heavily built, stooped, his big round head with its sparse white hair thrust forward. He wore an extraordinary outfit, a sort of blue boiler suit, open-necked, a shirt and spotted bow tie beneath. David was astonished by how old Winston Churchill had become; the pictures of him on the "Wanted" posters dated from years ago. The Head of the British Resistance walked slowly around the desk and sat down heavily. He looked pale, exhausted. Only when he had seated himself did Churchill turn and look at the three men standing by their chairs. It was a fierce, challenging look, the blue eyes still keen, the big square chin and the lower lip thrust out aggressively though the skin at the neck beneath was loose and wrinkled. Frank leaned forward, in a sort of stoop of his own, staring at Churchill in astonishment and terror. The tall man in the suit went and stood beside Churchill's desk.

"So, you got here," Churchill growled in the deep, lisping voice David remembered from thirties newsreels.

"Yes, sir," he answered.

"At much cost in life and trouble, Mr. Colville tells me." He nodded at the man in the suit, who was staring at them expressionlessly.

"I'm afraid so, sir," David said.

"Hitler is dead," Churchill said gravely. "You have heard?"

"Yes, sir."

"That evil man." There was weariness in his voice. "Who knows what will happen in Germany now? Perhaps they will make peace with what is left of Russia." The eyes flashed. "But Germany is still a terrible enemy." He looked at Colville. "They are still here, on the Isle of Wight, in Senate House, no doubt they have representatives in these wretched camps where they have taken the Jews. Britain is still under their fist, Nazi fingers in every dark corner of the state." He scowled, knitting his brows, lost in thought for a moment. Then he looked directly at Frank. David tensed, leaning an inch closer to his friend.

"Dr. Muncaster," Churchill said evenly. "It seems the Germans want you as badly as the Americans." Frank began to breathe fast; David saw his legs were trembling slightly. He thought angrily, they've set all this up to shock him, the secrecy, the waiting, Churchill appearing suddenly. It's all to scare him into talking. He put an arm on Frank's. "It's all right," he said soothingly.

"Leave him!" Churchill snapped. He glowered at David, then looked at Frank again. Something in his mobile face softened and he said, more quietly, "Here, Dr. Muncaster, come and sit down. John, bring across that chair." Churchill beckoned to Frank to sit. "I won't harm you," he said with a sort of gentle impatience. "I merely want to speak with you."

David realized that if Frank went over and sat down it would be very hard to get a cyanide pill to him. The two soldiers by the door had been watching them closely all the time. He would have to make a sudden dash, Frank would have to be ready. But Frank looked as though he might faint. Then, slowly and reluctantly, he stepped forward and sat opposite Churchill, staring at him with a sort of terrified fascination.

Churchill asked, "Do you know where you are, young man?"

Colville murmured, "We thought it better not to tell them, sir."

"Did you indeed?" Churchill gave him a glare. "Bloody security." He turned back to Frank, and spoke proudly. "You are at Chartwell, in Kent. This used to be my country house. It's my son Randolph's now. He pretends to be working with *them*, it means they leave this place alone." A shadow crossed his face. "Poor Randolph, they think him dishonorable; he has paid that price for me." He leaned back in his chair. "I come here as often as I can, it helps me think. Though my guardians believe it is dangerous, eh, Jock?" He looked at the tall man again, laughing throatily, then turned back to Frank. "What d'you think of my house, eh?"

"I saw the view this morning, sir," Frank said, hesitantly. "It's beautiful."

"Finest view in England!" Churchill smiled. "They tell me you have been ill. In hospital. A breakdown of some sort," he added gently.

"Yes, sir." Frank looked down.

"It's nothing to be ashamed of. I myself have suffered from depression all my life. My black dog, I call it." He paused. "Sometimes I have wanted to end it all."

Frank looked up at him in surprise. "Have you, sir?"

"I have. But the answer is action, always action." Churchill's look was suddenly fierce. "But perhaps you do not see it that way."

Frank took a deep breath. "I've always been too afraid to act."

He and Churchill looked at each other for a long moment. David was conscious of a clock ticking somewhere. Then Churchill said, quietly, "You found something out, didn't you? A scientific matter. My advisers believe it may be important. Some sort of breakthrough in weapons science the Americans have made."

"I'm sorry, sir. I can't tell you. I can only tell the Americans."

"Who know it already." Churchill nodded. "You do not wish the knowledge to spread." Churchill's voice took on a stern note. "Even to us, your country's friends."

"I'm sorry, I *can't* tell you. I was promised I wouldn't be asked." He gave David an anguished look.

"He was promised," David said. "We were told that was what the Americans wanted. It was the only way he would come with us, sir. Frank — Dr. Muncaster — feels the knowledge is too dangerous to spread."

Churchill glared at him. "Speak when you're spoken to! Damned impertinence! What are you, a junior civil servant?"

David put his hand over his pocket. If he could reach . . .

Churchill looked back at Frank. He was trembling but he looked Churchill straight back in the eye. Churchill pursed his lips. There was silence for almost a minute. David felt sweat trickling down his brow. Then Churchill said, "Dr. Muncaster, you are an honorable man." He turned to Colville. "The agreed arrangements will go ahead. Our promise to the Americans and to this man will be kept. The submarine is still off Brighton, isn't it? It is a debt of honor. To America, whose support under its new President is vital, and to this man. I will not have a promise I made broken, an innocent man sacrificed!" Churchill banged his fist on the desk, glowering at Colville.

"Actually, sir," Colville replied, "I agree with you. But a lot on the military side don't."

"Bugger them." Churchill looked at Frank, then Ben and David. He addressed Frank, very quietly. "You would not let the Germans take you alive, would you?"

"No, sir."

"You are quite certain?"

"Yes."

Churchill looked at Ben and David. "And that goes for you all?"

"Aye," Ben said, looking at Churchill directly.

"Yes, sir," David answered. "One of us has already died."

Churchill turned to Colville. "Then get them to Brighton. Right now." He got up, slowly, grasping his stick, and came around the table. Frank stood. Churchill gave an odd, quick, rubbery smile, as though his emotions were about to break through. Then he shook his hand. "Good luck to you," he said. He made his way over to David and Ben and shook their hands too. "I wish you all a safe journey," he said. Then he lumbered slowly to the door, which Colville opened for him, and went out. The two guards followed, leaving them alone.

Ben sat down again. "Jesus bloody Christ," he said.

David went over to Frank, who was staring across the desk at where Churchill had been sitting. "You all right?" he asked.

"Yes," Frank said quietly. "I think so." He looked between them and said quietly, "Thank you."

Ben said, "Can we trust him?"

Frank said, "Yes. I saw it, in his eyes. We can."

A movement outside caught David's eye. A little group of people was walking across the lawn, toward the house. Among them, he saw Natalia.

CHAPTER FIFTY-ONE

The car drove along deep Sussex lanes, between high banks lined with trees. They had made good time driving south from Chartwell; it was early on Monday morning and the roads were almost deserted. David remembered his first journey to Birmingham to see Frank. Only a fortnight ago, it seemed like another world. He had still worked at the Office then. He thought of its routines and customs, people like Dabb and Hubbold. He understood now how stifled and crushed he had felt without realizing it, before Charlie died even. His stomach lurched as he thought of Carol, her career over, too, and his dead friend, Geoff. He was sitting next to Natalia, her warmth pressed against him. He glanced at her and she smiled. His heart had lifted when he saw her from Churchill's window. Now he felt desire again. Why did the sexual urge, which God knew hadn't troubled him that much before in his life, keep returning now? Was it partly because, as Ben had said, you looked for solace in times of danger? But it was more than that, he knew; he was, like Natalia, in the end, rootless, in a time when rootlessness was dangerous: rootless and alone.

After the meeting with Churchill, they had spent a day resting at Chartwell. They had not been allowed to leave their room, so David had not seen Natalia again. Outside, they heard a constant murmur of voices, ringing telephones, sometimes running feet. At sunset the thick curtains had been drawn over the windows again.

In the evening they had a briefing meeting with an officer they had not met before. They were told that the following morning they would travel by car to Brighton. They were given yet another set of identities. The four of them—David, Ben, Natalia, and Frank—were to be a funeral party, going to Brighton for the interment of an elderly aunt.

They would stay in a boarding house while final arrangements were made for the American submarine waiting in the Channel to pick them up; they weren't to be told exactly where from yet. David and Ben and Frank were all to be cousins, and Natalia David's wife; with her accent, she could hardly pass as an Englishwoman's niece. David supposed Frank wasn't in a fit state to pass as anybody's husband, and maybe they knew Ben's secret and thought him unsuitable for the part. Sarah, they were told, was already in Brighton, and the boardinghouse owners had just been contacted to say the party was on its way. Sarah would be told, but they must pretend not to know her.

They had set off from Chartwell at nine on Monday the eighth, in a big black Volvo. David realized that the reason they only phoned their people in Brighton yesterday was because, until Churchill's decision, they might not have been going at all. Frank might have been under interrogation now, or even dead. Churchill had made his decision partly because Frank had touched his sense of honor; he wondered if that had been the deciding factor, the turning point. He looked at the back of Frank's head; like the other three men he wore a dark, heavy coat and black bowler. He still found it incredible that Frank had stood up to Winston Churchill, actually told him to his face that he wouldn't reveal his secret.

"What did ye think of Churchill, then?" Ben asked the company. "I could've fallen off my chair when he came in."

"He is very old," Natalia said. "I saw him in the corridor yesterday and it brought it home. Old and very tired."

"He's almost eighty." David thought she was right, he had looked ancient, desperately burdened and weary.

Ben said, "It's working people that carry the burden of getting rid of these Fascists. One of our leaders should be in charge, Attlee or Bevan. Or Harry Pollitt."

"Churchill has been a leader against Fascism since the thirties," Natalia replied quietly.

"To preserve the Empire. Though even he knows that one's lost now."

"He understood," Frank said suddenly.

Ben looked at him. "What d'ye mean?"

"He understood me."

There was silence; nobody quite knew how to answer. The car crested a hill and in the distance, across miles of undulating downland dotted with sheep, David saw the sea, blue and sparkling under the wide sky. Frank leaned forward, stared at it and smiled.

They arrived at the hotel, parking the car outside. They got out and took their suitcases from the boot, looking carefully around the narrow street. The weather was very clear and cold, no wind. The sea was at the end of the road, blue and dead calm. Ben came and stood beside David, leaning close. He said, very quietly, "There aren't going to be any problems involving your wife and Natalia, are there?"

David turned, frowning. Ben met his gaze firmly. "You ken what I mean. She's probably waiting for you inside. We can't afford any problems among ourselves, not till we're safe away."

David picked up his suitcase. "There won't be any," he said stiffly.

There was no sign of Sarah in the gloomy little reception hall of the Channel View Hotel, only a weary-looking middle-aged woman behind the desk. David gave their cover names in low, serious tones, appropriate for mourners. He knew the woman was with the Resistance but you could never be sure who might be listening. She leaned over the desk, smiling nervously. "It's all right. Our last commercial traveler has just gone. And we've taken no bookings for tomorrow. Though you need to keep to your cover identities, just in case."

David asked, "Is my wife here?"

She smiled again. "You're her husband? Yes. She's fine. She's here under the name Mrs. Hardcastle, a widow. She doesn't know you're coming, we were instructed not to tell her in advance. She's gone out for a walk. She often goes for walks during the day, it gets her out of her room. She'll be back for lunch." She smiled. "We've been a bit lax, letting her come and go. But we didn't want to keep her cooped up here, she looked so sad."

Ben asked, "Do you know how long we're staying?"

"My husband has just gone out. He'll be back soon, he might have some more information. Go upstairs and unpack, I'll call you when he gets back." She handed out keys from a pegboard on the wall behind her. "I'm Jane, by the way." She smiled again. "I think you'll all be away very soon."

They carried their bags up the dark, creaking staircase. Frank was beside David. "How are you?" David asked him.

"I'll be all right." He nodded with a kind of wonder. "The sea. I've always liked the sea. It made me think, we're nearly there, after everything. We might just do it. Mightn't we, David?"

David had been given a key with the number 16 on it, for him and Natalia. The two of them stopped outside the room, while Ben and Frank went into the one next door. Natalia smiled at David uncertainly.

"I suppose we'd better go in," she said.

The room was small and dingy, the window giving a view of the backs of neighboring buildings. It was dominated by a large double bed with a candlewick bedspread in an unpleasant shade of yellow. David put his suitcase on it and looked awkwardly at Natalia. She smiled tightly. "So, Sarah is out."

"Yes."

"How do you feel now, about seeing her again?"

David sat on the bed. "I don't know. Scared, I suppose." He laughed sadly. "Ironic, isn't it, according to our papers you're my wife now."

"You will go back to her, won't you?"

"We've been through so much, I've put her through so much. She needs me. But..."

Natalia sat beside him, looking at him with those slightly Oriental, green eyes. "You will go back to her in the end," she said sadly. "Because you are loyal."

"I don't know."

She didn't answer. He asked, "If we get to America, have they planned anything for you?"

She looked at him, the sun shining through the window on that lustrous brown hair. "They told me, before I came to join you at Chartwell, that I am to go to America with you. I need to rest. Perhaps I will do some more painting. I have been doing this work for a long time. They said I am in danger of becoming burned out."

"Are you?" His heart leapt at the thought that Natalia was coming too.

"This mission has been different," she said. "You know, all these years since my husband died I have had nobody. Oh, little affairs here and there but nothing serious, just work. But then I met you." She stood up. "People like me are especially useful to the Resistance. People without nationality, identity, family. I have been full of hate, anger, it has been all that's kept me going for years." Tears came into her eyes. "Now—yes, I'm tired. Meeting you helped me realize that."

"I've realized a lot since I met you."

She smiled. "Perhaps you are a little in love?"

"Yes, yes I am."

"I used to look forward so much to seeing you, those evenings in Soho. Your people, you especially, seemed so—honest. Many of those I have had to deal with these last seven years were not, they wanted money and power. You just wanted freedom, the end of all this evil." There were tears in her eyes. She leaned over and took his hand lightly. "But your wife was in the way then, as she is now."

A knock made them both jump. They looked at each other. David went and opened the door. He feared it would be Sarah, that she would see Natalia with him in tears, but it was Ben. He looked at them sharply. "Jane's husband's back. He wants to see us. We're all next door. Come on through."

"Give us a minute."

Ben shut the door. Natalia went over to the little washbasin and quickly washed and dried her face. "He's worried, isn't he? About—complications?"

He reached out his hand but she only shook her head and walked past him, touching his arm gently before opening the door.

*   *   *

Ben and Frank's room was identical to theirs except that there were two single beds. A fat man in shirt sleeves, a lick of brown hair drawn across his bald head, stood by the window. He looked at David and Natalia with a touch of impatience. Frank and Ben were sitting side by side on one of the beds. Opposite them, on the other bed, a large map of the coastline was spread out.

The man said, "I'm Bert. We need to get on at once. I don't like leaving Jane downstairs alone, not when there's something like this on."

"All right, pal," Ben said soothingly.

"This is like any war, there's periods when it's quiet and nothing's happening, but everyone needs to be ready at a moment's notice. Just like that." Bert clicked his fingers sharply, then looked at David. "Where's your wife?"

"Jane said she went out for a walk."

Bert sighed. "All right." He sounded annoyed. "We've all been waiting for days, with no word from London about when you were coming, then everything goes mad yesterday. You're on your way tonight."

"The American submarine knows we're here?" Natalia asked quietly.

"Yes. They've been wondering what the hell's going on, too."

"How do you contact them?" Natalia asked.

"We've a radio. Not here, in the town." He looked at each of them in turn. "It's fixed now, you all travel to Rottingdean tonight, after dark. The sub will be waiting out at sea. You get picked up at one a.m. The weather forecast's good, it's going to stay cold and dry with a calm sea." He stepped over to the map lying on the bed. "Come and look here." David and Natalia went and stood at the foot of the bed. He glanced at her; she looked composed and concentrated again.

Bert asked, "Does anyone know this coast at all? No? Well, see those gray areas? That's the cliffs, a sheer drop to the sea, there's just a path between them and the water at high tide, it's called the Undercliff Walk. The cliffs start just east of Brighton, here, and carry on to this gap in the cliffs—see, there? That's Rottingdean village, three miles east. There's a bay there, a cove, Rottingdean Gap. Then the cliffs rise again on the other side."

"What sort of place is this Rottingdean?" Ben asked.

"Small, an old fishing village, tourists come in the summer and there are people who've retired there. Posh, some of them; Rudyard Kipling lived there. It'll be very quiet late on a Monday night. You get down to the cove, where there's a small beach between the cliffs, a little before midnight. There'll be a boat ready to row you out to sea."

David said, "And then they take us away."

Bert nodded. "It's a spy sub, the Americans are often nosing around the Channel, seeing what messages they can pick up. They don't usually risk taking any of our people off, though, in case something goes wrong and there's a diplomatic incident." He looked at Frank, his face puzzled. "But they seem to want him very badly."

"Yes." Frank's voice sounded composed. "They do."

Ben asked, "Do you know where we're goin' tae, in America?"

Bert shook his head. "No idea. Somewhere along the East Coast, I suppose, to start with."

"What if there's patrol vessels?" Ben pressed.

"We'll have people watching the sea from the cliffs either side of Rottingdean. We haven't noticed any increased naval activity in the Channel—in any case, the Germans wouldn't tell the British authorities about this one. The waters off the coast are quite shallow, so the sub will have to come in on the surface and wait for you about a mile offshore. It'll be risky for them, and it means it's important you row out and reach them on time. Anyway, our people should be able to see any boats out at sea. If that happens, the mission gets called off and you come back here." He took a deep breath. "Everyone understand?"

"All clear," Ben said. The others nodded. Bert took the map and folded it.

"Right. We'll have another briefing later; my contact in town will have some more details this afternoon. Thank God it's getting too near Christmas for the shops to bother with reps, the last one's gone home now. All the same, I want you all to stay in the hotel. Keep to your cover stories. We do get casual visitors occasionally even at this time of year and we don't want anyone noticing anything unusual. All right? Now,

I've got to go and help Jane get lunch." He smiled awkwardly. "It's best to keep to normal routines so far as we can. Lunch will be ready in an hour."

Natalia asked him, "Have you done this many times before?"

"We've put people up for a few days. Some Jews, week before last. Nothing as big as this though."

Natalia looked at David, took a deep breath. She said. "I didn't sleep last night. I wouldn't mind getting some rest now. David, perhaps you could go to the lounge for a couple of hours. Then you can meet your wife when she returns."

"Yes," Ben said. "Good idea." He spoke lightly but gave David a determined nod. Frank too was looking at him, a concentrated stare.

"I'll show you where the lounge is," Bert said. "You can see the street from there." He smiled. "You can watch for her."

Bert took David downstairs. At the bottom he glanced back up, then said quietly, "That Muncaster, he was in a loony bin, wasn't he? Will he be able to go through with this? He won't go nuts or anything? This is very important for some reason, to us and the Yanks."

"No," David said. "I think he's all right."

"I hope so." Bert raised the flap in the desk and headed through to the back room.

David went into the lounge. There were several armchairs, well worn, the arms greasy, a writing desk, a television, and a bookcase with an assortment of pulp novels. He went and looked out of the window, trying to calm himself, to think.

He heard the door open quietly behind him. He wondered if it was Natalia, if she had changed her mind, but it was Frank who entered. He closed the door and stood uncertainly against it.

He said, "I wanted to thank you for what you offered to do, yesterday. If—if it had gone differently, with Churchill."

David smiled awkwardly. "I wouldn't have let them break their promise."

"You might have had a problem, reaching me with the pill."

"I'd have done it, or Ben would."

"We've made it to Brighton," Frank said.

"Yes. Yes, we have."

"I've always loved the sea, ever since I went to the seaside on holiday when I was small. You used to swim in competitions, didn't you?"

"When I was at school. I gave it up at Oxford, took up rowing, remember? But I still go to the pool sometimes — well, I did." He sighed. "I always used to like diving down into the deep water, into the silence."

"Yes. Silent, peaceful. Another world. Maybe I'll learn to swim in America." Frank looked down for a moment, then back up at David. "Your wife should be back soon."

"Yes."

Frank shifted nervously from foot to foot, then said, "Natalia — she's a good woman. A very good woman."

"I know."

"I won't say anything, about what I saw the night of the raid. But Sarah is your wife —"

"It's not your business, Frank," David said, quietly.

He sighed. "No. No, I suppose it isn't." He paused. "I keep thinking about Geoff."

"I know."

"He paid the biggest price."

They were silent a moment, then David said, "The secret, the nuclear secret your brother told you —"

"I shouldn't have told you it was that. I'm sorry —"

"No," David said. "I've been thinking — what is it? What is this thing that's cost us all so much? It's just that" — he groped for words — "I feel it would help me now, to deal with everything, with Geoff's death, if I knew. After all, after tonight either we'll be with people who know it all already, or —"

"Or we'll be dead. I know."

David said, "I'm sorry, I shouldn't have asked. I'm not thinking straight today —"

"Edgar was very drunk that night," Frank said, very quietly. "I didn't want him in my flat, I didn't want to see him again. But he had to show

539

he was better than me, he always did. I remember he said, 'Do you know what I do, what my work is?' Then he told me, leaning right in so I couldn't avoid hearing. He said it was the atom bomb. I never believed they'd actually built it, you see, despite that film of the mushroom cloud. I thought for once our government and the Germans were right to say it had been faked. Because the uranium, the explosive material inside the bomb, the amount of ore you'd need would be colossal, unimaginable."

David said, "The ore the Americans get from Canada."

Frank looked startled. "How do you know about that?"

"It was an issue that came up at the Dominions Office. It was one of the subjects I stole papers on, for the Resistance."

Frank said, "Everyone who worked in science in the academic world had been talking about the atom bomb since they found it was theoretically possible, back in 1938. But Edgar told me the Americans have been experimenting for years, for most of the forties, and they'd actually refined a new type of uranium, an isotope, as it's called, and a few suitcases full would be enough to destroy a city. He told me the basics and because I'm a scientist, too, I understood; it only took a few minutes. Just a few minutes." He shook his head. "You see, if anyone who wanted to build a bomb knew what Edgar had told me, it would save them years of research. Years and years. The Germans could do it. I remember Edgar boasted that just one of the bombs the Americans have got — just one — could destroy central London in an instant."

"Jesus Christ," David said.

"Afterwards, he realized what he'd done and told me to forget it." Frank laughed, and for a moment David heard something wild, deranged in his tone. Then Frank said, his voice low, "That was what made me angrier than anything else, that was what made me lose control and push him away. But I pushed him so hard he went out of the window. And then I suppose I went mad."

"Hearing that would be enough to drive anyone mad, I should think."

Frank smiled sadly. "But I was a little mad before. Not so much now."

"I think we're all a bit mad in this terrible world."

"Perhaps," Frank said. "You can't understand what a relief it is to tell someone everything. I know you won't say a word. I think perhaps I'll go and lie down for a bit." He laughed nervously. "We probably won't be getting much sleep tonight, eh?"

"No." David looked at him.

"I'll see you later." Frank hesitated, then added, "Good luck."

David stood looking at the closed door for a moment, then turned back and stared out of the window. And then he saw Sarah, walking toward him up the street. She wore strange clothes and her hair was short, a different color, red. Her strong-boned face looked exhausted, drained. *What have I done to her?* he thought.

CHAPTER FIFTY-TWO

The fog had gripped the capital for three days now; it felt as though it would never end. Gunther had bought a white facemask in a chemist's. It didn't make much difference though; the fog made his throat and nasal passages painfully sore and he had an almost constant headache. He didn't take painkillers, they made little difference and he thought they dulled the mind. On the evening after the news of Hitler's death Gunther groped his way home late in the evening. Goebbels, the new Führer, had made a speech extolling all that Hitler had achieved — the restoration of German greatness, her mastery of Europe, her destruction of Stalin and the settling of accounts with the Jews. The fulfillment of Germany's historic destiny. He had spoken of the magnificent funeral that would be held in Berlin in a week's time; in the meantime Hitler's body would lie in state at the Reich Chancellery, where already huge crowds were starting to queue outside. But Goebbels had said nothing of the continuing war in the East. It had been left to Himmler, in a broadcast of his own a couple of hours later, to speak in his slow, toneless voice of Germany's need to destroy each and every last stronghold of the Russian subhumans.

Every radio and television in the embassy had people crowding around it. And already SS and army people were grouping together, talking quietly. Gunther sensed that if there was to be a struggle for power, it would come quickly.

Gessler, after his initial shock at the Führer's passing, had quickly recovered control of himself, refocused. He took Gunther up to his office, sat behind his desk, confident and energetic again. He said, "If there's any change in policy toward the Russian war, or moves against the SS, we are ready to strike. In the name of Adolf Hitler and his legacy."

"This could turn into a civil war," Gunther said quietly.

"They'll lose. The whole boneheaded upper-class stiff-necked lot of them. We've got a million SS forces, all the Gauleiters and most Party members on our side."

"Has Speer said anything?"

"Not yet."

"What about Bormann?"

Gessler waved a hand dismissively. "Now Hitler's dead he counts for nothing. Bormann doesn't matter." He leaned forward. "But our mission does, more than ever now. I should have some more news very soon, about where Muncaster's people are being picked up." He smiled. "I have a phone call booked to Heydrich himself. I will let you know the result. I am Heydrich and Reichsführer Himmler's lieutenant in this embassy now, more than ever."

Later that afternoon Gunther had interrogated Drax again; he had told him about how they had abducted Muncaster from the hospital. He said, a note of satisfaction in his exhausted, rasping voice, that the cell system the Resistance used meant nobody in each operating group knew anyone outside their own cell. Drax told him about the woman who had accompanied them. She was from Eastern Europe and called Natalia; that was all he knew. Again, it was barely more than Gunther already had in his file; even her name was probably a pseudonym. He could see from the weary satisfaction in Drax's eyes that he knew these tidbits would not help Gunther. Throughout the conversation he had coughed, putting his hand to his bandaged chest, which obviously hurt him. The doctor told Gunther that Drax had internal bleeding and would probably not last long. They should get him across to Special Branch soon, so they could at least question him about the Civil Service spy ring before he died.

Gunther told him, "MI5 are unraveling the network in your Civil Service. As usually happens in a wide-ranging inquiry, they've found a couple of people who have caved in. One of the names they gave us was a very senior man in the Foreign Office. Sir Harold Jackson." Gunther saw from the flicker in Drax's eyes that he recognized the name. "When Special Branch went out to arrest him at his house in Hertfordshire, he and his wife stood on the doorstep and fired at them with shotguns, then turned them on themselves. We think he was the leader of your cell."

Drax did not respond. Gunther smiled thinly. "Well, that side of things doesn't really matter to us. We'll hand you over to Special Branch shortly and they can talk to you further about it."

"Why haven't you handed me over already? Why did you question me again? You haven't got Frank Muncaster and the others yet, have you?"

"We will, soon."

"You're a quiet man, aren't you?" Drax said, his blue eyes bright in his deathly pale face. "You like to sound so reasonable. But what you did earlier, to Carol, my parents, you're from hell!"

Gunther stood up and leaned over Drax, whose breath already stank of his approaching death. "Does it never occur to you, Mr. Drax, that if you had spent your life getting on with your work, living an ordinary life, and minding your own business like an ordinary, reasonable man, none of what happened to your parents or your work colleague would have occurred? It was your decision to betray your government, to join a bunch of murderous thugs. Yours." He stood up. "You don't see it, do you, people like you? That all you're doing is standing against the tide of historical destiny. Which, by the way, is about to drown you."

He got up and walked out of the cell.

In the evening, Gessler had more news for him. Radio traffic from Sussex suggested a lot of Resistance communications there. "I have serious resources working on the Isle of Wight. They've all been turned over to me. By Heydrich, earlier." His thin chest expanded with pride for a moment and Gunther realized that if it came to a conflict between the SS and the army Gessler would fight to the end for the SS vision, as he himself would. Gessler said, "We'll get them. We'll get them all." Then he frowned. "Speer's made a speech in Berlin now, by the way, about the need to slow down recruitment of foreign workers for the war industries. And he spoke about employing women — yes, women — to reduce our demands for labor from France and other countries under the 1940 Treaties."

"He's trying to stem the discontent there."

Gessler shook his head. "There's more to it than that. He's softening us up for a peace with what's left of Russia. Him and Goebbels. Goebbels understood the Jewish threat, but never the Russian one. Well, we'll see about that." He looked at Gunther. "I don't think there'll be any developments on our mission for a some hours. Then things will probably move very fast. Go home to your flat and wait for news. Try and get some sleep," he added. "You look exhausted."

After he had groped his way home through the fog Gunther sat and watched the BBC. The newscaster spoke in respectful, sepulchral tones of Germany's loss; although it was night and snowing in Berlin long queues had indeed already formed outside the Chancellery. The news was followed by a respectful biography of Goebbels. Gunther switched the television off and thought about the difference Hitler's death would make in Britain. The British would hope for a stable regime under Goebbels, and no doubt for a settlement with Russia. Looking for an easy life as usual, he reflected bitterly. The British didn't understand race, they understood national and Imperial pride and that was halfway to racial pride but they had never gone the whole way down that road. With time, if Mosley took the premiership, perhaps. He thought of civil war in Germany, the army against the SS. Even if the SS won, Germany would be terribly weakened. And after all they had achieved.

He had had a Christmas card from his son yesterday, a picture of a Christmas tree in Sevastopol, a letter inside. Michael said his mother and stepfather had been forced to have their Ukrainian servant arrested for stealing silver spoons that had once belonged to Gunther's mother. She was to be hanged. Michael had said it was a shame but his mother had told him these things are necessary.

Gunther thought of Hans, his twin. He remembered that first

Christmas when he came home from the Russian front. He remembered them speaking, with sad conviction, of how the Russian war was a historic climax of the fight between inferior and superior races. The racial hotchpotch of Eastern Europe which the Germans had stormed through was an abomination, a cesspit. Races couldn't mix, must never mix. Hans had spoken of how he had seen thousands of Russian prisoners, captured in the great 1941 pincer movements, penned into giant encampments on the steppe, surrounded by barbed wire and armed guards and left to die of hunger and thirst. He had seen the prisoners digging holes in the earth to escape the rain and cold. "You could smell the camps for miles," he had said. "They just reverted to an animal state."

And yet, Gunther thought, the Russians were still fighting. And with some help from the Americans soon, from what Adlai Stevenson said. All Germany's resources, all these years, had been plowed into that war. If they had had better generals, what things they could be doing with Russia's resources. If they finally won in Russia they could still build a new Europe, every country allied to Germany, but devoted to its own race and nationality. Perhaps then Germany could use its great rockets to go into space, perhaps put men on the moon. One day, he thought, we will.

He slept for several hours, an exhausted, dreamless sleep. He was wakened at seven a.m. by the telephone, Gessler's assistant summoning him back to the embassy. He put on his white facemask and stumbled his way back through the fog. It was only just getting light and few were about yet; there was complete silence all around. He felt suddenly disoriented, as though he were alone in a great, endless void. He fixed his attention on the faint yellow glow of a streetlight ahead and told himself angrily that he must stay calm, not give way to ridiculous fantasies. This was just bad weather, the lights and machinery of civilization were all around, just temporarily hidden by the smog. One day, given long enough, no doubt German scientists would be able to change the weather, too.

Gessler, in his office, was full of confidence once more, eyes shining bright behind his pince-nez. Gunther noticed that his desk was tidy again. He waved a piece of paper on which he had scribbled some numbers. "We've located the submarine, Hoth," he said triumphantly. "We know where it's going to surface! They're being picked up tonight."

Gunther felt his heart lift. "How? How did we get this?"

"Partly thanks to you!" Gessler beamed. Gunther was his golden boy now. "It was you that guessed a submarine would be picking them up, you that tricked Drax into revealing that it would be somewhere an hour from London. Every listening station on the Isle of Wight has been searching for transmissions concerning a submarine pickup since yesterday, and now they've just got it! Intelligence people, our SS people. There's been a sudden burst of radio traffic. Muncaster and four others are being picked up from a cove at a little place called Rottingdean, in Sussex, at one a.m. tomorrow morning. Unless the weather gets rough, which we're told it won't."

"They managed to decipher the message?"

"Yes. Thank God the British have given us all their Bletchley Park technology since 1940; smart that we made that a secret part of the Treaty. The Americans still have no idea we've broken their codes. Muncaster and his people will be sitting ducks." He beamed.

"And we're telling the British nothing."

"No. Nor anyone outside the SS." Gunther leaned back in his chair. He said slowly, "So now, with luck, Muncaster will fall right into our hands."

"Yes. There's no fog on the coast, the weather will be bright and clear. A boat will take them off the beach at half past midnight, some local man. He'll ferry them out to the submarine. It'll be on the surface. Risky for a foreign sub, shows how important this is to the Americans."

Gunther felt a moment of pure, joyous satisfaction. He ticked the names off on his fingers: "Muncaster, Hall, Fitzgerald and this Natalia woman. The fifth is probably Fitzgerald's wife." He looked at Gessler. "How will we do it, sir?"

Gessler folded his hands across his flat stomach. "It'll be our operation, an SS mission out of the embassy. I want to send you down there, with some good men, half a dozen if I can lay my hands on them. I thought of sending Kapp, who was at Drax's interrogation."

Gunther nodded agreement. "He looked a useful man."

"I've been studying the maps, and we're sending someone down to spy out the land now. The place, Rottingdean, is nothing more than a village in a fold between the cliffs, just a small cove. You hide there and then get Muncaster and his people when they arrive." He looked at Gunther seriously. "But we'll have to play it carefully, we don't want the British getting any wind of this." His tone became less enthusiastic. "They were going to start transporting the Jews on to the Isle of Wight today but the fog's put paid to that. From what I hear they're going to leave it till after the New Year now. I wonder if that could be politics. There's rumor that Rommel told Beaverbrook there wasn't any hurry with the transports."

Gunther frowned. "The army have never objected to Jew transports before."

"No, but they've often needed a push from above, from the Führer, heaven rest him. You know what they're like, saying it's a distraction from winning the Russian war, taking up resources." He stared at Gunther again. "Everything has changed with the Führer's death. If there is going to be—God forbid—a change in policy in Berlin, the Waffen SS are ready to fight the army. And if that turns into a long struggle, I'm told that what Muncaster knows could be very important."

Gessler looked at Gunther seriously. "Heydrich knows what it is and he's told me now. It's about nuclear weapons. The Bomb. The biggest prize of all, and it could be about to fall into SS hands. So that's why the mission is even more of a priority now. I was authorized to tell you." Gessler smiled. "See how trusted you are."

To be able to do this, Gunther thought, for Germany, for his son, the memory of his beloved brother. "Thank you," he said quietly.

Gessler coughed. "William Syme will be coming with you."

Gunther sat up. "Is that wise, sir? If Muncaster were to say something, if Syme even got a hint of what he knows—"

"We need an Englishman there. The local police will be told there's something going on and to steer clear, they'll be reassured that a Special Branch man will be coming down to deal with it. And Syme knows as much as anyone about Muncaster and his crew. And if he did get any knowledge he shouldn't—well, we spoke before about the option of disposing of him."

Gunther felt an unexpected stab of regret. Gessler noticed, and inclined his head. "I thought you didn't like him."

"I don't. But he's helped us a lot on this." Gunther took a deep breath. "But if it comes to that, it won't be a problem."

"I want you to keep Syme close, during tomorrow's operation and afterwards. I want you to bring him back here to the embassy. With Muncaster and his friends." His eyes stared into Gunther's. "Do you have any difficulties with that?"

Did they mean to kill Syme after all? Had they decided he knew too much already? It seemed hard, but this was war. "No, sir," he answered.

"When you bring Muncaster in I want you to assess him first, Hoth, weigh up the best ways to interrogate him before he gets sent to Berlin. Remember he's not—normal."

"Yes, sir." This was the sort of work Gunther was confident with; and it would be interesting to discover how Muncaster's mind worked, how and why it had malfunctioned. A thought occurred to him. "What about the Bennett woman?"

Gessler waved a hand. "Oh, we turned her over to the British yesterday afternoon. She'll probably get a secret trial, then five years in Holloway," he laughed. "Five years and a finger gone. Do they give women corporal punishment here? I can't remember. Anyway, they'll probably think what we've done to her is enough."

"What about Drax?"

"Special Branch have him. We let his parents go. I doubt he'll last long now."

CHAPTER FIFTY-THREE

Sarah had been for another walk. She had done so much walking these last few days that Brighton, so alien at first, was becoming familiar. This morning, in the winter sunshine, she had gone to Hove, through the grand early-Victorian squares along the seafront. The shops, their Christmas decorations looking oddly out of place at the seaside, were half empty. All the newspapers carried pictures of crowds in the Chancellery in Berlin, passing Hitler's open coffin. He lay, eyes closed, his face dead white, whiter than his mustache and hair.

Then, walking back to the hotel, she saw David looking out of the window at her. She felt a momentary surge of joy, then anxiety because he looked so thin, so much older, his cheeks sunken. Then anger filled her. She looked away from him as she mounted the steps to the hotel, slowly, though her heart was pounding.

Jane was sitting at the reception desk. She looked relieved to see Sarah. She leaned forward with a smile and whispered, "They've arrived. Your husband, he's in the lounge." Her expression changed to puzzlement when Sarah didn't smile in return, only said curtly, "I'll go in."

David was standing in the middle of the room. He looked at Sarah for a long moment, then walked quickly over and put his arms around her. "I'm so sorry," he said. "I couldn't let you know we were coming, we only knew ourselves yesterday—"

She didn't respond, just stood like a statue, so full of conflicting emotions she felt that if she relaxed she might fall in pieces to the floor. David stepped back a pace, still holding her by the shoulders. He said, "Are you—are you all right? What's happened to your hair?"

She shrugged off his hands and said, her voice so cold it surprised her, "Well, I was taken prisoner by the Germans, who told me you were a

Resistance spy, and interrogated at Senate House." She took a deep breath. "Then I was sent home, abducted by your people, one of whom killed a policeman in our house, by the way, then dumped here to wait for you and some strangers so we could all be sent to God knows where. They cut and dyed my hair because the Special Branch and the Germans will be looking for me." Her voice rose in rage. "And I'll never see my family again. Apart from that I'm fine. Who the hell are these other people, by the way?"

David said, "There's a man and woman from the Resistance, and Frank Muncaster, my old friend from university. You remember, I've told you about him. What's this about the Germans—you mean they arrested you? Our people didn't tell me, just that you were safe." He looked at her, his blue eyes wide with fear. "What happened there, did they—"

"Hurt me? No, they didn't, because I didn't know anything. I still bloody don't." She shrugged off his grip. Her voice rose again. "Answer my bloody question! What's going on? What are Frank Muncaster and these other people doing here?"

David raised his hands in a calming gesture. "Frank's a scientist. Something terrible happened to him; he ended up in a mental hospital in Birmingham. The Americans want him, very badly. Because of something he knows. So we—we lifted him. We brought him to London and now we've managed to get him down here. Sarah." He spoke with sudden eagerness. "Tonight we'll all be on a submarine to America."

She stared at him blankly. "A *submarine*?"

"Yes. I'm sorry all this happened, Sarah, but they chose me for this mission because I knew Frank, because he trusted me."

"And does he really? Trust you?" Her voice was sharp with sarcasm now.

"Yes. Yes, he does."

She stared at him. "And he's a mental case. Well, he'd have to be to trust you, wouldn't he?" She was still surprised by her own biting fury but she had had enough, more than any wife could take.

"Sarah—I came back for you—they found out I'd been a spy, but I tried to get home for you..."

Sarah took a long, deep breath. "This man in London, Jackson, he told me you'd been spying for the Resistance, giving them information from the Dominions Office. You involved that poor woman, Carol Bennett! Is that why you made friends with her? The day before I was arrested I went to Highgate and confronted her because I thought you were having an affair. The poor silly woman's in love with you, did you know that? I should think she's been arrested by now, like I was."

David looked on the verge of tears. He said, "Geoff's dead."

She started, shocked. "Dead? How?"

"We were hiding in a house up in London. Geoff was part of our team; he came with us to get Frank from the hospital. The house was raided, the couple sheltering us were killed and Geoff was too."

"Oh, Jesus Christ." Sarah collapsed into one of the armchairs.

David knelt beside her. "It's so important we get Frank to America. It's a big thing, Sarah, really big. He's got information—I can't tell you what—but it could help the Germans. The Gestapo are after it, it'll help the SS if there's a power struggle now Hitler's dead."

"How long were you and Geoff doing this? Spying?"

"Geoff joined the Resistance before me. He recruited me two years ago."

"After Charlie died."

"Not long after, yes..."

Her tone changed, sadness replacing the anger. "And you kept it all from me. I knew there was something, you'd been moving away from me ever since Charlie died. So what was I, just cover, the little wife at home?"

He shook his head vigorously. "No, no. You mustn't think that. When I started they said it was better you knew nothing, in case things ever went wrong and you were questioned." He looked at her, pleadingly. "And they were right, weren't they? You didn't know anything and that protected you."

She said, with a quiet, angry passion, "Didn't it ever occur to you that if I knew I might want to help you?"

"I didn't think you'd agree with what I was doing. You were always criticizing the Resistance for violence. Because people get killed in the struggle."

"Well, maybe you could have changed my mind, if you'd ever bothered to try. I've changed it on my own, anyway. I know now you've got to fight." Her eyes were full of sorrow. "Even though I know the violence will corrupt you all, because it always does."

"It's been hard—"

Her voice rose angrily again. "You decided to keep me out of it, as you've kept me out of everything since Charlie died."

He said, "I never realized—what it must have been like for you, in the house, alone. I'm sorry—"

"Don't pretend it was for my sake you didn't tell me, don't pretend it wasn't the easier thing for you to do. I've been blind for years," she added, bleakly. "Because I loved you so much." She stared into his miserable face. Her voice rose again. "Was that why you started working for them, because Charlie was dead and I wasn't enough? Because you *needed something else?*"

He shouted back, "No! It was because the persecutions had started and I'm Jewish!"

"What do you mean?" She stared at him blankly. "What on earth are you talking about?"

He came closer, gripping Sarah's wrists. "My mother's family came to Ireland from Eastern Europe. Long before she met Dad. I didn't know until she died, Mum and Dad kept it secret so I wouldn't experience prejudice. Dad persuaded me to go on keeping it secret." He looked at her levelly. "He was right. If they'd known who she was then later I'd've been kicked out of the Civil Service, I'd be in one of those detention camps now. You know the rules; half a Jew is still a Jew."

She pushed his hands away, stood up, and began walking up and down the room. She felt stunned. "You're a Jew. You've known that since before you met me and you kept it secret." She broke off. "You're not circumcised—"

"Mum wasn't a believer. Nor was Dad. I'm not a Jew and I'm not a

Catholic—according to any reasonable interpretation anyway. But where's reason these days?"

She stopped, looked at him. "All this time I've been married to a Jew. And you didn't tell me."

He asked, "Would it have mattered to you?"

She looked taken aback. "I'd have been surprised. Of course I would. But—you know me, you know I've always hated anti-Semitism."

"But even before 1940, we were all brought up with prejudice," he said quietly. "It's always there, anti-Semitism sometimes comes out when you least expect it—"

She shouted, "Not with *me!* Have you forgotten how my mum and dad brought me up?"

"But Irene—"

"Irene married a bigoted fool! You know what I think of him! But you didn't trust me. All these secrets. You never trusted me with any of it. Never."

He stood up, stepped toward her again. "I'm sorry. I was just so used to nobody knowing. Sometimes for a while I'd forget it myself until the persecutions started. And everything else, it was all to protect you."

"The support I could have given you, the help, the *love,*" she said despairingly. "None of that mattered, did it?"

"I thought it was for the best."

Sarah thought it a miserable answer, nothing of love in it. She stood for a long moment facing her husband. Part of her wanted to reach out and stroke his face, soothe his desperate unhappiness; another part wanted to hit him. She closed her eyes for a moment. Then she turned practical; it was the only way she could cope at the moment and God knew there were enough questions about practicalities, too. She took a deep breath. "What's going to happen tonight?"

David took a deep breath. "A boat will be waiting to pick us all up a few miles from here at half past midnight. It'll take us to an American submarine in the Channel. You, me, Frank, and the two others I'm with. They're all upstairs now."

"Frank was in a lunatic asylum. Is he fit to go? Does he want to go?"

"Yes. He's better than he was."

"Who are these other two?"

"Ben, he was a nurse at his hospital, and—and Natalia, she's the one in charge of our group." His voice faltered for a moment, and he took a deep breath. "Part of our cover is that Natalia and I are supposed to be husband and wife, and Ben and Frank my cousins; we're all supposed to have come down here for an old aunt's funeral. You and I are not supposed to know each other, by the way, we have to pretend."

"Pretend?" Sarah laughed bitterly.

He said, quietly, "I'm so sorry, Sarah. For everything. I..."

Just then there was a knock at the door. Jane came in. She looked scared. She said, "I'm sorry, but please, please keep your voices down. You can be heard upstairs, and in the hotel next door, these walls are thin." She looked at David, her eyes wide with fear. "What you shouted out earlier—"

"About being Jewish?" David nodded fiercely. "Yes, that's dangerous, isn't it?"

"It's all right," Sarah said. "I'll go up to my room." She looked at David. "Don't come after me."

Jane followed her out, and said, "Please don't think I'm interfering, only—you've got to be ready to go off tonight. You can't be arguing and fighting, not tonight."

Sarah realized just how frightened Jane was. Her life was at stake here, too.

In her room Sarah closed the door, sat on the bed and put her head in her hands. It had been as bad as she had feared, worse. She recognized that inside she had been hoping against hope for some explanation from David that would somehow make everything all right again. But he had lived in a world of deception and lies, not just since becoming a spy, but long before she'd met him. She had a feeling that even now he hadn't told her everything. How could she ever believe him again?

CHAPTER FIFTY-FOUR

Frank and Ben had been playing chess again. Ben, soundly beaten, seemed determined to win at least one game but Frank had got bored and said he needed a break. He went and looked out of the window. He saw a tall woman walk up the empty street and turn toward the hotel. Then she stopped in her tracks, staring in at the ground-floor window. She seemed to hunch her body a little before going on to climb the front steps, passing out of view. Frank turned and said quietly, "Someone's arrived. I think it might be David's wife."

Ben was sitting on his bed, the chessboard on a little table. He joined Frank by the window.

"She's gone now," Frank said.

"What was she like?"

"Quite tall. Red-haired. Funny, not that pretty. I'd have expected David to marry someone pretty."

"Love disnae always go like that," Ben said. "Romance is no' like in the films. Ye dinnae choose who ye love." There was a sadness in his voice. Frank thought, all I know of love is from the films. He sat on his bed again. Ben had given him another pill on the way to the hotel, but the odd peacefulness he had felt since his encounter with Churchill was more than that. It had been astonishing; the old man had seemed somehow to understand him. Frank was certain now that the Resistance people wouldn't try to take his secret. But he knew the safety of their little group here was as precarious as it had been in London. And tonight, when they tried to get on the submarine, that would be the most dangerous time of all.

Ben was looking at him curiously. "You all right there?"

"Yes."

"You've been awfy quiet."

"What will happen to me if we get to America?"

Ben lit a cigarette. "They'll ask all about what your brother told you, that's for sure. But you won't be telling them anything they don't know."

"I wonder what they'll do with me then."

"Maybe they'll give you a job working on the atom bomb. They love their superweapons, the Americans. Almost as bad as the Germans."

Frank shook his head. "I couldn't do that."

"I know. I wis just joking."

Frank pursed his lips. "I don't want to see my brother again," he said. "I hope they don't decide to—well—put me out of the way, because of what I know. Or put me back in a hospital."

"No, pal. You'll be a hero, coming over to them, escaping the Germans. Maybe they'll set you up in some nice, sunny, quiet wee town in California." But Frank knew Ben had no more idea than he did of what the Americans would do with him.

"I wanted to die, before, but now—I think I'd like to live, if I can. But not back in a hospital."

"You won't. I know it was hard there. There won't be such harsh conditions under communism. Hell, there'll be nae reason for people to get mental."

Frank didn't reply. He had grown to like and admire Ben now he knew the risks he had run to save him, but he wished he didn't get so misty-eyed about communism. "Now that bastard Hitler's dead," Ben added, "things'll change. You wait..."

Then, through the floor, they heard shouting, a woman's voice. Next David shouting back. "*No! It was because the persecutions had started and I'm Jewish!*"

Frank and Ben looked at each other in astonishment. Ben whistled. "That's a turn-up for the book. David? Jewish?" He looked at Frank. "Did you know?"

"I'd no idea."

Ben frowned. "They'd better stop yellin' at each other like that, sound travels."

But there was no more shouting, just murmuring voices. Then they heard a door shut downstairs, and footsteps mounting the stairs rapidly.

"They've got to get themselves sorted out," Ben said anxiously. "We need to be on the ball tonight."

Frank didn't answer. An odd feeling of betrayal had stolen over him, just as it had when he had overheard David and Natalia making love in the O'Shea house. David was Jewish? All the time he knew David, he'd had this secret, too. He told himself it was stupid; David owed him no confidences. "Everyone thought David's parents were Irish," he said.

"They must have had Jewish blood and kept it quiet." Ben sighed. "People fake their ancestry all over the place these days. There's parts of Scotland now, SNP strongholds, where if you've English blood you don't talk about it." He made an angry, scornful sound. "Nationalism, what a world we've let it make."

"It's strange. It feels—a shock. I suppose it doesn't matter if someone is Jewish, does it?"

"No. A lot of the best Communists have been Jews. Karl Marx himself, for example."

"Capitalists too," Frank said with a quiet smile. "Like the Rothschilds. And scientists, like Einstein. You know, the Nazi idea that there's a conspiracy between the Bolsheviks and Jewish capitalists always seemed so crazy. Each hates the other's system."

"That's because Fascist ideology never makes sense, not if you ever really stop to think about it."

"Nothing does make sense, much," Frank observed sadly.

Ben looked at him seriously. "You know David and Natalia were—well, you saw, when we all ran from the O'Sheas', didn't you?"

"Yes," Frank answered heavily, "I saw. Do you think David told his wife? Downstairs, just now?"

"I'm not sure. I don't think so, or they'd have been shouting about that, too. But we can't have the two of them going off like fireworks all over the place. I may have to have a word." He looked at Frank. "You're a bit down in the mouth about it. Did ye have a bit of a fancy for Natalia yerself?"

Frank smiled sadly. "No. She's very attractive, but she's"—he laughed awkwardly—"real. I've only ever thought about film stars, unattainable people, in that way." He had reddened with embarrassment. "What about you? Do you like her?"

"She's a good leader. Clearheaded, fast. But no, she's"—Ben smiled wryly—"no' my type."

"Haven't you got someone?" Frank asked. Ben had always seemed so focused on action, on what needed to be done next, that Frank hadn't thought of him having a private life.

Ben folded his arms on his chest. "No. Never met the right girl. Never met the right anybody." He gave a sad little laugh.

"What would they be like if you did?"

"Someone ma own class. But—nicer, gentler."

Frank frowned. There was something odd in the way Ben had put it, but he couldn't quite grasp what. He said, "I can't imagine what being married's like. My father died before I was born. In the trenches."

"My parents are still alive, somewhere. Sod the pair o' them."

"You didn't get on?"

"Let's just say I wisnae what they expected."

"Married couples. I've only really met colleagues' wives at the university. Christmas parties, things like that. Some seem happy, others you can see are miserable. You can't blame David's wife for being upset. If she never knew anything. That he was a spy, or Jewish—"

"Not our business, Frankie boy. All that matters is keepin' everyone focused. You too."

"Can you not give me a pill tonight? I want to be alert. In the fog, I got—confused."

"You sure? You won't get twitchy?"

"Not if we just leave it for a few hours." Frank smiled weakly. "I'll have one on the sub."

Ben looked at Frank seriously. "Okay. But whatever happens, you stay with us this time."

"I will."

*   *   *

Half an hour later Frank heard footsteps in the corridor outside again, then Bert's voice and a woman's. There was a knock at the door and Bert and Jane came in, followed by the woman Frank had seen from the window, David's wife. She looked tired, angry too. Bert was carrying his big map, rolled under his arm. He said, "We need to meet and talk about tonight. Get all the arrangements clear."

"I'll get the others." Jane went out. Ben stepped forward, extending a hand. "You must be Sarah, David's wife," he said cheerfully, for once playing down the Glasgow accent. "I'm Ben."

Sarah shook his hand. Her expression was wary, her pleasant voice cool as she asked, "How long have you been with my husband?"

"First met him a fortnight ago, believe it or not. Feels like years though, doesn't it, Frank?"

Sarah looked at Frank intently. He imagined her thinking: *you're* the one who brought all this about. Then she forced a smile and reached out her hand. "How do you do. My husband used to talk about you, the letters you wrote." She shook his hand gently; she had noticed its deformity.

Frank said, "David's been a good friend. For a long time."

"Please, sit down, sorry it's all untidy," Ben said, all cheery politeness. "Two fellas sharing a room, you know what that can get like." He took a stray sock off the bed. Sarah sat down. The door opened and Bert and Jane came back in, followed by David and then Natalia. David looked at his wife. She stared back angrily. She turned to Natalia, smiling uncertainly. "I'm Sarah Fitzgerald," she said.

"Natalia." The two women shook hands, Natalia looking at Sarah coolly. Frank realized Sarah didn't know about her and David; he hadn't told her. Bert spread the map on the other bed.

"Right," he said. "Tonight at ten thirty, Natalia will drive you all over to Rottingdean. There's the coast road, here on the map, but we think it's safer for you to drive north into the country and then come down into Rottingdean from there." He pointed at the map. "All clear so far?" Everyone nodded. Bert continued. "There's a path that leads under the cliffs from Brighton, too, but that's exposed, no cover at all if anything goes wrong. When you get to Rottingdean you go to a house in the village where our man will meet you. You'll all change into dark clothes, so you won't be seen so easily, and then walk down to the cove. They'll be thick clothes, it'll be very cold out at sea."

"It looks like a small place," Sarah said, looking at the map.

"It is. There's a lot of posh houses up around the green, mostly retired people. Rottingdean's always had a lot of writers and artists, people like that. Then along the High Street there's shops, smaller houses. That's where our man lives, he's a retired fisherman. It's a quiet place, nobody will be about on a cold December night. Then you make your way down to the cove." He looked around the little group. "From that point on, you're all at risk, there'd be no cover story to explain a group of people going down to the beach at night in December."

Sarah shook her head slightly. David asked, "What is it?"

"Nothing. I was just thinking how many identities I've had the last few days, how many sets of clothes." She looked at Bert. "You people have a lot of resources, don't you? More than I'd ever thought."

"None of it has been easy," Natalia said, coldly. "I can promise you that. Everyone involved has exposed themselves to danger." She hesitated, then added, "People have died."

Sarah met her gaze, "I know. I've seen two people killed in front of me in less than a fortnight."

Natalia nodded at Frank. "Getting this man away is very important indeed. That's what matters tonight, the rest of us are just passengers. It's as well to be clear about that."

Sarah stared back. "I understand very well. I know what danger is, I've learned that very fast. I'm not a fool, so please don't take me for one. Just tell me what to do."

Natalia inclined her head, a new respect in her look.

Bert said quietly, "Natalia is the leader, you all do as she says. So far as we know, we're safe. We've had people watching the cliffs, the village, the coastal path, and out to sea. Nothing unusual has been happening. When it gets dark we'll still have a few people on surveillance, from the cliffs. In case any unexpected boats appear."

Ben said, "It's important for everyone tae move quickly and quietly." He looked at Frank.

"Yes," Bert agreed. "The place will be asleep, you mustn't wake anyone up. It's going to be a quiet, clear night, there'll be a half-moon. The sea's like a millpond. Our man who'll take you to the cove has got a rowing boat and he'll start to row you out to the sub at twelve thirty. We've got precise coordinates, a spot about a mile out. Because the water's shallow inshore the sub will be on the surface. It'll take you on board. After that they'll go out to deeper water, dive, and take you to an American ship out in the Atlantic."

"And then it'll all be over," Frank said. He shook his head in wonder and disbelief.

Bert looked at him, then Sarah. Frank thought, We two are the weak ones, the others know how to fight.

Bert continued, "We have to think about what happens if things go wrong. Natalia, you, Ben, and David will have guns."

"They should only be used as a last resort," Natalia said. "Because of the noise."

Ben nodded agreement. "Aye. If we're attacked." He looked at Bert. "But whit if someone comes on us by accident, some wandering drunk or somethin'?"

"You'd have to silence them," Bert said. "Usual rules."

Sarah spoke up. "You mean kill them? Someone innocent?"

Natalia said, "Of course not. Who do you think we are? We knock them out and tie them up."

"I'm used tae doin' that," Ben said cheerfully.

Bert looked at Sarah. He said, "There's one last thing, Mrs. Fitzgerald. It's essential that if the worst comes to the worst none of you are taken alive. That's why everyone's been given cyanide pills."

She took a deep breath and looked at David.

He said, "I'm sorry, but if they caught us—"

"Dear God," she said quietly.

"Geoff had one," David told her. "But he didn't get the chance to use it. The fog caused a lot of confusion. That won't be a problem tonight."

Sarah looked around the group. "Do all of you have them?"

"I don't," Frank said.

"You'd be taken care of," Ben promised. "You know that."

"But you couldn't in the fog in London. No one could see me. Like David said, it was all confused."

Sarah looked at her husband again. Bert took a deep breath, reached into his pocket and pulled out a tiny circular pill.

"Let me," David said. He took it from Bert and held it out to Sarah. "We got this for you," he said. "It's only to be used if they're about to capture us." Suddenly his eyes filled with tears and Sarah had to make an effort not to cry too. She took a deep breath, then held out her hand. David laid the pill in her palm. He said, his voice choked, "You put it in your mouth and bite down. There's a tiny glass phial inside. It's instantaneous, you wouldn't feel a thing."

"So the two of us would go together in the end," she said, quiet sadness in her voice.

"Yes, we would."

This is what it's like for someone who's never thought of ending their life, Frank thought. It's hard. He glanced at Natalia. She was looking at David, her face expressionless.

They spent an hour going over the details until they had everything committed to memory. Eventually Bert picked up his map. Jane said, "We'll have something to eat in a little while. Nobody should go out for the rest of the day, please." Bert rolled up the map, and he and Jane went out.

The five of them were left sitting there. Sarah got up and moved to the door. She walked wearily, like someone wading through water. David followed, put his hand on her arm, but she said quietly, "I still need some time on my own. We'll talk later." She went to her room. After a moment David went out too. Frank heard his footsteps going downstairs.

"Will they be all right?" Ben asked.

"They'll have to be," Natalia said bluntly.

Frank looked at her. He thought how all his life he had been a watcher, an observer. Sometimes he had surprised himself how much he guessed about the lives, the thoughts of other people. And he had got to know these people well, this last week. He hadn't met Sarah until just now but he could see—surely anyone could—how much she loved David, how desperately she had been hurt. But he saw that Natalia loved David, too. Then, looking at her, another thought came to Frank, a quite different idea.

He stepped forward, his legs surprisingly stiff. "Natalia," he said. "Can I talk to you about something? On your own?"

Ben said quietly, "It's not our business."

"Please," Frank said.

Natalia looked surprised. Then she smiled and shrugged. "All right. Why not? We can go next door to my room."

She walked to the door, Frank following, Ben watching them go.

CHAPTER FIFTY-FIVE

Gunther walked steadily along the path that led from Brighton to Rottingdean, under the high chalk cliffs. His shoes, rubber-soled like those of Syme walking behind him and the SS man Kollwitz ahead, barely made a sound on the concrete path. They walked in silence as close as possible to the cliff itself, in case any Resistance people were watching the sea from the cliffs above. All wore heavy dark coats, thick black roll-neck sweaters, black gloves, and balaclavas. They had blackened their faces, too, with charcoal. Kollwitz, one of the four SS men accompanying the operation and a veteran of covert actions in Russia, said it could make all the difference in an ambush. Three other SS men were approaching Rottingdean from the other side, where the under-cliff walk continued on eastwards: Kapp, who had assisted with Drax's interrogation, Hauser from the basement, and Borsig, another veteran of Special Operations in Russia and like Kollwitz attached to SS Intelligence at the embassy. The two groups would meet at Rottingdean Gap, where there was a small pebbled beach connected to the village above by a path.

It was bitterly cold, a light but knifelike breeze blowing off the Channel. The tide was coming in, quietly and gently, for the sea was dead calm. In the moonlight Gunther could see the little white wavelets where the surf broke, not far below the path. A half-moon was high in a starry black sky, casting a long silver reflection on the sea. He remembered Michael talking about swimming in the Black Sea, how beautiful the shore looked with the mountains in the distance. He stumbled for a moment, catching his foot on a lump of chalk that had fallen from the cliff face. Syme reached out and grasped his arm in a firm grip, helping him right himself.

Gunther nodded his thanks. He swore inwardly; he should have been more careful. He was conscious of how much less fit he was than the other two men, how flabby.

They had spent the morning poring over maps in Gessler's office, assisted by a Special Branch man from Sussex, another of Syme's valuable connections. The man knew nothing except that the Branch were working with the Germans to intercept someone the Germans wanted and who would be in Rottingdean that night. The man had mentioned that Special Branch had their own concerns just now; since news of Hitler's death there had been several near riots in the Jewish detention camps, and police everywhere had been put on standby in case help was needed. Along with Gunther, Syme, and the Special Branch man, the four SS men Gessler had chosen for the operation had also been present. Two of them Gunther had not met before; Kollwitz was a young man in his late twenties, attached to SS Intelligence at the embassy. He had a youthful, strangely unmarked face, blond hair, and blank light-blue eyes. His colleague Borsig was also attached to Intelligence. He had a square, hard face with dark hair and heavy brows above eyes as sharp as a cat's. Kapp, the eager youngster who had been at Drax's interrogation, quick and lithe, had served in the East; Hauser, the officer in charge of the basement, was older and heavier, but still a strong, solid presence. All four were utterly loyal to the SS. Like Gunther, they wore suits for the meeting so as not to spook Syme's Special Branch contact, though they looked uncomfortable in them. Gessler alone wore his usual black uniform and cap. As embassy staff, the Germans all spoke good English.

Syme's colleague told them Rottingdean was small, little more than a village. Because it lay in a gap between the cliffs it had been an ancient haunt of smugglers. The Resistance were not strong there, the local people kept themselves to themselves. There was some tourist trade in the summer but the place would be very quiet on a cold December night. The local police had been told a Special Branch operation would be taking place on the beach and that they were to stay well away, even if shots were fired. However, by taking the cliff path Gunther's party need not actually go into Rottingdean at all. They could walk along from Brighton while the other three approached from the opposite direction.

Gessler thanked the Special Branch man and he left. The others gathered around the map. The Resistance people would probably have watchers on the cliffs along the coast, looking out over the Channel to spot any unusual activity on the sea, but they would have no reason to believe the Germans would be waiting for the fugitives on the beach. Gessler told them that according to the radio intercepts, a fisherman would meet Muncaster's party in the village and take them down to the beach, where a boat lay ready; they would then row out to sea to meet the submarine. They would have to walk from the village down a broad asphalt path to a short promenade, then down to the little pebbly beach. Gunther and Syme and the SS men would have to find cover and hide themselves on the promenade or the beach so that when Muncaster's party came down at half past midnight they could rush them, take them by surprise.

Kollwitz asked, "There will only be one boatman with them? There won't be other Resistance people there, or waiting on the beach?"

"No. That's clear from the radio intercepts," Gessler replied with satisfaction. "What few local people the Resistance have will be watching along the cliff tops. But go carefully, just in case they change their plans."

Kollwitz asked, "Is six of us enough?"

"You're the only experienced men we can spare."

"We are expecting six of them for the submarine, yes?" Borsig asked. "Two Resistance agents and three civilians—a man, a woman, and this lunatic? And the fisherman makes six." He shrugged. "Easy."

"Yes." Gessler's voice took on a note of bullying humor. "One for each of you. I think you should be able to handle them."

"The two Resistance people are handy," Syme cautioned. "I ran across them in the raid in London. A man and woman. But the others, yes, they're civilians."

"The civil servant, Fitzgerald, when I met him at the Dominions Office he looked fit," Gunther said. And he was in the 1940 war.

"They'll have guns," Kollwitz observed. "The Resistance pair certainly, perhaps Fitzgerald and the fisherman too."

Gunther nodded agreement. "Not Fitzgerald's wife, though, I think, she's one of these English pacifists." Kapp gave a grunt of contemptuous dismissal. "And not Muncaster."

"Lunatics can be strong," Borsig observed.

"Not this one," Syme said. "I've met him. He's a little pipsqueak, afraid of his own shadow."

Gunther looked around the SS men. "But remember, he is the one that matters. Berlin wants him alive. It might be useful to have the Resistance people as well, but the all others are of secondary importance."

Gessler stirred in his chair. "They may have suicide pills, so taking them by surprise is crucial. Securing their arms at once is very important. Get there early and choose a good spot. There'll be some moonlight, the weather forecast says it'll be a clear night."

Gunther looked at Syme. "You said it's a pebble beach?"

"Yes."

"Then it would be good to hide there if we can; we're bound to hear them coming."

Kollwitz nodded. "That is sound thinking. We've no idea where they are at this moment?"

Gunther shook his head. "It could be anywhere within easy reach of the Sussex coast. Rottingdean beach at half past midnight is the only place we're sure they'll be."

Hauser smiled, punching a meaty fist into his other hand. "It'll be like the old days in Russia. Stealing up on their Resistance groups."

Kollwitz looked around the others. "How are you on firearms?"

"I practice regularly on the range," Hauser replied complacently. "So does Comrade Kapp; I've seen him."

Gunther said, "I practice in Berlin, too." Though not, he thought, as regularly as he should.

Syme said, smugly, "I've got prizes from my firearms courses."

Gunther summed up: "So, we jump them, make sure they're disarmed, and remove any suicide pills they have. If you fire on them, shoot to wound if possible. And we all use English, so everyone understands." He inclined his head at Syme.

"Sturmbannführer Hoth is in charge," Gessler said. "He knows these people better than anyone, you obey all his orders. And remember, we want Muncaster alive." He tapped a finger on his desk for emphasis. "That's more important than anything. That order comes directly from Deputy Reichsführer Heydrich." He leaned across the desk and reached out a hand to Gunther. Gunther shook it. Gessler's eyes were full of triumphant emotion. "Good luck, Hoth," he said. "And thank you."

They traveled to Brighton after dark. During the day a light wind had got up in London and the fog, at last, was dispersing. As they drove out of the city in two cars, Gunther saw the streets illuminated properly for the first time in days. All the buildings shone with damp, windows and the tops of parked cars smeared with gray dirty grease. In many places women were out with buckets and mops, cleaning windows and steps. Even the icy puddles in the gutters looked dirty. By contrast the shop windows were full of Christmas decorations, fake white snow around their edges. Already a newspaper stand carried the legend: *Great London Smog Ends.*

With the fog gone they made good time. Soon they were out in the Surrey countryside. The car containing the three SS men who were to approach Rottingdean from the east took a turning toward Newhaven. There were two more cars waiting in a lane just outside Rottingdean, ready to pick them and the prisoners up later.

Gunther sat next to Syme in the back. Kollwitz drove. His blond hair was cropped and shaved a third of the way up his neck in the SS style; Gunther saw he had a spot coming. Beside him, Syme was cheerful. "They're talking about that new job for me," he told Gunther. "We're going to have a new, nationwide police intelligence service. MI5 are going to be integrated with us. About time. They'll scream like fuckin' stuck pigs but we uncovered the bleeding Civil Service spy ring for them." The Cockney accent was strong again, perhaps a sign of underlying stress in Syme, as the moment of truth approached. Gunther himself felt quite cool. Syme went on, "Looks like I could get promotion to superintendent, as well as a posting up North." He smiled, tapping the fingers of one hand up and down on his knee.

"Well done." But remembering the discussion with Gessler earlier, Gunther found it difficult to meet Syme's eye.

"You'll have to come back and visit me," Syme continued. "Tell you what, come over see the Coronation in the summer. How's that?"

"Yes," Gunther said. "Perhaps." Syme, for all his sharpness in other ways, had no idea that Gunther had always disliked him. Or perhaps he just didn't care.

They stepped from the cliff path out onto the promenade; it was small, less than a hundred yards long and perhaps two hundred and fifty wide. There were no lights, only the half-moon to guide them, but their eyes were accustomed to the dark now and they saw the promenade was deserted. On the landward side there was a high concrete wall, and behind that a little grassed area sloped gently up to a large building they had been told was the White Horse Hotel. There were no lights on there. Gunther saw there was a gap in the concrete wall where a steep paved path, perhaps a hundred yards long, led up to the coast road. On the other side of the path was another concrete wall and beyond that the cliffs began again, startlingly white.

Steps led down from the promenade to the beach, a strand of pebbles. Nearby a high stone groyne sloped gently down into the sea. In the dark lee of the groyne, a tiny light flashed three times. A pencil torch. It was the prearranged signal; the other three SS men were already there. Gunther sighed with relief.

Gunther, Syme, and Kollwitz walked down the steps onto the beach. The big round pebbles scrunched beneath their feet; there was no way of avoiding the noise. Borsig and Hauser and Kapp stepped away from the groyne to meet them. They were also dressed in heavy black camouflage. Kapp smiled, a brief flash of white teeth—he was enjoying this. "*Heil Hitler*," he said quietly. In Berlin, Goebbels had just commanded that

Hitler's name was to continue to be used as the National Greeting for all time. Nonetheless, Kollwitz added quietly, "And *Heil Himmler.*"

"All quiet?" Gunther asked.

"Yes. We walked along the path from Saltdean. When we got out of the car we saw a woman with a dog walking along the cliffs, looking out to sea. Probably Resistance. But she wouldn't see or hear us on that Undercliff path. We've been here half an hour; no sign of anyone."

"Too cold for lovers," Kapp murmured.

Gunther nodded. Nobody in their senses would come here on this bitter night. He shivered in the breeze from the sea, a little stronger here. The tide was well in, the thin line of gently hissing white surf surprisingly close. He glanced at his watch. Five past eleven.

Syme was also looking out to sea. He said, "Any chance the sub could see us from out there?"

"They're a mile out," Kollwitz answered. "I'd guess all they can see of this through a periscope is the dark gap in the cliffs. Besides, if they did see us take Muncaster's people they'd cut and run, they wouldn't want to cause a major diplomatic incident."

Borsig said, "We've found something. Come and look at this."

He led them down the side of the groyne. Near the surf they saw a large, humped shape, covered with a heavy gray tarpaulin. Borsig and Kapp lifted the cover; underneath was an upturned rowing boat. "That's big enough for six. There are oars underneath. This is the boat they're going to use," Kapp said, triumphantly.

"Yes." Gunther looked back up the beach, to the path where the British party would descend onto the noisy pebbles.

Borsig said, "If three of us get under the boat, and the other three crouch down behind it under the tarpaulin, between the boat and the groyne, when they arrive they'll walk right into our hands."

Gunther nodded, then smiled. "Yes, it's ideal. Who goes under?"

"You and Syme and Kapp," Borsig suggested. "Kapp and Syme are the thinnest, and if you dig away some of the pebbles you'll get a view of them coming down, then you can give the command signal. We'll all hear them coming, once they're on the beach, so when they arrive at the boat I suggest you knock on the side and we push it over onto them, you from below and us from behind. They'll be completely startled. Then we all jump out and grab them, one each, before they can move."

"Yes. Yes, that sounds right." Gunther looked at Borsig and Kollwitz. "You've planned ambushes before."

"Yes. In the East."

"I have too, in the Gestapo. But only in cities, usually against civilians. I'll be guided by you."

"Thank you. Now, let's lift the boat up."

"It'll be a bloody cold wait," Syme observed.

Kollwitz answered. "This is nothing. Try waiting in ambush in the Russian winter."

They took off the tarpaulin and lifted the boat. It was big and heavy but Borsig and Kollwitz lifted it easily enough. Kapp and Syme slipped under, moving the oars that had been placed under the boat to one side. Gunther felt his muscles protest as he lay down and scrabbled underneath.

"I'll give the side of the boat a kick as a signal," he said. "It's heavy. You three push hard."

Gunther dug away at the pebbles until he managed to make a small space between them and the bottom of the boat, enough for him to see through if he lay flat on his stomach. He looked up toward the path to the beach, a dark gap in the promenade. Under the boat it was pitch dark and there was a strong smell of seaweed. Already Gunther's feet felt like ice. Next to him Syme shifted his bony form, an elbow digging into his ribs. Always some part of Syme had to be twitching or moving. Gunther said, "Keep still, for God's sake. They'll hear the pebbles if you move about."

"All right. Sorry."

Gunther took off his watch to lay it next to his face. The luminous dial read 11.45. Three quarters of an hour to go until Muncaster's party arrived.

CHAPTER FIFTY-SIX

That afternoon, following the meeting with Bert, David went downstairs, back to the empty lounge. Jane, sitting at her desk in the hall, gave him an anxious smile as he passed.

He sat in an armchair and looked out of the window. What was he going to do? Sense and decency and old, bone-deep affection told him he belonged with Sarah. But would she have him now? And it was Natalia who offered him excitement, the chance of something new. More than that, she was someone who understood his past, his true origins.

After a while he went back upstairs, to the room he shared with her. He turned the handle, but the door was locked. He had a feeling Natalia was in there, but there was no sound, no answer to his knock. Then Sarah's door opened and she stood there, looking at him.

"Sarah."

She turned and went back into her room, but left the door open. He followed her in. She sat on the bed, looking at him bleakly. "Please don't say you're sorry again. I don't think I could stand that."

He closed the door and stood with his back to it. "What else can I say?"

"Nothing." She shook her head. "Nothing."

"About my being Jewish. I had to keep it quiet after 1940. All the more after Charlie came along—"

"You should have told me, David. It would have been a shock, a surprise, I'm not pretending otherwise, but it wouldn't have made any difference. And I could have supported you." She looked at him. "But that was just the start of the lies." Her eyes bore into his. "Whatever love you felt for me ended when Charlie died, didn't it?"

"No. But somehow his dying just—pulled us apart. I don't know why.

And then, when I joined the Resistance—I felt guilty for lying to you again, and that just made it all worse." He put two fingers to the bridge of his nose, squeezed hard. "I was a spoiled child and I'm a selfish man."

She answered quietly, "You believe in duty, self-sacrifice. I always admired you for that. But I don't want you to stay with me out of duty. And I don't know if I could ever trust you again."

He thought of his other secret, the last one. Natalia. She hadn't guessed about that. Poor Sarah, even now she didn't see it all. He took a deep breath. "You haven't said if you still love me."

"I don't think that's enough anymore."

He closed his eyes. She sighed, then stood up. "David, we mustn't discuss this now. That's what I wanted to say. Jane's worried. Whatever happens afterwards, now we have to concentrate on getting through tonight. We owe it to the others."

"Duty." David smiled, a sad twitch of the mouth.

"Yes, duty. And now I think you should go."

He left the room. Natalia's door was still locked. So he went back down to the lounge and sat once more staring out at the empty street. It struck him then that for the first time in their relationship Sarah was in charge.

At eight o'clock Jane called them down for dinner. Sarah had been lying on her bed, reading an Agatha Christie novel to try to keep her mind off everything. She took a deep breath and steeled herself to go downstairs. The other four—David, Frank, the Scotsman, and the woman with the Slavic accent—were already sitting around one of the tables. Bert was with them, reading a copy of the *Daily Express*. As Sarah approached Ben said jokingly that their next meal would be American food, on the sub.

Jane had made a beef stew, with potatoes and Brussels sprouts, tasteless like all the food Sarah had eaten in the hotel but hot and filling. Bert looked up from his paper. "It says here Goebbels is calling a conference of all the senior army officers. Himmler and Heydrich aren't invited. Looks like divisions among the Nazis are really starting."

"And they're reportin' that in the *Express*?" Ben said, surprised. "Beaverbrook's paper. Normally they cannae tell us enough about how strong and united our German allies are."

"Well, this government wants Goebbels to stop the Russian war. Even Mosley knows it's unwinnable."

"Do you think that could actually happen? Some sort of civil war in Germany?" Frank asked.

David had been quiet, but now he looked up. "Yes. Hitler held all the reins of power himself. There was always the risk everything would fall apart when he died. He said the Third Reich would last a thousand years and people believed him, but what Empire has ever lasted that long? Even the Roman Empire didn't. A few hundred years, that's the most any Empires have, and many a lot less."

"Like the British Empire," Ben said quietly.

"Yes." There was sadness in David's answer, even now.

Ben asked Bert, "I suppose there's still nothing in the paper about the Jews?"

"No. But the word I've heard is that plans to deport them to the Isle of Wight and then on to Germany are canceled indefinitely now."

"But Goebbels and Himmler both hate the Jews, as much as Hitler did. That's the one thing those bastards are united about."

"The British government are waiting to see what happens," Natalia said. "If Germany breaks down, and Britain wants to move closer to the Americans, better to have the Jews alive. A bargaining counter. Pawns. The fog was an excuse to cancel the transports, it came at the right time."

Sarah looked at her. She didn't like Natalia, she thought her hard and cold. So she was surprised when she went on to say, with feeling, "For now they're abandoned in those detention camps. They must be so cold in this weather, so cold."

Jane had come in with a tray, heavy with large bowls of steamed pudding and custard. As she served them she said, "They're not the same as us, they don't have the same loyalty to England."

Bert glared at his wife. "I thought you'd got that nonsense out of your head years ago, woman. When have the Jews ever been disloyal to this country? And saying they're not the same as us—you mean they haven't got pure English blood?"

"No. I'm sorry, I just..." Jane's words tailed off.

"I've nae English blood," Ben said, stressing his Glasgow accent, trying to lighten the tone.

Bert said, "Sorry, I should have said British, not English—"

"Dinna worry," Ben laughed. "I don't lose sleep over what mix of blood I've got. Though a Scot Nat would've been at you fast enough for saying English not British. Worrying about blood and ancestry, that's what's got Europe intae all this shit." He looked pointedly at Jane.

"I'm sorry. I'm glad they're not being deported. That's bad." Jane looked at Natalia. "And you're right, the poor beggars must be cold out in those barracks or wherever they're being held. It's just—I was brought up disliking Jews."

Natalia said, "It's colder still where they get sent to, in the East. Though they're not cold for long."

Frank looked at her. "What do you mean?"

"I believe the rumors they kill them in extermination camps are true." Natalia looked at David. A look passed between them. He met her eye. And then Sarah knew, she knew that David had told Natalia he was Jewish and she saw in their faces exactly what lay between them. She looked down quickly at her plate but she couldn't pick up a spoon, couldn't eat. She stood abruptly. "I don't feel very well. I'm going upstairs."

David said, "What's wrong?"

"I feel sick. I think it's just nerves, giving me a bit of a gippy tummy. I'll be all right if I lie down for a bit."

The last secret. The end. Sarah wished she could have run out of the hotel, back to London, back to Irene and her mother and father. She thought of her empty house, had a sudden horrible vision of Charlie there as a tiny, lonely ghost, wandering lost through the empty rooms. She cried and cried, but silently so that the others wouldn't hear.

*   *   *

To her surprise, perhaps because she was so exhausted, Sarah fell asleep. When Ben knocked on her door it was dark. He told her they were to go downstairs for a last briefing. It was almost ten o'clock. They gathered in the office behind the counter. David gave Sarah a smile, but she couldn't return it. Frank and Ben, noticing, exchanged glances. Natalia was watching David and Sarah carefully, her face expressionless. Sarah thought, she's worried there'll be some sort of outburst between us. But there mustn't be, I have to hold on.

Bert and Jane reported that everything was still quiet in Rotting-dean, the rendezvous was still on. The weather forecast said it would be clear and cold. Then Bert went to a safe on the wall and brought out two pistols. Sarah shuddered at the sight of them. They made her think of her father, the pistol he would have carried in the Great War. Bert handed one to Ben. Natalia said, "You know I have one already?"

"Yes." Bert looked at David. "You can handle a gun?"

"I was in the Norway campaign, remember?" He picked up the pistol and examined it. "I can use this." Then he grasped it firmly and put it in his pocket.

Bert turned to Sarah. He said quietly, "What about you, Mrs. Fitzgerald?"

She shook her head. "I couldn't. Anyway, I wouldn't know how." She took a deep breath, then reached into her pocket and pulled out the pel-let David had handed her earlier. She held it out. "But I'll use this, if I have to."

"We all must," Ben said quietly.

"Is there anything else we need to discuss before we leave?" Natalia asked. She looked around them all, her gaze lingering on Sarah. "Because from now on we have to be completely focused on our escape, on getting away."

Sarah nodded. "I know." She drew a deep breath. "I'm ready."

They left the hotel at half past ten, in the car. They drove out of Brighton, past the Pavilion, its domes outlined against the starry sky. Natalia was the driver, Ben beside her. David sat in the back, Frank between him and Sarah.

They drove north out of Brighton, into the empty, frosty countryside. For a while there was silence. Then Ben said, "The news says the fog's gone in London. But the casualty departments are full of people with asthma and bronchitis, animals died at the Smithfield cattle show. There was more about that than what's happening in Germany. They just say Goebbels is in charge. There's windy weather coming in tomorrow apparently, there's going to be heavy snow in Scotland."

"I went to school there," Frank said quietly.

Sarah turned to him. He looked very pale and frightened. But he was calm, not really like a lunatic at all though there was something odd, off-key, about him. She spoke to him gently. "And after that you went to Oxford, met David?" She could imagine David looking after Frank, protecting him.

"Yes. I'm sorry I've got you both in this mess."

"You got caught up in this by chance," David said. "Though it's just an extension of the madness the whole country, the whole world, has ended up in, isn't it?"

Frank turned and looked at David. "You're the best friend I ever had in my life," he said, suddenly.

"Come on, Frank," David said jokingly. "You're embarrassing me."

Frank turned back to Sarah, his eyes glinting in the dark interior of the car. "No, it's true, and this may be my last chance to say it. Your husband is a good man. He looks after people, protects them. There's not one in a hundred like him."

Silence descended again. After a while they turned south, heading back toward the sea.

CHAPTER FIFTY-SEVEN

They drove into Rottingdean, past some large houses to a village green with a pond in the center, a skin of ice on its surface, and a tall war memorial, a stone column topped with a cross. On a hill to the right Frank saw a large windmill, outlined against the starry sky. To the left the ground rose up to an ancient church. Frank remembered the kind, brave vicar in London; if it hadn't been for him, he knew, he would have wandered about in the fog until he was caught, and then—he took a long, deep breath.

A few cars were already parked outside the large houses surrounding the green, and Natalia drew quietly to a halt between two of them. They stepped out into the freezing air. There were a couple of streetlights, but nobody was in sight and the windows of all the houses were curtained and dark.

Natalia told them not to talk, just follow her, as quietly as possible. Frank felt his heart begin to pound as he walked beside David. Sarah and Ben were behind him and Natalia in front. They turned into a narrow street with shops on either side, some Christmas decorations in the windows. Beyond the end of the street, moonlight shone on the sea.

Frank remembered his talk with Natalia, when he had asked to see her that afternoon. In her room he had asked her, haltingly, to give David the chance to rebuild his marriage.

He had thought she might be rude or contemptuous, but she only said, in a kindly but definite tone, "You don't understand."

He answered, "I suppose that's true in a way. But I can see Sarah loves him, even though she's so angry now. And he has feelings for her, I'm sure he has."

Natalia lit a cigarette, inclined her head. "What if he feels more for me than for her?"

"If he just abandoned her in America, think of the guilt he'd feel. David doesn't forget people. He didn't forget me, remember, when you asked him to get me out of the asylum."

Natalia smiled sadly. "You are so like my brother. Your problem is not that you don't understand things, it's that you see too much. But you must leave me and David to decide what to do."

"I know," he answered quietly. Natalia looked out of the window, her arms crossed, her pose thoughtful, then turned back to face him.

"Don't say anything to the others, please. We all have to concentrate on our escape now."

Frank said, "I won't." He took a long, deep breath. "But there was something else I wanted to ask. About tonight."

Natalia turned into a tiny street of little cottages fronted with dark flint. She approached the second cottage. Like all the other buildings they had passed it was in darkness. But when she went up to the door it opened a crack; someone had been watching. She whispered the mission password, "Aztec."

The door opened wider and Natalia went in, the others following. For a moment they were in complete darkness. Then a light was switched on and they saw they were in a small room with battered furniture, photographs on the mantelpiece. A stocky man in his forties in a heavy blue jersey stood in the middle of the room. His face was lined and weatherbeaten, stubble on his seamed cheeks, but his small, dark eyes were sharp and alert as he looked them over. "Any problems?" he asked quietly. His deep voice had a strong country accent.

"None," Natalia said.

"Anyone about?"

"Nobody."

"We'll go through to the back."

They followed him into an untidy kitchen, smelling strongly of fish.

He drew a pair of dirty curtains shut and waved them toward a wooden dining table where hard chairs and a couple of stools had been drawn up. "Sit down." He joined them at the table, gnarled hands clasped together.

"All right," he said. "Give me your first names."

They told him. "I'm Eddie. I'm a fisherman," he said. "I'm going to row you out to the submarine. I've a big old rowing boat, I've left it down at the beach. Some of you will have to help me row, we're going out about a mile. I've got the bearings and a red torch to flash out to sea, when we get near. You'll see the sub as we approach; it's big. They're expecting us at one a.m., we need to get rowing out by twelve thirty. It's only just gone half past eleven, we've plenty of time." He nodded to the darkened kitchen window, and gave them a gap-toothed smile, his first sign of friendliness. "You need to know exactly where you're going if you're in a boat, there's an old submerged pier out there. I've fresh clothes for you here, heavy dark clothes. You'll need them, it's going to be very cold out at sea. Understand?"

They all nodded silently.

"We've had people walking up and down on the cliffs since morning with binoculars, there's no sign of anything unusual out to sea. And the village has been quiet all day." He looked around them once more, his eyes lingering on Frank, as most people's did. "Is everyone ready?"

"Yes," Natalia said.

"Has anyone any experience of rowing?"

David said, "I rowed for Oxford. Haven't done much since, but it'll come back."

"Good." Eddie picked up a pair of binoculars and slung them around his neck. "Go on up, then," he said. "Up and change. Men to the left room, women to the right."

They went upstairs. Frank and David and Ben changed into thick sweaters in a tiny bedroom, then heavy trousers, boots, and peaked caps. When they were finished Ben put his cap at a jaunty angle, grinned at them, and said, "All right, me hearties?" in a mock–Long John Silver accent. David managed the flicker of a smile. He looked at Frank. "We're going to be all right. We're almost there now."

Frank nodded. "You haven't said much since we arrived," David said. "Sure you're okay?"

"Yes," Frank answered quietly.

They went back outside. Eddie took the lead. They walked down the main street in silence, then at a signal from him they crossed the coast road, which ran at right angles to the High Street. There was a hotel opposite, a sign hanging from a pole creaking gently in the light breeze from the sea. Next to it a sharply angled stone path led down toward the water, between high concrete banks. They followed Eddie down. At the bottom of the path was a promenade, bounded by cliffs on both sides. Steps could be seen leading down from the promenade to the little beach. Eddie said, "Wait here a moment. I'll look around. Get your eyes accustomed to the dark."

He went forward, the rest of them standing at the end of the path, between the high banks. There was no light now, apart from the half-moon which made a long pencil of silvery light on the sea. Frank, looking at the others, felt a sudden sense of distance, as though none of this were anything to do with him anymore. He thought suddenly of his flat in Birmingham. He would never see it again. He realized he didn't care.

He heard Sarah speak quietly to David. "I was just thinking of Mrs. Templeman. I don't know why. I suppose I wonder what she'd think of it all."

"She'd think we were doing the right thing."

"And Charlie?"

"A great adventure." There was a catch in David's voice.

Eddie returned. "It looks all clear," he said quietly. "We're going to cross the promenade and go down the steps to the beach. Come on now, follow me. Slowly now, one at a time, don't rush."

David watched as Ben followed Eddie out onto the promenade. Frank was next, then Sarah. He was about step forward himself when he felt Natalia's hand on his arm. He looked around. He couldn't see her face properly in the shadowed mouth of the pathway but it looked serious, grave.

"Listen, David," she said quickly. "We've only a moment. I'm not coming with you."

He stared blankly. "What do you mean? You must—"

"I don't want to go to America. That's not where the struggle is. It's here, in Europe, the climax is coming at last. I have to be part of it. I'm going back to London. And you—you belong with your wife."

"But why—"

She put her finger to his lips. It tasted of the salty air. Her brown hair stirred in the breeze. "Your friend Frank came to see me." She smiled wryly. "What he said tipped the balance. And—I could never settle to a safe life again, even with you. Every time I thought I had one, you see, it was taken away."

Footsteps could be heard coming back from the promenade; the others would be wondering why they hadn't appeared. Natalia said, "Ben is in charge from now on." She grasped David's arms and kissed him quickly. He saw tears shining in those slightly slanted eyes. She said, quietly, *"Ich hob dich lieb."*

He held her. "What did you say?"

"It's what your mother said to you. It means 'I love you.' Forgive me for not telling you before. *Ich hob dich lieb,* David." And then she turned away and walked rapidly back up the path, disappearing from view quickly in her heavy dark clothes. Ben appeared beside him. One hand was in his pocket, where his gun was. "Whit the fuck's gaun' on?" he hissed.

"It's Natalia," David said. "She's not coming, she's staying behind."

"Jesus." Ben hesitated for a moment, looking up the path.

"She said you're in charge now. Come on," David added, quietly, a catch in his voice. "I never even knew her last name."

"Naebody did."

Then Sarah appeared at the mouth of the pathway, Frank and Eddie beside her. Eddie asked anxiously, "What happened?"

"Natalia's stayin' behind," Ben answered.

Sarah looked at her husband. "Why?"

Ben said, "Never mind. She's gone. I'm in charge now. Come on."

The five of them crossed the promenade and descended a flight of stone steps, clinging to a slippery metal rail. The whispering line of the surf was surprisingly close, the tide high. Eddie pointed over to a large, dark, concrete groyne about twenty yards away. The moonlight cast a shadow beside it. "The boat's over there," he said quietly. "Let's go and get it upright. It's gone a quarter past twelve."

They walked the short distance to the boat, their feet crunching on the shingle. It was hard keeping their balance in the dark; Sarah almost slipped and David took her arm. She looked at him and nodded thanks.

Then all hell broke loose. The boat heaved up from below, knocking Eddie and Ben to the ground. A sudden blur of dark figures surrounded them and strong arms grasped David's hands, pulling them behind him. Looking wildly to his left and right he saw that Sarah and Frank were similarly pinioned, held by men dressed in black clothes, with black balaclavas and blackened faces. A fourth man was dragging Eddie to his feet, while another struggled on the ground with Ben. Ben was strong but his assailant was stronger and a moment later he too was hauled to his feet, arms behind him.

There was a sixth man with them, stouter than the others. He stood by the boat, looking around. "There's one missing," he said in a German accent. "The Resistance woman." He walked over to David, looked at him, nodded briefly. "Mr. Fitzgerald. I recognize you from your photographs. Where is she?"

"Who?"

"The other woman who should be with you."

"She didn't come," David said.

The German frowned, puzzled. He took off his balaclava. "Then who leads you?"

Ben said, "I dae, ye fuckin' fat Nazi cunt." The tall thin man holding him twisted his arm violently, making him cry out. "Commie poof," the man spat, and David realized he was British. Eddie and Frank stood still, unmoving. Eddie's eyes were full of rage but Frank's were unfocused, looking straight ahead at the sea. David thought, it's what he's expected all along and he was right. We're not going to be able to save him after all.

Sarah said, "That's the man who interrogated me at Senate House. He's dangerous, David!"

David looked into the man's face. Under the streaks of charcoal it looked fat and puffy, but the mouth was a thin line and the eyes were clear and questing.

"Who betrayed us?" David asked.

The German smiled. "I tricked your friend Geoffrey Drax into letting some information drop. But mostly I worked it out myself, with the help of certain radio intercepts."

"Geoff? My God. He's alive?"

"No longer, I think. He was badly hurt. I am sorry, he was brave." He turned and went over to Frank. "Dr. Muncaster?" he asked quietly. "Remember me?"

"Yes," Frank answered, just as softly.

Gunther nodded at the tall thin man holding Ben. "And you'll remember Inspector Syme, who came with me to the hospital. You gave us a good run. This must have been a difficult time for you, a great strain." He spoke sympathetically. David thought, the bastard's weighing him up for interrogation already.

Gunther sighed. "Well, it's over now, Frank, you did your best. Relax, talk to us a little when we get you back to London, that's all you need to do." He turned to the others and said, "Hold them while I search them." Methodically, he went through each of the prisoners' pockets. He found Ben's gun, and David's, and handed them to Kollwitz and Kapp. He also dug out the suicide pills. He held them in the palm of his hand, then looked at Frank. "You do not have one?" he asked.

Frank shook his head.

"They were probably scared he'd top himself the first chance he got, like he tried at the hospital," Syme said mockingly.

Gunther turned to Ben. "Is that right?"

"Yes." Ben looked at Frank. "I'm sorry, pal."

Frank turned his head, his face working for a moment. "It's okay," he mumbled.

"Right," Gunther said briskly. "Get them tied up." He nodded at Sarah. "Start with her. I'll cover you." He took out a gun. "Don't try anything, Mrs. Fitzgerald, or I'll shoot you dead. You're dispensable, you see. You've dyed your hair, haven't you? You Resistance people, you are always so thorough. Now, keep your hands behind you." He produced several coils of strong wire from his pocket.

When her hands were tied Sarah's captor pushed her roughly down on the pebbles and stood back. Then Gunther turned to Eddie. He had not uttered a word so far but as his hands were tied he said, "My father and uncle died in the Great War, they're buried in Flanders. I'm only glad they took some of your people with them." His captor hit Eddie sharply on the side of the head before shoving him down on the shingle beside Sarah and tying his hands. Gunther looked at Frank, David, and Ben, each still held with arms pinned behind them. Gunther nodded at Frank. "Him next." David saw Frank was shaking, breathing fast. Gunther pointed the gun at his leg. "I won't kill you, we need you alive. But if you try anything I will shoot you in the knee."

David watched as the tall German holding Frank released his hands and took a coil of wire from Gunther. David thought, he and Ben would be next and then it would be over for all of them. The man holding him leaned forward and whispered in his ear, "I was with Sturmbannführer Hoth when he interrogated your friend, Drax." He chuckled. "He is so subtle, a master."

David turned his head away, looked down to where Sarah and Eddie lay trussed up, the two Germans standing guard above them.

Suddenly two shots rang out, echoing around the cliffs, and both of the Germans staggered and fell. One crashed to the pebbles but the other fell across the prone figures of Eddie and Sarah; David saw a wash of blood spill out over them. Gunther whirled around. "Get the prisoners in front of you!" he yelled to his three remaining men.

David was dragged around, pushed next to Frank and Ben. The three of them faced the promenade, forming a human shield for the two Germans and the Englishman holding them from behind. Gunther ran around behind them as well, feet crashing on the pebbles. Everyone was breathing hard, their breath visible in the cold air. David thought, Natalia's here, she stayed behind to see us safe and saw the ambush. Natalia, who was a crack shot.

"How many shooters?" Gunther's voice was a furious din.

Frank's captor answered, his voice with its heavy German accent steady. "Only one, I think. I saw two flashes, same place."

"I want you to try and get him. I'll hold Muncaster and cover you as well. Do you think you can do it, Kollwitz? I know it's open ground."

The German nodded at the groyne. "I can use the moonlight shadow for some cover." Turning his head, David saw the man called Kollwitz look at Gunther with cold, clear, fearless eyes.

"Thank you," Gunther said.

David watched as Kollwitz ran to the groyne, zigzagging, crouched over, moving astonishingly fast. He glanced down at Sarah, one dead German sprawled over her, the other beside her. Their guns lay where they had fallen on the pebbles. There was a blotchy darkness on Sarah's face, which David realized must be blood from the German. She stared up at him, she was breathing hard but her face was set. She gave him a brief nod. Eddie's face was turned toward the promenade from where the shots had come.

Kollwitz had almost reached the top of the groyne when another shot rang out, echoing over the beach. This time David saw a flash of light from behind the promenade rails. Gunther saw it too; he fired at it instantly. Frank flinched away. David heard a cry from the promenade, a woman's cry. He sagged in the arms of the man holding him. Gunther turned to Ben, his charcoal-streaked face furious. "It's her, isn't it, the Resistance woman? You posted her there on watch. That's two of my men dead, you lying bastard."

Ben didn't reply. David watched as the dark, crouched figure of Kollwitz climbed the steps. He saw him walk up and down the promenade, as though he were looking for something, then wave his hands as a signal they were safe. David thought, is Natalia lying up there dead? He saw the dark figure of the German walk back down the steps and toward them. He was carrying another gun as well as his own. He said to Gunther, "Looks like you hit him, sir. There was a gun on the promenade and there's a trail of blood leading to the path to the coast road. A lot, he's hurt."

"She's hurt," Gunther corrected him. "It was the woman. It'll take her time to get back to her people, even if she makes it."

"I thought it better not to follow," Kollwitz said. "She's harmless now."

Gunther nodded. He drew a deep breath. "Right, let's get the rest of them tied up. You next," he said to Frank, letting go his arms as he felt for another piece of wire in his pocket. Frank stood shivering violently.

And then he started to run. He almost overbalanced on the pebbles but he righted himself and stumbled on, toward the whispering line of the surf. It was surprisingly close now; the tide must be almost full.

Syme, who was holding Ben, laughed. "What are you doing, you silly cunt?"

Gunther, though, raised his gun. "Stop!" he cried out urgently. "What are you trying to do?" Frank stumbled on, almost in the sea now. Gunther lowered his pistol, aimed at Frank's legs, and fired. Frank went down with a groan. Gunther stepped across the pebbles and leaned over him, turned him around. David saw Frank's face, white with pain.

"Why did you do that?" Gunther asked. His voice was irritable, like that of a schoolmaster whose pupil had done something stupid. Frank didn't reply. Gunther looked at his leg. "It's just a flesh wound," he said, his voice reassuring now. "We'll look after you." He took off the thick scarf he was wearing and began tying it tightly around Frank's calf to make a tourniquet. Gunther called to Syme, "Come over here, help me get him up. Kollwitz and Kapp, watch the other two."

Kollwitz stepped into Syme's place, holding Ben's arms behind him, as the lanky Special Branch man stepped over to Gunther. Together they pulled Frank to his feet. The German let Syme take Frank's full weight. Frank stood on one leg, leaning on Syme, his trousers black with blood below the tourniquet. Gunther took a pencil torch from his pocket and shone it full in Frank's face. It was white and set, his eyes wide and staring. "Don't put any weight on your bad leg," Gunther said. "We'll help you over to the boat, you can sit down on it."

Frank put all his weight on his uninjured left leg. Then he took a long, shuddering breath and bared his teeth at Gunther in a wide, mirthless smile, the old Muncaster rictus. But there was something different this time; Frank was holding something between his teeth. Gunther shouted, "No!" as Frank clenched his jaws together hard and David heard the faint crunch of breaking glass. Frank's body jerked convulsively and he fell forward, deliberately throwing himself at the German to unbalance him and Syme. Gunther's feet skittered on the slippery pebbles and he fell backwards, Frank falling on top of him. David thought, Natalia must have given him her pill. He must have talked her into it. He must've put it in his mouth when they left the car in Rottingdean; that was why he hardly spoke after that. And now he was dead, Frank was dead.

Taking advantage of everyone's shock, Ben shoved himself violently backwards at the German holding his arms, Kollwitz. His captor lost his balance and staggered, letting Ben break away. David dug his heels into the pebbles and tried to do the same to the man holding him, but his captor braced himself and held on, letting out an angry grunt. Kollwitz had righted himself and was reaching for his pistol but Ben was quicker; he threw himself at one of the guns lying beside Sarah and Eddie, then raised his weapon and shot the fair-haired German full in the chest. As he went down David's captor pushed him away and aimed his gun at Ben. He and Ben fired at the same time. They hit each other. Both crashed to the pebbles, the German dead with a bullet hole in his forehead, Ben writhing on the ground, clutching his shoulder.

The beach was strewn with bodies now, dead and injured and bound. Gunther was struggling to push Frank's corpse off him. Only David and Syme were left standing now, facing each other. Syme reached into his pocket and pulled his gun on David. "Don't you fuckin' move, sunshine," he said fiercely, his accent suddenly broad Cockney. "Hands in the air!"

David lifted his arms above his head, staring Syme in the eye.

With a grunt Gunther pushed Frank's body off him but he did not stand. Instead he knelt, crouching over the body of the man he had hunted across England. He shone the torch in Frank's face again. David saw Frank's eyes, as still and unseeing as Charlie's had been that terrible day, the Muncaster grin frozen on his face, tiny shards of glass glinting on his teeth. Gunther reached out and held Frank's shoulders, then bowed his head. Syme looked at David. "Right, you fucker, hands behind your back. Let's get you tied up. You can still be of use to Special Branch. Hoth, you cover me." Gunther looked at him with unseeing eyes for a moment. *"Will you bleedin' cover me?"* Syme repeated, his voice ringing across the beach.

"Yes — yes." Gunther pulled himself together and fumbled for his gun, pointing it at David. On the ground nearby, just beyond Sarah and Eddie, Ben was still groaning, clutching his shoulder. His gun lay beside him on the sand. Syme turned toward him, his face furious. "Stop making that noise, you cunt!"

"I've got half ma fuckin' arm shot off," Ben shouted.

"I'll bloody shut you up for good!" Syme stepped toward him, pistol raised, walking past where Sarah and Eddie lay. Then David saw Sarah brace herself and kick up and out with both feet, right into Syme's groin. He yelled and doubled over, dropping his gun, which fell by Sarah's face. He reached down for it but she stretched out and bit him, with all her force, on the hand. He screamed, "Fucking bitch!" and staggered away, tripping and falling down on the pebbles with a howl.

David lunged forward and picked up Syme's gun. As he did so he heard a bullet ricochet off a pebble nearby, saw sparks from the bullet. Gunther. He turned swiftly and shot the German in the arm, Gunther's gun flying outwards in a spray of blood. Gunther looked down at his arm in astonishment, then at David as he walked over and pointed Syme's gun at the center of the German's broad, charcoal-smeared forehead. Behind him Ben was still groaning, and Syme was curled over in a fetal position, sobbing with pain. Perhaps Sarah's heavy Wellington boots had burst his balls; David hoped so. His wife had saved him.

He looked into the German's eyes. They looked, not hard and wicked as David had expected, nor frightened, but sorrowful and unutterably weary. David was suddenly aware of how cold he was, his feet were like ice and the hand holding the gun almost numb.

The German stood there, seeming not to care about the blood gushing down his coat from his ruined arm. He gave David a sad, lopsided smile and shook his head slightly. He said quietly, "You won't win. You just held our victory up a little. That's all you can ever do." Then, louder, he shouted, "For Germany!" And there was a bang and a flash as David shot him between the eyes. Gunther fell back with a crash and lay still, his forehead shattered, blood and brains seeping out, white and black in the moonlight, the lopsided smile still on his face, as though he knew best even now. Beside him Frank lay, mouth still locked in the Muncaster grin. David looked back at Syme, who was struggling shakily to his feet, hands between his legs. David pointed the gun at Syme and he raised his hands. Still watching him, David reached over and gently closed Frank's eyes.

Suddenly he heard the crunch of running feet: Syme was running away, slowly and painfully, toward the promenade. David fired at him but missed, the cold numbness in his hand affecting his aim. Syme loped painfully on. He reached the steps to the promenade and began to climb them. David fired again and this time he hit him; Syme went down. But he was still alive; he began crawling painfully up the steps. His leg muscles aching from the cold, David started to run toward him, but from the ground nearby Eddie called out, "No! You've got to get us into the boat! There's just time to reach the submarine! But only just!"

David stood irresolute for a moment. He looked at his watch. It was quarter to one. All that horror and killing had lasted only half an hour. Syme had reached the top of the steps now, and was crawling onto the promenade. David raised his gun again but Sarah called out, "No, David! Leave him! You have to help us get away! And Ben's hurt!"

Eddie said, "If we're not there soon the sub will go! Untie us, quick!"

David thought of Natalia, hoped desperately that she had got away. Then he looked into Sarah's eyes and nodded. He went over to Ben. He looked in a bad way, grimacing with pain, blood leaking from a nasty shoulder wound. David could see white, exposed bone. Ben said, "I cannae feel my arm."

"We'll get you safe on the sub."

Ben looked around the bodies on the beach. "We beat thae fuckin' Nazis, eh?"

"Yes. Yes, we did."

He looked down toward the water. "Frank's dead, isn't he? What happened? I didn't see."

"He had a poison pill after all. Natalia gave it to him."

Tears came to Ben's eyes. "Poor Frankie. Poor wee man."

Frozen, soaked and shocked as they were, David and Eddie pulled away in the boat as fast as they could. The breeze was stronger out at sea, bitterly cold. Ben lay in the bottom of the boat. Sarah had opened his coat and had taken off her own jumper, pressing it down on Ben's shoulder to staunch the flow of blood.

They were already some distance from the shore. Looking back, David saw the line of chalk cliffs that stretched to the east, the Seven Sisters. For a second he thought he saw something move on top of the cliffs. "Eddie," he said. "Can I have the binoculars?"

"What is it?" he asked sharply.

"I thought I saw someone, up on the cliffs."

"Be quick." Eddie handed David the binoculars. Resting one arm on the rowlock, he scanned the top of the cliffs. He caught a glimpse of two figures, one a woman with long hair, leaning on the other one, a man. The woman was waving out to sea. He thought, it's Natalia, she made it. She's found one of the Resistance watchers.

"Anyone?" Eddie asked anxiously.

"I thought I saw a woman waving. It might have been Natalia." He glanced at Sarah, but she didn't look up from tending Ben. "He's unconscious now," she said. "He's in a bad way."

Eddie and David pulled as fast as they could. Eddie had a compass on the seat beside him, kept guiding David to change course slightly. Out on the calm sea the silence was unnerving after the shots and cries on the beach. David looked at his watch. Almost quarter past. "Not far," Eddie said. "Steady, now."

David looked at him. "Will you come with us? To America."

The fisherman spat in the water. "Not likely. I've been a Sussex man all my life." He gave his gap-toothed grin again. "Do you know, since the 1940 Treaty put those duties on trade between Britain and Europe, smuggling's started up again. French perfume, that's a favorite. Haven't earned too bad a living since."

"Will it be safe for you to go back?" Sarah asked. "If he survives, Syme could identify you."

"I've friends all along the coast, most of them Resistance. I'll be all right."

"Why did you join?" David asked.

"Don't like being told what to do by Nazis and Fascists. It's as simple as that, my friend. That's all it needs to be."

"If you've the courage," Sarah said.

It was unbearably cold; David could barely feel his hands on the oars. He looked at Sarah again. "How's Ben now?"

"Quiet." She looked at him and said. "Why didn't Natalia come with us?"

David didn't answer, lowering his head over the oars. Then he felt a hand on his arm. He looked up. Sarah smiled at him, through the blood on her face, her old reassuring smile, the smile he had never deserved. He smiled back, sadly. Then Eddie sat up, pointing. "Look!" he shouted. "Over there!"

They all turned to look.

Ahead of them they made out an enormous shape in the water, dark, like a whale. Eddie took out his torch and flashed a series of red signals. After a moment red flashes appeared in return. They rowed harder. They made out a giant cigar-shaped object, its flanks wet and slippery. They saw deck rails, a long gun barrel. As they came up to it the submarine towered over them; they made out a conning tower bristling with periscopes, dark-clad figures moving in front. The conning-tower hatch opened and a powerful light shone on them, blinding them for a second.

David shouted out the password. "Aztec!"

The boat bumped against the side of the submarine, its dark flanks glistening above them in the moonlight. A rope was thrown across the rail by one of the figures beside the conning tower; Eddie caught it and made it fast.

"Aztec it is," a confident American voice shouted back. "Let's get you safe aboard!"

EPILOGUE

October 1953
Ten months later

They arrived secretly at Chartwell early in the morning, three large unmarked cars driving steadily along the lanes, stirring up clouds of autumn leaves. As a conference room they used the big dining room with its views over the lawns and the lake, sitting around the table. There were no civil servants present, only a note taker for each side: Jock Colville for the British Resistance and a clerk from the Prime Minister's office for the government.

Colville hadn't seen Beaverbrook in person since 1940. The Prime Minister was subdued, with none of his usual energy and bombast, his round little shoulders slumped, his lined face pale. He was accompanied by three of his senior Cabinet ministers. Foreign Secretary Rab Butler greeted the Resistance negotiators with bonhomie as though they were old friends who had happened not to meet at the club for a while. Ben Greene, though, the Coalition Labour leader, already looked a defeated man, his huge fat body slumped over the table. Only Enoch Powell showed defiance. His thin white face was full of angry contempt, his voice coldly severe throughout the meeting though his eyes, as always, burned passionately.

The Resistance was represented, besides Churchill, by three key politicians who had followed him since the time of the 1940 Peace Treaty. Clement Attlee and Harold Macmillan were both sadly formal toward the men who had put them beyond the law, and had wanted to capture and kill them; Aneurin Bevan, though, could not hide an air of triumph.

Colville had worried about Churchill, for the old man was failing. He had had a stroke earlier in the year, and though he had recovered physically the mental slowing and lack of focus that had begun to show in recent years were growing. But sometimes, as on this morning, Churchill could still gather his resources of energy to remarkable effect. He left much of the talking to his colleagues, but dominated the table, gloweringly contemptuously at his old foes, his interventions always sharp and decisive.

Events had moved fast since Hitler's death the previous December. Goebbels, despite initial hesitation, had been unwilling to defy the SS determination to fight the Russian war to the end. In March a group of army officers, in alliance with Albert Speer and influential German business leaders, banded together with sections of the Nazi Party who realized the Russian war was unwinnable. They launched a military coup, assassinating Goebbels, and promising a permanent settlement with "Russian interests" before the war brought Germany and Europe to total ruin. A temporary ceasefire with Russia had been agreed. But Himmler and his million-strong SS forces had immediately launched a counter-coup with the support of most of the Nazi party. Civil war had erupted across Germany, the fighting men on the two sides treating each other with the same savagery they had shown previously to the conquered peoples, German civilians fleeing to the countryside or cowering in cellars. In Russia, too, Wehrmacht and Waffen SS forces had begun fighting each other. Hitler had held all power in his hands for twenty years and with him gone the whole ramshackle, rivalry-ridden structure had collapsed. Taking advantage, the Russians abrogated the ceasefire and began marching west.

The army had hoped for a quick victory but the civil war had lasted over six months, the army winning control of each German region slowly and painfully. They had the support of the navy and most of the civilian population, and it was an open secret that the Americans, with Adlai Stevenson now in office as President, were sending supplies to the army through Hamburg. But under Himmler, who had declared himself the new Führer, and his deputy Heydrich, SS forces had everywhere fought to the last man. A week ago Vienna had fallen, leaving the remaining Nazi forces besieged in their last redoubts in the Bavarian and Austrian Alps, running out of food and fuel. The Eastern Front had completely collapsed and the forces of the Russian Federation were sweeping westward, further and faster than anyone could have expected. They had uncovered terrible things, labor camps as bad as anything Stalin had created, and vast extermination camps, gassing plants and crematoria. They now had control of most of the Ukraine and parts of eastern Poland. A week ago they had broken through into the Crimean peninsula, from where rumors were coming of savage massacres of German settlers. Without the threat of German forces behind them the European satellite regimes were tottering and falling; everywhere in the east ethnic Germans, even those who had lived there peacefully for centuries, were being massacred or fleeing west. In France secret talks were under way between the Petain–Laval government and the French Resistance; the French Jews had been freed from the detention camps where they had been held for months. In Italy, Mussolini had been removed by his own Fascist Party, and in Spain General Franco had just been overthrown and shot by a group of army officers. There was confusion, and in places fighting, across Europe. In Britain there had been a pitched battle in Senate House, Rommel and the army people against the SS. The army had won. Rommel was still ambassador; the SS faction had all been killed or imprisoned. Rommel promised elections in Germany, once the civil war was over. And now Britain's turn had come.

Round the Chartwell dining table, Beaverbrook offered Churchill a senior role in a Government of National Unity, all the men present forming a new government, Mosley and the Fascists excluded. Churchill brusquely refused, insisting the British Resistance alone was morally entitled to govern. They would deal with any of Mosley's people who resisted them, then call elections.

"The Fascists will want to hold on to the power they have," Beaverbrook said. "Best to have us on your side to negotiate with them."

"You are no longer of any account," Bevan answered brutally. "And what power they have, you gave them."

Beaverbrook looked stunned. He said, "We used to be friends, Nye."

"That was my mistake. A long time ago."

Beaverbrook spread his arms wide. "The Jews will be released from their camps. I've already said so publicly. I never wanted them detained in the first place."

"And all of their homes and property will be returned to them," Churchill insisted. "Those supporters of Mosley, and yours, who moved into their houses will be booted out."

"That could be complicated—"

"Booted out!" Churchill shouted. "The whole bloody lot of them!"

"Very well. And I've promised I'll sack Mosley as Home Secretary. That proves our goodwill."

"But will Mosley go quietly?" Attlee asked. He had said little so far, puffing quietly on his pipe, though his eyes followed every move. "His people are unhappy about releasing the Jews. It's just as well you put the camps under army control. If the Auxiliary Police were still running them, they might have disobeyed your orders."

"I'll disband the Auxies." Beaverbrook's voice rose. "But if they and Mosley's people resist a change of government, you'll need the old police force, the army, all the forces of law and order, on your side. Do you think they'll obey you if my people and I aren't there? We've governed this country for twelve years. Half of your people are Socialists, you've fought the police and army on the streets. What if the forces of law and order resist you? Are you going to arm the Reds to fight them? Factory workers and miners?"

"They're fighting already," Bevan answered quietly. Attlee nodded.

Churchill looked at Beaverbrook. "When you go, those with sense will realize that the days of authoritarian government are over, and they'll jump from your bandwagon onto ours to save their skins. It's happening already." He leaned across the table. "And those who don't, the fanatics, Mosley's Blackshirts, they will be dealt with, with whatever force it takes. The tide has turned, Max, as I knew it would in the end. As Bevan just said, you count for nothing now."

"What happens to India?" Powell snapped. He looked directly at Churchill. "You've opposed Indian independence all your life. You called Gandhi a half-naked fakir. But these people, your people"—he gestured at Attlee and Bevan—"they want to hand it over."

"We can't hold India down anymore," Churchill replied heavily. "Perhaps I was wrong. In any case, I lost."

Powell stared furiously around the table. "India is *ours*," he said in his sharp, hard nasal voice. Colville wondered if, in the end, Powell, the fiercest nationalist of them all, would go down fighting with Mosley.

But Beaverbrook wouldn't. The old man spoke now, his broad lips trembling slightly. "If I agree to go, what happens to me?" he asked. "To the others around this table?"

Churchill didn't answer for a moment. Then he said, "If you agree to go quietly, we'll let you go quietly."

"Go back to your country house," Bevan taunted him mockingly.

"No, you'll have to leave the country, Max," Churchill said. He waved a hand. "Maybe Canada will have you back, I don't know."

"My newspapers—"

"You give them up," Bevan said, his voice rising. "Two or three proprietors foisting their prejudices on a nation is not a free press. We'll sell your papers, each one to someone different."

Beaverbrook blustered. "You want to send me into exile because you know people will rally around me—"

"No," Attlee said bluntly. "Because you're poison. You always were."

By the time Beaverbrook and his people left to consult the rest of their Cabinet, the Resistance leaders knew they had won. The others were jubilant but Churchill looked tired. After a few minutes he asked the others to leave him alone with Colville. When they had gone he got up, slowly and painfully, and went to sit in an armchair. "Whiskey, Jock," he said wearily. "Pour one for yourself." He stuck a cigar between his teeth, lit it, and bit down on it hard.

Colville stood beside him. Churchill stared out of the window at the leaf-strewn lawn, his face somber. "There will be fighting," he said. "Maybe very soon. Mosley won't just go. Little Beaverbrook's people are unimportant now, as I said, but Mosley and his men have guns. And some of the Auxiliaries will support him."

"Not all," Colville answered. "Some have come over to us already. Remember that Inspector Syme, who was involved in the Muncaster affair? He was hit in the leg, but survived?" Churchill grunted and nodded. "He approached us last month, he knows a lot of the key people who can be expected to jump our way. We might give him a role in the new police force, behind the scenes."

"The devils we have to deal with," Churchill growled. He seemed sunk in gloom, his "black dog" had entered the room again. He said, "Who knows, Beaverbrook may even tell his people to come and arrest us tonight."

"They won't, sir. They know they're finished. They'll try to save their own skins now, hold on to what they can. It might be an idea, though, to ask the Americans to say they would welcome a change of government in Britain. They said it of France yesterday."

"Good idea." Churchill nodded, encouraged. "Telephone the White House now."

Colville hesitated. "It'll need to be put carefully. Stevenson is different from the isolationist Presidents, but he's frightened of a revolution in Europe. And Beaverbrook was right. When the Fascists resist we will need to—what did they say in the Spanish Civil War? Arm the workers?"

"They're armed already. And Attlee and Bevan's people are committed to free elections, they always have been." Churchill nodded. "And soon, we shall have them again." He glowered at Colville. "What about these Russian rumors? That Khrushchev has been overthrown?"

"I think they may be true, sir. Sections of the KGB and state industries say they've taken over Moscow and are going to create a capitalist state, like the one the Germans planned for Russia east of Astrakhan, only bigger, and nationalist. It'll be popular. The Russians don't want communism back."

"Who's in charge of this?"

"A couple of unknowns. The mayor of Moscow and a KGB man. My guess is such a regime would be pretty corrupt. The Soviet Union certainly was. Poland and the Baltics have declared their independence, by the way. They're fighting both Germans and Russians."

Churchill shook his head sadly. "So it will go on, at least for a time, the endless suffering. If only we had stood firm in 1940, it could all have been over by now." He bowed his head.

Colville asked, "Will you stand for Prime Minister in the election here?"

"I don't know. Old age is the devil. Especially without my Clemmie." Churchill was silent a moment, then looked sharply up at Colville. "But if I don't it should be Macmillan for the Conservatives, not Eden. Anthony's not up to it."

"It could be Bevan for Labour. A lot of their people want him, say Attlee is too old, too moderate. They could win. Full-blooded socialism."

"If that's what the people choose, it is up to them. So long as these vile years of bloodshed and oppression can be brought to an end." Churchill relapsed into silence again, staring into space. After a minute Colville said gently, "Would you like me to leave you, sir? Set up the call to Washington?"

"The Muncaster affair," Churchill said. "The man who knew the secrets of the atom bomb. You remember him?"

"Yes, sir. He died in that shootout in Sussex."

Churchill grunted. "A brave man. Took his secret to the grave rather than let the Germans have it." He looked at Colville sharply. "There were those of us who badly wanted to prize the secret out of him, hoping to set up our own nuclear program."

Colville sighed. "Well, the secret will spread eventually, it must. God help civilization then."

Churchill shook his head. "We were so afraid the Germans might get hold of what Muncaster knew, remember? But it wouldn't have mattered in the end, would it? They'd never have had time to develop the Bomb before their whole regime collapsed into civil war."

"We didn't know that then," Colville said. "We didn't know it would all fall to pieces so soon."

Churchill grunted. "Well, only America has the Bomb now. The mission succeeded. What happened to the rest of those people, by the way? That woman from—where was it?"

"Slovakia. She went back there in the spring. Just before the Slovak army rose against the Fascists."

"There's still fighting there, isn't there?"

"Yes. It's pretty savage, I hear."

"And the others? The English civil servant and the Scot? I met them with Muncaster that morning, I remember. The Englishman's wife got away too, didn't she?"

"Yes. They were all questioned pretty closely in America, I know that. Muncaster's older brother was dead by then. He had a stroke, in custody."

"That whole family gone, then?"

"Yes. There were some questions about the Scot—he was a Communist. I think he got sent to Canada. He lost an arm in that fight. The other man and his wife got a clean bill of health, permission to stay in the States. I don't know what happened to them after that." He smiled. "Maybe they'll come back now."

Churchill sat up. He looked more cheerful now. He banged a fist on the arm of his chair. "Yes. The exiles will be returning soon. To help us rebuild. Rebuild! We need them all now."

ACKNOWLEDGMENTS

All novels, perhaps historical novels especially, are to some extent collaborative efforts. *Dominion* has benefited from the help of others more than most. First and foremost I must thank my wonderful editor and agent, Maria Rejt of Mantle/Macmillan, and Antony Topping of Greene & Heaton, and their excellent staff—especially Sophie Orme, Ali Blackburn, and Susan Opie at Mantle and Chris Wellbelove at Greene & Heaton, who managed to track down a crucial 1999 Channel 4 documentary on the Great Smog of 1952.

My thanks to Maria and Antony are all the greater for their support when, following a long period of debilitating illness, which put the book behind schedule, I was diagnosed this year with bone-marrow cancer. Along with treatment, their faith in the book and in me has allowed it to be finished in time for October 2012 publication.

Becky Smith once again did an astonishingly speedy and accurate job of typing. Olivia Williams carried out some crucial research for me in London when I was not well enough to go there, and I am grateful for the excellent job she did.

Once again, I thank the group of friends who read the book in manuscript and commented on it comprehensively and perceptively as usual: Roz Brody, Mike Holmes, Jan King, and William Shaw.

Lou Taylor, Professor of Dress and Textile History, and Dr. Gillian Scott, both of the School of Humanities, University of Brighton, were very generous with their time in discussing aspects of social history and fashion during the period from the 1930s to the 1950s, which helped greatly in my construction of an alternate universe.

My warm thanks to Dr. Françoise Hutton for discussing the type of medication Frank might have been on, and the modern history of mental hospitals.

Robert Edwards was very helpful in sharing his great knowledge of Sussex for the scenes set there. Martin Foster advised me, a complete ignoramus on the subject, on some basics of radio communication.

For the second book running, Rear Admiral John Lippiett, Chief Executive of the Mary Rose Trust, helped me with naval matters, which are important at the end of the story, and I am grateful to him for taking time out from his work in completing the final stages of the new Mary Rose Museum, which will be opening in 2013. (I can reassure him that in my planned next novel, Matthew Shardlake will keep his feet firmly on dry land.) The Museum Appeal has done wonders in raising funds, but is still £400,000 short of its target. When finished, it will have on display the greatest store of Tudor artifacts anywhere in the world, in a magnificent setting. More information and pictures can be found at www.maryrose.org. Donations for the final stages of the project can be sent via the website or to The Mary Rose Trust, HM Naval Base, Portsmouth PO1 3LX.

Alan Purdie at the British Legion was very helpful in providing details which helped me construct the 1952 Remembrance Day Ceremony in Chapter One. It is a very different Remembrance Day in my alternate universe, but I hope I managed to retain something of the atmosphere of respect which the ceremony deserves.

Any errors of fact in the book are, of course, my own responsibility.

Thanks to my friend Robyn Young for discussions of history and the strategy of book writing, and support when times were tough. Thanks also to Paul Tempest and Peter Allinson for lending me their house to work in while building works were taking place in mine. And last but not least, to Graham Brown of Fullertons for frequent bouts of photocopying and limitless supplies of stationery.

BIBLIOGRAPHICAL NOTE

Dominion involved a greater range of background reading than any previous novel I have written.

On British social and political history from the 1930s to the 1950s, the most useful works were Angus Calder's *The People's War: Britain 1939–45* (1971), still I think the best social history of wartime Britain. Also very useful were Juliet Gardiner's *The Thirties: An Intimate History* (2010), and *Wartime Britain 1939–45* (2004), and Richard Overy's *The Morbid Age: Britain between the Wars* (2009).

Peter Hennessy's *Never Again: Britain 1945–51* (1992) and *Having It So Good: Britain in the Fifties* (2000) are packed with fascinating information. David Kynaston's *Austerity Britain 1945–51* (2008) and *Family Britain 1951–57* (2010) were also very helpful. I think Kynaston's insight that, culturally, Britain in the decade following the Second World War retreated into a 1930s view on many social issues, is crucial. In the first decade after the war there were highly censorious attitudes to subjects like illegitimacy, homosexuality, and divorce, and the belief that women belonged in the home returned after the war. In my alternate universe Britain in 1952 is even more like the 1930s, and without the social reforms and full employment created by the Attlee government of 1945–51.

On particular topics, Juliet Nicolson's *The Great Silence* (2009) is a moving and evocative account of Britain coming to terms with the terrible losses of the First World War, which so affected Sarah's family in my book. Barbara Tate's *West End Girls* (2010) is a fascinating and extraordinary memoir of life in a Soho brothel of the period, and Dilys's establishment in *Dominion* owes it much. The Channel 4 documentary *Killer Fog* (1999) tells the extraordinary story of the Great Smog of 1952 evocatively and with compassion for the many who died. Rupert Alla-son's *The Branch* (1983) was a very useful brief introduction to the his-tory of the Special Branch; though I suspect the author would disagree with my portrayal of how the Branch might have developed in an authoritarian Britain, I see it as perfectly probable.

Many novels helped me in reimagining the period, notably those of Patrick Hamilton. (The roadhouse where David and his party stop on the way to Birmingham owes something to the Kings Head in the third volume of his Gorse trilogy [1952–1955].) Norman Collins's wonderful though sadly forgotten novel *London Belongs to Me* (1945) brings Lon-don uniquely to life during the traumatic years 1938–40. *Noblesse Oblige*, ed. Nancy Mitford (1956) includes her hilarious essay on snobbery and the use of language in contemporary society.

The story of Britain between the 1930s and 1950s is partly the story of empire in decline. Jan Morris's *Farewell the Trumpets* (1976), the final volume of her Pax Britannica Trilogy, was particularly useful and evoca-tive. I read a number of accounts of Civil Service life during the period, of which the most useful was undoubtedly Joe Garner's *The Common-wealth Office, 1925–68* (1968). Andrew Stewart's *Britain and the Domin-ions in the Second World War* (2008) is a useful and informative recent academic study. Peter Hennessy's *Whitehall* (1989) was also very helpful.

For Churchill and the crisis of May 1940, Roy Jenkins's *Churchill* (2001) is I think the best single-volume biography to date. John Charm-ley's *Churchill: The End of Glory* (1993) is exhaustively well informed though exhaustingly biased against Churchill. On the other hand, Mad-husree Mukerjee's *Churchill's Secret War* (2010), telling of his extraordi-nary callousness when it came to the Bengal famine of 1942, was a necessary douche of cold water for one like me who, remembering Churchill's role in 1940, can perhaps incline to being too reverential.

On the Cabinet discussions over whether to make peace in 1940 I found Andrew Roberts's *Eminent Churchillians* (1994) and *The Holy Fox: A Life of Lord Halifax* (1991) very useful, along with John Lukacs's *Five Days in London: May 1940* (2001) and Ian Kershaw's *Fateful Choices* (2007). Richard Overy's *The Battle of Britain* was very helpful at the early stages of my research. I had originally considered setting this book in a Britain where the proposed German invasion of Britain in 1940, Operation Sealion, had actually taken place. There has been much debate as to whether it could have succeeded and Overy's book finally convinced me that it could not.

There was a substantial minority in Britain who in 1939–40, for various reasons, opposed undertaking what would inevitably be total mobilization for a life-or-death struggle against Nazi Germany. Many were pacifists; a few were Scottish Nationalists; the most important were anti-Semites and outright Nazis. Particularly helpful on these various individuals and groups were Thomas Linehan's *British Fascism 1918–39* (2000), and Richard Griffiths's *Fellow Travelers of the Right: British Enthusiasts for Nazi Germany 1933–39* (1993) together with his *Patriotism Perverted: Captain Ramsay, the Right Club and British Anti-Semitism 1939–40* (1998). This book tells the story of one of the leading pro-Nazi and anti-Semitic figures, who ended up detained in prison along with Oswald Mosley and who, while there, was much exercised, like the Scottish National Party, by the question of Scottish women being sent to work in England. (Ramsay was a Scottish Conservative MP.) The SNP's opposition to Scots being conscripted to fight the war against Nazism can be verified in studies, such as Peter Lynch's *The History of the Scottish National Party* (Cardiff, 2002).

On the history of British anti-Semitism, I found Anthony Julius's *Trials of the Diaspora: A History of Anti-Semitism in England* (2010) to be very fair and informative in the sections leading up to 1945, though the postwar sections are, in my view, neither. Anne Chisholm and Michael Davie's biography *Beaverbrook: A Life* (1992) convinced me that if there was one outstanding candidate to run a regime such as the one portrayed in this book it was Beaverbrook.

On the subject of mental hospitals in the 1950s — that decade must have been one of the worst in which to be mentally ill, with experimental and sometimes dangerous new treatments introduced and before the radical reforms of the 1960s — I found Diana Gittins's *Madness in Its Place: Narratives of Severalls Hospital 1913–97* (1998) especially helpful, along with Dilys Smith's *Park Prewett Hospital: The History 1898–1984* (1986) and Derek McCarthy's *Certified and Detained: A True Account* (2009). Interestingly all three books describe an identical regime, though from widely different points of view. Bartley Green is fictitious but, I think, representational.

The Great Smog of December 1952 was caused by unusual weather conditions over southern England, at a period when London was still belching out tons of coal smoke from homes and power stations (the weather that week was unusually cold) as well as, increasingly, traffic fumes. It was the worst smog in the capital's history. It is now estimated that 12,000 people died, mostly from respiratory diseases. Atmospheric conditions and pollution levels would have been the same in my alternate universe. In the real world, the government covered up the number who died, but the smog was instrumental in bringing about the Clean Air Act a few years later.

In looking at how a British Resistance Movement might have fought a collaborationist regime, the closest (though not exact) parallel has to be the French Resistance. I found John F. Sweets's *Choices in Vichy France* (1994) and Matthew Cobb's *The Resistance* (2009) especially helpful.

The United States in this novel is neutral and at peace with Japan, as I believe could have happened if Britain had fallen or surrendered in 1940. This would have strengthened the predominantly Republican isolationist movement in America, which in turn could have led to Roosevelt losing the 1940 Presidential election. If, as in this book, a Democrat was at last again elected in 1952, the most likely candidate would have been the man who lost to Eisenhower in 1952 and 1956, Adlai Stevenson. Porter McKeever's biography, *Adlai Stevenson* (1989), tells the story of one of history's narrow losers who, in this book, becomes a winner.

Inevitably, *Dominion* involved much reading about Nazi Germany. I think the best recent study of the regime is Richard Evans's three-volume history: *The Coming of the Third Reich* (2003), *The Third Reich in Power* (2005), and *The Third Reich at War* (2008). Toby Thacker's *Joseph Goebbels; Life and Death* (2010) was very useful on the man who in my book succeeds Hitler, and on the politics of the regime generally. Mark Mazower's *Hitler's Empire: Nazi Rule in Occupied Europe* is an excellent study, not least of the various crazy and murderous Nazi plans for the future of Russia. James Taylor and Warren Shaw's *Dictionary of the Third Reich* (1987) was indispensable. Warren Shaw's son, my friend William Shaw, was one of those who read the book in manuscript; *Dominion* therefore owes something to two generations of the same family.

Russia's War (1997) by Richard Overy, the range of whose scholarship on the Second World War is matched only by his readability, is I think the best short account of Germany's militarily unwinnable war against the Soviet Union. Rodric Braithwaite's *Moscow 1941: A City and Its People at War* (2006) is an enthralling account of Germany's first defeat at the Battle of Moscow. In my alternate universe, German forces are able—with Britain gone from the field—to begin their offensive against Russia earlier and with more troops, and take Moscow, but then become, as I think they inevitably would, bogged down in Russia's vastness. Lizzie Collingham's *The Taste of War: World War II and the Battle for Food* (2011) is an enthralling and important account of the role of food supplies in the winning and losing of the Second World War, again not least in Russia.

On the development of nuclear weapons and rocketry, Michael Neufeld's *Von Braun: Dreamer of Space, Engineer of War* (2007) and James P. Delgado's *Nuclear Dawn: The Atomic Bomb from the Manhattan Project to the Cold War* (2009) were very helpful for a non-scientist. C. P. Snow's *The New Men* (1954) is a fascinating novel by a wartime Civil Service insider about Britain's efforts to manufacture a nuclear bomb.

John Cornwell's *Hitler's Pope* (1999) is the best of all too many accounts of how the Vatican of Pope Pius XII collaborated with the Nazi regime and its puppets and did next to nothing to stop the Holocaust in Catholic countries, despite the efforts of some courageous local Catholics. I found the story of the extent of the Catholic Church hierarchy's collaborationist attitude to Nazi and Fascist mass murder shocking enough in the context of the Spanish Civil War: in that of the Second World War it seems an almost indelible stain.

Which brings me, finally, to the tragic story of Slovakia and the Holocaust. The events that Natalia relates to David all happened in Slovakia in the real world, as in the alternate one. A collaborationist, nationalist anti-Semitic regime led by a Catholic priest, Father Tiso, and his second in command, the murderous Fascist Vojtech Tuka, used its own party paramilitaries, the Hlinka Guard, to load Slovak Jews onto the trains which were to carry them to the death camps in the first major deportations of the Holocaust, and also sent troops to fight in Russia. Some Slovak Catholics approved the deportations, others protested so vigorously that the deportations were — though too late for most — suspended. There is a good literature on the subject. Karen Henderson's *Slovakia: The Escape from Invisibility* (2002) is a useful introduction to the country's modern history. Mark W. Axworthy's *Axis Slovakia: Hitler's Slavic Wedge 1938–45* (2002) tells the story of the Tiso regime. Kathryn Winter's *Katarina* (1998), Gerta Vrbová's *Trust and Deceit: A Tale of Survival in Slovakia and Hungary 1939–1945* (2006), and her husband Rudolf Vrba's *I Escaped from Auschwitz* (2006) tell the story from the point of view of Slovak Jews. Vrba's story is one of the most extraordinary memoirs of the Second World War. Finally the papers in *Racial Violence Past and Present* (Slovak National Museum and Museum of Jewish Culture, Bratislava 2003) are a warning from history to Europe today.

Finally, and more happily, I cannot end without mentioning Robert Harris's *Fatherland* (1992) — for me the best alternate history novel ever written.

HISTORICAL NOTE

I was born in 1952, the year in which *Dominion* is set. My parents met through the wartime naval posting of my father, an English Midlander, to Scotland, my mother's home. So I am, like many British people of my generation, a child of wartime population movements.

Winston Churchill was Prime Minister when I was born, and throughout my childhood he was a revered figure. By the time I came to political awareness at the start of the 1970s, and abandoned, to their amusement and bemusement, my parents' Conservatism for the left-wing sympathies I have retained ever since, I found a different view of Churchill in the new circles I moved in. He was, many said, a warmonger, a ferocious imperialist who opposed any progress toward Indian independence, a fanatical anti-Socialist, hammer of the workers in the General Strike of 1926, and sender of troops to shoot down miners at Tonypandy in 1910. All of these accusations are true except, oddly, the last, despite its persistence.[1]

There were, I think, several Churchills—not surprising for a man whose political career spanned sixty-four years and who spent his life promoting highly original ideas, some crazy, some brilliant. First there was the radical Liberal, on the left of his party, of the years before 1914. Then during and after the Great War appeared the second Churchill, the ferocious anti-Socialist and anti-Communist Conservative, unshakeable opponent of Indian political advancement, on that subject a reactionary even by the standards of his own party at the time. But from 1935 on there emerged a third Churchill, the anti-Nazi who saw that Hitler meant war and that appeasement would end in disaster. He

---

1. R. Jenkins, *Churchill* (2001), 197–200.

genuinely loathed the fanatic nationalism and anti-Semitism of the Nazis and their destruction of democracy. This Churchill appeared on anti-appeasement platforms with Labour and trade union leaders like Ernest Bevin, and in 1940 allied with Labour against large parts of his own party in his determination to rally the nation to fight the war to the last, and his speeches, personality, and human skills inspired both politicians and people to do just that. In old age, during his second premiership of 1951–55, a fourth Churchill appeared, his politics turned centrist and consensual, and who in 1949 admitted to Jawaharlal Nehru that he had done him great wrong.[2]

It is of course undeniable that throughout his days Churchill was an old-fashioned British imperialist, and that ideas of British exceptionalism were at the forefront of his wartime speeches. So it may seem odd that in this book, whose overarching theme is the dangers and evils of politics based on nationalism and race, Churchill appears as a heroic figure. But it should be remembered that Churchill was never a narrow nationalist, and in 1940–45 he always saw Britain in the context of the wider European and world struggle. This is shown in his June 1940 speech which I have chosen as the aphorism for this book; he saw with vivid clarity the darkness that Nazism and the Nazis had brought to Europe and which would continue to spread if they were not stopped.

I have always been fascinated by the notion of alternate history—how the world might have changed had one seminal event turned out differently. And sometimes, as in May 1940, the history of the world does indeed seem to turn on a sixpence. Of course the story told here, of the events that followed Churchill failing to become Prime Minister, is only *an* alternate history, not *the* alternate history, for there can be no such thing. Every imagined change to history, every road not taken, opens up probabilities and likelihoods to the historian, but never certainties. I think, however, that Churchill was right in believing that if Britain had accepted German

---

2. M. Mukerjee, *Churchill's Secret War* (2010), 276.

peace overtures in 1940 it would inevitably have become dominated by Nazi Germany. The world I have created is only one of the scenarios that might have followed, though I believe a likely one.

And so, to turn to that crucial moment in the history of the real world, when Churchill became Prime Minister instead of Lord Halifax. Between 1935, when Fascist aggression in Europe began with Mussolini's invasion of Ethiopia, and March 1939, when Hitler finally destroyed Czechoslovakia, the policy of appeasement was supported by a majority within the ruling British National Government, a coalition with a large majority which had been in power since 1931. It was overwhelmingly Conservative but included a small number of important Labour and Liberal defectors.

Appeasement was not then a dirty word—it meant, broadly, to seek peace by negotiating peaceful solutions to international problems. People were appeasers from a number of often very different motives. One should never underestimate the importance of the memory of the horrors of the Great War, and the perfectly reasonable dread that with advancing technology, especially in the air, a second European war would be even more cataclysmic and involve the bombing of civilians with high explosives and, it was feared, poison gas. Stanley Baldwin was right when he said, in 1932, that "the bomber will always get through."

Then there were those who thought the Treaty of Versailles, severing German territories from the Reich in a treaty that otherwise idolized the principle of national self-determination, unfair. And there were many, particularly Conservatives, who while they disliked the Nazi regime, and thought its leaders common and thuggish, felt it was not up to them to interfere in German domestic affairs and saw the Nazis as a bulwark against the threat of communism. Lord Halifax, just before visiting Hitler as Foreign Secretary in 1937, wrote that "Nationalism and Racialism is a powerful force but I can't feel that it's either unnatural or immoral!," and added this comment shortly after: "I cannot myself doubt that these fellows are genuine haters of communism."[3]

---

3. A. Roberts, *The Holy Fox* (1991), 67.

We know now, more accurately than people did in the 1930s, how appallingly murderous the regime that Lenin and Stalin had created actually was, but in the 1930s it was no possible military threat to the West. The widespread fears on the British right of communism spreading at home were a chimera.

Then there were others who positively admired Nazism. Lloyd George, Prime Minister during the Great War, called Hitler also "unquestionably a great leader" and "the greatest German of the age."[4] There were Oswald Mosley's Blackshirts, supported for a time by Lord Rothermere's *Daily Mail,* and Hitler had influential admirers in business and on the wealthy aristocratic right. There were very few Labour politicians who had any good words for the Nazis, but there were one or two, notably Ben Greene, quite an important figure for a while in the 1930s. In *Dominion* he becomes Labour leader in the pro-Treaty coalition.

Then there were the pacifists, whose opposition to war in any form was total, even after the Second World War began. Pacifism within the Labour Party had been strong in the early 1930s, but declined as Fascist aggression grew, particularly with the Spanish Civil War. Pacifism remained as a force, though, both within and outside the Labour Party. The position taken by people like Vera Brittain and the minority of some twenty Labour MPs who formed the Parliamentary Peace Aims Group was courageous given the atmosphere of the time, but the Peace Aims Group would undoubtedly have voted for a treaty in 1940, and lived—though perhaps not for long—to regret it.

At Munich in 1938, Chamberlain believed that by ceding the predominantly German-speaking areas of Czechoslovakia to Hitler, he had met the Führer's last demand. When, the following spring, Hitler occupied the remaining Czech lands and set up Slovakia as a puppet state, Chamberlain realized he had been deceived. When he went on to invade Poland in September 1939 Chamberlain declared war, but he was a reluctant and ineffective war leader. His long-held hopes for peace gone, he became a tragic figure. When, in spring 1940, Chamberlain said that

---

4. R. Griffiths, *Fellow Travelers of the Right* (1980), 223–24.

Hitler had "missed the bus" for a spring offensive only for the Germans immediately to invade Denmark and Norway, and British military operations in Norway ended in disaster, his position as Prime Minister came under threat. A large minority of Conservative MPs voted against the government or abstained in the Norway Debate in Parliament in May 1940. Chamberlain turned to the Labour leaders with the offer of a coalition; they agreed to serve, but only under a different Conservative leader. Chamberlain realized he would have to go.

Thus followed the fateful meeting of 9 May 1940 between Chamberlain, the Conservative Chief Whip David Margesson, and the two leading candidates for the succession, Halifax and Churchill. Each of the participants left a record of what happened, which differ considerably in detail but not in essentials.[5] Edward Wood, Lord Halifax, Chamberlain's Foreign Secretary, had the premiership for the asking. He was patrician, experienced, trusted, reliable, and respected, though he had been a leading appeaser and there was sometimes an odd element of passivity in his nature. He was supported by the bulk of the Conservative party, Chamberlain, and the King. His junior minister, Rab Butler, had spent the previous evening imploring him to accept the premiership. Labour sat on their hands between the two candidates. Churchill, on the other hand, who had been brought back into the Cabinet when war was declared, was tough, pugnacious, brilliantly creative, and popular with the public; but had a reputation among Conservatives as serially disloyal, an ex-Liberal, an unreliable adventurer who had (as he did) some questionable friends.

But Halifax did not press for the position, and agreed to serve under Churchill. He seems to have realized that he did not have the personality to fight the titanic struggle that was coming; the very next day the Germans invaded the Low Countries and France. He also suffered at times of crisis from agonizing, probably psychosomatic, stomach pains. Honorably, he stood aside. Churchill became Prime Minister and entered

---

5. Roberts, *op. cit.*, chapter 21, is the best account.

the House of Commons to loud cheers from the Labour benches, but few from the Conservatives. They took a long time to learn to love him.

Churchill immediately appointed a new War Cabinet, the central core of ministers to direct the war. Besides himself, Halifax and Chamberlain remained for the Conservatives—other prominent appeasers were cast out (Sir Samuel Hoare suddenly found himself ambassador to Franco's Spain)—and Churchill appointed two Labour members, the party leader Clement Attlee and his deputy Arthur Greenwood. This was more than Labour were strictly entitled to, given their level of parliamentary representation, but it was a shrewd move—Churchill had not been a politician for forty years for nothing—because both were anti-appeasers who could be relied on to support him in prosecuting the war vigorously. It gave him a majority in the War Cabinet, and Chamberlain too, though now terminally ill, showed a new resolution.

This was needed. By the end of May 1940 British and French forces were in full retreat, the British to Dunkirk. At this point Germany made peace overtures, as they did again later in 1940, the thrust of which was that Hitler, who had never wanted war against his fellow Aryan nation, would leave the British Empire alone in return for a free hand in Europe. Halifax wanted these overtures to be followed up; it seemed the war in the West was lost and perhaps now was the time to try to settle and avoid further bloodshed. Churchill argued, though, that a peace treaty would inevitably lead to German domination of Britain and that with her navy and air force, supported (though in some cases not wholeheartedly) by the Empire and with the protection of the Channel, she should fight on and face invasion if need be. Churchill won the day and obtained support of the full Cabinet. The rest is history.

Had Halifax become Prime Minister, the outcome would likely have been very different. He would have appointed a different War Cabinet, with a different balance. It might well have negotiated peace when France surrendered. If that had happened I think both the Labour and Conservative parties would have split, a Labour minority following most

Conservatives into a pro-Treaty coalition. I believe King George VI would have stayed—constitutionally he would have had to support the decision of his government—and carried on as King, however reluctantly as the regime hardened. I have never bought the idea that the Germans, had Britain surrendered or been defeated, would have restored King Edward VIII, though certainly the Nazis played with that idea. True, Edward was pro-Nazi, but many in Britain loathed him for abdicating and he was such an irresponsible and foolish man that, as King, he would have been a headache to any government.

Deciding who Britain's political leaders might have been in the years that followed is difficult. Even if people are long dead one is reluctant to label them unfairly. Faced with the realities of what the Treaty brought about in the circumstances of this book, I think Halifax would have resigned in guilt and despair. Chamberlain died late in 1940 and as for the other leading candidate to succeed Halifax, Sir Samuel Hoare, I am conscious that his firsthand experience of fascism in Spain turned him into an anti-Fascist. I have portrayed Herbert Morrison, who was anti-Fascist but saw himself as a realist and was always consumed by the lust for power, as leading the Labour pro-Treaty minority but, like Halifax, later resigning in despair. Lloyd George, however, I am sure would have loved a late return to power and there is no question of his sympathies with Hitler.

As for the man who succeeds Lloyd George in *Dominion*, if one is looking for an appeaser in love with power, fanatical about a united British Empire setting up tariffs against the rest of the world, and a man who was irredeemably corrupt and unscrupulous (he left his native Canada under a cloud over the circumstances in which he had made a business fortune), the obvious candidate has to be Max Aitken, Lord Beaverbrook. Clement Attlee, who did not say such things lightly, described him as the only evil person he had ever met, a judgment shared by others,[6] although Churchill was, from time to time, friendly with him. To be fair, Beaverbrook was never an active anti-Semite, but nor did he

---

6. R. Pearce, *Attlee* (1997), 97.

like Jews and nor was the issue particularly important to him. From the Great War until the early 1930s he was the epitome of the newspaper magnate who successfully interfered in politics, until Stanley Baldwin courageously squashed him when he described newspaper proprietors as having "power without responsibility, the prerogative of the harlot throughout the ages." No single newspaper proprietor had such power again until the years following Margaret Thatcher's victory in 1979 when she, followed by Tony Blair (and Alex Salmond of the SNP), handed ever-increasing amounts of influence to Rupert Murdoch.

Enoch Powell was always the most fanatic of British nationalists, and though in the 1960s he became the ultimate British isolationist, while at the Conservative Research Department in the late 1940s he was a passionate imperialist. He sent a paper to Churchill, then the Leader of the Opposition, in 1946 advising the military reconquest of India, which made Churchill worry about his sanity, though Rab Butler managed to reassure him.[7] Powell seems to me an obvious candidate for India Secretary. Rab Butler later became a leading Conservative moderate, but he was the most passionate of appeasers before 1939, a fact which earned him the lasting enmity of Harold Macmillan, who hated fascism.

The Scottish Nationalist Party was formed in 1934 through the merger of two small parties, the right-wing Scottish Party and the leftish National Party of Scotland. The new party, which remained very small, included elements sympathetic to fascism, but had no common policies on the serious issues of the day—mass unemployment, the continuing Depression, and the darkening international scene—beyond the dream, common to all nationalist and Fascist parties throughout Europe, that the expression of nationhood would release some sort of a mystical "national spirit" that would somehow resolve all problems. The struggle against fascism was no priority for them; in 1939 the Party Conference voted to oppose conscription. Their leader, Douglas Young, was imprisoned for his refusal to be conscripted on the grounds that there existed

---

7. R. Butler, *The Art of the Possible*, 143, quoted in D. Sandbrook, *Never Had It So Good* (2005), 85–86.

no Scottish government to decide on it. The SNP's 1939 resolution and subsequent behavior show the unimportance fighting fascism had for them, while the rest of the British people, like my Scottish mother and English father, were either working their fingers to the bone on the home front or serving in the forces to fight the greatest threat civilization has ever faced.

In my alternative universe I see the SNP splitting, with right-wing elements supporting the Beaverbrook government in return for national symbols like the return of the Stone of Scone and vague promises of autonomy or independence. As Gunther says in the book, the co-option of local nationalists from Brittany to Croatia was an important element in Nazi policy throughout Europe.

During the 1980s, a new school of thought appeared, criticizing Churchill's decision to fight the war at all costs. This time it came from the political right. In 1993 the academic John Charmley wrote a book, *Churchill: The End of Glory*,[8] which stimulated Alan Clark, the ever-controversial Conservative MP, to write a *Times* article questioning whether Britain might have been better to make peace with Hitler in 1940. This exaggerated Charmley's position, but nonetheless his book questions Churchill's policy of fighting the war at all costs: "In international affairs it was the Soviets and the Americans who divided the world between them; in domestic politics it was the Socialists who reaped the benefits of the efforts of the Great (1940–45) Coalition."[9]

To take the last point first, the Attlee government of 1945–51 was put in office not by Churchill, but the electorate. Whether the creation of the welfare state, full employment, and the nationalization of part of the economy was a good or a bad thing is a matter of judgment. (I have portrayed in my book what I think conditions for ordinary people under a government that opposed these things would have looked like.) But peace with Hitler—which would certainly have involved Britain aligning itself with

---

8. J. Charmley, *Churchill: The End of Glory. A Political Biography* (1993).
9. Ibid., Preface, *xvii*.

German foreign policy in Europe—was likely, I think, to lead to the end of democracy, let alone glory, in Britain. What, for example, would have happened (as in my book appears likely in a 1950 election) if a party or group opposed to the Treaty looked like being elected?

Charmley accepts that the Empire by 1939, particularly India, was going to be difficult to hold on to for long, and blames Churchill for his failure to see the facts. This is fair enough. However, a government which accepted the peace terms available in 1940 would inevitably have had to rely more, economically, on the Empire; unrest in India could only have got worse with Britain tied to the Nazis; the breakup of the "old" Commonwealth would have been a distinct possibility. The New Zealanders, in particular, would have loathed links with the Nazis.

It is true (and the strongest argument used by those who disagree that the Second World War was "the good war"), that Stalin's victory made the Soviet Union the second power in the world, and gave it control over Eastern Europe, which suffered murderous oppression and economic exploitation from his regime in the postwar years. Even so, had Hitler been allowed a free hand in Eastern Europe and Russia, the fate of those countries would have been even worse. It took the efforts of Britain, Russia, and the USA to end the war in Europe in 1945. By then, the Holocaust had taken place and twenty million Soviet citizens, many of them civilians, as well as two million Poles and many other people from Eastern Europe, were dead. If the struggle in the East had continued with Russia fighting Hitler alone, the war would have gone on for years and the slaughter would have been infinitely greater yet. Hitler planned to kill the populations of Leningrad and Moscow, perhaps seven million people, and either enslave or murder Russians and Poles who could not show Aryan ancestry.

The war in Russia was, I think, always militarily unwinnable; the country was just too vast, and the population totally hostile. This was not because the Russians loved Stalin but because Hitler planned to kill or enslave all of them, so they fought, quite simply, for their lives, as did the Poles, who fought back vigorously against attempts to settle part of their country with the Germans. I think the result would have been as I have portrayed it in my book: Europe east of Germany as a vast slaughterhouse, conventional warfare combined with an endless guerrilla conflict; Vietnam on an almost unimaginable scale. If people think that the preservation of some hypothetical British glory would have been worth that, it is not a notion I can share.

There is also the question of the effect of a British surrender on America. America would then have had no potential military toehold in Europe and might well have turned its back on the continent and done a deal with the Japanese. This in turn would have made the Japanese war against China, which reproduced many of the features of the German–Soviet war in its scale and murderousness, all the more protracted.

Therefore, despite the horrors of Stalin's rule in the Soviet Union and Eastern Europe which followed Russian victory, I think a British surrender would have made world conditions even worse, to say nothing of the consequent continuation of Fascist rule in Western Europe.

Hitler believed that his Reich would last a thousand years. This was never likely. He deliberately built up the regime as a series of conflicting factions with himself at its head. And physically he is unlikely to have lasted long—most historians agree that by the last year of his life he was showing symptoms of early, rapidly developing Parkinson's disease. In my book, by 1952 the disease has taken its most rapid and serious path. If Hitler had died or become disabled there would have been a struggle for the succession between the regime's competing factions, not least the army and the SS. In the real world sections of the army tried to assassinate Hitler in 1944, by which time it was clear the war was lost. The 1944 Bomb Plot failed: had it succeeded a civil war between army and SS was a likely outcome.[10] This would, I think, have been even more likely had Hitler died in 1952; I have postulated a larger group of opponents in the army than existed in 1944, based on their having fought an unwinnable war in Russia for a further eight years.

The Nazi regime was, contrary to myth, always unstable at its heart.

---

10. R. Evans, *The Third Reich at War* (2008), 645.

So, too, was Stalin's dictatorship; following his death the regime changed greatly and became far less murderous, though it remained, economically, monolithically Communist, and brutal to any people or satellite countries that stepped out of line.

And so, at the end, I think the Second World War was, still, the good war. Western Europe did indeed, for many years, enter the "broad sunlit uplands" which Churchill foresaw. But nothing lasts forever, and at the time of writing, August 2012, Europe faces both economic and political crisis. And across the continent, in response, forces of nationalism and xenophobia are on the rise again. European history in the first half of the twentieth century was, apart from Russia, a story of nationalism triumphant. The rivalries between big-nation nationalisms culminated in the war of 1914 and nationalist spirit kept that war going for four years despite its unprecedented slaughter. Courageous figures like Lord Lansdowne in Britain, who talked of a settlement, were thrust aside, or worse. After the Great War came the Treaty of Versailles, which glorified small-nation nationalism. New states sprang up from the wreckage of the old Empires, most of which promptly began discriminating against the new minorities within their borders, not least the Jews, and ended up as nationalist dictatorships. And in both large and small European countries nationalism gave birth to its monster children, fascism, based on the organized worship of the nation and Nazism, which worshipped not just nationality but race.

After the Second World War nationalism did not die. One only needs to look for example at de Gaulle's France, or the anti-Communist movements in Eastern Europe, but for the most part it was far less fierce, less xenophobic. But now it is back in its rawest form; all across Europe, in France, Hungary, Greece, Finland, even Holland, and most worryingly perhaps in Russia, fiercely nationalist, anti-immigrant, and sometimes openly Fascist nationalist parties are significant forces in politics again. And the terrible story of Yugoslavia in the 1990s reminds us just how murderous European nationalisms can still become.

*   *   *

I find it heartbreaking—literally heartbreaking—that my own country, Britain, which was less prone to domestic nationalist extremism between the wars than most, is increasingly falling victim to the ideologies of nationalist parties. The larger ones are not racialist, but they share the belief that national identity is the issue of fundamental, overriding importance in politics; it is the atavistic notion that nationhood can, somehow, allow people to bound free from the oppression—nationalism always defines itself against some enemy "other"—and solve all their problems. UKIP promises a future that will somehow be miraculously golden if Britain simply walks away from the European Union. (To what? To trade with whom?) At least they have the honesty to be clear that they envisage a particular type of political economy, based on that other modern dogma which has failed so often and disastrously, not least in Russia, that "pure" free markets can end economic problems.

Far larger, and more dangerous, is the threat to all of Britain posed by the Scottish National Party, which now sits in power in the devolved government in Edinburgh. As they always have been, the SNP are a party without politics in the conventional sense, willing to tack to the political right (as the 1970s) or the left (as in the 1980s and 1990s) or the center (as today) if they think it will help them win independence. They will promise anything to anyone in their pursuit of power. They are very shrewd political manipulators. In power, they present themselves as competent, progressive democrats (which many are) but behind that, as always, lies the appeal to the mystic glories of independence, which is what the party has always been for. Once ruling an independent state, they will not easily be dislodged. How people who regard themselves as progressive can support a party whose biggest backers include the right-wing Souter family who own Stagecoach, and Rupert Murdoch, escapes me completely. Like all who think they will be able to ride a nationalist tiger, they will find themselves sadly mistaken.

The SNP have no real position on the crucial questions of political economy that affect people's lives, and never have; their whole basis has always been the old myth that released national consciousness will somehow make all well. They promise a low-regulation, low-corporate-tax regime to please the right, and a strong welfare state to please the left. The wasting asset of oil will not resolve the problem that, as any calculation shows, an independent Scotland will start its life in deficit.

It does not take more than a casual glance at its history to show that the SNP have never had any interest in the practical consequences of independence. They care about the ideal of a nation, not the people who live in it. They ignore or fudge vital questions about the economy and EC membership. In recent times, before the Euro crisis, they cheerfully talked of an independent Scotland joining the euro (they evade the huge issue of whether an independent Scotland, as well possibly as the remainder of the UK, would have to reapply for EU membership, a legal minefield). Before 2008 they spoke of the banking sector, of all things, as the core of an independent Scottish economy, forecasting a Scottish future comparable to that of Ireland and Iceland, shortly before both countries went so catastrophically bust. Now they talk of keeping the pound but following an independent economic policy. (How would that work? Why should the rest of the UK agree effectively to write a blank check? How would that be independence exactly?) But the practical problems of the real world have never been of interest to parties based on nationalism; on the contrary populist politicians like Alex Salmond ask people to turn their backs on real social and economic questions and seek comfort in a romanticized past and shared—often imagined—grievances. National problems are always someone else's fault. The unscrambling of the British economy and British debt after three hundred years of intimate unity is impossible to calculate using any accounting formula. Arguments are already leading to bitterness and growing national hostility on both sides of the border. That is what nationalism does, and what it feeds off. And all the arguments, all the ill feeling, are tragically unnecessary.

Meanwhile the SNP are trying to manipulate the independence referendum to secure a maximum vote for themselves, by holding it in the anniversary year of the Battle of Bannockburn and lowering the voting age to include sixteen- and seventeen-year-olds, because polls have shown that age group is most likely to vote for them. This smacks dangerously of electoral manipulation by a ruling party to stay in power and increase its power. God knows we have seen enough of that in modern European history. John Gray has recently written that while the dictatorships of the 1930s are unlikely to return, "toxic democracies based on nationalism and xenophobia" could emerge in a number of countries and be in power for long periods.[11] Scots are proud, rightly, of seeing their country in a European context. This, today, is the context.

Scotland and England have been politically and economically united for over three centuries. They have not been at war as states since the sixteenth century. The civil wars of the seventeenth and the Jacobite wars of the eighteenth centuries, though they had strong nationalist elements too, were both essentially about the nature of kingship and its relation to Parliament, society, and religion within all the nations of the British Isles. This is not a historical narrative the SNP would approve, of course. They want a people drugged on historical legend, replete with holy national sites (such as Bannockburn) and myths. These things are the dead, empty heart of nationalism, always said to be unique in every country, always drearily similar. The British people have intimately shared everything, good and bad, involved in the experiences of the first Industrial Revolution, the rise and fall of the British Empire, and two world wars. Economic division in Britain has been, since the 1930s, not between Scotland and England but between southeast England and the rest. There are probably millions like me who are British Anglo-Scots and wish to be allowed to remain so.

Prejudices between the Scots and English have on the whole been mild in recent history. In my view, at least, the Scots and English are very good at knocking the rough corners off each other's national cultures. But, beneath the empty populist bonhomie of Alex Salmond, the prospective breakup of Britain is already creating a new culture of hostility and bitterness on both sides of the border. I hope with all my heart

---

11. J. Gray, *A Point of View: The Trouble with Freedom*, BBC Radio (24 Aug 2012).

that Scotland votes to remain in Britain, because then at least one nationalist specter that has grown during my lifetime will vanish from Europe. If this book can persuade even one person of the dangers of nationalist politics in Scotland as in the rest of Europe, and to vote "no" in the referendum on Scottish independence, it will have made the whole labor worthwhile. The recent record of other parties in Scotland has not been good; that is never a reason to vote for something worse, and to do so irrevocably; and a party which is often referred to by its members, as the SNP is, as the "National Movement"[12] should send a chill down the spine of anyone who remembers what those words have so often meant in Europe.

August 2013

A year has passed since I wrote the Historical Note to Dominion. Politics and economics in Europe remain unsettled, and parties promising populist nationalist solutions of various kinds remain a dark shadow. In Scotland, the independence referendum is due on September 18, 2014, a year from now. The question is not whether Scotland could survive as an independent state—it could—but whether independence and national-identity politics are the best option for its people's future.

There has been a devolved Scottish parliament since 1999. It has wide-ranging powers, and the Labour-Liberal coalition of 1999–2007 enacted many measures that the Scottish people (and I personally) consider generally beneficial. The irony is that the powers available under devolution (and more are in the pipeline) have never been fully used—for example, the power to vary, and soon to set, Scotland's income tax. The Scottish National Party has run the Scottish government with a large majority since 2011 but has done virtually nothing;

---

12. D. Torrance, *Salmond: Against the Odds* (2011), xi.

instead, Scottish politics have been put on hold while the SNP government pushes for independence.

Independence, however, would bring economic risks that the SNP has tried to conceal, meeting challenges with evasion and insult. Fortunately, canny Scots are increasingly realizing that the SNP is simply not being straight with them about the risks to their future. The leaking of an internal SNP government document showed that despite that party's public optimism about an independent Scottish economy, privately it realizes that declining reserves of oil, and the costs of setting up a new state, would mean an independent Scottish government would have problems affording state pensions and unemployment benefits. The SNP government's claim that it relied on legal advice when it said that Scotland could automatically join the European Union as a separate member proved untrue; renegotiating EU membership remains a legal minefield. The question of what currency an independent Scotland would use remains entirely unresolved.

Meanwhile, the SNP has used Scottish government money for propaganda in ways far from the Scottish democratic tradition. The National Tourism Agency in 2013 produced an official history for visitors that, instead of highlighting Britain's victory against the Nazis in 1945, considered the election of the SNP's first MP that year more important, and followed up with a chronicle of party "achievements." And the party is about to produce its "White Paper" prospectus for independence to every Scottish household at taxpayer expense.

What are its aims? A dogmatic commitment to national independence and nothing else. Why else conceal the economic realities from the people? This is the world of nation-state first, people second. It is far from new politics, this tragic song of twentieth- and now twenty-first-century Europe.

Scottish culture has, I think, a grand tradition of practical hardheadedness. Where the heart is concerned, the country has a strong sense of national pride. The SNP will, I believe, try to drum up an exaggerated, distorted, exclusivist version of that pride more and more over the next year, seeking to identify Scottishness with independence—and, of course, with its own party. But patriotism, as Edith Cavell said, is not enough. When it places mythic, atavistic nationalism above all, it is destructive and dangerous. Is this sort of narrow inwardness the best of Scotland? I do not think so.

It is perfectly possible, in an increasingly multicultural world, to be loyal to more than one identity—to be Scottish and British. The peoples of the UK have achieved much together before and can continue to do so. And in this deeply troubled world, we should all be looking higher than national-identity politics.

I would therefore urge Scots to use both head and heart and vote no in 2014, and to donate toward, support, or at least look at the arguments presented by the all-party and nonparty "No" campaign, Better Together (bettertogether.net).

ABOUT THE AUTHOR

After a career as an attorney, C. J. Sansom now writes full time. He has written five Matthew Shardlake novels, including *Dissolution*, which P. D. James picked as one of her five favorite mysteries in the *Wall Street Journal*; *Dark Fire*, winner of the CW Ellis Peters Historical Dagger Award; *Sovereign*; *Revelation*, a *USA Today* Best Book of the Year for 2009; and the #1 international bestseller *Heartstone*, a novel which the *Washington Post* claimed "ranks with Iain Pears's *An Instance of the Fingerpost* (1998) among the very best of recent historical thrillers." Sansom is also the author of *Winter in Madrid*, a novel set in the aftermath of the Spanish Civil War. His books have been sold in twenty-five countries. Sansom lives in Brighton, England.

MULHOLLAND BOOKS

You won't be able to put down these Mulholland books.

THE THICKET *by Joe R. Lansdale*

BREED *by Chase Novak*

DARWIN'S BLADE *by Dan Simmons*

S. *created by J.J. Abrams and written by Doug Dorst*

THE LOST GIRLS OF ROME *by Donato Carrisi*

SEAL TEAM SIX: HUNT THE FALCON *by Don Mann with Ralph Pezzullo*

THE RIGHT HAND *by Derek Haas*

THE SHINING GIRLS *by Lauren Beukes*

GUN MACHINE *by Warren Ellis*

DOMINION *by C. J. Sansom*

SAY YOU'RE SORRY *by Michael Robotham*

SHE'S LEAVING HOME *by William Shaw*

WE ARE HERE *by Michael Marshall*

THE STOLEN ONES *by Richard Montanari*

WATCHING YOU *by Michael Robotham*

Visit mulhollandbooks.com for
your daily suspense fiction fix.

Download the FREE Mulholland Books app.